Joseph Heller was born in 1923 in Brooklyn, New York. He served as a bombadier in the Second World War, afterwards attending the colleges of New York, Columbia and Oxford, the last on a Fullbright scholarship. He then taught for two years at Pennsylvania State University, before returning to New York, where he began a successful career in the advertising departments of, progressively, *Time, Look* and *McCall's*. It was during this time that he had the idea for *Catch-22*. Working on the novel in spare moments and evenings at home, it took him eight years to complete and was first published in 1961.

His second novel, *Something Happened*, was published in 1971, *Good as Gold* in 1979, and *God Knows* in 1984. He is also the author of the play *We Bombed in New Haven*. Joseph Heller now lives in East Hampton, New York.

Also by Joseph Heller

CATCH-22

Since this extraordinary novel was first published in 1961, almost two million copies have been sold in the Corgi edition alone. Without question, *Catch-22* is one of the great novels of the century, an opinion shared by countless reviewers, as the following extracts confirm:

'A book of enormous richness and art, of deep thought and brilliant writing' *Spectator*

'A wild, moving, shocking, hilarious, raging, exhilarating, giant roller-coaster of a book' New York *Herald Tribune*

'Devastatingly original novel, with a deep felicity of comic invention . . . deeply impressive' *Irish Times*

'Brilliant' *Queen*

'Extremely funny, sad, frightening – and above all, funny' *Sunday Telegraph*

'The greatest satirical work in English since "Erewhon"' *Observer*

There was only one catch . . .
and that was Catch-22

CATCH-22

Joseph Heller

CORGI BOOKS

CATCH-22

A CORGI BOOK   0 552 01500 8

Originally published in Great Britain by Jonathan Cape Ltd

PRINTING HISTORY
Jonathan Cape edition published 1962
Corgi edition published 1964
Corgi edition reprinted 1964 (twice)
Corgi edition reprinted 1965
Corgi edition reprinted 1966 (twice)
Corgi edition reprinted 1967
Corgi edition reprinted 1968 (twice)
Corgi edition reissued 1969
Corgi edition reprinted 1970 (three times)
Corgi edition reprinted 1971 (twice)
Corgi edition reprinted 1972
Corgi edition reprinted 1973
Corgi edition reissued 1974
Corgi edition reprinted 1974
Corgi edition reprinted 1975 (twice)
Corgi edition reprinted 1976 (three times)
Corgi edition reprinted 1977
Corgi edition reprinted 1978 (twice)
Corgi edition reprinted 1979 (twice)
Corgi edition reprinted 1980 (three times)
Corgi edition reprinted 1981
Corgi edition reprinted 1982
Corgi edition reprinted 1983
Corgi edition reprinted 1984
Corgi edition reprinted 1985
Black Swan edition published 1985
Black Swan edition reprinted 1986
Corgi edition reprinted 1987
Black Swan edition reprinted 1988
Corgi edition reprinted 1988
Corgi edition reprinted 1989

Corgi Books are published by Transworld Publishers Ltd.,
61–63 Uxbridge Road, Ealing, London W5 5SA,
in Australia by Transworld Publishers (Australia) Pty. Ltd.,
15–23 Helles Avenue, Moorebank, NSW 2170, and in New
Zealand by Transworld Publishers (N.Z.) Ltd., Cnr. Moselle
and Waipareira Avenues, Henderson, Auckland.

Printed and bound in Great Britain by
Hazell Watson & Viney Limited
Member of BPCC Limited
Aylesbury, Bucks, England

CATCH-22

To my mother,
and to Shirley,
and my children, Erica and Ted

1   The Texan

It was love at first sight.

The first time Yossarian saw the chaplain he fell madly in love with him.

Yossarian was in the hospital with a pain in his liver that fell just short of being jaundice. The doctors were puzzled by the fact that it wasn't quite jaundice. If it became jaundice they could treat it. If it didn't become jaundice and went away they could discharge him. But this just being short of jaundice all the time confused them.

Each morning they came around, three brisk and serious men with efficient mouths and inefficient eyes, accompanied by brisk and serious Nurse Duckett, one of the ward nurses who didn't like Yossarian. They read the chart at the foot of the bed and asked impatiently about the pain. They seemed irritated when he told them it was exactly the same.

'Still no movement?' the full colonel demanded.

The doctors exchanged a look when he shook his head.

'Give him another pill.'

Nurse Duckett made a note to give Yossarian another pill, and the four of them moved along to the next bed. None of the nurses liked Yossarian. Actually, the pain in his liver had gone away, but Yossarian didn't say anything and the doctors never suspected. They just suspected that he had been moving his bowels and not telling anyone.

Yossarian had everything he wanted in the hospital. The food wasn't too bad, and his meals were brought to him in bed. There were extra rations of fresh meat, and during the hot part of the afternoon he and the others were served chilled fruit juice or chilled chocolate milk. Apart from the doctors and the nurses, no one ever disturbed him. For a little while in the morning he had to censor letters, but he was free after that to spend the rest of each day lying around idly with a clear conscience. He was comfortable in the hospital, and it was easy to stay on because he always ran a temperature of 101. He was even more comfortable than Dunbar, who had to keep falling down on his face in order to get *his* meals brought to him in bed.

After he had made up his mind to spend the rest of the war in the hospital, Yossarian wrote letters to everyone he knew saying that he was in the hospital but never mentioning why. One day he had a better idea. To everyone he knew he wrote that he was going on a very dangerous mission. 'They asked for volunteers. It's very dangerous, but someone has to do it. I'll write you the instant I get back.' And he had not written anyone since.

All the officer patients in the ward were forced to censor letters written by all the enlisted-men patients, who were kept in residence in wards of their own. It was a monotonous job, and Yossarian was disappointed to learn that the lives of enlisted men were only slightly more interesting than the lives of officers. After the first day he had no curiosity at all. To break the monotony he invented games. Death to all modifiers, he declared one day, and out of every letter that passed through his hands went every adverb and every adjective. The next day he made war on articles. He reached a much higher plane of creativity the following day when he blacked out everything in the letters but *a*, *an* and *the*. That

14

erected more dynamic intralinear tensions, he felt, and in just about every case left a message far more universal. Soon he was proscribing parts of salutations and signatures and leaving the text untouched. One time he blacked out all but the salutation 'Dear Mary' from a letter, and at the bottom he wrote, 'I yearn for you tragically. R. O. Shipman, Chaplain, U.S. Army.' R. O. Shipman was the group chaplain's name.

When he had exhausted all possibilities in the letters, he began attacking the names and addresses on the envelopes, obliterating whole homes and streets, annihilating entire metropolises with careless flicks of his wrist as though he were God. Catch-22 required that each censored letter bear the censoring officer's name. Most letters he didn't read at all. On those he didn't read at all he wrote his own name. On those he did read he wrote, 'Washington Irving.' When that grew monotonous he wrote, 'Irving Washington.' Censoring the envelopes had serious repercussions, produced a ripple of anxiety on some ethereal military echelon that floated a C.I.D. man back into the ward posing as a patient. They all knew he was a C.I.D. man because he kept inquiring about an officer named Irving or Washington and because after his first day there he wouldn't censor letters. He found them too monotonous.

It was a good ward this time, one of the best he and Dunbar had ever enjoyed. With them this time was the twenty-four-year-old fighter-pilot captain with the sparse golden mustache who had been shot into the Adriatic Sea in midwinter and not even caught cold. Now the summer was upon them, the captain had not been shot down, and he said he had the grippe. In the bed on Yossarian's right, still lying amorously on his belly, was the startled captain with malaria in his blood and a mosquito bite on his ass. Across the aisle from Yossarian was Dunbar, and next to Dunbar was the artillery captain with whom Yossarian had stopped playing chess. The captain was a good chess player, and the games were always interesting. Yossarian had stopped playing chess with him because the games were so interesting they were foolish. Then there was the educated Texan from Texas who looked like someone in Technicolor and felt, patriotically, that people of means – decent folk – should be given more votes than drifters, whores, criminals, degenerates, atheists and indecent folk – people without means.

Yossarian was unspringing rhythms in the letters the day they brought the Texan in. It was another quiet, hot, untroubled day. The heat pressed heavily on the roof, stifling sound. Dunbar was lying motionless on his back again with his eyes staring up at the ceiling like a doll's. He was working hard at increasing his life span. He did it by cultivating boredom. Dunbar was working so hard at increasing his life span that Yossarian thought he was dead. They put the Texan in a bed in the middle of the ward, and it wasn't long before he donated his views.

Dunbar sat up like a shot. 'That's it,' he cried excitedly. 'There was something missing – all the time I knew there was something missing – and now I know what it is.' He banged his fist down into his palm. 'No patriotism,' he declared.

'You're right,' Yossarian shouted back. 'You're right, you're right, you're right. The hot dog, the Brooklyn Dodgers. Mom's apple pie. That's what everyone's fighting for. But who's fighting for the decent folk? Who's fighting for more votes for the decent folk? There's no patriotism, that's what it is. And no matriotism, either.'

The warrant officer on Yossarian's left was unimpressed. 'Who gives a shit?' he asked tiredly, and turned over on his side to go to sleep.

The Texan turned out to be good-natured, generous and likable. In three days no one could stand him.

He sent shudders of annoyance scampering up ticklish spines, and everybody fled from him – everybody but the soldier in white, who had no choice. The soldier in white was encased from head to toe in plaster and gauze. He had two useless legs and two useless arms. He had been smuggled into the ward during the night, and the men had no idea he was among them until they awoke in the morning and saw the two strange legs hoisted from the hips, the two strange arms anchored up perpendicularly, all four limbs pinioned strangely in air by lead weights suspended darkly above him that never moved. Sewn into the bandages over the insides of both elbows were zippered lips through which he was fed clear fluid from a clear jar. A silent zinc pipe rose from the cement on his groin and was coupled to a slim rubber hose that carried waste from his kidneys and dripped it efficiently into a clear, stoppered jar on the floor. When the jar on the floor was full, the jar feeding his elbow was empty, and the two were simply switched quickly so that the stuff could drip back into him. All they ever really saw of the soldier in white was a frayed black hole over his mouth.

The soldier in white had been filed next to the Texan, and the Texan sat sideways on his own bed and talked to him throughout the morning, afternoon and evening in a pleasant, sympathetic drawl. The Texan never minded that he got no reply.

Temperatures were taken twice a day in the ward. Early each morning and late each afternoon Nurse Cramer entered with a jar full of thermometers and worked her way up one side of the ward and down the other, distributing a thermometer to each patient. She managed the soldier in white by inserting a thermometer into the hole over his mouth and leaving it balanced there on the lower rim. When she returned to the man in the first bed, she took his thermometer and recorded his temperature, and then moved on to the next bed and continued around the ward again. One afternoon when she had completed her first circuit of the ward and came a second time to the soldier in white, she read his thermometer and discovered that he was dead.

'Murderer,' Dunbar said quietly.

The Texan looked up at him with an uncertain grin.

'Killer,' Yossarian said.

17

'What are you fellas talkin' about?' the Texan asked nervously.

'You murdered him,' said Dunbar.

'You killed him,' said Yossarian.

The Texan shrank back. 'You fellas are crazy. I didn't even touch him.'

'You murdered him,' said Dunbar.

'I heard you kill him,' said Yossarian.

'You killed him because he was a nigger,' Dunbar said.

'You fellas are crazy,' the Texan cried. 'They don't allow niggers in here. They got a special place for niggers.'

'The sergeant smuggled him in,' Dunbar said.

'The Communist sergeant,' said Yossarian.

'And you knew it.'

The warrant officer on Yossarian's left was unimpressed by the entire incident of the soldier in white. The warrant officer was unimpressed by everything and never spoke at all unless it was to show irritation.

The day before Yossarian met the chaplain, a stove exploded in the mess hall and set fire to one side of the kitchen. An intense heat flashed through the area. Even in Yossarian's ward, almost three hundred feet away, they could hear the roar of the blaze and the sharp cracks of flaming timber. Smoke sped past the orange-tinted windows. In about fifteen minutes the crash trucks from the airfield arrived to fight the fire. For a frantic half hour it was touch and go. Then the firemen began to get the upper hand. Suddenly there was the monotonous old drone of bombers returning from a mission, and the firemen had to roll up their hoses and speed back to the field in case one of the planes crashed and caught fire. The planes landed safely. As soon as the last one was down, the firemen wheeled their trucks around and raced back up the hill to resume their fight with the fire at the hospital. When they got there, the blaze was out. It had died of its own accord, expired completely without even an ember to be watered down, and there was nothing for the disappointed firemen to do but drink tepid coffee and hang around trying to screw the nurses.

The chaplain arrived the day after the fire. Yossarian was busy expurgating all but romance words from the letters when the chaplain sat down in a chair between the beds and asked him how he was feeling. He had placed himself a bit to one side, and the captain's bars on the tab of his shirt collar were all the insignia Yossarian could see. Yossarian had no idea who he was and just took it for granted that he was either another doctor or another madman.

'Oh, pretty good,' he answered. 'I've got a slight pain in my liver and I haven't been the most regular of fellows, I guess, but all in all I must admit that I feel pretty good.'

'That's good,' said the chaplain.

'Yes,' Yossarian said. 'Yes, that is good.'

'I meant to come around sooner,' the chaplain said, 'but I really haven't been well.'

'That's too bad,' Yossarian said.

'Just a head cold,' the chaplain added quickly.

'I've got a fever of a hundred and one,' Yossarian added just as quickly.

'That's too bad,' said the chaplain.

'Yes,' Yossarian agreed. 'Yes, that is too bad.'

The chaplain fidgeted. 'Is there anything I can do for you?' he asked after a while.

'No, no.' Yossarian sighed. 'The doctors are doing all that's humanly possible, I suppose.'

'No, no.' The chaplain colored faintly. 'I didn't mean anything like that. I meant cigarettes . . . or books . . . or . . . toys.'

'No, no,' Yossarian said. 'Thank you. I have everything I need, I suppose – everything but good health.'

'That's too bad.'

'Yes,' Yossarian said. 'Yes, that is too bad.'

The chaplain stirred again. He looked from side to side a few times, then gazed up at the ceiling, then down at the floor. He drew a deep breath.

'Lieutenant Nately sends his regards,' he said.

Yossarian was sorry to hear they had a mutual friend. It seemed there was a basis to their conversation after all. 'You know Lieutenant Nately?' he asked regretfully.

'Yes, I know Lieutenant Nately quite well.'

'He's a bit loony, isn't he?'

The chaplain's smile was embarrassed. 'I'm afraid I couldn't say. I don't think I know him that well.'

'You can take my word for it,' Yossarian said. 'He's as goofy as they come.'

The chaplain weighed the next silence heavily and then shattered it with an abrupt question. 'You are Captain Yossarian, aren't you?'

'Nately had a bad start. He came from a good family.'

'Please excuse me,' the chaplain persisted timorously. 'I may be committing a very grave error. Are you Captain Yossarian?'

'Yes,' Captain Yossarian confessed. 'I am Captain Yossarian.'

'Of the 256th Squadron?'

'Of the fighting 256th Squadron,' Yossarian replied. 'I didn't know there were any other Captain Yossarians. As far as I know, I'm the only Captain Yossarian I know, but that's only as far as I know.'

'I see,' the chaplain said unhappily.

'That's two to the fighting eighth power,' Yossarian pointed out, 'if you're thinking of writing a symbolic poem about our squadron.'

'No,' mumbled the chaplain. 'I'm not thinking of writing a symbolic poem about your squadron.'

Yossarian straightened sharply when he spied the tiny silver cross on the other side of the chaplain's collar. He was thoroughly astonished, for he had never really talked with a chaplain before.

'You're a chaplain,' he exclaimed ecstatically. 'I didn't know you were a chaplain.'

'Why, yes,' the chaplain answered. 'Didn't you know I was a chaplain?'

'Why, no. I didn't know you were a chaplain.' Yossarian stared at him with a big, fascinated grin. 'I've never really seen a chaplain before.'

The chaplain flushed again and gazed down at this hands. He was a slight man of about thirty-two with tan hair and brown diffident eyes. His face was narrow and rather pale. An innocent nest of ancient pimple pricks lay in the basin of each cheek. Yossarian wanted to help him.

'Can I do anything at all to help you?' the chaplain asked.

Yossarian shook his head, still grinning. 'No, I'm sorry. I have everything I need and I'm quite comfortable. In fact, I'm not even sick.'

'That's good.' As soon as the chaplain said the words, he was sorry and shoved his knuckles into his mouth with a giggle of alarm, but Yossarian remained silent and disappointed him. 'There are other men in the group I must visit,' he apologized finally. 'I'll come to see you again, probably tomorrow.'

'Please do that,' Yossarian said.

'I'll come only if you want me to,' the chaplain said, lowering his head shyly. 'I've noticed that I make many of the men uncomfortable.'

Yossarian glowed with affection. 'I want you to,' he said. 'You won't make me uncomfortable.'

The chaplain beamed gratefully and then peered down at a slip of paper he had been concealing in his hand all the while. He counted along the beds in the ward, moving his lips, and then centered his attention dubiously on Dunbar.

'May I inquire,' he whispered softly, 'if that is Lieutenant Dunbar?'

'Yes,' Yossarian answered loudly, 'that is Lieutenant Dunbar.'

'Thank you,' the chaplain whispered. 'Thank you very much. I must visit with him. I must visit with every member of the group who is in the hospital.'

'Even those in other wards?' Yossarian asked.

'Even those in other wards.'

'Be careful in those other wards, Father,' Yossarian warned. 'That's where they keep the mental cases. They're filled with lunatics.'

'It isn't necessary to call me Father,' the chaplain explained. 'I'm an Anabaptist.'

'I'm dead serious about those other wards,' Yossarian continued grimly. 'M.P.s won't protect you, because they're craziest of all. I'd go with you myself, but I'm scared stiff. Insanity is contagious. This is the only sane ward in the whole hospital. Everybody is crazy but us. This is probably the only sane ward in the whole world, for that matter.'

The chaplain rose quickly and edged away from Yossarian's bed, and then nodded with a conciliating smile and promised to conduct himself with appropriate caution. 'And now I must visit with Lieutenant Dunbar,' he said. Still he lingered, remorsefully. 'How is Lieutenant Dunbar?' he asked at last.

'As good as they go,' Yossarian assured him. 'A true prince. One of the finest, least dedicated men in the whole world.'

'I didn't mean that,' the chaplain answered, whispering again. 'Is he very sick?'

'No, he isn't very sick. In fact, he isn't sick at all.'

'That's good.' The chaplain sighed with relief.

'Yes,' Yossarian said. 'Yes, that is good.'

'A chaplain,' Dunbar said when the chaplain had visited him and gone. 'Did you see that? A chaplain.'

'Wasn't he sweet?' said Yossarian. 'Maybe they should give him three votes.'

'Who's they?' Dunbar demanded suspiciously.

In a bed in the small private section at the end of the ward, always working ceaselessly behind the green plyboard partition, was the solemn middle-aged colonel who was visited every day by a gentle, sweet-faced woman with curly ashblond hair who was not a nurse and not a Wac and not a Red Cross girl but who nevertheless appeared faithfully at the hospital in Pianosa each afternoon wearing pretty pastel summer dresses that were very smart and white leather pumps with heels half high at the base of nylon seams that were inevitably straight. The colonel was in Communications, and he was kept busy day and night transmitting glutinous messages from the interior into square pads of gauze which he sealed meticulously and delivered to a covered white pail that stood on the night table beside his bed. The colonel was gorgeous. He had a cavernous mouth, cavernous cheeks, cavernous, sad mildewed eyes. His face was the color of clouded silver. He coughed quietly, gingerly, and dabbed the pads slowly at his lips with a distaste that had become automatic.

The colonel dwelt in a vortex of specialists who were still specializing in trying to determine what was troubling him. They hurled lights in his eyes to see if he could see, rammed needles into nerves to hear if he could feel. There was a urologist for his urine, a lymphologist for his lymph, an endocrinologist for his endocrines, a psychologist for his psyche, a dermatologist for his derma; there was a pathologist for his pathos, a cystologist for his cysts, and a bald and pedantic cetologist from the zoology department at Harvard who had been shanghaied ruthlessly into the Medical Corps by a faulty anode in an I.B.M. machine and spent his sessions with the dying colonel trying to discuss *Moby Dick* with him.

The colonel had really been investigated. There was not an organ of his body that had not been drugged and derogated, dusted and dredged, fingered and photographed, removed, plundered and replaced. Neat, slender and erect, the woman touched him often as she sat by his bedside and was the epitome of stately sorrow each time she smiled. The colonel was tall, thin and stooped. When he rose to walk, he bent forward even more, making a deep cavity of his body, and placed his feet down very carefully, moving ahead by inches from the knees down. There were violet pools under his eyes. The woman spoke softly, softer than the colonel coughed, and none of the men in the ward ever heard her voice.

In less than ten days the Texan cleared the ward. The

artillery captain broke first, and after that the exodus started. Dunbar, Yossarian and the fighter captain all bolted the same morning. Dunbar stopped having dizzy spells, and the fighter captain blew his nose. Yossarian told the doctors that the pain in his liver had gone away. It was as easy as that. Even the warrant officer fled. In less than ten days, the Texan drove everybody in the ward back to duty – everybody but the C.I.D. man, who had caught cold from the fighter captain and come down with pneumonia.

2   Clevinger

In a way the C.I.D. man was pretty lucky, because outside the hospital the war was still going on. Men went mad and were rewarded with medals. All over the world, boys on every side of the bomb line were laying down their lives for what they had been told was their country, and no one seemed to mind, least of all the boys who were laying down their young lives. There was no end in sight. The only end in sight was Yossarian's own, and he might have remained in the hospital until doomsday had it not been for that patriotic Texan with his infundibuliform jowls and his lumpy, rumpleheaded, indestructible smile cracked forever across the front of his face like the brim of a black ten-gallon hat. The Texan wanted everybody in the ward to be happy but Yossarian and Dunbar. He was really very sick.

But Yossarian couldn't be happy, even though the Texan didn't want him to be, because outside the hospital there was still nothing funny going on. The only thing going on was a war, and no one seemed to notice but Yossarian and Dunbar. And when Yossarian tried to remind people, they drew away from him and thought he was crazy. Even Clevinger, who should have known better but didn't, had told him he was crazy the last time

they had seen each other, which was just before
Yossarian had fled into the hospital.

Clevinger had stared at him with apoplectic rage and
indignation and, clawing the table with both hands, had
shouted, 'You're crazy!'

'Clevinger, what do you want from people?' Dunbar
had replied wearily above the noises of the officers'
club.

'I'm not joking,' Clevinger persisted.

'They're trying to kill me,' Yossarian told him calmly.

'No one's trying to kill you,' Clevinger cried.

'Then why are they shooting at me?' Yossarian asked.

'They're shooting at *everyone*,' Clevinger answered.
'They're trying to kill everyone.'

'And what difference does that make?'

Clevinger was already on the way, half out of his chair
with emotion, his eyes moist and his lips quivering and
pale. As always occurred when he quarreled over principles in which he believed passionately, he would end
up gasping furiously for air and blinking back bitter
tears of conviction. There were many principles in which
Clevinger believed passionately. He was crazy.

'Who's they?' he wanted to know. 'Who, specifically,
do you think is trying to murder you?'

'Every one of them,' Yossarian told him.

'Every one of whom?'

'Every one of whom do you think?'

'I haven't any idea.'

'Then how do you know they aren't?'

'Because . . .' Clevinger sputtered, and turned speechless with frustration.

Clevinger really thought he was right, but Yossarian
had proof, because strangers he didn't know shot at him
with cannons every time he flew up into the air to drop
bombs on them, and it wasn't funny at all. And if that
wasn't funny, there were lots of things that weren't even
funnier. There was nothing funny about living like a bum
in a tent in Pianosa between fat mountains behind him
and a placid blue sea in front that could gulp down a

person with a cramp in the twinkling of an eye and ship him back to shore three days later, all charges paid, bloated, blue and putrescent, water draining out through both cold nostrils.

The tent he lived in stood right smack up against the wall of the shallow, dull-colored forest separating his own squadron from Dunbar's. Immediately alongside was the abandoned railroad ditch that carried the pipe that carried the aviation gasoline down to the fuel trucks at the airfield. Thanks to Orr, his roommate, it was the most luxurious tent in the squadron. Each time Yossarian returned from one of his holidays in the hospital or rest leaves in Rome, he was surprised by some new comfort Orr had installed in his absence – running water, wood-burning fireplace, cement floor. Yossarian had chosen the site, and he and Orr had raised the tent together. Orr, who was a grinning pygmy with pilot's wings and thick, wavy brown hair parted in the middle, furnished all the knowledge, while Yossarian, who was taller, stronger, broader and faster, did most of the work. Just the two of them lived there, although the tent was big enough for six. When summer came, Orr rolled up the side flaps to allow a breeze that never blew to flush away the air baking inside.

Immediately next door to Yossarian was Havermeyer, who liked peanut brittle and lived all by himself in the two-man tent in which he shot tiny field mice every night with huge bullets from the .45 he had stolen from the dead man in Yossarian's tent. On the other side of Havermeyer stood the tent McWatt no longer shared with Clevinger, who had still not returned when Yossarian came out of the hospital. McWatt shared his tent now with Nately, who was away in Rome courting the sleepy whore he had fallen so deeply in love with there who was bored with her work and bored with him too. McWatt was crazy. He was a pilot and flew his plane as low as he dared over Yossarian's tent as often as he could, just to see how much he could frighten him, and loved to go buzzing with a wild, close roar over the

27

wooden raft floating on empty oil drums out past the sand bar at the immaculate white beach where the men went swimming naked. Sharing a tent with a man who was crazy wasn't easy, but Nately didn't care. He was crazy, too, and had gone every free day to work on the officers' club that Yossarian had not helped build.

Actually, there were many officers' clubs that Yossarian had not helped build, but he was proudest of the one on Pianosa. It was a sturdy and complex monument to his powers of determination. Yossarian never went there to help until it was finished; then he went there often, so pleased was he with the large, fine, rambling shingled building. It was truly a splendid structure, and Yossarian throbbed with a mighty sense of accomplishment each time he gazed at it and reflected that none of the work that had gone into it was his.

There were four of them seated together at a table in the officers' club the last time he and Clevinger had called each other crazy. They were seated in back near the crap table on which Appleby always managed to win. Appleby was as good at shooting crap as he was at playing ping-pong, and he was as good at playing ping-pong as he was at everything else. Everything Appleby did, he did well. Appleby was a fairhaired boy from Iowa who believed in God, Motherhood and the American Way of Life, without ever thinking about any of them, and everybody who knew him liked him.

'I hate that son of a bitch,' Yossarian growled.

The argument with Clevinger had begun a few minutes earlier when Yossarian had been unable to find a machine gun. It was a busy night. The bar was busy, the crap table was busy, the ping-pong table was busy. The people Yossarian wanted to machine-gun were busy at the bar singing sentimental old favorites that nobody else ever tired of. Instead of machine-gunning them, he brought his heel down hard on the ping-pong ball that came rolling toward him off the paddle of one of the two officers playing.

'That Yossarian,' the two officers laughed, shaking

their heads, and got another ball from the box on the shelf.

'That Yossarian,' Yossarian answered them.

'Yossarian,' Nately whispered cautioningly.

'You see what I mean?' asked Clevinger.

The officers laughed again when they heard Yossarian mimicking them. 'That Yossarian,' they said more loudly.

'That Yossarian,' Yossarian echoed.

'Yossarian, please,' Nately pleaded.

'You see what I mean?' asked Clevinger. 'He has anti-social aggressions.'

'Oh, shut up,' Dunbar told Clevinger. Dunbar liked Clevinger because Clevinger annoyed him and made the time go slow.

'Appleby isn't even here,' Clevinger pointed out triumphantly to Yossarian.

'Who said anything about Appleby?' Yossarian wanted to know.

'Colonel Cathcart isn't here, either.'

'Who said anything about Colonel Cathcart?'

'What son of a bitch *do* you hate, then?'

'What son of a bitch *is* here?'

'I'm not going to argue with you,' Clevinger decided. 'You don't know who you hate.'

'Whoever's trying to poison me,' Yossarian told him.

'Nobody's trying to poison you.'

'They poisoned my food twice, didn't they? Didn't they put poison in my food during Ferrara and during the Great Big Siege of Bologna?'

'They put poison in *everybody's* food,' Clevinger explained.

'And what difference does *that* make?'

'And it wasn't even poison!' Clevinger cried heatedly, growing more emphatic as he grew more confused.

As far back as Yossarian could recall, he explained to Clevinger with a patient smile, somebody was always hatching a plot to kill him. There were people who cared for him and people who didn't, and those who didn't hated him and were out to get him. They hated him because he was Assyrian. But they couldn't touch him, he told Clevinger, because he had a sound mind in a pure body and was as strong as an ox. They couldn't touch him because he was Tarzan, Mandrake, Flash Gordon. He was Bill Shakespeare. He was Cain, Ulysses, the Flying Dutchman; he was Lot in Sodom, Deirdre of the Sorrows, Sweeney in the nightingales among trees. He was miracle ingredient Z-247. He was –

'Crazy!' Clevinger interrupted, shrieking. 'That's what you are! Crazy!'

'– immense. I'm a real, slam-bang, honest-to-goodness, three-fisted humdinger. I'm a bona fide supraman.'

'Superman?' Clevinger cried. 'Superman?'

'Supraman,' Yossarian corrected.

'Hey, fellas, cut it out,' Nately begged with embarrassment. 'Everybody's looking at us.'

'You're crazy,' Clevinger shouted vehemently, his eyes filling with tears. 'You've got a Jehovah complex.'

'I think everyone is Nathaniel.'

Clevinger arrested himself in mid-declamation, suspiciously. 'Who's Nathaniel?'

'Nathaniel who?' inquired Yossarian innocently.

Clevinger skirted the trap neatly. 'You think everybody is Jehovah. You're no better than Raskolnikov –'

'Who?'

'– yes, Raskolnikov, who –'

'Raskolnikov!'

'– who – I mean it – who felt he could justify killing an old woman –'

'No better than?'

'– yes, justify, that's right – with an ax! And I can prove it to you!' Gasping furiously for air, Clevinger enumerated Yossarian's symptoms: an unreasonable belief that everybody around him was crazy, a homicidal impulse to machine-gun strangers, retrospective falsification, an unfounded suspicion that people hated him and were conspiring to kill him.

But Yossarian knew he was right, because, as he explained to Clevinger, to the best of his knowledge he had never been wrong. Everywhere he looked was a nut, and it was all a sensible young gentleman like himself could do to maintain his perspective amid so much madness. And it was urgent that he did, for he knew his life was in peril.

Yossarian eyed everyone he saw warily when he returned to the squadron from the hospital. Milo was away, too, in Smyrna for the fig harvest. The mess hall ran smoothly in Milo's absence. Yossarian had responded ravenously to the pungent aroma of spicy lamb while he was still in the cab of the ambulance bouncing down along the knotted road that lay like a broken suspender between the hospital and the squadron. There was shish-kabob for lunch, huge, savory hunks of spitted meat sizzling like the devil over charcoal after marinating seventy-two hours in a secret mixture Milo had stolen from a crooked trader in the Levant, served with Iranian rice and asparagus tips Parmesan, followed by cherries jubilee for dessert and then steaming cups of fresh coffee with Benedictine and brandy. The meal was served in enormous helpings on damask tablecloths by the skilled Italian waiters Major — de Coverley had kidnaped from the mainland and given to Milo.

Yossarian gorged himself in the mess hall until he thought he would explode and then sagged back in a contented stupor, his mouth filmy with a succulent residue. None of the officers in the squadron had ever eaten so well as they ate regularly in Milo's mess hall, and Yossarian wondered awhile if it wasn't perhaps all worth it. But then he burped and remembered that they were trying to kill him, and he sprinted out of the mess hall wildly and ran looking for Doc Daneeka to have himself taken off combat duty and sent home. He found Doc Daneeka in sunlight, sitting on a high stool outside his tent.

'Fifty missions,' Doc Daneeka told him, shaking his head. 'The colonel wants fifty missions.'

'But I've only got forty-four!'

Doc Daneeka was unmoved. He was a sad, birdlike man

with the spatulate face and scrubbed, tapering features of a well-groomed rat.

'Fifty missions,' he repeated, still shaking his head. 'The colonel wants fifty missions.'

3   Havermeyer

Actually, no one was around when Yossarian returned
from the hospital but Orr and the dead man in
Yossarian's tent. The dead man in Yossarian's tent was
a pest, and Yossarian didn't like him, even though he
had never seen him. Having him lying around all day
annoyed Yossarian so much that he had gone to the
orderly room several times to complain to Sergeant
Towser, who refused to admit that the dead man even
existed, which, of course, he no longer did. It was still
more frustrating to try to appeal directly to Major
Major, the long and bony squadron commander, who
looked a little bit like Henry Fonda in distress and went
jumping out the window of his office each time
Yossarian bullied his way past Sergeant Towser to
speak to him about it. The dead man in Yossarian's tent
was simply not easy to live with. He even disturbed Orr,
who was not easy to live with, either, and who, on the
day Yossarian came back was tinkering with the faucet
that fed gasoline into the stove he had started building
while Yossarian was in the hospital.

'What are you doing?' Yossarian asked guardedly
when he entered the tent, although he saw at once.

'There's a leak here,' Orr said. 'I'm trying to fix it.'

'Please stop it,' said Yossarian. 'You're making me nervous.'

'When I was a kid,' Orr replied, 'I used to walk around all day with crab apples in my cheeks. One in each cheek.'

Yossarian put aside the musette bag from which he had begun removing his toilet articles and braced himself suspiciously. A minute passed. 'Why?' he found himself forced to ask finally.

Orr tittered triumphantly. 'Because they're better than horse chestnuts,' he answered.

Orr was kneeling on the floor of the tent. He worked without pause, taking the faucet apart, spreading all the tiny pieces out carefully, counting and then studying each one interminably as though he had never seen anything remotely similar before, and then reassembling the whole apparatus, over and over and over and over again, with no loss of patience or interest, no sign of fatigue, no indication of ever concluding. Yossarian watched him tinkering and felt certain he would be compelled to murder him in cold blood if he did not stop. His eyes moved toward the hunting knife that had been slung over the mosquito-net bar by the dead man the day he arrived. The knife hung beside the dead man's empty leather gun holster, from which Havermeyer had stolen the gun.

'When I couldn't get crab apples,' Orr continued, 'I used horse chestnuts. Horse chestnuts are about the same size as crab apples and actually have a better shape, although the shape doesn't matter a bit.'

'Why did you walk around with crab apples in your cheeks?' Yossarian asked again. 'That's what I asked.'

'Because they've got a better shape than horse chestnuts,' Orr answered. 'I just told you that.'

'Why,' swore Yossarian at him approvingly, 'you evil-eyed, mechanically-aptituded, disaffiliated son of a bitch, did you walk around with *anything* in your cheeks?'

'I didn't,' Orr said, 'walk around with *anything* in my

cheeks. I walked around with crab apples in my cheeks. When I couldn't get crab apples I walked around with horse chestnuts. In my cheeks.'

Orr giggled. Yossarian made up his mind to keep his mouth shut and did. Orr waited. Yossarian waited longer.

'One in each cheek,' Orr said.

'Why?'

Orr pounced. 'Why what?'

Yossarian shook his head, smiling, and refused to say.

'It's a funny thing about this valve,' Orr mused aloud.

'What is?' Yossarian asked.

'Because I wanted –'

Yossarian knew. 'Jesus Christ! Why did you want –'

'– apple cheeks.'

'– apple cheeks?' Yossarian demanded.

'I wanted apple cheeks,' Orr repeated. 'Even when I was a kid I wanted apple cheeks someday, and I decided to work at it until I got them, and by God, I did work at it until I got them, and that's how I did it, with crab apples in my cheeks all day long.' He giggled again. 'One in each cheek.'

'Why did you want apple cheeks?'

'I didn't want apple cheeks,' Orr said. 'I wanted big cheeks. I didn't care about the color so much, but I wanted them big. I worked at it just like one of those crazy guys you read about who go around squeezing rubber balls all day long just to strengthen their hands. In fact, I *was* one of those crazy guys. I used to walk around all day with rubber balls in my hands, too.'

'Why?'

'Why what?'

'Why did you walk around all day with rubber balls in your hands?'

'Because rubber balls –' said Orr.

'– are better than crab apples?'

Orr sniggered as he shook his head. 'I did it to protect my good reputation in case anyone ever caught me walking around with crab apples in my cheeks. With rubber balls in my hands I could deny there were crab apples in my cheeks. Every time someone asked me why I was walking around with crab apples in my cheeks, I'd just open my hands and show them it was rubber balls I was walking around with, not crab apples, and that they were in my hands, not my cheeks. It was a good story. But I never knew if it got across or not, since it's pretty tough to make people understand you when you're talking to them with two crab apples in your cheeks.'

Yossarian found it pretty tough to understand him then, and he wondered once again if Orr wasn't talking to him with the tip of his tongue in one of his apple cheeks.

Yossarian decided not to utter another word. It would be futile. He knew Orr, and he knew there was not a chance in hell of finding out from him then why he had wanted big cheeks. It would do no more good to ask than it had done to ask him why that whore had kept beating him over the head with her shoe that morning in Rome in the cramped vestibule outside the open door of Nately's whore's kid sister's room. She was a tall, strapping girl with long hair and incandescent blue veins converging populously beneath her cocoa-colored skin where the flesh was most tender, and she kept cursing and shrieking and jumping high up into the air on her bare feet to keep right on hitting him on the top of his head with the spiked heel of her shoe. They were both naked, and raising a rumpus that brought everyone in the apartment into the hall to watch, each couple in a bed-room doorway, all of them naked except the aproned and sweatered old woman, who clucked reprovingly, and the lecherous, dissipated old man, who cackled aloud hilariously through the whole episode with a kind of avid and superior glee. The girl shrieked and Orr giggled. Each time she landed with the heel of her shoe, Orr giggled louder, infuriating her still further so that she flew up still higher into the air for another shot at his noodle, her wondrously full breasts soaring all over the place like billowing pennants in a strong wind and her

36

buttocks and strong thighs shim-sham-shimmying this way and that way like some horrifying bonanza. She shrieked and Orr giggled right up to the time she shrieked and knocked him cold with a good solid crack on the temple that made him stop giggling and sent him off to the hospital in a stretcher with a hole in his head that wasn't very deep and a very mild concussion that kept him out of combat only twelve days.

Nobody could find out what had happened, not even the cackling old man and clucking old woman, who were in a position to find out everything that happened in that vast and endless brothel with its multitudinous bedrooms on facing sides of the narrow hallways going off in opposite directions from the spacious sitting room with its shaded windows and single lamp. Every time she met Orr after that, she'd hoist her skirts up over her tight white elastic panties and, jeering coarsely, bulge her firm, round belly out at him, cursing him contemptuously and then roaring with husky laughter as she saw him giggle fearfully and take refuge behind Yossarian. Whatever he had done or tried to do or failed to do behind the closed door of Nately's whore's kid sister's room was still a secret. The girl wouldn't tell Nately's whore or any of the other whores or Nately or Yossarian. Orr might tell, but Yossarian had decided not to utter another word.

'Do you want to know why I wanted big cheeks?' Orr asked.

Yossarian kept his mouth shut.

'Do you remember,' Orr said, 'that time in Rome when that girl who can't stand you kept hitting me over the head with the heel of her shoe? Do you want to know why she was hitting me?'

It was still impossible to imagine what he could have done to make her angry enough to hammer him over the head for fifteen or twenty minutes, yet not angry enough to pick him up by the ankles and dash his brains out. She was certainly tall enough, and Orr was certainly short enough. Orr had buck teeth and bulging eyes to go with his big cheeks and was even smaller than young Huple, who lived on the wrong side of the railroad tracks in the tent in the administration area in which Hungry Joe lay screaming in his sleep every night.

The administration area in which Hungry Joe had pitched his tent by mistake lay in the center of the squadron between the ditch, with its rusted railroad tracks, and the tilted black bituminous road. The men could pick up girls along that road if they promised to take them where they wanted to go, buxom, young, homely, grinning girls with missing teeth whom they could drive off the road and lie down in the wild grass with, and Yossarian did whenever he could, which was not nearly as often as Hungry Joe, who could get a jeep but couldn't drive, begged him to try. The tents of the enlisted men in the squadron stood on the other side of the road alongside the open-air movie theater in which, for the daily amusement of the dying, ignorant armies clashed by night on a collapsible screen, and to which another U.S.O. troupe came that same afternoon.

The U.S.O. troupes were sent by General P. P. Peckem, who had moved his headquarters up to Rome and had nothing better to do while he schemed against General Dreedle. General Peckem was a general with whom neatness definitely counted. He was a spry, suave and very precise general who knew the circumference of the equator and always wrote 'enhanced' when he meant 'increased.' He was a prick, and no one knew this better than General Dreedle, who was incensed by General Peckem's recent directive requiring all tents in the Mediterranean theater of operations to be pitched along parallel lines with entrances facing back proudly toward the Washington Monument. To General Dreedle, who ran a fighting outfit, it seemed a lot of crap. Furthermore, it was none of General Peckem's goddam business how the tents in General Dreedle's wing were pitched. There then followed a hectic jurisdictional dispute between these overlords that was decided in General Dreedle's favor by ex-P.F.C. Wintergreen, mail clerk at Twenty-seventh Air Force Headquarters. Wintergreen determined the outcome by throwing all communications from General Peckem into the waste-basket. He found them too prolix. General Dreedle's views, expressed in less pretentious literary style, pleased ex-P.F.C. Wintergreen and were sped along by him in zealous observance of regulations. General Dreedle was victorious by default.

To regain whatever status he had lost, General Peckem began sending out more U.S.O. troupes than he had ever sent out before and assigned to Colonel Cargill himself the responsibility of generating enough enthusiasm for them.

But there was no enthusiasm in Yossarian's group. In Yossarian's group there was only a mounting number of enlisted men and officers who found their way solemnly to Sergeant Towser several times a day to ask if the orders sending them home had come in. They were men who had finished their fifty missions. There were more of them now than when Yossarian had gone into the hospital, and they were still waiting. They worried and bit their nails. They were grotesque, like useless young men in a depression. They moved sideways, like crabs. They were waiting for the orders sending them home to safety to return from Twenty-seventh Air Force Headquarters in Italy, and while they waited they had nothing to do but worry and bite their nails and find their way solemnly to Sergeant Towser several times a day to ask if the order sending them home to safety had come.

They were in a race and knew it, because they knew from bitter experience that Colonel Cathcart might raise the number of missions again at any time. They had nothing better to do than wait. Only Hungry Joe had something better to do each time he finished his missions. He had screaming nightmares and won fist fights with Huple's cat. He took his camera to the front row of every U.S.O. show and tried to shoot pictures up the skirt of the yellowheaded singer with two big ones in a sequined dress that always seemed ready to burst. The pictures never came out.

Colonel Cargill, General Peckem's troubleshooter, was a forceful, ruddy man. Before the war he had been an alert, hard-hitting, aggressive marketing executive. He was a very bad marketing executive. Colonel Cargill was so awful a marketing executive that his services were much sought after by firms eager to establish losses for tax purposes. Throughout the civilized world, from Battery Park to Fulton Street, he was known as a dependable man for a fast tax write-off. His prices were high, for failure often did not come easily. He had to start at the top and work his way down, and with sympathetic friends in Washington, losing money was no simple matter. It took months of hard work and careful misplanning. A person misplaced, disorganized, miscalculated, overlooked everything and opened every loophole, and just when he thought he had it made, the government gave him a lake or a forest or an oilfield and spoiled everything. Even with such handicaps, Colonel Cargill could be relied on to run the most prosperous enterprise into the ground. He was a self-made man who owed his lack of success to nobody.

'Men,' Colonel Cargill began in Yossarian's squadron, measuring his pauses carefully. 'You're American officers. The officers of no other army in the world can make that statement. Think about it.'

Sergeant Knight thought about it and then politely informed Colonel Cargill that he was addressing the enlisted men and that the officers were to be found waiting for him on the other side of the squadron. Colonel Cargill thanked him crisply and glowed with self-satisfaction as he strode across the area. It made him proud to observe that twenty-nine months in the service had not blunted his genius for ineptitude.

'Men,' he began his address to the officers, measuring his pauses carefully. 'You're American officers. The officers of no other army in the world can make that statement. Think about it.' He waited a moment to permit them to think about it. 'These people are your guests!' he shouted suddenly. 'They've traveled over

40

three thousand miles to entertain you. How are they going to feel if nobody wants to go out and watch them? What's going to happen to their morale? Now, men, it's no skin off my behind. But that girl that wants to play the accordion for you today is old enough to be a mother. How would you feel if your own mother traveled over three thousand miles to play the accordion for some troops that didn't want to watch her? How is that kid whose mother that accordion player is old enough to be going to feel when he grows up and learns about it? We all know the answer to that one. Now, men, don't misunderstand me. This is all voluntary, of course. I'd be the last colonel in the world to order you to go to that U.S.O. show and have a good time, but I want every one of you who isn't sick enough to be in a hospital to go to that U.S.O. show right now and have a good time, and *that's an order!*'

Yossarian did feel almost sick enough to go back into the hospital, and he felt even sicker three combat missions later when Doc Daneeka still shook his melancholy head and refused to ground him.

'You think you've got troubles?' Doc Daneeka rebuked him grievingly. 'What about me? I lived on peanuts for eight years while I learned how to be a doctor. After the peanuts, I lived on chicken feed in my own office until I could build up a practice decent enough to even pay expenses. Then, just as the shop was finally starting to show a profit, they drafted me. I don't know what you're complaining about.'

Doc Daneeka was Yossarian's friend and would do just about nothing in his power to help him. Yossarian listened very carefully as Doc Daneeka told him about Colonel Cathcart at Group, who wanted to be a general, about General Dreedle at Wing and General Dreedle's nurse, and about all the other generals at Twenty-seventh Air Force Headquarters, who insisted on only forty missions as a completed tour of duty.

'Why don't you just smile and make the best of it?' he advised Yossarian glumly. 'Be like Havermeyer.'

Yossarian shuddered at the suggestion. Havermeyer was a lead bombardier who never took evasive action going in to the target and thereby increased the danger of all the men who flew in the same formation with him.

'Havermeyer, why the hell don't you ever take evasive action?' they would demand in a rage after the mission.

'Hey, you men leave Captain Havermeyer alone,' Colonel Cathcart would order. 'He's the best damned bombardier we've got.'

Havermeyer grinned and nodded and tried to explain how he dumdummed the bullets with a hunting knife before he fired them at the field mice in his tent every night. Havermeyer *was* the best damned bombardier they had, but he flew straight and level all the way from the I.P. to the target, and even far beyond the target until he saw the falling bombs strike ground and explode in a darting spurt of abrupt orange that flashed beneath the swirling pall of smoke and pulverized debris geysering up wildly in huge, rolling waves of gray and black. Havermeyer held mortal men rigid in six planes as steady and still as sitting ducks while he followed the bombs all the way down through the plexiglass nose with deep interest and gave the German gunners below all the time they needed to set their sights and take their aim and pull their triggers or lanyards or switches or whatever the hell they did pull when *they* wanted to kill people they didn't know.

Havermeyer was a lead bombardier who never missed. Yossarian was a lead bombardier who had been demoted because he no longer gave a damn whether he missed or not. He had decided to live forever or die in the attempt, and his only mission each time he went up was to come down alive.

The men had loved flying behind Yossarian, who used to come barreling in over the target from all directions and every height, climbing and diving and twisting and turning so steeply and sharply that it was all the pilots of the other five planes could do to stay in formation with him, leveling out only for the two or three seconds it took for the bombs to drop and then zooming off again with an aching howl of engines, and wrenching his flight through the air so violently as he wove his way through the filthy barrages of flak that the six planes were soon flung out all over the sky like prayers, each one a push-over for the German fighters, which was just fine with Yossarian, for there were no German fighters any more and he did not want any exploding planes near his when they exploded. Only when all the *Sturm und Drang* had been left far behind would he tip his flak helmet back wearily on his sweating head and stop barking directions to McWatt at the controls, who had nothing better to wonder about at a time like that than where the bombs had fallen.

'Bomb bay clear,' Sergeant Knight in the back would announce.

'Did we hit the bridge?' McWatt would ask.

'I couldn't see, sir, I kept getting bounced around back here pretty hard and I couldn't see. Everything's covered with smoke now and I can't see.'

'Hey, Aarfy, did the bombs hit the target?'

'What target?' Captain Aardvaark, Yossarian's plump, pipe-smoking navigator would say from the confusion of maps he had created at Yossarian's side in the nose of the ship. 'I don't think we're at the target yet. Are we?'

'Yossarian, did the bombs hit the target?'

'What bombs?' answered Yossarian, whose only concern had been the flak.

'Oh, well,' McWatt would sing, 'what the hell.'

Yossarian did not give a damn whether he hit the target or not, just as long as Havermeyer or one of the other lead bombardiers did and they never had to go back. Every now and then someone grew angry enough at Havermeyer to throw a punch at him.

'I said you men leave Captain Havermeyer alone,' Colonel Cathcart warned them all angrily. 'I said he's the best damned bombardier we've got, didn't I?'

Havermeyer grinned at the colonel's intervention and

shoved another piece of peanut brittle inside his face.

Havermeyer had grown very proficient at shooting field mice at night with the gun he had stolen from the dead man in Yossarian's tent. His bait was a bar of candy and he would presight in the darkness as he sat waiting for the nibble with a finger of his other hand inside a loop of the line he had run from the frame of his mosquito net to the chain of the unfrosted light bulb overhead. The line was taut as a banjo string, and the merest tug would snap it on and blind the shivering quarry in a blaze of light. Havermeyer would chortle exultantly as he watched the tiny mammal freeze and roll its terrified eyes about in frantic search of the intruder. Havermeyer would wait until the eyes fell upon his own and then he laughed aloud and pulled the trigger at the same time, showering the rank, furry body all over the tent with a reverberating crash and dispatching its timid soul back to his or her Creator.

Late one night, Havermeyer fired a shot at a mouse that brought Hungry Joe bolting out at him barefoot, ranting at the top of his screechy voice and emptying his own .45 into Havermeyer's tent as he came charging down one side of the ditch and up the other and vanished all at once inside one of the slit trenches that had appeared like magic beside every tent the morning after Milo Minderbinder had bombed the squadron. It was just before dawn during the Great Big Siege of Bologna, when tongueless dead men peopled the night hours like living ghosts and Hungry Joe was half out of his mind because he had finished his missions again and was not scheduled to fly. Hungry Joe was babbling incoherently when they fished him out from the dank bottom of the slit trench, babbling of snakes, rats and spiders. The others flashed their searchlights down just to make sure. There was nothing inside but a few inches of stagnant rain water.

'You see?' cried Havermeyer. 'I told you. I told you he was crazy, didn't I?'

4   Doc Daneeka

Hungry Joe was crazy, and no one knew it better than
Yossarian, who did everything he could to help him.
Hungry Joe just wouldn't listen to Yossarian. Hungry Joe
just wouldn't listen because he thought Yossarian was
crazy.

'Why should he listen to you?' Doc Daneeka inquired
of Yossarian without looking up.

'Because he's got troubles.'

Doc Daneeka snorted scornfully. 'He thinks he's got
troubles? What about me?' Doc Daneeka continued
slowly with a gloomy sneer. 'Oh, I'm not complaining. I
know there's a war on. I know a lot of people are going to
have to suffer for us to win it. But why must I be one of
them? Why don't they draft some of these old doctors
who keep shooting their kissers off in public about what
big sacrifices the medical game stands ready to make? I
don't want to make sacrifices. I want to make dough.'

Doc Daneeka was a very neat, clean man whose idea
of a good time was to sulk. He had a dark complexion
and a small, wise, saturnine face with mournful pouches
under both eyes. He brooded over his health continually
and went almost daily to the medical tent to have his
temperature taken by one of the two enlisted men there

who ran things for him practically on their own, and ran it so efficiently that he was left with little else to do but sit in the sunlight with his stuffed nose and wonder what other people were so worried about. Their names were Gus and Wes and they had succeeded in elevating medicine to an exact science. All men reporting on sick call with temperatures above 102 were rushed to the hospital. All those except Yossarian reporting on sick call with temperatures below 102 had their gums and toes painted with gentian violet solution and were given a laxative to throw away into the bushes. All those reporting on a sick call with temperatures of exactly 102 were asked to return in an hour to have their temperatures taken again. Yossarian, with his temperature of 101, could go to the hospital whenever he wanted to because he was not afraid of them.

The system worked just fine for everybody, especially for Doc Daneeka, who found himself with all the time he needed to watch old Major — de Coverley pitching horseshoes in his private horseshoe-pitching pit, still wearing the transparent eye patch Doc Daneeka had fashioned for him from the strip of celluloid stolen from Major Major's orderly room window months before when Major — de Coverley had returned from Rome with an injured cornea after renting two apartments there for the officers and enlisted men to use on their rest leaves. The only time Doc Daneeka ever went to the medical tent was the time he began to feel he was a very sick man each day and stopped in just to have Gus and Wes look him over. They could never find anything wrong with him. His temperature was always 96.8, which was perfectly all right with them, as long as he didn't mind. Doc Daneeka did mind. He was beginning to lose confidence in Gus and Wes and was thinking of having them both transferred back to the motor pool and replaced by someone who *could* find something wrong.

Doc Daneeka was personally familiar with a number of things that were drastically wrong. In addition to his health, he worried about the Pacific Ocean and flight time. Health was something no one ever could be sure of for a long enough time. The Pacific Ocean was a body of water surrounded on all sides by elephantiasis and other dread diseases to which, if he ever displeased Colonel Cathcart by grounding Yossarian, he might suddenly find himself transferred. And flight time was the time he had to spend in airplane flight each month in order to get his flight pay. Doc Daneeka hated to fly. He felt imprisoned in an airplane. In an airplane there was absolutely no place in the world to go except to another part of the airplane. Doc Daneeka had been told that people who enjoyed climbing into an airplane were really giving vent to a subconscious desire to climb back into the womb. He had been told this by Yossarian, who made it possible for Dan Daneeka to collect his flight pay each month without ever climbing back into the womb. Yossarian would persuade McWatt to enter Doc Daneeka's name on his flight log for training missions or trips to Rome.

'You know how it is,' Doc Daneeka had wheedled, with a sly, conspiratorial wink. 'Why take chances when I don't have to?'

'Sure,' Yossarian agreed.

'What difference does it make to anyone if I'm in the plane or not?'

'No difference.'

'Sure, that's what I mean,' Doc Daneeka said. 'A little grease is what makes this world go round. One hand washes the other. Know what I mean? You scratch my back, I'll scratch yours.'

Yossarian knew what he meant.

'That's not what I meant,' Doc Daneeka said, as Yossarian began scratching his back. 'I'm talking about co-operation. Favors. You do a favor for me, I'll do one for you. Get it?'

'Do one for me,' Yossarian requested.

'Not a chance,' Doc Daneeka answered.

There was something fearful and minute about Doc Daneeka as he sat despondently outside his tent in the sunlight as often as he could, dressed in khaki summer trousers and a short-sleeved summer shirt that was bleached almost to an antiseptic gray by the daily laundering to which he had it subjected. He was like a man who had grown frozen with horror once and had never come completely unthawed. He sat all tucked up into himself, his slender shoulders huddled halfway around his head, his suntanned hands with their luminous silver fingernails massaging the backs of his bare, folded arms gently as though he were cold. Actually, he was a very warm, compassionate man who never stopped feeling sorry for himself.

'Why me?' was his constant lament, and the question was a good one.

Yossarian knew it was a good one because Yossarian was a collector of good questions and had used them to disrupt the educational sessions Clevinger had once conducted two nights a week in Captain Black's intelligence tent with the corporal in eyeglasses who everybody knew was probably a subversive. Captain Black knew he was a subversive because he wore eyeglasses and used words like *panacea* and *utopia*, and because he disapproved of Adolf Hitler, who had done such a great job of combating un-American activities in Germany. Yossarian attended the educational sessions because he wanted to find out why so many people were working so hard to kill him. A handful of other men were also interested, and the questions were many and good when Clevinger and the subversive corporal finished and made the mistake of asking if there were any.

'Who is Spain?'

'Why is Hitler?'

'When is right?'

'Where was that stooped and mealy-colored old man I used to call Poppa when the merry-go-round broke down?'

'How was trump at Munich?'

'Ho-ho beriberi.'

and

'Balls!'

all rang out in rapid succession, and then there was Yossarian with the question that had no answer:

'Where are the Snowdens of yesteryear?'

The question upset them, because Snowden had been killed over Avignon when Dobbs went crazy in mid-air and seized the controls away from Huple.

The corporal played it dumb. 'What?' he asked.

'Where are the Snowdens of yesteryear?'

'I'm afraid I don't understand.'

'*Où sont les Neigedens d'antan?*' Yossarian said to make it easier for him.

'*Parlez en anglais*, for Christ's sake,' said the corporal. '*Je ne parle pas français*.'

'Neither do I,' answered Yossarian, who was ready to pursue him through all the words in the world to wring the knowledge from him if he could, but Clevinger intervened, pale, thin, and laboring for breath, a humid coating of tears already glistening in his under-nourished eyes.

Group Headquarters was alarmed, for there was no telling what people might find out once they felt free to ask whatever questions they wanted to. Colonel Cathcart sent Colonel Korn to stop it, and Colonel Korn succeeded with a rule governing the asking of questions. Colonel Korn's rule was a stroke of genius, Colonel Korn explained in his report to Colonel Cathcart. Under Colonel Korn's rule, the only people permitted to ask questions were those who never did. Soon the only people attending were those who never asked questions, and the sessions were discontinued altogether, since Clevinger, the corporal and Colonel Korn agreed that it was neither possible nor necessary to educate people who never questioned anything.

Colonel Cathcart and Lieutenant Colonel Korn lived and worked in the Group Headquarters building, as did all the members of the headquarters staff, with the exception of the chaplain. The Group Headquarters building was an enormous, windy, antiquated structure

49

built of powdery red stone and banging plumbing. Behind the building was the modern skeet-shooting range that had been constructed by Colonel Cathcart for the exclusive recreation of the officers at Group and at which every officer and enlisted man on combat status now, thanks to General Dreedle, had to spend a minimum of eight hours a month.

Yossarian shot skeet, but never hit any. Appleby shot skeet and never missed. Yossarian was as bad at shooting skeet as he was at gambling. He could never win money gambling either. Even when he cheated he couldn't win, because the people he cheated against were always better at cheating too. These were two disappointments to which he had resigned himself: he would never be a skeet shooter, and he would never make money.

'It takes brains not to make money,' Colonel Cargill wrote in one of the homiletic memoranda he regularly prepared for circulation over General Peckem's signature. 'Any fool can make money these days and most of them do. But what about people with talent and brains? Name, for example, one poet who makes money.'

'T. S. Eliot,' ex-P.F.C. Wintergreen said in his mail-sorting cubicle at Twenty-seventh Air Force Headquarters, and slammed down the telephone without identifying himself.

Colonel Cargill, in Rome was perplexed.

'Who was it?' asked General Peckem.

'I don't know,' Colonel Cargill replied.

'What did he want?'

'I don't know.'

'Well, what did he say?'

' "T. S. Eliot," ' Colonel Cargill informed him.

'What's that?'

' "T. S. Eliot," ' Colonel Cargill repeated.

'Just "T. S. –" '

'Yes, sir. That's all he said. Just "T. S. Eliot." '

'I wonder what it means,' General Peckem reflected. Colonel Cargill wondered, too.

'T. S. Eliot,' General Peckem mused.

50

'T. S. Eliot,' Colonel Cargill echoed with the same funereal puzzlement.

General Peckem roused himself after a moment with an unctuous and benignant smile. His expression was shrewd and sophisticated. His eyes gleamed maliciously. 'Have someone get me General Dreedle,' he requested Colonel Cargill. 'Don't let him know who's calling.'

Colonel Cargill handed him the phone.

'T. S. Eliot,' General Peckem said, and hung up.

'Who was it?' asked Colonel Moodus.

General Dreedle, in Corsica, did not reply. Colonel Moodus was General Dreedle's son-in-law, and General Dreedle, at the insistence of his wife and against his own better judgment, had taken him into the military business. General Dreedle gazed at Colonel Moodus with level hatred. He detested the very sight of his son-in-law, who was his aide and therefore in constant attendance upon him. He had opposed his daughter's marriage to Colonel Moodus because he disliked attending weddings. Wearing a menacing and pre-occupied scowl, General Dreedle moved to the full-length mirror in his office and stared at his stocky reflection. He had a grizzled, broad-browed head with iron-gray tufts over his eyes and a blunt and belligerent jaw. He brooded in ponderous speculation over the cryptic message he had just received. Slowly his face softened with an idea, and he curled his lips with wicked pleasure.

'Get Peckem,' he told Colonel Moodus. 'Don't let the bastard know who's calling.'

'Who was it?' asked Colonel Cargill, back in Rome.

'That same person,' General Peckem replied with a definite trace of alarm. 'Now he's after me.'

'What did he want?'

'I don't know.'

'What did he say?'

'The same thing.'

' "T. S. Eliot"?'

'Yes, "T. S. Eliot." That's all he said.' General Peckem had a hopeful thought. 'Perhaps it's a new code or something, like the colors of the day. Why don't you have someone check with Communications and see if it's a new code or something or the colors of the day?'

Communications answered that T. S. Eliot was not a new code or the colors of the day.

Colonel Cargill had the next idea. 'Maybe I ought to phone Twenty-seventh Air Force Headquarters and see if they know anything about it. They have a clerk up there named Wintergreen I'm pretty close to. He's the one who tipped me off that our prose was too prolix.'

Ex-P.F.C. Wintergreen told Cargill that there was no record at Twenty-seventh Air Force Headquarters of a T. S. Eliot.

'How's our prose these days?' Colonel Cargill decided to inquire while he had ex-P.F.C. Wintergreen on the phone. 'It's much better now, isn't it?'

'It's still too prolix,' ex-P.F.C. Wintergreen replied.

'It wouldn't surprise me if General Dreedle were behind the whole thing,' General Peckem confessed at last. 'Remember what he did to that skeet-shooting range?'

General Dreedle had thrown open Colonel Cathcart's private skeet-shooting range to every officer and enlisted man in the group on combat duty. General Dreedle wanted his men to spend as much time out on the skeet-shooting range as the facilities and their flight schedule would allow. Shooting skeet eight hours a month was excellent training for them. It trained them to shoot skeet.

Dunbar loved shooting skeet because he hated every minute of it and the time passed so slowly. He had figured out that a single hour on the skeet-shooting range with people like Havermeyer and Appleby could be worth as much as eleven-times-seventeen years.

'I think you're crazy,' was the way Clevinger had responded to Dunbar's discovery.

'Who wants to know?' Dunbar answered.

'I mean it,' Clevinger insisted.

'Who cares?' Dunbar answered.

'I really do. I'll even go so far as to concede that life seems longer i –'

'– is longer i –'

'– is longer – Is longer? All right, is longer if it's filled with periods of boredom and discomfort, b –'

'Guess how fast?' Dunbar said suddenly.

'Huh?'

'They go,' Dunbar explained.

'Who?'

'Years.'

'Years.'

'Years,' said Dunbar. 'Years, years, years.'

'Clevinger, why don't you let Dunbar alone?' Yossarian broke in. 'Don't you realize the toll this is taking?'

'It's all right,' said Dunbar magnanimously. 'I have some decades to spare. Do you know how long a year takes when it's going away?'

'And you shut up also,' Yossarian told Orr, who had begun to snigger.

'I was just thinking about that girl,' Orr said. 'That girl in Sicily. That girl in Sicily with the bald head.'

'You'd *better* shut up also,' Yossarian warned him.

'It's your fault,' Dunbar said to Yossarian. 'Why don't you let him snigger if he wants to? It's better than having him talking.'

'All right. Go ahead and snigger if you want to.'

'Do you know how long a year takes when it's going away?' Dunbar repeated to Clevinger. 'This long.' He snapped his fingers. 'A second ago you were stepping into college with your lungs full of fresh air. Today you're an old man.'

'Old?' asked Clevinger with surprise. 'What are you talking about?'

'Old.'

'I'm not old.'

'You're inches away from death every time you go on a mission. How much older can you be at your age? A half minute before that you were stepping into high school, and an unhooked brassiere was as close as you ever hoped to get to Paradise. Only a fifth of a second before that you were a small kid with a ten-week summer vacation that lasted a hundred thousand years and still ended too soon. Zip! They go rocketing by so fast. How the hell else are you ever going to slow time down?' Dunbar was almost angry when he finished.

'Well, maybe it is true,' Clevinger conceded unwillingly in a subdued tone. 'Maybe a long life does have to be filled with many unpleasant conditions if it's to seem long. But in that event, who wants one?'

'I do,' Dunbar told him.

'Why?' Clevinger asked.

'What else is there?'

5   Chief White Halfoat

Doc Daneeka lived in a splotched gray tent with Chief White Halfoat, whom he feared and despised.

'I can just picture his liver,' Doc Daneeka grumbled.

'Picture my liver,' Yossarian advised him.

'There's nothing wrong with your liver.'

'That shows how much you don't know,' Yossarian bluffed, and told Doc Daneeka about the troublesome pain in his liver that had troubled Nurse Duckett and Nurse Cramer and all the doctors in the hospital because it wouldn't become jaundice and wouldn't go away.

Doc Daneeka wasn't interested. 'You think you've got troubles?' he wanted to know. 'What about me? You should've been in my office the day those newlyweds walked in.'

'What newlyweds?'

'Those newlyweds that walked into my office one day. Didn't I ever tell you about them? She was lovely.'

So was Doc Daneeka's office. He had decorated his waiting room with goldfish and one of the finest suites of cheap furniture. Whatever he could he bought on credit, even the goldfish. For the rest, he obtained money from greedy relatives in exchange for shares of the profits.

His office was in Staten Island in a two-family firetrap just four blocks away from the ferry stop and only one block south of a supermarket, three beauty parlors, and two corrupt druggists. It was a corner location, but nothing helped. Population turnover was small, and people clung through habit to the same physicians they had been doing business with for years. Bills piled up rapidly, and he was soon faced with the loss of his most precious medical instruments: his adding machine was repossessed, and then his typewriter. The goldfish died. Fortunately, just when things were blackest, the war broke out.

'It was a godsend,' Doc Daneeka confessed solemnly. 'Most of the other doctors were soon in the service, and things picked up overnight. The corner location really started paying off, and I soon found myself handling more patients than I could handle competently. I upped my kickback fee with those two drugstores. The beauty parlors were good for two, three abortions a week. Things couldn't have been better, and then look what happened. They had to send a guy from the draft board around to look me over. I was Four-F. I had examined myself pretty thoroughly and discovered that I was unfit for military service. You'd think my word would be enough, wouldn't you, since I was a doctor in good standing with my county medical society and with my local Better Business Bureau. But no, it wasn't, and they sent this guy around just to make sure I really did have one leg amputated at the hip and was helplessly bedridden with incurable rheumatoid arthritis. Yossarian, we live in an age of distrust and deteriorating spiritual values. It's a terrible thing,' Doc Daneeka protested in a voice quavering with strong emotion. 'It's a terrible thing when even the word of a licensed physician is suspected by the country he loves.'

Doc Daneeka had been drafted and shipped to Pianosa as a flight surgeon, even though he was terrified of flying.

'I don't have to go looking for trouble in an airplane,'

he noted, blinking his beady, brown, offended eyes myopically. 'It comes looking for me. Like that virgin I'm telling you about that couldn't have a baby.'

'What virgin?' Yossarian asked. 'I thought you were telling me about some newlyweds.'

'That's the virgin I'm telling you about. They were just a couple of young kids, and they'd been married, oh, a little over a year when they came walking into my office without an appointment. You should have seen her. She was so sweet and young and pretty. She even blushed when I asked about her periods. I don't think I'll ever stop loving that girl. She was built like a dream and wore a chain around her neck with a medal of Saint Anthony hanging down inside the most beautiful bosom I never saw. "It must be a terrible temptation for Saint Anthony," I joked – just to put her at ease, you know. "Saint Anthony?" her husband said. "Who's Saint Anthony?" "Ask your wife," I told him. "She can tell you who Saint Anthony is." "Who is Saint Anthony?" he asked her. "Who?" she wanted to know. "Saint Anthony," he told her. "Saint Anthony?" she said. "Who's Saint Anthony?" When I got a good look at her inside my examination room I found she was still a virgin. I spoke to her husband alone while she was pulling her girdle back on and hooking it onto her stockings. "Every night," he boasted. A real wise guy, you know. "I never miss a night," he boasted. He meant it, too. "I even been puttin' it to her mornings before the breakfasts she makes me before we go to work," he boasted. There was only one explanation. When I had them both together again I gave them a demonstration of intercourse with the rubber models I've got in my office. I've got these rubber models in my office with all the reproductive organs of both sexes that I keep locked up in separate cabinets to avoid a scandal. I mean I used to have them. I don't have anything any more, not even a practice. The only thing I have now is this low temperature that I'm really starting to worry about. Those two kids I've got working for me in the medical tent aren't worth a damn as diagnosticians. All they know how to do is complain. They think they've got troubles? What about me? They should have been in my office that day with those two newlyweds looking at me as though I were telling them something nobody'd ever heard of before. You never saw anybody so interested. "You mean like this?" he asked me, and worked the models for himself awhile. You know, I can see where a certain type of person might get a big kick out of doing just that. "That's it," I told him. "Now, you go home and try it my way for a few months and see what happens. Okay?" "Okay," they said, and paid me in cash without any argument. "Have a good time," I told them, and they thanked me and walked out together. He had his arm around her waist as though he couldn't wait to get her home and put it to her again. A few days later he came back all by himself and told my nurse he had to see me right away. As soon as we were alone, he punched me in the nose.'

'He did what?'

'He called me a wise guy and punched me in the nose. "What are you, a wise guy?" he said, and knocked me flat on my ass. Pow! Just like that. I'm not kidding.'

'I know you're not kidding,' Yossarian said. 'But why did he do it?'

'How should I know why he did it?' Doc Daneeka retorted with annoyance.

'Maybe it had something to do with Saint Anthony?'

Doc Daneeka looked at Yossarian blankly. 'Saint Anthony?' he asked with astonishment. 'Who's Saint Anthony?'

'How should I know?' answered Chief White Halfoat, staggering inside the tent just then with a bottle of whiskey cradled in his arm and sitting himself down pugnaciously between the two of them.

Doc Daneeka rose without a word and moved his chair outside the tent, his back bowed by the compact kit of injustices that was his perpetual burden. He could not bear the company of his room-mate.

Chief White Halfoat thought he was crazy. 'I don't

know what's the matter with that guy,' he observed reproachfully. 'He's got no brains, that's what's the matter with him. If he had any brains he'd grab a shovel and start digging. Right here in the tent, he'd start digging, right under my cot. He'd strike oil in no time. Don't he know how that enlisted man struck oil with a shovel back in the States? Didn't he ever hear what happened to that kid – what was the name of that rotten rat bastard pimp of a snotnose back in Colorado?'

'Wintergreen.'

'Wintergreen.'

'He's afraid,' Yossarian explained.

'Oh, no. Not Wintergreen.' Chief White Halfoat shook his head with undisguised admiration. 'That stinking little punk wise-guy son of a bitch ain't afraid of nobody.'

'Doc Daneeka's afraid. That's what's the matter with him.'

'What's he afraid of?'

'He's afraid of you,' Yossarian said. 'He's afraid you're going to die of pneumonia.'

'He'd *better* be afraid,' Chief White Halfoat said. A deep, low laugh rumbled through his massive chest. 'I will, too, the first chance I get. You just wait and see.'

Chief White Halfoat was a handsome, swarthy Indian from Oklahoma with a heavy, hard-boned face and tousled black hair, a half-blooded Creek from Enid who, for occult reasons of his own, had made up his mind to die of pneumonia. He was a glowering, vengeful, disillusioned Indian who hated foreigners with names like Cathcart, Korn, Black and Havermeyer and wished they'd all go back to where their lousy ancestors had come from.

'You wouldn't believe it, Yossarian,' he ruminated, raising his voice deliberately to bait Doc Daneeka, 'but this used to be a pretty good country to live in before they loused it up with their goddam piety.'

Chief White Halfoat was out to revenge himself upon the white man. He could barely read or write and had been assigned to Captain Black as assistant intelligence officer.

'How could I learn to read or write?' Chief White Halfoat demanded with simulated belligerence, raising his voice again so that Doc Daneeka would hear. 'Every place we pitched our tent, they sank an oil well. Every time they sank a well, they hit oil. And every time they hit oil, they made us pack up our tent and go someplace else. We were human divining rods. Our whole family had a natural affinity for petroleum deposits, and soon every oil company in the world had technicians chasing us around. We were always on the move. It was one hell of a way to bring a child up, I can tell you. I don't think I ever spent more than a week in one place.'

His earliest memory was of a geologist.

'Every time another White Halfoat was born,' he continued, 'the stock market turned bullish. Soon whole drilling crews were following us around with all their equipment just to get the jump on each other. Companies began to merge just so they could cut down on the number of people they had to assign to us. But the crowd in back of us kept growing. We never got a good night's sleep. When we stopped, they stopped. When we moved, they moved, chuckwagons, bulldozers, derricks, generators. We were a walking business boom, and we began to receive invitations from some of the best hotels just for the amount of business we would drag into town with us. Some of those invitations were mighty generous, but we couldn't accept any because we were Indians and all the best hotels that were inviting us wouldn't accept Indians as guests. Racial prejudice is a terrible thing, Yossarian. It really is. It's a terrible thing to treat a decent, loyal Indian like a nigger, kike, wop or spic.' Chief White Halfoat nodded slowly with conviction.

'Then, Yossarian, it finally happened – the beginning of the end. They began to follow us around from in front. They would try to guess where we were going to stop next and would begin drilling before we even got there, so we couldn't stop. As soon as we'd begin to unroll our blankets, they would kick us off. They had confidence in us. They wouldn't even wait to strike oil before they kicked us off. We were so tired we almost didn't care the day our time ran out. One morning we found ourselves completely surrounded by oilmen waiting for us to come their way so they could kick us off. Everywhere you looked there was an oilman on a ridge, waiting there like Indians getting ready to attack. It was the end. We couldn't stay where we were because we had just been kicked off. And there was no place left for us to go. Only the Army saved me. Luckily, the war broke out just in the nick of time, and a draft board picked me right up out of the middle and put me down safely in Lowery Field, Colorado. I was the only survivor.'

Yossarian knew he was lying, but did not interrupt as Chief White Halfoat went on to claim that he had never heard from his parents again. That didn't bother him too much, though, for he had only their word for it that they were his parents, and since they had lied to him about so many other things, they could just as well have been lying to him about that too. He was much better acquainted with the fate of a tribe of first cousins who had wandered away north in a diversionary movement and pushed inadvertently into Canada. When they tried to return, they were stopped at the border by American immigration authorities who would not let them back into the country. They could not come back in because they were red.

It was a horrible joke, but Doc Daneeka didn't laugh until Yossarian came to him one mission later and pleaded again, without any real expectation of success, to be grounded. Doc Daneeka snickered once and was soon immersed in problems of his own, which included Chief White Halfoat, who had been challenging him all that morning to Indian wrestle, and Yossarian, who decided right then and there to go crazy.

'You're wasting your time,' Doc Daneeka was forced to tell him.

'Can't you ground someone who's crazy?'

'Oh, sure. I have to. There's a rule saying I have to ground anyone who's crazy.'

'Then why don't you ground me? I'm crazy. Ask Clevinger.'

'Clevinger? Where is Clevinger? You find Clevinger and I'll ask him.'

'Then ask any of the others. They'll tell you how crazy I am.'

'They're crazy.'

'Then why don't you ground them?'

'Why don't they ask me to ground them?'

'Because they're crazy, that's why.'

'Of course they're crazy,' Doc Daneeka replied. 'I just told you they're crazy, didn't I? And you can't let crazy people decide whether you're crazy or not, can you?'

Yossarian looked at him soberly and tried another approach. 'Is Orr crazy?'

'He sure is,' Doc Daneeka said.

'Can you ground him?'

'I sure can. But first he has to ask me to. That's part of the rule.'

'Then why doesn't he ask you to?'

'Because he's crazy,' Doc Daneeka said. 'He has to be crazy to keep flying combat missions after all the close calls he's had. Sure, I can ground Orr. But first he has to ask me to.'

'That's all he has to do to be grounded?'

'That's all. Let him ask me.'

'And then you can ground him?' Yossarian asked.

'No. Then I can't ground him.'

'You mean there's a catch?'

'Sure there's a catch,' Doc Daneeka replied. 'Catch-22. Anyone who wants to get out of combat duty isn't really crazy.'

There was only one catch and that was Catch-22, which specified that a concern for one's own safety in the face of dangers that were real and immediate was the process of a rational mind. Orr was crazy and could be grounded. All he had to do was ask; and as soon as he did, he would no longer be crazy and would have to fly more missions. Orr would be crazy to fly more missions and sane if he didn't, but if he was sane he had to fly them. If he flew them he was crazy and didn't have to; but if he didn't want to he was sane and had to. Yossarian was moved very deeply by the absolute simplicity of this clause of Catch-22 and let out a respectful whistle.

'That's some catch, that Catch-22,' he observed.

'It's the best there is,' Doc Daneeka agreed.

Yossarian saw it clearly in all its spinning reasonableness. There was an elliptical precision about its perfect pairs of parts that was graceful and shocking, like good modern art, and at times Yossarian wasn't quite sure that he saw it at all, just the way he was never quite sure about good modern art or about the flies Orr saw in Appleby's eyes. He had Orr's word to take for the flies in Appleby's eyes.

'Oh, they're there, all right,' Orr had assured him about the flies in Appleby's eyes after Yossarian's fist fight with Appleby in the officers' club, 'although he probably doesn't even know it. That's why he can't see things as they really are.'

'How come he doesn't know it?' inquired Yossarian.

'Because he's got flies in his eyes,' Orr explained with exaggerated patience. 'How can he see he's got flies in his eyes if he's got flies in his eyes?'

It made as much sense as anything else, and Yossarian was willing to give Orr the benefit of the doubt because Orr was from the wilderness outside New York City and knew so much more about wildlife than Yossarian did, and because Orr, unlike Yossarian's mother, father, sister, brother, aunt, uncle, in-law, teacher, spiritual leader, legislator, neighbor and newspaper, had never lied to him about anything crucial before. Yossarian had mulled his newfound knowledge about Appleby over in private for a day or two and then decided, as a good deed, to pass the word along to Appleby himself.

'Appleby, you've got flies in your eyes,' he whispered helpfully as they passed by each other in the doorway of the parachute tent on the day of the weekly milk run to Parma.

'What?' Appleby responded sharply, thrown into confusion by the fact that Yossarian had spoken to him at all.

'You've got flies in your eyes,' Yossarian repeated. 'That's probably why you can't see them.'

Appleby retreated from Yossarian with a look of loathing bewilderment and sulked in silence until he was in the jeep with Havermeyer riding down the long, straight road to the briefing room, where Major Danby, the fidgeting group operations officer, was waiting to conduct the preliminary briefing with all the lead pilots, bombardiers and navigators. Appleby spoke in a soft voice so that he would not be heard by the driver or by Captain Black, who was stretched out with his eyes closed in the front seat of the jeep.

'Havermeyer,' he asked hesitantly. 'Have I got flies in my eyes?'

Havermeyer blinked quizzically. 'Sties?' he asked.

'No, flies,' he was told.

Havermeyer blinked again. 'Flies?'

'In my eyes.'

'You must be crazy,' Havermeyer said.

'No, I'm not crazy. Yossarian's crazy. Just tell me if I've got flies in my eyes or not. Go ahead. I can take it.'

Havermeyer popped another piece of peanut brittle into his mouth and peered very closely into Appleby's eyes.

'I don't see any,' he announced.

Appleby heaved an immense sigh of relief. Havermeyer had tiny bits of peanut brittle adhering to his lips, chin and cheeks.

'You've got peanut brittle crumbs on your face,' Appleby remarked to him.

'I'd rather have peanut brittle crumbs on my face than flies in my eyes,' Havermeyer retorted.

The officers of the other five planes in each flight arrived in trucks for the general briefing that took place thirty minutes later. The three enlisted men in each crew were not briefed at all, but were carried directly out on the airfield to the separate planes in which they were scheduled to fly that day, where they waited around with the ground crew until the officers with whom they had been scheduled to fly swung off the rattling tailgates of the trucks delivering them and it was time to climb aboard and start up. Engines rolled over disgruntedly on lollipop-shaped hardstands, resisting first, then idling smoothly awhile, and then the planes lumbered around and nosed forward lamely over the pebbled ground like sightless, stupid, crippled things until they taxied into the line at the foot of the landing strip and took off swiftly, one behind the other, in a zooming, rising roar, banking slowly into formation over mottled treetops, and circling the field at even speed until all the flights of six had been formed and then setting course over cerulean water on the first leg of the journey to the target in northern Italy or France. The planes gained altitude steadily and were above nine thousand feet by the time they crossed into enemy territory. One of the surprising things always was the sense of calm and utter silence, broken only by the test rounds fired from the machine guns, by an occasional toneless, terse remark over the intercom, and, at last, by the sobering pronouncement of the bombardier in each plane that they were at the I.P. and about to turn toward the target. There was always sunshine, always a tiny sticking in the throat from the rarefied air.

The B-25s they flew in were stable, dependable, dull-green ships with twin rudders and engines and wide wings. Their single fault, from where Yossarian sat as a bombardier, was the tight crawlway separating the bombardier's compartment in the plexiglass nose from the nearest escape hatch. The crawlway was a narrow, square, cold tunnel hollowed out beneath the flight controls, and a large man like Yossarian could squeeze through only with difficulty. A chubby, moon-faced navigator with little reptilian eyes and a pipe like Aarfy's had trouble, too, and Yossarian used to chase him back from the nose as they turned toward the target, now minutes away. There was a time of tension then, a time of waiting with nothing to hear and nothing to see and nothing to do but wait as the antiaircraft guns below took aim and made ready to knock them all sprawling into infinite sleep if they could.

The crawlway was Yossarian's lifeline to outside from a plane about to fall, but Yossarian swore at it with seething antagonism, reviled it as an obstacle put there by providence as part of the plot that would destroy him. There was room for an additional escape hatch right there in the nose of a B-25, but there was no escape hatch. Instead there was the crawlway, and since the mess on the mission over Avignon he had learned to detest every mammoth inch of it, for it slung him seconds and seconds away from his parachute, which was too bulky to be taken up front with him, and seconds and seconds more after that away from the escape hatch on the floor between the rear of the elevated flight deck and the feet of the faceless top turret gunner mounted high above. Yossarian longed to be where Aarfy could be once Yossarian had chased him back from the nose; Yossarian longed to sit on the floor in a huddled ball right on top of the escape hatch inside a sheltering igloo of extra flak suits that he would have been happy to carry along with him, his parachute already hooked to his harness where it belonged, one fist clenching the red-handled rip cord, one fist gripping the emergency hatch release that would spill him earthward into the air at the first dreadful squeal of destruction. That was where he wanted to be if he had to be there at all, instead of hung out there in front like some goddam cantilevered goldfish in some goddam cantilevered goldfish bowl while the goddam foul black tiers of flak were bursting and booming and billowing all around and above and below him in a climbing, cracking, staggered, banging, phantasmagorical, cosmological wickedness that jarred and tossed and shivered, clattered and

66

pierced, and threatened to annihilate them all in one splinter of a second in one vast flash of fire.

Aarfy had been no use to Yossarian as a navigator or as anything else, and Yossarian drove him back from the nose vehemently each time so that they would not clutter up each other's way if they had to scramble suddenly for safety. Once Yossarian had driven him back from the nose, Aarfy was free to cower on the floor where Yossarian longed to cower, but he stood bolt upright instead with his stumpy arms resting comfortably on the backs of the pilot's and co-pilot's seats, pipe in hand, making affable small talk to McWatt and whoever happened to be co-pilot and pointing out amusing trivia in the sky to the two men, who were too busy to be interested. McWatt was too busy responding at the controls to Yossarian's strident instructions as Yossarian slipped the plane in on the bomb run and then whipped them all away violently around the ravenous pillars of exploding shells with curt, shrill, obscene commands to McWatt that were much like the anguished, entreating nightmare yelpings of Hungry Joe in the dark. Aarfy would puff reflectively on his pipe throughout the whole chaotic clash, gazing with unruffled curiosity at the war through McWatt's window as though it were a remote disturbance that could not affect him. Aarfy was a dedicated fraternity man who loved cheerleading and class reunions and did not have brains enough to be afraid. Yossarian did have brains enough and was, and the only thing that stopped him from abandoning his post under fire and scurrying back through the crawlway like a yellow-bellied rat was his unwillingness to entrust the evasive action out of the target area to anybody else. There was nobody else in the world he would honor with so great a responsibility. There was nobody else he knew who was as big a coward. Yossarian was the best man in the group at evasive action, but had no idea why.

There was no established procedure for evasive action. All you needed was fear, and Yossarian had plenty of that, more fear than Orr or Hungry Joe, more fear than Dunbar, who had resigned himself submissively to the idea that he must die someday. Yossarian had not resigned himself to that idea, and he bolted for his life wildly on each mission the instant his bombs were away, hollering, '*Hard, hard, hard, hard, you bastard, hard!*' at McWatt and hating McWatt viciously all the time as though McWatt were to blame for their being up there at all to be rubbed out by strangers, and everybody else in the plane kept off the intercom, except for the pitiful time of the mess on the mission to Avignon when Dobbs went crazy in mid-air and began weeping pathetically for help.

'Help him, help him,' Dobbs sobbed. 'Help him, help him.'

'Help who? Help who?' called back Yossarian, once he had plugged his headset back into the intercom system, after it had been jerked out when Dobbs wrested the controls away from Huple and hurled them all down suddenly into the deafening, paralyzing, horrifying dive which had plastered Yossarian helplessly to the ceiling of the plane by the top of his head and from which Huple had rescued them just in time by seizing the controls back from Dobbs and leveling the ship out almost as suddenly right back in the middle of the buffeting layer of cacophonous flak from which they had escaped successfully only a moment before. *Oh, God! Oh, God, oh, God*, Yossarian had been pleading wordlessly as he dangled from the ceiling of the nose of the ship by the top of his head, unable to move.

'The bombardier, the bombardier,' Dobbs answered in a cry when Yossarian spoke. 'He doesn't answer, he doesn't answer. Help the bombardier, help the bombardier.'

'I'm the bombardier,' Yossarian cried back at him. 'I'm the bombardier. I'm all right. I'm all right.'

'Then help him, help him,' Dobbs begged. 'Help him, help him.'

And Snowden lay dying in back.

6   Hungry Joe

Hungry Joe did have fifty missions, but they were no help. He had his bags packed and was waiting again to go home. At night he had eerie, ear-splitting nightmares that kept everyone in the squadron awake but Huple, the fifteen-year-old pilot who had lied about his age to get into the Army and lived with his pet cat in the same tent with Hungry Joe. Huple was a light sleeper, but claimed he never heard Hungry Joe scream. Hungry Joe was sick.

'So what?' Doc Daneeka snarled resentfully. 'I had it made, I tell you. Fifty grand a year I was knocking down, and almost all of it tax-free, since I made my customers pay me in cash. I had the strongest trade association in the world backing me up. And look what happened. Just when I was all set to really start stashing it away, they had to manufacture fascism and start a war horrible enough to affect even me. I gotta laugh when I hear someone like Hungry Joe screaming his brains out every night. I really gotta laugh. *He's* sick? How does he think I feel?'

Hungry Joe was too firmly embedded in calamities of his own to care how Doc Daneeka felt. There were the noises, for instance. Small ones enraged him and he hollered himself hoarse at Aarfy for the wet, sucking sounds he made puffing on his pipe, at Orr for tinkering, at McWatt for the explosive snap he gave each card he turned over when he dealt at blackjack or poker, at Dobbs for letting his teeth chatter as he went blundering clumsily about bumping into things. Hungry Joe was a throbbing, ragged mass of motile irritability. The steady ticking of a watch in a quiet room crashed like torture against his unshielded brain.

'Listen, kid,' he explained harshly to Huple very late one evening, 'if you want to live in this tent, you've got to do like I do. You've got to roll your wrist watch up in a pair of wool socks every night and keep it on the bottom of your foot locker on the other side of the room.'

Huple thrust his jaw out defiantly to let Hungry Joe know he couldn't be pushed around and then did exactly as he had been told.

Hungry Joe was a jumpy, emaciated wretch with a fleshless face of dingy skin and bone and twitching veins squirming subcutaneously in the blackened hollows behind his eyes like severed sections of snake. It was a desolate, cratered face, sooty with care like an abandoned mining town. Hungry Joe ate voraciously, gnawed incessantly at the tips of his fingers, stammered, choked, itched, sweated, salivated, and sprang from spot to spot fanatically with an intricate black camera with which he was always trying to take pictures of naked girls. They never came out. He was always forgetting to put film in the camera or turn on lights or remove the cover from the lens opening. It wasn't easy persuading naked girls to pose, but Hungry Joe had the knack.

'Me big man,' he would shout. 'Me big photographer from *Life* magazine. Big picture on heap big cover. *Si, si, si!* Hollywood star. Multi *dinero*. Multi divorces. Multi ficky-fick all day long.'

Few women anywhere could resist such wily cajolery, and prostitutes would spring to their feet eagerly and hurl themselves into whatever fantastic poses he requested for them. Women killed Hungry Joe. His response to them as sexual beings was one of frenzied worship and idolatry. They were lovely, satisfying, maddening manifestations of the miraculous, instruments of pleasure too powerful to be measured, too keen to be endured, and too exquisite to be intended for employment by base, unworthy man. He could interpret their naked presence in his hands only as a cosmic oversight destined to be rectified speedily, and he was driven always to make what carnal use of them he could in the fleeting moment or two he felt he had before Someone caught wise and whisked them away. He could never decide whether to furgle them or photograph them, for he had found it impossible to do both simultaneously. In fact, he was finding it almost impossible to do either, so scrambled were his powers of performance by the compulsive need for haste that invariably possessed him. The pictures never came out, and Hungry Joe never got in. The odd thing was that in civilian life Hungry Joe really had been a photographer for *Life* magazine.

He was a hero now, the biggest hero the Air Force had, Yossarian felt, for he had flown more combat tours of duty than any other hero the Air Force had. He had flown six combat tours of duty. Hungry Joe had finished flying his first combat tour of duty when twenty-five missions were all that were necessary for him to pack his bags, write happy letters home and begin hounding Sergeant Towser humorously for the arrival of the orders rotating him back to the States. While he waited, he spent each day shuffling rhythmically around the entrance of the operations tent, making boisterous wisecracks to everybody who came by and jocosely calling Sergeant Towser a lousy son of a bitch every time Sergeant Towser popped out of the orderly room.

Hungry Joe had finished flying his first twenty-five missions during the week of the Salerno beachhead, when Yossarian was laid up in the hospital with a burst of clap he had caught on a low-level mission over a Wac in bushes on a supply flight to Marrakech. Yossarian did his best to catch up with Hungry Joe and almost did, flying six missions in six days, but his twenty-third mission was to Arezzo, where Colonel Nevers was killed, and that was as close as he had ever been able to come to going home. The next day Colonel Cathcart was there, brimming with tough pride in his new outfit and celebrating his assumption of command by raising the number of missions required from twenty-five to thirty. Hungry Joe unpacked his bags and rewrote the happy letters home. He stopped hounding Sergeant Towser humorously. He began hating Sergeant Towser, focusing all blame upon him venomously, even though he knew Sergeant Towser had nothing to do with the arrival of Colonel Cathcart or the delay in the processing of shipping orders that might have rescued him seven days earlier and five times since.

Hungry Joe could no longer stand the strain of waiting for shipping orders and crumbled promptly into ruin every time he finished another tour of duty. Each time he was taken off combat status, he gave a big party for the little circle of friends he had. He broke out the bottles of bourbon he had managed to buy on his four-day weekly circuits with the courier plane and laughed, sang, shuffled and shouted in a festival of inebriated ecstasy until he could no longer keep awake and receded peacefully into slumber. As soon as Yossarian, Nately and Dunbar put him to bed he began screaming in his sleep. In the morning he stepped from his tent looking haggard, fearful and guilt-ridden, an eaten shell of a human building rocking perilously on the brink of collapse.

The nightmares appeared to Hungry Joe with celestial punctuality every single night he spent in the squadron throughout the whole harrowing ordeal when he was not flying combat missions and was waiting once again for the orders sending him home that never came. Impressionable men in the squadron like Dobbs and Captain Flume were so deeply disturbed by Hungry Joe's shrieking nightmares that they would begin to have shrieking nightmares of their own, and the piercing obscenities they flung into the air every night from their separate places in the squadron rang against each other in the darkness romantically like the mating calls of songbirds with filthy minds. Colonel Korn acted decisively to arrest what seemed to him to be the beginning of an unwholesome trend in Major Major's squadron. The solution he provided was to have Hungry Joe fly the courier ship once a week, removing him from the squadron for four nights, and the remedy, like all Colonel Korn's remedies, was successful.

Every time Colonel Cathcart increased the number of missions and returned Hungry Joe to combat duty, the nightmares stopped and Hungry Joe settled down into a normal state of terror with a smile of relief. Yossarian read Hungry Joe's shrunken face like a headline. It was good when Hungry Joe looked bad and terrible when Hungry Joe looked good. Hungry Joe's inverted set of responses was a curious phenomenon to everyone but Hungry Joe, who denied the whole thing stubbornly.

'Who dreams?' he answered, when Yossarian asked him what he dreamed about.

'Joe, why don't you go see Doc Daneeka?' Yossarian advised.

'Why should I go see Doc Daneeka? I'm not sick.'

'What about your nightmares?'

'I don't have nightmares,' Hungry Joe lied.

'Maybe he can do something about them.'

'There's nothing wrong with nightmares,' Hungry Joe answered. 'Everybody has nightmares.'

Yossarian thought he had him. 'Every night?' he asked.

'Why not every night?' Hungry Joe demanded.

And suddenly it all made sense. Why not every night, indeed? It made sense to cry out in pain every night. It made more sense than Appleby, who was a stickler for regulations and had ordered Kraft to order Yossarian to take his Atabrine tablets on the flight overseas after Yossarian and Appleby had stopped talking to each other. Hungry Joe made more sense than Kraft, too, who was dead, dumped unceremoniously into doom over Ferrara by an exploding engine after Yossarian took his flight of six planes in over the target a second time. The group had missed the bridge at Ferrara again for the seventh straight day with the bombsight that could put bombs into a pickle barrel at forty thousand feet, and one whole week had already passed since Colonel Cathcart had volunteered to have his men destroy the bridge in twenty-four hours. Kraft was a skinny, harmless kid from Pennsylvania who wanted only to be liked, and was destined to be disappointed in even so humble and degrading an ambition. Instead of being liked, he was dead, a bleeding cinder on the barbarous pile whom nobody had heard in those last precious moments while the plane with one wing plummeted. He had lived innocuously for a little while and then had gone down in flame over Ferrara on the seventh day, while God was resting, when McWatt turned and Yossarian guided him in over the target on a second bomb run because Aarfy was confused and Yossarian had been unable to drop his bombs the first time.

'I guess we do have to go back again, don't we?' McWatt had said somberly over the intercom.

'I guess we do,' said Yossarian.

'Do we?' said McWatt.

'Yeah.'

'Oh, well,' sang McWatt, 'what the hell.'

And back they had gone while the planes in the other flights circled safely off in the distance and every crashing cannon in the Hermann Goering Division below was busy crashing shells this time only at them.

Colonel Cathcart had courage and never hesitated to volunteer his men for any target available. No target was too dangerous for his group to attack, just as no shot was too difficult for Appleby to handle on the ping-pong table. Appleby was a good pilot and a superhuman ping-pong player with flies in his eyes who never lost a point. Twenty-one serves were all it ever took for Appleby to disgrace another opponent. His prowess on the ping-pong table was legendary, and Appleby won every game he started until the night Orr got tipsy on gin and juice and smashed open Appleby's forehead with his paddle after Appleby had smashed back each of Orr's first five serves. Orr leaped on top of the table after hurling his paddle and came sailing off the other end in a running broad jump with both feet planted squarely in Appleby's face. Pandemonium broke loose. It took almost a full minute for Appleby to disentangle himself from Orr's flailing arms and legs and grope his way to his feet, with Orr held off the ground before him by the shirt front in one hand and his other arm drawn back in a fist to smite him dead, and at that moment Yossarian stepped forward and took Orr away from him. It was a night of surprises for Appleby, who was as large as Yossarian and as strong and who swung at Yossarian as hard as he could with a punch that flooded Chief White Halfoat with such joyous excitement that he turned and busted Colonel Moodus in the nose with a punch that filled General Dreedle with such mellow gratification that he had Colonel Cathcart throw the chaplain out of the officers' club and orderd Chief White Halfoat moved into Doc Daneeka's tent, where he could be under a doctor's care twenty-four hours a day and be kept in good enough physical condition to bust Colonel Moodus in the nose again whenever General Dreedle wanted him to. Sometimes General Dreedle made special trips down from Wing Headquarters with Colonel Moodus and his nurse just to have Chief White Halfoat bust his son-in-law in the nose.

Chief White Halfoat would much rather have remained in the trailer he shared with Captain Flume, the silent, haunted squadron public-relations officer who spent most of each evening developing the pictures he took during the day to be sent out with his publicity releases. Captain Flume spent as much of each evening as he could working in his darkroom and then lay down on his cot with his fingers crossed and a rabbit's foot around his neck and tried with all his might to stay awake. He lived in mortal fear of Chief White Halfoat. Captain Flume was obsessed with the idea that Chief White

Halfoat would tiptoe up to his cot one night when he was sound asleep and slit his throat open for him from ear to ear. Captain Flume had obtained this idea from Chief White Halfoat himself, who did tiptoe up to his cot one night as he was dozing off, to hiss portentously that one night when he, Captain Flume, was sound asleep he, Chief White Halfoat, was going to slit his throat open for him from ear to ear. Captain Flume turned to ice, his eyes, flung open wide, staring directly up into Chief White Halfoat's, glinting drunkenly only inches away.

'Why?' Captain Flume managed to croak finally.

'Why not?' was Chief White Halfoat's answer.

Each night after that, Captain Flume forced himself to keep awake as long as possible. He was aided immeasurably by Hungry Joe's nightmares. Listening so intently to Hungry Joe's maniacal howling night after night, Captain Flume grew to hate him and began wishing that Chief White Halfoat would tiptoe up to *his* cot one night and slit *his* throat open for him from ear to ear. Actually, Captain Flume slept like a log most nights and merely *dreamed* he was awake. So convincing were these dreams of lying awake that he woke from them each morning in complete exhaustion and fell right back to sleep.

Chief White Halfoat had grown almost fond of Captain Flume since his amazing metamorphosis. Captain Flume had entered his bed that night a buoyant extrovert and left it the next morning a brooding introvert, and Chief White Halfoat proudly regarded the new Captain Flume as his own creation. He had never intended to slit Captain Flume's throat open for him from ear to ear. Threatening to do so was merely his idea of a joke, like dying of pneumonia, busting Colonel Moodus in the nose or challenging Doc Daneeka to Indian wrestle. All Chief White Halfoat wanted to do when he staggered in drunk each night was go right to sleep, and Hungry Joe often made that impossible. Hungry Joe's nightmares gave Chief White Halfoat the heebie-jeebies, and he often wished that someone would tiptoe into Hungry

Joe's tent, lift Huple's cat off his face and slit his throat open for him from ear to ear, so that everybody in the squadron but Captain Flume could get a good night's sleep.

Even though Chief White Halfoat kept busting Colonel Moodus in the nose for General Dreedle's benefit, he was still outside the pale. Also outside the pale was Major Major, the squadron commander, who had found *that* out the same time he found out that he was squadron commander from Colonel Cathcart, who came blasting into the squadron in his hopped-up jeep the day after Major Duluth was killed over Perugia. Colonel Cathcart slammed to a screeching stop inches short of the railroad ditch separating the nose of his jeep from the lopsided basketball court on the other side, from which Major Major was eventually driven by the kicks and shoves and stones and punches of the men who had almost become his friends.

'You're the new squadron commander,' Colonel Cathcart had bellowed across the ditch at him. 'But don't think it means anything, because it doesn't. All it means is that you're the new squadron commander.'

And Colonel Cathcart had roared away as abruptly as he'd come, whipping the jeep around with a vicious spinning of wheels that sent a spray of fine grit blowing into Major Major's face. Major Major was immobilized by the news. He stood speechless, lanky and gawking, with a scuffed basketball in his long hands as the seeds of rancor sown so swiftly by Colonel Cathcart took root in the soldiers around him who had been playing basketball with him and who had let him come as close to making friends with them as anyone had ever let him come before. The whites of his moony eyes grew large and misty as his mouth struggled yearningly and lost against the familiar, impregnable loneliness drifting in around him again like suffocating fog.

Like all the other officers at Group Headquarters except Major Danby, Colonel Cathcart was infused with the democratic spirit: he believed that all men were created equal, and he therefore spurned all men outside Group Headquarters with equal fervor. Nevertheless, he believed in his men. As he told them frequently in the briefing room, he believed they were at least ten missions better than any other outfit and felt that any who did not share this confidence he had placed in them could get the hell out. The only way they could get the hell out, though, as Yossarian learned when he flew to visit ex-P.F.C. Wintergreen, was by flying the extra ten missions.

'I still don't get it,' Yossarian protested. 'Is Doc Daneeka right or isn't he?'

'How many did he say?'

'Forty.'

'Daneeka was telling the truth,' ex-P.F.C. Wintergreen admitted. 'Forty missions is all you have to fly as far as Twenty-seventh Air Force Headquarters is concerned.'

Yossarian was jubilant. 'Then I can go home, right? I've got forty-eight.'

'No, you can't go home,' ex-P.F.C. Wintergreen corrected him. 'Are you crazy or something?'

'Why not?'

'Catch-22.'

'Catch-22?' Yossarian was stunned. 'What the hell has Catch-22 got to do with it?'

'Catch-22,' Doc Daneeka answered patiently, when Hungry Joe had flown Yossarian back to Pianosa, 'says you've always got to do what your commanding officer tells you to.'

'But Twenty-seventh Air Force says I can go home with forty missions.'

'But they don't say you have to go home. And regulations do say you have to obey every order. That's the catch. Even if the colonel were disobeying a Twenty-seventh Air Force order by making you fly more missions, you'd still have to fly them, or you'd be guilty of disobeying an order of his. And then Twenty-seventh Air Force Headquarters would really jump on you.'

Yossarian slumped with disappointment. 'Then I really

have to fly the fifty missions, don't I?' he grieved.

'The fifty-five,' Doc Daneeka corrected him.

'What fifty-five?'

'The fifty-five missions the colonel now wants all of you to fly.'

Hungry Joe heaved a huge sigh of relief when he heard Doc Daneeka and broke into a grin. Yossarian grabbed Hungry Joe by the neck and made him fly them both right back to ex-P.F.C. Wintergreen.

'What would they do to me,' he asked in confidential tones, 'if I refused to fly them?'

'We'd probably shoot you,' ex-P.F.C. Wintergreen replied.

'*We?*' Yossarian cried in surprise. 'What do you mean, *we*? Since when are you on their side?'

'If you're going to be shot, whose side do you expect me to be on?' ex-P.F.C. Wintergreen retorted.

Yossarian winced. Colonel Cathcart had raised him again.

7 McWatt

Ordinarily, Yossarian's pilot was McWatt, who, shaving in loud red, clean pajamas outside his tent each morning, was one of the odd, ironic, incomprehensible things surrounding Yossarian. McWatt was the craziest combat man of them all probably, because he was perfectly sane and still did not mind the war. He was a short-legged, wide-shouldered, smiling young soul who whistled bouncy show tunes continuously and turned over cards with sharp snaps when he dealt at blackjack or poker until Hungry Joe disintegrated into quaking despair finally beneath their cumulative impact and began ranting at him to stop snapping the cards.

'You son of a bitch, you only do it because it hurts me,' Hungry Joe would yell furiously, as Yossarian held him back soothingly with one hand. 'That's the only reason he does it, because he likes to hear me scream – you goddam son of a bitch!'

McWatt crinkled his fine, freckled nose apologetically and vowed not to snap the cards any more, but always forgot. McWatt wore fleecy bedroom slippers with his red pajamas and slept between freshly pressed colored bedsheets like the one Milo had retrieved half of for him from the grinning thief with the sweet tooth in exchange for none of the pitted dates Milo had borrowed from Yossarian. McWatt was deeply impressed with Milo, who, to the amusement of Corporal Snark, his mess sergeant, was already buying eggs for seven cents apiece and selling them for five cents. But McWatt was never as impressed with Milo as Milo had been with the letter Yossarian had obtained for his liver from Doc Daneeka.

'What's this?' Milo had cried out in alarm, when he came upon the enormous corrugated carton filled with packages of dried fruit and cans of fruit juices and desserts that two of the Italian laborers Major — de Coverley had kidnaped for his kitchen were about to carry off to Yossarian's tent.

'This is Captain Yossarian, sir,' said Corporal Snark with a superior smirk. Corporal Snark was an intellectual snob who felt he was twenty years ahead of his time and did not enjoy cooking down to the masses. 'He has a letter from Doc Daneeka entitling him to all the fruit and fruit juices he wants.'

'What's this?' cried out Yossarian, as Milo went white and began to sway.

'This is Lieutenant Milo Minderbinder, sir,' said Corporal Snark with a derisive wink. 'One of our new pilots. He became mess officer while you were in the hospital this last time.'

'What's this?' cried out McWatt, late in the afternoon, as Milo handed him half his bedsheet.

'It's half of the bedsheet that was stolen from your tent this morning,' Milo explained with nervous self-satisfaction, his rusty mustache twitching rapidly. 'I'll bet you didn't even know it was stolen.'

'Why should anyone want to steal half a bedsheet?' Yossarian asked.

Milo grew flustered. 'You don't understand,' he protested.

And Yossarian also did not understand why Milo needed so desperately to invest in the letter from Doc Daneeka, which came right to the point. 'Give Yossarian all the dried fruit and fruit juices he wants,' Doc Daneeka had written. 'He says he has a liver condition.'

'A letter like this,' Milo mumbled despondently, 'could ruin any mess officer in the world.' Milo had come to Yossarian's tent just to read the letter again, following his carton of lost provisions across the squadron like a mourner. 'I have to give you as much as you ask for. Why, the letter doesn't even say you have to eat all of it yourself.'

'And it's a good thing it doesn't,' Yossarian told him, 'because I never eat any of it. I have a liver condition.'

'Oh, yes, I forgot,' said Milo, in a voice lowered deferentially. 'Is it bad?'

'Just bad enough,' Yossarian answered cheerfully.

'I see,' said Milo. 'What does that mean?'

'It means that it couldn't be better . . .'

'I don't think I understand.'

'. . . .without being worse. Now do you see?'

'Yes, now I see. But I still don't think I understand.'

'Well, don't let it trouble you. Let it trouble me. You see, I don't really have a liver condition. I've just got the symptoms. I have a Garnett-Fleischaker syndrome.'

'I see,' said Milo. 'And what is a Garnett-Fleischaker syndrome?'

'A liver condition.'

'I see,' said Milo, and began massaging his black eyebrows together wearily with an expression of interior pain, as though waiting for some stinging discomfort he was experiencing to go away. 'In that case,' he continued finally, 'I suppose you do have to be very careful about what you eat, don't you?'

'Very careful indeed,' Yossarian told him. 'A good Garnett-Fleischaker syndrome isn't easy to come by, and I don't want to ruin mine. That's why I never eat any fruit.'

'Now I do see,' said Milo. 'Fruit is bad for your liver?'

'No, fruit is good for my liver. That's why I never eat any.'

'Then what do you do with it?' demanded Milo, plodding

along doggedly through his mounting confusion to fling out the question burning on his lips. 'Do you sell it?'

'I give it away.'

'To who?' cried Milo, in a voice cracking with dismay.

'To anyone who wants it,' Yossarian shouted back.

Milo let out a long, melancholy wail and staggered back, beads of perspiration popping out suddenly all over his ashen face. He tugged on his unfortunate mustache absently, his whole body trembling.

'I give a great deal of it to Dunbar,' Yossarian went on.

'Dunbar?' Milo echoed numbly.

'Yes. Dunbar can eat all the fruit he wants and it won't do him a damned bit of good. I just leave the carton right out there in the open for anyone who wants any to come and help himself. Aarfy comes here to get prunes because he says he never gets enough prunes in the mess hall. You might look into that when you've got some time because it's no fun having Aarfy hanging around here. Whenever the supply runs low I just have Corporal Snark fill me up again. Nately always takes a whole load of fruit along with him whenever he goes to Rome. He's in love with a whore there who hates me and isn't at all interested in him. She's got a kid sister who never leaves them alone in bed together, and they live in an apartment with an old man and woman and a bunch of other girls with nice fat thighs who are always kidding around also. Nately brings them a whole cartonful every time he goes.'

'Does he sell it to them?'

'No, he gives it to them.'

Milo frowned. 'Well, I suppose that's very generous of him,' he remarked with no enthusiasm.

'Yes, very generous,' Yossarian agreed.

'And I'm sure it's perfectly legal,' said Milo, 'since the food is yours once you get it from me. I suppose that with conditions as hard as they are, these people are very glad to get it.'

'Yes, very glad,' Yossarian assured him. 'The two girls sell it all on the black market and use the money to buy flashy costume jewelry and cheap perfume.'

Milo perked up. 'Costume jewelry!' he exclaimed. 'I didn't know that. How much are they paying for cheap perfume?'

'The old man uses his share to buy raw whiskey and dirty pictures. He's a lecher.'

'A lecher?'

'You'd be surprised.'

'Is there much of a market in Rome for dirty pictures?' Milo asked.

'You'd be surprised. Take Aarfy, for instance. Knowing him, you'd never suspect, would you?'

'That he's a lecher?'

'No, that he's a navigator. You know Captain Aardvaark, don't you? He's that nice guy who came up to you your first day in the squadron and said, "Aardvaark's my name, and navigation is my game." He wore a pipe in his face and probably asked you what college you went to. Do you know him?'

Milo was paying no attention. 'Let me be your partner,' he blurted out imploringly.

Yossarian turned him down, even though he had no doubt that the truckloads of fruit *would* be theirs to dispose of any way they saw fit once Yossarian had requisitioned them from the mess hall with Doc Daneeka's letter. Milo was crestfallen, but from that moment on he trusted Yossarian with every secret but one, reasoning shrewdly that anyone who would not steal from the country he loved would not steal from anybody. Milo trusted Yossarian with every secret but the location of the holes in the hills in which he began burying his money once he returned from Smyrna with his planeload of figs and learned from Yossarian that a C.I.D. man had come to the hospital. To Milo, who had been gullible enough to volunteer for it, the position of mess officer was a sacred trust.

'I didn't even realize we weren't serving enough prunes,' he had admitted that first day. 'I suppose it's because I'm still so new. I'll raise the question with my first chef.'

Yossarian eyed him sharply. 'What first chef?' he demanded. 'You don't have a first chef.'

'Corporal Snark,' Milo explained, looking away a little guiltily. 'He's the only chef I have, so he really is my first chef, although I hope to move him over to the administrative side. Corporal Snark tends to be a little too creative, I feel. He thinks being a mess sergeant is some sort of art form and is always complaining about having to prostitute his talents. Nobody is asking him to do any such thing! Incidentally, do you happen to know why he was busted to private and is only a corporal now?'

'Yes,' said Yossarian. 'He poisoned the squadron.'

Milo went pale again. 'He did *what*?'

'He mashed hundreds of cakes of GI soap into the sweet potatoes just to show that people have the taste of Philistines and don't know the difference between good and bad. Every man in the squadron was sick. Missions were canceled.'

'Well!' Milo exclaimed, with thin-lipped disapproval. 'He certainly found out how wrong *he* was, didn't he?'

'On the contrary,' Yossarian corrected. 'He found out how *right* he was. We packed it away by the plateful and clamored for more. We all knew we were sick, but we had no idea we'd been poisoned.'

Milo sniffed in consternation twice, like a shaggy brown hare. 'In that case, I certainly do want to get him over to the administrative side. I don't want anything like that happening while I'm in charge. You see,' he confided earnestly, 'what I hope to do is give the men in this squadron the best meals in the whole world. That's really something to shoot at, isn't it? If a mess officer aims at anything less, it seems to me, he has no right being mess officer. Don't you agree?'

Yossarian turned slowly to gaze at Milo with probing distrust. He saw a simple, sincere face that was incapable of subtlety or guile, an honest, frank face with disunited large eyes, rusty hair, black eyebrows and an unfortunate reddish-brown mustache. Milo had a long, thin nose with sniffing, damp nostrils heading sharply off to the right, always pointing away from where the rest of him was looking. It was the face of a man of hardened integrity who could no more consciously violate the moral principles on which his virtue rested than he could transform himself into a despicable toad. One of these moral principles was that it was never a sin to charge as much as the traffic would bear. He was capable of mighty paroxysms of righteous indignation, and he was indignant as could be when he learned that a C.I.D. man was in the area looking for him.

'He's not looking for you,' Yossarian said, trying to placate him. 'He's looking for someone up in the hospital who's been signing Washington Irving's name to the letters he's been censoring.'

'I never signed Washington Irving's name to any letters,' Milo declared.

'Of course not.'

'But that's just a trick to get me to confess I've been making money in the black market.' Milo hauled violently at a disheveled hunk of his off-colored mustache. 'I don't like guys like that. Always snooping around people like us. Why doesn't the government get after ex-P.F.C. Wintergreen, if it wants to do some good? He's got no respect for rules and regulations and keeps cutting prices on me.'

Milo's mustache was unfortunate because the separated halves never matched. They were like Milo's disunited eyes, which never looked at the same thing at the same time. Milo could see more things than most people, but he could see none of them too distinctly. In contrast to his reaction to news of the C.I.D. man, he learned with calm courage from Yossarian that Colonel Cathcart had raised the number of missions to fifty-five.

'We're at war,' he said. 'And there's no use complaining about the number of missions we have to fly. If the colonel says we have to fly fifty-five missions, we have to fly them.'

'Well, I don't have to fly them,' Yossarian vowed. 'I'll go see Major Major.'

'How can you? Major Major never sees anybody.'

'Then I'll go back into the hospital.'

'You just came out of the hospital ten days ago,' Milo reminded him reprovingly. 'You can't keep running into the hospital every time something happens you don't like. No, the best thing to do is fly the missions. It's our duty.'

Milo had rigid scruples that would not even allow him to borrow a package of pitted dates from the mess hall that day of McWatt's stolen bedsheet, for the food at the mess hall was all still the property of the government.

'But I can borrow it from you,' he explained to Yossarian, 'since all this fruit is yours once you get it from me with Doctor Daneeka's letter. You can do whatever you want to with it, even sell it at a high profit instead of giving it away free. Wouldn't you want to do that together?'

'No.'

Milo gave up. 'Then lend me one package of pitted dates,' he requested. 'I'll give it back to you. I swear I will, and there'll be a little something extra for you.'

Milo proved good as his word and handed Yossarian a quarter of McWatt's yellow bedsheet when he returned with the unopened package of dates and with the grinning thief with the sweet tooth who had stolen the bedsheet from McWatt's tent. The piece of bedsheet now belonged to Yossarian. He had earned it while napping, although he did not understand how. Neither did McWatt.

'What's this?' cried McWatt, staring in mystification at the ripped half of his bedsheet.

'It's half of the bedsheet that was stolen from your tent this morning,' Milo explained. 'I'll bet you didn't even know it was stolen.'

'Why should anyone want to steal half a bedsheet?' Yossarian asked.

Milo grew flustered. 'You don't understand,' he protested. 'He stole the whole bedsheet, and I got it back with the package of pitted dates you invested. That's why the quarter of the bedsheet is yours. You made a very handsome return on your investment, particularly since you've gotten back every pitted date you gave me.' Milo next addressed himself to McWatt. 'Half the bedsheet is yours because it was all yours to begin with, and I really don't understand what you're complaining about, since you wouldn't have any part of it if Captain Yossarian and I hadn't intervened in your behalf.'

'Who's complaining?' McWatt exclaimed. 'I'm just trying to figure out what I can do with half a bedsheet.'

'There are lots of things you can do with half a bedsheet.' Milo assured him. 'The remaining quarter of the bedsheet I've set aside for myself as a reward for my enterprise, work and initiative. It's not for myself, you understand, but for the syndicate. That's something you might do with half the bedsheet. You can leave it in the syndicate and watch it grow.'

'What syndicate?'

'The syndicate I'd like to form someday so that I can give you men the good food you deserve.'

'You want to form a syndicate?'

'Yes, I do. No, a mart. Do you know what a mart is?'

'It's a place where you buy things, isn't it?'

'And sell things,' corrected Milo.

'And sell things.'

'All my life I've wanted a mart. You can do lots of things if you've got a mart. But you've got to have a mart.'

'You want a mart?'

'And every man will have a share.'

Yossarian was still puzzled, for it was a business matter, and there was much about business matters that always puzzled him.

'Let me try to explain it again,' Milo offered with growing weariness and exasperation, jerking his thumb toward the thief with the sweet tooth, still grinning beside him. 'I knew he wanted the dates more than the bedsheet. Since he doesn't understand a word of English, I made it a point to conduct the whole transaction in English.'

'Why didn't you just hit him over the head and take the

bedsheet away from him?' Yossarian asked.

Pressing his lips together with dignity, Milo shook his head. 'That would have been most unjust,' he scolded firmly. 'Force is wrong, and two wrongs never make a right. It was much better my way. When I held the dates out to him and reached for the bedsheet, he probably thought I was offering to trade.'

'What were you doing?'

'Actually, I *was* offering to trade, but since he doesn't understand English, I can always deny it.'

'Suppose he gets angry and wants the dates?'

'Why, we'll just hit him over the head and take them away from him,' Milo answered without hesitation. He looked from Yossarian to McWatt and back again. 'I really can't see what everyone is complaining about. We're all much better off than before. Everybody is happy but this thief, and there's no sense worrying about him, since he doesn't even speak our language and deserves whatever he gets. Don't you understand?'

But Yossarian still didn't understand either how Milo could buy eggs in Malta for seven cents apiece and sell them at a profit in Pianosa for five cents.

8   Lieutenant Scheisskopf

Not even Clevinger understood how Milo could do that, and Clevinger knew everything. Clevinger knew everything about the war except why Yossarian had to die while Corporal Snark was allowed to live, or why Corporal Snark had to die while Yossarian was allowed to live. It was a vile and muddy war, and Yossarian could have lived without it – lived forever, perhaps. Only a fraction of his countrymen would give up their lives to win it, and it was not his ambition to be among them. To die or not to die, that was the question, and Clevinger grew limp trying to answer it. History did not demand Yossarian's premature demise, justice could be satisfied without it, progress did not hinge upon it, victory did not depend on it. That men would die was a matter of necessity; *which* men would die, though, was a matter of circumstance, and Yossarian was willing to be the victim of anything but circumstance. But that was war. Just about all he could find in its favor was that it paid well and liberated children from the pernicious influence of their parents.

Clevinger knew so much because Clevinger was a genius with a pounding heart and blanching face. He was a gangling, gawky, feverish, famish-eyed brain. As a Harvard undergraduate he had won prizes in scholarship for just about everything, and the only reason he had not won prizes in scholarship for everything else was that he was too busy signing petitions, circulating petitions and challenging petitions, joining discussion groups and resigning from discussion groups, attending youth congresses, picketing other youth congresses and organizing student committees in defense of dismissed faculty members. Everyone agreed that Clevinger was certain to go far in the academic world. In short, Clevinger was one of those people with lots of intelligence and no brains, and everyone knew it except those who soon found it out.

In short, he was a dope. He often looked to Yossarian like one of those people hanging around modern museums with both eyes together on one side of a face. It was an illusion, of course, generated by Clevinger's predilection for staring fixedly at one side of a question and never seeing the other side at all. Politically, he was a humanitarian who did know right from left and was trapped uncomfortably between the two. He was constantly defending his Communist friends to his right-wing enemies and his right-wing friends to his Communist enemies, and he was thoroughly detested by both groups, who never defended him to anyone because they thought he was a dope.

He was a very serious, very earnest and very conscientious dope. It was impossible to go to a movie with him without getting involved afterwards in a discussion on empathy, Aristotle, universals, messages and the obligations of the cinema as an art form in a materialistic society. Girls he took to the theater had to wait until the first intermission to find out from him whether or not they were seeing a good or a bad play, and then found out at once. He was a militant idealist who crusaded against racial bigotry by growing faint in its presence. He knew everything about literature except how to enjoy it.

Yossarian tried to help him. 'Don't be a dope,' he had

counseled Clevinger when they were both at cadet school in Santa Ana, California.

'I'm going to tell him,' Clevinger insisted, as the two of them sat high in the reviewing stands looking down on the auxiliary parade-ground at Lieutenant Scheisskopf raging back and forth like a beardless Lear.

'Why me?' Lieutenant Scheisskopf wailed.

'Keep still, idiot,' Yossarian advised Clevinger avuncularly.

'You don't know what you're talking about,' Clevinger objected.

'I know enough to keep still, idiot.'

Lieutenant Scheisskopf tore his hair and gnashed his teeth. His rubbery cheeks shook with gusts of anguish. His problem was a squadron of aviation cadets with low morale who marched atrociously in the parade competition that took place every Sunday afternoon. Their morale was low because they did not want to march in parades every Sunday afternoon and because Lieutenant Scheisskopf had appointed cadet officers from their ranks instead of permitting them to elect their own.

'I *want* someone to tell me,' Lieutenant Scheisskopf beseeched them all prayerfully. 'If any of it is my fault, I *want* to be told.'

'He *wants* someone to tell him,' Clevinger said.

'He wants everyone to keep still, idiot,' Yossarian answered.

'Didn't you hear him?' Clevinger argued.

'I heard him,' Yossarian replied. 'I heard him say very loudly and very distinctly that he wants every one of us to keep our mouths shut if we know what's good for us.'

'I won't punish you,' Lieutenant Scheisskopf swore.

'He says he won't punish me,' said Clevinger.

'He'll castrate you,' said Yossarian.

'I swear I won't punish you,' said Lieutenant Scheisskopf. 'I'll be grateful to the man who tells me the truth.'

'He'll hate you,' said Yossarian. 'To his dying day he'll hate you.'

Lieutenant Scheisskopf was an R.O.T.C. graduate who was rather glad that war had broken out, since it gave him an opportunity to wear an officer's uniform every day and say 'Men' in a clipped, military voice to the bunches of kids who fell into his clutches every eight weeks on their way to the butcher's block. He was an ambitious and humorless Lieutenant Scheisskopf, who confronted his responsibilities soberly and smiled only when some rival officer at the Santa Ana Army Air Force Base came down with a lingering disease. He had poor eyesight and chronic sinus trouble, which made war especially exciting for him, since he was in no danger of going overseas. The best thing about him was his wife and the best thing about his wife was a girl friend named Dori Duz who did whenever she could and had a Wac uniform that Lieutenant Scheisskopf's wife put on every weekend and took off every weekend for every cadet in her husband's squadron who wanted to creep into her.

Dori Duz was a lively little tart of copper-green and gold who loved doing it best in toolsheds, phone booths, field houses and bus kiosks. There was little she hadn't tried and less she wouldn't. She was shameless, slim, nineteen and aggressive. She destroyed egos by the score and made men hate themselves in the morning for the way she found them, used them and tossed them aside. Yossarian loved her. She was a marvelous piece of ass who found him only fair. He loved the feel of springy muscle beneath her skin everywhere he touched her the only time she'd let him. Yossarian loved Dori Duz so much that he couldn't help flinging himself down passionately on top of Lieutenant Scheisskopf's wife every week to revenge himself upon Lieutenant Scheisskopf for the way Lieutenant Scheisskopf was revenging himself upon Clevinger.

Lieutenant Scheisskopf's wife was revenging herself upon Lieutenant Scheisskopf for some unforgettable crime of his she couldn't recall. She was a plump, pink, sluggish girl who read good books and kept urging

Yossarian not to be so bourgeois without the r. She was never without a good book close by, not even when she was lying in bed with nothing on her but Yossarian and Dori Duz's dog tags. She bored Yossarian, but he was in love with her, too. She was a crazy mathematics major from the Wharton School of Business who could not count to twenty-eight each month without getting into trouble.

'Darling, we're going to have a baby again,' she would say to Yossarian every month.

'You're out of your goddam head,' he would reply.

'I mean it, baby,' she insisted.

'So do I.'

'Darling, we're going to have a baby again,' she would say to her husband.

'I haven't the time,' Lieutenant Scheisskopf would grumble petulantly. 'Don't you know there's a parade going on?'

Lieutenant Scheisskopf cared very deeply about winning parades and about bringing Clevinger up on charges before the Action Board for conspiring to advocate the overthrow of the cadet officers Lieutenant Scheisskopf had appointed. Clevinger was a troublemaker and a wise guy. Lieutenant Scheisskopf knew that Clevinger might cause even more trouble if he wasn't watched. Yesterday it was the cadet officers; tomorrow it might be the world. Clevinger had a mind, and Lieutenant Scheisskopf had noticed that people with minds tended to get pretty smart at times. Such men were dangerous, and even the new cadet officers whom Clevinger had helped into office were eager to give damning testimony against him. The case against Clevinger was open and shut. The only thing missing was something to charge him with.

It could not be anything to do with parades, for Clevinger took the parades almost as seriously as Lieutenant Scheisskopf himself. The men fell out for the parades early each Sunday afternoon and groped their way into ranks of twelve outside the barracks. Groaning with hangovers, they limped in step to their station on the main paradeground, where they stood motionless in the heat for an hour or two with the men from the sixty or seventy other cadet squadrons until enough of them had collapsed to call it a day. On the edge of the field stood a row of ambulances and teams of trained stretcher bearers with walkie-talkies. On the roofs of the ambulances were spotters with binoculars. A tally clerk kept score. Supervising this entire phase of the operation was a medical officer with a flair for accounting who okayed pulses and checked the figures of the tally clerk. As soon as enough unconscious men had been collected in the ambulances, the medical officer signaled the bandmaster to strike up the band and end the parade. One behind the other, the squadrons marched up the field, executed a cumbersome turn around the reviewing stand and marched down the field and back to their barracks.

Each of the parading squadrons was graded as it marched past the reviewing stand, where a bloated colonel with a big fat mustache sat with the other officers. The best squadron in each wing won a yellow pennant on a pole that was utterly worthless. The best squadron on the base won a red pennant on a longer pole that was worth even less, since the pole was heavier and was that much more of a nuisance to lug around all week until some other squadron won it the following Sunday. To Yossarian, the idea of pennants as prizes was absurd. No money went with them, no class privileges. Like Olympic medals and tennis trophies, all they signified was that the owner had done something of no benefit to anyone more capably than everyone else.

The parades themselves seemed equally absurd. Yossarian hated a parade. Parades were so martial. He hated hearing them, hated seeing them, hated being tied up in traffic by them. He hated being made to take part in them. It was bad enough being an aviation cadet without having to act like a soldier in the blistering heat every Sunday afternoon. It was bad enough being an aviation cadet because it was obvious now that the war would not be over before he had finished his training. That was the only reason he had volunteered for cadet training in the first place. As a soldier who had qualified for aviation cadet training, he had weeks and weeks of waiting for assignment to a class, weeks and weeks more to become a bombardier-navigator, weeks and weeks more of operational training after that to prepare him for overseas duty. It seemed inconceivable then that the war could last that long, for God was on his side, he had been told, and God, he had also been told, could do whatever He wanted to. But the war was not nearly over, and his training was almost complete.

Lieutenant Scheisskopf longed desperately to win parades and sat up half the night working on it while his wife waited amorously for him in bed thumbing through Krafft-Ebing to her favorite passages. He read books on marching. He manipulated boxes of chocolate soldiers until they melted in his hands and then maneuvered in ranks of twelve a set of plastic cowboys he had bought from a mail-order house under an assumed name and kept locked away from everyone's eyes during the day. Leonardo's exercises in anatomy proved indispensable. One evening he felt the need for a live model and directed his wife to march around the room.

'Naked?' she asked hopefully.

Lieutenant Scheisskopf smacked his hands over his eyes in exasperation. It was the despair of Lieutenant Scheisskopf's life to be chained to a woman who was incapable of looking beyond her own dirty, sexual desires to the titanic struggles for the unattainable in which noble man could become heroically engaged.

'Why don't you ever whip me?' she pouted one night.

'Because I haven't the time,' he snapped at her impatiently. 'I haven't the time. Don't you know there's a parade going on?'

And he really did not have the time. There it was Sunday already, with only seven days left in the week to get ready for the next parade. He had no idea where the hours went. Finishing last in three successive parades had given Lieutenant Scheisskopf an unsavory reputation, and he considered every means of improvement, even nailing the twelve men in each rank to a long two-by-four beam of seasoned oak to keep them in line. The plan was not feasible, for making a ninety-degree turn would have been impossible without nickel-alloy swivels inserted in the small of every man's back, and Lieutenant Scheisskopf was not sanguine at all about obtaining that many nickel-alloy swivels from Quartermaster or enlisting the co-operation of the surgeons at the hospital.

The week after Lieutenant Scheisskopf followed Clevinger's recommendation and let the men elect their own cadet officers, the squadron won the yellow pennant. Lieutenant Scheisskopf was so elated by his unexpected achievement that he gave his wife a sharp crack over the head with the pole when she tried to drag him into bed to celebrate by showing their contempt for the sexual mores of the lower middle classes in Western civilization. The next week the squadron won the red flag, and Lieutenant Scheisskopf was beside himself with rapture. And the week after that his squadron made history by winning the red pennant two weeks in a row! Now Lieutenant Scheisskopf had confidence enough in his powers to spring his big surprise. Lieutenant Scheisskopf had discovered in his extensive research that the hands of marchers, instead of swinging freely, as was then the popular fashion, ought never to be moved more than three inches from the center of the thigh, which meant, in effect, that they were scarcely to be swung at all.

Lieutenant Scheisskopf's preparations were elaborate and clandestine. All the cadets in his squadron were sworn to secrecy and rehearsed in the dead of night on the auxiliary paradeground. They marched in darkness that was pitch and bumped into each other blindly, but they did not panic, and they were learning to march without swinging their hands. Lieutenant Scheisskopf's first thought had been to have a friend of his in the sheet metal shop sink pegs of nickel alloy into each man's thighbones and link them to the wrists by strands of copper wire with exactly three inches of play, but there wasn't time – there was never enough time – and good copper wire was hard to come by in wartime. He remembered also that the men, so hampered, would be unable to fall properly during the impressive fainting ceremony preceding the marching and that an inability to faint properly might affect the unit's rating as a whole.

And all week long he chortled with repressed delight at the officers' club. Speculation grew rampant among his closest friends.

'I wonder what that Shithead is up to,' Lieutenant Engle said.

Lieutenant Scheisskopf responded with a knowing smile to the queries of his colleagues. 'You'll find out Sunday,' he promised. 'You'll find out.'

Lieutenant Scheisskopf unveiled his epochal surprise that Sunday with all the aplomb of an experienced impresario. He said nothing while the other squadrons ambled past the reviewing stand crookedly in their customary manner. He gave no sign even when the first ranks of his own squadron hove into sight with their swingless marching and the first stricken gasps of alarm were hissing from his startled fellow officers. He held back even then until the bloated colonel with the big fat mustache whirled upon him savagely with a purpling face, and then he offered the explanation that made him immortal.

'Look, Colonel,' he announced. 'No hands.'

And to an audience stilled with awe, he distributed certified photostatic copies of the obscure regulation on which he had built his unforgettable triumph. This was Lieutenant Scheisskopf's finest hour. He won the parade, of course, hands down, obtaining permanent possession of the red pennant and ending the Sunday parades altogether, since good red pennants were as hard to come by in wartime as good copper wire. Lieutenant Scheisskopf was made First Lieutenant Scheisskopf on the spot and began his rapid rise through the ranks. There were few who did not hail him as a true military genius for his important discovery.

'That Lieutenant Scheisskopf,' Lieutenant Travers remarked. 'He's a military genius.'

'Yes, he really is,' Lieutenant Engle agreed. 'It's a pity the schmuck won't whip his wife.'

'I don't see what that has to do with it,' Lieutenant Travers answered coolly. 'Lieutenant Bemis whips Mrs. Bemis beautifully every time they have sexual intercourse, and he isn't worth a farthing at parades.'

'I'm talking about flagellation,' Lieutenant Engle retorted. 'Who gives a damn about parades?'

Actually, no one but Lieutenant Scheisskopf really gave a damn about the parades, least of all the bloated colonel with the big fat mustache, who was chairman of the Action Board and began bellowing at Clevinger the moment Clevinger stepped gingerly into the room to plead innocent to the charges Lieutenant Scheisskopf had lodged against him. The colonel beat his fist down upon the table and hurt his hand and became so further enraged with Clevinger that he beat his fist down upon the table even harder and hurt his hand some more. Lieutenant Scheisskopf glared at Clevinger with tight lips, mortified by the poor impression Clevinger was making.

'In sixty days you'll be fighting Billy Petrolle,' the colonel with the big fat mustache roared. 'And you think it's a big fat joke.'

'I don't think it's a joke, sir,' Clevinger replied.

'Don't interrupt.'

'Yes, sir.'

'And say "sir" when you do,' ordered Major Metcalf.

'Yes, sir.'

'Weren't you just ordered not to interrupt?' Major Metcalf inquired coldly.

'But I didn't interrupt, sir,' Clevinger protested.

'No. And you didn't say "sir," either. Add that to the charges against him,' Major Metcalf directed the corporal who could take shorthand. 'Failure to say "sir" to superior officers when not interrupting them.'

'Metcalf,' said the colonel, 'you're a goddam fool. Do you know that?'

Major Metcalf swallowed with difficulty. 'Yes, sir.'

'Then keep your goddam mouth shut. You don't make sense.'

There were three members of the Action Board, the bloated colonel with the big fat mustache, Lieutenant Scheisskopf and Major Metcalf, who was trying to develop a steely gaze. As a member of the Action Board, Lieutenant Scheisskopf was one of the judges who would weigh the merits of the case against Clevinger as presented by the prosecutor. Lieutenant Scheisskopf was also the prosecutor. Clevinger had an officer defending him. The officer defending him was Lieutenant Scheisskopf.

It was all very confusing to Clevinger, who began vibrating in terror as the colonel surged to his feet like a gigantic belch and threatened to rip his stinking, cowardly body apart limb from limb. One day he had stumbled while marching to class; the next day he was formally charged with 'breaking ranks while in formation, felonious assault, indiscriminate behavior, mopery, high treason, provoking, being a smart guy, listening to classical music and so on.' In short, they threw the book at him, and there he was, standing in dread before the bloated colonel, who roared once more that in sixty days he would be fighting Billy Petrolle and demanded to know how the hell he would like being washed out and shipped to the Solomon Islands to bury bodies. Clevinger replied with courtesy that he would not like it; he was a dope who would rather be a corpse than bury one. The colonel sat down and settled back, calm and cagey suddenly, and ingratiatingly polite.

'What did you mean,' he inquired slowly, 'when you said we couldn't punish you?'

'When, sir?'

'I'm asking the questions. You're answering them.'

'Yes, sir. I –'

'Did you think we brought you here to ask questions and for me to answer them?'

'No, sir. I –'

'What did we bring you here for?'

'To answer questions.'

'You're goddam right,' roared the colonel. 'Now suppose you start answering some before I break your goddam head. Just what the hell did you mean, you bastard, when you said we couldn't punish you?'

'I don't think I ever made that statement, sir.'

'Will you speak up, please? I couldn't hear you.'

'Yes, sir. I –'

'Will you speak up, please? He couldn't hear you.'

'Yes, sir. I –'

'Metcalf.'

'Sir?'

'Didn't I tell you to keep your stupid mouth shut?'

'Yes, sir.'

'Then keep your stupid mouth shut when I tell you to keep your stupid mouth shut. Do you understand? Will you speak up, please? I couldn't hear you.'

'Yes, sir. I –'

'Metcalf, is that your foot I'm stepping on?'

'No, sir. It must be Lieutenant Scheisskopf's foot.'

'It isn't my foot,' said Lieutenant Scheisskopf.

'Then maybe it is my foot after all,' said Major Metcalf.

'Move it.'

'Yes, sir. You'll have to move your foot first, colonel. It's on top of mine.'

'Are you telling me to move my foot?'

'No, sir. Oh, no, sir.'

'Then move your foot and keep your stupid mouth shut. Will you speak up, please? I still couldn't hear you.'

'Yes, sir. I said that I didn't say that you couldn't punish me.'

'Just what the hell are you talking about?'

'I'm answering your question, sir.'

'What question?'

' "Just what the hell did you mean, you bastard, when you said we couldn't punish you?" ' said the corporal who could take shorthand, reading from his steno pad.

'All right,' said the colonel. 'Just what the hell *did* you mean?'

'I didn't say you couldn't punish me, sir.'

'When?' asked the colonel.

'When what, sir?'

'Now you're asking me questions again.'

'I'm sorry, sir. I'm afraid I don't understand your question.'

'When didn't you say we couldn't punish you? Don't you understand my question?'

'No, sir. I don't understand.'

'You've just told us that. Now suppose you answer my question.'

'But how can I answer it?'

'That's another question you're asking me.'

'I'm sorry, sir. But I don't know how to answer it. I never said you couldn't punish me.'

'Now you're telling us when you did say it. I'm asking you to tell us when you didn't say it.'

Clevinger took a deep breath. 'I always didn't say you couldn't punish me, sir.'

'That's much better, Mr. Clevinger, even though it is a barefaced lie. Last night in the latrine. Didn't you whisper that we couldn't punish you to that other dirty son of a bitch we don't like? What's his name?'

'Yossarian, sir,' Lieutenant Scheisskopf said.

'Yes, Yossarian. That's right. Yossarian. Yossarian? Is that his name? Yossarian? What the hell kind of a name is Yossarian?'

Lieutenant Scheisskopf had the facts at his finger tips. 'It's Yossarian's name, sir,' he explained.

'Yes, I suppose it is. Didn't you whisper to Yossarian that we couldn't punish you?'

'Oh, no, sir. I whispered to him that you couldn't find me guilty –'

'I may be stupid,' interrupted the colonel, 'but the

distinction escapes me. I guess I *am* pretty stupid, because the distinction escapes me.'

'W –'

'You're a windy son of a bitch, aren't you? Nobody asked you for clarification and you're giving me clarification. I was making a statement, not asking for clarification. You are a windy son of a bitch, aren't you?'

'No, sir.'

'*No*, sir? Are you calling me a goddam liar?'

'Oh, no, sir.'

'Then you're a windy son of a bitch, aren't you?'

'No, sir.'

'Are you trying to pick a fight with me?'

'No, sir.'

'Are you a windy son of a bitch?'

'No, sir.'

'Goddammit, you *are* trying to pick a fight with me. For two stinking cents I'd jump over this big fat table and rip your stinking, cowardly body apart limb from limb.'

'Do it! Do it!' cried Major Metcalf.

'Metcalf, you stinking son of a bitch. Didn't I tell you to keep your stinking, cowardly, stupid mouth shut?'

'Yes, sir. I'm sorry, sir.'

'Then suppose *you* do it.'

'I was only trying to learn, sir. The only way a person can learn is by trying.'

'Who says so?'

'Everybody says so, sir. Even Lieutenant Scheisskopf says so.'

'Do you say so?'

'Yes, sir,' said Lieutenant Scheisskopf. 'But everybody says so.'

'Well, Metcalf, suppose you try keeping that stupid mouth of yours shut, and maybe that's the way you'll learn how. Now, where were we? Read me back the last line.'

' "Read me back the last line," ' read back the corporal who could take shorthand.

'Not my last line, stupid!' the colonel shouted. 'Somebody else's.'

103

' "Read me back the last line." ' read back the corporal.

'That's *my* last line again!' shrieked the colonel, turning purple with anger.

'Oh, no, sir,' corrected the corporal. 'That's *my* last line. I read it to you just a moment ago. Don't you remember, sir? It was only a moment ago.'

'Oh, my God! Read me back *his* last line, stupid. Say, what the hell's your name, anyway?'

'Popinjay, sir.'

'Well, you're next, Popinjay. As soon as his trial ends, your trial begins. Get it?'

'Yes, sir. What will I be charged with?'

'What the hell difference does that make? Did you hear what he asked me? You're going to learn, Popinjay – the minute we finish with Clevinger you're going to learn. Cadet Clevinger, what did – You are Cadet Clevinger, aren't you, and not Popinjay?'

'Yes, sir.'

'Good. What did –'

'I'm Popinjay, sir.'

'Popinjay, is your father a millionaire, or a member of the Senate?'

'No, sir.'

'Then you're up shit creek, Popinjay, without a paddle. He's not a general or a high-ranking member of the Administration, is he?'

'No, sir.'

'That's good. What does your father do?'

'He's dead, sir.'

'That's very good. You really are up the creek, Popinjay. Is Popinjay really your name? Just what the hell kind of a name is Popinjay anyway? I don't like it.'

'It's Popinjay's name, sir,' Lieutenant Scheisskopf explained.

'Well, I don't like it, Popinjay, and I just can't wait to rip your stinking, cowardly body apart limb from limb. Cadet Clevinger, will you please repeat what the hell it was you did or didn't whisper to Yossarian late last night in the latrine?'

'Yes, sir. I said that you couldn't find me guilty –'

'We'll take it from there. Precisely what did you mean, Cadet Clevinger, when you said we couldn't find you guilty?'

'I didn't say you couldn't find me guilty, sir.'

'When?'

'When what, sir?'

'Goddammit, are you going to start pumping me again?'

'No, sir. I'm sorry, sir.'

'Then answer the question. When didn't you say we couldn't find you guilty?'

'Late last night in the latrine, sir.'

'Is that the only time you didn't say it?'

'No, sir. I always didn't say you couldn't find me guilty, sir. What I did say to Yossarian was –'

'Nobody asked you what you did say to Yossarian. We asked you what you didn't say to him. We're not at all interested in what you did say to Yossarian. Is that clear?'

'Yes, sir.'

'Then we'll go on. What did you say to Yossarian?'

'I said to him, sir, that you couldn't find me guilty of the offense with which I am charged and still be faithful to the cause of . . .'

'Of what? You're mumbling.'

'Stop mumbling.'

'Yes, sir.'

'And mumble "sir" when you do.'

'Metcalf, you bastard!'

'Yes, sir,' mumbled Clevinger. 'Of justice, sir. That you couldn't find –'

'Justice?' The colonel was astounded. 'What is justice?'

'Justice, sir –'

'That's not what justice is,' the colonel jeered, and began pounding the table again with his big fat hand. 'That's what Karl Marx is. I'll tell you what justice is. Justice is a knee in the gut from the floor on the chin at

105

night sneaky with a knife brought up down on the magazine of a battleship sandbagged underhanded in the dark without a word of warning. Garroting. That's what justice is when we've all got to be tough enough and rough enough to fight Billy Petrolle. From the hip. Get it?'

'No, sir.'

'Don't sir me!'

'Yes, sir.'

'And say "sir" when you don't,' ordered Major Metcalf.

Clevinger was guilty, of course, or he would not have been accused, and since the only way to prove it was to find him guilty, it was their patriotic duty to do so. He was sentenced to walk fifty-seven punishment tours. Popinjay was locked up to be taught a lesson, and Major Metcalf was shipped to the Solomon Islands to bury bodies. A punishment tour for Clevinger was fifty minutes of a weekend hour spent pacing back and forth before the provost marshal's building with a ton of an unloaded rifle on his shoulder.

It was all very confusing to Clevinger. There were many strange things taking place, but the strangest of all, to Clevinger, was the hatred, the brutal, uncloaked, inexorable hatred of the members of the Action Board, glazing their unforgiving expressions with a hard, vindictive surface, glowing in their narrowed eyes malignantly like inextinguishable coals. Clevinger was stunned to discover it. They would have lynched him if they could. They were three grown men and he was a boy, and they hated him and wished him dead. They had hated him before he came, hated him while he was there, hated him after he left, carried their hatred for him away malignantly like some pampered treasure after they separated from each other and went to their solitude.

Yossarian had done his best to warn him the night before. 'You haven't got a chance, kid,' he told him glumly. 'They hate Jews.'

'But I'm not Jewish,' answered Clevinger.

'It will make no difference,' Yossarian promised, and Yossarian was right. 'They're after everybody.'

Clevinger recoiled from their hatred as though from a blinding light. These three men who hated him spoke his language and wore his uniform, but he saw their loveless faces set immutably into cramped, mean lines of hostility and understood instantly that nowhere in the world, not in all the fascist tanks or planes or submarines, not in the bunkers behind the machine guns or mortars or behind the blowing flame throwers, not even among all the expert gunners of the crack Hermann Goering Antiaircraft Division or among the grisly connivers in all the beer halls in Munich and everywhere else, were there men who hated him more.

9   Major Major Major Major

Major Major Major Major had had a difficult time from the start.

Like Minniver Cheevy, he had been born too late – exactly thirty-six hours too late for the physical well-being of his mother, a gentle, ailing woman who, after a full day and a half's agony in the rigors of childbirth, was depleted of all resolve to pursue further the argument over the new child's name. In the hospital corridor, her husband moved ahead with the unsmiling determination of someone who knew what he was about. Major Major's father was a towering, gaunt man in heavy shoes and a black woolen suit. He filled out the birth certificate without faltering, betraying no emotion at all as he handed the completed form to the floor nurse. The nurse took it from him without comment and padded out of sight. He watched her go, wondering what she had on underneath.

Back in the ward, he found his wife lying vanquished beneath the blankets like a desiccated old vegetable, wrinkled, dry and white, her enfeebled tissues absolutely still. Her bed was at the very end of the ward, near a cracked window thickened with grime. Rain splashed from a moiling sky and the day was dreary and cold. In other parts of the hospital chalky people with aged, blue lips were dying on time. The man stood erect beside the bed and gazed down at the woman a long time.

'I have named the boy Caleb,' he announced to her finally in a soft voice. 'In accordance with your wishes.' The woman made no answer, and slowly the man smiled. He had planned it all perfectly, for his wife was asleep and would never know that he had lied to her as she lay on her sickbed in the poor ward of the county hospital.

From this meager beginning had sprung the ineffectual squadron commander who was now spending the better part of each working day in Pianosa forging Washington Irving's name to official documents. Major Major forged diligently with his left hand to elude identification, insulated against intrusion by his own undesired authority and camouflaged in his false mustache and dark glasses as an additional safeguard against detection by anyone chancing to peer in through the dowdy celluloid window from which some thief had carved out a slice. In between these two low points of his birth and his success lay thirty-one dismal years of loneliness and frustration.

Major Major had been born too late and too mediocre. Some men are born mediocre, some men achieve mediocrity, and some men have mediocrity thrust upon them. With Major Major it had been all three. Even among men lacking all distinction he inevitably stood out as a man lacking more distinction than all the rest, and people who met him were always impressed by how unimpressive he was.

Major Major had three strikes on him from the beginning – his mother, his father and Henry Fonda, to whom he bore a sickly resemblance almost from the moment of his birth. Long before he even suspected who Henry Fonda was, he found himself the subject of unflattering comparisons everywhere he went. Total strangers saw fit to deprecate him, with the result that he was stricken early with a guilty fear of people and an obsequious impulse to apologize to society for the fact that he was not Henry Fonda. It was not an easy task for him to go through life looking something like Henry Fonda, but he never once thought of quitting, having inherited his perseverance from his father, a lanky man with a good sense of humor.

Major Major's father was a sober God-fearing man whose idea of a good joke was to lie about his age. He was a long-limbed farmer, a God-fearing, freedom-loving, law-abiding rugged individualist who held that federal aid to anyone but farmers was creeping socialism. He advocated thrift and hard work and disapproved of loose women who turned him down. His specialty was alfalfa, and he made a good thing out of not growing any. The government paid him well for every bushel of alfalfa he did not grow. The more alfalfa he did not grow, the more money the government gave him, and he spent every penny he didn't earn on new land to increase the amount of alfalfa he did not produce. Major Major's father worked without rest at not growing alfalfa. On long winter evenings he remained indoors and did not mend harness, and he sprang out of bed at the crack of noon every day just to make certain that the chores would not be done. He invested in land wisely and soon was not growing more alfalfa than any other man in the county. Neighbors sought him out for advice on all subjects, for he had made much money and was therefore wise. 'As ye sow, so shall ye reap,' he counseled one and all, and everyone said, 'Amen.'

Major Major's father was an outspoken champion of economy in government, provided it did not interfere with the sacred duty of government to pay farmers as much as they could get for all the alfalfa they produced that no one else wanted or for not producing any alfalfa at all. He was a proud and independent man who was opposed to unemployment insurance and never hesitated to whine, whimper, wheedle, and extort for as much as he could get from whomever he could. He was a devout man whose pulpit was everywhere.

'The Lord gave us good farmers two strong hands so

110

that we could take as much as we could grab with both of them,' he preached with ardor on the courthouse steps or in front of the A & P as he waited for the bad-tempered gum-chewing young cashier he was after to step outside and give him a nasty look. 'If the Lord didn't want us to take as much as we could get,' he preached, 'He wouldn't have given us two good hands to take it with.' And the others murmured, 'Amen.'

Major Major's father had a Calvinist's faith in predestination and could perceive distinctly how everyone's misfortunes but his own were expressions of God's will. He smoked cigarettes and drank whiskey, and he thrived on good wit and stimulating intellectual conversation, particularly his own when he was lying about his age or telling that good one about God and his wife's difficulties in delivering Major Major. The good one about God and his wife's difficulties had to do with the fact that it had taken God only six days to produce the whole world, whereas his wife had spent a full day and a half in labor just to produce Major Major. A lesser man might have wavered that day in the hospital corridor, a weaker man might have compromised on such excellent substitutes as Drum Major, Minor Major, Sergeant Major, or C. Sharp Major, but Major Major's father had waited fourteen years for just such an opportunity, and he was not a person to waste it. Major Major's father had a good joke about opportunity. 'Opportunity only knocks once in this world,' he would say. Major Major's father repeated this good joke at every opportunity.

Being born with a sickly resemblance to Henry Fonda was the first of a long series of practical jokes of which destiny was to make Major Major the unhappy victim throughout his joyless life. Being born Major Major Major was the second. The fact that he had been born Major Major Major was a secret known only to his father. Not until Major Major was enrolling in kindergarten was the discovery of his real name made, and then the effects were disastrous. The news killed his mother, who just lost her will to live and wasted away and died, which was just fine with his father, who had decided to marry the bad-tempered girl at the A & P if he had to and who had not been optimistic about his chances of getting his wife off the land without paying her some money or flogging her.

On Major Major himself the consequences were only slightly less severe. It was a harsh and stunning realization that was forced upon him at so tender an age, the realization that he was not, as he had always been led to believe, Caleb Major, but instead was some total stranger named Major Major Major about whom he knew absolutely nothing and about whom nobody else had ever heard before. What playmates he had withdrew from him and never returned, disposed, as they were, to distrust all strangers, especially one who had already deceived them by pretending to be someone they had known for years. Nobody would have anything to do with him. He began to drop things and to trip. He had a shy and hopeful manner in each new contact, and he was always disappointed. Because he needed a friend so desperately, he never found one. He grew awkwardly into a tall, strange, dreamy boy with fragile eyes and a very delicate mouth whose tentative, groping smile collapsed instantly into hurt disorder at every fresh rebuff.

He was polite to his elders, who disliked him. Whatever his elders told him to do, he did. They told him to look before he leaped, and he always looked before he leaped. They told him never to put off until the next day what he could do the day before, and he never did. He was told to honor his father and his mother, and he honored his father and his mother. He was told that he should not kill, and he did not kill, until he got into the Army. Then he was told to kill, and he killed. He turned the other cheek on every occasion and always did unto others exactly as he would have had others do unto him. When he gave to charity, his left hand never knew what his right hand was doing. He never once took the name of the Lord his God in vain, committed adultery or

112

coveted his neighbor's ass. In fact, he loved his neighbor and never even bore false witness against him. Major Major's elders disliked him because he was such a flagrant nonconformist.

Since he had nothing better to do well in, he did well in school. At the state university he took his studies so seriously that he was suspected by the homosexuals of being a Communist and suspected by the Communists of being a homosexual. He majored in English history, which was a mistake.

'English history!' roared the silver-maned senior Senator from his state indignantly. 'What's the matter with American history? American history is as good as any history in the world!'

Major Major switched immediately to American literature, but not before the F.B.I. had opened a file on him. There were six people and a Scotch terrier inhabiting the remote farmhouse Major Major called home, and five of them and the Scotch terrier turned out to be agents for the F.B.I. Soon they had enough derogatory information on Major Major to do whatever they wanted to with him. The only thing they could find to do with him, however, was take him into the Army as a private and make him a major four days later so that Congressmen with nothing else on their minds could go trotting back and forth through the streets of Washington, D.C., chanting, 'Who promoted Major Major? Who promoted Major Major?'

Actually, Major Major had been promoted by an I.B.M. machine with a sense of humor almost as keen as his father's. When war broke out, he was still docile and compliant. They told him to enlist, and he enlisted. They told him to apply for aviation cadet training, and he applied for aviation cadet training, and the very next night found himself standing barefoot in icy mud at three o'clock in the morning before a tough and belligerent sergeant from the Southwest who told them he could beat hell out of any man in his outfit and was ready to prove it. The recruits in his squadron had all been shaken roughly awake only minutes before by the sergeant's corporals and told to assemble in front of the administration tent. It was still raining on Major Major. They fell into ranks in the civilian clothes they had brought into the Army with them three days before. Those who had lingered to put shoes and socks on were sent back to their cold, wet, dark tents to remove them, and they were all barefoot in the mud as the sergeant ran his stony eyes over their faces and told them he could beat hell out of any man in his outfit. No one was inclined to dispute him.

Major Major's unexpected promotion to major the next day plunged the belligerent sergeant into a bottomless gloom, for he was no longer able to boast that he could beat hell out of any man in his outfit. He brooded for hours in his tent like Saul, receiving no visitors, while his elite guard or corporals stood discouraged watch outside. At three o'clock in the morning he found his solution, and Major Major and the other recruits were again shaken roughly awake and ordered to assemble barefoot in the drizzly glare at the administration tent, where the sergeant was already waiting, his fists clenched on his hips cockily, so eager to speak that he could hardly wait for them to arrive.

'Me and Major Major,' he boasted, in the same tough, clipped tones of the night before, 'can beat hell out of any man in my outfit.'

The officers on the base took action on the Major Major problem later that same day. How could they cope with a major like Major Major? To demean him personally would be to demean all other officers of equal or lesser rank. To treat him with courtesy, on the other hand, was unthinkable. Fortunately, Major Major had applied for aviation cadet training. Orders transferring him away were sent to the mimeograph room late in the afternoon, and at three o'clock in the morning Major Major was again shaken roughly awake, bidden Godspeed by the sergeant and placed aboard a plane heading west.

Lieutenant Scheisskopf turned white as a sheet when Major Major reported to him in California with bare feet and mudcaked toes. Major Major had taken it for granted that he was being shaken roughly awake again to stand barefoot in the mud and had left his shoes and socks in the tent. The civilian clothing in which he reported for duty to Lieutenant Scheisskopf was rumpled and dirty. Lieutenant Scheisskopf, who had not yet made his reputation as a parader, shuddered violently at the picture Major Major would make marching barefoot in his squadron that coming Sunday.

'Go to the hospital quickly,' he mumbled, when he had recovered sufficiently to speak, 'and tell them you're sick. Stay there until your allowance for uniforms catches up with you and you have some money to buy some clothes. And some shoes. Buy some shoes.'

'Yes, sir.'

'I don't think you have to call me "sir," sir,' Lieutenant Scheisskopf pointed out. 'You outrank me.'

'Yes, sir. I may outrank you, sir, but you're still my commanding officer.'

'Yes, sir, that's right,' Lieutenant Scheisskopf agreed. 'You may outrank me, sir, but I'm still your commanding officer. So you better do what I tell you, sir, or you'll get into trouble. Go to the hospital and tell them you're sick, sir. Stay there until your uniform allowance catches up with you and you have some money to buy some uniforms.'

'Yes, sir.'

'And some shoes, sir. Buy some shoes the first chance you get, sir.'

'Yes, sir. I will, sir.'

'Thank you, sir.'

Life in cadet school for Major Major was no different than life had been for him all along. Whoever he was with always wanted him to be with someone else. His instructors gave him preferred treatment at every stage in order to push him along quickly and be rid of him. In almost no time he had his pilot's wings and found himself overseas, where things began suddenly to improve. All his life, Major Major had longed for but one thing, to be absorbed, and in Pianosa, for a while, he finally was. Rank meant little to the men on combat duty, and relations between officers and enlisted men were relaxed and informal. Men whose names he didn't even know said 'Hi' and invited him to go swimming or play basketball. His ripest hours were spent in the day-long basketball games no one gave a damn about winning. Score was never kept, and the number of players might vary from one to thirty-five. Major Major had never played basketball or any other game before, but his great, bobbing height and rapturous enthusiasm helped make up for his innate clumsiness and lack of experience. Major Major found true happiness there on the lopsided basketball court with the officers and enlisted men who were almost his friends. If there were no winners, there were no losers, and Major Major enjoyed every gamboling moment right up till the day Colonel Cathcart roared up in his jeep after Major Duluth was killed and made it impossible for him ever to enjoy playing basketball there again.

'You're the new squadron commander,' Colonel Cathcart had shouted rudely across the railroad ditch to him. 'But don't think it means anything, because it doesn't. All it means is that you're the new squadron commander.'

Colonel Cathcart had nursed an implacable grudge against Major Major for a long time. A superfluous major on his rolls meant an untidy table of organization and gave ammunition to the men at Twenty-seventh Air Force Headquarters who Colonel Cathcart was positive were his enemies and rivals. Colonel Cathcart had been praying for just some stroke of good luck like Major Duluth's death. He had been plagued by one extra major; he now had an opening for one major. He appointed Major Major squadron commander and roared away in his jeep as abruptly as he had come.

For Major Major, it meant the end of the game. His face flushed with discomfort, and he was rooted to the spot in disbelief as the rain clouds gathered above him again. When he turned to his teammates, he encountered a reef of curious, reflective faces all gazing at him woodenly with morose and inscrutable animosity. He shivered with shame. When the game resumed, it was not good any longer. When he dribbled, no one tried to stop him; when he called for a pass, whoever had the ball passed it; and when he missed a basket, no one raced him for the rebound. The only voice was his own. The next day was the same, and the day after that he did not come back.

Almost on cue, everyone in the squadron stopped talking to him and started staring at him. He walked through life self-consciously with downcast eyes and burning cheeks, the object of contempt, envy, suspicion, resentment and malicious innuendo everywhere he went. People who had hardly noticed his resemblance to Henry Fonda before now never ceased discussing it, and there were even those who hinted sinisterly that Major Major had been elevated to squadron commander *because* he resembled Henry Fonda. Captain Black, who had aspired to the position himself, maintained that Major Major really *was* Henry Fonda but was too chickenshit to admit it.

Major Major floundered bewilderedly from one embarrassing catastrophe to another. Without consulting him, Sergeant Towser had his belongings moved into the roomy trailer Major Duluth had occupied alone, and when Major Major came rushing breathlessly into the orderly room to report the theft of his things, the young corporal there scared him half out of his wits by leaping to his feet and shouting 'Attention!' the moment he appeared. Major Major snapped to attention with all the rest in the orderly room, wondering what important personage had entered behind him. Minutes passed in rigid silence, and the whole lot of them might have stood there at attention till doomsday if Major Danby had not dropped by from Group to congratulate Major Major twenty minutes later and put them all at ease.

Major Major fared even more lamentably at the mess hall, where Milo, his face fluttery with smiles, was waiting to usher him proudly to a small table he had set up in front and decorated with an embroidered tablecloth and a nosegay of posies in a pink cut-glass vase. Major Major hung back with horror, but he was not bold enough to resist with all the others watching. Even Havermeyer had lifted his head from his plate to gape at him with his heavy, pendulous jaw. Major Major submitted meekly to Milo's tugging and cowered in disgrace at his private table throughout the whole meal. The food was ashes in his mouth, but he swallowed every mouthful rather than risk offending any of the men connected with its preparation. Alone with Milo later, Major Major felt protest stir for the first time and said he would prefer to continue eating with the other officers. Milo told him it wouldn't work.

'I don't see what there is to work,' Major Major argued. 'Nothing ever happened before.'

'You were never the squadron commander before.'

'Major Duluth was the squadron commander and he always ate at the same table with the rest of the men.'

'It was different with Major Duluth, sir.'

'In what way was it different with Major Duluth?'

'I wish you wouldn't ask me that, sir,' said Milo.

'Is it because I look like Henry Fonda?' Major Major mustered the courage to demand.

'Some people say you *are* Henry Fonda,' Milo answered.

'Well, I'm not Henry Fonda,' Major Major exclaimed, in a voice quavering with exasperation. 'And I don't look the least bit like him. And even if I do look like Henry Fonda, what difference does that make?'

'It doesn't make any difference. That's what I'm trying to tell you, sir. It's just not the same with you as it was with Major Duluth.'

And it just wasn't the same, for when Major Major, at the next meal, stepped from the food counter to sit with the others at the regular tables, he was frozen in his tracks by the impenetrable wall of antagonism thrown up by their faces and stood petrified with his tray quivering in his hands until Milo glided forward wordlessly to rescue him, by leading him tamely to his private table. Major Major gave up after that and always ate at his table alone with his back to the others. He was certain they resented him because he seemed too good to eat with them now that he was squadron commander. There was never any conversation in the mess tent when Major Major was present. He was conscious that other officers tried to avoid eating at the same time, and everyone was greatly relieved when he stopped coming there altogether and began taking his meals in his trailer.

Major Major began forging Washington Irving's name to official documents the day after the first C.I.D. man showed up to interrogate him about somebody at the hospital who had been doing it and gave him the idea. He had been bored and dissatisfied in his new position. He had been made squadron commander but had no idea what he was supposed to do as squadron commander, unless all he was supposed to do was forge Washington Irving's name to official documents and listen to the isolated clinks and thumps of Major — de Coverley's horseshoes falling to the ground outside the window of his small office in the rear of the orderly-room tent. He was hounded incessantly by an impression of vital duties left unfulfilled and waited in vain for his responsibilities to overtake him. He seldom went out unless it was absolutely necessary, for he could not get used to being stared at. Occasionally, the monotony was broken by some officer or enlisted man Sergeant Towser referred to him on some matter that Major Major was unable to cope with and referred right back to Sergeant Towser for sensible disposition. Whatever he was supposed to get done as squadron commander apparently was getting done without any assistance from him. He grew moody and depressed. At times he thought seriously of going with all his sorrows to see the chaplain, but the chaplain seemed so overburdened with miseries of his own that Major Major shrank from adding to his troubles. Besides, he was not quite sure if chaplains were for squadron commanders.

He had never been quite sure about Major — de Coverley, either, who, when he was not away renting apartments or kidnaping foreign laborers, had nothing more pressing to do than pitch horseshoes. Major Major often paid strict attention to the horseshoes falling softly against the earth or riding down around the small steel pegs in the ground. He peeked out at Major — de Coverley for hours and marveled that someone so august had nothing more important to do. He was often tempted to join Major — de Coverley, but pitching horseshoes all day long seemed almost as dull as signing 'Major Major Major' to official documents, and Major — de Coverley's countenance was so forbidding that Major Major was in awe of approaching him.

Major Major wondered about his relationship to Major — de Coverley and about Major — de Coverley's relationship to him. He knew that Major — de Coverley was his executive officer, but he did not know what that meant, and he could not decide whether in Major — de Coverley he was blessed with a lenient superior or cursed with a delinquent subordinate. He did not want to ask Sergeant Towser, of whom he was secretly afraid, and there was no one else he could ask, least of all Major — de Coverley. Few people ever dared approach Major — de Coverley about anything and the only officer foolish enough to pitch one of his horseshoes was stricken the very next day with the worst case of Pianosan crud that Gus or Wes or even Doc Daneeka had ever seen or even heard about. Everyone was positive the disease had been inflicted upon the poor officer in retribution by Major — de Coverley, although no one was sure how.

Most of the official documents that came to Major Major's desk did not concern him at all. The vast majority consisted of allusions to prior communications which Major Major had never seen or heard of. There was never any need to look them up, for the instructions were invariably to disregard. In the space of a single productive minute, therefore, he might endorse twenty separate documents each advising him to pay absolutely no attention to any of the others. From General Peckem's office on the mainland came prolix bulletins each day headed by such cheery homilies as 'Procrastination is the Thief of Time' and 'Cleanliness is Next to Godliness.'

General Peckem's communications about cleanliness and procrastination made Major Major feel like a filthy procrastinator, and he always got those out of the way as quickly as he could. The only official documents that interested him were those occasional ones pertaining to the unfortunate second lieutenant who had been killed on the mission over Orvieto less than two hours after he arrived on Pianosa and whose partly unpacked belongings were still in Yossarian's tent. Since the unfortunate lieutenant had reported to the operations tent instead of to the orderly room, Sergeant Towser had decided that it would be safest to report him as never having reported to the squadron at all, and the occasional documents relating to him dealt with the fact that he seemed to have vanished into thin air, which, in one way, was exactly what did happen to him. In the long run, Major Major was grateful for the official documents that came to his desk, for sitting in his office signing them all day long was a lot better than sitting in his office all day long not signing them. They gave him something to do.

Inevitably, every document he signed came back with a fresh page added for a new signature by him after intervals of from two to ten days. They were always much thicker than formerly, for in between the sheet bearing his last endorsement and the sheet added for his new endorsement were the sheets bearing the most recent endorsements of all the other officers in scattered locations who were also occupied in signing their names to that same official document. Major Major grew despondent as he watched simple communications swell prodigiously into huge manuscripts. No matter how many times he signed one, it always came back for still another signature, and he began to despair of ever being free of any of them. One day – it was the day after the C.I.D. man's first visit – Major Major signed Washington Irving's name to one of the documents instead of his own, just to see how it would feel. He liked it. He liked it so much that for the rest of that afternoon he did the same with all the official documents. It was an act of impulsive frivolity and rebellion for which he knew afterward he would be punished severely. The next morning he entered his office in trepidation and waited to see what would happen. Nothing happened.

He had sinned, and it was good, for none of the documents to which he had signed Washington Irving's name ever came back! Here, at last, was progress, and Major Major threw himself into his new career with uninhibited gusto. Signing Washington Irving's name to official documents was not much of a career, perhaps, but it was less monotonous than signing 'Major Major Major.' When Washington Irving did grow monotonous, he could reverse the order and sign Irving Washington until that grew monotonous. And he was getting something done, for none of the documents signed with either of these names ever came back to the squadron.

What did come back, eventually, was a *second* C.I.D. man, masquerading as a pilot. The men knew he was a C.I.D. man because he confided to them he was and urged each of them not to reveal his true identity to any of the other men to whom he had already confided that he was a C.I.D. man.

'You're the only one in the squadron who knows I'm a C.I.D. man,' he confided to Major Major, 'and it's absolutely essential that it remain a secret so that my efficiency won't be impaired. Do you understand?'

'Sergeant Towser knows.'

'Yes, I know. I had to tell him in order to get in to see you. But I know he won't tell a soul under any circumstances.'

'He told me,' said Major Major. 'He told me there was a C.I.D. man outside to see me.'

'That bastard. I'll have to throw a security check on him. I wouldn't leave any top-secret documents lying around here if I were you. At least not until I make my report.'

'I don't get any top-secret documents,' said Major Major.

'That's the kind I mean. Lock them in your cabinet where Sergeant Towser can't get his hands on them.'

'Sergeant Towser has the only key to the cabinet.'

'I'm afraid we're wasting time,' said the second C.I.D. man rather stiffly. He was a brisk, pudgy, high-strung person whose movements were swift and certain. He took a number of photostats out of a large red expansion envelope he had been hiding conspicuously beneath a leather flight jacket painted garishly with pictures of airplanes flying through orange bursts of flak and with orderly rows of little bombs signifying fifty-five combat missions flown. 'Have you ever seen any of these?'

Major Major looked with a blank expression at copies of personal correspondence from the hospital on which the censoring officer had written 'Washington Irving' or 'Irving Washington.'

'No.'

'How about these?'

Major Major gazed next at copies of official documents addressed to him to which he had been signing the same signatures.

'No.'

'Is the man who signed these names in your squadron?'

'Which one? There are two names here.'

'Either one. We figure that Washington Irving and Irving Washington are one man and that he's using two names just to throw us off the track. That's done very often you know.'

'I don't think there's a man with either of those names in my squadron.'

A look of disappointment crossed the second C.I.D. man's face. 'He's a lot cleverer than we thought,' he observed. 'He's using a third name and posing as someone else. And I think . . . yes, I think I know what that third name is.' With excitement and inspiration, he held another photostat out for Major Major to study. 'How about this?'

Major Major bent forward slightly and saw a copy of the piece of V mail from which Yossarian had blacked out everything but the name Mary and on which he had written, 'I yearn for you tragically. R. O. Shipman, Chaplain, U.S. Army.' Major Major shook his head.

'I've never seen it before.'

'Do you know who R. O. Shipman is?'

'He's the group chaplain.'

'That locks it up,' said the second C.I.D. man. 'Washington Irving is the group chaplain.'

Major Major felt a twinge of alarm. 'R. O. Shipman is the group chaplain,' he corrected.

'Are you sure?'

'Yes.'

'Why should the group chaplain write this on a letter?'

'Perhaps somebody else wrote it and forged his name.'

'Why should somebody want to forge the group chaplain's name?'

'To escape detection.'

'You may be right,' the second C.I.D. man decided after an instant's hesitation, and smacked his lips crisply. 'Maybe we're confronted with a gang, with two men working together who just happen to have opposite names. Yes, I'm sure that's it. One of them here in the squadron, one of them up at the hospital and one of them with the chaplain. That makes three men, doesn't it? Are you absolutely sure you never saw any of these official documents before?'

'I would have signed them if I had.'

'With whose name?' asked the second C.I.D. man cunningly. 'Yours or Washington Irving's?'

'With my own name,' Major Major told him. 'I don't even know Washington Irving's name.'

The second C.I.D. man broke into a smile.

'Major, I'm glad you're in the clear. It means we'll be able to work together, and I'm going to need every man I can get. Somewhere in the European theater of operations is a man who's getting his hands on communications addressed to you. Have you any idea who it can be?'

'No.'

'Well, I have a pretty good idea,' said the second C.I.D. man, and leaned forward to whisper confidentially. 'That bastard Towser. Why else would he go around shooting his mouth off about me? Now, you keep your eyes open and let me know the minute you hear anyone even talking about Washington Irving. I'll throw a security check on the chaplain and everyone else around here.'

The moment he was gone, the first C.I.D. man jumped into Major Major's office through the window and wanted to know who the second C.I.D. man was. Major Major barely recognized him.

'He was a C.I.D. man,' Major Major told him.

'Like hell he was,' said the first C.I.D. man. 'I'm the C.I.D. man around here.'

Major Major barely recognized him because he was wearing a faded maroon corduroy bathrobe with open seams under both arms, linty flannel pajamas, and worn house slippers with one flapping sole. This was regulation hospital dress, Major Major recalled. The man had added about twenty pounds and seemed bursting with good health.

'I'm really a very sick man,' he whined. 'I caught cold in the hospital from a fighter pilot and came down with a very serious case of pneumonia.'

'I'm very sorry,' Major Major said.

'A lot of good that does me,' the C.I.D. man sniveled. 'I don't want your sympathy. I just want you to know what I'm going through. I came down to warn you that Washington Irving seems to have shifted his base of operations from the hospital to your squadron. You haven't heard anyone around here talking about Washington Irving, have you?'

'As a matter of fact, I have,' Major Major answered.

'That man who was just in here. He was talking about Washington Irving.'

'Was he really?' the first C.I.D. man cried with delight. 'This might be just what we needed to crack the case wide open! You keep him under surveillance twenty-four hours a day while I rush back to the hospital and write my superiors for further instructions.' The C.I.D. man jumped out of Major Major's office through the window and was gone.

A minute later, the flap separating Major Major's office from the orderly room flew open and the second C.I.D. man was back, puffing frantically in haste. Gasping for breath, he shouted. 'I just saw a man in red pajamas jumping out of your window and go running up the road! Didn't you see him?'

'He was here talking to me,' Major Major answered.

'I thought that looked mighty suspicious, a man jumping out the window in red pajamas.' The man paced about the small office in vigorous circles. 'At first I thought it was you, hightailing it for Mexico. But now I see it wasn't you. He didn't say anything about Washington Irving, did he?'

'As a matter of fact,' said Major Major, 'he did.'

'He did?' cried the second C.I.D. man. 'That's fine! This might be just the break we needed to crack the case wide open. Do you know where we can find him?'

'At the hospital. He's really a very sick man.'

'That's great!' exclaimed the second C.I.D. man. 'I'll go right up there after him. It would be best if I went incognito. I'll go explain the situation at the medical tent and have them send me there as a patient.'

'They won't send me to the hospital as a patient unless I'm sick,' he reported back to Major Major. 'Actually, I am pretty sick. I've been meaning to turn myself in for a checkup, and this will be a good opportunity. I'll go back

126

to the medical tent and tell them I'm sick, and I'll get sent to the hospital that way.'

'Look what they did to me,' he reported back to Major Major with purple gums. His distress was inconsolable. He carried his shoes and socks in his hands, and his toes had been painted with gentian-violet solution, too. 'Who ever heard of a C.I.D. man with purple gums?' he moaned.

He walked away from the orderly room with his head down and tumbled into a slit trench and broke his nose. His temperature was still normal, but Gus and Wes made an exception of him and sent him to the hospital in an ambulance.

Major Major had lied, and it was good. He was not really surprised that it was good, for he had observed that people who did lie were, on the whole, more resourceful and ambitious and successful than people who did not lie. Had he told the truth to the second C.I.D. man, he would have found himself in trouble. Instead he had lied and he was free to continue his work.

He became more circumspect in his work as a result of the visit from the second C.I.D. man. He did all his signing with his left hand and only while wearing the dark glasses and false mustache he had used unsuccessfully to help him begin playing basketball again. As an additional precaution, he made a happy switch from Washington Irving to John Milton. John Milton was supple and concise. Like Washington Irving, he could be reversed with good effect whenever he grew monotonous. Furthermore, he enabled Major Major to double his output, for John Milton was so much shorter than either his own name or Washington Irving's and took so much less time to write. John Milton proved fruitful in still one more respect. He was versatile, and Major Major soon found himself incorporating the signature in fragments of imaginary dialogues. Thus, typical endorsements on the official documents might read, 'John, Milton is a sadist' or 'Have you seen Milton, John?' One signature of which he was especially proud read, 'Is anybody in the John, Milton?' John Milton threw open whole new vistas filled with charming, inexhaustible possibilities that promised to ward off monotony forever. Major Major went back to Washington Irving when John Milton grew monotonous.

Major Major had bought the dark glasses and false mustache in Rome in a final, futile attempt to save himself from the swampy degradation into which he was steadily sinking. First there had been the awful humiliation of the Great Loyalty Oath Crusade, when not one of the thirty or forty people circulating competitive loyalty oaths would even allow him to sign. Then, just when that was blowing over, there was the matter of Clevinger's plane disappearing so mysteriously in thin air with every member of the crew, and blame for the strange mishap centering balefully on him because he had never signed any of the loyalty oaths.

The dark glasses had large magenta rims. The false black mustache was a flamboyant organ grinder's, and he wore them both to the basketball game one day when he felt he could endure his loneliness no longer. He affected an air of jaunty familiarity as he sauntered to the court and prayed silently that he would not be recognized. The others pretended not to recognize him, and he began to have fun. Just as he finished congratulating himself on his innocent ruse he was bumped hard by one of his opponents and knocked to his knees. Soon he was bumped hard again, and it dawned on him that they did recognize him and that they were using his disguise as a license to elbow, trip and maul him. They did not want him at all. And just as he did realize this, the players on his team fused instinctively with the players on the other team into a single, howling, bloodthirsty mob that descended upon him from all sides with foul curses and swinging fists. They knocked him to the ground, kicked him while he was on the ground, attacked him again after he had struggled blindly to his feet. He covered his face with his hands and could not see. They swarmed all over each other in their frenzied compulsion to bludgeon him, kick him, gouge him, trample him. He was pummeled spinning to the edge of the ditch and sent slithering down on his head and shoulders. At the bottom he found his footing, clambered up the other wall and staggered away beneath the hail of hoots and stones with which they pelted him until he lurched into shelter around a corner of the orderly room tent. His paramount concern throughout the entire assault was to keep his dark glasses and false mustache in place so that he might continue pretending he was somebody else and be spared the dreaded necessity of having to confront them with his authority.

Back in his office, he wept; and when he finished weeping he washed the blood from his mouth and nose, scrubbed the dirt from the abrasions on his cheek and forehead, and summoned Sergeant Towser.

'From now on,' he said, 'I don't want anyone to come in to see me while I'm here. Is that clear?'

'Yes, sir,' said Sergeant Towser. 'Does that include me?'

'Yes.'

'I see. Will that be all?'

'Yes.'

'What shall I say to the people who do come to see you while you're here?'

'Tell them I'm in and ask them to wait.'

'Yes, sir. For how long?'

'Until I've left.'

'And then what shall I do with them?'

'I don't care.'

'May I send them in to see you after you've left?'

'Yes.'

'But you won't be here then, will you?'

'No.'

'Yes, sir. Will that be all?'

'Yes.'

'Yes, sir.'

'From now on,' Major Major said to the middle-aged enlisted man who took care of his trailer, 'I don't want you to come here while I'm here to ask me if there's anything you can do for me. Is that clear?'

'Yes, sir,' said the orderly. 'When should I come here to find out if there's anything you want me to do for you?'

'When I'm not here.'

'Yes, sir. And what should I do?'

'Whatever I tell you to.'

'But you won't be here to tell me. Will you?'

'No.'

'Then what should I do?'

'Whatever has to be done.'

'Yes, sir.'

'That will be all,' said Major Major.

'Yes, sir,' said the orderly. 'Will that be all?'

'No,' said Major Major. 'Don't come in to clean, either. Don't come in for anything unless you're sure I'm not here.'

'Yes, sir. But how can I always be sure?'

'If you're not sure, just assume that I am here and go away until you are sure. Is that clear?'

'Yes, sir.'

'I'm sorry to have to talk to you in this way, but I have to. Goodbye.'

'Goodbye, sir.'

'And thank you. For everything.'

'Yes, sir.'

'From now on,' Major Major said to Milo Minderbinder, 'I'm not going to come to the mess hall any more. I'll have all my meals brought to me in my trailer.'

'I think that's a good idea, sir,' Milo answered. 'Now I'll be able to serve you special dishes that the others will never know about. I'm sure you'll enjoy them. Colonel Cathcart always does.'

'I don't want any special dishes. I want exactly what you serve all the other officers. Just have whoever brings it knock once on my door and leave the tray on the step. Is that clear?'

'Yes, sir,' said Milo. 'That's very clear. I've got some live Maine lobsters hidden away that I can serve you

130

tonight with an excellent Roquefort salad and two frozen éclairs that were smuggled out of Paris only yesterday together with an important member of the French underground. Will that do for a start?'

'No.'

'Yes, sir. I understand.'

For dinner that night Milo served him broiled Maine lobster with excellent Roquefort salad and two frozen éclairs. Major Major was annoyed. If he sent it back, though, it would only go to waste or to somebody else, and Major Major had a weakness for broiled lobster. He ate with a guilty conscience. The next day for lunch there was terrapin Maryland with a whole quart of Dom Pérignon 1937, and Major Major gulped it down without a thought.

After Milo, there remained only the men in the orderly room, and Major Major avoided them by entering and leaving every time through the dingy celluloid window of his office. The window unbuttoned and was low and large and easy to jump through from either side. He managed the distance between the orderly room and his trailer by darting around the corner of the tent when the coast was clear, leaping down into the railroad ditch and dashing along with head bowed until he attained the sanctuary of the forest. Abreast of his trailer, he left the ditch and wove his way speedily toward home through the dense underbrush, in which the only person he ever encountered was Captain Flume, who, drawn and ghostly, frightened him half to death one twilight by materializing without warning out of a patch of dewberry bushes to complain that Chief White Halfoat had threatened to slit his throat open from ear to ear.

'If you ever frighten me like that again,' Major Major told him, 'I'll slit your throat open from ear to ear.'

Captain Flume gasped and dissolved right back into the patch of dewberry bushes, and Major Major never set eyes on him again.

When Major Major looked back on what he had accomplished, he was pleased. In the midst of a few

131

foreign acres teeming with more than two hundred people, he had succeeded in becoming a recluse. With a little ingenuity and vision, he had made it all but impossible for anyone in the squadron to talk to him, which was just fine with everyone, he noticed, since no one wanted to talk to him anyway. No one, it turned out, but that madman Yossarian, who brought him down with a flying tackle one day as he was scooting along the bottom of the ditch to his trailer for lunch.

The last person in the squadron Major Major wanted to be brought down with a flying tackle by was Yossarian. There was something inherently disreputable about Yossarian, always carrying on so disgracefully about that dead man in his tent who wasn't even there and then taking off all his clothes after the Avignon mission and going around without them right up to the day General Dreedle stepped up to pin a medal on him for his heroism over Ferrara and found him standing in formation stark naked. No one in the world had the power to remove the dead man's disorganized effects from Yossarian's tent. Major Major had forfeited the authority when he permitted Sergeant Towser to report the lieutenant who had been killed over Orvieto less than two hours after he arrived in the squadron as never having arrived in the squadron at all. The only one with any right to remove his belongings from Yossarian's tent, it seemed to Major Major, was Yossarian himself, and Yossarian, it seemed to Major Major, had no right.

Major Major groaned after Yossarian brought him down with a flying tackle, and tried to wiggle to his feet. Yossarian wouldn't let him.

'Captain Yossarian,' Yossarian said, 'requests permission to speak to the major at once about a matter of life or death.'

'Let me up, please,' Major Major bid him in cranky discomfort. 'I can't return your salute while I'm lying on my arm.'

Yossarian released him. They stood up slowly. Yossarian saluted again and repeated his request.

'Let's go to my office,' Major Major said. 'I don't think this is the best place to talk.'

'Yes, sir,' answered Yossarian.

They smacked the gravel from their clothing and walked in constrained silence to the entrance of the orderly room.

'Give me a minute or two to put some mercurochrome on these cuts. Then have Sergeant Towser send you in.'

'Yes, sir.'

Major Major strode with dignity to the rear of the orderly room without glancing at any of the clerks and typists working at the desks and filing cabinets. He let the flap leading to his office fall closed behind him. As soon as he was alone in his office, he raced across the room to the window and jumped outside to dash away. He found Yossarian blocking his path. Yossarian was waiting at attention and saluted again.

'Captain Yossarian requests permission to speak to the major at once about a matter of life or death,' he repeated determinedly.

'Permission denied,' Major Major snapped.

'That won't do it.'

Major Major gave in. 'All right,' he conceded wearily. 'I'll talk to you. Please jump inside my office.'

'After you.'

They jumped inside the office. Major Major sat down, and Yossarian moved around in front of his desk and told him that he did not want to fly any more combat missions. What *could he do*? Major Major asked himself. All he could do was what he had been instructed to do by Colonel Korn and hope for the best.

'Why not?' he asked.

'I'm afraid.'

'That's nothing to be ashamed of,' Major Major counseled him kindly. 'We're all afraid.'

'I'm not ashamed,' Yossarian said. 'I'm just afraid.'

'You wouldn't be normal if you were never afraid. Even the bravest men experience fear. One of the biggest jobs we all face in combat is to overcome our fear.'

'Oh, come on, Major. Can't we do without that horse-shit?'

Major Major lowered his gaze sheepishly and fiddled with his fingers. 'What do you want me to tell you?'

'That I've flown enough missions and can go home.'

'How many have you flown?'

'Fifty-one.'

'You've only got four more to fly.'

'He'll raise them. Every time I get close he raises them.'

'Perhaps he won't this time.'

'He never sends anyone home, anyway. He just keeps them around waiting for rotation orders until he doesn't have enough men left for the crews, and then raises the number of missions and throws them all back on combat status. He's been doing that ever since he got here.'

'You mustn't blame Colonel Cathcart for any delay with the orders,' Major Major advised. 'It's Twenty-seventh Air Force's responsibility to process the orders promptly once they get them from us.'

'He could still ask for replacements and send us home when the orders did come back. Anyway, I've been told that Twenty-seventh Air Force wants only forty missions and that it's only his own idea to get us to fly fifty-five.'

'I wouldn't know anything about that,' Major Major answered. 'Colonel Cathcart is our commanding officer and we must obey him. Why don't you fly the four more missions and see what happens?'

'I don't want to.'

What could you do? Major Major asked himself again. What could you do with a man who looked you squarely in the eye and said he would rather die than be killed in combat, a man who was at least as mature and intelligent as you were and who you had to pretend was not? What could you say to him?

'Suppose we let you pick your missions and fly milk

runs,' Major Major said. 'That way you can fly the four missions and not run any risks.'

'I don't want to fly milk runs. I don't want to be in the war any more.'

'Would you like to see our country lose?' Major Major asked.

'We won't lose. We've got more men, more money and more material. There are ten million men in uniform who could replace me. Some people are getting killed and a lot more are making money and having fun. Let somebody else get killed.'

'But suppose everybody on our side felt that way.'

'Then I'd certainly be a damned fool to feel any other way. Wouldn't I?'

What could you possibly say to him? Major Major wondered forlornly. One thing he could not say was that there was nothing he could do. To say there was nothing he could do would suggest he *would* do something if he could and imply the existence of an error of injustice in Colonel Korn's policy. Colonel Korn had been most explicit about that. He must never say there was nothing he could do.

'I'm sorry,' he said. 'But there's nothing I can do.'

10 Wintergreen

Clevinger was dead. That was the basic flaw in his philosophy. Eighteen planes had let down through a beaming white cloud off the coast of Elba one afternoon on the way back from the weekly milk run to Parma; seventeen came out. No trace was ever found of the other, not in the air or on the smooth surface of the jade waters below. There was no debris. Helicopters circled the white cloud till sunset. During the night the cloud blew away, and in the morning there was no more Clevinger.

The disappearance was astounding, as astounding, certainly, as the Grand Conspiracy of Lowery Field, when all sixty-four men in a single barrack vanished one payday and were never heard of again. Until Clevinger was snatched from existence so adroitly, Yossarian had assumed that the men had simply decided unanimously to go AWOL the same day. In fact, he had been so encouraged by what appeared to be a mass desertion from sacred responsibility that he had gone running outside in elation to carry the exciting news to ex-P.F.C. Wintergreen.

'What's so exciting about it?' ex-P.F.C. Wintergreen sneered obnoxiously, resting his filthy GI shoe on his spade and lounging back in a surly slough against the wall of one of the deep, square holes it was his military specialty to dig.

Ex-P.F.C. Wintergreen was a snide little punk who enjoyed working at cross-purposes. Each time he went AWOL, he was caught and sentenced to dig and fill up holes six feet deep, wide and long for a specified length of time. Each time he finished his sentence, he went AWOL again. Ex-P.F.C. Wintergreen accepted his role of digging and filling up holes with all the uncomplaining dedication of a true patriot.

'It's not a bad life,' he would observe philosophically. 'And I guess somebody has to do it.'

He had wisdom enough to understand that digging holes in Colorado was not such a bad assignment in wartime. Since the holes were in no great demand, he could dig them and fill them up at a leisurely pace, and he was seldom overworked. On the other hand, he was busted down to buck private each time he was court-martialed. He regretted this loss of rank keenly.

'It was kind of nice being a P.F.C.,' he reminisced yearningly. 'I had status – you know what I mean? – and I used to travel in the best circles.' His face darkened with resignation. 'But that's all behind me now,' he guessed. 'The next time I go over the hill it will be as a buck private, and I just know it won't be the same.' There was no future in digging holes. 'The job isn't even steady. I lose it each time I finish serving my sentence. Then I have to go over the hill again if I want it back. And I can't even keep doing that. There's a catch. Catch-22. The next time I go over the hill, it will mean the stockade. I don't know what's going to become of me. I might even wind up overseas if I'm not careful.' He did not want to keep digging holes for the rest of his life, although he had no objection to doing it as long as there was a war going on and it was part of the war effort. 'It's a matter of duty,' he observed, 'and we each have our own to perform. My duty is to keep digging these holes, and I've been doing such a good job of it that I've just been

137

recommended for the Good Conduct Medal. Your duty is to screw around in cadet school and hope the war ends before you get out. The duty of the men in combat is to win the war, and I just wish they were doing their duty as well as I've been doing mine. It wouldn't be fair if I had to go overseas and do their job too, would it?'

One day ex-P.F.C. Wintergreen struck open a water pipe while digging in one of his holes and almost drowned to death before he was fished out nearly unconscious. Word spread that it was oil, and Chief White Halfoat was kicked off the base. Soon every man who could find a shovel was outside digging frenziedly for oil. Dirt flew everywhere; the scene was almost like the morning in Pianosa seven months later after the night Milo bombed the squadron with every plane he had accumulated in his M & M syndicate, and the airfield, bomb dump and repair hangars as well, and all the survivors were outside hacking cavernous shelters into the solid ground and roofing them over with sheets of armor plate stolen from the repair sheds at the field and with tattered squares of waterproof canvas stolen from the side flaps of each other's tents. Chief White Halfoat was transferred out of Colorado at the first rumor of oil and came to rest finally in Pianosa as a replacement for Lieutenant Coombs, who had gone out on a mission as a guest one day just to see what combat was like and had died over Ferrara in the plane with Kraft. Yossarian felt guilty each time he remembered Kraft, guilty because Kraft had been killed on Yossarian's second bomb run, and guilty because Kraft had got mixed up innocently also in the Splendid Atabrine Insurrection that had begun in Puerto Rico on the first leg of their flight overseas and ended in Pianosa ten days later with Appleby striding dutifully into the orderly room the moment he arrived to report Yossarian for refusing to take his Atabrine tablets. The sergeant there invited him to be seated.

'Thank you, Sergeant, I think I will,' said Appleby. 'About how long will I have to wait? I've still got a lot to get done today so that I can be fully prepared bright and early tomorrow morning to go into combat the minute they want me to.'

'Sir?'

'What's that, Sergeant?'

'What was your question?'

'About how long will I have to wait before I can go in to see the major?'

'Just until he goes out to lunch,' Sergeant Towser replied. 'Then you can go right in.'

'But he won't be there then. Will he?'

'No, sir. Major Major won't be back in his office until after lunch.'

'I see,' Appleby decided uncertainly. 'I think I'd better come back after lunch, then.'

Appleby turned from the orderly room in secret confusion. The moment he stepped outside, he thought he saw a tall, dark officer who looked a little like Henry Fonda come jumping out of the window of the orderly-room tent and go scooting out of sight around the corner. Appleby halted and squeezed his eyes closed. An anxious doubt assailed him. He wondered if he were suffering from malaria, or, worse, from an overdose of Atabrine tablets. Appleby had been taking four times as many Atabrine tablets as the amount prescribed because he wanted to be four times as good a pilot as everyone else. His eyes were still shut when Sergeant Towser tapped him lightly on the shoulder and told him he could go in now if he wanted to, since Major Major had just gone out. Appleby's confidence returned.

'Thank you, Sergeant. Will he be back soon?'

'He'll be back right after lunch. Then you'll have to go right out and wait for him in front till he leaves for dinner. Major Major never sees anyone in his office while he's in his office.'

'Sergeant, what did you just say?'

'I said that Major Major never sees anyone in his office while he's in his office.'

Appleby stared at Sergeant Towser intently and

attempted a firm tone. 'Sergeant, are you trying to make a fool out of me just because I'm new in the squadron and you've been overseas a long time?'

'Oh, no, sir,' answered the sergeant deferentially. 'Those are my orders. You can ask Major Major when you see him.'

'That's just what I intend to do, Sergeant. When can I see him?'

'Never.'

Crimson with humiliation, Appleby wrote down his report about Yossarian and the Atabrine tablets on a pad the sergeant offered him and left quickly, wondering if perhaps Yossarian were not the only man privileged to wear an officer's uniform who was crazy.

By the time Colonel Cathcart had raised the number of missions to fifty-five, Sergeant Towser had begun to suspect that perhaps every man who wore a uniform was crazy. Sergeant Towser was lean and angular and had find blond hair so light it was almost without color, sunken cheeks, and teeth like large white marshmallows. He ran the squadron and was not happy doing it. Men like Hungry Joe glowered at him with blameful hatred, and Appleby subjected him to vindictive discourtesy now that he had established himself as a hot pilot and a ping-pong player who never lost a point. Sergeant Towser ran the squadron because there was no one else in the squadron to run it. He had no interest in war or advancement. He was interested in shards and Hepplewhite furniture.

Almost without realizing it, Sergeant Towser had fallen into the habit of thinking of the dead man in Yossarian's tent in Yossarian's own terms – as a dead man in Yossarian's tent. In reality, he was no such thing. He was simply a replacement pilot who had been killed in combat before he had officially reported for duty. He had stopped at the operations tent to inquire the way to the orderly-room tent and had been sent right into action because so many men had completed the thirty-five missions required then that Captain Piltchard and Captain

Wren were finding it difficult to assemble the number of crews specified by Group. Because he had never officially gotten into the squadron, he could never officially be gotten out, and Sergeant Towser sensed that the multiplying communications relating to the poor man would continue reverberating forever.

His name was Mudd. To Sergeant Towser, who deplored violence and waste with equal aversion, it seemed like such an abhorrent extravagance to fly Mudd all the way across the ocean just to have him blown into bits over Orvieto less than two hours after he arrived. No one could recall who he was or what he had looked like, least of all Captain Piltchard and Captain Wren, who remembered only that a new officer had shown up at the operations tent just in time to be killed and who colored uneasily every time the matter of the dead man in Yossarian's tent was mentioned. The only one who might have seen Mudd, the men in the same plane, had all been blown to bits with him.

Yossarian, on the other hand, knew exactly who Mudd was. Mudd was the unknown soldier who had never had a chance, for that was the only thing anyone ever did know about all the unknown soldiers – they never had a chance. They had to be dead. And this dead one was really unknown, even though his belongings still lay in a tumble on the cot in Yossarian's tent almost exactly as he had left them three months earlier the day he never arrived – all contaminated with death less than two hours later, in the same way that all was contaminated with death in the very next week during the Great Big Siege of Bologna when the moldy odor of mortality hung wet in the air with the sulphurous fog and every man scheduled to fly was already tainted.

There was no escaping the mission to Bologna once Colonel Cathcart had volunteered his group for the ammunition dumps there that the heavy bombers on the Italian mainland had been unable to destroy from their higher altitudes. Each day's delay deepened the awareness and deepened the gloom. The clinging, overpowering conviction of death spread steadily with the continuing rainfall, soaking mordantly into each man's ailing countenance like the corrosive blot of some crawling disease. Everyone smelled of formaldehyde. There was nowhere to turn for help, not even to the medical tent, which had been ordered closed by Colonel Korn so that no one could report for sick call, as the men had done on the one clear day with a mysterious epidemic of diarrhea that had forced still another postponement. With sick call suspended and the door to the medical tent nailed shut, Doc Daneeka spent the intervals between rain perched on a high stool, wordlessly absorbing the bleak outbreak of fear with a sorrowing neutrality, roosting like a melancholy buzzard below the ominous, hand-lettered sign tacked up on the closed door of the medical tent by Captain Black as a joke and left hanging there by Doc Daneeka because it was no joke. The sign was bordered in dark crayon and read: 'CLOSED UNTIL FURTHER NOTICE. DEATH IN THE FAMILY.'

The fear flowed everywhere, into Dunbar's squadron, where Dunbar poked his head inquiringly through the entrance of the medical tent there one twilight and spoke respectfully to the blurred outline of Dr. Stubbs, who was sitting in the dense shadows inside before a bottle of whiskey and a bell jar filled with purified drinking water.

'Are you all right?' he asked solicitously.

'Terrible,' Dr. Stubbs answered.

'What are you doing here?'

'Sitting.'

'I thought there was no more sick call.'

'There ain't.'

'Then why are you sitting here?'

'Where else should I sit? At the goddam officers' club with Colonel Cathcart and Korn? Do you know what I'm doing here?'

'Sitting.'

'In the squadron, I mean. Not in the tent. Don't be such a goddam wise guy. Can you figure out what a doctor is doing here in the squadron?'

'They've got the doors to the medical tents nailed shut in the other squadrons,' Dunbar remarked.

'If anyone sick walks through my door I'm going to ground him,' Dr. Stubbs vowed. 'I don't give a damn what they say.'

'You can't ground anyone,' Dunbar reminded. 'Don't you know the orders?'

'I'll knock him flat on his ass with an injection and really ground him.' Dr. Stubbs laughed with sardonic amusement at the prospect. 'They think they can order sick call out of existence. The bastards. Ooops, there it goes again.' The rain began falling again, first in the trees, then in the mud puddles, then, faintly, like a soothing murmur, on the tent top. 'Everything's wet,' Dr. Stubbs observed with revulsion. 'Even the latrines and urinals are backing up in protest. The whole goddam world smells like a charnel house.'

The silence seemed bottomless when he stopped talking. Night fell. There was a sense of vast isolation.

'Turn on the light,' Dunbar suggested.

'There is no light. I don't feel like starting my generator. I used to get a big kick out of saving people's lives. Now I wonder what the hell's the point, since they all have to die anyway.'

'Oh, there's a point, all right,' Dunbar assured him.

'Is there? What is the point?'

'The point is to keep them from dying for as long as you can.'

'Yeah, but what's the point, since they all have to die anyway?'

'The trick is not to think about that.'

'Never mind the trick. What the hell's the point?'

Dunbar pondered in silence for a few moments. 'Who the hell knows?'

Dunbar didn't know. Bologna should have exulted Dunbar, because the minutes dawdled and the hours dragged like centuries. Instead it tortured him, because he knew he was going to be killed.

'Do you really want some more codeine?' Dr. Stubbs asked.

143

'It's for my friend Yossarian. He's sure he's going to be killed.'

'Yossarian? Who the hell is Yossarian? What the hell kind of a name is Yossarian, anyway? Isn't he the one who got drunk and started that fight with Colonel Korn at the officers' club the other night?'

'That's right. He's Assyrian.'

'That crazy bastard.'

'He's not so crazy,' Dunbar said. 'He swears he's not going to fly to Bologna.'

'That's just what I mean,' Dr. Stubbs answered. 'That crazy bastard may be the only sane one left.'

11   Captain Black

Corporal Kolodny learned about it first in a phone call
from Group and was so shaken by the news that he
crossed the intelligence tent on tiptoe to Captain Black,
who was resting drowsily with his bladed shins up on
the desk, and relayed the information to him in a
shocked whisper.

Captain Black brightened immediately. 'Bologna?' he
exclaimed with delight. 'Well, I'll be damned.' He broke
into loud laughter. 'Bologna, huh?' He laughed again
and shook his head in pleasant amazement. 'Oh, boy! I
can't wait to see those bastards' faces when they find
out they're going to Bologna. Ha, ha, ha!'

It was the first really good laugh Captain Black had
enjoyed since the day Major Major outsmarted him and
was appointed squadron commander, and he rose with
torpid enthusiasm and stationed himself behind the
front counter in order to wring the most enjoyment from
the occasion when the bombardiers arrived for their
map kits.

'That's right, you bastards, Bologna,' he kept repeating to all the bombardiers who inquired incredulously if
they were really going to Bologna. 'Ha! Ha! Ha! Eat your
livers, you bastards. This time you're really in for it.'

Captain Black followed the last of them outside to observe with relish the effect of the knowledge upon all of the other officers and enlisted men who were assembling with their helmets, parachutes and flak suits around the four trucks idling in the center of the squadron area. He was a tall, narrow, disconsolate man who moved with a crabby listlessness. He shaved his pinched, pale face every third or fourth day, and most of the time he appeared to be growing a reddish-gold mustache over his skinny upper lip. He was not disappointed in the scene outside. There was consternation darkening every expression, and Captain Black yawned deliciously, rubbed the last lethargy from his eyes and laughed gloatingly each time he told someone else to eat his liver.

Bologna turned out to be the most rewarding event in Captain Black's life since the day Major Duluth was killed over Perugia and he was almost selected to replace him. When word of Major Duluth's death was radioed back to the field, Captain Black responded with a surge of joy. Although he had never really contemplated the possibility before, Captain Black understood at once that he was the logical man to succeed Major Duluth as squadron commander. To begin with, he was the squadron intelligence officer, which meant he was more intelligent than everyone else in the squadron. True, he was not on combat status, as Major Duluth had been and as all squadron commanders customarily were; but this was really another powerful argument in his favor, since his life was in no danger and he would be able to fill the post for as long as his country needed him. The more Captain Black thought about it, the more inevitable it seemed. It was merely a matter of dropping the right word in the right place quickly. He hurried back to his office to determine a course of action. Settling back in his swivel chair, his feet up on the desk and his eyes closed, he began imagining how beautiful everything would be once he was squadron commander.

While Captain Black was imagining, Colonel Cathcart

146

was acting, and Captain Black was flabbergasted by the speed with which, he concluded, Major Major had outsmarted him. His great dismay at the announcement of Major Major's appointment as squadron commander was tinged with an embittered resentment he made no effort to conceal. When fellow administrative officers expressed astonishment at Colonel Cathcart's choice of Major Major, Captain Black muttered that there was something funny going on; when they speculated on the political value of Major Major's resemblance to Henry Fonda, Captain Black asserted that Major Major really *was* Henry Fonda; and when they remarked that Major Major was somewhat odd, Captain Black announced that he was a Communist.

'They're taking over everything,' he declared rebelliously. 'Well, you fellows can stand around and let them if you want to, but I'm not going to. I'm going to do something about it. From now on I'm going to make every son of a bitch who comes to my intelligence tent sign a loyalty oath. And I'm not going to let that bastard Major Major sign one even if he wants to.'

Amost overnight the Glorious Loyalty Oath Crusade was in full flower, and Captain Black was enraptured to discover himself spearheading it. He had really hit on something. All the enlisted men and officers on combat duty had to sign a loyalty oath to get their map cases from the intelligence tent, a second loyalty oath to receive their flak suits and parachutes from the parachute tent, a third loyalty oath for Lieutenant Balkington, the motor vehicle officer, to be allowed to ride from the squadron to the airfield in one of the trucks. Every time they turned around there was another loyalty oath to be signed. They signed a loyalty oath to get their pay from the finance officer, to obtain their PX supplies, to have their hair cut by the Italian barbers. To Captain Black, every officer who supported his Glorious Loyalty Oath Crusade was a competitor, and he planned and plotted twenty-four hours a day to keep one step ahead. He would stand second to none in his devotion to country. When other officers had followed his urging and introduced loyalty oaths of their own, he went them one better by making every son of a bitch who came to his intelligence tent sign two loyalty oaths, then three, then four; then he introduced the pledge of allegiance, and after that 'The Star-Spangled Banner,' one chorus, two choruses, three choruses, four choruses. Each time Captain Black forged ahead of his competitors, he swung upon them scornfully for their failure to follow his example. Each time they followed his example, he retreated with concern and racked his brain for some new stratagem that would enable him to turn upon them scornfully again.

Without realizing how it had come about, the combat men in the squadron discovered themselves dominated by the administrators appointed to serve them. They were bullied, insulted, harassed and shoved about all day long by one after the other. When they voiced objection, Captain Black replied that people who were loyal would not mind signing all the loyalty oaths they had to. To anyone who questioned the effectiveness of the loyalty oaths, he replied that people who really did owe allegiance to their country would be proud to pledge it as often as he forced them to. And to anyone who questioned the morality, he replied that 'The Star-Spangled Banner' was the greatest piece of music ever composed. The more loyalty oaths a person signed, the more loyal he was; to Captain Black it was as simple as that, and he had Corporal Kolodny sign hundreds with his name each day so that he could always prove he was more loyal than anyone else.

'The important thing is to keep them pledging,' he explained to his cohorts. 'It doesn't matter whether they mean it or not. That's why they make little kids pledge allegiance even before they know what "pledge" and "allegiance" mean.'

To Captain Piltchard and Captain Wren, the Glorious Loyalty Oath Crusade was a glorious pain in the ass, since it complicated their task of organizing the crews for each combat mission. Men were tied up all over the squadron signing, pledging and singing, and the missions took hours longer to get under way. Effective emergency action became impossible, but Captain Piltchard and Captain Wren were both too timid to raise any outcry against Captain Black, who scrupulously enforced each day the doctrine of 'Continual Reaffirmation' that he had originated, a doctrine designed to trap all those men who had become disloyal since the last time they had signed a loyalty oath the day before. It was Captain Black who came with advice to Captain Piltchard and Captain Wren as they pitched about in their bewildering predicament. He came with a delegation and advised them bluntly to make each man sign a loyalty oath before allowing him to fly on a combat mission.

'Of course, it's up to you,' Captain Black pointed out.'Nobody's trying to pressure you. But everyone else is making them sign loyalty oaths, and it's going to look mighty funny to the F.B.I if you two are the only ones who don't care enough about your country to make them sign loyalty oaths, too. If you want to get a bad reputation, that's nobody's business but your own. All we're trying to do is help.'

Milo was not convinced and absolutely refused to deprive Major Major of food, even if Major Major was a Communist, which Milo secretly doubted. Milo was by nature opposed to any innovation that threatened to disrupt the normal course of affairs. Milo took a firm moral stand and absolutely refused to participate in the Glorious Loyalty Oath Crusade until Captain Black called upon him with his delegation and requested him to.

'National defense is *everybody's* job,' Captain Black replied to Milo's objection. 'And this whole program is voluntary, Milo – don't forget that. The men don't *have* to sign Piltchard and Wren's loyalty oath if they don't want to. But we need you to starve them to death if they don't. It's just like Catch-22. Don't you get it? You're not against Catch-22, are you?'

Doc Daneeka was adamant.

149

'What makes you so sure Major Major is a Communist?'

'You never heard him denying it until we began accusing him, did you? And you don't see him signing any of our loyalty oaths.'

'You aren't letting him sign any.'

'Of course not,' Captain Black explained. 'That would defeat the whole purpose of our crusade. Look, you don't have to play ball with us if you don't want to. But what's the point of the rest of us working so hard if you're going to give Major Major medical attention the minute Milo begins starving him to death? I just wonder what they're going to think up at Group about the man who's undermining our whole security program. They'll probably transfer you to the Pacific.'

Doc Daneeka surrendered swiftly. 'I'll go tell Gus and Wes to do whatever you want them to.'

Up at Group, Colonel Cathcart had already begun wondering what was going on.

'It's that idiot Black off on a patriotism binge,' Colonel Korn reported with a smile. 'I think you'd better play ball with him for a while, since you're the one who promoted Major Major to squadron commander.'

'That was your idea,' Colonel Cathcart accused him petulantly. 'I never should have let you talk me into it.'

'And a very good idea it was, too,' retorted Colonel Korn, 'since it eliminated that superfluous major that's been giving you such an awful black eye as an administrator. Don't worry, this will probably run its course soon. The best thing to do now is send Captain Black a letter of total support and hope he drops dead before he does too much damage.' Colonel Korn was struck with a whimsical thought. 'I wonder! You don't suppose that imbecile will try to turn Major Major out of his trailer, do you?'

'The next thing we've got to do is turn that bastard Major Major out of his trailer,' Captain Black decided. 'I'd like to turn his wife and kids out into the woods, too. But we can't. He has no wife and kids. So we'll just have to make do with what we have and turn him out. Who's in charge of the tents?'

'He is.'

'You see?' cried Captain Black. 'They're taking over *everything*! Well, I'm not going to stand for it. I'll take this matter right to Major — de Coverley himself if I have to. I'll have Milo speak to him about it the minute he gets back from Rome.'

Captain Black had boundless faith in the wisdom, power and justice of Major — de Coverley, even though he had never spoken to him before and still found himself without the courage to do so. He deputized Milo to speak to Major — de Coverley for him and stormed about impatiently as he waited for the tall executive officer to return. Along with everyone else in the squadron, he lived in profound awe and reverence of the majestic, white-haired major with craggy face and Jehovean bearing, who came back from Rome finally with an injured eye inside a new celluloid eye patch and smashed his whole Glorious Crusade to bits with a single stroke.

Milo carefully said nothing when Major — de Coverley stepped into the mess hall with his fierce and austere dignity the day he returned and found his way blocked by a wall of officers waiting in line to sign loyalty oaths. At the far end of the food counter, a group of men who had arrived earlier were pledging allegiance to the flag, with trays of food balanced in one hand, in order to be allowed to take seats at the table. Already at the tables, a group that had arrived still earlier was singing 'The Star-Spangled Banner' in order that they might use the salt and pepper and ketchup there. The hubbub began to subside slowly as Major — de Coverley paused in the doorway with a frown of puzzled disapproval, as though viewing something bizarre. He started forward in a straight line, and the wall of officers before him parted like the Red Sea. Glancing neither left nor right, he strode indomitably up to the steam counter and, in a clear, full-bodied voice that was gruff with age and resonant with ancient eminence and authority, said:

'Gimme eat.'

Instead of eat, Corporal Snark gave Major — de Coverley a loyalty oath to sign. Major — de Coverley swept it away with mighty displeasure the moment he recognized what it was, his good eye flaring up blindingly with fiery disdain and his enormous old corrugated face darkening in mountainous wrath.

'Gimme eat, I said,' he ordered loudly in harsh tones that rumbled ominously through the silent tent like claps of distant thunder.

Corporal Snark turned pale and began to tremble. He glanced toward Milo pleadingly for guidance. For several terrible seconds there was not a sound. Then Milo nodded.

'Give him eat,' he said.

Corporal Snark began giving Major — de Coverley eat. Major — de Coverley turned from the counter with his tray full and came to a stop. His eyes fell on the groups of other officers gazing at him in mute appeal, and, with righteous belligerence, he roared:

'Give *everybody* eat!'

'Give *everybody* eat!' Milo echoed with joyful relief, and the Glorious Loyalty Oath Crusade came to an end.

Captain Black was deeply disillusioned by this treacherous stab in the back from someone in high place upon whom he had relied so confidently for support. Major — de Coverley had let him down.

'Oh, it doesn't bother me a bit,' he responded cheerfully to everyone who came to him with sympathy. 'We completed our task. Our purpose was to make everyone we don't like afraid and to alert people to the danger of Major Major, and we certainly succeeded at that. Since we weren't going to let him sign loyalty oaths anyway, it doesn't really matter whether we have them or not.'

Seeing everyone in the squadron he didn't like afraid once again throughout the appalling, interminable Great Big Siege of Bologna reminded Captain Black nostalgically of the good old days of his Glorious Loyalty

Oath Crusade when he had been a man of real consequence, and when even big shots like Milo Minderbinder, Doc Daneeka and Piltchard and Wren had trembled at his approach and groveled at his feet. To prove to newcomers that he really had been a man of consequence once, he still had the letter of commendation he had received from Colonel Cathcart.

12   Bologna

Actually, it was not Captain Black but Sergeant Knight
who triggered the solemn panic of Bologna, slipping
silently off the truck for two extra flak suits as soon as
he learned the target and signaling the start of the grim
procession back into the parachute tent that degenerated into a frantic stampede finally before all the extra
flak suits were gone.

'Hey, what's going on?' Kid Sampson asked nervously.
'Bologna can't be that rough, can it?'

Nately, sitting trancelike on the floor of the truck, held
his grave young face in both hands and did not answer
him.

It was Sergeant Knight and the cruel series of post-
ponements, for just as they were climbing up into their
planes that first morning, along came a jeep with the
news that it was raining in Bologna and that the mission
would be delayed. It was raining in Pianosa too by the
time they returned to the squadron, and they had the
rest of that day to stare woodenly at the bomb line on the
map under the awning of the intelligence tent and
ruminate hypnotically on the fact that there was no
escape. The evidence was there vividly in the narrow
red ribbon tacked across the mainland: the ground

forces in Italy were pinned down forty-two insurmountable miles south of the target and could not possibly capture the city in time. Nothing could save the men in Pianosa from the mission to Bologna. They were trapped.

Their only hope was that it would never stop raining, and they had no hope because they all knew it would. When it did stop raining in Pianosa, it rained in Bologna. When it stopped raining in Bologna, it began again in Pianosa. If there was no rain at all, there were freakish, inexplicable phenomena like the epidemic of diarrhea or the bomb line that moved. Four times during the first six days they were assembled and briefed and then sent back. Once, they took off and were flying in formation when the control tower summoned them down. The more it rained, the worse they suffered. The worse they suffered, the more they prayed that it would continue raining. All through the night, men looked at the sky and were saddened by the stars. All through the day, they looked at the bomb line on the big, wobbling easel map of Italy that blew over in the wind and was dragged in under the awning of the intelligence tent every time the rain began. The bomb line was a scarlet band of narrow satin ribbon that delineated the forwardmost position of the Allied ground forces in every sector of the Italian mainland.

The morning after Hungry Joe's fist fight with Huple's cat, the rain stopped falling in both places. The landing strip began to dry. It would take a full twenty-four hours to harden; but the sky remained cloudless. The resentments incubating in each man hatched into hatred. First they hated the infantrymen on the mainland because they had failed to capture Bologna. Then they began to hate the bomb line itself. For hours they stared relentlessly at the scarlet ribbon on the map and hated it because it would not move up high enough to encompass the city. When night fell, they congregated in the darkness with flashlights, continuing their macabre vigil at the bomb line in brooding entreaty as though hoping to move the ribbon up by the collective weight of their sullen prayers.

'I really can't believe it,' Clevinger exclaimed to Yossarian in a voice rising and falling in protest and wonder. 'It's a complete reversion to primitive superstition. They're confusing cause and effect. It makes as much sense as knocking on wood or crossing your fingers. They really believe that we wouldn't have to fly that mission tomorrow if someone would only tiptoe up to the map in the middle of the night and move the bomb line over Bologna. Can you imagine? You and I must be the only rational ones left.'

In the middle of the night Yossarian knocked on wood, crossed his fingers, and tiptoed out of his tent to move the bomb line up over Bologna.

Corporal Kolodny tiptoed stealthily into Captain Black's tent early the next morning, reached inside the mosquito net and gently shook the moist shoulder blade he found there until Captain Black opened his eyes.

'What are you waking me up for?' whimpered Captain Black.

'They captured Bologna, sir,' said Corporal Kolodny. 'I thought you'd want to know. Is the mission canceled?'

Captain Black tugged himself erect and began scratching his scrawny long thighs methodically. In a little while he dressed and emerged from his tent, squinting, cross and unshaven. The sky was clear and warm. He peered without emotion at the map. Sure enough, they had captured Bologna. Inside the intelligence tent, Corporal Kolodny was already removing the maps of Bologna from the navigation kits. Captain Black seated himself with a loud yawn, lifted his feet to the top of his desk and phoned Colonel Korn.

'What are you waking me up for?' whimpered Colonel Korn.

'They captured Bologna during the night, sir. Is the mission canceled?'

'What are you talking about, Black?' Colonel Korn growled. 'Why should the mission be canceled?'

'Because they captured Bologna, sir. Isn't the mission canceled?'

'Of course the mission is canceled. Do you think we're bombing our own troops now?'

'What are you waking me up for?' Colonel Cathcart whimpered to Colonel Korn.

'They captured Bologna,' Colonel Korn told him. 'I thought you'd want to know.'

'Who captured Bologna?'

'We did.'

Colonel Cathcart was overjoyed, for he was relieved of the embarrasing commitment to bomb Bologna without blemish to the reputation for valor he had earned by volunteering his men to do it. General Dreedle was pleased with the capture of Bologna, too, although he was angry with Colonel Moodus for waking him up to tell him about it. Headquarters was also pleased and decided to award a medal to the officer who captured the city. There was no officer who had captured the city, so they gave the medal to General Peckem instead, because General Peckem was the only officer with sufficient initiative to ask for it.

As soon as General Peckem had received his medal, he began asking for increased responsibility. It was General Peckem's opinion that all combat units in the theater should be placed under the jurisdiction of the Special Service Corps, of which General Peckem himself was the commanding officer. If dropping bombs on the enemy was not a special service, he reflected aloud frequently with the martyred smile of sweet reasonableness that was his loyal confederate in every dispute, then he could not help wondering what in the world was. With amiable regret, he declined the offer of a combat post under General Dreedle.

'Flying combat missions *for* General Dreedle is not exactly what I had in mind,' he explained indulgently with a smooth laugh. 'I was thinking more in terms of *replacing* General Dreedle, or perhaps of something *above* General Dreedle where I could exercise supervision over a great many *other* generals too. You see, my most precious abilities are mainly administrative ones. I have a happy facility for getting different people to agree.'

'He has a happy facility for getting different people to agree what a prick he is,' Colonel Cargill confided invidiously to ex-P.F.C. Wintergreen in the hope that ex-P.F.C. Wintergreen would spread the unfavourable report along through Twenty-seventh Air Force Headquarters. 'If anyone deserves that combat post, I do. It was even my idea that we ask for the medal.'

'You really want to go into combat?' ex-P.F.C. Wintergreen inquired.

'Combat?' Colonel Cargill was aghast. 'Oh, no – you misunderstand me. Of course, I wouldn't actually *mind* going into combat, but my best abilities are mainly administrative ones. I too have a happy facility for getting different people to agree.'

'He too has a happy facility for getting different people to agree what a prick he is,' ex-P.F.C. Wintergreen confided with a laugh to Yossarian, after he had come to Pianosa to learn if it was really true about Milo and the Egyptian cotton. 'If anyone deserves a promotion, I do.' Actually, he had risen already to ex-corporal, having shot through the ranks shortly after his transfer to Twenty-seventh Air Force Headquarters as a mail clerk and been busted right down to private for making odious audible comparisons about the commissioned officers for whom he worked. The heady taste of success had infused him further with morality and fired him with ambition for loftier attainments. 'Do you want to buy some Zippo lighters?' he asked Yossarian. 'They were stolen right from quartermaster.'

'Does Milo know you're selling cigarette lighters?'

'What's it his business? Milo's not carrying cigarette lighters too now, is he?'

'He sure is,' Yossarian told him. 'And his aren't stolen.'

'That's what you think,' ex-P.F.C. Wintergreen answered with a laconic snort. 'I'm selling mine for a buck apiece. What's he getting for his?'

'A dollar and a penny.'

Ex-P.F.C. Wintergreen snickered triumphantly. 'I beat him every time,' he gloated. 'Say, what about all that Egyptian cotton he's stuck with? How much did he buy?'

'All.'

'In the whole world? Well, I'll be damned!' ex-P.F.C. Wintergreen crowed with malicious glee. 'What a dope! You were in Cairo with him. Why'd you let him do it?'

'Me?' Yossarian answered with a shrug. 'I have no influence on him. It was those teletype machines they have in all the good restaurants there. Milo had never seen a stock ticker before, and the quotation for Egyptian cotton happpened to be coming in just as he asked the headwaiter to explain it to him. "Egyptian cotton?" Milo said with that look of his. "How much is Egyptian cotton selling for?" The next thing I knew he had bought the whole goddam harvest. And now he can't unload any of it.'

'He has no imagination. I can unload plenty of it in the black market if he'll make a deal.'

'Milo knows the black market. There's no demand for cotton.'

'But there is a demand for medical supplies. I can roll the cotton up on wooden toothpicks and peddle them as sterile swabs. Will he sell to me at a good price?'

'He won't sell to you at any price,' Yossarian answered. 'He's pretty sore at you for going into competition with him. In fact, he's pretty sore at everybody for getting diarrhea last weekend and giving his mess hall a bad name. Say, you can help us.' Yossarian suddenly seized his arm. 'Couldn't you forge some official orders on that mimeograph machine of yours and get us out of flying to Bologna?'

Ex-P.F.C. Wintergreen pulled away slowly with a look of scorn. 'Sure I could,' he explained with pride. 'But I would never dream of doing anything like that.'

'Why not?'

'Because it's your job. We all have our jobs to do. My job is to unload these Zippo lighters at a profit if I can and pick up some cotton from Milo. Your job is to bomb the ammunition dumps at Bologna.'

'But I'm going to be killed at Bologna,' Yossarian pleaded. 'We're all going to be killed.'

'Then you'll just have to be killed,' replied ex-P.F.C. Wintergreen. 'Why can't you be a fatalist about it the way I am? If I'm destined to unload these lighters at a profit and pick up some Egyptian cotton cheap from Milo, then that's what I'm going to do. And if you're destined to be killed over Bologna, then you're going to be killed, so you might just as well go out and die like a man. I hate to say this, Yossarian, but you're turning into a chronic complainer.'

Clevinger agreed with ex-P.F.C. Wintergreen that it was Yossarian's job to get killed over Bologna and was livid with condemnation when Yossarian confessed that it was he who had moved the bomb line and caused the mission to be canceled.

'Why the hell not?' Yossarian snarled, arguing all the more vehemently because he suspected he was wrong. 'Am I supposed to get my ass shot off just because the colonel wants to be a general?'

'What about the men on the mainland?' Clevinger demanded with just as much emotion. 'Are they supposed to get their asses shot off just because you don't want to go? Those men are entitled to air support!'

'But not necessarily by me. Look, they don't care who knocks out those ammunition dumps. The only reason we're going is because that bastard Cathcart volunteered us.'

'Oh, I know all that,' Clevinger assured him, his gaunt face pale and his agitated brown eyes swimming in sincerity. 'But the fact remains that those ammunition dumps are still standing. You know very well that I don't approve of Colonel Cathcart any more than you do.' Clevinger paused for emphasis, his mouth quivering, and then beat his fist down softly against his sleeping bag. 'But it's not for us to determine what targets must be destroyed or who's to destroy them or –'

'Or who gets killed doing it? And why?'

'Yes, even that. We have no right to question –'

'You're insane!'

'– no right to question –'

'Do you really mean that it's not my business how or why I get killed and that it is Colonel Cathcart's? Do you really mean that?'

'Yes, I do,' Clevinger insisted, seeming unsure. 'There are men entrusted with winning the war who are in a much better position than we are to decide what targets have to be bombed.'

'We are talking about two different things,' Yossarian answered with exaggerated weariness. 'You are talking about the relationship of the Air Corps to the infantry, and I am talking about the relationship of me to Colonel Cathcart. You are talking about winning the war, and I am talking about winning the war and keeping alive.'

'Exactly,' Clevinger snapped smugly. 'And which do you think is more important?'

'To whom?' Yossarian shot back. 'Open your eyes, Clevinger. It doesn't make a damned bit of difference *who* wins the war to someone who's dead.'

Clevinger sat for a moment as though he'd been slapped. 'Congratulations!' he exclaimed bitterly, the thinnest milk-white line enclosing his lips tightly in a bloodless, squeezing ring. 'I can't think of another attitude that could be depended upon to give greater comfort to the enemy.'

'The enemy,' retorted Yossarian with weighted precision, 'is anybody who's going to get you killed, no matter *which* side he's on, and that includes Colonel Cathcart. And don't you forget that, because the longer you remember it, the longer you might live.'

But Clevinger did forget it, and now he was dead. At the time, Clevinger was so upset by the incident that Yossarian did not dare tell him he had also been responsible for the epidemic of diarrhea that had caused the other unnecessary postponement. Milo was even more upset by the possibility that someone had poisoned his squadron again, and he came bustling fretfully to Yossarian for assistance.

'Please find out from Corporal Snark if he put laundry soap in the sweet potatoes again,' he requested furtively. 'Corporal Snark trusts you and will tell you the truth if you give him your word you won't tell anyone else. As soon as he tells you, come and tell me.'

'Of course I put laundry soap in the sweet potatoes,' Corporal Snark admitted to Yossarian. 'That's what you asked me to do, isn't it? Laundry soap is the best way.'

'He swears to God he didn't have a thing to do with it,' Yossarian reported back to Milo.

Milo pouted dubiously. 'Dunbar says there is no God.'

There was no hope left. By the middle of the second week, everyone in the squadron began to look like Hungry Joe, who was not scheduled to fly and screamed horribly in his sleep. He was the only one who could sleep. All night long, men moved through the darkness outside their tents like tongueless wraiths with cigarettes. In the daytime they stared at the bomb line in futile, drooping clusters or at the still figure of Doc Daneeka sitting in front of the closed door of the medical tent beneath the morbid hand-lettered sign. They began to invent humorless, glum jokes of their own and disastrous rumors about the destruction awaiting them at Bologna.

Yossarian sidled up drunkenly to Colonel Korn at the officers' club one night to kid with him about the new Lepage gun that the Germans had moved in.

'What Lepage gun?' Colonel Korn inquired with curiosity.

'The new three-hundred-and-forty-four-millimeter Lepage glue gun,' Yossarian answered. 'It glues a whole formation of planes together in mid-air.'

Colonel Korn jerked his elbow free from Yossarian's clutching fingers in startled affront. 'Let go of me, you idiot!' he cried out furiously, glaring with vindictive approval as Nately leaped upon Yossarian's back and pulled him away. 'Who is that lunatic, anyway?'

Colonel Cathcart chortled merrily. 'That's the man you made me give a medal to after Ferrara. You had me promote him to captain, too, remember? It serves you right.'

Nately was lighter than Yossarian and had great difficulty maneuvering Yossarian's lurching bulk across the room to an unoccupied table. 'Are you crazy?' Nately kept hissing with trepidation. 'That was Colonel Korn. Are you crazy?'

Yossarian wanted another drink and promised to leave quietly if Nately brought him one. Then he made Nately bring him two more. When Nately finally coaxed him to the door, Captain Black came stomping in from outside, banging his sloshing shoes down hard on the wood floor and spilling water from his eaves like a high roof.

'Boy, are you bastards in for it!' he announced exuberantly, splashing away from the puddle forming at his feet. 'I just got a call from Colonel Korn. Do you know what they've got waiting for you at Bologna? Ha! Ha! They've got the new Lepage glue gun. It glues a whole formation of planes together in mid-air.'

'My God, it's true!' Yossarian shrieked, and collapsed against Nately in terror.

'There is no God,' answered Dunbar calmly, coming up with a slight stagger.

'Hey, give me a hand with him, will you? I've got to get him back in his tent.'

'Says who?'

'Says me. Gee, look at the rain.'

'We've got to get a car.'

'Steal Captain Black's car,' said Yossarian. 'That's what I always do.'

'We can't steal anybody's car. Since you began stealing the nearest car every time you wanted one, nobody leaves the ignition on.'

'Hop in,' said Chief White Halfoat, driving up drunk in

a covered jeep. He waited until they had crowded inside and then spurted ahead with a suddenness that rolled them all over backward. He roared with laughter at their curses. He drove straight ahead when he left the parking lot and rammed the car into the embankment on the other side of the road. The others piled forward in a helpless heap and began cursing him again. 'I forgot to turn,' he explained.

'Be careful, will you?' Nately cautioned. 'You'd better put your headlights on.'

Chief White Halfoat pulled back in reverse, made his turn and shot away up the road at top speed. The wheels were sibilant on the whizzing black-top surface.

'Not so fast,' urged Nately.

'You'd better take me to your squadron first so I can help you put him to bed. Then you can drive me back to my squadron.'

'Who the hell are you?'

'Dunbar.'

'Hey, put your headlights on,' Nately shouted. 'And watch the road!'

'They are on. Isn't Yossarian in this car? That's the only reason I let the rest of you bastards in.' Chief White Halfoat turned completely around to stare into the back seat.

'Watch the road!'

'Yossarian? Is Yossarian in here?'

'I'm here, Chief. Let's go home. What makes you so sure? You never answered my question.'

'You see? I told you he was here.'

'What question?'

'Whatever it was we were talking about.'

'Was it important?'

'I don't remember if it was important or not. I wish to God I knew what it was.'

'There is no God.'

'That's what we were talking about,' Yossarian cried. 'What makes you so sure?'

'Hey, are you sure your headlights are on?' Nately called out.

'They're on, they're on. What does he want from me? It's all this rain on the windshield that makes it look dark from back there.'

'Beautiful, beautiful rain.'

'I hope it never stops raining. Rain, rain, go a –'

'– way. Come a –'

'– again some oth –'

'– er day. Little Yo-Yo wants –'

'– to play. In –'

'– the meadow, in –'

Chief White Halfoat missed the next turn in the road and ran the jeep all the way up to the crest of a steep embankment. Rolling back down, the jeep turned over on its side and settled softly in the mud. There was a frightened silence.

'Is everyone all right?' Chief White Halfoat inquired in a hushed voice. No one was injured, and he heaved a long sigh of relief. 'You know, that's my trouble,' he groaned. 'I never listen to anybody. Somebody kept telling me to put my headlights on, but I just wouldn't listen.'

'I kept telling you to put your headlights on.'

'I know, I know. And I just wouldn't listen, would I? I wish I had a drink. I *do* have a drink. Look. It's not broken.'

'It's raining in,' Nately noticed. 'I'm getting wet.'

Chief White Halfoat got the bottle of rye open, drank and handed it off. Lying tangled up on top of each other, they all drank but Nately, who kept groping ineffectually for the door handle. The bottle fell against his head with a clunk, and whiskey poured down his neck. He began writhing convulsively.

'Hey, we've got to get out of here!' he cried. 'We'll all drown.'

'Is anybody in there?' asked Clevinger with concern, shining a flashlight down from the top.

'It's Clevinger!' they shouted, and tried to pull him in through the window as he reached down to aid them.

'Look at them!' Clevinger exclaimed indignantly to McWatt, who sat grinning at the wheel of the staff car.

'Lying there like a bunch of drunken animals. You too, Nately? You ought to be ashamed! Come on – help me get them out of here before they all die of pneumonia.'

'You know, that don't sound like such a bad idea,' Chief White Halfoat reflected. 'I think I will die of pneumonia.'

'Why?'

'Why not?' answered Chief White Halfoat, and lay back in the mud contentedly with the bottle of rye cuddled in his arms.

'Oh, now look what he's doing!' Clevinger exclaimed with irritation. 'Will you get up and get into the car so we can all go back to the squadron?'

'We can't all go back. Someone has to stay here to help the Chief with this car he signed out of the motor pool.'

Chief White Halfoat settled back in the staff car with an ebullient, prideful chuckle. 'That's Captain Black's car,' he informed them jubilantly. 'I stole it from him at the officers' club just now with an extra set of keys he thought he lost this morning.'

'Well, I'll be damned! That calls for a drink.'

'Haven't you had enough to drink?' Clevinger began scolding as soon as McWatt started the car. 'Look at you. You don't care if you drink yourselves to death or drown yourselves to death, do you?'

'Just as long as we don't fly ourselves to death.'

'Hey, open it up, open it up,' Chief White Halfoat urged McWatt. 'And turn off the headlights. That's the only way to do it.'

'Doc Daneeka is right,' Clevinger went on. 'People don't know enough to take care of themselves. I really am disgusted with all of you.'

'Okay, fatmouth, out of the car,' Chief White Halfoat ordered. 'Everybody get out of the car but Yossarian. Where's Yossarian?'

'Get the hell off me.' Yossarian laughed, pushing him away. 'You're all covered with mud.'

Clevinger focused on Nately. 'You're the one who really surprises me. Do you know what you smell like?

Instead of trying to keep him out of trouble, you get just as drunk as he is. Suppose he got in another fight with Appleby?' Clevinger's eyes opened wide with alarm when he heard Yossarian chuckle. 'He didn't get in another fight with Appleby, did he?'

'Not this time,' said Dunbar.

'No, not this time. This time I did even better.'

'This time he got in a fight with Colonel Korn.'

'He didn't!' gasped Clevinger.

'He did?' exclaimed Chief White Halfoat with delight. 'That calls for a drink.'

'But that's terrible!' Clevinger declared with deep apprehension. 'Why in the world did you have to pick on Colonel Korn? Say, what happened to the lights? Why is everything so dark?'

'I turned them off,' answered McWatt. 'You know, Chief White Halfoat is right. It's much better with the headlights off.'

'Are you crazy?' Clevinger screamed, and lunged forward to snap the headlights on. He whirled around upon Yossarian in near hysteria. 'You see what you're doing? You've got them all acting like you! Suppose it stops raining and we have to fly to Bologna tomorrow. You'll be in fine physical condition.'

'It won't ever gonna stop raining. No, sir, a rain like this really might go on forever.'

'It has stopped raining!' someone said, and the whole car fell silent.

'You poor bastards,' Chief White Halfoat murmured compassionately after a few moments had passed.

'Did it really stop raining?' Yossarian asked meekly.

McWatt switched off the windshield wipers to make certain. The rain had stopped. The sky was starting to clear. The moon was sharp behind a gauzy brown mist.

'Oh, well,' sang McWatt soberly. 'What the hell.'

'Don't worry fellas,' Chief White Halfoat said. 'The landing strip is too soft to use tomorrow. Maybe it'll start raining again before the field dries out.'

'You goddam stinking lousy son of a bitch,' Hungry Joe

screamed from his tent as they sped into the squadron.

'Jesus, is he back here tonight? I thought he was still in Rome with the courier ship.'

'Oh! Ooooh! Oooooooh!' Hungry Joe screamed.

Chief White Halfoat shuddered. 'That guy gives me the willies,' he confessed in a grouchy whisper. 'Hey, whatever happened to Captain Flume?'

'There's a guy that gives me the willies. I saw him in the woods last week eating wild berries. He never sleeps in his trailer any more. He looked like hell.'

'Hungry Joe's afraid he'll have to replace somebody who goes on sick call, even though there is no sick call. Did you see him the other night when he tried to kill Havermeyer and fell into Yossarian's slit trench?'

'Ooooh!' screamed Hungry Joe. 'Oh! Ooooh! Ooooooh!'

'It sure is a pleasure not having Flume around in the mess hall any more. No more of that "Pass the salt, Walt." '

'Or "Pass the bread, Fred." '

'Or "Shoot me a beet, Pete." '

'Keep away, keep away,' Hungry Joe screamed. 'I said keep away, keep away, you goddam stinking lousy son of a bitch.'

'At least we found out what he dreams about,' Dunbar observed wryly. 'He dreams about goddam stinking lousy sons of bitches.'

Late that night Hungry Joe dreamed that Huple's cat was sleeping on his face, suffocating him, and when he woke up, Huple's cat *was* sleeping on his face. His agony was terrifying, the piercing, unearthly howl with which he split the moonlit dark vibrating in its own impact for seconds afterward like a devastating shock. A numbing silence followed, and then a riotous din rose from inside his tent.

Yossarian was among the first ones there. When he burst through the entrance, Hungry Joe had his gun out and was struggling to wrench his arm free from Huple to shoot the cat, who kept spitting and feinting at him ferociously to distract him from shooting Huple. Both humans were in their GI underwear. The unfrosted light bulb overhead was swinging crazily on its loose wire, and the jumbled black shadows kept swirling and bobbing chaotically, so that the entire tent seemed to be reeling. Yossarian reached out instinctively for balance and then launched himself forward in a prodigious dive that crushed the three combatants to the ground beneath him. He emerged from the melee with the scruff of a neck in each hand – Hungry Joe's neck and the cat's. Hungry Joe and the cat glared at each other savagely. The cat spat viciously at Hungry Joe, and Hungry Joe tried to hit it with a haymaker.

'A fair fight,' Yossarian decreed, and all the others who had come running to the uproar in horror began cheering ecstatically in a tremendous overflow of relief. 'We'll have a fair fight,' he explained officially to Hungry Joe and the cat after he had carried them both outside, still holding them apart by the scruffs of their necks. 'Fists, fangs and claws. But no guns,' he warned Hungry Joe. 'And no spitting,' he warned the cat sternly. 'When I turn you both loose, go. Break clean in the clinches and come back fighting. Go!'

There was a huge, giddy crowd of men who were avid for any diversion, but the cat turned chicken the moment Yossarian released him and fled from Hungry Joe ignominiously like a yellow dog. Hungry Joe was declared the winner. He swaggered away happily with the proud smile of a champion, his shriveled head high and his emaciated chest out. He went back to bed victorious and dreamed again that Huple's cat was sleeping on his face, suffocating him.

13   Major — de Coverley

Moving the bomb line did not fool the Germans, but it did
fool Major — de Coverley, who packed his musette bag,
commandeered an airplane and, under the impression
that Florence too had been captured by the Allies, had
himself flown to that city to rent two apartments for the
officers and the enlisted men in the squadron to use
on rest leaves. He had still not returned by the time
Yossarian jumped back outside Major Major's office
and wondered whom to appeal to next for help.

Major — de Coverley was a splendid, awe-inspiring,
grave old man with a massive leonine head and an angry
shock of wild white hair that raged like a blizzard
around his stern, patriarchal face. His duties as squadron executive officer did consist entirely, as both Doc
Daneeka and Major Major had conjectured, of pitching
horseshoes, kidnaping Italian laborers, and renting
apartments for the enlisted men and officers to use on
rest leaves, and he excelled at all three.

Each time the fall of a city like Naples, Rome or
Florence seemed imminent, Major — de Coverley would
pack his musette bag, commandeer an airplane and a
pilot, and have himself flown away, accomplishing all
this without uttering a word, by the sheer force of his

solemn, domineering visage and the peremptory gestures of his wrinkled finger. A day or two after the city fell, he would be back with leases on two large and luxurious apartments there, one for the officers and one for the enlisted men, both already staffed with competent, jolly cooks and maids. A few days after that, newspapers would appear throughout the world with photographs of the first American soldiers bludgeoning their way into the shattered city through rubble and smoke. Inevitably, Major — de Coverley was among them, seated straight as a ramrod in a jeep he had obtained from somewhere, glancing neither right nor left as the artillery fire burst about his invincible head and lithe young infantrymen with carbines went loping up along the sidewalks in the shelter of burning buildings or fell dead in doorways. He seemed eternally indestructible as he sat there surrounded by danger, his features molded firmly into that same fierce, regal, just and forbidding countenance which was recognized and revered by every man in the squadron.

To German intelligence, Major — de Coverley was a vexatious enigma; not one of the hundreds of American prisoners would ever supply any concrete information about the elderly white-haired officer with the gnarled and menacing brow and blazing, powerful eyes who seemed to spearhead every important advance so fearlessly and successfully. To American authorities his identity was equally perplexing; a whole regiment of crack CID men had been thrown into the front lines to find out who he was, while a battalion of combat-hardened public-relations officers stood on red alert twenty-four hours a day with orders to begin publicizing him the moment he was located.

In Rome, Major — de Coverley had outdone himself with the apartments. For the officers, who arrived in groups of four or five, there was an immense double room for each in a new white stone building, with three spacious bathrooms with walls of shimmering aquamarine tile and one skinny maid named Michaela who tittered at everything and kept the apartment in spotless order. On the landing below lived the obsequious owners. On the landing above lived the beautiful rich black-haired countess and her beautiful rich black-haired daughter-in-law, both of whom would put out only for Nately, who was too shy to want them, and for Aarfy, who was too stuffy to take them and tried to dissuade them from ever putting out for anyone but their husbands, who had chosen to remain in the north with the family's business interests.

'They're really a couple of good kids,' Aarfy confided earnestly to Yossarian, whose recurring dream it was to have the nude milk-white female bodies of both these beautiful rich black-haired good kids lying stretched out in bed erotically with him at the same time.

The enlisted men descended upon Rome in gangs of twelve or more with Gargantuan appetites and heavy crates filled with canned food for the women to cook and serve to them in the dining room of their own apartment on the sixth floor of a red brick building with a clinking elevator. There was always more activity at the enlisted men's place. There were always more enlisted men, to begin with, and more women to cook and serve and sweep and scrub, and then there were always the gay and silly sensual young girls that Yossarian had found and brought there and those that the sleepy enlisted men returning to Pianosa after their exhausting seven-day debauch had brought there on their own and were leaving behind for whoever wanted them next. The girls had shelter and food for as long as they wanted to stay. All they had to do in return was hump any of the men who asked them to, which seemed to make everything just about perfect for them.

Every fourth day or so Hungry Joe came crashing in like a man in torment, hoarse, wild, and frenetic, if he had been unlucky enough to finish his missions again and was flying the courier ship. Most times he slept at the enlisted men's apartment. Nobody was certain how many rooms Major — de Coverley had rented, not even the stout black-bodiced woman in corsets on the first floor from whom he had rented them. They covered the whole top floor, and Yossarian knew they extended down to the fifth floor as well, for it was in Snowden's room on the fifth floor that he had finally found the maid in the lime-colored panties with a dust mop the day after Bologna, after Hungry Joe had discovered him in bed with Luciana at the officers' appartment that same morning and had gone running like a fiend for his camera.

The maid in the lime-colored panties was a cheerful, fat, obliging woman in her mid-thirties with squashy thighs and swaying hams in lime-colored panties that she was always rolling off for any man who wanted her. She had a plain broad face and was the most virtuous woman alive: she laid for *everybody*, regardless of race, creed, color or place of national origin, donating herself sociably as an act of hospitality, procrastinating not even for the moment it might take to discard the cloth or broom or dust mop she was clutching at the time she was grabbed. Her allure stemmed from her accessibility; like Mt. Everest, she was there, and the men climbed on top of her each time they felt the urge. Yossarian was in love with the maid in the lime-colored panties because she seemed to be the only woman left he could make love to without falling in love with. Even the bald-headed girl in Sicily still evoked in him strong sensations of pity, tenderness and regret.

Despite the multiple perils to which Major — de Coverley exposed himself each time he rented apartments, his only injury had occurred, ironically enough, while he was leading the triumphal procession into the open city of Rome, where he was wounded in the eye by a flower fired at him from close range by a seedy, cackling, intoxicated old man, who, like Satan himself, had then bounded up on Major — de Coverley's car with malicious glee, seized him roughly and contemptuously by his venerable white head and kissed him mockingly on each cheek with a mouth reeking with sour fumes of wine, cheese and garlic, before dropping back into the joyous celebrating throngs with a hollow, dry, excoriating laugh. Major — de Coverley, a Spartan in adversity, did not flinch once throughout the whole hideous ordeal. And not until he had returned to Pianosa, his business in Rome completed, did he seek medical attention for his wound.

He resolved to remain binocular and specified to Doc Daneeka that his eye patch be transparent so that he could continue pitching horseshoes, kidnaping Italian laborers and renting apartments with unimpaired vision. To the men in the squadron, Major — de Coverley was a colossus, although they never dared tell him so. The only one who ever did dare address him was Milo Minderbinder, who approached the horseshoe-pitching pit with a hard-boiled egg his second week in the squadron and held it aloft for Major — de Coverley to see. Major — de Coverley straightened with astonishment at Milo's effrontery and concentrated upon him the full fury of his storming countenance with its rugged overhang of gullied forehead and huge crag of a humpbacked nose that came charging out of his face wrathfully like a Big Ten fullback. Milo stood his ground, taking shelter behind the hard-boiled egg raised protectively before his face like a magic charm. In time the gale began to subside, and the danger passed.

'What is that?' Major — de Coverley demanded at last.

'An egg,' Milo answered

'What kind of an egg?' Major — de Coverley demanded.

'A hard-boiled egg,' Milo answered.

'What kind of a hard-boiled egg?' Major — de Coverley demanded.

'A fresh hard-boiled egg,' Milo answered.

'Where did the fresh egg come from?' Major — de Coverley demanded.

'From a chicken,' Milo answered.

'Where is the chicken?' Major — de Coverley demanded.

'The chicken is in Malta,' Milo answered.

'How many chickens are there in Malta?'

'Enough chickens to lay fresh eggs for every officer in the squadron at five cents apiece from the mess fund,' Milo answered.

'I have a weakness for fresh eggs,'Major — de Coverley confessed.

'If someone put a plane at my disposal, I could fly down there once a week in a squadron plane and bring back all the fresh eggs we need,' Milo answered. 'After all, Malta's not so far away.

'Malta's not so far away,' Major — de Coverley observed. 'You could probably fly down there once a week in a squadron plane and bring back all the fresh eggs we need.'

'Yes,' Milo agreed. 'I suppose I could do that, if someone wanted me to and put a plane at my disposal.'

'I like my fresh eggs fried,' Major — de Coverley remembered. 'In fresh butter.'

'I can find all the fresh butter we need in Sicily for twenty-five cents a pound,' Milo answered. 'Twenty-five cents a pound for fresh butter is a good buy. There's enough money in the mess fund for butter too, and we could probably sell some to the other squadrons at a profit and get back most of what we pay for our own.'

'What's your name, son?' asked Major — de Coverley.

'My name is Milo Minderbinder, sir. I am twenty-seven years old.'

'You're a good mess officer, Milo.'

'I'm not the mess officer, sir.'

'You're a good mess officer, Milo.'

'Thank you, sir. I'll do everything in my power to be a good mess officer.'

'Bless you, my boy. Have a horseshoe.'

'Thank you, sir. What should I do with it?'

'Throw it.'

'Away?'

'At the peg there. Then pick it up and throw it at this peg. It's a game, see? You get the horseshoe back.'

'Yes, sir. I see. How much are horseshoes selling for?'

The smell of a fresh egg snapping exotically in a pool of fresh butter carried a long way on the Mediterranean trade winds and brought General Dreedle racing back with a voracious appetite, accompanied by his nurse, who accompanied him everywhere, and his son-in-law, Colonel Moodus. In the beginning General Dreedle devoured all his meals in Milo's mess hall. Then the other three squadrons in Colonel Cathcart's group turned their mess halls over to Milo and gave him an airplane and a pilot each so that he could buy fresh eggs and fresh butter for them too. Milo's planes shuttled back and forth seven days a week as every officer in the four squadrons began devouring fresh eggs in an insatiable orgy of fresh-egg eating. General Dreedle devoured fresh eggs for breakfast, lunch and dinner – between meals he devoured more fresh eggs – until Milo located abundant sources of fresh veal, beef, duck, baby lamb chops, mushroom caps, broccoli, South African rock lobster tails, shrimp, hams, puddings, grapes, ice cream, strawberries and artichokes. There were three other bomb groups in General Dreedle's combat wing, and they each jealously dispatched their own planes to Malta for fresh eggs, but discovered that fresh eggs were selling there for seven cents apiece. Since they could buy them from Milo for five cents apiece, it made more sense to turn over their mess halls to his syndicate, too, and give him the planes and pilots needed to ferry in all the other good food he promised to supply as well.

Everyone was elated with this turn of events, most of all Colonel Cathcart, who was convinced he had won a feather in his cap. He greeted Milo jovially each time they met and, in an excess of contrite generosity, impulsively recommended Major Major for promotion. The recommendation was rejected at once at Twenty-seventh Air Force Headquarters by ex-P.F.C. Wintergreen, who scribbled a brusque, unsigned reminder that the Army had only one Major Major Major Major and did not intend to lose him by promotion just to please Colonel Cathcart. Colonel Cathcart was stung by the blunt rebuke and skulked guiltily about his room in smarting repudiation. He blamed Major Major for this black eye and decided to bust him down to lieutenant that very same day.

'They probably won't let you,' Colonel Korn remarked with a condescending smile, savoring the situation. 'For precisely the same reasons that they wouldn't let you promote him. Besides, you'd certainly look foolish trying to bust him down to lieutenant right after you tried to promote him to my rank.'

Colonel Cathcart felt hemmed in on every side. He had been much more successful in obtaining a medal for Yossarian after the debacle of Ferrara, when the bridge spanning the Po was still standing undamaged seven days after Colonel Cathcart had volunteered to destroy it. Nine missions his men had flown there in six days, and the bridge was not demolished until the tenth mission on the seventh day, when Yossarian killed Kraft and his crew by taking his flight of six planes in over the target a second time. Yossarian came in carefully on his second bomb run because he was brave then. He buried his head in his bombsight until his bombs were away; when he looked up, everything inside the ship was suffused in a weird orange glow. At first he thought that his own plane was on fire. Then he spied the plane with the burning engine directly above him and screamed to McWatt through the intercom to turn left hard. A second later, the wing of Kraft's plane blew off. The flaming wreck dropped, first the fuselage, then the spinning wing, while a shower of tiny metal fragments began tap dancing on the roof of Yossarian's own plane and the incessant *cachung! cachung! cachung!* of the flak was still thumping all around him.

Back on the ground, every eye watched grimly as he walked in dull dejection up to Captain Black outside the green clapboard briefing room to make his intelligence report and learned that Colonel Cathcart and Colonel Korn were waiting to speak to him inside. Major Danby stood barring the door, waving everyone else away in ashen silence. Yossarian was leaden with fatigue and longed to remove his sticky clothing. He stepped into the briefing room with mixed emotions, uncertain how he was supposed to feel about Kraft and the others, for they had all died in the distance of a mute and secluded agony at a moment when he was up to his own ass in the same vile, excruciating dilemma of duty and damnation.

Colonel Cathcart, on the other hand, was all broken up by the event. 'Twice?' he asked.

'I would have missed it the first time,' Yossarian replied softly, his face lowered.

Their voices echoed slightly in the long, narrow bungalow.

'But *twice*?' Colonel Cathcart repeated, in vivid disbelief.

'I would have missed it the first time,' Yossarian repeated.

'But Kraft would be alive.'

'And the bridge would still be up.'

'A trained bombardier is supposed to drop his bombs the first time,' Colonel Cathcart reminded him. 'The other five bombardiers dropped their bombs the first time.'

'And missed the target,' Yossarian said. 'We'd have had to go back there again.'

'And maybe you would have gotten it the first time then.'

'And maybe I wouldn't have gotten it at all.'

'But maybe there wouldn't have been any losses.'

'And maybe there would have been more losses, with the bridge still left standing. I thought you wanted the bridge destroyed.'

'Don't contradict me,' Colonel Cathcart said. 'We're all in enough trouble.'

'I'm not contradicting you, sir.'

'Yes you are. Even that's a contradiction.'

'Yes, sir. I'm sorry.'

Colonel Cathcart cracked his knuckles violently. Colonel Korn, a stocky, dark, flaccid man with a shapeless paunch, sat completely relaxed on one of the benches in the front row, his hands clasped comfortably over the top of his bald and swarthy head. His eyes were amused behind his glinting rimless spectacles.

'We're trying to be perfectly objective about this,' he prompted Colonel Cathcart.

'We're trying to be perfectly objective about this,' Colonel Cathcart said to Yossarian with the zeal of sudden inspiration. 'It's not that I'm being sentimental or anything. I don't give a damn about the men or the airplane. It's just that it looks so lousy on the report. How am I going to cover up something like this in the report?'

'Why don't you give me a medal?' Yossarian suggested timidly.

'For going around twice?'

'You gave one to Hungry Joe when he cracked up that airplane by mistake.'

Colonel Cathcart snickered ruefully. 'You'll be lucky if we don't give you a court-martial.'

'But I got the bridge the second time around,' Yossarian protested. 'I thought you wanted the bridge destroyed.'

'Oh, I don't know what I wanted,' Colonel Cathcart cried out in exasperation. 'Look, of course I wanted the bridge destroyed. That bridge has been a source of trouble to me ever since I decided to send you men out to get it. But why couldn't you do it the first time?'

'I didn't have enough time. My navigator wasn't sure we had the right city.'

'The right city?' Colonel Cathcart was baffled. 'Are you trying to blame it all on Aarfy now?'

'No, sir. It was my mistake for letting him distract me. All I'm trying to say is that I'm not infallible.'

'Nobody is infallible,' Colonel Cathcart said sharply, and then continued vaguely, with an afterthought: 'Nobody is indispensable, either.'

There was no rebuttal. Colonel Korn stretched sluggishly. 'We've got to reach a decision,' he observed casually to Colonel Cathcart.

'We've got to reach a decision,' Colonel Cathcart said

to Yossarian. 'And it's all your fault. Why did you have to go around twice? Why couldn't you drop your bombs the first time like all the others?'

'I would have missed the first time.'

'It seems to me that *we're* going around twice,' Colonel Korn interrupted with a chuckle.

'But what are we going to do?' Colonel Cathcart exclaimed with distress. 'The others are all waiting outside.'

'Why don't we give him a medal?' Colonel Korn proposed.

'For going around twice? What can we give him a medal for?'

'For going around twice,' Colonel Korn answered with a reflective, self-satisfied smile. 'After all, I suppose it did take a lot of courage to go over that target a second time with no other planes around to divert the anti-aircraft fire. And he did hit the bridge. You know, that might be the answer – to act boastfully about something we ought to be ashamed of. That's a trick that never seems to fail.'

'Do you think it will work?'

'I'm sure it will. And let's promote him to captain, too, just to make certain.'

'Don't you think that's going a bit farther than we have to?'

'No, I don't think so. It's best to play safe. And a captain's not much difference.'

'All right,' Colonel Cathcart decided. 'We'll give him a medal for being brave enough to go around over the target twice. And we'll make him a captain, too.'

Colonel Korn reached for his hat.

'Exit smiling,' he joked, and put his arm around Yossarian's shoulders as they stepped outside the door.

14   Kid Sampson

By the time of the mission to Bologna, Yossarian was
brave enough not to go around over the target even once,
and when he found himself aloft finally in the nose of Kid
Sampson's plane, he pressed in the button of his throat
mike and asked,

'Well? What's wrong with the plane?'

Kid Sampson let out a shriek. 'Is something wrong
with the plane? What's the matter?'

Kid Sampson's cry turned Yossarian to ice. 'Is something the matter?' he yelled in horror. 'Are we bailing
out?'

'I don't know!' Kid Sampson shot back in anguish,
wailing excitedly. 'Someone said we're bailing out! Who
is this, anyway? Who is this?'

'This is Yossarian in the nose! Yossarian in the nose. I
heard you say there was something the matter. Didn't
you say there was something the matter?'

'I thought you said there was something wrong. Everything seems okay. Everything is all right.'

Yossarian's heart sank. Something was terribly wrong
if everything was all right and they had no excuse for
turning back. He hesitated gravely.

'I can't hear you,' he said.

'I said everything is all right.'

The sun was blinding white on the porcelain-blue water below and on the flashing edges of the other airplanes. Yossarian took hold of the colored wires leading into the jackbox of the intercom system and tore them loose.

'I still can't hear you,' he said.

He heard nothing. Slowly he collected his map case and his three flak suits and crawled back to the main compartment. Nately, sitting stiffly in the co-pilot's seat, spied him through the corner of his eye as he stepped up on the flight deck behind Kid Sampson. He smiled at Yossarian wanly, looking frail and exceptionally young and bashful in the bulky dungeon of his earphones, hat, throat mike, flak suit and parachute. Yossarian bent close to Kid Sampson's ear.

'I still can't hear you,' he shouted above the even drone of the engines.

Kid Sampson glanced back at him with surprise. Kid Sampson had an angular, comical face with arched eyebrows and a scrawny blond mustache.

'What?' he called out over his shoulder.

'I still can't hear you,' Yossarian repeated.

'You'll have to talk louder,' Kid Sampson said. 'I still can't hear you.'

'I said I still can't hear you!' Yossarian yelled.

'I can't help it,' Kid Sampson yelled back at him. 'I'm shouting as loud as I can.'

'I couldn't hear you over my intercom,' Yossarian bellowed in mounting helplessness. 'You'll have to turn back.'

'For an intercom?' asked Kid Sampson incredulously.

'Turn back,' said Yossarian, 'before I break your head.'

Kid Sampson looked for moral support toward Nately, who stared away from him pointedly. Yossarian outranked them both. Kid Sampson resisted doubtfully for another moment and then capitulated eagerly with a triumphant whoop.

'That's just fine with me,' he announced gladly, and blew out a shrill series of whistles up into his mustache. 'Yes sirree, that's just fine with old Kid Sampson.' He whistled again and shouted over the intercom, 'Now hear this, my little chickadees. This is Admiral Kid Sampson talking. This Admiral Kid Sampson squawking, the pride of the Queen's marines. Yessiree. We're turning back, boys, by crackee, *we're turning back!*'

Nately ripped off his hat and earphones in one jubilant sweep and began rocking back and forth happily like a handsome child in a high chair. Sergeant Knight came plummeting down from the top gun turret and began pounding them all on the back with delirious enthusiasm. Kid Sampson turned the plane away from the formation in a wide, graceful arc and headed toward the airfield. When Yossarian plugged his headset into one of the auxiliary jackboxes, the two gunners in the rear section of the plane were both singing 'La Cucaracha.'

Back at the field, the party fizzled out abruptly. An uneasy silence replaced it, and Yossarian was sober and self-conscious as he climbed down from the plane and took his place in the jeep that was already waiting for them. None of the men spoke at all on the drive back through the heavy, mesmerizing quiet blanketing mountains, sea and forests. The feeling of desolation persisted when they turned off the road at the squadron. Yossarian got out of the car last. After a minute, Yossarian and a gentle warm wind were the only things stirring in the haunting tranquillity that hung like a drug over the vacated tents. The squadron stood insensate, bereft of everything human but Doc Daneeka, who roosted dolorously like a shivering turkey buzzard beside the closed door of the medical tent, his stuffed nose jabbing away in thirsting futility at the hazy sunlight streaming down around him. Yossarian knew Doc Daneeka would not go swimming with him. Doc Daneeka would never go swimming again; a person could swoon or suffer a mild coronary occlusion in an inch or two of water and drown to death, be carried out to sea by an undertow, or made vulnerable to poliomyelitis or meningococcus infection through chilling or over-exertion. The threat of Bologna to others had instilled in Doc Daneeka an even more poignant solicitude for his own safety. At night now, he heard burglars.

Through the lavender gloom clouding the entrance of the operations tent, Yossarian glimpsed Chief White Halfoat, diligently embezzling whiskey rations, forging the signatures of nondrinkers and pouring off the alcohol with which he was poisoning himself into separate bottles rapidly in order to steal as much as he could before Captain Black roused himself with recollection and came hurrying over indolently to steal the rest himself.

The jeep started up again softly. Kid Sampson, Nately and the others wandered apart in a noiseless eddy of motion and were sucked away into the cloying yellow stillness. The jeep vanished with a cough. Yossarian was alone in a ponderous, primeval lull in which everything green looked black and everything else was imbued with the color of pus. The breeze rustled leaves in a dry and diaphanous distance. He was restless, scared and sleepy. The sockets of his eyes felt grimy with exhaustion. Wearily he moved inside the parachute tent with its long table of smoothed wood, a nagging bitch of a doubt burrowing painlessly inside a conscience that felt perfectly clear. He left his flak suit and parachute there and crossed back past the water wagon to the intelligence tent to return his map case to Captain Black, who sat drowsing in his chair with his skinny long legs up on his desk and inquired with indifferent curiosity why Yossarian's plane had turned back. Yossarian ignored him. He set the map down on the counter and walked out.

Back in his own tent, he squirmed out of his parachute harness and then out of his clothes. Orr was in Rome, due back that same afternoon from the rest leave he had won by ditching his plane in the waters off Genoa.

Nately would already be packing to replace him, entranced to find himself still alive and undoubtedly impatient to resume his wasted and heartbreaking courtship of his prostitute in Rome. When Yossarian was undressed, he sat down on his cot to rest. He felt much better as soon as he was naked. He never felt comfortable in clothes. In a little while he put fresh undershorts back on and set out for the beach in his moccasins, a khaki-colored bath towel draped over his shoulders.

The path from the squadron led him around a mysterious gun emplacement in the woods; two of the three enlisted men stationed there lay sleeping on the circle of sand bags and the third sat eating a purple pomegranate, biting off large mouthfuls between his churning jaws and spewing the ground roughage out away from him into the bushes. When he bit, red juice ran out of his mouth. Yossarian padded ahead into the forest again, caressing his bare, tingling belly adoringly from time to time as though to reassure himself it was all still there. He rolled a piece of lint out of his navel. Along the ground suddenly, on both sides of the path, he saw dozens of new mushrooms the rain had spawned poking their nodular fingers up through the clammy earth like lifeless stalks of flesh, sprouting in such necrotic profusion everywhere he looked that they seemed to be proliferating right before his eyes. There were thousands of them swarming as far back into the underbrush as he could see, and they appeared to swell in size and multiply in number as he spied them. He hurried away from them with a shiver of eerie alarm and did not slacken his pace until the soil crumbled to dry sand beneath his feet and they had been left behind. He glanced back apprehensively, half expecting to find the limp white things crawling after him in sightless pursuit or snaking up through the treetops in a writhing and ungovernable mutative mass.

The beach was deserted. The only sounds were hushed ones, the bloated gurgle of the stream, the respirating hum of the tall grass and shrubs behind him, the apathetic moaning of the dumb, translucent waves. The surf was always small, the water clear and cool. Yossarian left his things on the sand and moved through the knee-high waves until he was completely immersed. On the other side of the sea, a bumpy sliver of dark land lay wrapped in mist, almost invisible. He swam languorously out to the raft, held on a moment, and swam languorously back to where he could stand on the sand bar. He submerged himself head first into the green water several times until he felt clean and wide-awake and then stretched himself out face down in the sand and slept until the planes returning from Bologna were almost overhead and the great, cumulative rumble of their many engines came crashing in through his slumber in an earth-shattering roar.

He woke up blinking with a slight pain in his head and opened his eyes upon a world boiling in chaos in which everything was in proper order. He gasped in utter amazement at the fantastic sight of the twelve flights of planes organized calmly into exact formation. The scene was too unexpected to be true. There were no planes spurting ahead with wounded, none lagging behind with damage. No distress flares smoked in the sky. No ship was missing but his own. For an instant he was paralyzed with a sensation of madness. Then he understood, and almost wept at the irony. The explanation was simple: clouds had covered the target before the planes could bomb it, and the mission to Bologna was still to be flown.

He was wrong. There had been no clouds. Bologna had been bombed. Bologna was a milk run. There had been no flak there at all.

15   Piltchard & Wren

Captain Piltchard and Captain Wren, the inoffensive
joint squadron operations officers, were both mild, soft-
spoken men of less than middle height who enjoyed flying combat missions and begged nothing more of life and
Colonel Cathcart than the opportunity to continue flying
them. They had flown hundreds of combat missions and
wanted to fly hundreds more. They assigned themselves
to every one. Nothing so wonderful as war had ever
happened to them before; and they were afraid it might
never happen to them again. They conducted their
duties humbly and reticently, with a minimum of fuss,
and went to great lengths not to antagonize anyone.
They smiled quickly at everyone they passed. When they
spoke, they mumbled. They were shifty, cheerful, subservient men who were comfortable only with each other
and never met anyone else's eye, not even Yossarian's
eye at the open-air meeting they called to reprimand him
publicly for making Kid Sampson turn back from the
mission to Bologna.

'Fellas,' said Captain Piltchard, who had thinning
dark hair and smiled awkwardly. 'When you turn back
from a mission, try to make sure it's for something
important, will you? Not for something unimportant . . .

like a defective intercom ... or something like that. Okay? Captain Wren has more he wants to say to you on that subject.'

'Captain Piltchard's right, fellas,' said Captain Wren. 'And that's all I'm going to say to you on that subject. Well, we finally got to Bologna today, and we found out it's a milk run. We were all a little nervous, I guess, and didn't do too much damage. Well, listen to this. Colonel Cathcart got permission for us to go back. And tomorrow we're really going to paste those ammunition dumps. Now, what do you think about that?'

And to prove to Yossarian that they bore him no animosity, they even assigned him to fly lead bombardier with McWatt in the first formation when they went back to Bologna the next day. He came in on the target like a Havermeyer, confidently taking no evasive action at all, and suddenly they were shooting the living shit out of him!

Heavy flak was everywhere! He had been lulled, lured and trapped, and there was nothing he could do but sit there like an idiot and watch the ugly black puffs smashing up to kill him. There was nothing he could do until his bombs dropped but look back into the bombsight, where the fine cross-hairs in the lens were glued magnetically over the target exactly where he had placed them, intersecting perfectly deep inside the yard of his block of camouflaged warehouses before the base of the first building. He was trembling steadily as the plane crept ahead. He could hear the hollow *boom-boom-boom-boom* of the flak pounding all around him in overlapping measures of four, the sharp, piercing crack! of a single shell exploding suddenly very close by. His head was bursting with a thousand dissonant impulses as he prayed for the bombs to drop. He wanted to sob. The engines droned on monotonously like a fat, lazy fly. At last the indices on the bombsight crossed, tripping away the eight 500-pounders one after the other. The plane lurched upward buoyantly with the lightened load. Yossarian bent away from the bombsight crookedly to watch the indicator on

188

his left. When the pointer touched zero, he closed the bomb bay doors and, over the intercom, at the very top of his voice, shrieked:

'Turn right hard!'

McWatt responded instantly. With a grinding howl of engines, he flipped the plane over on one wing and wrung it around remorselessly in a screaming turn away from the twin spires of flak Yossarian had spied stabbing toward them. Then Yossarian had McWatt climb and keep climbing higher and higher until they tore free finally into a calm, diamond-blue sky that was sunny and pure everywhere and laced in the distance with long white veils of tenuous fluff. The wind strummed soothingly against the cylindrical panes of his windows, and he relaxed exultantly only until they picked up speed again and then turned McWatt left and plunged him right back down, noticing with a transitory spasm of elation the mushrooming clusters of flak leaping open high above him and back over his shoulder to the right, exactly where he could have been if he had not turned left and dived. He leveled McWatt out with another harsh cry and whipped him upward and around again into a ragged blue patch of unpolluted air just as the bombs he had dropped began to strike. The first one fell in the yard, exactly where he had aimed, and then the rest of the bombs from his own plane and from the other planes in his flight burst open on the ground in a charge of rapid orange flashes across the tops of the buildings, which collapsed instantly in a vast, churning wave of pink and gray and coal-black smoke that went rolling out turbulently in all directions and quaked convulsively in its bowels as though from great blasts of red and white and golden sheet lightning.

'Well, will you look at that,' Aarfy marveled sonorously right beside Yossarian, his plump, orbicular face sparkling with a look of bright enchantment. 'There must have been an ammunition dump down there.'

Yossarian had forgotten about Aarfy. 'Get out!' he shouted at him. 'Get out of the nose!'

Aarfy smiled politely and pointed down toward the target in a generous invitation for Yossarian to look. Yossarian began slapping at him insistently and signaled wildly toward the entrance of the crawlway.

'Get back in the ship!' he cried frantically. 'Get back in the ship!'

Aarfy shrugged amiably. 'I can't hear you,' he explained.

Yossarian seized him by the straps of his parachute harness and pushed him backward toward the crawlway just as the plane was hit with a jarring concussion that rattled his bones and made his heart stop. He knew at once they were all dead.

'Climb!' he screamed into the intercom at McWatt when he saw he was still alive. 'Climb, you bastard! Climb, climb, climb, climb!'

The plane zoomed upward again in a climb that was swift and straining, until he leveled it out with another harsh shout at McWatt and wrenched it around once more in a roaring, merciless forty-five-degree turn that sucked his insides out in one enervating sniff and left him floating fleshless in mid-air until he leveled McWatt out again just long enough to hurl him back around toward the right and then down into a screeching dive. Through endless blobs of ghostly black smoke he sped, the hanging smut wafting against the smooth plexiglass nose of the ship like an evil, damp, sooty vapor against his cheeks. His heart was hammering again in aching terror as he hurtled upward and downward through the blind gangs of flak charging murderously into the sky at him, then sagging inertly. Sweat gushed from his neck in torrents and poured down over his chest and waist with the feeling of warm slime. He was vaguely aware for an instant that the planes in his formation were no longer there, and then he was aware of only himself. His throat hurt like a raw slash from the strangling intensity with which he shrieked each command to McWatt. The engines rose to a deafening, agonized, ululating bellow each time McWatt changed direction. And far out in front the bursts of flak were still swarming into the sky from new batteries of guns poking around for accurate altitude as they waited sadistically for him to fly into range.

The plane was slammed again suddenly with another loud, jarring explosion that almost rocked it over on its back, and the nose filled immediately with sweet clouds of blue smoke. *Something was on fire!* Yossarian whirled to escape and smacked into Aarfy, who had struck a match and was placidly lighting his pipe. Yossarian gaped at his grinning, moon-faced navigator in utter shock and confusion. It occurred to him that one of them was mad.

'Jesus Christ!' he screamed at Aarfy in tortured amazement. 'Get the hell out of the nose! Are you crazy? Get out!'

'What?' said Aarfy.

'Get out!' Yossarian yelled hysterically, and began clubbing Aarfy backhanded with both fists to drive him away. 'Get out!'

'I still can't hear you,'Aarfy called back innocently with an expression of mild and reproving perplexity. 'You'll have to talk a little louder.'

'Get out of the nose!' Yossarian shrieked in frustration. 'They're trying to kill us! Don't you understand? They're trying to kill us!'

'Which way should I go, goddam it?' McWatt shouted furiously over the intercom in a suffering, high-pitched voice. 'Which way should I go?'

'Turn left! *Left*, you goddam dirty son of a bitch! Turn left *hard!*'

Aarfy crept up close behind Yossarian and jabbed him sharply in the ribs with the stem of his pipe. Yossarian flew up toward the ceiling with a whinnying cry, then jumped completely around on his knees, white as a sheet and quivering with rage. Aarfy winked encouragingly and jerked his thumb back toward McWatt with a humorous *moue*.

'What's eating *him*?' he asked with a laugh.

191

Yossarian was struck with a weird sense of distortion. 'Will you get out of here?' he yelped beseechingly, and shoved Aarfy over with all his strength. 'Are you deaf or something? Get back in the plane!' And to McWatt he screamed, 'Dive! *Dive!*'

Down they sank once more into the crunching, thudding, voluminous barrage of bursting antiaircraft shells as Aarfy came creeping back behind Yossarian and jabbed him sharply in the ribs again. Yossarian shied upward with another whinnying gasp.

'I still couldn't hear you,' Aarfy said.

'I said get *out of* here!' Yossarian shouted, and broke into tears. He began punching Aarfy in the body with both hands as hard as he could. 'Get *away* from me! Get *away!*'

Punching Aarfy was like sinking his fists into a limp sack of inflated rubber. There was no resistance, no response at all from the soft, insensitive mass, and after a while Yossarian's spirit died and his arms dropped helplessly with exhaustion. He was overcome with a humiliating feeling of impotence and was ready to weep in self-pity.

'What did you say?' Aarfy asked.

'Get *away* from me,' Yossarian answered, pleading with him now. 'Go back in the plane.'

'I still can't hear you.'

'Never mind,' wailed Yossarian, 'never mind. Just leave me alone.'

'Never mind what?'

Yossarian began hitting himself in the forehead. He seized Aarfy by the shirt front and struggling to his feet for traction, dragged him to the rear of the nose compartment and flung him down like a bloated and unwieldy bag in the entrance of the crawlway. A shell banged open with a stupendous clout right beside his ear as he was scrambling back toward the front, and some undestroyed recess of his intelligence wondered that it did not kill them all. They were climbing again. The engines were howling again as though in pain, and the air inside the plane was acrid with the smell of machinery and fetid with the stench of gasoline. The next thing he knew, *it was snowing!*

Thousands of tiny bits of white paper were falling like snowflakes inside the plane, milling around his head so thickly that they clung to his eyelashes when he blinked in astonishment and fluttered against his nostrils and lips each time he inhaled. When he spun around in his bewilderment, Aarfy was grinning proudly from ear to ear like something inhuman as he held up a shattered paper map for Yossarian to see. A large chunk of flak had ripped up from the floor through Aarfy's colossal jumble of maps and had ripped out through the ceiling inches away from their heads. Aarfy's joy was sublime.

'Will you look at this?' he murmured, waggling two of his stubby fingers playfully into Yossarian's face through the hole in one of his maps. 'Will you look at this?'

Yossarian was dumbfounded by his state of rapturous contentment. Aarfy was like an eerie ogre in a dream, incapable of being bruised or evaded, and Yossarian dreaded him for a complex of reasons he was too petrified to untangle. Wind whistling up through the jagged gash in the floor kept the myriad bits of paper circulating like alabaster particles in a paperweight and contributed to a sensation of lacquered, waterlogged unreality. Everything seemed strange, so tawdry and grotesque. His head was throbbing from a shrill clamor that drilled relentlessly into both ears. It was McWatt, begging for directions in an incoherent frenzy. Yossarian continued staring in tormented fascination at Aarfy's spherical countenance beaming at him so serenely and vacantly through the drifting whorls of white paper bits and concluded that he was a raving lunatic just as eight bursts of flak broke open successively at eye level off to the right, then eight more, and then eight more, the last group pulled over toward the left so that they were almost directly in front.

'Turn left hard!' he hollered to McWatt, as Aarfy kept

grinning, and McWatt did turn left hard, but the flak turned left hard with them, catching up fast, and Yossarian hollered, 'I said *hard, hard, hard, hard, you bastard, hard!*'

And McWatt bent the plane around even harder still, and suddenly, miraculously, they were out of range. The flak ended. The guns stopped booming at them. And they were alive.

Behind him, men were dying. Strung out for miles in a stricken, tortuous, squirming line, the other flights of planes were making the same hazardous journey over the target, threading their swift way through the swollen masses of new and old burst of flak like rats racing in a pack through their own droppings. One was on fire, and flapped lamely off by itself, billowing gigantically like a monstrous blood-red star. As Yossarian watched, the burning plane floated over on its side and began spiraling down slowly in wide, tremulous, narrowing circles, its huge flaming burden blazing orange and flaring out in back like a long, swirling cape of fire and smoke. There were parachutes, one, two, three. . .four, and then the plane gyrated into a spin and fell the rest of the way to the ground, fluttering insensibly inside its vivid pyre like a shred of colored tissue paper. One whole flight of planes from another squadron had been blasted apart.

Yossarian sighed barrenly, his day's work done. He was listless and sticky. The engines crooned mellifluously as McWatt throttled back to loiter and allow the rest of the planes in his flight to catch up. The abrupt stillness seemed alien and artificial, a little insidious. Yossarian unsnapped his flak suit and took off his helmet. He sighed again, restlessly, and closed his eyes and tried to relax.

'Where's Orr?' someone asked suddenly over his intercom.

Yossarian bounded up with a one-syllable cry that crackled with anxiety and provided the only rational explanation for the whole mysterious phenomenon of the flak at Bologna: *Orr!* He lunged forward over the bombsight to search downward through the plexiglass for some reassuring sign of Orr, who drew flak like a magnet and who had undoubtedly attracted the crack batteries of the whole Hermann Goering Division to Bologna overnight from wherever the hell they had been stationed the day before when Orr was still in Rome. Aarfy launched himself forward an instant later and cracked Yossarian on the bridge of the nose with the sharp rim of his flak helmet. Yossarian cursed him as his eyes flooded with tears.

'There he is,' Aarfy orated funereally, pointing down dramatically at a hay wagon and two horses standing before the barn of a gray stone farmhouse. 'Smashed to bits. I guess their numbers were all up.'

Yossarian swore at Aarfy again and continued searching intently, cold with a compassionate kind of fear now for the little bouncy and bizarre buck-toothed tentmate who had smashed Appleby's forehead open with a ping-pong racket and who was scaring the daylights out of Yossarian once again. At last Yossarian spotted the two-engined, twin-ruddered plane as it flew out of the green background of the forests over a field of yellow farmland. One of the propellers was feathered and perfectly still, but the plane was maintaining altitude and holding a proper course. Yossarian muttered an unconscious prayer of thankfulness and then flared up at Orr savagely in a ranting fusion of resentment and relief.

'That bastard!' he began. 'That goddam stunted, red faced, big-cheeked, curlyheaded, buck-toothed rat bastard son of a bitch!'

'What?' said Aarfy.

'That dirty goddam midget-assed, apple-cheeked, goggle-eyed, undersized, buck-toothed, grinning, crazy sonofabitchin-bastard!' Yossarian sputtered.

'What?'

'*Never mind!*'

'I still can't hear you,' Aarfy answered.

Yossarian swung himself around methodically to face Aarfy. 'You prick,' he began.

'Me?'

'You pompous, rotund, neighborly, vacuous, complacent. . .'

Aarfy was unperturbed. Calmly he struck a wooden match and sucked noisily at his pipe with an eloquent air of benign and magnanimous forgiveness. He smiled sociably and opened his mouth to speak. Yossarian put his hand over Aarfy's mouth and pushed him away wearily. He shut his eyes and pretended to sleep all the way back to the field so that he would not have to listen to Aarfy or see him.

At the briefing room Yossarian made his intelligence report to Captain Black and then waited in muttering suspense with all the others until Orr chugged into sight overhead finally with his one good engine still keeping him aloft gamely. Nobody breathed. Orr's landing gear would not come down. Yossarian hung around only until Orr had crash-landed safely, and then stole the first jeep he could find with a key in the ignition and raced back to his tent to begin packing feverishly for the emergency rest leave he had decided to take in Rome, where he found Luciana and her invisible scar that same night.

16 Luciana

He found Luciana sitting alone at a table in the Allied
officers' night club, where the drunken Anzac major
who had brought her there had been stupid enough to
desert her for the ribald company of some singing comrades at the bar.

'All right, I'll dance with you,' she said, before
Yossarian could even speak. 'But I won't let you sleep
with me.'

'Who asked you?' Yossarian asked her.

'You don't want to sleep with me?' she exclaimed with
surprise.

'I don't want to dance with you.'

She seized Yossarian's hand and pulled him out on the
dance floor. She was a worse dancer than even he was,
but she threw herself about to the synthetic jitterbug
music with more uninhibited pleasure than he had ever
observed until he felt his legs falling asleep with boredom and yanked her off the dance floor toward the table
at which the girl he should have been screwing was still
sitting tipsily with one hand around Aarfy's neck, her
orange satin blouse still hanging open slovenly below
her full white lacy brassière as she made dirty sex talk
ostentatiously with Huple, Orr, Kid Sampson and Hungry

Joe. Just as he reached them, Luciana gave him a forceful, unexpected shove that carried them both well beyond the table, so that they were still alone. She was a tall, earthy, exuberant girl with long hair and a pretty face, a buxom, delightful, flirtatious girl.

'All right,' she said, 'I will let you buy me dinner. But I won't let you sleep with me.'

'Who asked you?' Yossarian asked with surprise.

'You don't want to sleep with me?'

'I don't want to buy you dinner.'

She pulled him out of the night club into the street and down a flight of steps into a black-market restaurant filled with lively, chirping, attractive girls who all seemed to know each other and with the self-conscious military officers from different countries who had come there with them. The food was elegant and expensive, and the aisles were overflowing with great streams of flushed and merry proprietors, all stout and balding. The bustling interior radiated with enormous, engulfing waves of fun and warmth.

Yossarian got a tremendous kick out of the rude gusto with which Luciana ignored him completely while she shoveled away her whole meal with both hands. She ate like a horse until the last plate was clean, and then she placed her silverware down with an air of conclusion and settled back lazily in her chair with a dreamy and congested look of sated gluttony. She drew a deep, smiling, contented breath and regarded him amorously with a melting gaze.

'Okay, Joe,' she purred, her glowing dark eyes drowsy and grateful. 'Now I will let you sleep with me.'

'My name is Yossarian.'

'Okay, Yossarian,' she answered with a soft repentant laugh. 'Now I will let you sleep with me.'

'Who asked you?' said Yosssarian.

Luciana was stunned. 'You don't want to sleep with me?'

Yossarian nodded emphatically, laughing, and shot his hand up under her dress. The girl came to life with a horrified start. She jerked her legs away from him instantly, whipping her bottom around. Blushing with alarm and embarrassment, she pushed her skirt back down with a number of prim, sidelong glances about the restaurant.

'Now I will let you sleep with me,' she explained cautiously in a manner of apprehensive indulgence. 'But not now.'

'I know. When we get back to my room.'

The girl shook her head, eyeing him mistrustfully and keeping her knees pressed together. 'No, now I must go home to my mamma, because my mamma does not like me to dance with soldiers or let them take me to dinner, and she will be very angry with me if I do not come home now. But I will let you write down for me where you live. And tomorrow morning I will come to your room for ficky-fick before I go to my work at the French office. *Capisci?*'

'Bullshit!' Yossarian exclaimed with angry disappointment.

'*Cosa vuol dire* bullshit?' Luciana inquired with a blank look.

Yossarian broke into loud laughter. He answered her finally in a tone of sympathetic good humor. 'It means that I want to escort you now to wherever the hell I have to take you next so that I can rush back to that night club before Aarfy leaves with that wonderful tomato he's got without giving me a chance to ask about an aunt or friend she must have who's just like her.'

'*Come?*'

'*Subito, subito,*' he taunted her tenderly. 'Mamma is waiting. Remember?'

'*Si, si.* Mamma.'

Yossarian let the girl drag him through the lovely Roman spring night for almost a mile until they reached a chaotic bus depot honking with horns, blazing with red and yellow lights and echoing with the snarling vituperations of unshaven bus drivers pouring loathsome, hair-raising curses out at each other, at their passengers and at the strolling, unconcerned knots of pedestrians clogging their paths, who ignored them until they were bumped by the buses and began shouting curses back. Luciana vanished aboard one of the diminutive green vehicles, and Yossarian hurried as fast as he could all the way back to the cabaret and the bleary-eyed bleached blond in the open orange satin blouse. She seemed infatuated with Aarfy, but he prayed intensely for her luscious aunt as he ran, or for a luscious girl friend, sister, cousin, or mother who was just as libidinous and depraved. She would have been perfect for Yossarian, a debauched, coarse, vulgar, amoral, appetizing slattern whom he had longed for and idolized for months. She was a real find. She paid for her own drinks, and she had an automobile, an apartment and a salmon-colored cameo ring that drove Hungry Joe clean out of his senses with its exquisitely carved figures of a naked boy and girl on a rock. Hungry Joe snorted and pranced and pawed at the floor in salivating lust and groveling need, but the girl would not sell him the ring, even though he offered her all the money in all their pockets and his complicated black camera thrown in. She was not interested in money or cameras. She was interested in fornication.

  She was gone when Yossarian got there. They were all gone, and he walked right out and moved in wistful dejection through the dark, emptying streets. Yossarian was not often lonely when he was by himself, but he was lonely now in his keen envy of Aarfy, who he knew was in bed that very moment with the girl who was just right for Yossarian, and who could also make out any time he wanted to, *if* he ever wanted to, with either or both of the two slender, stunning, aristocratic women who lived in the apartment upstairs and fructified Yossarian's sex fantasies whenever he had sex fantasies, the beautiful rich black-haired countess with the red, wet, nervous lips and her beautiful rich black-haired daughter-in-law. Yossarian was madly in love with all of them as he made his way back to the officers' apartment, in love with Luciana, with the prurient intoxicated girl in the unbuttoned satin blouse, and with the beautiful rich countess and her beautiful rich daughter-in-law, both of whom would never let him touch them or even flirt with them. They doted kittenishly on Nately and deferred passively to Aarfy, but they thought Yossarian was crazy and recoiled from him with distasteful contempt each time he made an indecent proposal or tried to fondle them when they passed on the stairs. They were both superb creatures with pulpy, bright, pointed tongues and mouths like round warm plums, a little sweet and sticky, a little rotten. They had class; Yossarian was not sure what class was, but he knew that they had it and he did not, and that they knew it, too. He could picture, as he walked, the kind of underclothing they wore against their svelte feminine parts, filmy, smooth, clinging garments of deepest black or of opalescent pastel radiance with flowering lace borders fragrant with the tantalizing fumes of pampered flesh and scented bath salts rising in a germinating cloud from their blue-white breasts. He wished again that he was where Aarfy was, making obscene, brutal, cheerful love with a juicy drunken tart who didn't give a tinker's dam about him and would never think of him again.

But Aarfy was already back in the apartment when Yossarian arrived, and Yossarian gaped at him with that same sense of persecuted astonishment he had suffered that same morning over Bologna at his malign and cabalistic and irremovable presence in the nose of the plane.

'What are you doing here?' he asked.

'That's right, ask him!' Hungry Joe exclaimed in a rage. 'Make him tell you what he's doing here!'

With a long, theatrical moan, Kid Sampson made a pistol of his thumb and forefinger and blew his own brains out. Huple, chewing away on a bulging wad of bubble gum, drank everything in with a callow, vacant expression on his fifteen-year-old face. Aarfy was tapping the bowl of his pipe against his palm leisurely as he paced back and forth in corpulent self-approval, obviously delighted by the stir he was causing.

'Didn't you go home with that girl?' Yossarian demanded.

'Oh, sure, I went home with her,' Aarfy replied. 'You didn't think I was going to let her try to find her way home alone, did you?'

'Wouldn't she let you stay with her?'

'Oh, she wanted me to stay with her, all right.' Aarfy chuckled. 'Don't you worry about good old Aarfy. But I wasn't going to take advantage of a sweet kid like that just because she'd had a little too much to drink. What kind of a guy do you think I am?'

'Who said anything about taking advantage of her?' Yossarian railed at him in amazement. 'All she wanted to do was get into bed with someone. That's the only thing she kept talking about all night long.'

'That's because she was a little mixed up,' Aarfy explained. 'But I gave her a little talking to and really put some sense into her.'

'You bastard!' Yossarian exclaimed, and sank down tiredly on the divan beside Kid Sampson. 'Why the hell didn't you give her to one of us if you didn't want her?'

'You see?' Hungry Joe asked. 'There's something wrong with him.'

Yossarian nodded and looked at Aarfy curiously. 'Aarfy, tell me something. Don't you ever screw any of them?'

Aarfy chuckled again with conceited amusement. 'Oh sure, I prod them. Don't you worry about me. But never any nice girls. I know what kind of girls to prod and what kind of girls not to prod, and I never prod any nice girls. This one was a sweet kid. You could see her family had money. Why, I even got her to throw that ring of hers away right out the car window.'

Hungry Joe flew into the air with a screech of intolerable pain. 'You did *what*?' he screamed. 'You did *what*?' He began whaling away at Aarfy's shoulders and arms with both fists, almost in tears. 'I ought to *kill* you for what you did, you lousy bastard. He's *sinful*, that's what he is. He's got a dirty mind, ain't he? Ain't he got a dirty mind?'

'The dirtiest,' Yossarian agreed.

'What are you fellows talking about?' Aarfy asked with genuine puzzlement, tucking his face away protectively inside the cushioning insulation of his oval shoulders. 'Aw, come on, Joe,' he pleaded with a smile of mild discomfort. 'Quit punching me, will you?'

But Hungry Joe would not quit punching until Yossarian picked him up and pushed him away toward his bedroom. Yossarian moved listlessly into his own room, undressed and went to sleep. A second later it was morning, and someone was shaking him.

'What are you waking me up for?' he whimpered.

It was Michaela, the skinny maid with the merry disposition and homely sallow face, and she was waking him up because he had a visitor waiting just outside the door. *Luciana!* He could hardly believe it. And she was alone in the room with him after Michaela had departed, lovely, hale and statuesque, steaming and rippling with an irrepressible affectionate vitality even as she remained in one place and frowned at him irately. She stood like a youthful female colossus with her magnificent columnar legs apart on high white shoes with wedged heels, wearing a pretty green dress and swinging a large, flat white leather pocketbook, with which she cracked him hard across the face when he leaped out of bed to grab her. Yossarian staggered backward out of range in a daze, clutching his stinging cheek with bewilderment.

'Pig!' She spat out at him viciously, her nostrils flaring in a look of savage disdain. '*Vive com' un animale!*'

With a fierce, guttural, scornful, disgusted oath, she strode across the room and threw open the three tall casement windows, letting inside an effulgent flood of sunlight and crisp fresh air that washed through the stuffy room like an invigorating tonic. She placed her pocketbook on a chair and began tidying the room, picking his things up from the floor and off the tops of the furniture, throwing his socks, handkerchief and underwear into an empty drawer of the dresser and hanging his shirt and trousers up in the closet.

Yossarian ran out of the bedroom into the bathroom and brushed his teeth. He washed his hands and face and combed his hair. When he ran back, the room was in order and Luciana was almost undressed. Her expression was relaxed. She left her earrings on the dresser and padded barefoot to the bed wearing just a pink rayon chemise that came down to her hips. She glanced about the room prudently to make certain there was nothing she had overlooked in the way of neatness and then drew back the coverlet and stretched herself out luxuriously with an expression of feline expectation. She beckoned to him longingly, with a husky laugh.

'Now,' she announced in a whisper, holding both arms out to him eagerly. 'Now I will let you sleep with me.'

She told him some lies about a single weekend in bed with a slaughtered fiancé in the Italian Army, and they all turned out to be true, for she cried, 'finito!' almost as soon as he started and wondered why he didn't stop, until he had finitoed too and explained to her.

He lit cigarettes for both of them. She was enchanted by the deep suntan covering his whole body. He wondered about the pink chemise that she would not remove. It was cut like a man's undershirt, with narrow shoulder straps, and concealed the invisible scar on her back that she refused to let him see after he had made her tell him it was there. She grew tense as fine steel when he traced the mutilated contours with his finger tip from a pit in her shoulder blade almost to the base of her spine. He winced at the many tortured nights she had spent in the hospital, drugged or in pain, with the ubiquitous, ineradicable odors of ether, fecal matter and disinfectant, of human flesh mortified and decaying amid the white uniforms, the rubber-soled shoes, and the eerie night lights glowing dimly until dawn in the corridors. She had been wounded in an air raid.

'*Dove?*' he asked, and he held his breath in suspense.

'*Napoli.*'

'*Germans?*'

'*Americani.*'

His heart cracked, and he fell in love. He wondered if she would marry him.

'*Tu sei pazzo,*' she told him with a pleasant laugh.

'Why am I crazy?' he asked.

'*Perchè non posso sposare.*'

'Why can't you get married?'

'Because I am not a virgin,' she answered.

'What has that got to do with it?'

'Who will marry me? No one wants a girl who is not a virgin.'

'I will. I'll marry you.'

'*Ma non posso sposarti.*'

'Why can't you marry me?'

'*Perchè sei pazzo.*'

'Why am I crazy?'

'*Perchè vuoi sposarmi.*'

Yossarian wrinkled his forehead with quizzical amusement. 'You won't marry me because I'm crazy, and you say I'm crazy because I want to marry you? Is that right?'

'*Si.*'

'*Tu sei pazz'!*' he told her loudly.

'*Perchè?*' she shouted back at him indignantly, her unavoidable round breasts rising and falling in a saucy huff beneath the pink chemise as she sat up in bed indignantly. 'Why am I crazy?'

'Because you won't marry me.'

'*Stupido!*' she shouted back at him, and smacked him loudly and flamboyantly on the chest with the back of her hand. '*Non posso sposarti! Non capisci? Non posso sposarti.*'

'Oh, sure, I understand. And why can't you marry me?'

'*Perchè sei pazzo!*'

'And why am I crazy?'

'*Perchè vuoi sposarmi.*'

'Because I want to marry you. *Carina, ti amo,*' he explained, and he drew her gently back down to the pillow. '*Ti amo molto.*'

'*Tu sei pazzo,*' she murmured in reply, flattered.

'*Perchè?*'

'Because you say you love me. How can you love a girl who is not a virgin?'

'Because I can't marry you.'

She bolted right up again in a threatening rage. 'Why can't you marry me?' she demanded, ready to clout him again if he gave an uncomplimentary reply. 'Just because I am not a virgin?'

'No, no, darling. Because *you're* crazy.'

She stared at him in blank resentment for a moment and then tossed her head back and roared appreciatively with hearty laughter. She gazed at him with new approval when she stopped, the lush, responsive tissues of her dark face turning darker still and blooming somnolently with a swelling and beautifying infusion of blood. Her eyes grew dim. He crushed out both their cigarettes, and they turned into each other wordlessly in an engrossing kiss just as Hungry Joe came meandering into the room without knocking to ask if Yossarian wanted to go out with him to look for girls. Hungry Joe stopped on a dime when he saw them and shot out of the room. Yossarian shot out of bed even faster and began shouting at Luciana to get dressed. The girl was dumfounded. He pulled her roughly out of bed by her arm and flung her away toward her clothing, then raced for the door in time to slam it shut as Hungry Joe was running back in with his camera. Hungry Joe had his leg wedged in the door and would not pull it out.

'Let me in!' he begged urgently, wriggling and squirming maniacally. 'Let me in !' He stopped struggling for a moment to gaze up into Yossarian's face through the crack in the door with what he must have supposed was a beguiling smile. 'Me no Hungry Joe,' he explained earnestly. 'Me heap big photographer from *Life* magazine. Heap big picture on heap big cover. I make you big

Hollywood star, Yossarian. Multi *dinero*. Multi divorces. Multi ficky-fic all day long. *Si, si, si!'*

Yossarian slammed the door shut when Hungry Joe stepped back a bit to try to shoot a picture of Luciana dressing. Hungry Joe attacked the stout wooden barrier fanatically, fell back to reorganize his energies and hurled himself forward fanatically again. Yossarian slithered into his own clothes between assaults. Luciana had her green-and-white summer dress on and was holding the skirt bunched up above her waist. A wave of misery broke over him as he saw her about to vanish inside her panties forever. He reached out to grasp her and drew her to him by the raised calf of her leg. She hopped forward and molded herself against him. Yossarian kissed her ears and her closed eyes romantically and rubbed the backs of her thighs. She began to hum sensually a moment before Hungry Joe hurled his frail body against the door in still one more desperate attack and almost knocked them both down. Yossarian pushed her away.

'*Vite! Vite!*' he scolded her. 'Get your things on!'

'What the hell are you talking about?' she wanted to know.

'Fast! Fast! Can't you understand English? Get your clothes on fast!'

'*Stupido!*' she snarled back at him. '*Vite* is French, not Italian. *Subito, subito!* That's what you mean. *Subito!*'

'*Si, si.* That's what I mean. *Subito, subito!*'

'*Si, si,*' she responded co-operatively, and ran for her shoes and earrings.

Hungry Joe had paused in his attack to shoot pictures through the closed door. Yossarian could hear the camera shutter clicking. When both he and Luciana were ready, Yossarian waited for Hungry Joe's next charge and yanked the door open on him unexpectedly. Hungry Joe spilled forward into the room like a floundering frog. Yossarian skipped nimbly around him, guiding Luciana along behind him through the apartment and out into the hallway. They bounced down the stairs with a great roistering clatter, laughing out loud breathlessly and knocking their hilarious heads together each time they paused to rest. Near the bottom they met Nately coming up and stopped laughing. Nately was drawn, dirty and unhappy. His tie was twisted and his shirt was rumpled, and he walked with his hands in his pockets. He wore a hangdog, hopeless look.

'What's the matter, kid?' Yossarian inquired compassionately.

'I'm flat broke again,' Nately replied with a lame and distracted smile. 'What am I going to do?'

Yossarian didn't know. Nately had spent the last thirty-two hours at twenty dollars an hour with the apathetic whore he adored, and he had nothing left of his pay or of the lucrative allowance he received every month from his wealthy and generous father. That meant he could not spend time with her any more. She would not allow him to walk beside her as she strolled the pavements soliciting other servicemen, and she was infuriated when she spied him trailing her from a distance. He was free to hang around her apartment if he cared to, but there was no certainty that she would be there. And she would give him nothing unless he could pay. She found sex uninteresting. Nately wanted the assurance that she was not going to bed with anyone unsavory or with someone he knew. Captain Black always made it a point to buy her each time he came to Rome, just so he could torment Nately with the news that he had thrown his sweetheart another hump and watch Nately eat his liver as he related the atrocious indignities to which he had forced her to submit.

Luciana was touched by Nately's forlorn air, but broke loudly into robust laughter again the moment she stepped outside into the sunny street with Yossarian and heard Hungry Joe beseeching them from the window to come back and take their clothes off, because he really was a photographer from *Life* magazine. Luciana fled mirthfully along the sidewalk in her high white wedgies, pulling Yossarian along in tow with the same

208

lusty and ingenuous zeal she had displayed in the dance hall the night before and at every moment since. Yossarian caught up and walked with his arm around her waist until they came to the corner and she stepped away from him. She straightened her hair in a mirror from her pocketbook and put lipstick on.

'Why don't you ask me to let you write my name and address on a piece of paper so that you will be able to find me again when you come to Rome?' she suggested.

'Why don't you let me write your name and address down on a piece of paper?' he agreed.

'Why?' she demanded belligerently, her mouth curling suddenly into a vehement sneer and her eyes flashing with anger. 'So you can tear it up into little pieces as soon as I leave?'

'Who's going to tear it up?' Yossarian protested in confusion. 'What the hell are you talking about?'

'You will,' she insisted. 'You'll tear it up into little pieces the minute I'm gone and go walking away like a big shot because a tall, young, beautiful girl like me, Luciana, let you sleep with her and did not ask you for money.'

'How much money are you asking me for?' he asked her.

'*Stupido!*' she shouted with emotion. 'I am not asking you for any money!' She stamped her foot and raised her arm in a turbulent gesture that made Yossarian fear she was going to crack him in the face again with her great pocketbook. Instead, she scribbled her name and address on a slip of paper and thrust it at him. 'Here,' she taunted him sardonically, biting on her lip to still a delicate tremor. 'Don't forget. Don't forget to tear it into tiny pieces as soon as I am gone.'

Then she smiled at him serenely, squeezed his hand and, with a whispered regretful '*Addio*,' pressed herself against him for a moment and then straightened and walked away with unconscious dignity and grace.

The minute she was gone, Yossarian tore the slip of paper up and walked away in the other direction, feeling very much like a big shot because a beautiful young girl like Luciana had slept with him and did not ask for money. He was pretty pleased with himself until he looked up in the dining room of the Red Cross building and found himself eating breakfast with dozens and dozens of other servicemen in all kinds of fantastic uniforms, and then all at once he was surrounded by images of Luciana getting out of her clothes and into her clothes and caressing and haranguing him tempestuously in the pink rayon chemise she wore in bed with him and would not take off. Yossarian choked on his toast and eggs at the enormity of his error in tearing her long, lithe, nude, young vibrant limbs into tiny peices of paper so impudently and dumping her down so smugly into the gutter from the curb. He missed her terribly already. There were so many strident faceless people in uniform in the dining room with him. He felt an urgent desire to be alone with her again soon and sprang up impetuously from his table and went running outside and back down the street toward the apartment in search of the tiny bits of paper in the gutter, but they had all been flushed away by a street cleaner's hose.

He couldn't find her again in the Allied officers' night club that evening or in the sweltering, burnished, hedonistic bedlam of the black-market restaurant with its vast bobbing wooden trays of elegant food and its chirping flock of bright and lovely girls. He couldn't even find the restaurant. When he went to bed alone, he dodged flak over Bologna again in a dream, with Aarfy hanging over his shoulder abominably in the plane with a bloated sordid leer. In the morning he ran looking for Luciana in all the French offices he could find, but nobody knew what he was talking about, and then he ran in terror, so jumpy, distraught and disorganized that he just had to keep running in terror somewhere, to the enlisted men's apartment for the squat maid in the lime-colored panties, whom he found dusting in Snowden's room on the fifth floor in her drab brown sweater and heavy dark skirt. Snowden was still alive then, and

Yossarian could tell it was Snowden's room from the name stenciled in white on the blue duffel bag he tripped over as he plunged through the doorway at her in a frenzy of creative desperation. The woman caught him by the wrists before he could fall as he came stumbling toward her in need and pulled him along down on top of her as she flopped over backward onto the bed and enveloped him hospitably in her flaccid and consoling embrace, her dust mop aloft in her hand like a banner as her broad, brutish congenial face gazed up at him fondly with a smile of unperjured friendship. There was a sharp elastic snap as she rolled the lime-colored panties off beneath them both without disturbing him.

He stuffed money into her hand when they were finished. She hugged him in gratitude. He hugged her. She hugged him back and then pulled him down on top of her on the bed again. He stuffed more money into her hand when they were finished this time and ran out of the room before she could begin hugging him in gratitude again. Back at his own apartment, he threw his things together as fast as he could, left for Nately what money he had, and ran back to Pianosa on a supply plane to apologize to Hungry Joe for shutting him out of the bedroom. The apology was unnecessary, for Hungry Joe was in high spirits when Yossarian found him. Hungry Joe was grinning from ear to ear, and Yossarian turned sick at the sight of him, for he understood instantly what the high spirits meant.

'Forty missions,' Hungry Joe announced readily in a voice lyrical with relief and elation. 'The colonel raised them again.'

Yossarian was stunned. 'But I've got thirty-two, goddammit! Three more and I would have been through.'

Hungry Joe shrugged indifferently. 'The colonel wants forty missions, ' he repeated.

Yossarian shoved him out of the way and ran right into the hospital.

17   The soldier in white

Yossarian ran right into the hospital, determined to remain there forever rather than fly one mission more than the thirty-two missions he had. Ten days after he changed his mind and came out, the colonel raised the missions to forty-five and Yossarian ran right back in, determined to remain in the hospital forever rather than fly one mission more than the six missions more he had just flown.

Yossarian could run into the hospital whenever he wanted to because of his liver and because of his eyes; the doctors couldn't fix his liver condition and couldn't meet his eyes each time he told them he had a liver condition. He could enjoy himself in the hospital, just as long as there was no one really very sick in the same ward. His system was sturdy enough to survive a case of someone else's malaria or influenza with scarcely any discomfort at all. He could come through other people's tonsilectomies without suffering any postoperative distress, and even endure their hernias and hemorrhoids with only mild nausea and revulsion. But that was just about as much as he could go through without getting sick. After that he was ready to bolt. He could relax in the hospital, since no one there expected him to do anything. All he was expected to do in the hospital was die or get better, and since he was perfectly all right to begin with, getting better was easy.

Being in the hospital was better than being over Bologna or flying over Avignon with Huple and Dobbs at the controls and Snowden dying in back.

There were usually not nearly as many sick people inside the hospital as Yossarian saw outside the hospital, and there were generally fewer people inside the hospital who were seriously sick. There was a much lower death rate inside the hospital than outside the hospital, and a much healthier death rate. Few people died unnecessarily. People knew a lot more about dying inside the hospital and made a much neater, more orderly job of it. They couldn't dominate Death inside the hospital, but they certainly made her behave. They had taught her manners. They couldn't keep Death out, but while she was in she had to act like a lady. People gave up the ghost with delicacy and taste inside the hospital. There was none of that crude, ugly ostentation about dying that was so common outside the hospital. They did not blow up in mid-air like Kraft or the dead man in Yossarian's tent, or freeze to death in the blazing summertime the way Snowden had frozen to death after spilling his secret to Yossarian in the back of the plane.

'I'm cold,' Snowden had whimpered. 'I'm cold.'

'There, there,' Yossarian had tried to comfort him. 'There, there.'

They didn't take it on the lam weirdly inside a cloud the way Clevinger had done. They didn't explode into blood and clotted matter. They didn't drown or get struck by lightning, mangled by machinery or crushed in landslides. They didn't get shot to death in hold-ups, strangled to death in rapes, stabbed to death in saloons, bludgeoned to death with axes by parents or children or die summarily by some other act of God. Nobody choked to death. People bled to death like gentlemen in an operating room or expired without comment in an oxygen tent. There was none of that tricky now-you-see-me-

213

now-you-don't business so much in vogue outside the hospital, none of that now-I-am-and-now-I-ain't. There were no famines or floods. Children didn't suffocate in cradles or iceboxes or fall under trucks. No one was beaten to death. People didn't stick their heads into ovens with the gas on, jump in front of subway trains or come plummeting like dead weights out of hotel windows with a *whoosh!*, accelerating at the rate of sixteen feet per second to land with a hideous *plop!* on the sidewalk and die disgustingly there in public like an alpaca sack full of hairy strawberry ice cream, bleeding, pink toes awry.

All things considered, Yossarian often preferred the hospital, even though it had its faults. The help tended to be officious, the rules, if heeded, restrictive, and the management meddlesome. Since sick people were apt to be present, he could not always depend on a lively young crowd in the same ward with him, and the entertainment was not always good. He was forced to admit that the hospitals had altered steadily for the worse as the war continued and one moved closer to the battlefront, the deterioration in the quality of the guests becoming most marked within the combat zone itself where the effects of booming wartime conditions were apt to make themselves conspicuous immediately. The people got sicker and sicker the deeper he moved into combat, until finally in the hospital that last time there had been the soldier in white, who could not have been any sicker without being dead, and he soon was.

The soldier in white was constructed entirely of gauze, plaster and a thermometer, and the thermometer was merely an adornment left balanced in the empty dark hole in the bandages over his mouth early each morning and late each afternoon by Nurse Cramer and Nurse Duckett right up to the afternoon Nurse Cramer read the thermometer and discovered he was dead. Now that Yossarian looked back, it seemed that Nurse Cramer, rather than the talkative Texan, had murdered the soldier in white; if she had not read the thermometer and reported what she had found, the soldier in white might still be lying there alive exactly as he had been lying there all along, encased from head to toe in plaster and gauze with both strange, rigid legs elevated from the hips and both strange arms strung up perpendicularly, all four bulky limbs in casts, all four strange, useless limbs hoisted up in the air by taut wire cables and fantastically long lead weights suspended darkly above him. Lying there that way might not have been much of a life, but it was all the life he had, and the decision to terminate it, Yossarian felt, should hardly have been Nurse Cramer's.

The soldier in white was like an unrolled bandage with a hole in it or like a broken block of stone in a harbor with a crooked zinc pipe jutting out. The other patients in the ward, all but the Texan, shrank from him with a tenderhearted aversion from the moment they set eyes on him the morning after the night he had been sneaked in. They gathered soberly in the farthest recess of the ward and gossiped about him in malicious, offended undertones, rebelling against his presence as a ghastly imposition and resenting him malevolently for the nauseating truth of which he was bright reminder. They shared a common dread that he would begin moaning.

'I don't know what I'll do if he does begin moaning,' the dashing young fighter pilot with the golden mustache had grieved forlornly. 'It means he'll moan during the night, too, because he won't be able to tell time.'

No sound at all came from the soldier in white all the time he was there. The ragged round hole over his mouth was deep and jet black and showed no sign of lip, teeth, palate or tongue. The only one who ever came close enough to look was the affable Texan, who came close enough several times a day to chat with him about more votes for the decent folk, opening each conversation with the same unvarying greeting: 'What do you say, fella? How you coming along?' The rest of the men avoided them both in their regulation maroon corduroy bathrobes and unraveling flannel pajamas, wondering gloomily who the soldier in white was, why he was there and what he was really like inside.

'He's all right, I tell you,' the Texan would report back to them encouragingly after each of his social visits.

'Deep down inside he's really a regular guy. He's feeling a little shy and insecure now because he doesn't know anybody here and can't talk. Why don't you all just step right up to him and introduce yourselves? He won't hurt you.'

'What the goddam hell are you talking about?' Dunbar demanded. 'Does he even know what you're talking about?'

'Sure he knows what I'm talking about. He's not stupid. There ain't nothing wrong with him.'

'Can he hear you?'

'Well, I don't know if he can hear me or not, but I'm sure he knows what I'm talking about.'

'Does that hole over his mouth ever move?'

'Now, what kind of a crazy question is that?' the Texan asked uneasily.

'How can you tell if he's breathing if it never moves?'

'How can you tell it's a he?'

'Does he have pads over his eyes underneath that bandage over his face?'

'Does he ever wiggle his toes or move the tips of his fingers?'

The Texan backed away in mounting confusion. 'Now, what kind of a crazy question is that? You fellas must all be crazy or something. Why don't you just walk right up to him and get acquainted? He's a real nice guy, I tell you.'

The soldier in white was more like a stuffed and sterilized mummy than a real nice guy. Nurse Duckett and Nurse Cramer kept him spick-and-span. They brushed his bandages often with a whiskbroom and scrubbed the plaster casts on his arms, legs, shoulders, chest and pelvis with soapy water. Working with a round tin of metal polish, they waxed a dim gloss on the

216

dull zinc pipe rising from the cement on his groin. With damp dish towels they wiped the dust several times a day from the slim black rubber tubes leading in and out of him to the two large stoppered jars, one of them, hanging on a post beside his bed, dripping fluid into his arm constantly through a slit in the bandages while the other, almost out of sight on the floor, drained the fluid away through the zinc pipe rising from his groin. Both young nurses polished the glass jars unceasingly. They were proud of their housework. The more solicitous of the two was Nurse Cramer, a shapely, pretty, sexless girl with a wholesome unattractive face. Nurse Cramer had a cute nose and a radiant, blooming complexion dotted with fetching sprays of adorable freckles that Yossarian detested. She was touched very deeply by the soldier in white. Her virtuous, pale-blue, saucerlike eyes flooded with leviathan tears on unexpected occasions and made Yossarian mad.

'How the hell do you know he's even in there?' he asked her.

'Don't you dare talk to me that way!' she replied indignantly.

'Well, how do you? You don't even know if it's really him.'

'Who?'

'Whoever's supposed to be in all those bandages. You might really be weeping for somebody else. How do you know he's even alive?'

'What a terrible thing to say!' Nurse Cramer exclaimed. 'Now, you get right into bed and stop making jokes about him.'

'I'm not making jokes. Anybody might be in there. For all we know, it might even be Mudd.'

'What are you talking about?' Nurse Cramer pleaded with him in a quavering voice.

'Maybe that's where the dead man is.'

'What dead man?'

'I've got a dead man in my tent that nobody can throw out. His name is Mudd.'

Nurse Cramer's face blanched and she turned to Dunbar desperately for aid. 'Make him stop saying things like that,' she begged.

'Maybe there's no one inside,' Dunbar suggested helpfully. 'Maybe they just sent the bandages here for a joke.'

She stepped away from Dunbar in alarm. 'You're crazy,' she cried, glancing about imploringly. 'You're both crazy.'

Nurse Duckett showed up then and chased them all back to their own beds while Nurse Cramer changed the stoppered jars for the soldier in white. Changing the jars for the soldier in white was no trouble at all, since the same clear fluid was dripped back inside him over and over again with no apparent loss. When the jar feeding the inside of his elbow was just about empty, the jar on the floor was just about full, and the two were simply uncoupled from their respective hoses and reversed quickly so that the liquid could be dripped right back into him. Changing the jars was no trouble to anyone but the men who watched them changed every hour or so and were baffled by the procedure.

'Why can't they hook the two jars up to each other and eliminate the middleman?' the artillery captain with whom Yossarian had stopped playing chess inquired. 'What the hell do they need him for?'

'I wonder what he did to deserve it,' the warrant officer with malaria and a mosquito bite on his ass lamented after Nurse Cramer had read her thermometer and discovered that the soldier in white was dead.

'He went to war,' the fighter pilot with the golden mustache surmised.

'We all went to war,' Dunbar countered.

'That's what I mean,' the warrant officer with malaria continued. 'Why him? There just doesn't seem to be any logic to this system of rewards and punishment. Look what happened to me. If I had gotten syphillis or a dose of clap for my five minutes of passion on the beach instead of this damned mosquito bite, I could see justice.

But malaria? *Malaria*? Who can explain malaria as a consequence of fornication?' The warrant officer shook his head in numb astonishment.

'What about me?' Yossarian said. 'I stepped out of my tent in Marrakech one night to get a bar of candy and caught your dose of clap when that Wac I never even saw before hissed me into the bushes. All I really wanted was a bar of candy, but who could turn it down?'

'That sounds like my dose of clap, all right,' the warrant officer agreed. 'But I've still got somebody else's malaria. Just for once I'd like to see all these things sort of straightened out, with each person getting exactly what he deserves. It might give me some confidence in this universe.'

'I've got somebody else's three hundred thousand dollars,' the dashing young fighter captain with the golden mustache admitted. 'I've been goofing off since the day I was born. I cheated my way through prep school and college, and just about all I've been doing ever since is shacking up with pretty girls who think I'd make a good husband. I've got no ambition at all. The only thing I want to do after the war is marry some girl who's got more money than I have and shack up with lots more pretty girls. The three hundred thousand bucks was left to me before I was born by a grandfather who made a fortune selling on an international scale. I know I don't deserve it, but I'll be damned if I give it back. I wonder who it really belongs to.'

'Maybe it belongs to my father,' Dunbar conjectured. 'He spent a lifetime at hard work and never could make enough money to even send my sister and me through college. He's dead now, so you might as well keep it.'

'Now, if we can just find out who my malaria belongs to we'd be all set. It's not that I've got anything against malaria. I'd just as soon goldbrick with malaria as with anything else. It's only that I feel an injustice has been committed. Why should I have somebody else's malaria and you have my dose of clap?'

'I've got more than your dose of clap,' Yossarian told

him. 'I've got to keep flying combat missions because of that dose of yours until they kill me.'

'That makes it even worse. What's the justice in that?'

'I had a friend named Clevinger two and a half weeks ago who used to see plenty of justice in it.'

'It's the highest kind of justice of all, ' Clevinger had gloated, clapping his hands with a merry laugh. 'I can't help thinking of the *Hippolytus* of Euripedes, where the early licentiousness of Theseus is probably responsible for the asceticism of the son that helps bring about the tragedy that ruins them all. If nothing else, that episode with the Wac should teach you the evil of sexual immorality.'

'It teaches me the evil of candy.'

'Can't you see that you're not exactly without blame for the predicament you're in?' Clevinger had continued with undisguised relish. 'If you hadn't been laid up in the hospital with venereal disease for ten days back there in Africa, you might have finished your twenty-five missions in time to be sent home before Colonel Nevers was killed and Colonel Cathcart came to replace him.'

'And what about you?' Yossarian had replied. 'You never got clap in Marrakech and you're in the same predicament.'

'I don't know,' confessed Clevinger, with a trace of mock concern. 'I guess I must have done something very bad in my time.'

'Do you really believe that?'

Clevinger laughed. 'No, of course not. I just like to kid you along a little.'

There were too many dangers for Yossarian to keep track of. There was Hitler, Mussolini and Tojo, for example, and they were all out to kill him. There was Lieutenant Scheisskopf with his fanaticism for parades and there was the bloated colonel with his big fat mustache and his fanaticism for retribution, and they wanted to kill him, too. There was Appleby, Havermeyer, Black and Korn. There was Nurse Cramer and Nurse Duckett, who he was almost certain wanted him dead, and there was the Texan and the C.I.D. man, about whom he had no doubt. There were bartenders, bricklayers and bus conductors all over the world who wanted him dead, landlords and tenants, traitors and patriots, lynchers, leeches and lackeys, and they were all out to bump him off. That was the secret Snowden had spilled to him on the mission to Avignon — they were out to get him; and Snowden had spilled it all over the back of the plane.

There were lymph glands that might do him in. There were kidneys, nerve sheaths and corpuscles. There were tumors of the brain. There was Hodgkin's disease, leukemia, amyotrophic lateral sclerosis. There were fertile red meadows of epithelial tissue to catch and coddle a cancer cell. There were diseases of the skin, diseases of the bone, diseases of the lung, diseases of the stomach, diseases of the heart, blood and arteries. There were diseases of the head, diseases of the neck, diseases of the chest, diseases of the intestines, diseases of the crotch. There even were diseases of the feet. There were billions of conscientious body cells oxidating away day and night like dumb animals at their complicated job of keeping him alive and healthy, and every one was a potential traitor and foe. There were so many diseases that it took a truly diseased mind to even think about them as often as he and Hungry Joe did.

Hungry Joe collected lists of fatal diseases and arranged them in alphabetical order so that he could put his finger without delay on any one he wanted to worry about. He grew very upset whenever he misplaced some or when he could not add to his list, and he would go rushing in a cold sweat to Doc Daneeka for help.

'Give him Ewing's tumor,' Yossarian advised Doc Daneeka, who would come to Yossarian for help in handling Hungry Joe, 'and follow it up with melanoma. Hungry Joe likes lingering diseases, but he likes the fulminating ones even more.'

Doc Daneeka had never heard of either. 'How do you manage to keep up on so many diseases like that?' he inquired with high professional esteem.

221

'I learn about them at the hospital when I study the *Reader's Digest*.'

Yossarian had so many ailments to be afraid of that he was sometimes tempted to turn himself in to the hospital for good and spend the rest of his life stretched out there inside an oxygen tent with a battery of specialists and nurses seated at one side of his bed twenty-four hours a day waiting for something to go wrong and at least one surgeon with a knife poised at the other, ready to jump forward and begin cutting away the moment it became necessary. Aneurisms, for instance; how else could they ever defend him in time against an aneurism of the aorta? Yossarian felt much safer inside the hospital than outside the hospital, even though he loathed the surgeon and his knife as much as he had ever loathed anyone. He could start screaming inside a hospital and people would at least come running to try to help; outside the hospital they would throw him in prison if he ever started screaming about all the things he felt everyone ought to start screaming about, or they would put him in the hospital. One of the things he wanted to start screaming about was the surgeon's knife that was almost certain to be waiting for him and everyone else who lived long enough to die. He wondered often how he would ever recognize the first chill, flush, twinge, ache, belch, sneeze, stain, lethargy, vocal slip, loss of balance or lapse of memory that would signal the inevitable beginning of the inevitable end.

He was afraid also that Doc Daneeka would still refuse to help him when he went to him again after jumping out of Major Major's office, and he was right.

'You think you've got something to be afraid about?' Doc Daneeka demanded, lifting his delicate immaculate dark head up from his chest to gaze at Yossarian irascibly for a moment with lachrymose eyes. 'What about me? My precious medical skills are rusting away here on this lousy island while other doctors are cleaning up. Do you think I enjoy sitting here day after day refusing to help you? I wouldn't mind it so much if I could refuse to help you back in the States or in some place like Rome. But saying no to you here isn't easy for me, either.'

'Then stop saying no. Ground me.'

'I can't ground you,' Doc Daneeka mumbled. 'How many times do you have to be told?'

'Yes you can. Major Major told me you're the only one in the squadron who *can* ground me.'

Doc Daneeka was stunned. 'Major Major told you that? When?'

'When I tackled him in the ditch.'

'Major Major told you that? In a ditch?'

'He told me in his office after we left the ditch and jumped inside. He told me not to tell anyone he told me, so don't start shooting your mouth off.'

'Why that dirty, scheming liar!' Doc Daneeka cried. 'He wasn't supposed to tell anyone. Did he tell you how I could ground you?'

'Just by filling out a little slip of paper saying I'm on the verge of a nervous collapse and sending it to Group. Dr. Stubbs grounds men in his squadron all the time, so why can't you?'

'And what happens to the men after Stubbs does ground them?' Doc Daneeka retorted with a sneer. 'They go right back on combat status, don't they? And he finds himself right up the creek. Sure, I can ground you by filling out a slip saying you're unfit to fly. But there's a catch.'

'Catch-22?'

'Sure. If I take you off combat duty, Group has to approve my action, and Group isn't going to. They'll put you right back on combat status, and then where will I be? On my way to the Pacific Ocean, probably. No, thank you. I'm not going to take any chances for you.'

'Isn't it worth a try?' Yossarian argued. 'What's so hot about Pianosa?'

'Pianosa is terrible. But it's better than the Pacific Ocean. I wouldn't mind being shipped someplace civilized where I might pick up a buck or two in abortion

223

money every now and then. But all they've got in the
Pacific is jungles and monsoons, I'd rot there.'

'You're rotting here.'

Doc Daneeka flared up angrily. 'Yeah? Well, at least
I'm going to come out of this war alive, which is a lot
more than you're going to do.'

'That's just what I'm trying to tell you, goddammit. I'm
asking you to save my life.'

'It's not my business to save lives,' Doc Daneeka
retorted sullenly.

'What is your business?'

'I don't know what my business is. All they ever told
me was to uphold the ethics of my profession and never
give testimony against another physician. Listen. You
think you're the only one whose life is in danger? What
about me? Those two quacks I've got working for me in
the medical tent still can't find out what's wrong with
me.'

'Maybe it's Ewing's tumor,' Yossarian muttered sarcastically.

'Do you really think so?' Doc Daneeka exclaimed with
fright.

'Oh, I don't know,' Yossarian answered impatiently. 'I
just know I'm not going to fly any more missions. They
wouldn't really shoot me, would they? I've got fifty-one.'

'Why don't you at least finish the fifty-five before you
take a stand?' Doc Daneeka advised. 'With all your
bitching, you've never finished a tour of duty even once.'

'How the hell can I? The colonel keeps raising them
every time I get close.'

'You never finish your missions because you keep running into the hospital or going off to Rome. You'd be in a
much stronger position if you had your fifty-five finished
and then refused to fly. Then maybe I'd see what I could
do.'

'Do you promise?'

'I promise.'

'What do you promise?'

'I promise that maybe I'll think about doing something

to help if you finish your fifty-five missions and if you get McWatt to put my name on his flight log again so that I can draw my flight pay without going up in a plane. I'm afraid of airplanes. Did you read about that airplane crash in Idaho three weeks ago? Six people killed. It was terrible. I don't know why they want me to put in four hours' flight time every month in order to get my flight pay. Don't I have enough to worry about without worrying about being killed in an airplane crash too?'

'I worry about the airplane crashes also,' Yossarian told him. 'You're not the only one.'

'Yeah, but I'm also pretty worried about that Ewing's tumor,' Doc Daneeka boasted. 'Do you think that's why my nose is stuffed all the time and why I always feel so chilly? Take my pulse.'

Yossarian also worried about Ewing's tumor and melanoma. Catastrophes were lurking everywhere, too numerous to count. When he contemplated the many diseases and potential accidents threatening him, he was positively astounded that he had managed to survive in good health for as long as he had. It was miraculous. Each day he faced was another dangerous mission against mortality. And he had been surviving them for twenty-eight years.

18 The soldier who saw everything twice

Yossarian owed his good health to exercise, fresh air, teamwork and good sportsmanship; it was to get away from them all that he had first discovered the hospital. When the physical-education officer at Lowery Field ordered everyone to fall out for calisthenics one afternoon, Yossarian, the private, reported instead at the dispensary with what he said was a pain in his right side.

'Beat it,' said the doctor on duty there, who was doing a crossword puzzle.

'We can't tell him to beat it,' said a corporal. 'There's a new directive out about abdominal complaints. We have to keep them under observation five days because so many of them have been dying after we make them beat it.'

'All right,' grumbled the doctor. 'Keep him under observation five days and *then* make him beat it.'

They took Yossarian's clothes away and put him in a ward, where he was very happy when no one was snoring nearby. In the morning a helpful young English intern popped in to ask him about his liver.

'I think it's my appendix that's bothering me,' Yossarian told him.

226

'Your appendix is no good,' the Englishman declared with jaunty authority. 'If your appendix goes wrong, we can take it out and have you back on active duty in almost no time at all. But come to us with a liver complaint and you can fool us for weeks. The liver, you see, is a large, ugly mystery to us. If you've ever eaten liver you know what I mean. We're pretty sure today that the liver exists and we have a fairly good idea of what it does whenever it's doing what it's supposed to be doing. Beyond that, we're really in the dark. After all, what is a liver? My father, for example, died of cancer of the liver and was never sick a day of his life right up till the moment it killed him. Never felt a twinge of pain. In a way, that was too bad, since I hated my father. Lust for my mother, you know.'

'What's an English medical officer doing on duty here?' Yossarian wanted to know.

The officer laughed. 'I'll tell you all about that when I see you tomorrow morning. And throw that silly ice bag away before you die of pneumonia.'

Yossarian never saw him again. That was one of the nice things about all the doctors at the hospital; he never saw any of them a second time. They came and went and simply disappeared. In place of the English intern the next day, there arrived a group of doctors he had never seen before to ask him about his appendix.

'There's nothing wrong with my appendix,' Yossarian informed them. 'The doctor yesterday said it was my liver.'

'Maybe it is his liver,' replied the white-haired officer in charge. 'What does his blood count show?'

'He hasn't had a blood count.'

'Have one taken right away. We can't afford to take chances with a patient in his condition. We've got to keep ourselves covered in case he dies.' He made a notation on his clipboard and spoke to Yossarian. 'In the meantime, keep that ice bag on. It's very important.'

'I don't have an ice bag on.'

'Well, get one. There must be an ice bag around here

somewhere. And let someone know if the pain becomes unendurable.'

At the end of ten days, a new group of doctors came to Yossarian with bad news; he was in perfect health and had to get out. He was rescued in the nick of time by a patient across the aisle who began to see everything twice. Without warning, the patient sat up in bed and shouted.

'I see everything twice!'

A nurse screamed and an orderly fainted. Doctors came running up from every direction with needles, lights, tubes, rubber mallets and oscillating metal tines. They rolled up complicated instruments on wheels. There was not enough of the patient to go around, and specialists pushed forward in line with raw tempers and snapped at their colleagues in front to hurry up and give somebody else a chance. A colonel with a large forehead and horn-rimmed glasses soon arrived at a diagnosis.

'It's meningitis,' he called out emphatically, waving the others back. 'Although Lord knows there's not the slightest reason for thinking so.'

'Then why pick meningitis?' inquired a major with a suave chuckle. 'Why not, let's say, acute nephritis?'

'Because I'm a meningitis man, that's why, and not an acute-nephritis man,' retorted the colonel. 'And I'm not going to give him up to any of you kidney birds without a struggle. I was here first.'

In the end, the doctors were all in accord. They agreed they had no idea what was wrong with the soldier who saw everything twice, and they rolled him away into a room in the corridor and quarantined everyone else in the ward for fourteen days.

Thanksgiving Day came and went without any fuss while Yossarian was still in the hospital. The only bad thing about it was the turkey for dinner, and even that was pretty good. It was the most rational Thanksgiving he had ever spent, and he took a sacred oath to spend every future Thanksgiving Day in the cloistered shelter of a hospital. He broke his sacred oath the very next year, when he spent the holiday in a hotel room instead in intellectual conversation with Lieutenant Scheisskopf's wife, who had Dori Duz's dog tags on for the occasion and who henpecked Yossarian sententiously for being cynical and callous about Thanksgiving, even though she didn't believe in God just as much as he didn't.

'I'm probably just as good an atheist as you are,' she speculated boastfully. 'But even I feel that we all have a great deal to be thankful for and that we shouldn't be ashamed to show it.'

'Name one thing I've got to be thankful for,' Yossarian challenged her without interest.

'Well. . .' Lieutenant Scheisskopf's wife mused and paused a moment to ponder dubiously. 'Me.'

'Oh, come on,' he scoffed.

She arched her eyebrows in surprise. 'Aren't you thankful for me?' she asked. She frowned peevishly, her pride wounded. 'I don't have to shack up with you, you know,' she told him with cold dignity. 'My husband has a whole squadron full of aviation cadets who would be only too happy to shack up with their commanding officer's wife just for the added fillip it would give them.'

Yossarian decided to change the subject. 'Now you're changing the subject,' he pointed out diplomatically. 'I'll bet I can name two things to be miserable about for every one you can name to be thankful for.'

'Be thankful you've got me,' she insisted.

'I am, honey. But I'm also goddam good and miserable that I can't have Dori Duz again, too. Or the hundreds of other girls and women I'll see and want in my short lifetime and won't be able to go to bed with even once.'

'Be thankful you're healthy.'

'Be bitter you're not going to stay that way.'

'Be glad you're even alive.'

'Be *furious* you're going to die.'

'Things could be much worse,' she cried.

'They could be one hell of a lot better,' he answered heatedly.

229

'You're naming only one thing,' she protested. 'You said you could name two.'

'And don't tell me God works in mysterious ways,' Yossarian continued, hurtling on over her objection. 'There's nothing so mysterious about it. He's not working at all. He's playing. Or else He's forgotten all about us. That's the kind of God you people talk about – a country bumpkin, a clumsy, bungling, brainless, conceited, uncouth hayseed. Good God, how much reverence can you have for a Supreme Being who finds it necessary to include such phenomena as phlegm and tooth decay in His divine system of creation? What in the world was running through that warped, evil, scatalogical mind of His when He robbed old people of the power to control their bowel movements? Why in the world did He ever create pain?'

'Pain?' Lieutenant Scheisskopf's wife pounced upon the word victoriously. 'Pain is a useful symptom. Pain is a warning to us of bodily dangers.'

'And who created the dangers?' Yossarian demanded. He laughed caustically. 'Oh, He was really being charitable to us when He gave us pain! Why couldn't He have used a doorbell instead to notify us, or one of His celestial choirs? Or a system of blue-and-red neon tubes right in the middle of each person's forehead. Any jukebox manufacturer worth his salt could have done that. Why couldn't He?'

'People would certainly look silly walking around with red neon tubes in the middle of their foreheads.'

'They certainly look beautiful now writhing in agony or stupefied with morphine, don't they? What a colossal, immortal blunderer! When you consider the opportunity and power He had to really do a job, and then look at the stupid, ugly little mess He made of it instead, His sheer incompetence is almost staggering. It's obvious He never met a payroll. Why, no self-respecting businessman would hire a bungler like Him as even a shipping clerk!'

Lieutenant Scheisskopf's wife had turned ashen in

230

disbelief and was ogling him with alarm. 'You'd better not talk that way about Him, honey,' she warned him reprovingly in a low and hostile voice. 'He might punish you.'

'Isn't He punishing me enough?' Yossarian snorted resentfully. 'You know, we mustn't let Him get away with it. Oh, no, we certainly mustn't let Him get away scot free for all the sorrow He's caused us. Someday I'm going to make Him pay. I know when. On the Judgment Day. Yes, that's the day I'll be close enough to reach out and grab that little yokel by His neck and –'

'Stop it! Stop it!' Lieutenant Scheisskopf's wife screamed suddenly, and began beating him ineffectually about the head with both fists. 'Stop it!'

Yossarian ducked behind his arm for protection while she slammed away at him in feminine fury for a few seconds, and then he caught her determinedly by the wrists and forced her gently back down on the bed. 'What the hell are you getting so upset about?' he asked her bewilderedly in a tone of contrite amusement. 'I thought you didn't believe in God.'

'I don't,' she sobbed, bursting violently into tears. 'But the God I don't believe in is a good God, a just God, a merciful God. He's not the mean and stupid God you make Him out to be.'

Yossarian laughed and turned her arms loose. 'Let's have a little more religious freedom between us,' he proposed obligingly. 'You don't believe in the God you want to, and I won't believe in the God I want to. Is that a deal?'

That was the most illogical Thanksgiving he could ever remember spending, and his thoughts returned wishfully to his halcyon fourteen-day quarantine in the hospital the year before; but even that idyll had ended on a tragic note; he was still in good health when the quarantine period was over, and they told him again that he had to get out and go to war. Yossarian sat up in bed when he heard the bad news and shouted.

'I see everything twice!'

Pandemonium broke loose in the ward again. The specialists came running up from all directions and ringed him in a circle of scrutiny so confining that he could feel the humid breath from their various noses blowing uncomfortably upon the different sectors of his body. They went snooping into his eyes and ears with tiny beams of light, assaulted his legs and feet with rubber hammers and vibrating forks, drew blood from his veins, held anything handy up for him to see on the periphery of his vision.

The leader of this team of doctors was a dignified, solicitous gentleman who held one finger up directly in front of Yossarian and demanded, 'How many fingers do you see?'

'Two,' said Yossarian.

'How many fingers do you see now?' asked the doctor, holding up two.

'Two,' said Yossarian.

'And how many now?' asked the doctor, holding up none.

'Two,' said Yossarian.

The doctor's face wreathed with a smile. 'By jove, he's right,' he declared jubilantly. 'He *does* see everything twice.'

They rolled Yossarian away on a stretcher into the room with the other soldier who saw everything twice and quarantined everyone else in the ward for another fourteen days.

'I see everything twice!' the soldier who saw everything twice shouted when they rolled Yossarian in.

'I see everything twice!' Yossarian shouted back at him just as loudly, with a secret wink.

'The walls! The walls!' the other soldier cried. 'Move back the walls!'

'The walls! The walls!' Yossarian cried. 'Move back the walls!'

One of the doctors pretended to shove the wall back. 'Is that far enough?'

The soldier who saw everything twice nodded weakly

and sank back on his bed. Yossarian nodded weakly too, eying his talented roommate with great humility and admiration. He knew he was in the presence of a master. His talented roommate was obviously a person to be studied and emulated. During the night, his talented roommate died, and Yossarian decided that he had followed him far enough.

'I see everything once!' he cried quickly.

A new group of specialists came pounding up to his bedside with their instruments to find out if it was true.

'How many fingers do you see?' asked the leader, holding up one.

'One.'

The doctor held up two fingers. 'How many fingers do you see now?'

'One.'

The doctor held up ten fingers. 'And how many now?'

'One.'

The doctor turned to the other doctors with amazement. 'He does see everything once!' he exclaimed. 'We made him all better.'

'And just in time, too,' announced the doctor with whom Yossarian next found himself alone, a tall, torpedo-shaped congenial man with an unshaven growth of brown beard and a pack of cigarettes in his shirt pocket that he chain-smoked insouciantly as he leaned against the wall. 'There are some relatives here to see you. Oh, don't worry,' he added with a laugh. 'Not your relatives. It's the mother, father and brother of that chap who died. They've traveled all the way from New York to see a dying soldier, and you're the handiest one we've got.'

'What are you talking about?' Yossarian asked suspiciously. 'I'm not dying.'

'Of course you're dying. We're all dying. Where the devil else do you think you're heading?'

'They didn't come to see me,' Yossarian objected. 'They came too see their son.'

'They'll have to take what they can get. As far as

we're concerned, one dying boy is just as good as any other, or just as bad. To a scientist, all dying boys are equal. I have a proposition for you. You let them come in and look you over for a few minutes and I won't tell anyone you've been lying about your liver symptoms.'

Yossarian drew back from him farther. 'You know about that?'

'Of course I do. Give us some credit.' The doctor chuckled amiably and lit another cigarette. 'How do you expect anyone to believe you have a liver condition if you keep squeezing the nurses' tits every time you get a chance? You're going to have to give up sex if you want to convince people you've got an ailing liver.'

'That's a hell of a price to pay just to keep alive. Why didn't you turn me in if you knew I was faking?'

'Why the devil should I?' asked the doctor with a flicker of surprise. 'We're all in this business of illusion together. I'm always willing to lend a helping hand to a fellow conspirator along the road to survival if he's willing to do the same for me. These people have come a long way, and I'd rather not disappoint them. I'm sentimental about old people.'

'But they came to see their son.'

'They came too late. Maybe they won't even notice the difference.'

'Suppose they start crying.'

'They probably will start crying. That's one of the reasons they came. I'll listen outside the door and break it up if it starts getting tacky.'

'It all sounds a bit crazy,' Yossarian reflected. 'What do they want to watch their son die for, anyway?'

'I've never been able to figure that one out,' the doctor admitted, 'but they always do. Well, what do you say? All you've got to do is lie there a few minutes and die a little. Is that asking so much?'

'All right,' Yossarian gave in. 'If it's just for a few minutes and you promise to wait right outside.' He warmed to his role. 'Say, why don't you wrap a bandage around me for effect?'

'That sounds like a splendid idea,' applauded the doctor.

They wrapped a batch of bandages around Yossarian. A team of medical orderlies installed tan shades on each of the two windows and lowered them to douse the room in depressing shadows. Yossarian suggested flowers and the doctor sent an orderly out to find two small bunches of fading ones with a strong and sickening smell. When everything was in place, they made Yossarian get back into bed and lie down. Then they admitted the visitors.

The visitors entered uncertainly as though they felt they were intruding, tiptoeing in with stares of meek apology, first the grieving mother and father, then the brother, a glowering heavy-set sailor with a deep chest. The man and woman stepped into the room stiffly side by side as though right out of a familiar, though esoteric, anniversary daguerrotype on a wall. They were both short, sere and proud. They seemed made of iron and old, dark clothing. The woman had a long, brooding oval face of burnt umber, with coarse graying black hair parted severely in the middle and combed back austerely behind her neck without curl, wave or ornamentation. Her mouth was sullen and sad, her lined lips compressed. The father stood very rigid and quaint in a double-breasted suit with padded shoulders that were much too tight for him. He was broad and muscular on a small scale and had a magnificently curled silver mustache on his crinkled face. His eyes were creased and rheumy, and he appeared tragically ill at ease as he stood awkwardly with the brim of his black felt fedora held in his two brawny laborer's hands out in front of his wide lapels. Poverty and hard work had inflicted iniquitous damage on both. The brother was looking for a fight. His round white cap was cocked at an insolent tilt, his hands were clenched, and he glared at everything in the room with a scowl of injured truculence.

The three creaked forward timidly, holding themselves close to each other in a stealthy, funereal group and inching forward almost in step, until they arrived at the side of the bed and stood staring down at Yossarian. There was a gruesome and excruciating silence that threatened to endure forever. Finally Yossarian was unable to bear it any longer and cleared his throat. The old man spoke at last.

'He looks terrible,' he said.

'He's sick, Pa.'

'Giuseppe,' said the mother, who had seated herself in a chair with her veinous fingers clasped in her lap.

'My name is Yossarian,' Yossarian said.

'His name is Yossarian, Ma. Yossarian, don't you recognize me? I'm your brother John. Don't you know who I am?'

'Sure I do. You're my brother John.'

'He does recognize me! Pa, he knows who I am. Yossarian, here's Papa. Say hello to Papa.'

'Hello, Papa,' said Yossarian.

'Hello, Giuseppe.'

'His name is Yossarian, Pa.'

'I can't get over how terrible he looks,' the father said.

'He's very sick, Pa. The doctor says he's going to die.'

'I didn't know whether to believe the doctor or not,' the father said. 'You know how crooked those guys are.'

'Giuseppe,' the mother said again, in a soft, broken chord of muted anguish.

'His name is Yossarian. Ma. She don't remember things too good any more. How're they treating you in here, kid? They treating you pretty good?'

'Pretty good,' Yossarian told him.

'That's good. Just don't let anybody in here push you around. You're just as good as anybody else in here even though you are Italian. You've got rights, too.'

Yossarian winced and closed his eyes so that he would not have to look at his brother John. He began to feel sick.

'*Now* see how terrible he looks,' the father observed.

'Giuseppe,' the mother said.

'Ma, his name is Yossarian,' the brother interrupted

236

her impatiently. 'Can't you remember?'

'It's all right,' Yossarian interrupted him. 'She can call me Giuseppe if she wants to.'

'Giuseppe,' she said to him.

'Don't worry, Yossarian,' the brother said. 'Everything is going to be all right.'

'Don't worry, Ma,' Yossarian said. 'Everything is going to be all right.'

'Did you have a priest?' the brother wanted to know.

'Yes,' Yossarian lied, wincing again.

'That's good,' the brother decided. 'Just as long as you're getting everything you've got coming to you. We came all the way from New York. We were afraid we wouldn't get here in time.'

'In time for what?'

'In time to see you before you died.'

'What difference would it make?'

'We didn't want you to die by yourself.'

'What difference would it make?'

'He must be getting delirious,' the brother said. 'He keeps saying the same thing over and over again.'

'That's really very funny,' the old man replied. 'All the time I thought his name was Giuseppe, and now I find out his name is Yossarian. That's really very funny.'

'Ma, make him feel good,' the brother urged. 'Say something to cheer him up.'

'Giuseppe.'

'It's not Giuseppe, Ma. It's Yossarian.'

'What difference does it make?' the mother answered in the same mourning tone, without looking up. 'He's dying.'

Her tumid eyes filled with tears and she began to cry, rocking back and forth slowly in her chair with her hands lying in her lap like fallen moths. Yossarian was afraid she would start wailing. The father and brother began crying also. Yossarian remembered suddenly why they were all crying, and he began crying too. A doctor Yossarian had never seen before stepped inside the room and told the visitors courteously that they had to go. The father drew himself up formally to say goodbye.

'Giuseppe,' he began.

'Yossarian,' corrected the son.

'Yossarian,' said the father.

'Giuseppe,' corrected Yossarian.

'Soon you're going to die.'

Yossarian began to cry again. The doctor threw him a dirty look from the rear of the room, and Yossarian made himself stop.

The father continued solemnly with his head lowered. 'When you talk to the man upstairs,' he said, 'I want you to tell Him something for me. Tell Him it ain't right for people to die when they're young. I mean it. Tell Him if they got to die at all, they got to die when they're old. I want you to tell Him that. I don't think He knows it ain't right, because He's supposed to be good and it's been going on for a long, long time. Okay?'

'And don't let anybody up there push you around,' the brother advised. 'You'll be just as good as anybody else in heaven, even though you are Italian.'

'Dress warm,' said the mother, who seemed to know.

19 Colonel Cathcart

Colonel Cathcart was a slick, successful, slipshod, unhappy man of thirty-six who lumbered when he walked and wanted to be a general. He was dashing and dejected, poised and chagrined. He was complacent and insecure, daring in the administrative stratagems he employed to bring himself to the attention of his superiors and craven in his concern that his schemes might all backfire. He was handsome and unattractive, a swashbuckling, beefy, conceited man who was putting on fat and was tormented chronically by prolonged seizures of apprehension. Colonel Cathcart was conceited because he was a full colonel with a combat command at the age of only thirty-six; and Colonel Cathcart was dejected because although he was already thirty-six he was still only a full colonel.

Colonel Cathcart was impervious to absolutes. He could measure his own progress only in relationship to others, and his idea of excellence was to do something at least as well as all the men his own age who were doing the same thing even better. The fact that there were thousands of men his own age and older who had not even attained the rank of major enlivened him with foppish delight in his own remarkable worth; on the other hand, the fact that there were men of his own age and younger who were already generals contaminated him with an agonizing sense of failure and made him gnaw at his fingernails with an unappeasable anxiety that was even more intense than Hungry Joe's.

Colonel Cathcart was a very large, pouting, broad-shouldered man with close-cropped curly dark hair that was graying at the tips and an ornate cigarette holder that he purchased the day before he arrived in Pianosa to take command of his group. He displayed the cigarette holder grandly on every occasion and had learned to manipulate it adroitly. Unwittingly, he had discovered deep within himself a fertile aptitude for smoking with a cigarette holder. As far as he could tell, his was the only cigarette holder in the whole Mediterranean theater of operations, and the thought was both flattering and disquieting. He had no doubts at all that someone as debonair and intellectual as General Peckem approved of his smoking with a cigarette holder, even though the two were in each other's presence rather seldom, which in a way was very lucky, Colonel Cathcart recognized with relief, since General Peckem might not have approved of his cigarette holder at all. When such misgivings assailed Colonel Cathcart, he choked back a sob and wanted to throw the damned thing away, but he was restrained by his unswerving conviction that the cigarette holder never failed to embellish his masculine, martial physique with a high gloss of sophisticated heroism that illuminated him to dazzling advantage among all the other full colonels in the American Army with whom he was in competition. Although how could he be sure?

Colonel Cathcart was indefatigable that way, an industrious, intense, dedicated military tactician who calculated day and night in the service of himself. He was his own sarcophagus, a bold and infallible diplomat who was always berating himself disgustedly for all the chances he had missed and kicking himself regretfully for all the errors he had made. He was tense, irritable, bitter and smug. He was a valorous opportunist who pounced hoggishly upon every opportunity Colonel Korn discovered for him and trembled in damp despair immediately afterwards at the possible consequences he might suffer. He collected rumors greedily and treasured gossip. He believed all the news he heard and had faith in none. He was on the alert constantly for every signal, shrewdly sensitive to relationships and situations that did not exist. He was someone in the know who was always striving pathetically to find out what was going on. He was a blustering, intrepid bully who brooded inconsolably over the terrible ineradicable impressions he knew he kept making on people of prominence who were scarcely aware that he was even alive.

Everybody was persecuting him. Colonel Cathcart lived by his wits in an unstable, arithmetical world of black eyes and feathers in his cap, of overwhelming imaginary triumphs and catastrophic imaginary defeats. He oscillated hourly between anguish and exhilaration, multiplying fantastically the grandeur of his victories and exaggerating tragically the seriousness of his defeats. Nobody ever caught him napping. If word reached him that General Dreedle or General Peckem had been seen smiling, frowning, or doing neither, he could not make himself rest until he had found an acceptable interpretation and grumbled mulishly until Colonel Korn persuaded him to relax and take things easy.

Lieutenant Colonel Korn was a loyal, indispensable ally who got on Colonel Cathcart's nerves. Colonel Cathcart pledged eternal gratitude to Colonel Korn for the ingenious moves he devised and was furious with him afterward when he realized they might not work. Colonel Cathcart was greatly indebted to Colonel Korn and did not like him at all. The two were very close. Colonel Cathcart was jealous of Colonel Korn's intelligence and had to remind himself often that Colonel Korn was still only a lieutenant colonel, even though he was almost ten years older than Colonel Cathcart, and that Colonel Korn had obtained his education at a state university. Colonel Cathcart bewailed the miserable fate that had given him for an invaluable assistant someone as common as Colonel Korn. It was degrading to have to depend so thoroughly on a person who had been educated at a state university. If someone did have to become indispensable to him, Colonel Cathcart lamented, it could just as easily have been someone wealthy and well groomed, someone from a better family who was more mature than Colonel Korn and who did not treat Colonel Cathcart's desire to become a general as frivolously as Colonel Cathcart secretly suspected Colonel Korn secretly did.

Colonel Cathcart wanted to be a general so desperately he was willing to try anything, even religion, and he summoned the chaplain to his office late one morning the week after he had raised the number of missions to sixty and pointed abruptly down toward his desk to his copy of *The Saturday Evening Post.* The colonel wore his khaki shirt collar wide open, exposing a shadow of tough black bristles of beard on his egg-white neck, and had a spongy hanging underlip. He was a person who never tanned, and he kept out of the sun as much as possible to avoid burning. The colonel was more than a head taller than the chaplain and over twice as broad, and his swollen, overbearing authority made the chaplain feel frail and sickly by contrast.

'Take a look, Chaplain,' Colonel Cathcart directed, screwing a cigarette into his holder and seating himself affluently in the swivel chair behind his desk. 'Let me know what you think.'

The chaplain looked down at the open magazine compliantly and saw an editorial spread dealing with an American bomber group in England whose chaplain said prayers in the briefing room before each mission. The chaplain almost wept with happiness when he realized the colonel was not going to holler at him. The two had hardly spoken since the tumultuous evening Colonel Cathcart had thrown him out of the officers'

club at General Dreedle's bidding after Chief White
Halfoat had punched Colonel Moodus in the nose. The
chaplain's initial fear had been that the colonel intended
reprimanding him for having gone back into the officers'
club without permission the evening before. He had
gone there with Yossarian and Dunbar after the two had
come unexpectedly to his tent in the clearing in the
woods to ask him to join them. Intimidated as he was by
Colonel Cathcart, he nevertheless found it easier to brave
his displeasure than to decline the thoughtful invitation
of his two new friends, whom he had met on one of his
hospital visits just a few weeks before and who had
worked so effectively to insulate him against the myriad
social vicissitudes involved in his official duty to live on
closest terms of familiarity with more than nine hundred
unfamiliar officers and enlisted men who thought him
an odd duck.

The chaplain glued his eyes to the pages of the magazine. He studied each photograph twice and read the
captions intently as he organized his response to the
colonel's question into a grammatically complete sentence that he rehearsed and reorganized in his mind a
considerable number of times before he was able finally
to muster the courage to reply.

'I think that saying prayers before each mission is a
very moral and highly laudatory procedure, sir,' he
offered timidly, and waited.

'Yeah,' said the colonel. 'But I want to know if you
think they'll work here.'

'Yes, sir,' answered the chaplain after a few moments.
'I should think they would.'

'Then I'd like to give it a try.' The colonel's ponderous,
farinaceous cheeks were tinted suddenly with glowing
patches of enthusiasm. He rose to his feet and began
walking around excitedly. 'Look how much good they've
done for these people in England. Here's a picture of a
colonel in *The Saturday Evening Post* whose chaplain
conducts prayers before each mission. If the prayers
work for him, they should work for us. Maybe if we say

prayers, they'll put *my* picture in *The Saturday Evening Post.*'

The colonel sat down again and smiled distantly in lavish contemplation. The chaplain had no hint of what he was expected to say next. With a pensive expression on his oblong, rather pale face, he allowed his gaze to settle on several of the high bushels filled with red plum tomatoes that stood in rows against each of the walls. He pretended to concentrate on a reply. After a while he realized that he was staring at rows and rows of bushels of red plum tomatoes and grew so intrigued by the question of what bushels brimming with red plum tomatoes were doing in a group commander's office that he forgot completely about the discussion of prayer meetings until Colonel Cathcart, in a genial digression, inquired:

'Would you like to buy some, Chaplain? They come right off the farm Colonel Korn and I have up in the hills. I can let you have a bushel wholesale.'

'Oh, no, sir. I don't think so.'

'That's quite all right,' the colonel assured him liberally. 'You don't have to. Milo is glad to snap up all we can produce. These were picked only yesterday. Notice how firm and ripe they are, like a young girl's breasts.'

The chaplain blushed, and the colonel understood at once that he had made a mistake. He lowered his head in shame, his cumbersome face burning. His fingers felt gross and unwieldy. He hated the chaplain venomously for being a chaplain and making a coarse blunder out of an observation that in any other circumstances, he knew, would have been considered witty and urbane. He tried miserably to recall some means of extricating them both from their devastating embarrassment. He recalled instead that the chaplain was only a captain, and he straightened at once with a shocked and outraged gasp. His cheeks grew tight with fury at the thought that he had just been duped into humiliation by a man who was almost the same age as he was and still only a captain, and he swung upon the chaplain avengingly with a look of such murderous antagonism that the chaplain began to tremble. The colonel punished him sadistically with a long, glowering, malignant, hateful, silent stare.

'We were speaking about something else,' he reminded the chaplain cuttingly at last. 'We were not speaking about the firm, ripe breasts of beautiful young girls but about something else entirely. We were speaking about conducting religious services in the briefing room before each mission. Is there any reason why we can't?'

'No, sir,' the chaplain mumbled.

'Then we'll begin with this afternoon's mission.' The colonel's hostility softened gradually as he applied himself to details. 'Now, I want you to give a lot of thought to the kind of prayers we're going to say. I don't want anything heavy or sad. I'd like you to keep it light and snappy, something that will send the boys out feeling pretty good. Do you know what I mean? I don't want any of this Kingdom of God or Valley of Death stuff. That's all too negative. What are you making such a sour face for?'

'I'm sorry, sir,' the chaplain stammered. 'I happened to be thinking of the Twenty-third Psalm just as you said that.'

'How does that one go?'

'That's the one you were just referring to, sir. "The Lord is my shepherd; I –" '

'That's the one I was just referring to. It's out. What else have you got?'

' "Save me, O God; for the waters are come in unto –" '

'No waters,' the colonel decided, blowing ruggedly into his cigarette holder after flipping the butt down into his combed-brass ash tray. 'Why don't we try something musical? How about the harps on the willows?'

'That has the rivers of Babylon in it, sir,' the chaplain replied. ' ". . .there we sat down, yea, we wept, when we remembered Zion." '

'Zion? Let's forget about that one right now. I'd like to

245

know how that one even got in there. Haven't you got anything humorous that stays away from waters and valleys and God? I'd like to keep away from the subject of religion altogether if we can.'

The chaplain was apologetic. 'I'm sorry, sir, but just about all the prayers I know are rather somber in tone and make at least some passing reference to God.'

'Then let's get some new ones. The men are already doing enough bitching about the missions I send them on without our rubbing it in with any sermons about God or death or Paradise. Why can't we take a more positive approach? Why can't we all pray for something good, like a tighter bomb pattern, for example? Couldn't we pray for a tighter bomb pattern?'

'Well, yes, sir, I suppose so,' the chaplain answered hesitantly. 'You wouldn't even need me if that's all you wanted to do. You could do that yourself.'

'I know I could,' the colonel responded tartly. 'But what do you think you're here for? I could shop for my own food, too, but that's Milo's job, and that's why he's doing it for every group in the area. Your job is to lead us in prayer, and from now on you're going to lead us in a prayer for a tighter bomb pattern before every mission. Is that clear? I think a tighter bomb pattern is something really worth praying for. It will be a feather in all our caps with General Peckem. General Peckem feels it makes a much nicer aerial photograph when the bombs explode close together.'

'General Peckem, sir?'

'That's right, Chaplain,' the colonel replied, chuckling paternally at the chaplain's look of puzzlement. 'I wouldn't want this to get around, but it looks like General Dreedle is finally on the way out and that General Peckem is slated to replace him. Frankly, I'm not going to be sorry to see that happen. General Peckem is a very good man, and I think we'll all be much better off under him. On the other hand, it might never take place, and we'd still remain under General Dreedle. Frankly, I wouldn't be sorry to see that happen either, because General Dreedle is another very good man, and I think we'll all be much better off under him too. I hope you're going to keep all this under your hat, Chaplain. I wouldn't want either one to get the idea I was throwing my support on the side of the other.'

'Yes, sir.'

'That's good,' the colonel exclaimed, and stood up jovially. 'But all this gossip isn't getting us into *The Saturday Evening Post*, eh, Chaplain? Let's see what kind of procedure we can evolve. Incidentally, Chaplain, not a word about this beforehand to Colonel Korn. Understand?'

'Yes, sir.'

Colonel Cathcart began tramping back and forth reflectively in the narrow corridors left between his bushels of plum tomatoes and the desk and wooden chairs in the center of the room. 'I suppose we'll have to keep you waiting outside until the briefing is over, because all that information is classified. We can slip you in while Major Danby is synchronizing the watches. I don't think there's anything secret about the right time. We'll allocate about a minute and a half for you in the schedule. Will a minute and a half be enough?'

'Yes, sir. If it doesn't include the time necessary to excuse the atheists from the room and admit the enlisted men.'

Colonel Cathcart stopped in his tracks. 'What atheists?' he bellowed defensively, his whole manner changing in a flash to one of virtuous and belligerent denial. 'There are no atheists in my outfit! Atheism is against the law, isn't it?'

'No, sir.'

'It isn't?' The colonel was surprised. 'Then it's un-American, isn't it?'

'I'm not sure, sir,' answered the chaplain.

'Well, I am!' the colonel declared. 'I'm not going to disrupt our religious services just to accommodate a bunch of lousy atheists. They're getting no special privileges from me. They can stay right where they are and pray with the rest of us. And what's all this about enlisted men? Just how the hell do they get into this act?'

The chaplain felt his face flush. 'I'm sorry, sir. I just assumed you would want the enlisted men to be present, since they would be going along on the same mission.'

'Well, I don't. They've got a God and a chaplain of their own, haven't they?'

'No, sir.'

'What are you talking about? You mean they pray to the same God we do?'

'Yes, sir.'

'And He *listens*?'

'I think so, sir.'

'Well, I'll be damned,' remarked the colonel, and he snorted to himself in quizzical amusement. His spirits drooped suddenly a moment later, and he ran his hand nervously over his short, black, graying curls. 'Do you really think it's a good idea to let the enlisted men in?' he asked with concern.

'I should think it only proper, sir.'

'I'd like to keep them out,' confided the colonel, and began cracking his knuckles savagely as he wandered back and forth. 'Oh, don't get me wrong, Chaplain. It isn't that I think the enlisted men are dirty, common and inferior. It's that we just don't have enough room. Frankly, though, I'd just as soon the officers and enlisted men didn't fraternize in the briefing room. They see enough of each other during the mission, it seems to me. Some of my very best friends are enlisted men, you understand, but that's about as close as I care to let them come. Honestly now, Chaplain, you wouldn't want your sister to marry an enlisted man, would you?'

'My sister is an enlisted man, sir,' the chaplain replied.

The colonel stopped in his tracks again and eyed the chaplain sharply to make certain he was not being ridiculed. 'Just what do you mean by that remark, Chaplain? Are you trying to be funny?'

'Oh, no, sir,' the chaplain hastened to explain with a

look of excruciating discomfort. 'She's a master sergeant in the Marines.'

The colonel had never liked the chaplain and now he loathed and distrusted him. He experienced a keen premonition of danger and wondered if the chaplain too were plotting against him, if the chaplain's reticent, unimpressive manner were really just a sinister disguise masking a fiery ambition that, 'way down deep, was crafty and unscrupulous. There was something funny about the chaplain, and the colonel soon detected what it was. The chaplain was standing stiffly at attention, for the colonel had forgotten to put him at ease. Let him stay that way, the colonel decided vindictively, just to show him who was boss and to safeguard himself against any loss of dignity that might devolve from his acknowledging the omission.

Colonel Cathcart was drawn hypnotically toward the window with a massive, dull stare of moody introspection. The enlisted men were always treacherous, he decided. He looked downward in mournful gloom at the skeet-shooting range he had ordered built for the officers on his headquarters staff, and he recalled the mortifying afternoon General Dreedle had tongue-lashed him ruthlessly in front of Colonel Korn and Major Danby and ordered him to throw open the range to all the enlisted men and officers on combat duty. The skeet-shooting range had been a real black eye for him, Colonel Cathcart was forced to conclude. He was positive that General Dreedle had never forgotten it, even though he was positive that General Dreedle didn't even remember it, which was really very unjust, Colonel Cathcart lamented, since the idea of a skeet-shooting range itself should have been a real feather in his cap, even though it had been such a real black eye. Colonel Cathcart was helpless to assess exactly how much ground he had gained or lost with his goddam skeet-shooting range and wished that Colonel Korn were in his office right then to evaluate the entire episode for him still one more time and assuage his fears.

It was all very perplexing, all very discouraging. Colonel Cathcart took the cigarette holder out of his mouth, stood it on end inside the pocket of his shirt, and began gnawing on the fingernails of both hands grievously. Everybody was against him, and he was sick to his soul that Colonel Korn was not with him in this moment of crisis to help him decide what to do about the prayer meetings. He had almost no faith at all in the chaplain, who was still only a captain. 'Do you think,' he asked, 'that keeping the enlisted men out might interfere with our chances of getting results?'

The chaplain hesitated, feeling himself on unfamiliar ground again. 'Yes, sir,' he replied finally. 'I think it's conceivable that such an action could interfere with your chances of having the prayers for a tighter bomb pattern answered.'

'I wasn't even thinking about that!' cried the colonel, with his eyes blinking and splashing like puddles. 'You mean that God might even decide to punish me by giving us a *looser* bomb pattern?'

'Yes, sir,' said the chaplain. 'It's conceivable He might.'

'The hell with it, then,' the colonel asserted in a huff of independence. 'I'm not going to set these damned prayer meetings up just to make things *worse* than they are.' With a scornful snicker, he settled himself behind his desk, replaced the empty cigarette holder in his mouth and lapsed into parturient silence for a few moments. 'Now I think about it,' he confessed, as much to himself as to the chaplain, 'having the men pray to God probably wasn't such a hot idea anyway. The editors of *The Saturday Evening Post* might not have co-operated.'

The colonel abandoned his project with remorse, for he had conceived it entirely on his own and had hoped to unveil it as a striking demonstration to everyone that he had no real need for Colonel Korn. Once it was gone, he was glad to be rid of it, for he had been troubled from the start by the danger of instituting the plan without first checking it out with Colonel Korn. He heaved an immense sigh of contentment. He had a much higher opinion of himself now that his idea was abandoned, for he had made a very wise decision, he felt, and, most important, he had made this wise decision without consulting Colonel Korn.

'Will that be all, sir?' asked the chaplain.

'Yeah,' said Colonel Cathcart. 'Unless you've got something else to suggest.'

'No, sir. Only. . .'

The colonel lifted his eyes as though affronted and studied the chaplain with aloof distrust. 'Only what, Chaplain?'

'Sir,' said the chaplain, 'some of the men are very upset since you raised the number of missions to sixty. They've asked me to speak to you about it.'

The colonel was silent. The chaplain's face reddened to the roots of his sandy hair as he waited. The colonel kept him squirming a long time with a fixed, uninterested look devoid of all emotion.

'Tell them there's a war going on,' he advised finally in a flat voice.

'Thank you, sir, I will,' the chaplain replied in a flood of gratitude because the colonel had finally said something. 'They were wondering why you couldn't requisition some of the replacement crews that are waiting in Africa to take their places and then let them go home.'

'That's an administrative matter,' the colonel said. 'It's none of their business.' He pointed languidly toward the wall. 'Help yourself to a plum tomato, Chaplain. Go ahead, it's on me.'

'Thank you, sir. Sir –'

'Don't mention it. How do you like living out there in the woods, Chaplain? Is everything hunky dory?'

'Yes, sir.'

'That's good. You get in touch with us if you need anything.'

'Yes, sir. Thank you, sir. Sir –'

'Thanks for dropping around, Chaplain. I've got some work to do now. You'll let me know if you can think of

251

anything for getting our names into *The Saturday Evening Post,* won't you?'

'Yes, sir, I will.' The chaplain braced himself with a prodigious effort of the will and plunged ahead brazenly. 'I'm particularly concerned about the condition of one of the bombardiers, sir. Yossarian.'

The colonel glanced up quickly with a start of vague recognition. 'Who?' he asked in alarm.

'Yossarian, sir.'

'Yossarian?'

'Yes, sir. Yossarian. He's in a very bad way, sir. I'm afraid he won't be able to suffer much longer without doing something desperate.'

'Is that a fact, Chaplain?'

'Yes, sir. I'm afraid it is.'

The colonel thought about it in heavy silence for a few moments. 'Tell him to trust in God,' he advised finally.

'Thank you, sir,' said the chaplain. 'I will.'

20 Corporal Whitcomb

The late-August morning sun was hot and steamy, and
there was no breeze on the balcony. The chaplain moved
slowly. He was downcast and burdened with self-
approach when he stepped without noise from the colonel's office on his rubber-soled and rubber-heeled
brown shoes. He hated himself for what he construed to
be his own cowardice. He had intended to take a much
stronger stand with Colonel Cathcart on the matter of
the sixty missions, to speak out with courage, logic and
eloquence on a subject about which he had begun to feel
very deeply. Instead he had failed miserably, had
choked up once again in the face of opposition from a
stronger personality. It was a familiar, ignominious
experience, and his opinion of himself was low.

He choked up even more a second later when he spied
Colonel Korn's tubby monochrome figure trotting up the
curved, wide, yellow stone staircase toward him in
lackadaisical haste from the great dilapidated lobby
below with its lofty walls of cracked dark marble and
circular floor of cracked grimy tile. The chaplain was
even more frightened of Colonel Korn than he was of
Colonel Cathcart. The swarthy, middle-aged lieutenant
colonel with the rimless, icy glasses and faceted, bald,

domelike pate that he was always touching sensitively with the tips of his splayed fingers disliked the chaplain and was impolite to him frequently. He kept the chaplain in a constant state of terror with his curt, derisive tongue and his knowing, cynical eyes that the chaplain was never brave enough to meet for more than an accidental second. Inevitably, the chaplain's attention, as he cowered meekly before him, focused on Colonel Korn's midriff, where the shirttails bunching up from inside his sagging belt and ballooning down over his waist gave him an appearance of slovenly girth and made him seem inches shorter than his middle height. Colonel Korn was an untidy disdainful man with an oily skin and deep, hard lines running almost straight down from his nose between his crepuscular jowls and his square, clefted chin. His face was dour, and he glanced at the chaplain without recognition as the two drew close on the staircase and prepared to pass.

'Hiya, Father,' he said tonelessly without looking at the chaplain. 'How's it going?'

'Good morning, sir,' the chaplain replied, discerning wisely that Colonel Korn expected nothing more in the way of a response.

Colonel Korn was proceeding up the stairs without slackening his pace, and the chaplain resisted the temptation to remind him again that he was not a Catholic but an Anabaptist, and that it was therefore neither necessary nor correct to address him as Father. He was almost certain now that Colonel Korn remembered and that calling him Father with a look of such bland innocence was just another one of Colonel Korn's methods of taunting him because he was only an Anabaptist.

Colonel Korn halted without warning when he was almost by and came whirling back down upon the chaplain with a glare of infuriated suspicion. The chaplain was petrified.

'What are you doing with that plum tomato, Chaplain?' Colonel Korn demanded roughly.

The chaplain looked down his arm with surprise at the

plum tomato Colonel Cathcart had invited him to take. 'I got it in Colonel Cathcart's office, sir,' he managed to reply.

'Does the colonel know you took it?'

'Yes, sir. He gave it to me.'

'Oh, in that case I guess it's okay,' Colonel Korn said, mollified. He smiled without warmth, jabbing the crumpled folds of his shirt back down inside his trousers with his thumbs. His eyes glinted keenly with a private and satisfying mischief. 'What did Colonel Cathcart want to see you about, Father?' he asked suddenly.

The chaplain was tongue-tied with indecision for a moment. 'I don't think I ought –'

'Saying prayers to the editors of *The Saturday Evening Post*?'

The chaplain almost smiled. 'Yes, sir.'

Colonel Korn was enchanted with his own intuition. He laughed disparagingly. 'You know, I was afraid he'd begin thinking about something so ridiculous as soon as he saw this week's *Saturday Evening Post*. I hope you succeeded in showing him what an atrocious idea it is.'

'He has decided against it, sir.'

'That's good. I'm glad you convinced him that the editors of *The Saturday Evening Post* were not likely to run that same story twice just to give some publicity to some obscure colonel. How are things in the wilderness, Father? Are you able to manage out there?'

'Yes, sir. Everything is working out.'

'That's good. I'm happy to hear you have nothing to complain about. Let us know if you need anything to make you comfortable. We all want you to have a good time out there.'

'Thank you, sir. I will.'

Noise of a growing stir rose from the lobby below. It was almost lunchtime, and the earliest arrivals were drifting into the headquarters mess halls, the enlisted men and officers separating into different dining halls on facing sides of the archaic rotunda. Colonel Korn stopped smiling.

'You had lunch with us here just a day or so ago, didn't you, Father?' he asked meaningfully.

'Yes, sir. The day before yesterday.'

'That's what I thought,' Colonel Korn said, and paused to let his point sink in. 'Well, take it easy, Father. I'll see you around when it's time for you to eat here again.'

'Thank you, sir.'

The chaplain was not certain at which of the five officers' and five enlisted men's mess halls he was scheduled to have lunch that day, for the system of rotation worked out for him by Colonel Korn was complicated, and he had forgotten his records back in his tent. The chaplain was the only officer attached to Group Headquarters who did not reside in the moldering red stone Group Headquarters building itself or in any of the smaller satellite structures that rose about the grounds in disjuncted relationship. The chaplain lived in a clearing in the woods about four miles away between the officers' club and the first of the four squadron areas that stretched away from Group Headquarters in a distant line. The chaplain lived alone in a spacious, square tent that was also his office. Sounds of revelry traveled to him at night from the officers' club and kept him awake often as he turned and tossed on his cot in passive, half-voluntary exile. He was not able to gauge the effect of the mild pills he took occasionally to help him sleep and felt guilty about it for days afterward.

The only one who lived with the chaplain in his clearing in the woods was Coporal Whitcomb, his assistant. Corporal Whitcomb, an atheist, was a disgruntled subordinate who felt he could do the chaplain's job much better than the chaplain was doing it and viewed himself, therefore, as an under-privileged victim of social inequity. He lived in a tent of his own as spacious and square as the chaplain's. He was openly rude and contemptuous to the chaplain once he discovered that the chaplain would let him get away with it. The borders of the two tents in the clearing stood no more than four or five feet apart.

It was Colonel Korn who had mapped out this way of life for the chaplain. One good reason for making the chaplain live outside the Group Headquarters building was Colonel Korn's theory that dwelling in a tent as most of his parishioners did would bring him into closer communication with them. Another good reason was the fact that having the chaplain around Headquarters all the time made the other officers uncomfortable. It was one thing to maintain liaison with the Lord, and they were all in favor of that; it was something else, though, to have Him hanging around twenty-four hours a day. All in all, as Colonel Korn described it to Major Danby, the jittery and goggle-eyed group operations officer, the chaplain had it pretty soft; he had little more to do than listen to the troubles of others, bury the dead, visit the bedridden and conduct religious services. And there were not so many dead for him to bury any more, Colonel Korn pointed out, since opposition from German fighter planes had virtually ceased and since close to ninety per cent of what fatalities there still were, he estimated, perished behind the enemy lines or disappeared inside the clouds, where the chaplain had nothing to do with disposing of the remains. The religious services were certainly no great strain, either, since they were conducted only once a week at the Group Headquarters building and were attended by very few of the men.

Actually, the chaplain was learning to love it in his clearing in the woods. Both he and Corporal Whitcomb had been provided with every convenience so that neither might ever plead discomfort as a basis for seeking permission to return to the Headquarters building. The chaplain rotated his breakfasts, lunches and dinners in separate sets among the eight squadron mess halls and ate every fifth meal in the enlisted men's mess at Group Headquarters and every tenth meal at the officers' mess there. Back home in Wisconsin the chaplain had been very fond of gardening, and his heart welled with a glorious impression of fertility and fruition each time he contemplated the low, prickly boughs of the stunted

trees and the waist-high weeds and thickets by which he
was almost walled in. In the spring he had longed to
plant begonias and zinnias in a narrow bed around his
tent but had been deterred by his fear of Corporal
Whitcomb's rancor. The chaplain relished the privacy
and isolation of his verdant surroundings and the rev-
erie and meditation that living there fostered. Fewer
people came to him with their troubles than formerly,
and he allowed himself a measure of gratitude for that
too. The chaplain did not mix freely and was not comfortable in conversation. He missed his wife and his
three small children, and she missed him.

What displeased Corporal Whitcomb most about the
chaplain, apart from the fact that the chaplain believed
in God, was his lack of initiative and aggressiveness.
Corporal Whitcomb regarded the low attendance at
religious services as a sad reflection of his own status.
His mind germinated feverishly with challenging new
ideas for sparking the great spiritual revival of which he
dreamed himself the architect – box lunches, church
socials, form letters to the families of men killed and
injured in combat, censorship, Bingo. But the chaplain
blocked him. Corporal Whitcomb bridled with vexation
beneath the chaplain's restraint, for he spied room for
improvement everywhere. It was people like the chaplain, he concluded, who were responsible for giving religion such a bad name and making pariahs out of them
both. Unlike the chaplain, Corporal Whitcomb detested
the seclusion of the clearing in the woods. One of the
first things he intended to do after he deposed the chaplain was move back into the Group Headquarters building, where he could be right in the thick of things.

When the chaplain drove back into the clearing after
leaving Colonel Korn, Corporal Whitcomb was outside
in the muggy haze talking in conspiratorial tones to a
strange chubby man in a maroon corduroy bathrobe and
gray flannel pajamas. The chaplain recognized the bathrobe and pajamas as official hospital attire. Neither
of the two men gave him any sign of recognition. The

stranger's gums had been painted purple; his corduroy bathrobe was decorated in back with a picture of a B-25 nosing through orange bursts of flak and in front with six neat rows of tiny bombs signifying sixty combat missions flown. The chaplain was so struck by the sight that he stopped to stare. Both men broke off their conversation and waited in stony silence for him to go. The chaplain hurried inside his tent. He heard, or imagined he heard, them tittering.

Corporal Whitcomb walked in a moment later and demanded, 'What's doing?'

'There isn't anything new,' the chaplain replied with averted eyes. 'Was anyone here to see me?'

'Just that crackpot Yossarian again. He's a real troublemaker, isn't he?'

'I'm not so sure he's a crackpot,' the chaplain observed.

'That's right, take his part,' said Corporal Whitcomb in an injured tone, and stamped out.

The chaplain could not believe that Corporal Whitcomb was offended again and had really walked out. As soon as he did realize it, Corporal Whitcomb walked back in.

'You always side with other people,' Corporal Whitcomb accused. 'You don't back up your men. That's one of the things that's wrong with you.'

'I didn't intend to side with him,' the chaplain apologized. 'I was just making a statement.'

'What did Colonel Cathcart want?'

'It wasn't anything important. He just wanted to discuss the possibility of saying prayers in the briefing room before each mission.'

'All right, don't tell me,' Corporal Whitcomb snapped and walked out again.

The chaplain felt terrible. No matter how considerate he tried to be, it seemed he always managed to hurt Corporal Whitcomb's feelings. He gazed down remorsefully and saw that the orderly forced upon him by Colonel Korn to keep his tent clean and attend to his belongings had neglected to shine his shoes again.

Corporal Whitcomb came back in. 'You never trust me with information,' he whined truculently. 'You don't have confidence in your men. That's another one of the things that's wrong with you.'

'Yes, I do,' the chaplain assured him guiltily. 'I have lots of confidence in you.'

'Then how about those letters?'

'No, not now,' the chaplain pleaded, cringing. 'Not the letters. Please don't bring that up again. I'll let you know if I have a change of mind.'

Corporal Whitcomb looked furious. 'Is that so? Well, it's all right for you to just sit there and shake your head while I do all the work. Didn't you see the guy outside with all those pictures painted on his bathrobe?'

'Is he here to see me?'

'No,' Corporal Whitcomb said, and walked out.

It was hot and humid inside the tent, and the chaplain felt himself turning damp. He listened like an unwilling eavesdropper to the muffled, indistinguishable drone of the lowered voices outside. As he sat inertly at the rickety bridge table that served as a desk, his lips were closed, his eyes were blank, and his face, with its pale ochre hue and ancient, confined clusters of minute acne pits, had the color and texture of an uncracked almond shell. He racked his memory for some clue to the origin of Corporal Whitcomb's bitterness toward him. In some way he was unable to fathom, he was convinced he had done him some unforgivable wrong. It seemed incredible that such lasting ire as Corporal Whitcomb's could have stemmed from his rejection of Bingo or the form letters home to the families of the men killed in combat. The chaplain was despondent with an acceptance of his own ineptitude. He had intended for some weeks to have a heart-to-heart talk with Corporal Whitcomb in order to find out what was bothering him, but was already ashamed of what he might find out.

Outside the tent, Corporal Whitcomb snickered. The other man chuckled. For a few precarious seconds, the chaplain tingled with a weird, occult sensation of having experienced the identical situation before in some prior time or existence. He endeavored to trap and nourish the impression in order to predict, and perhaps even control, what incident would occur next, but the afflatus melted away unproductively, as he had known beforehand it would. *Déjà vu.* The subtle, recurring confusion between illusion and reality that was characteristic of paramnesia fascinated the chaplain, and he knew a number of things about it. He knew, for example, that it was called paramnesia, and he was interested as well in such corollary optical phenomena as *jamais vu*, never seen, and *presque vu*, almost seen. There were terrifying, sudden moments when objects, concepts and even people that the chaplain had lived with almost all his life inexplicably took on an unfamiliar and irregular aspect that he had never seen before and which made them totally strange: *jamais vu*. And there were other moments when he almost saw absolute truth in brilliant flashes of clarity that almost came to him: *presque vu*. The episode of the naked man in the tree at Snowden's funeral mystified him thoroughly. It was not *déjà vu*, for at the time he had experienced no sensation of ever having seen a naked man in a tree at Snowden's funeral before. It was not *jamais vu*, since the apparition was not of someone, or something, familiar appearing to him in an unfamiliar guise. And it was certainly not *presque vu*, for the chaplain did see him.

A jeep started up with a backfire directly outside and roared away. Had the naked man in the tree at Snowden's funeral been merely a hallucination? Or had it been a true revelation? The chaplain trembled at the mere idea. He wanted desperately to confide in Yossarian, but each time he thought about the occurrence he decided not to think about it any further, although now that he did think about it he could not be sure that he ever really *had* thought about it.

Corporal Whitcomb sauntered back in wearing a shiny new smirk and leaned his elbow impertinently against the center pole of the chaplain's tent.

'Do you know who that guy in the red bathrobe was?' he asked boastfully. 'That was a C.I.D. man with a fractured nose. He came down here from the hospital on official business. He's conducting an investigation.'

The chaplain raised his eyes quickly in obsequious commiseration. 'I hope you're not in any trouble. Is there anything I can do?'

'No, I'm not in any trouble,' Corporal Whitcomb replied with a grin. 'You are. They're going to crack down on you for signing Washington Irving's name to all those letters you've been signing Washington Irving's name to. How do you like that?'

'I haven't been signing Washington Irving's name to any letters,' said the chaplain.

'You don't have to lie to me,' Corporal Whitcomb answered. 'I'm not the one you have to convince.'

'But I'm not lying.'

'I don't care whether you're lying or not. They're going to get you for intercepting Major Major's correspondence, too. A lot of that stuff is classified information.'

'What correspondence?' asked the chaplain plaintively in rising exasperation. 'I've never even seen any of Major Major's correspondence.'

'You don't have to lie to me,' Corporal Whitcomb replied. 'I'm not the one you have to convince.'

'But I'm not lying!' protested the chaplain.

'I don't see why you have to shout at me,' Corporal Whitcomb retorted with an injured look. He came away from the center pole and shook his finger at the chaplain for emphasis. 'I just did you the biggest favor anybody ever did you in your whole life, and you don't even realize it. Every time he tries to report you to his superiors, somebody up at the hospital censors out the details. He's been going batty for weeks trying to turn you in. I just put a censor's okay on his letter without even reading it. That will make a very good impression for you up at C.I.D. headquarters. It will let them know that we're not the least bit afraid to have the whole truth about you come out.'

The chaplain was reeling with confusion. 'But you aren't authorized to censor letters, are you?'

'Of course not,' Corporal Whitcomb answered. 'Only officers are ever authorized to do that. I censored it in your name.'

'But I'm not authorized to censor letters either. Am I?'

'I took care of that for you, too.' Corporal Whitcomb assured him. 'I signed somebody else's name for you.'

'Isn't that forgery?'

'Oh, don't worry about that either. The only one who might complain in a case of forgery is the person whose name you forged, and I looked out for your interests by picking a dead man. I used Washington Irving's name.' Corproal Whitcomb scrutinized the chaplain's face closely for some sign of rebellion and then breezed ahead confidently with concealed irony. 'That was pretty quick thinking on my part, wasn't it?'

'I don't know,' the chaplain wailed softly in a quavering voice, squinting with grotesque contortions of anguish and incomprehension. 'I don't think I understand all you've been telling me. How will it make a good impression for me if you signed Washington Irving's name instead of my own?'

'Because they're convinced that you are Washington Irving. Don't you see? They'll know it was you.'

'But isn't that the very belief we want to dispel? Won't this help them prove it?'

'If I thought you were going to be so stuffy about it, I wouldn't even have tried to help,' Corporal Whitcomb declared indignantly, and walked out. A second later he walked back in. 'I just did you the biggest favor anybody ever did you in your whole life and you don't even know it. You don't know how to show your appreciation. That's another one of the things that's wrong with you.'

'I'm sorry,' the chaplain apologized contritely. 'I really am sorry. It's just that I'm so completely stunned by all you're telling me that I don't even realize what I'm saying. I'm really very grateful to you.'

'Then how about letting me send out those form

letters?' Corporal Whitcomb demanded immediately. 'Can I begin working on the first drafts?'

The chaplain's jaw dropped in astonishment. 'No, no,' he groaned. 'Not now.'

Corporal Whitcomb was incensed. 'I'm the best friend you've got and you don't even know it,' he asserted belligerently, and walked out of the chaplain's tent. He walked back in. 'I'm on your side and you don't even realize it. Don't you know what serious trouble you're in? That C.I.D. man has gone rushing back to the hospital to write a brand-new report on you about that tomato.'

'What tomato?' the chaplain asked, blinking.

'The plum tomato you were hiding in your hand when you first showed up here. There it is. The tomato you're still holding in your hand right this very minute!'

The captain unclenched his fingers with surprise and saw that he was still holding the plum tomato he had obtained in Colonel Cathcart's office. He set it down quickly on the bridge table. 'I got this tomato from Colonel Cathcart,' he said, and was struck by how ludicrous his explanation sounded. 'He insisted I take it.'

'You don't have to lie to me,' Corporal Whitcomb answered. 'I don't care whether you stole it from him or not.'

'Stole it?' the chaplain exclaimed with amazement. 'Why should I want to steal a plum tomato?'

'That's exactly what had us both stumped,' said Corporal Whitcomb. 'And then the C.I.D. man figured out you might have some important secret papers hidden away inside it.'

The chaplain sagged limply beneath the mountainous weight of his despair. 'I don't have any important secret papers hidden away inside it,' he stated simply. 'I didn't even want it to begin with. Here, you can have it and see for yourself.'

'I don't want it.'

'Please take it away,' the chaplain pleaded in a voice that was barely audible. 'I want to be rid of it.'

'I don't want it,' Corporal Whitcomb snapped again,

and stalked out with an angry face, suppressing a smile of great jubilation at having forged a powerful new alliance with the C.I.D. man and at having succeeded again in convincing the chaplain that he was really displeased.

Poor Whitcomb, sighed the chaplain, and blamed himself for his assistant's malaise. He sat mutely in a ponderous, stultifying melancholy, waiting expectantly for Corporal Whitcomb to walk back in. He was disappointed as he heard the peremptory crunch of Corporal Whitcomb's footsteps recede into silence. There was nothing he wanted to do next. He decided to pass up lunch for a Milky Way and a Baby Ruth from his foot locker and a few swallows of luke-warm water from his canteen. He felt himself surrounded by dense, overwhelming fogs of possibilities in which he could perceive no glimmer of light. He dreaded what Colonel Cathcart would think when the news that he was suspected of being Washington Irving was brought to him, then fell to fretting over what Colonel Cathcart was already thinking about him for even having broached the subject of sixty missions. There was so much unhappiness in the world, he reflected, bowing his head dismally beneath the tragic thought, and there was nothing he could do about anybody's, least of all his own.

21   General Dreedle

Colonel Cathcart was not thinking anything at all about the chaplain, but was tangled up in a brand-new, menacing problem of his own: *Yossarian!*

Yossarian! The mere sound of that execrable, ugly name made his blood run cold and his breath come in labored gasps. The chaplain's first mention of the name *Yossarian!* had tolled deep in his memory like a portentous gong. As soon as the latch of the door had clicked shut, the whole humiliating recollection of the naked man in formation came cascading down upon him in a mortifying, choking flood of stinging details. He began to perspire and tremble. There was a sinister and unlikely coincidence exposed that was too diabolical in implication to be anything less than the most hideous of omens. The name of the man who had stood naked in ranks that day to receive his Distinguished Flying Cross from General Dreedle had also been – *Yossarian!* And now it was a man named Yossarian who was threatening to make trouble over the sixty missions he had just ordered the men in his group to fly. Colonel Cathcart wondered gloomily if it was the same Yossarian.

He climbed to his feet with an air of intolerable woe and began moving about his office. He felt himself in the presence of the mysterious. The naked man in formation, he conceded cheerlessly, had been a real black eye for him. So had the tampering with the bomb line before the mission to Bologna and the seven-day delay in destroying the bridge at Ferrara, even though destroying the bridge at Ferrara finally, he remembered with glee, had been a real feather in his cap, although losing a plane there the second time around, he recalled in dejection, had been another black eye, even though he had won another real feather in his cap by getting a medal approved for the bombardier who had gotten him the real black eye in the first place by going around over the target twice. That bombardier's name, he remembered suddenly with another stupefying shock, had also been *Yossarian!* Now there were *three!* His viscous eyes bulged with astonishment and he whipped himself around in alarm to see what was taking place behind him. A moment ago there had been no Yossarians in his life; now they were multiplying like hobgoblins. He tried to make himself grow calm. Yossarian was not a common name; perhaps there were not really three Yossarians but only two Yossarians, or maybe even only one Yossarian – *but that really made no difference!* The colonel was still in grave peril. Intuition warned him that he was drawing close to some immense and inscrutable cosmic climax, and his broad, meaty, towering frame tingled from head to toe at the thought that Yossarian, whoever he would eventually turn out to be, was destined to serve as his nemesis.

Colonel Cathcart was not superstitious, but he did believe in omens, and he sat right back down behind his desk and made a cryptic notation on his memorandum pad to look into the whole suspicious business of the Yossarians right away. He wrote his reminder to himself in a heavy and decisive hand, amplifying it sharply with a series of coded punctuation marks and underlining the whole message twice, so that it read:

Yossarian! ! ! (?)!

The colonel sat back when he had finished and was extremely pleased with himself for the prompt action he had just taken to meet this sinister crisis. *Yossarian* – the very sight of the name made him shudder. There were so many esses in it. It just had to be subversive. It was like the word *subversive* itself. It was like *seditious* and *insidious* too, and like *socialist, suspicious, fascist* and *Communist*. It was an odious, alien, distasteful name, that just did not inspire confidence. It was not at all like such clean, crisp, honest, American names as Cathcart, Peckem and Dreedle.

Colonel Cathcart rose slowly and began drifting about his office again. Almost unconsciously, he picked up a plum tomato from the top of one of the bushels and took a voracious bite. He made a wry face at once and threw the rest of the plum tomato into his waste-basket. The colonel did not like plum tomatoes, not even when they were his own, and these were not even his own. These had been purchased in different market places all over Pianosa by Colonel Korn under various identities, moved up to the colonel's farmhouse in the hills in the dead of night, and transported down to Group Headquarters the next morning for sale to Milo, who paid Colonel Cathcart and Colonel Korn premium prices for them. Colonel Cathcart often wondered if what they were doing with the plum tomatoes was legal, but Colonel Korn said it was, and he tried not to brood about it too often. He had no way of knowing whether or not the house in the hills was legal, either, since Colonel Korn had made all the arrangements. Colonel Cathcart did not know if he owned the house or rented it, from whom he had acquired it or how much, if anything, it was costing. Colonel Korn was the lawyer, and if Colonel Korn assured him that fraud, extortion, currency manipulation, embezzlement, income tax evasion and black-market speculations were legal, Colonel Cathcart was in no position to disagree with him.

All Colonel Cathcart knew about his house in the hills was that he had such a house and hated it. He was never so bored as when spending there the two or three days every other week necessary to sustain the illusion that his damp and drafty stone farmhouse in the hills was a golden palace of carnal delights. Officers' clubs everywhere pulsated with blurred but knowing accounts of lavish, hushed-up drinking and sex orgies there and of secret, intimate nights of ecstasy with the most beautiful, the most tantalizing, the most readily aroused and most easily satisfied Italian courtesans, film actresses, models and countesses. No such private nights of ecstasy or hushed-up drinking and sex orgies ever occurred. They might have occurred if either General Dreedle or General Peckem had once evinced an interest in taking part in orgies with him, but neither ever did, and the colonel was certainly not going to waste his time and energy making love to beautiful women unless there was something in it for him.

The colonel dreaded his dank lonely nights at his farmhouse and the dull, uneventful days. He had much more fun back at Group, browbeating everyone he wasn't afraid of. However, as Colonel Korn kept reminding him, there was not much glamour in having a farmhouse in the hills if he never used it. He drove off to his farmhouse each time in a mood of self-pity. He carried a shotgun in his jeep and spent the monotonous hours there shooting it at birds and at the plum tomatoes that did grow there in untended rows and were too much trouble to harvest.

Among those officers of inferior rank toward whom Colonel Cathcart still deemed it prudent to show respect, he included Major — de Coverley, even though he did not want to and was not sure he even had to. Major — de Coverley was as great a mystery to him as he was to Major Major and to everyone else who ever took notice of him. Colonel Cathcart had no idea whether to look up or look down in his attitude toward Major — de Coverley. Major — de Coverley was only a major, even though he was ages older than Colonel Cathcart; at the same time, so many other people treated Major —

de Coverley with such profound and fearful veneration that Colonel Cathcart had a hunch they might know something. Major — de Coverley was an ominous, incomprehensible presence who kept him constantly on edge and of whom even Colonel Korn tended to be wary. Everyone was afraid of him, and no one knew why. No one even knew Major — de Coverley's first name, because no one had ever had the temerity to ask him. Colonel Cathcart knew that Major — de Coverley was away and he rejoiced in his absence until it occurred to him that Major — de Coverley might be away somewhere conspiring against him, and then he wished that Major — de Coverley were back in his squadron where he belonged so that he could be watched.

In a little while Colonel Cathcart's arches began to ache from pacing back and forth so much. He sat down behind his desk again and resolved to embark upon a mature and systematic evaluation of the entire military situation. With the businesslike air of a man who knows how to get things done, he found a large white pad, drew a straight line down the middle and crossed it near the top, dividing the page into two blank columns of equal width. He rested a moment in critical rumination. Then he huddled over his desk, and at the head of the left column, in a cramped and finicky hand, he wrote, '*Black Eyes!!!*' At the top of the right column he wrote, '*Feathers in My Cap!!! !!*' He leaned back once more to inspect his chart admiringly from an objective perspective. After a few seconds of solemn deliberation, he licked the tip of his pencil carefully and wrote under '*Black Eyes!!!*,' after intent intervals:

> *Ferrara*
>
> *Bologna (bomb line moved on map during)*
>
> *Skeet range*
>
> *Naked man in formation (after Avignon)*

Then he added:

Food poisoning (during Bologna)

and

Moaning (epidemic of during Avignon briefing)

Then he added:

Chaplain (hanging around officers' club every night)

He decided to be charitable about the chaplain, even though he did not like him, and under '*Feathers in My Cap!!! !!*' he wrote:

Chaplain (hanging around officers' club every night)

The two chaplain entries, therefore, neutralized each other. Alongside '*Ferrara*' and '*Naked man in formation (after Avignon)*' he then wrote:

Yossarian!

Alongside '*Bologna (bomb line moved on map during)*' '*Food poisoning (during Bologna)*' and '*Moaning (epidemic of during Avignon briefing)*' he wrote in a bold, decisive hand:

?

Those entries labeled '?' were the ones he wanted to investigate immediately to determine if Yossarian had played any part in them.

Suddenly his arm began to shake, and he was unable to write any more. He rose to his feet in terror, feeling sticky and fat, and rushed to the open window to gulp in fresh air. His gaze fell on the skeet-range, and he reeled away with a sharp cry of distress, his wild and feverish eyes scanning the walls of his office frantically as though they were swarming with Yossarians.

Nobody loved him. General Dreedle hated him, although General Peckem liked him, although he couldn't be sure, since Colonel Cargill, General Peckem's aide, undoubtedly had ambitions of his own and was probably sabotaging him with General Peckem at every opportunity. The only good colonel, he decided, was a dead colonel, except for himself. The only colonel he trusted was Colonel Moodus, and even *he* had an in with his father-in-law. Milo, of course, had been the big feather in his cap, although having his group bombed by Milo's planes had probably been a terrible black eye for him, even though Milo had ultimately stilled all protest by disclosing the huge net profit the syndicate had realized on the deal with the enemy and convincing everyone that bombing his own men and planes had therefore really been a commendable and very lucrative blow on the side of private enterprise. The colonel was insecure about Milo because other colonels were trying to lure him away, and Colonel Cathcart still had that lousy Big Chief White Halfoat in his group who that lousy, lazy Captain Black claimed was the one really responsible for the bomb line's being moved during the Big Siege of Bologna. Colonel Cathcart liked Big Chief White Halfoat because Big Chief White Halfoat kept punching that lousy Colonel Moodus in the nose every time he got drunk and Colonel Moodus was around. He wished that Big Chief White Halfoat would begin punching Colonel Korn in his fat face, too. Colonel Korn was a lousy smart aleck. Someone at Twenty-seventh Air Force Headquarters had it in for him and sent back every report he wrote with a blistering rebuke, and Colonel Korn had bribed a clever mail clerk there named Wintergreen to try to find out who it was. Losing the plane over Ferrara the second time around had not done him any good, he had to admit, and neither had having that other plane disappear inside that cloud – *that was one he hadn't even written down!* He tried to recall, longingly, if Yossarian had been lost in that plane in the cloud and realized that Yossarian could not possibly have been lost in that plane in the cloud if he was still around now raising such a big stink about having to fly a lousy five missions more.

Maybe sixty missions were too many for the men to fly, Colonel Cathcart reasoned, if Yossarian objected to flying them, but he then remembered that forcing his men to fly more missions than everyone else was the most tangible achievement he had going for him. As Colonel Korn often remarked, the war was crawling with group commanders who were merely doing their duty, and it required just some sort of dramatic gesture like making his group fly more combat missions than any other bomber group to spotlight his unique qualities of leadership. Certainly none of the generals seemed to object to what he was doing, although as far as he could detect they weren't particularly impressed either, which made him suspect that perhaps sixty combat missions were not nearly enough and that he ought to increase the number at once to seventy, eighty, a hundred, or even two hundred, three hundred, or six thousand!

Certainly he would be much better off under somebody suave like General Peckem than he was under somebody boorish and insensitive like General Dreedle, because General Peckem had the discernment, the intelligence and the Ivy League background to appreciate and enjoy him at his full value, although General Peckem had never given the slightest indication that he appreciated or enjoyed him at all. Colonel Cathcart felt perceptive enough to realize that visible signals of recognition were never necessary between sophisticated, self-assured people like himself and General Peckem who could warm to each other from a distance with innate mutual understanding. It was enough that they were of like kind, and he knew it was only a matter of waiting discreetly for preferment until the right time, although it rotted Colonel Cathcart's self-esteem to observe that General Peckem never deliberately sought him out and that he labored no harder to impress Colonel Cathcart with his epigrams and erudition than he did to impress anyone else in earshot, even enlisted men. Either Colonel Cathcart wasn't getting through to

General Peckem or General Peckem was not the scintillating, discriminating, intellectual, forward-looking personality he pretended to be and it was really General Dreedle who was sensitive, charming, brilliant and sophisticated and under whom he would certainly be much better off, and suddenly Colonel Cathcart had absolutely no conception of how strongly he stood with anyone and began banging on his buzzer with his fist for Colonel Korn to come running into his office and assure him that everybody loved him, that Yossarian was a figment of his imagination, and that he was making wonderful progress in the splendid and valiant campaign he was waging to become a general.

Actually, Colonel Cathcart did not have a chance in hell of becoming a general. For one thing, there was ex-P.F.C. Wintergreen, who also wanted to be a general and who always distorted, destroyed, rejected or misdirected any correspondence by, for or about Colonel Cathcart that might do him credit. For another, there already was a general, General Dreedle who knew that General Peckem was after his job but did not know how to stop him.

General Dreedle, the wing commander, was a blunt, chunky, barrel-chested man in his early fifties. His nose was squat and red, and he had lumpy white, bunched-up eyelids circling his small gray eyes like haloes of bacon fat. He had a nurse and a son-in-law, and he was prone to long, ponderous silences when he had not been drinking too much. General Dreedle had wasted too much of his time in the Army doing his job well, and now it was too late. New power alignments had coalesced without him and he was at a loss to cope with them. At unguarded moments his hard and sullen face slipped into a somber, preoccupied look of defeat and frustration. General Dreedle drank a great deal. His moods were arbitrary and unpredictable. 'War is hell,' he declared frequently, drunk or sober, and he really meant it, although that did not prevent him from making a good living out of it or from taking his son-in-law into the business with him, even though the two bickered constantly.

'That bastard,' General Dreedle would complain about his son-in-law with a contemptuous grunt to anyone who happened to be standing beside him at the curve of the bar of the officers' club. 'Everything he's got he owes to me. I made him, that lousy son of a bitch! He hasn't got brains enough to get ahead on his own.'

'He thinks he knows everything,' Colonel Moodus would retort in a sulking tone to his own audience at the other end of the bar. 'He can't take criticism and he won't listen to advice.'

'All he can do is give advice,' General Dreedle would observe with a rasping snort. 'If it wasn't for me, he'd still be a corporal.'

General Dreedle was always accompanied by both Colonel Moodus and his nurse, who was as delectable a piece of ass as anyone who saw her had ever laid eyes on. General Dreedle's nurse was chubby, short and blond. She had plump dimpled cheeks, happy blue eyes, and neat curly turned-up hair. She smiled at everyone and never spoke at all unless she was spoken to. Her bosom was lush and her complexion clear. She was irresistible, and men edged away from her carefully. She was succulent, sweet, docile and dumb, and she drove everyone crazy but General Dreedle.

'You should see her naked,' General Dreedle chortled with croupy relish, while his nurse stood smiling proudly right at his shoulder. 'Back at Wing she's got a uniform in my room made of purple silk that's so tight her nipples stand out like bing cherries. Milo got me the fabric. There isn't even room enough for panties or a brassière underneath. I make her wear it some nights when Moodus is around just to drive him crazy.' General Dreedle laughed hoarsely. 'You should see what goes on inside that blouse of hers every time she shifts her weight. She drives him out of his mind. The first time I catch him putting a hand on her or any other woman I'll bust the horny bastard right down to private and put him on K.P. for a year.'

'He keeps her around just to drive me crazy,' Colonel Moodus accused aggrievedly at the other end of the bar. 'Back at Wing she's got a uniform made out of purple silk that's so tight her nipples stand out like bing cherries. There isn't even room for panties or a brassière underneath. You should hear that rustle every time she shifts her weight. The first time I make a pass at her or any other girl he'll bust me right down to private and put me on K.P. for a year. She drives me out of my mind.'

'He hasn't gotten laid since we shipped overseas,' confided General Dreedle, and his square grizzled head bobbed with sadistic laughter at the fiendish idea. 'That's one of the reasons I never let him out of my sight, just so he can't get to a woman. Can you imagine what that poor son of a bitch is going through?'

'I haven't been to bed with a woman since we shipped overseas,' Colonel Moodus whimpered tearfully. 'Can you imagine what I'm going through?'

General Dreedle could be as intransigent with anyone else when displeased as he was with Colonel Moodus. He had no taste for sham, tact or pretension, and his credo as a professional soldier was unified and concise: he believed that the young men who took orders from him should be willing to give up their lives for the ideals, aspirations and idiosyncrasies of the old men he took orders from. The officers and enlisted men in his command had identity for him only as military quantities. All he asked was that they do their work; beyond that, they were free to do whatever they pleased. They were free, as Colonel Cathcart was free, to force their men to fly sixty missions if they chose, and they were free, as Yossarian had been free, to stand in formation naked if they wanted to, although General Dreedle's granite jaw swung open at the sight and he went striding dictatorially right down the line to make certain that there really was a man wearing nothing but moccasins waiting at attention in ranks to receive a medal from him. General Dreedle was speechless. Colonel Cathcart began to faint when he spied Yossarian, and Colonel

Korn stepped up behind him and squeezed his arm in a strong grip. The silence was grotesque. A steady warm wind flowed in from the beach, and an old cart filled with dirty straw rumbled into view on the main road, drawn by a black donkey and driven by a farmer in a flopping hat and faded brown work clothes who paid no attention to the formal military ceremony taking place in the small field on his right.

At last General Dreedle spoke. 'Get back in the car,' he snapped over his shoulder to his nurse, who had followed him down the line. The nurse toddled away with a smile toward his brown staff car, parked about twenty yards away at the edge of the rectangular clearing. General Dreedle waited in austere silence until the car door slammed and then demanded, 'Which one is this?'

Colonel Moodus checked his roster. 'This one is Yossarian, Dad. He gets a Distinguished Flying Cross.'

'Well, I'll be damned,' mumbled General Dreedle, and his ruddy monolithic face softened with amusement. 'Why aren't you wearing clothes, Yossarian?'

'I don't want to.'

'What do you mean you don't want to? Why the hell don't you want to?'

'I just don't want to, sir.'

'Why isn't he wearing clothes?' General Dreedle demanded over his shoulder of Colonel Cathcart.

'He's talking to you,' Colonel Korn whispered over Colonel Cathcart's shoulder from behind, jabbing his elbow sharply into Colonel Cathcart's back.

'Why isn't he wearing clothes?' Colonel Cathcart demanded of Colonel Korn with a look of acute pain, tenderly nursing the spot where Colonel Korn had just jabbed him.

'Why isn't he wearing clothes?' Colonel Korn demanded of Captain Piltchard and Captain Wren.

'A man was killed in his plane over Avignon last week and bled all over him,' Captain Wren replied. 'He swears he's never going to wear a uniform again.'

'A man was killed in his plane over Avignon last week

277

and bled all over him,' Colonel Korn reported directly to General Dreedle. 'His uniform hasn't come back from the laundry yet.'

'Where are his other uniforms?'

'They're in the laundry, too.'

'What about his underwear?' General Dreedle demanded.

'All his underwear's in the laundry, too,' answered Colonel Korn.

'That sounds like a lot of crap to me,' General Dreedle declared.

'It is a lot of crap, sir,' Yossarian said.

'Don't you worry, sir,' Colonel Cathcart promised General Dreedle with a threatening look at Yossarian. 'You have my personal word for it that this man will be severely punished.'

'What the hell do I care if he's punished or not?' General Dreedle replied with surprise and irritation. 'He's just won a medal. If he wants to receive it without any clothes on, what the hell business is it of yours?'

'Those are my sentiments exactly, sir!' Colonel Cathcart echoed with resounding enthusiasm and mopped his brow with a damp white handkerchief. 'But would you say that, sir, even in the light of General Peckem's recent memorandum on the subject of appropriate military attire in combat areas?'

'Peckem?' General Dreedle's face clouded.

'Yes, sir, sir,' said Colonel Cathcart obsequiously. 'General Peckem even recommends that we send our men into combat in full-dress uniform so they'll make a good impression on the enemy when they're shot down.'

'Peckem?' repeated General Dreedle, still squinting with bewilderment. 'Just what the hell does Peckem have to do with it?'

Colonel Korn jabbed Colonel Cathcart sharply again in the back with his elbow.

'Absolutely nothing, sir!' Colonel Cathcart responded sprucely, wincing in extreme pain and gingerly rubbing the spot where Colonel Korn had just jabbed him again.

'And that's exactly why I decided to take absolutely no action at all until I first had an opportunity to discuss it with you. Shall we ignore it completely, sir?'

General Dreedle ignored him completely, turning away from him in baleful scorn to hand Yossarian his medal in its case.

'Get my girl back from the car,' he commanded Colonel Moodus crabbily, and waited in one spot with his scowling face down until his nurse had rejoined him.

'Get word to the office right away to kill that directive I just issued ordering the men to wear neckties on the combat missions,' Colonel Cathcart whispered to Colonel Korn urgently out of the corner of his mouth.

'I told you not to do it,' Colonel Korn snickered. 'But you just wouldn't listen to me.'

'Shhhh!' Colonel Cathcart cautioned. 'Goddammit, Korn, what did you do to my back?'

Colonel Korn snickered again.

General Dreedle's nurse always followed General Dreedle everywhere he went, even into the briefing room just before the mission to Avignon, where she stood with her asinine smile at the side of the platform and bloomed like a fertile oasis at General Dreedle's shoulder in her pink-and-green uniform. Yossarian looked at her and fell in love, desperately. His spirits sank, leaving him empty inside and numb. He sat gazing in clammy want at her full red lips and dimpled cheeks as he listened to Major Danby describe in a monotonous, didactic male drone the heavy concentrations of flak awaiting them at Avignon, and he moaned in deep despair suddenly at the thought that he might never see again this lovely woman to whom he had never spoken a word and whom he now loved so pathetically. He throbbed and ached with sorrow, fear and desire as he stared at her; she was so beautiful. He worshiped the ground she stood on. He licked his parched, thirsting lips with a sticky tongue and moaned in misery again, loudly enough this time to attract the startled, searching glances of the men sitting around him on the rows of crude wooden benches in their chocolate-coloured coveralls and stitched white parachute harnesses.

Nately turned to him quickly with alarm. 'What is it?' he whispered. 'What's the matter?'

Yossarian did not hear him. He was sick with lust and mesmerized with regret. General Dreedle's nurse was only a little chubby, and his senses were stuffed to congestion with the yellow radiance of her hair and the unfelt pressure of her soft short fingers, with the rounded, untasted wealth of her nubile breasts in her Army-pink shirt that was opened wide at the throat and with the rolling, ripened, triangular confluences of her belly and thighs in her tight, slick forest-green gabardine officer's pants. He drank her in insatiably from head to painted toenail. He never wanted to lose her. 'Oooooooooooooh,' he moaned again, and this time the whole room rippled at his quavering, drawn-out cry. A wave of startled uneasiness broke over the officers on the dais, and even Major Danby, who had begun synchronizing the watches, was distracted momentarily as he counted out the seconds and almost had to begin again. Nately followed Yossarian's transfixed gaze down the long frame auditorium until he came to General Dreedle's nurse. He blanched with trepidation when he guessed what was troubling Yossarian.

'Cut it out, will you?' Nately warned in a fierce whisper.

'Ooooooooooooooooooooh,' Yossarian moaned a fourth time, this time loudly enough for everyone to hear him distinctly.

'Are you crazy?' Nately hissed vehemently. 'You'll get into trouble.'

'Ooooooooooooooooooooh,' Dunbar answered Yossarian from the opposite end of the room.

Nately recognized Dunbar's voice. The situation was now out of control, and he turned away with a small moan. 'Ooh.'

'Ooooooooooooooooooooh,' Dunbar moaned back at him.

'Oooooooooooooooooooooh,' Nately moaned out loud in exasperation when he realized that he had just moaned.

'Oooooooooooooooooooooh,' Dunbar moaned back at him again.

'Oooooooooooooooooooooh,' someone entirely new chimed in from another section of the room, and Nately's hair stood on end.

Yossarian and Dunbar both replied while Nately cringed and hunted about futilely for some hole in which to hide and take Yossarian with him. A sprinkling of people were smothering laughter. An elfin impulse possessed Nately and he moaned intentionally the next time there was a lull. Another new voice answered. The flavor of disobedience was titillating, and Nately moaned deliberately again, the next time he could squeeze one in edgewise. Still another new voice echoed him. The room was boiling irrepressibly into bedlam. An eerie hubbub of voices was rising. Feet were scuffled, and things began to drop from people's fingers – pencils, computers, map cases, clattering steel flak helmets. A number of men who were not moaning were now giggling openly, and there was no telling how far the unorganized insurrection of moaning might have gone if General Dreedle himself had not come forward to quell it, stepping out determinedly in the center of the platform directly in front of Major Danby, who, with his earnest, persevering head down, was still concentrating on his wrist watch and saying, '. . . twenty-five seconds . . . twenty . . . fifteen . . .' General Dreedle's great, red domineering face was gnarled with perplexity and oaken with awesome resolution.

'That will be all, men,' he ordered tersely, his eyes glaring with disapproval and his square jaw firm, and that's all there was. 'I run a fighting outfit,' he told them sternly, when the room had grown absolutely quiet and the men on the benches were all cowering sheepishly, 'and there'll be no more moaning in this group as long as I'm in command. Is that clear?'

It was clear to everybody but Major Danby, who was

still concentrating on his wrist watch and counting down the seconds aloud. '... four ... three ... two ... one ... time!' called out Major Danby, and raised his eyes triumphantly to discover that no one had been listening to him and that he would have to begin all over again. 'Ooooh,' he moaned in frustration.

'*What was that?*' roared General Dreedle incredulously, and whirled around in a murderous rage upon Major Danby, who staggered back in terrified confusion and began to quail and perspire. '*Who is this man?*'

'M-major Danby, sir,' Colonel Cathcart stammered. 'My group operations officer.'

'Take him out and shoot him,' ordered General Dreedle. 'S-sir?'

'I said take him out and shoot him. Can't you hear?'

'Yes, sir!' Colonel Cathcart responded smartly, swallowing hard, and turned in a brisk manner to his chauffeur and his meteorologist. 'Take Major Danby out and shoot him.'

'S-sir?' his chauffeur and his meteorologist stammered.

'I said take Major Danby out and shoot him,' Colonel Cathcart snapped. 'Can't you hear?'

The two young lieutenants nodded lumpishly and gaped at each other in stunned and flaccid reluctance, each waiting for the other to initiate the procedure of taking Major Danby outside and shooting him. Neither had ever taken Major Danby outside and shot him before. They inched their way dubiously toward Major Danby from opposite sides. Major Danby was white with fear. His legs collapsed suddenly and he began to fall, and the two young lieutenants sprang forward and seized him under both arms to save him from slumping to the floor. Now that they had Major Danby, the rest seemed easy, but there were no guns. Major Danby began to cry. Colonel Cathcart wanted to rush to his side and comfort him, but did not want to look like a sissy in front of General Dreedle. He remembered that Appleby and Havermeyer always brought their .45 automatics

282

on the missions, and he began to scan the rows of men in search of them.

As soon as Major Danby began to cry, Colonel Moodus, who had been vacillating wretchedly on the sidelines, could restrain himself no longer and stepped out diffidently toward General Dreedle with a sickly air of self-sacrifice. 'I think you'd better wait a minute, Dad,' he suggested hesitantly. 'I don't think you can shoot him.'

General Dreedle was infuriated by his intervention. 'Who the hell says I can't?' he thundered pugnaciously in a voice loud enough to rattle the whole building. Colonel Moodus, his face flushing with embarrassment, bent close to whisper into his ear. 'Why the hell can't I?' General Dreedle bellowed. Colonel Moodus whispered some more. 'You mean I can't shoot anyone I want to?' General Dreedle demanded with uncompromising indignation. He pricked up his ears with interest as Colonel Moodus continued whispering. 'Is that a fact?' he inquired, his rage tamed by curiosity.

'Yes, Dad. I'm afraid it is.'

'I guess you think you're pretty goddam smart, don't you?' General Dreedle lashed out at Colonel Moodus suddenly.

Colonel Moodus turned crimson again. 'No, Dad, it isn't –'

'All right, let the insubordinate son of a bitch go,' General Dreedle snarled, turning bitterly away from his son-in-law and barking peevishly at Colonel Cathcart's chauffeur and Colonel Cathcart's meteorologist. 'But get him out of this building and keep him out. And let's continue this goddam briefing before the war ends. I've never seen so much incompetence.'

Colonel Cathcart nodded lamely at General Dreedle and signaled his men hurriedly to push Major Danby outside the building. As soon as Major Danby had been pushed outside, though, there was no one to continue the briefing. Everyone gawked at everyone else in oafish surprise. General Dreedle turned puple with rage as nothing happened. Colonel Cathcart had no idea what to do. He was about to begin moaning aloud when Colonel Korn came to the rescue by stepping forward and taking control. Colonel Cathcart sighed with enormous, tearful relief, almost overwhelmed with gratitude.

'Now, men, we're going to synchronize our watches,' Colonel Korn began promptly in a sharp, commanding manner, rolling his eyes flirtatiously in General Dreedle's direction. 'We're going to synchronize our watches one time and one time only, and if it doesn't come off in that one time, General Dreedle and I are going to want to know why. Is that clear?' He fluttered his eyes toward General Dreedle again to make sure his plug had registered. 'Now set your watches for nine-eighteen.'

Colonel Korn synchronized their watches without a single hitch and moved ahead with confidence. He gave the men the colors of the day and reviewed the weather conditions with an agile, flashy versatility, casting side-long, simpering looks at General Dreedle every few seconds to draw increased encouragement from the excellent impression he saw he was making. Preening and pruning himself effulgently and strutting vain-gloriously about the platform as he picked up momentum, he gave the men the colors of the day again and shifted nimbly into a rousing pep talk on the importance of the bridge at Avignon to the war effort and the obligation of each man on the mission to place love of country above love of life. When his inspiring dissertation was finished, he gave the men the colors of the day still one more time, stressed the angle of approach and reviewed the weather conditions again. Colonel Korn felt himself at the full height of his powers. He *belonged* in the spotlight.

Comprehension dawned slowly on Colonel Cathcart; when it came, he was struck dumb. His face grew longer and longer as he enviously watched Colonel Korn's treachery continue, and he was almost afraid to listen when General Dreedle moved up beside him and, in a whisper blustery enough to be heard throughout the room, demanded,

'Who is that man?'

Colonel Cathcart answered with wan foreboding, and General Dreedle then cupped his hand over his mouth and whispered something that made Colonel Cathcart's face glow with immense joy. Colonel Korn saw and quivered with uncontainable rapture. Had he just been promoted in the field by General Dreedle to full colonel? He could not endure the suspense. With a masterful flourish, he brought the briefing to a close and turned expectantly to receive ardent congratulations from General Dreedle – who was already striding out of the building without a glance backward, trailing his nurse and Colonel Moodus behind him. Colonel Korn was stunned by this disappointing sight, but only for an instant. His eyes found Colonel Cathcart, who was still standing erect in a grinning trance, and he rushed over jubilantly and began pulling on his arm.

'What'd he say about me?' he demanded excitedly in a fervor of proud and blissful anticipation. 'What did General Dreedle say?'

'He wanted to know who you were.'

'I know that. I know that. But what'd he say about me? What'd he say?'

'You make him sick.'

22 Milo the mayor

That was the mission on which Yossarian lost his nerve.
Yossarian lost his nerve on the mission to Avignon
because Snowden lost his guts, and Snowden lost his
guts because their pilot that day was Huple, who was
only fifteen years old, and their co-pilot was Dobbs, who
was even worse and who wanted Yossarian to join with
him in a plot to murder Colonel Cathcart. Huple was a
good pilot, Yossarian knew, but he was only a kid, and
Dobbs had no confidence in him, either, and wrested the
controls away without warning after they had dropped
their bombs, going berserk in mid-air and tipping the
plane over into that heart-stopping, ear-splitting, indes-
cribably petrifying fatal dive that tore Yossarian's
earphones free from their connection and hung him
helplessly to the roof of the nose by the top of his head.

Oh, God! Yossarian had shrieked soundlessly as he
felt them all falling. *Oh, God! Oh, God! Oh, God! Oh, God!*
he had shrieked beseechingly through lips that could not
open as the plane fell and he dangled without weight by
the top of his head until Huple managed to seize the
controls back and leveled the plane out down inside the
crazy, craggy, patchwork canyon of crashing antiaircraft fire from which they had climbed away and from

286

which they would now have to escape again. Almost at once there was a thud and a hole the size of a big fist in the plexiglass. Yossarian's cheeks were stinging with shimmering splinters. There was no blood

'What happened? What happened?' he cried, and trembled violently when he could not hear his own voice in his ears. He was cowed by the empty silence on the intercom and almost too horrified to move as he crouched like a trapped mouse on his hands and knees and waited without daring to breathe until he finally spied the gleaming cylindrical jack plug of his headset swinging back and forth in front of his eyes and jammed it back into its receptable with fingers that rattled. *Oh, God!* he kept shrieking with no abatement of terror as the flak thumped and mushroomed all about him. *Oh, God!*

Dobbs was weeping when Yossarian jammed his jack plug back into the intercom system and was able to hear again.

'Help him, help him,' Dobbs was sobbing. 'Help him, help him.'

'Help who? Help who?' Yossarian called back. 'Help who?'

'The bombardier, the bombardier,' Dobbs cried. 'He doesn't answer. Help the bombardier, help the bombardier.'

'I'm the bombardier,' Yossarian cried back at him. 'I'm the bombardier. I'm all right. I'm all right.'

'Then help him, help him,' Dobbs wept. 'Help him, help him.'

'Help who? Help who?'

'The radio-gunner,' Dobbs begged. 'Help the radio-gunner.'

'I'm cold,' Snowden whimpered feebly over the intercom system then in a bleat of plaintive agony. 'Please help me. I'm cold.'

And Yossarian crept out through the crawlway and climbed up over the bomb bay and down into the rear section of the plane where Snowden lay on the floor wounded and freezing to death in a yellow splash of sunlight near the new tail gunner lying stretched out on the floor beside him in a dead faint.

Dobbs was the worst pilot in the world and knew it, a shattered wreck of a virile young man who was continually striving to convince his superiors that he was no longer fit to pilot a plane. None of his superiors would listen, and it was the day the number of missions was raised to sixty that Dobbs stole into Yossarian's tent while Orr was out looking for gaskets and disclosed the plot he had formulated to murder Colonel Cathcart. He needed Yossarian's assistance.

'You want us to kill him in cold blood?' Yossarian objected.

'That's right,' Dobbs agreed with an optimistic smile, encouraged by Yossarian's ready grasp of the situation. 'We'll shoot him to death with the Luger I brought back from Sicily that nobody knows I've got.'

'I don't think I could do it,' Yossarian concluded, after weighing the idea in silence awhile.

Dobbs was astonished. 'Why not?'

'Look. Nothing would please me more than to have the son of a bitch break his neck or get killed in a crash or to find out that someone else had shot him to death. But I don't think I could kill him.'

'He'd do it to you,' Dobbs argued. 'In fact, you're the one who told me he *is* doing it to us by keeping us in combat so long.'

'But I don't think I could do it to him. He's got a right to live, too, I guess.'

'Not as long as he's trying to rob you and me of our right to live. What's the matter with you?' Dobbs was flabbergasted. 'I used to listen to you arguing that same thing with Clevinger. And look what happened to him. Right inside that cloud.'

'Stop shouting, will you?' Yossarian shushed him.

'I'm not shouting!' Dobbs shouted louder, his face red with revolutionary fervor. His eyes and nostrils were running, and his palpitating crimson lower lip was splattered with a foamy dew. 'There must have been close to a hundred men in the group who had finished their fifty-five missions when he raised the number to sixty. There must have been at least another hundred like you with just a couple more to fly. He's going to kill us all if we let him go on forever. We've got to kill him first.'

Yossarian nodded expressionlessly, without committing himself. 'Do you think we could get away with it?'

'I've got it all worked out. I –'

'Stop shouting, for Christ's sake!'

'I'm not shouting. I've got it –'

'Will you stop shouting!'

'I've got it all worked out,' Dobbs whispered, gripping the side of Orr's cot with white-knuckled hands to constrain them from waving. 'Thursday morning when he's due back from that goddam farmhouse of his in the hills, I'll sneak up through the woods to that hairpin turn in the road and hide in the bushes. He has to slow down there, and I can watch the road in both directions to make sure there's no one else around. When I see him coming, I'll shove a big log out into the road to make him stop his jeep. Then I'll step out of the bushes with my Luger and shoot him in the head until he's dead. I'll bury the gun, come back down through the woods to the squadron and go about my business just like everybody else. What could possibly go wrong?'

Yossarian had followed each step attentively. 'Where do I come in?' he asked in puzzlement.

'I couldn't do it without you,' Dobbs explained. 'I need you to tell me to go ahead.'

Yossarian found it hard to believe him. 'Is that all you want me to do? Just tell you to go ahead?'

'That's all I need from you,' Dobbs answered. 'Just tell me to go ahead and I'll blow his brains out all by myself the day after tomorrow.' His voice was accelerating with emotion and rising again. 'I'd like to shoot Colonel Korn in the head, too, while we're at it, although I'd like to spare Major Danby, if that's all right with you. Then

289

I'd murder Appleby and Havermeyer also, and after we finish murdering Appleby and Havermeyer I'd like to murder McWatt.'

'McWatt?' cried Yossarian, almost jumping up in horror. 'McWatt's a friend of mine. What do you want from McWatt?'

'I don't know,' Dobbs confessed with an air of floundering embarrassment. 'I just thought that as long as we were murdering Appleby and Havermeyer we might as well murder McWatt too. Don't you want to murder McWatt?'

Yossarian took a firm stand. 'Look, I might keep interested in this if you stop shouting it all over the island and if you stick to killing Colonel Cathcart. But if you're going to turn this into a blood bath, you can forget about me.'

'All right, all right,' Dobbs sought to placate him. 'Just Colonel Cathcart. Should I do it? Tell me to go ahead.'

Yossarian shook his head. 'I don't think I could tell you to go ahead.'

Dobbs was frantic. 'I'm willing to compromise,' he pleaded vehemently. 'You don't have to tell me to go ahead. Just tell me it's a good idea. Okay? Is it a good idea?'

Yossarian still shook his head. 'It would have been a great idea if you had gone ahead and done it without even speaking to me. Now it's too late. I don't think I can tell you anything. Give me some more time. I might change my mind.'

'Then it *will* be too late.'

Yossarian kept shaking his head. Dobbs was disappointed. He sat for a moment with a hangdog look, then spurted to his feet suddenly and stamped away to have another impetuous crack at persuading Doc Daneeka to ground him, knocking over Yossarian's washstand with his hip when he lurched around and tripping over the fuel line of the stove Orr was still constructing. Doc Daneeka withstood Dobb's blustering and gesticulating attack with a series of impatient nods and sent him to the medical tent to describe his symptoms to Gus and Wes, who painted his gums purple with gentian-violet solution the moment he started to talk. They painted his toes purple, too, and forced a laxative down his throat when he opened his mouth again to complain, and then they sent him away.

Dobbs was in even worse shape than Hungry Joe, who could at least fly missions when he was not having nightmares. Dobbs was almost as bad as Orr, who seemed happy as an undersized, grinning lark with his deranged and galvanic giggle and shivering warped buck teeth and who was sent along for a rest leave with Milo and Yossarian on the trip to Cairo for eggs when Milo bought cotton instead and took off at dawn for Istanbul with his plane packed to the gun turrets with exotic spiders and unripened red bananas. Orr was one of the homeliest freaks Yossarian had ever encountered, and one of the most attractive. He had a raw bulgy face, with hazel eyes squeezing from their sockets like matching brown halves of marbles and thick, wavy particolored hair sloping up to a peak on the top of his head like a pomaded pup tent. Orr was knocked down into the water or had an engine shot out almost every time he went up, and he began jerking on Yossarian's arm like a wild man after they had taken off for Naples and come down in Sicily to find the scheming, cigar-smoking, ten-year-old pimp with the two twelve-year-old virgin sisters waiting for them in town in front of the hotel in which there was room for only Milo. Yossarian pulled back from Orr adamantly, gazing with some concern and bewilderment at Mt. Etna instead of Mt. Vesuvius and wondering what they were doing in Sicily instead of Naples as Orr kept entreating him in a tittering, stuttering, concupiscent turmoil to go along with him behind the scheming ten-year-old pimp to his two twelve-year-old virgin sisters who were not really virgins and not really sisters and who were really only twenty-eight.

'Go with him,' Milo instructed Yossarian laconically. 'Remember your mission.'

'All right,' Yossarian yielded with a sigh, remembering

his mission. 'But at least let me try to find a hotel room first so I can get a good night's sleep afterward.'

'You'll get a good night's sleep with the girls,' Milo replied with the same air of intrigue. 'Remember your mission.'

But they got no sleep at all, for Yossarian and Orr found themselves jammed into the same double bed with the two twelve-year-old twenty-eight-year-old prostitutes, who turned out to be oily and obese and who kept waking them up all night long to ask them to switch partners. Yossarian's perceptions were soon so fuzzy that he paid no notice to the beige turban the fat one crowding into him kept wearing until late the next morning when the scheming ten-year-old pimp with the Cuban panatella snatched it off in public in a bestial caprice that exposed in the brilliant Sicilian daylight her shocking, mis-shapen and denudate skull. Vengeful neighbors had shaved her hair to the gleaming bone because she had slept with Germans. The girl screeched in feminine outrage and waddled comically after the scheming ten-year-old pimp, her grisly, bleak, violated scalp slithering up and down ludicrously around the queer darkened wart of her face like something bleached and obscene. Yossarian had never laid eyes on anything so bare before. The pimp spun the turban high on his finger like a trophy and kept himself skipping inches ahead of her finger tips as he led her in a tantalizing circle around the square congested with people who were howling with laughter and pointing to Yossarian with derision when Milo strode up with a grim look of haste and puckered his lips reprovingly at the unseemly spectacle of so much vice and frivolity. Milo insisted on leaving at once for Malta.

'We're sleepy,' Orr whined

'That's your own fault,' Milo censured them both selfrighteously. 'If you had spent the night in your hotel room instead of with these immoral girls, you'd both feel as good as I do today.'

'You told us to go with them,' Yossarian retorted

accusingly. 'And we didn't have a hotel room. You were the only one who could get a hotel room.'

'That wasn't my fault, either,' Milo explained haughtily. 'How was I supposed to know all the buyers would be in town for the chick-pea harvest?'

'You knew it,' Yossarian charged. 'That explains why we're here in Sicily instead of Naples. You've probably got the whole damned plane filled with chick-peas already.'

'Shhhhhh!' Milo cautioned sternly, with a meaningful glance toward Orr. 'Remember your mission.'

The bomb bay, the rear and tail sections of the plane and most of the top turret gunner's section were all filled with bushels of chick-peas when they arrived at the airfield to take off for Malta.

Yossarian's mission on the trip was to distract Orr from observing where Milo bought his eggs, even though Orr was a member of Milo's syndicate and, like every other member of Milo's syndicate, owned a share. His mission was silly, Yossarian felt, since it was common knowledge that Milo bought his eggs in Malta for seven cents apiece and sold them to the mess halls in his syndicate for five cents apiece.

'I just don't trust him,' Milo brooded in the plane, with a backward nod toward Orr, who was curled up like a tangled rope on the low bushels of chick-peas, trying torturedly to sleep. 'And I'd just as soon buy my eggs when he's not around to learn my business secrets. What else don't you understand?'

Yossarian was riding beside him in the co-pilot's seat. 'I don't understand why you buy eggs for seven cents apiece in Malta and sell them for five cents.'

'I do it to make a profit.'

'But how can you make a profit? You lose two cents an egg.'

'But I make a profit of three and a quarter cents an egg by selling them for four and a quarter cents an egg to the people in Malta I buy them from for seven cents an egg. Of course, I don't make the profit. The syndicate makes the profit. And everybody has a share.'

293

Yossarian felt he was beginning to understand. 'And the people you sell the eggs to at four and a quarter cents apiece make a profit of two and three quarter cents apiece when they sell them back to you at seven cents apiece. Is that right? Why don't you sell the eggs directly to you and eliminate the people you buy them from?'

'Because I'm the people I buy them from,' Milo explained. 'I make a profit of three and a quarter cents apiece when I sell them to me and a profit of two and three quarter cents apiece when I buy them back from me. That's a total profit of six cents an egg. I lose only two cents an egg when I sell them to the mess halls at five cents apiece, and that's how I can make a profit buying eggs for seven cents apiece and selling them for five cents apiece. I pay only one cent apiece at the hen when I buy them in Sicily.'

'In Malta,' Yossarian corrected. 'You buy your eggs in Malta, not Sicily.'

Milo chortled proudly. 'I don't buy eggs in Malta,' he confessed, with an air of slight and clandestine amusement that was the only departure from industrious sobriety Yossarian had ever seen him make. 'I buy them in Sicily for one cent apiece and transfer them to Malta secretly at four and a half cents apiece in order to get the price of eggs up to seven cents apiece when people come to Malta looking for them.'

'Why do people come to Malta for eggs when they're so expensive there?'

'Because they've always done it that way.'

'Why don't they look for eggs in Sicily?'

'Because they've never done it that way.'

'Now I really don't understand. Why don't you sell your mess halls the eggs for seven cents apiece instead of for five cents apiece?'

'Because my mess halls would have no need for me then. Anyone can buy seven-cents-apiece eggs for seven cents apiece.'

'Why don't they bypass you and buy the eggs directly

from you in Malta at four and a quarter cents apiece?'

'Because I wouldn't sell it to them.'

'Why wouldn't you sell it to them?'

'Because then there wouldn't be as much room for profit. At least this way I can make a bit for myself as a middleman.'

'Then you do make a profit for yourself,' Yossarian declared.

'Of course I do. But it all goes to the syndicate. And everybody has a share. Don't you understand? It's exactly what happens with those plum tomatoes I sell to Colonel Cathcart.'

'*Buy*,' Yossarian corrected him. 'You don't *sell* plum tomatoes to Colonel Cathcart and Colonel Korn. You *buy* plum tomatoes from them.'

'No, *sell*,' Milo corrected Yossarian. 'I distributed my plum tomatoes in markets all over Pianosa under an assumed name so that Colonel Cathcart and Colonel Korn can buy them up from me under their assumed names at four cents apiece and sell them back to me the next day for the syndicate at five cents apiece. They make a profit of one cent apiece, I make a profit of three and a half cents apiece, and everybody comes out ahead.'

'Everybody but the syndicate,' said Yossarian with a snort. 'The syndicate is paying five cents apiece for plum tomatoes that cost you only half a cent apiece. How does the syndicate benefit?'

'The syndicate benefits when I benefit,' Milo explained, 'because everybody has a share. And the syndicate gets Colonel Cathcart's and Colonel Korn's support so that they'll let me go out on trips like this one. You'll see how much profit that can mean in about fifteen minutes when we land in Palermo.'

'Malta,' Yossarian corrected him. 'We're flying to Malta now, not Palermo.'

'No, we're flying to Palermo,' Milo answered. 'There's an endive exporter in Palermo I have to see for a minute about a shipment of mushrooms to Bern that were damaged by mold.'

'Milo, how do you do it?' Yossarian inquired with laughing amazement and admiration. 'You fill out a flight plane for one place and then you go to another. Don't the people in the control towers ever raise hell?'

'They all belong to the syndicate,' Milo said. 'And they know that what's good for the syndicate is good for the country, because that's what makes Sammy run. The men in the control towers have a share, too, and that's why they always have to do whatever they can to help the syndicate.'

'Do I have a share?'

'Everybody has a share.'

'Does Orr have a share?'

'Everybody has a share.'

'And Hungry Joe? He has a share, too?'

'Everybody has a share.'

'Well, I'll be damned,' mused Yossarian, deeply impressed with the idea of a share for the very first time.

Milo turned toward him with a faint glimmer of mischief. 'I have a sure-fire plan for cheating the federal government out of six thousand dollars. We can make three thousand dollars apiece without any risk to either of us. Are you interested?'

'No.'

Milo looked at Yossarian with profound emotion. 'That's what I like about you,' he exclaimed. 'You're honest! You're the only one I know that I can really trust. That's why I wish you'd try to be of more help to me. I really was disappointed when you ran off with those two tramps in Catania yesterday.'

Yossarian stared at Milo in quizzical disbelief. 'Milo, you told me to go with them. Don't you remember?'

'That wasn't my fault,' Milo answered with dignity. 'I had to get rid of Orr some way once we reached town. It will be a lot different in Palermo. When we land in Palermo, I want you and Orr to leave with the girls right from the airport.'

'With what girls?'

'I radioed ahead and made arrangements with a four-year-old pimp to supply you and Orr with two eight-year-old virgins who are half Spanish. He'll be waiting at the airport in a limousine. Go right in as soon as you step out of the plane.'

'Nothing doing,' said Yossarian, shaking his head. 'The only place I'm going is to sleep.'

Milo turned livid with indignation, his slim long nose flickering spasmodically between his black eyebrows and his unbalanced orange-brown mustache like the pale, thin flame of a single candle. 'Yossarian, remember your mission,' he reminded reverently.

'To hell with my mission,' Yossarian responded indifferently. 'And to hell with the syndicate too, even though I do have a share. I don't want any eight-year-old virgins, even if they are half Spanish.'

'I don't blame you. But these eight-year-old virgins are really only thirty-two. And they're not really half Spanish but only one-third Estonian.'

'I don't care for any virgins.'

'And they're not even virgins,' Milo continued persuasively. 'The one I picked out for you was married for a short time to an elderly schoolteacher who slept with her only on Sundays, so she's really almost as good as new.'

But Orr was sleepy, too, and Yossarian and Orr were both at Milo's side when they rode into the city of Palermo from the airport and discovered that there was no room for the two of them at the hotel there either, and, more important, that Milo was mayor.

The weird, implausible reception for Milo began at the airfield, where civilian laborers who recognized him halted in their duties respectively to gaze at him with full expressions of controlled exuberance and adulation. News of his arrival preceded him into the city, and the outskirts were already crowded with cheering citizens as they sped by in their small uncovered truck. Yossarian and Orr were mystified and mute and pressed close against Milo for security.

Inside the city, the welcome for Milo grew louder as

the truck slowed and eased deeper toward the middle of town. Small boys and girls had been released from school and were lining the sidewalks in new clothes, waving tiny flags. Yossarian and Orr were absolutely speechless now. The streets were jammed with joyous throngs, and strung overhead were huge banners bearing Milo's picture. Milo had posed for these pictures in a drab peasant's blouse with a high collar, and his scrupulous, paternal countenance was tolerant, wise, critical and strong as he stared out at the populace omnisciently with his undisciplined mustache and disunited eyes. Sinking invalids blew kisses to him from windows. Aproned shopkeepers cheered ecstatically from the narrow doorways of their shops. Tubas crumped. Here and there a person fell and was trampled to death. Sobbing old women swarmed through each other frantically around the slow-moving truck to touch Milo's shoulder or press his hand. Milo bore the tumultuous celebrations with benevolent grace. He waved back to everyone in elegant reciprocation and showered generous handfuls of foil-covered Hershey kisses to the rejoicing multitudes. Lines of lusty young boys and girls skipped along behind him with their arms linked, chanting in hoarse and glassy-eyed adoration, 'Mi-lo! Mi-lo! Mi-lo!'

Now that his secret was out, Milo relaxed with Yossarian and Orr and inflated opulently with a vast, shy pride. His cheeks turned flesh-colored. Milo had been elected mayor of Palermo – and of nearby Carini, Monreale, Bagheria, Termini Imerese, Cefali, Mistretta and Nicosia as well – because he had brought Scotch to Sicily.

Yossarian was amazed. 'The people here like to drink Scotch that much?'

'They don't drink any of the Scotch,' Milo explained 'Scotch is very expensive, and these people here are very poor.'

'Then why do you import it to Sicily if nobody drinks any?'

'To build up a price. I move the Scotch here from Malta to make more room for profit when I sell it back to me for somebody else. I created a whole new industry here. Today Sicily is the third largest exporter of Scotch in the world, and *that's* why they elected me mayor.'

'How about getting us a hotel room if you're such a hot-shot?' Orr grumbled impertinently in a voice slurred with fatigue.

Milo responded contritely. 'That's just what I'm going to do,' he promised. 'I'm really sorry about forgetting to radio ahead for hotel rooms for you two. Come along to my office and I'll speak to my deputy mayor about it right now.'

Milo's office was a barbershop, and his deputy mayor was a pudgy barber from whose obsequious lips cordial greetings foamed as effusively as the lather he began whipping up in Milo's shaving cup.

'Well, Vittorio,' said Milo, settling back lazily in one of Vittorio's barber chairs, 'how were things in my absence this time?'

'Very sad, Signor Milo, very sad. But now that you are back, the people are all happy again.'

'I was wondering about the size of the crowds. How come all the hotels are full?'

'Because so many people from other cities are here to see you, Signor Milo. And because we have all the buyers who have come into town for the artichoke auction.'

Milo's hand soared up perpendicularly like an eagle and arrested Vittorio's shaving brush. 'What's artichoke?' he inquired.

'Artichoke, Signor Milo? An artichoke is a very tasty vegetable that is popular everywhere. You must try some artichokes while you are here, Signor Milo. We grow the best in the world.'

'Really?' said Milo. 'How much are artichokes selling for this year?'

'It looks like a very good year for artichokes. The crops were very bad.'

'Is that a fact?' mused Milo, and was gone, sliding from

his chair so swiftly that his striped barber's apron retained his shape for a second or two after he had gone before it collapsed. Milo had vanished from sight by the time Yossarian and Orr rushed after him to the doorway.

'Next?' barked Milo's deputy mayor officiously. 'Who's next?'

Yossarian and Orr walked from the barbershop in dejection. Deserted by Milo, they trudged homelessly through the reveling masses in futile search of a place to sleep. Yossarian was exhausted. His head throbbed with a dull, debilitating pain, and he was irritable with Orr, who had found two crab apples somewhere and walked with them in his cheeks until Yossarian spied them there and made him take them out. Then Orr found two horse chestnuts somewhere and slipped those in until Yossarian detected them and snapped at him again to take the crap apples out of his mouth. Orr grinned and replied that they were not crab apples but horse chestnuts and that they were not in his mouth but in his hands, but Yossarian was not able to understand a single word he said because of the horse chestnuts in his mouth and made him take them out anyway. A sly light twinkled in Orr's eyes. He rubbed his forehead harshly with his knuckles, like a man in an alcoholic stupor, and snickered lewdly.

'Do you remember that girl –' He broke off to snicker lewdly again. 'Do you remember that girl who was hitting me over the head with that shoe in that apartment in Rome, when we were both naked?' he asked with a look of cunning expectation. He waited until Yossarian nodded cautiously. 'If you let me put the chestnuts back in my mouth I'll tell you why she was hitting me. Is that a deal?'

Yossarian nodded, and Orr told him the whole fantastic story of why the naked girl in Nately's whore apartment was hitting him over the head with her shoe, but Yossarian was not able to understand a single word because the horse chestnuts were back in his mouth.

Yossarian roared with exasperated laughter at the trick, but in the end there was nothing for them to do when night fell but eat a damp dinner in a dirty restaurant and hitch a ride back to the airfield, where they slept on the chill metal floor of the plane and turned and tossed in groaning torment until the truck drivers blasted up less than two hours later with their crates of artichokes and chased them out onto the ground while they filled up the plane. A heavy rain began falling. Yossarian and Orr were dripping wet by the time the trucks drove away and had no choice but to squeeze themselves back into the plane and roll themselves up like shivering anchovies between the jolting corners of the crates of artichokes that Milo flew up to Naples at dawn and exchanged for the cinnamon sticks, cloves, vanilla beans and pepper pods that he rushed right back down south with that same day to Malta, where, it turned out, he was Assistant Governor-General. There was no room for Yossarian and Orr in Malta either. Milo was Major Sir Milo Minderbinder in Malta and had a gigantic office in the governor-general's building. His mahogany desk was immense. In a panel of the oak wall, between crossed British flags, hung a dramatic arresting photograph of Major Sir Milo Minderbinder in the dress uniform of the Royal Welsh Fusiliers. His mustache in the photograph was clipped and narrow, his chin was chiseled, and his eyes were sharp as thorns. Milo had been knighted, commissioned a major in the Royal Welsh Fusiliers and named Assistant Governor-General of Malta because he had brought the egg trade there. He gave Yossarian and Orr generous permission to spend the night on the thick carpet in his office, but shortly after he left a sentry in battle dress appeared and drove them from the building at the tip of his bayonet, and they rode out exhaustedly to the airport with a surly cab driver, who overcharged them, and went to sleep inside the plane again, which was filled now with leaking gunny sacks of cocoa and freshly ground coffee and reeking with an odor so rich that they were both outside retching violently against the landing gear when Milo was chauffeured up the first thing the next morning, looking fit as a fiddle, and took right off for Oran, where there was again no room at the hotel for Yossarian and Orr, and where Milo was Vice-Shah. Milo had at his disposal sumptuous quarters inside a salmon-pink palace, but Yossarian and Orr were not allowed to accompany him inside because they were Christian infidels. They were stopped at the gates by gargantuan Berber guards with scimitars and chased away. Orr was snuffling and sneezing with a crippling head cold. Yossarian's broad back was bent and aching. He was ready to break Milo's neck, but Milo was Vice-Shah of Oran and his person was sacred. Milo was not only the Vice-Shah of Oran, as it turned out, but also the Caliph of Baghdad, the Imam of Damascus, and the Sheik of Araby. Milo was the corn god, the rain god and the rice god in backward regions where such crude gods were still worshiped by ignorant and superstitious people, and deep inside the jungles of Africa, he intimated with becoming modesty, large graven images of his mustached face could be found overlooking primitive stone altars red with human blood. Everywhere they touched he was acclaimed with honor, and it was one triumphal ovation after another for him in city after city until they finally doubled back through the Middle East and reached Cairo, where Milo cornered the market on cotton that no one else in the world wanted and brought himself promptly to the brink of ruin. In Cairo there was at last room at the hotel for Yossarian and Orr. There were soft beds for them with fat fluffed-up pillows and clean, crisp sheets. There were closets with hangers for their clothes. There was water to wash with. Yossarian and Orr soaked their rancid, unfriendly bodies pink in a steaming-hot tub and then went from the hotel with Milo to eat shrimp cocktails and filet mignon in a very fine restaurant with a stock ticker in the lobby that happened to be clicking out the latest quotation for Egyptian cotton when Milo inquired of the captain of waiters what kind of machine it was. Milo had never imagined a machine so beautiful as a stock ticker before.

'Really?' he exclaimed when the captain of waiters had finished his explanation. 'And how much is Egyptian cotton selling for?' The captain of waiters told him, and Milo bought the whole crop.

But Yossarian was not nearly so frightened by the Egyptian cotton Milo bought as he was by the bunches of green red bananas Milo had spotted in the native market place as they drove into the city, and his fears proved justified, for Milo shook him awake out of a deep sleep just after twelve and shoved a partly peeled banana toward him. Yossarian choked back a sob.

'Taste it,' Milo urged, following Yossarian's writhing face around with the banana insistently.

'Milo, you bastard,' moaned Yossarian, 'I've got to get some sleep.'

'Eat it and tell me if it's good,' Milo persevered. 'Don't tell Orr I gave it to you. I charged him two piasters for his.'

Yossarian ate the banana submissively and closed his eyes after telling Milo it was good, but Milo shook him awake again and instructed him to get dressed as quickly as he could, because they were leaving at once for Pianosa.

'You and Orr have to load the bananas into the plane right away,' he explained. 'The man said to watch out for spiders while you're handling the bunches.'

'Milo, can't we wait until morning?' Yossarian pleaded. 'I've got to get some sleep.'

'They're ripening very quickly,' answered Milo, 'and we don't have a minute to lose. Just think how happy the men back at the squadron will be when they get these bananas.'

But the men back at the squadron never even saw any of the bananas, for it was a seller's market for bananas in Istanbul and a buyer's market in Beirut for the caraway seeds Milo rushed with to Bengasi after selling the bananas, and when they raced back into Pianosa breathlessly six days later at the conclusion of Orr's rest leave, it was with a load of best white eggs from Sicily that Milo said were from Egypt and sold to his mess halls for only *four* cents apiece so that all the commanding officers in his syndicate would implore him to speed right back to Cairo for more bunches of green red bananas to sell in Turkey for the caraway seeds in demand in Bengasi. And everybody had a share.

23 Nately's old man

The only one back in the squadron who did see any of Milo's red bananas was Aarfy, who picked up two from an influential fraternity brother of his in the Quartermaster Corps when the bananas ripened and began streaming into Italy through normal black-market channels and who was in the officers' apartment with Yossarian the evening Nately finally found his whore again after so many fruitless weeks of mournful searching and lured her back to the apartment with two girl friends by promising them thirty dollars each.

'Thirty dollars each?' remarked Aarfy slowly, poking and patting each of the three strapping girls skeptically with the air of a grudging connoisseur. 'Thirty dollars is a lot of money for pieces like these. Besides, I never paid for it in my life.'

'I'm not asking you to pay for it,' Nately assured him quickly. 'I'll pay for them all. I just want you guys to take the other two. Won't you help me out?'

Aarfy smirked complacently and shook his soft round head. 'Nobody has to pay for it for good old Aarfy. I can get all I want any time I want it. I'm just not in the mood right now.'

'Why don't you just pay all three and send the other

two away?' Yossarian suggested.

'Because then mine will be angry with me for making her work for her money,' Nately replied with an anxious look at his girl, who was glowering at him restlessly and starting to mutter. 'She says that if I really like her I'd send her away and go to bed with one of the others.'

'I have a better idea,' boasted Aarfy. 'Why don't we keep the three of them here until after the curfew and then threaten to push them out into the street to be arrested unless they give us all their money? We can even threaten to push them out the window.'

'Aarfy!' Nately was aghast.

'I was only trying to help,' said Aarfy sheepishly. Aarfy was always trying to help Nately because Nately's father was rich and prominent and in an excellent position to help Aarfy after the war. 'Gee whiz,' he defended himself querulously. 'Back in school we were always doing things like that. I remember one day we tricked these two dumb high-school girls from town into the fraternity house and made them put out for all the fellows there who wanted them by threatening to call up their parents and say they were putting out for us. We kept them trapped in bed there for more than ten hours. We even smacked their faces a little when they started to complain. Then we took away their nickels and dimes and chewing gum and threw them out. Boy, we used to have fun in that fraternity house,' he recalled peacefully, his corpulent cheeks aglow with the jovial, rubicund warmth of nostalgic recollection. 'We used to ostracize everyone, even each other.'

But Aarfy was no help to Nately now as the girl Nately had fallen so deeply in love with began swearing at him sullenly with rising, menacing resentment. Luckily, Hungry Joe burst in just then, and everything was all right again, except that Dunbar staggered in drunk a minute later and began embracing one of the other giggling girls at once. Now there were four men and three girls, and the seven of them left Aarfy in the apartment and climbed into a horse-drawn cab, which remained at the curb at a dead halt while the girls demanded their money in advance. Nately gave them ninety dollars with a gallant flourish, after borrowing twenty dollars from Yossarian, thirty-five dollars from Dunbar and seventeen dollars from Hungry Joe. The girls grew friendlier then and called an address to the driver, who drove them at a clopping pace halfway across the city into a section they had never visited before and stopped in front of an old, tall building on a dark street. The girls led them up four steep, very long flights of creaking wooden stairs and guided them through a doorway into their own wonderful and resplendent tenement apartment, which burgeoned miraculously with an infinite and proliferating flow of supple young naked girls and contained the evil and debauched ugly old man who irritated Nately constantly with his caustic laughter and the clucking, proper old woman in the ash-gray woolen sweater who disapproved of everything immoral that occurred there and tried her best to tidy up.

The amazing place was a fertile, seething cornucopia of female nipples and navels. At first, there were just their own three girls, in the dimly-lit, drab brown sitting room that stood at the juncture of three murky hallways leading in separate directions to the distant recesses of the strange and marvelous bordello. The girls disrobed at once, pausing in different stages to point proudly to their garish underthings and bantering all the while with the gaunt and dissipated old man with the shabby long white hair and slovenly white unbuttoned shirt who sat cackling lasciviously in a musty blue armchair almost in the exact center of the room and bade Nately and his companions welcome with a mirthful and sardonic formality. Then the old woman trudged out to get a girl for Hungry Joe, dipping her captious head sadly, and returned with two big-bosomed beauties, one already undressed and the other in only a transparent pink half slip that she wiggled out of while sitting down. Three more naked girls sauntered in from a different direction and remained to chat, then two others. Four more girls passed through the room in an indolent group, engrossed in conversation; three were barefoot and one wobbled perilously on a pair of unbuckled silver dancing shoes that did not seem to be her own. One more girl appeared wearing only panties and sat down, bringing the total congregating there in just a few minutes to eleven, all but one of them completely unclothed.

There was bare flesh lounging everywhere, most of it plump, and Hungry Joe began to die. He stood stock still in rigid, cataleptic astonishment while the girls ambled in and made themselves comfortable. Then he let out a piercing shriek suddenly and bolted toward the door in a headlong dash back toward the enlisted men's apartment for his camera, only to be halted in his tracks with another frantic shriek by the dreadful, freezing premonition that this whole lovely, lurid, rich and colorful pagan paradise would be snatched away from him irredeemably if he were to let it out of his sight for even an instant. He stopped in the doorway and sputtered, the wiry veins and tendons in his face and neck pulsating violently. The old man watched him with victorious merriment, sitting in his musty blue armchair like some satanic and hedonistic deity on a throne, a stolen U.S. Army blanket wrapped around his spindly legs to ward off a chill. He laughed quietly, his sunken, shrewd eyes sparkling perceptively with a cynical and wanton enjoyment. He had been drinking. Nately reacted on sight with bristling enmity to this wicked, depraved and unpatriotic old man who was old enough to remind him of his father and who made disparaging jokes about America.

'America,' he said, 'will lose the war. And Italy will win it.'

'America is the strongest and most prosperous nation on earth,' Nately informed him with lofty fervor and dignity. 'And the American fighting man is second to none.'

'Exactly,' agreed the old man pleasantly, with a hint

308

of taunting amusement. 'Italy, on the other hand, is one of the least prosperous nations on earth. And the Italian fighting man is probably second to all. And that's exactly why my country is doing so well in this war while your country is doing so poorly.'

Nately guffawed with surprise, then blushed apologetically for his impoliteness. 'I'm sorry I laughed at you,' he said sincerely, and he continued in a tone of respectful condescension. 'But Italy was occupied by the Germans and is now being occupied by us. You don't call that doing very well, do you?'

'But of course I do,' exclaimed the old man cheerfully. 'The Germans are being driven out, and we are still here. In a few years you will be gone, too, and we will still be here. You see, Italy is really a very poor and weak country, and that's what makes us so strong. Italian soldiers are not dying any more. But American and German soldiers are. I call that doing extremely well. Yes, I am quite certain that Italy will survive this war and still be in existence long after your own country has been destroyed.'

Nately could scarcely believe his ears. He had never heard such shocking blasphemies before, and he wondered with instinctive logic why G-men did not appear to lock the traitorous old man up. 'America is not going to be destroyed!' he shouted passionately.

'Never?' prodded the old man softly.

'Well. . .' Nately faltered.

The old man laughed indulgently, holding in check a deeper, more explosive delight. His goading remained gentle. 'Rome was destroyed, Greece was destroyed, Persia was destroyed, Spain was destroyed. All great countries are destroyed. Why not yours? How much longer do you really think your own country will last? Forever? Keep in mind that the earth itself is destined to be destroyed by the sun in twenty-five million years or so.'

Nately squirmed uncomfortably. 'Well, forever is a long time, I guess.'

'A million years?' persisted the jeering old man with keen, sadistic zest. 'A half million? The frog is almost five hundred million years old. Could you really say with much certainty that America, with all its strength and prosperity, with its fighting man that is second to none, and with its standard of living that is the highest in the world, will last as long as. . .the frog?'

Nately wanted to smash his leering face. He looked about imploringly for help in defending his country's future against the obnoxious calumnies of this sly and sinful assailant. He was disappointed. Yossarian and Dunbar were busy in a far corner pawing orgiastically at four or five frolicsome girls and six bottles of red wine, and Hungry Joe had long since tramped away down one of the mystic hallways, propelling before him like a ravening despot as many of the broadest-hipped young prostitutes as he could contain in his frail wind-milling arms and cram into one double bed.

Nately felt himself at an embarrassing loss. His own girl sat sprawled out gracelessly on an overstuffed sofa with an expression of otiose boredom. Nately was unnerved by her torpid indifference to him, by the same sleepy and inert poise that he remembered so vividly, so sweetly, and so miserably from the first time she had seen him and ignored him at the packed penny-ante blackjack game in the living room of the enlisted men's apartment. Her lax mouth hung open in a perfect O, and God alone knew at what her glazed and smoky eyes were staring in such brute apathy. The old man waited tranquilly, watching him with a discerning smile that was both scornful and sympathetic. A lissome, blond, sinuous girl with lovely legs and honey-colored skin laid herself out contentedly on the arm of the old man's chair and began molesting his angular, pale, dissolute face languidly and coquettishly. Nately stiffened with resentment and hostility at the sight of such lechery in a man so old. He turned away with a sinking heart and wondered why he simply did not take his own girl and go to bed.

This sordid, vulturous, diabolical old man reminded

Nately of his father because the two were nothing at all alike. Nately's father was a courtly white-haired gentleman who dressed impeccably; this old man was an uncouth bum. Nately's father was a sober, philosophical and responsible man; this old man was fickle and licentious. Nately's father was discreet and cultured; this old man was a boor. Nately's father believed in honor and knew the answer to everything; this old man believed in nothing and had only questions. Nately's father had a distinguished white mustache; this old man had no mustache at all. Nately's father – and everyone else's father Nately had ever met – was dignified, wise and venerable; this old man was utterly repellent, and Nately plunged back into debate with him, determined to repudiate his vile logic and insinuations with an ambitious vengence that would capture the attention of the bored, phlegmatic girl he had fallen so intensely in love with and win her admiration forever.

'Well, frankly, I don't know how long America is going to last,' he proceeded dauntlessly. 'I suppose we can't last forever if the world itself is going to be destroyed someday. But I do know that we're going to survive and triumph for a long, long time.'

'For how long?' mocked the profane old man with a gleam of malicious elation. 'Not even as long as the frog?'

'Much longer than you or me,' Nately blurted out lamely.

'Oh, is that all! That won't be very much longer then, considering that you're so gullible and brave and that I am already such an old, old man.'

'How old are you?' Nately asked, growing intrigued and charmed with the old man in spite of himself.

'A hundred and seven.' The old man chuckled heartily at Nately's look of chagrin. 'I see you don't believe that either.'

'I don't believe anything you tell me,' Nately replied, with a bashful mitigating smile. 'The only thing I do believe is that America is going to win the war.'

311

'You put so much stock in *winning* wars,' the grubby iniquitous old man scoffed. 'The real trick lies in *losing* wars, in knowing which wars can be *lost*. Italy has been losing wars for centuries, and just see how splendidly we've done nonetheless. France wins wars and is in a continual state of crisis. Germany loses and prospers. Look at our own recent history. Italy won a war in Ethiopia and promptly stumbled into serious trouble. Victory gave us such insane delusions of grandeur that we helped start a world war we hadn't a chance of winning. But now that we are losing again, everything has taken a turn for the better, and we will certainly come out on top again if we succeed in being defeated.'

Nately gaped at him in undisguised befuddlement. 'Now I really don't understand what you're saying. You talk like a madman.'

'But I live like a sane one. I was a fascist when Mussolini was on top, and I am an anti-fascist now that he has been deposed. I was fanatically pro-German when the Germans were here to protect us against the Americans, and now that the Americans are here to protect us against the Germans I am fanatically pro-American. I can assure you, my outraged young friend' – the old man's knowing, disdainful eyes shone even more effervescently as Nately's stuttering dismay increased – 'that you and your country will have a no more loyal partisan in Italy than me – but only as long as you *remain* in Italy.'

'But,' Nately cried out in disbelief, 'you're a turncoat! A time-server! A shameful, unscrupulous opportunist!'

'I am a hundred and seven years old,' the old man reminded him suavely.

'Don't you have any principles?'

'Of course not.'

'No morality?'

'Oh, I am a very moral man,' the villainous old man assured him with satiric seriousness, stroking the bare hip of a buxom black-haired girl with pretty dimples who had stretched herself out seductively on the other arm of his chair. He grinned at Nately sarcastically as he sat between both naked girls in smug and threadbare splendor, with a sovereign hand on each.

'I can't believe it,' Nately remarked grudgingly, trying stubbornly not to watch him in relationship to the girls. 'I simply can't believe it.'

'But it's perfectly true. When the Germans marched into the city, I danced in the streets like a youthful ballerina and shouted, "*Heil* Hitler!" until my lungs were hoarse. I even waved a small Nazi flag that I snatched away from a beautiful little girl while her mother was looking the other way. When the Germans left the city, I rushed out to welcome the Americans with a bottle of excellent brandy and a basket of flowers. The brandy was for myself, of course, and the flowers were to sprinkle upon our liberators. There was a very stiff and stuffy old major riding in the first car, and I hit him squarely in the eye with a red rose. A marvelous shot! You should have seen him wince.'

Nately gasped and was on his feet with amazement, the blood draining from his cheeks. 'Major — de Coverley!' he cried.

'Do you know him?' inquired the old man with delight. 'What a charming coincidence!'

Nately was too astounded even to hear him. 'So *you're* the one who wounded Major — de Coverley!' he exclaimed in horrified indignation. 'How could you do such a thing?'

The fiendish old man was unperturbed. 'How could I resist, you mean. You should have seen the arrogant old bore, sitting there so sternly in that car like the Almighty Himself, with his big, rigid head and his foolish, solemn face. What a tempting target he made! I got him in the eye with an American Beauty rose. I thought that was most appropriate. Don't you?'

'That was a *terrible* thing to do!' Nately shouted at him reproachfully. 'A vicious and criminal thing! Major — de Coverley is our squadron executive officer!'

'Is he?' teased the unregenerate old man, pinching his

pointy jaw gravely in a parody of repentance. 'In that case, you must give me credit for being impartial. When the Germans rode in, I almost stabbed a robust young Oberleutnant to death with a sprig of edelweiss.'

Nately was appalled and bewildered by the abominable old man's inability to perceive the enormity of his offence. 'Don't you realize what you've done?' he scolded vehemently. 'Major — de Coverley is a noble and wonderful person, and everyone admires him.'

'He's a silly old fool who really has no right acting like a silly young fool. Where is he today? Dead?'

Nately answered softly with somber awe. 'Nobody knows. He seems to have disappeared.'

'You see? Imagine a man his age risking what little life he has left for something so absurd as a country.'

Nately was instantly up in arms again. 'There is nothing so absurd about risking your life for your country!' he declared.

'Isn't there?' asked the old man. 'What is a country? A country is a piece of land surrounded on all sides by boundaries, usually unnatural. Englishmen are dying for England, Americans are dying for America, Germans are dying for Germany, Russians are dying for Russia. There are now fifty or sixty countries fighting in this war. Surely so many countries can't *all* be worth dying for.'

'Anything worth living for,' said Nately, 'is worth dying for.'

'And anything worth dying for,' answered the sacrilegious old man, 'is certainly worth living for. You know, you're such a pure and naive young man that I almost feel sorry for you. How old are you? Twenty-five? Twenty-six?'

'Nineteen,' said Nately. 'I'll be twenty in January.'

'If you live.' The old man shook his head, wearing, for a moment, the same touchy, meditating frown of the fretful and disapproving old woman. 'They are going to kill you if you don't watch out, and I can see now that you are not going to watch out. Why don't you use some sense and try to be more like me? You might live to be a hundred and seven, too.'

'Because it's better to die on one's feet than live on one's knees,' Nately retorted with triumphant and lofty conviction. 'I guess you've heard that saying before.'

'Yes, I certainly have,' mused the treacherous old man, smiling again. 'But I'm afraid you have it backward. It is better to *live* on one's feet than die on one's knees. *That* is the way the saying goes.'

'Are you sure?' Nately asked with sober confusion. 'It seems to make more sense my way.'

'No, it makes more sense my way. Ask your friends.'

Nately turned to ask his friends and discovered they had gone. Yossarian and Dunbar had both disappeared. The old man roared with contemptuous merriment at Nately's look of embarrassed surprise. Nately's face darkened with shame. He vacillated helplessly for a few seconds and then spun himself around and fled inside the nearest of the hallways in search of Yossarian and Dunbar, hoping to catch them in time and bring them back to the rescue with news of the remarkable clash between the old man and Major — de Coverley. All the doors in the hallways were shut. There was light under none. It was already very late. Nately gave up his search forlornly. There was nothing left for him to do, he realized finally, but get the girl he was in love with and lie down with her somewhere to make tender, courteous love to her and plan their future together; but she had gone off to bed, too, by the time he returned to the sitting room for her, and there was nothing left for him to do then but resume his abortive discussion with the loathsome old man, who rose from his armchair with jesting civility and excused himself for the night, abandoning Nately there with two bleary-eyed girls who could not tell him into which room his own whore had gone and who padded off to bed several seconds later after trying in vain to interest him in themselves, leaving him to sleep alone in the sitting room on the small, lumpy sofa.

Nately was a sensitive, rich, good-looking boy with

dark hair, trusting eyes, and a pain in his neck when he awoke on the sofa early the next morning and wondered dully where he was. His nature was invariably gentle and polite. He had lived for almost twenty years without trauma, tension, hate, or neurosis, which was proof to Yossarian of just how crazy he really was. His childhood had been a pleasant, though disciplined, one. He got on well with his brothers and sisters, and he did not hate his mother and father, even though they had both been very good to him.

Nately had been brought up to detest people like Aarfy, whom his mother characterized as climbers, and people like Milo, whom his father characterized as pushers, but he had never learned how, since he had never been permitted near them. As far as he could recall, his homes in Philadelphia, New York, Maine, Palm Beach, Southampton, London, Deauville, Paris and the south of France had always been crowded only with ladies and gentlemen who were not climbers or pushers. Nately's mother, a descendant of the New England Thorntons, was a Daughter of the American Revolution. His father was a Son of a Bitch.

'Always remember,' his mother had reminded him frequently, 'that you are a Nately. You are not a Vanderbilt, whose fortune was made by a vulgar tugboat captain, or a Rockefeller, whose wealth was amassed through unscrupulous speculations in crude petroleum; or a Reynolds or Duke, whose income was derived from the sale to the unsuspecting public of products containing cancer-causing resins and tars; and you are certainly not an Astor, whose family, I believe, still lets rooms. You are a Nately, and the Nately's have never done *any-thing* for their money.'

'What your mother means, son,' interjected his father affably one time with that flair for graceful and economical expression Nately admired so much, 'is that old money is better than new money and that the newly rich are never to be esteemed as highly as the newly poor. Isn't that correct, my dear?'

Nately's father brimmed continually with sage and

sophisticated counsel of that kind. He was as ebullient and ruddy as mulled claret, and Nately liked him a great deal, although he did not like mulled claret. When war. broke out, Nately's family decided that he would enlist in the armed forces, since he was too young to be placed in the diplomatic service, and since his father had it on excellent authority that Russia was going to collapse in a matter of weeks or months and that Hitler, Churchill, Roosevelt, Mussolini, Ghandi, Franco, Peron and the Emperor of Japan would then all sign a peace treaty and live together happily ever after. It was Nately's father's idea that he join the Air Corps, where he could train safely as a pilot while the Russians capitulated and the details of the armistice were worked out, and where, as an officer, he would associate only with gentlemen.

Instead, he found himself with Yossarian, Dunbar and Hungry Joe in a whore house in Rome, poignantly in love with an indifferent girl there with whom he finally did lie down the morning after the night he slept alone in the sitting room, only to be interrupted almost immediately by her incorrigible kid sister, who came bursting in without warning and hurled herself onto the bed jealously so that Nately could embrace her, too. Nately's whore sprang up snarling to whack her angrily and jerked her to her feet by her hair. The twelve-year-old girl looked to Nately like a plucked chicken or like a twig with the bark peeled off: her sapling body embarrassed everyone in her precocious attempts to imitate her elders, and she was always being chased away to put clothes on and ordered out into the street to play in the fresh air with the other children. The two sisters swore and spat at each other now savagely, raising a fluent, deafening commotion that brought a whole crowd of hilarious spectators swarming into the room. Nately gave up in exasperation. He asked his girl to get dressed and took her downstairs for breakfast. The kid sister tagged along, and Nately felt like the proud head of a family as the three of them ate respectably in a nearby open-air café. But Nately's whore was already bored by the time they started back, and she decided to go streetwalking with two other girls rather than spend more time with him. Nately and the kid sister followed meekly a block behind, the ambitious youngster to pick up valuable pointers, Nately to eat his liver in mooning frustration, and both were saddened when the girls were stopped by soldiers in a staff car and driven away.

Nately went back to the café and bought the kid sister chocolate ice cream until her spirits improved and then returned with her to the apartment, where Yossarian and Dunbar were flopped out in the sitting room with an exhausted Hungry Joe, who was still wearing on his battered face the blissful, numb, triumphant smile with which he had limped into view from his massive harem that morning like a person with numerous broken bones. The lecherous and depraved old man was delighted with Hungry Joe's split lips and black-and-blue eyes. He greeted Nately warmly, still wearing the same rumpled clothes of the evening before. Nately was profoundly upset by his seedy and disreputable appearance, and whenever he came to the apartment he wished that the corrupt, immoral old man would put on a clean Brooks Brothers shirt, shave, comb his hair, wear a tweed jacket, and grow a dapper white mustache so that Nately would not have to suffer such confusing shame each time he looked at him and was reminded of his father.

24 Milo

April had been the best month of all for Milo. Lilacs
bloomed in April and fruit ripened on the vine. Heart-
beats quickened and old appetites were renewed. I
April a livelier iris gleamed upon the burnished dove.
April was spring, and in the spring Milo Minderbinder's
fancy had lightly turned to thoughts of tangerines.

'Tangerines?'

'Yes, sir.'

'My men would love tangerines,' admitted the colonel
in Sardinia who commanded four squadrons of B-26s.

'There'll be all the tangerines they can eat that you're
able to pay for with money from your mess fund,' Milo
assured him.

'Casaba melons?'

'Are going for a song in Damascus.'

'I have a weakness for casaba melons. I've always
had a weakness for casaba melons.'

'Just lend me one plane from each squadron, just one
plane, and you'll have all the casabas you can eat that
you've money to pay for.'

'We buy from the syndicate?'

'And everybody has a share.'

'It's amazing, positively amazing. How can you do it?'

'Mass purchasing power makes the big difference. For example, breaded veal cutlets.'

'I'm not so crazy about breaded veal cutlets,' grumbled the skeptical B-25 commander in the north of Corsica.

'Breaded veal cutlets are very nutritious,' Milo admonished him piously. 'They contain egg yolk and bread crumbs. And so are lamb chops.'

'Ah, lamb chops,' echoed the B-25 commander. 'Good lamb chops?'

'The best,' said Milo, 'that the black market has to offer.'

'Baby lamb chops?'

'In the cutest little pink paper panties you ever saw. Are going for a song in Portugal.'

'I can't send a plane to Portugal. I haven't the authority.'

'I can, once you lend the plane to me. With a pilot to fly it. And don't forget – you'll get General Dreedle.'

'Will General Dreedle eat in my mess hall again?'

'Like a pig, once you start feeding him my best white fresh eggs fried in my pure creamery butter. There'll be tangerines too, and casaba melons, honeydews, fi..t of Dover sole, baked Alaska, and cockles and mussels.'

'And everybody has a share?'

'That,' said Milo, 'is the most beautiful part of it.'

'I don't like it,' growled the uncooperative fighter-plane commander, who didn't like Milo either.

'There's an unco-operative fighter-plane commander up north who's got it in for me,' Milo complained to General Dreedle. 'It takes just one person to ruin the whole thing, and then you wouldn't have your fresh eggs fried in my pure creamery butter anymore.'

General Dreedle had the unco-operative fighter-plane commander transferred to the Solomon Islands to dig graves and replaced him with a senile colonel with bursitis and a craving for litchi nuts who introduced Milo to the B-17 general on the mainland with a yearning for Polish sausage.

'Polish sausage is going for peanuts in Cracow,' Milo informed him.

'Polish sausage,' sighed the general nostalgically. 'You know, I'd give just about anything for a good hunk of Polish sausage. Just about anything.'

'You don't have to give *anything*. Just give me one plane for each mess hall and a pilot who will do what he's told. And a small down payment on your initial order as a token of good faith.'

'But Cracow is hundreds of miles behind the enemy lines. How will you get to the sausage?'

'There's an international Polish sausage exchange in Geneva. I'll just fly the peanuts into Switzerland and exchange them for Polish sausage at the open market rate. They'll fly the peanuts back to Cracow and I'll fly the Polish sausage back to you. You buy only as much Polish sausage as you want through the syndicate. There'll be tangerines too, with only a little artificial coloring added. And eggs from Malta and Scotch from Sicily. You'll be paying the money to yourself when you buy from the syndicate, since you'll own a share, so you'll really be getting everything you buy for nothing. Doesn't that makes sense?'

'Sheer genius. How in the world did you ever think of it?'

'My name is Milo Minderbinder. I am twenty-seven years old.'

Milo Minderbinder's planes flew in from everywhere, the pursuit planes, bombers, and cargo ships streaming into Colonel Cathcart's field with pilots at the controls who would do what they were told. The planes were decorated with flamboyant squadron emblems illustrating such laudable ideals as Courage, Might, Justice, Truth, Liberty, Love, Honor and Patriotism that were painted out at once by Milo's mechanics with a double coat of flat white and replaced in garish purple with the stenciled name M & M ENTERPRISES, FINE FRUITS AND PRODUCE. The 'M & M' in 'M & M ENTERPRISES' stood for Milo & Minderbinder, and the & was inserted, Milo revealed candidly, to nullify any impression that the syndicate was a one-man operation. Planes arrived for Milo from airfields in Italy, North Africa and England, and from Air Transport Command stations in Liberia, Ascension Island, Cairo, and Karachi. Pursuit planes were traded for additional cargo ships or retained for emergency invoice duty and small-parcel service; trucks and tanks were procured from the ground forces and used for short-distance road hauling. Everybody had a share, and men got fat and moved about tamely with toothpicks in their greasy lips. Milo supervised the whole expanding operation by himself. Deep otter-brown lines of preoccupation etched themselves permanently into his careworn face and gave him a harried look of sobriety and mistrust. Everybody but Yossarian thought Milo was a jerk, first for volunteering for the job of mess officer and next for taking it so seriously. Yossarian also thought that Milo was a jerk; but he also knew that Milo was a genius.

One day Milo flew away to England to pick up a load of Turkish halvah and came flying back from Madagascar leading four German bombers filled with yams, collards, mustard greens and black-eyed Georgia peas. Milo was dumbfounded when he stepped down to the ground and found a contingent of armed M.P.'s waiting to imprison the German pilots and confiscate their planes. *Confiscate!* The mere word was anathema to him, and he stormed back and forth in excoriating condemnation, shaking a piercing finger of rebuke in the guilt-ridden faces of Colonel Cathcart, Colonel Korn and the poor battle-scarred captain with the submachine gun who commanded the M.P.s.

'Is this Russia?' Milo assailed them incredulously at the top of his voice. '*Confiscate?*' he shrieked, as though he could not believe his own ears. 'Since when is it the policy of the American government to confiscate the private property of its citizens? Shame on you! Shame on all of you for even thinking such a horrible thought.'

'But Milo,' Major Danby interrupted timidly, 'we're at

war with Germany, and those are German planes.'

'They are no such thing!' Milo retorted furiously. 'Those planes belong to the syndicate, and everybody has a share. *Confiscate?* How can you possibly confiscate your own private property? *Confiscate*, indeed! I've never heard anything so depraved in my whole life.'

And sure enough, Milo was right, for when they looked, his mechanics had painted out the German swastikas on the wings, tails and fuselages with double coats of flat white and stenciled in the words M & M ENTERPRISES, FINE FRUITS AND PRODUCE. Right before their eyes he had transformed his syndicate into an international cartel.

Milo's argosies of plenty now filled the air. Planes poured in from Norway, Denmark, France, Germany, Austria, Italy, Yugoslavia, Romania, Bulgaria, Sweden, Finland, Poland – from everywhere in Europe, in fact, but Russia, with whom Milo refused to do business. When everybody who was going to had signed up with M & M Enterprises, Fine Fruits and Produce, Milo created a wholly owned subsidiary, M & M Fancy Pastry, and obtained more airplanes and more money from the mess funds for scones and crumpets from the British Isles, prune and cheese Danish from Copenhagen, éclairs, cream puffs, Napoleons and *petits fours* from Paris, Reims and Grenoble, *Kugelhopf*, pumpernickel and *Pfefferkuchen* from Berlin, *Linzer* and *Dobos Torten* from Vienna, *Strudel* from Hungary and *baklava* from Ankara. Each morning Milo sent planes aloft all over Europe and North Africa hauling long red tow signs advertising the day's specials in large square letters: 'EYE ROUND, 79¢. . .WHITING, 21¢.' He boosted cash income for the syndicate by leasing tow signs to Pet Milk, Gaines Dog Food, and Noxzema. In a spirit of civic enterprise, he regularly allotted a certain amount of free aerial advertising space to General Peckem for the propagation of such messages in the public interest as NEATNESS COUNTS, HASTE MAKES WASTE, and THE FAMILY THAT PRAYS TOGETHER STAYS TOGETHER. Milo purchased spot radio announcements on Axis Sally's and Lord Haw Haw's daily propaganda broadcasts from Berlin to keep things moving. Business boomed on every battlefront.

Milo's planes were a familiar sight. They had freedom of passage everywhere, and one day Milo contracted with the American military authorities to bomb the German-held highway bridge at Orvieto and with the German military authorities to defend the highway bridge at Orvieto with antiaircraft fire against his own attack. His fee for attacking the bridge for America was the total cost of the operation plus six per cent and his fee from Germany for defending the bridge was the same cost-plus-six agreement augmented by a merit bonus of a thousand dollars for every American plane he shot down. The consummation of these deals represented an important victory for private enterprise, he pointed out, since the armies of both countries were socialized institutions. Once the contracts were signed, there seemed to be no point in using the resources of the syndicate to bomb and defend the bridge, inasmuch as both governments had ample men and material right there to do so and were perfectly happy to contribute them, and in the end Milo realized a fantastic profit from both halves of his project for doing nothing more than signing his name twice.

The arrangements were fair to both sides. Since Milo did have freedom of passage everywhere, his planes were able to steal over in a sneak attack without alerting the german anti-aircraft gunners; and since Milo knew about the attack, he was able to alert the German antiaircraft gunners in sufficient time for them to begin firing accurately the moment the planes came into range. It was an ideal arrangement for everyone but the dead man in Yossarian's tent, who was killed over the target the day he arrived.

'I didn't kill him!' Milo kept replying passionately to Yossarian's angry protest. 'I wasn't even there that day, I tell you. Do you think I was down there on the ground firing an antiaircraft gun when the planes came over?'

'But you organized the whole thing, didn't you?' Yossarian shouted back at him in the velvet darkness cloaking the path leading past the still vehicles of the motor pool to the open-air movie theater.

'And I didn't organize anything,' Milo answered indignantly, drawing great agitated sniffs of air in through his hissing, pale, twitching nose. 'The Germans have the bridge, and we were going to bomb it, whether I stepped into the picture or not. I just saw a wonderful opportunity to make some profit out of the mission, and I took it. What's so terrible about that?'

'What's so terrible about it? Milo, a man in my tent was killed on that mission before he could even unpack his bags.'

'But I didn't kill him.'

'You got a thousand dollars extra for it.'

'But I didn't kill him. I wasn't even there, I tell you. I was in Barcelona buying olive oil and skinless and boneless sardines, and I've got the purchase orders to prove it. And I didn't get the thousand dollars. That thousand dollars went to the syndicate, and everybody got a share, even you.' Milo was appealing to Yossarian from the bottom of his soul. 'Look, I didn't start this war, Yossarian, no matter what that lousy Wintergreen is saying. I'm just trying to put it on a businesslike basis. Is anything wrong with that? You know, a thousand dollar's ain't such a bad price for a medium bomber and a crew. If I can persuade the Germans to pay me a thousand dollars for every plane they shoot down, why shouldn't I take it?'

'Because you're dealing with the enemy, that's why. Can't you understand that we're fighting a war? People are dying. Look around you, for Christ's sake!'

Milo shook his head with weary forbearance. 'And the Germans are not our enemies,' he declared. 'Oh I know what you're going to say. Sure, we're at war with them. But the Germans are also members in good standing of the syndicate, and it's my job to protect their rights as shareholders. Maybe they did start the war,

325

and maybe they are killing millions of people, but they pay their bills a lot more promptly than some allies of ours I could name. Don't you understand that I have to respect the sanctity of my contract with Germany? Can't you see it from my point of view?'

'No,' Yossarian rebuffed him harshly.

Milo was stung and made no effort to disguise his wounded feelings. It was a muggy, moonlit night filled with gnats, moths, and mosquitoes. Milo lifted his arm suddenly and pointed towards the open-air theater, where the milky, dust-filled beam bursting horizontally from the projector slashed a conelike swath in the blackness and draped in a fluorescent membrane of light the audience tilted on the seats there in hypnotic sags, their faces focused upward toward the aluminized movie screen. Milo's eyes were liquid with integrity, and his artless and uncorrupted face was lustrous with a shining mixture of sweat and insect repellent.

'Look at them,' he exclaimed in a voice choked with emotion. 'They're my friends, my countrymen, my comrades in arms. A fellow never had a better bunch of buddies. Do you think I'd do a single thing to harm them if I didn't have to? Haven't I got enough on my mind? Can't you see how upset I am already about all that cotton piling up on those piers in Egypt?' Milo's voice splintered into fragments, and he clutched at Yossarian's shirt front as though drowning. His eyes were throbbing visibly like brown caterpillars. 'Yossarian, what am I going to do with so much cotton? It's all your fault for letting me buy it.'

The cotton was piling up on the piers in Egypt, and nobody wanted any. Milo had never dreamed that the Nile Valley could be so fertile or that there would be no market at all for the crop he had bought. The mess halls in his syndicate would not help; they rose up in uncompromising rebellion against his proposal to tax them on a per capita basis in order to enable each man to own his own share of the Egyptian cotton crop. Even his reliable friends the Germans failed him in this crisis: they preferred ersatz. Milo's mess halls would not even help him store the cotton, and his warehousing costs sky-rocketed and contributed to the devastating drain upon his cash reserves. The profits from the Orvieto mission were sucked away. He began writing home for the money he had sent back in better days; soon that was almost gone. And new bales of cotton kept arriving on the wharves at Alexandria every day. Each time he succeeded in dumping some on the world market for a loss it was snapped up by canny Egyptian brokers in the Levant, who sold it back to him at the original price, so that he was really worse off than before.

M & M Enterprises verged on collapse. Milo cursed himself hourly for his monumental greed and stupidity in purchasing the entire Egyptian cotton crop, but a contract was a contract and had to be honored, and one night, after a sumptuous evening meal, all Milo's fighters and bombers took off, joined in formation directly overhead and began dropping bombs on the group. He had landed another contract with the Germans, this time to bomb his own outfit. Milo's planes separated in a well co-ordinated attack and bombed the fuel stocks and the ordnance dump, the repair hangars and the B-25 bombers resting on the lollipop-shaped hardstands at the field. His crews spared the landing strip and the mess halls so that they could land safely when their work was done and enjoy a hot snack before retiring. They bombed with their landing lights on, since no one was shooting back. They bombed all four squadrons, the officers' club and the Group Headquarters building. Men bolted from their tents in sheer terror and did not know in which direction to turn. Wounded soon lay screaming everywhere. A cluster of fragmentation bombs exploded in the yard of the officers' club and punched jagged holes in the side of the wooden building and in the bellies and backs of a row of lieutenants and captains standing at the bar. They doubled over in agony and dropped. The rest of the officers fled towards the two exits in panic and jammed up the doorways like a dense, howling dam of human flesh as they shrank from going farther.

Colonel Cathcart clawed and elbowed his way through the unruly, bewildered mass until he stood outside by himself. He stared up at the sky in stark astonishment and horror. Milo's planes, ballooning serenely in over the blossoming treetops with their bomb bay doors open and wing flaps down and with their monstrous, bug-eyed, blinding, fiercely flickering, eerie landing lights on, were the most apocalyptic sight he had ever beheld. Colonel Cathcart let go a stricken gasp of dismay and hurled himself headlong into his jeep, almost sobbing. He found the gas pedal and the ignition and sped toward the airfield as fast as the rocking car would carry him, his huge flabby hands clenched and bloodless on the wheel or blaring his horn tormentedly. Once he almost killed himself when he swerved with a banshee screech of tires to avoid plowing into a bunch of men running crazily toward the hills in their underwear with their stunned faces down and their thin arms pressed high around their temples as puny shields. Yellow, orange and red fires were burning on both sides of the road. Tents and trees were in flames, and Milo's planes kept coming around interminably with their blinking white landing lights on and their bomb bay doors open. Colonel Cathcart almost turned the jeep over when he slammed the brakes on at the control tower. He leaped from the car while it was still skidding dangerously and hurtled up the flight of steps inside, where three men were busy at the instruments and the controls. He bowled two of them aside in his lunge for the nickel-plated microphone, his eyes glittering wildly and his beefy face contorted with stress. He squeezed the microphone in a bestial grip and began shouting hysterically at the top of his voice,

'Milo, you son of a bitch! Are you crazy? What the hell are you doing? Come down! Come down!'

'Stop hollering so much, will you?' answered Milo, who was standing there right beside him in the control

tower with a microphone of his own. 'I'm right here.'
Milo looked at him with reproof and turned back to his
work. 'Very good, men, very good,' he chanted into his
microphone. 'But I see one supply shed still standing.
That will never do, Purvis – I've spoken to you about
that kind of shoddy work before. Now, you go right back
there this minute and try it again. And this time come in
slowly . . . slowly. Haste makes waste, Purvis. Haste
makes waste. If I've told you that once, I must have told
you that a hundred times. Haste makes waste.'

The loud-speaker overhead began squawking. 'Milo,
this is Alvin Brown. I've finished dropping my bombs.
What should I do now?'

'Strafe,' said Milo.

'*Strafe?*' Alvin Brown was shocked.

'We have no choice,' Milo informed him resignedly.
'It's in the contract.'

'Oh, okay, then,' Alvin Brown acquiesced. 'In that
case I'll strafe.'

This time Milo had gone too far. Bombing his own men
and planes was more than even the most phlegmatic
observer could stomach, and it looked like the end for
him. High-ranking government officials poured in to
investigate. Newspapers inveighed against Milo with
glaring headlines, and Congressmen denounced the
atrocity in stentorian wrath and clamored for punishment. Mothers with children in the service organized
into militant groups and demanded revenge. Not one
voice was raised in his defense. Decent people everywhere were affronted, and Milo was all washed up until
he opened his books to the public and disclosed the
tremendous profit he had made. He could reimburse the
government for all the people and property he had
destroyed and still have enough money left over to continue buying Egyptian cotton. Everybody, of course,
owned a share. And the sweetest part of the whole deal
was that there really was no need to reimburse the
government at all.

'In a democracy, the government is the people,' Milo

explained. 'We're people, aren't we? So we might just as well keep the money and eliminate the middleman. Frankly, I'd like to see the government get out of war altogether and leave the whole field to private industry. If we pay the government everything we owe it, we'll only be encouraging government control and discouraging other individuals from bombing their own men and planes. We'll be taking away their incentive.'

Milo was correct, of course, as everyone soon agreed but a few embittered misfits like Doc Daneeka, who sulked cantankerously and muttered offensive insinuations about the morality of the whole venture until Milo mollified him with a donation, in the name of the syndicate, of a lightweight aluminium collapsible garden chair that Doc Daneeka could fold up conveniently and carry outside his tent each time Chief White Halfoat came inside his tent and carry back inside his tent each time Chief White Halfoat came out. Doc Daneeka had lost his head during Milo's bombardment; instead of running for cover, he had remained out in the open and performed his duty, slithering along the ground through shrapnel, strafing and incendiary bombs like a furtive, wily lizard from casualty to casualty, administering tourniquets, morphine, splints and sulfanilamide with a dark and doleful visage, never saying one word more than he had to and reading in each man's bluing wound a dreadful portent of his own decay. He worked himself relentlessly into exhaustion before the long night was over and came down with a sniffle the next day that sent him hurrying querulously into the medical tent to have his temperature taken by Gus and Wes and to obtain a mustard plaster and vaporizer.

Doc Daneeka tended each moaning man that night with the same glum and profound and introverted grief he showed at the airfield the day of the Avignon mission when Yossarian climbed down the few steps of his plane naked, in a state of utter shock, with Snowden smeared abundantly all over his bare heels and toes, knees, arms and fingers, and pointed inside wordlessly toward where the young radio-gunner lay freezing to death on the floor beside the still younger tail-gunner who kept falling back into a dead faint each time he opened his eyes and saw Snowden dying.

Doc Daneeka draped a blanket around Yossarian's shoulders almost tenderly after Snowden had been removed from the plane and carried into an ambulance on a stretcher. He led Yossarian toward his jeep. McWatt helped, and the three drove in silence to the squadron medical tent, where McWatt and Doc Daneeka guided Yossarian inside to a chair and washed Snowden off him with cold wet balls of absorbent cotton. Doc Daneeka gave him a pill and a shot that put him to sleep for twelve hours. When Yossarian woke up and went to see him, Doc Daneeka gave him another pill and a shot that put him to sleep for another twelve hours. When Yossarian woke up again and went to see him, Doc Daneeka made ready to give him another pill and a shot.

'How long are you going to keep giving me those pills and shots?' Yossarian asked him.

'Until you feel better.'

'I feel all right now.'

Doc Daneeka's frail suntanned forehead furrowed with surprise. 'Then why don't you put some clothes on? Why are you walking around naked?'

'I don't want to wear a uniform any more.'

Doc Daneeka accepted the explanation and put away his hypodermic syringe. 'Are you sure you feel all right?'

'I feel fine. I'm just a little logy from all those pills and shots you've been giving me.'

Yossarian went about his business with no clothes on all the rest of that day and was still naked late the next morning when Milo, after hunting everywhere else, finally found him sitting up a tree a small distance in back of the quaint little military cemetery at which Snowden was being buried. Milo was dressed in his customary business attire – olive-drab trousers, a fresh olive-drab shirt and tie, with one silver first lieutenant's bar gleaming on the collar, and a regulation dress cap with a stiff leather bill.

'I've been looking all over for you,' Milo called up to Yossarian from the ground reproachfully.

'You should have looked for me in this tree,' Yossarian answered. 'I've been up here all morning.'

'Come on down and taste this and tell me if it's good. It's very important.'

Yossarian shook his head. He sat nude on the lowest limb of the tree and balanced himself with both hands grasping the bough directly above. He refused to budge, and Milo had no choice but to stretch both arms about the trunk in a distasteful hug and start climbing. He struggled upward clumsily with loud grunts and wheezes, and his clothes were squashed and crooked by the time he pulled himself up high enough to hook a leg over the limb and pause for breath. His dress cap was askew and in danger of falling. Milo caught it just in time when it began slipping. Globules of perspiration glistened like transparent pearls around his mustache and swelled like opaque blisters under his eyes. Yossarian watched him impassively. Cautiously Milo worked himself around in a half circle so that he could face Yossarian. He unwrapped tissue paper from something soft, round and brown and handed it to Yossarian.

'Please taste this and let me know what you think. I'd like to serve it to the men.'

'What is it?' asked Yossarian, and took a big bite.

'Chocolate-covered cotton.'

Yossarian gagged convulsively and sprayed his big mouthful of chocolate-covered cotton right into Milo's face. 'Here, take it back!' he spouted angrily. 'Jesus Christ! Have you gone crazy? You didn't even take the goddam seeds out.'

'Give it a chance, will you?' Milo begged. 'It can't be that bad. Is it really that bad?'

'It's even worse.'

'But I've got to make the mess halls feed it to the men.'

'They'll never be able to swallow it.'

'They've got to swallow it,' Milo ordained with dictatorial grandeur, and almost broke his neck when he let go with one arm to wave a righteous finger in the air.

'Come on out here,' Yossarian invited him. 'You'll be much safer, and you can see everything.'

Gripping the bough above with both hands, Milo began inching his way out on the limb sideways with utmost care and apprehension. His face was rigid with tension, and he sighed with relief when he found himself seated securely beside Yossarian. He stroked the tree affectionately. 'This is a pretty good tree,' he observed admiringly with proprietary gratitude.

'It's the tree of life,' Yossarian answered, waggling his toes, 'and of knowledge of good and evil, too.'

Milo squinted closely at the bark and branches. 'No it isn't,' he replied. 'It's a chestnut tree. I ought to know. I sell chestnuts.'

'Have it your way.'

They sat in the tree without talking for several seconds, their legs dangling and their hands almost straight up on the bough above, the one completely nude but for a pair of crepe-soled sandals, the other completely dressed in a coarse olive-drab woolen uniform with his tie knotted tight. Milo studied Yossarian diffidently through the corner of his eye, hesitating tactfully.

'I want to ask you something,' he said at last. 'You don't have any clothes on. I don't want to butt in or anything, but I just want to know. Why aren't you wearing your uniform?'

'I don't want to.'

Milo nodded rapidly like a sparrow pecking. 'I see, I see,' he stated quickly with a look of vivid confusion. 'I understand perfectly. I heard Appleby and Captain Black say you had gone crazy, and I just wanted to find out.' He hesitated politely again, weighing his next question. 'Aren't you ever going to put your uniform on again?'

'I don't think so.'

Milo nodded with spurious vim to indicate he still

understood and then sat silent, ruminating gravely with troubled misgiving. A scarlet-crested bird shot by below, brushing sure dark wings against a quivering bush. Yossarian and Milo were covered in their bower by tissue-thin tiers of sloping green and largely surrounded by other gray chestnut trees and a silver spruce. The sun was high overhead in a vast sapphire-blue sky beaded with low, isolated, puffy clouds of dry and immaculate white. There was no breeze, and the leaves about them hung motionless. The shade was feathery. Everything was at peace but Milo, who straightened suddenly with a muffled cry and began pointing excitedly.

'Look at that!' he exclaimed in alarm. 'Look at that! That's a funeral going on down there. That looks like the cemetery. Isn't it?'

Yossarian answered him slowly in a level voice. 'They're burying that kid who got killed in my plane over Avignon the other day. Snowden.'

'What happened to him?' Milo asked in a voice deadened with awe.

'He got killed.'

'That's terrible,' Milo grieved, and his large brown eyes filled with tears. 'That poor kid. It really is terrible.' He bit his trembling lip hard, and his voice rose with emotion when he continued. 'And it will get even worse if the mess halls don't agree to buy my cotton. Yossarian, what's the matter with them? Don't they realize it's their syndicate? Don't they know they've all got a share?'

'Did the dead man in my tent have a share?' Yossarian demanded caustically.

'Of course he did,' Milo assured him lavishly. 'Everybody in the squadron has a share.'

'He was killed before he even got into the squadron.'

Milo made a deft grimace of tribulation and turned away. 'I wish you'd stop picking on me about that dead man in your tent,' he pleaded peevishly. 'I told you I didn't have anything to do with killing him. Is it my fault that I saw this great opportunity to corner the market on

Egyptian cotton and got us into all this trouble? Was I supposed to know there was going to be a glut? I didn't even know what a glut was in those days. An opportunity to corner a market doesn't come along very often, and I was pretty shrewd to grab the chance when I had it.' Milo gulped back a moan as he saw six uniformed pall-bearers lift the plain pine coffin from the ambulance and set it gently down on the ground beside the yawning gash of the freshly dug grave. 'And now I can't get rid of a single penny's worth,' he mourned.

Yossarian was unmoved by the fustian charade of the burial ceremony, and by Milo's crushing bereavement. The chaplain's voice floated up to him through the distance tenuously in an unintelligible, almost inaudible monotone, like a gaseous murmur. Yossarian could make out Major Major by his towering and lanky aloofness and thought he recognized Major Danby mopping his brow with a handkerchief. Major Danby had not stopped shaking since his run-in with General Dreedle. There were strands of enlisted men molded in a curve around the three officers, as inflexible as lumps of wood, and four idle gravediggers in streaked fatigues lounging indifferently on spades near the shocking, incongruous heap of loose copper-red earth. As Yossarian stared, the chaplain elevated his gaze toward Yossarian beatifically, pressed his fingers down over his eyeballs in a manner of affliction, peered upward again toward Yossarian searchingly, and bowed his head, concluding what Yossarian took to be a climactic part of the funeral rite. The four men in fatigues lifted the coffin on slings and lowered it into the grave. Milo shuddered violently.

'I can't watch it,' he cried, turning away in anguish. 'I just can't sit here and watch while those mess halls let my syndicate die.' He gnashed his teeth and shook his head with bitter woe and resentment. 'If they had any loyalty, they would buy my cotton till it hurts so that they can keep right on buying my cotton till it hurts them some more. They would build fires and burn up their underwear and summer uniforms just to create bigger demand. But they won't do a thing. Yossarian, try eating the rest of this chocolate-covered cotton for me. Maybe it will taste delicious now.'

Yossarian pushed his hand away. 'Give up, Milo. People can't eat cotton.'

Milo's face narrowed cunningly. 'It isn't really cotton,' he coaxed. 'I was joking. It's really cotton candy, delicious cotton candy. Try it and see.'

'Now you're lying.'

'I never lie!' Milo rejoindered with proud dignity.

'You're lying now.'

'I only lie when it's necessary,' Milo explained defensively, averting his eyes for a moment and blinking his lashes winningly. 'This stuff is better than cotton candy, really it is. It's made out of real cotton. Yossarian, you've got to help me make the men eat it. Egyptian cotton is the finest cotton in the world.'

'But it's indigestible,' Yossarian emphasized. 'It will make them sick, don't you understand? Why don't you try living on it yourself if you don't believe me?'

'I did try,' admitted Milo gloomily. 'And it made me sick.'

The graveyard was yellow as hay and green as cooked cabbage. In a little while the chaplain stepped back, and the beige crescent of human forms began to break up sluggishly, like flotsam. The men drifted without haste or sound to the vehicles parked along the side of the bumpy dirt road. With their heads down disconsolately, the chaplain, Major Major and Major Danby moved toward their jeeps in an ostracized group, each holding himself friendlessly several feet away from the other two.

'It's all over,' observed Yossarian.

'It's the end,' Milo agreed despondently. 'There's no hope left. And all because I left them free to make their own decisions. That should teach me a lesson about discipline the next time I try something like this.'

'Why don't you sell your cotton to the government?'

Yossarian suggested casually, as he watched the four men in streaked fatigues shoveling heaping bladefuls of the copper-red earth back down inside the grave.

Milo vetoed the idea brusquely. 'It's a matter of principle,' he explained firmly. 'The government has no business in business, and I would be the last person in the world to ever try to involve the government in a business of mine. But the business of government is business,' he remembered alertly, and continued with elation. 'Calvin Coolidge said that, and Calvin Coolidge was a President, so it must be true. And the government does have the responsibility of buying all the Egyptian cotton I've got that no one else wants so that I can make a profit, doesn't it?' Milo's face clouded almost as abruptly, and his spirits descended into a state of sad anxiety. 'But how will I get the government to do it?'

'Bribe it,' Yossarian said.

'Bribe it!' Milo was outraged and almost lost his balance and broke his neck again. 'Shame on you!' he scolded severely, breathing virtuous fire down and upward into his rusty mustache through his billowing nostrils and prim lips. 'Bribery is against the law, and you know it. But it's not against the law to make a profit, is it? So it can't be against the law for me to bribe someone in order to make a fair profit, can it? No, of course not!' He fell to brooding again, with a meek, almost pitiable distress. 'But how will I know who to bribe?'

'Oh, don't you worry about that,' Yossarian comforted him with a toneless snicker as the engines of the jeeps and ambulance fractured the drowsy silence and the vehicles in the rear began driving away backward. 'You make the bribe big enough and they'll find you. Just make sure you do everything right out in the open. Let everyone know exactly what you want and how much you're willing to pay for it. The first time you act guilty or ashamed, you might get into trouble.'

'I wish you'd come with me,' Milo remarked. 'I won't feel safe among people who take bribes. They're no better than a bunch of crooks.'

'You'll be all right,' Yossarian assured him with confidence. 'If you run into trouble, just tell everybody that the security of the country requires a strong domestic Egyptian-cotton speculating industry.'

'It does,' Milo informed him solemnly. 'A strong Egyptian-cotton speculating industry means a much stronger America.'

'Of course it does. And if that doesn't work, point out the great number of American families that depend on it for income.'

'A great many American families do depend on it for income.'

'You see?' said Yossarian. 'You're much better at it than I am. You almost make it sound true.'

'It is true,' Milo exclaimed with a strong trace of old hauteur.

'That's what I mean. You do it with just the right amount of conviction.'

'You're sure you won't come with me?'

Yossarian shook his head.

Milo was impatient to get started. He stuffed the remainder of the chocolate-covered cotton ball into his shirt pocket and edged his way back gingerly along the branch to the smooth gray trunk. He threw this arms about the trunk in a generous and awkward embrace and began shinnying down, the sides of his leather-soled shoes slipping constantly so that it seemed many times he would fall and injure himself. Halfway down, he changed his mind and climbed back up. Bits of tree bark stuck to his mustache, and his straining face was flushed with exertion.

'I wish you'd put your uniform on instead of going around naked that way,' he confided pensively before he climbed back down again and hurried away. 'You might start a trend, and then I'll never get rid of all this goldarned cotton.'

25 The chaplain

It was already some time since the chaplain had first begun wondering what everything was all about. Was there a God? How could he be sure? Being an Anabaptist minister in the American Army was difficult enough under the best of circumstances; without dogma, it was almost intolerable.

People with loud voices frightened him. Brave, aggressive men of action like Colonel Cathcart left him feeling helpless and alone. Wherever he went in the Army, he was a stranger. Enlisted men and officers did not conduct themselves with him as they conducted themselves with other enlisted men and officers, and even other chaplains were not as friendly toward him as they were toward each other. In a world in which success was the only virtue, he had resigned himself to failure. He was painfully aware that he lacked the ecclesiastical aplomb and savoir-faire that enabled so many of his colleagues in other faiths and sects to get ahead. He was just not equipped to excel. He thought of himself as ugly and wanted daily to be home with his wife.

Actually, the chaplain was almost good-looking, with a pleasant, sensitive face as pale and brittle as sandstone. His mind was open on every subject.

Perhaps he really was Washington Irving, and perhaps he really had been signing Washington Irving's name to those letters he knew nothing about. Such lapses of memory were not uncommon in medical annals, he knew. There was no way of really knowing anything. He remembered very distinctly – or was under the impression he remembered very distinctly – his feeling that he had met Yossarian somewhere before the first time he *had* met Yossarian lying in bed in the hospital. He remembered experiencing the same disquieting sensation almost two weeks later when Yossarian appeared at his tent to ask to be taken off combat duty. By that time, of course, the chaplain *had* met Yossarian somewhere before, in that odd, unorthodox ward in which every patient seemed delinquent but the unfortunate patient covered from head to toe in white bandages and plaster who was found dead one day with a thermometer in his mouth. But the chaplain's impression of a prior meeting was of some occasion far more momentous and occult than that, of a significant encounter with Yossarian in some remote, submerged and perhaps even entirely spiritual epoch in which he had made the identical, foredooming admission that there was nothing, absolutely nothing, he could do to help him.

Doubts of such kind gnawed at the chaplain's lean, suffering frame insatiably. *Was* there a single true faith, or a life after death? How many angels *could* dance on the head of a pin, and with what matters *did* God occupy himself in all the infinite aeons before the Creation? Why was it necessary to put a protective seal on the brow of Cain if there *were* no other people to protect him from? *Did* Adam and Eve produce daughters? These were the great, complex questions of ontology that tormented him. Yet they never seemed nearly as crucial to him as the question of kindness and good manners. He was pinched perspiringly in the epistemological dilemma of the skeptic, unable to accept solutions to problems he was unwilling to dismiss as unsolvable. He was never without misery, and never without hope.

'Have you ever,' he inquired hesitantly of Yossarian that day in his tent as Yossarian sat holding in both hands the warm bottle of Coca-Cola with which the chaplain had been able to solace him, 'been in a situation which you felt you had been in before, even though you knew you were experiencing it for the first time?' Yossarian nodded perfunctorily, and the chaplain's breath quickened in anticipation as he made ready to join his will power with Yossarian's in a prodigious effort to rip away at last the voluminous black folds shrouding the eternal mysteries of existence. 'Do you have that feeling now?'

Yossarian shook his head and explained that *déjà vu* was just a momentary infinitesimal lag in the operation of two coactive sensory nerve centers that commonly functioned simultaneously. The chaplain scarcely heard him. He was disappointed, but not inclined to believe Yossarian, for he had been given a sign, a secret, enigmatic vision that he still lacked the boldness to divulge. There was no mistaking the awesome implications of the chaplain's revelation: it was either an insight of divine origin or a hallucination; he was either blessed or losing his mind. Both prospects filled him with equal fear and depression. It was neither *déjà vu, presque vu* nor *jamais vu*. It was possible that there were other *vus* of which he had never heard and that one of these other *vus* would explain succinctly the baffling phenomenon of which he had been both a witness and a part; it was even possible that none of what he thought had taken place, really *had* taken place, that he was dealing with an aberration of memory rather than of perception, that he never really *had* thought he had seen, that his impression now that he once had thought so was merely the *illusion* of an illusion, and that he was only now imagining that he had ever once imagined seeing a naked man sitting in a tree at the cemetery.

It was obvious to the chaplain now that he was not

particularly well suited to his work, and he often speculated whether he might not be happier serving in some other branch of the service, as a private in the infantry or field artillery, perhaps, or even as a paratrooper. He had no real friends. Before meeting Yossarian, there was no one in the group with whom he felt at ease, and he was hardly at ease with Yossarian, whose frequent rash and insubordinate outbursts kept him almost constantly on edge and in an ambiguous state of enjoyable trepidation. The chaplain felt safe when he was at the officers' club with Yossarian and Dunbar, and even with just Nately and McWatt. When he sat with them he had no need to sit with anyone else; his problem of where to sit was solved, and he was protected against the undesired company of all those fellow officers who invariably welcomed him with excessive cordiality when he approached and waited uncomfortably for him to go away. He made so many people uneasy. Everyone was always very friendly toward him, and no one was ever very nice; everyone spoke to him, and one one ever said anything. Yossarian and Dunbar were much more relaxed, and the chaplain was hardly uncomfortable with them at all. They even defended him the night Colonel Cathcart tried to throw him out of the officers' club again, Yossarian rising truculently to intervene and Nately shouting out, '*Yossarian!*' to restrain him. Colonel Cathcart turned white as a sheet at the sound of Yossarian's name, and, to everyone's amazement, retreated in horrified disorder until he bumped into General Dreedle, who elbowed him away with annoyance and ordered him right back to order the chaplain to start coming into the officers' club every night again.

The chaplain had almost as much trouble keeping track of his status at the officers' club as he had remembering at which of the ten mess halls in the group he was scheduled to eat his next meal. He would just as soon have remained kicked out of the officers' club, had it not been for the pleasure he was now finding there with his new companions. If the chaplain did not go to the officers' club at night, there was no place else he could go. He would pass the time at Yossarian's and Dunbar's table with a shy, reticent smile, seldom speaking unless addressed, a glass of thick sweet wine almost untasted before him as he toyed unfamiliarly with the tiny corncob pipe that he affected self-consciously and occasionally stuffed with tobacco and smoked. He enjoyed listening to Nately, whose maudlin, bittersweet lamentations mirrored much of his own romantic desolation and never failed to evoke in him resurgent tides of longing for his wife and children. The chaplain would encourage Nately with nods of comprehension or assent, amused by his candor and immaturity. Nately did not glory too immodestly that his girl was a prostitute, and the chaplain's awareness stemmed mainly from Captain Black, who never slouched past their table without a broad wink at the chaplain and some tasteless, wounding jibe about her to Nately. The chaplain did not approve of Captain Black and found it difficult not to wish him evil.

No one, not even Nately, seemed really to appreciate that he, Chaplain Robert Oliver Shipman, was not just a chaplain but a human being, that he *could* have a charming, passionate, pretty wife whom he loved almost insanely and three small blue-eyed children with strange, forgotten faces who would grow up someday to regard him as a freak and who might never forgive him for all the social embarrassment his vocation would cause them. Why couldn't anybody understand that he was not really a freak but a normal, lonely adult trying to lead a normal, lonely adult life? If they pricked him, didn't he bleed? And if he was tickled, didn't he laugh? It seemed never to have occurred to them that he, just as they, had eyes, hands, organs, dimensions, senses and affections, that he was wounded by the same kind of weapons they were, warmed and cooled by the same breezes and fed by the same kind of food, although, he was forced to concede, in a different mess hall for each successive meal. The only person who did seem to realize he had feelings was Corporal Whitcomb, who

343

had just managed to bruise them all by going over his head to Colonel Cathcart with his proposal for sending form letters of condolence home to the families of men killed or wounded in combat.

The chaplain's wife was the one thing in the world he *could* be certain of, and it would have been sufficient, if only he had been left to live his life out with just her and the children. The chaplain's wife was a reserved, diminutive, agreeable woman in her early thirties, very dark and very attractive, with a narrow waist, calm intelligent eyes, and small, bright, pointy teeth in a child-like face that was vivacious and petite; he kept forgetting what his children looked like, and each time he returned to their snapshots it was like seeing their faces for the first time. The chaplain loved his wife and children with such tameless intensity that he often wanted to sink to the ground helplessly and weep like a casta-way cripple. He was tormented inexorably by morbid fantasies involving them, by dire, hideous omens of illness and accident. His meditations were polluted with threats of dread diseases like Ewing's tumor and leukemia; he saw his infant son die two or three times every week because he had never taught his wife how to stop arterial bleeding; watched, in tearful, paralyzed silence, his whole family electrocuted, one after the other, at a baseboard socket because he had never told her that a human body would conduct electricity; all four went up in flames almost every night when the water heater exploded and set the two-story wooden house afire; in ghastly, heartless, revolting detail he saw his poor dear wife's trim and fragile body crushed to a viscous pulp against the brick wall of a market building by a half-witted drunken automobile driver and watched his hysterical five-year-old daughter being led away from the grisly scene by a kindly middle-aged gentleman with snow white hair who raped and murdered her repeatedly as soon as he had driven her off to a deserted sandpit, while his two younger children starved to death slowly in the house after his wife's mother, who had been baby-sitting, dropped dead from a heart attack when news of his wife's accident was given to her over the telephone. The chaplain's wife was a sweet, soothing, considerate woman, and he yearned to touch the warm flesh of her slender arm again and stroke her smooth black hair, to hear her intimate, comforting voice. She was a much stronger person than he was. He wrote brief, untroubled letters to her once a week, sometimes twice. He wanted to write urgent love letters to her all day long and crowd the endless pages with desperate, uninhibited confessions of his humble worship and need and with careful instructions for administering artificial respiration. He wanted to pour out to her in torrents of self-pity all his unbearable loneliness and despair and warn her never to leave the boric acid or the aspirin in reach of the children or to cross a street against the traffic light. He did not wish to worry her. The chaplain's wife was intuitive, gentle, compassionate and responsive. Almost inevitably, his reveries of reunion with her ended in explicits acts of love-making.

The chaplain felt most deceitful presiding at funerals, and it would not have astonished him to learn that the apparition in the tree that day was a manifestation of the Almighty's censure for the blasphemy and pride inherent in his function. To simulate gravity, feign grief and pretend supernatural intelligence of the hereafter in so fearsome and arcane a circumstance as death seemed the most criminal of offenses. He recalled – or was almost convinced he recalled – the scene at the cemetery perfectly. He could still see Major Major and Major Danby standing somber as broken stone pillars on either side of him, see almost the exact number of enlisted men and almost the exact places in which they had stood, see the four unmoving men with spades, the repulsive coffin and the large, loose, triumphant mound of reddish-brown earth, and the massive, still, depthless, muffling sky, so weirdly blank and blue that day it was almost poisonous. He would remember them forever, for they were all part and parcel of the most extraordinary event that had ever befallen him, an event perhaps marvelous, perhaps pathological – the vision of the naked man in the tree. How could he explain it? It was not already seen or never seen, and certainly not almost seen; neither *déjà vu, jamais vu* nor *presque vu* was elastic enough to cover it. Was it a ghost, then? The dead man's soul? An angel from heaven or a minion from hell? Or was the whole fantastic episode merely the figment of a diseased imagination, his own, of a deteriorating mind, a rotting brain? The possibility that there really had been a naked man in the tree – two men, actually, since the first had been joined shortly by a second man clad in a brown mustache and sinister dark garments from head to toe who bent forward ritualistically along the limb of the tree to offer the first man something to drink from a brown goblet – never crossed the chaplain's mind.

The chaplain was sincerely a very helpful person who was never able to help anyone, not even Yossarian when he finally decided to seize the bull by the horns and visit Major Major secretly to learn if, as Yossarian had said, the men in Colonel Cathcart's group really were being forced to fly more combat missions than anyone else. It was a daring, impulsive move on which the chaplain decided after quarreling with Corporal Whitcomb again and washing down with tepid canteen water his joyless lunch of Milky Way and Baby Ruth. He went to Major Major on foot so that Corproal Whitcomb would not see him leaving, stealing into the forest noiselessly until the two tents in his clearing were left behind, then dropping down inside the abandoned railroad ditch, where the footing was surer. He hurried along the fossilized wooden ties with accumulating mutinous anger. He had been browbeaten and humiliated successively that morning by Colonel Cathcart, Colonel Korn and Corporal Whitcomb. He just *had* to make himself felt in some respect! His slight chest was soon puffing for breath. He moved as swiftly as he could without breaking into a run, fearing his resolution might dissolve if he slowed. Soon he saw a uniformed figure coming toward him between the rusted rails. He clambered immediately up the side of the ditch, ducked inside a dense copse of low trees for concealment and sped along in his original direction a narrow, overgrown mossy path he found winding deep inside the shaded forest. It was tougher going there, but he plunged ahead with the same reckless and consuming determination, slipping and stumbling often and stinging his unprotected hands on the stubborn branches blocking his way until the bushes and tall ferns on both sides spread open and he lurched past an olive-drab military trailer on cinder blocks clearly visible through the thinning underbrush. He continued past a tent with a luminous pear-gray cat sunning itself outside and past another trailer on cinder blocks and then burst into the clearing of Yossarian's squadron. A salty dew had formed on his lips. He did not pause, but strode directly across the clearing into the orderly room, where he was welcomed by a gaunt, stoop-shouldered staff sergeant with prominent cheekbones and long, very light blond hair, who informed him graciously that he could go right in, since Major Major was out.

The chaplain thanked him with a curt nod and proceeded alone down the aisle between the desks and typewriters to the canvas partition in the rear. He bobbed through the triangular opening and found himself inside an empty office. The flap fell closed behind him. He was breathing hard and sweating profusely. The office remained empty. He thought he heard furtive whispering. Ten minutes passed. He looked about in stern displeasure, his jaws clamped together indomitably, and then turned suddenly to water as he remembered the staff sergeant's exact words: he could go right in, since Major Major was out. *The enlisted men were playing a practical joke!* The chaplain shrank back from the wall in terror, bitter tears springing to his eyes. A pleading whimper escaped his trembling lips. Major

347

Major was elsewhere, and the enlisted men in the other room had made him the butt of an inhuman prank. He could almost see them waiting on the other side of the canvas wall, bunched up expectantly like a pack of greedy, gloating omnivorous beasts of prey, ready with their barbaric mirth and jeers to pounce on him brutally the moment he reappeared. He cursed himself for his gullibility and wished in panic for something like a mask or a pair of dark glasses and a false mustache to disguise him, or for a forceful, deep voice like Colonel Cathcart's and broad, muscular shoulders and biceps to enable him to step outside fearlessly and vanquish his malevolent persecutors with an overbearing authority and self-confidence that would make them all quail and slink away cravenly in repentance. He lacked the courage to face them. The only other way out was the window. The coast was clear, and the chaplain jumped out of Major Major's office through the window, darted swiftly around the corner of the tent, and leaped down inside the railroad ditch to hide.

He scooted away with his body doubled over and his face contorted intentionally into a nonchalant, sociable smile in case anyone chanced to see him. He abandoned the ditch for the forest the moment he saw someone coming toward him from the opposite direction and ran through the cluttered forest frenziedly like someone pursued, his cheeks burning with disgrace. He heard loud, wild peals of derisive laughter crashing all about him and caught blurred glimpses of wicked, beery faces smirking far back inside the bushes and high overhead in the foliage of the trees. Spasms of scorching pains stabbed through his lungs and slowed him to a crippled walk. He lunged and staggered onward until he could go no farther and collapsed all at once against a gnarled apple tree, banging his head hard against the trunk as he toppled forward and holding on with both arms to keep from falling. His breathing was a rasping, moaning din in his ears. Minutes passed like hours before he finally recognized himself as the source of the turbulent roar that was overwhelming him. The pains in his chest abated. Soon he felt strong enough to stand. He cocked his ears craftily. The forest was quiet. There was no demonic laughter, no one was chasing him. He was too tired and sad and dirty to feel relieved. He straightened his disheveled clothing with fingers that were numb and shaking and walked the rest of the way to the clearing with rigid self-control. The chaplain brooded often about the danger of heart attack.

Corporal Whitcomb's jeep was still parked in the clearing. The chaplain tiptoed stealthily around the back of Corporal Whitcomb's tent rather than pass the entrance and risk being seen and insulted by him. Heaving a grateful sigh, he slipped quickly inside his own tent and found Corporal Whitcomb ensconced on his cot, his knees propped up. Corporal Whitcomb's mud-caked shoes were on the chaplain's blanket, and he was eating one of the chaplain's candy bars as he thumbed with sneering expression through one of the chaplain's Bibles.

'Where've you been?' he demanded rudely and disinterestedly, without looking up.

The chaplain colored and turned away evasively. 'I went for a walk through the woods.'

'All right,' Corporal Whitcomb snapped. 'Don't take me into your confidence. But just wait and see what happens to my morale.' He bit into the chaplain's candy bar hungrily and continued with a full mouth. 'You had a visitor while you were gone. Major Major.'

The chaplain spun around with surprise and cried: 'Major Major? Major Major was here?'

'That's who we're talking about, isn't it?'

'Where did he go?'

'He jumped down into that railroad ditch and took off like a frightened rabbit.' Corporal Whitcomb snickered. 'What a jerk!'

'Did he say what he wanted?'

'He said he needed your help in a matter of great importance.'

349

The chaplain was astounded. 'Major Major said *that*?'

'He didn't *say* that,' Corporal Whitcomb corrected with withering precision. 'He wrote it down in a sealed personal letter he left on your desk.'

The chaplain glanced at the bridge table that served as his desk and saw only the abominable orange-red pear-shaped plum tomato he had obtained that same morning from Colonel Cathcart, still lying on its side where he had forgotten it like an indestructible and incarnadine symbol of his own ineptitude. 'Where is the letter?'

'I threw it away as soon as I tore it open and read it.' Coporal Whitcomb slammed the Bible shut and jumped up. 'What's the matter? Won't you take my word for it?' He walked out. He walked right back in and almost collided with the chaplain, who was rushing out behind him on his way back to Major Major. 'You don't know how to delegate responsibility,' Corporal Whitcomb informed him sullenly. 'That's another one of the things that's wrong with you.'

The chaplain nodded penitently and hurried past, unable to make himself take the time to apologize. He could feel the skillful hand of fate motivating him imperatively. Twice that day already, he realized now, Major Major had come racing toward him inside the ditch; and twice that day the chaplain had stupidly postponed the destined meeting by bolting into the forest. He seethed with self-recrimination as he hastened back as rapidly as he could stride along the splintered, irregularly spaced railroad ties. Bits of grit and gravel inside his shoes and socks were grinding the tops of his toes raw. His pale, laboring face was screwed up unconsciously into a grimace of acute discomfort. The early August afternoon was growing hotter and more humid. It was almost a mile from his tent to Yossarian's squadron. The chaplain's summer-tan shirt was soaking with perspiration by the time he arrived there and rushed breathlessly back inside the orderly room tent, where he was halted peremptorily by the same treacherous, soft-spoken staff sergeant with round eyeglasses and gaunt cheeks, who requested him to remain outside because Major Major was inside and told him he would not be allowed inside until Major Major went out. The chaplain looked at him in an uncomprehending daze. Why did the sergeant hate him? he wondered. His lips were white and trembling. He was aching with thirst. What was the matter with people. Wasn't there tragedy enough? The sergeant put his hand out and held the chaplain steady.

'I'm sorry, sir,' he said regretfully in a low, courteous melancholy voice. 'But those are Major Major's orders. He never wants to see anyone.'

'He wants to see me,' the chaplain pleaded. 'He came to my tent to see me while I was here before.'

'Major Major did that?' the sergeant asked.

'Yes, he did. Please go in and ask him.'

'I'm afraid I can't go in, sir. He never wants to see me either. Perhaps if you left a note.'

'I don't want to leave a note. Doesn't he ever make an exception?'

'Only in extreme circumstances. The last time he left his tent was to attend the funeral of one of the enlisted men. The last time he saw anyone in his office was a time he was forced to. A bombardier named Yossarian forced –'

'Yossarian?' The chaplain lit up with excitement at this new coincidence. Was this another miracle in the making? 'But that's exactly whom I want to speak to him about! Did they talk about the number of missions Yossarian has to fly?'

'Yes, sir, that's exactly what they did talk about. Captain Yossarian had flown fifty-one missions, and he appealed to Major Major to ground him so that he wouldn't have to fly four more. Colonel Cathcart wanted only fifty-five missions then.'

'And what did Major Major say?'

'Major Major told him there was nothing he could do.' The chaplain's face fell. 'Major Major said that?'

'Yes, sir. In fact, he advised Yossarian to go see you for help. Are you certain you wouldn't like to leave a note, sir? I have a pencil and paper right here.'

The chaplain shook his head, chewing his clotted dry lower lip forlornly, and walked out. It was still so early in the day, and so much had already happened. The air was cooler in the forest. His throat was parched and sore. He walked slowly and asked himself ruefully what new misfortune could possibly befall him a moment before the mad hermit in the woods leaped out at him without warning from behind a mulberry bush. The captain screamed at the top of his voice.

The tall, cadaverous stranger fell back in fright at the chaplain's cry and shrieked, 'Don't hurt me!'

'Who are you?' the chaplain shouted.

'Please don't hurt me!' the man shouted back.

'I'm the chaplain!'

'Then why do you want to hurt me?'

'I don't want to hurt you!' the chaplain insisted with a rising hint of exasperation, even though he was still rooted to the spot. 'Just tell me who you are and what you want from me.'

'I just want to find out if Chief White Halfoat died of pneumonia yet,' the man shouted back. 'That's all I want. I live here. My name is Flume. I belong to the squadron, but I live here in the woods. You can ask anyone.'

The chaplain's composure began trickling back as he studied the queer, cringing figure intently. A pair of captain's bars ulcerated with rust hung on the man's ragged shirt collar. He had a hairy, tar-black mole on the underside of one nostril and a heavy rough mustache the color of poplar bark.

'Why do you live in the woods if you belong to the squadron?' the chaplain inquired curiously.

'I have to live in the woods,' the captain replied crabbily, as though the chaplain ought to know. He straightened slowly, still watching the chaplain guardedly although he towered above him by more than a full head.

'Don't you hear everybody talking about me? Chief
White Halfoat swore he was going to cut my throat some
night when I was fast asleep, and I don't dare lie down
in the squadron while he's still alive.'

The chaplain listened to the implausible explanation
distrustfully. 'But that's incredible,' he replied. 'That
would be premeditated murder. Why didn't you report
the incident to Major Major?'

'I did report the incident to Major Major,' said the
captain sadly 'and Major Major said *he* would cut my
throat if I ever spoke to him again.' The man studied the
chaplain fearfully. 'Are you going to cut my throat, too?'

'Oh, no, no, no,' the chaplain assured him. 'Of course
not. Do you really live in the forest?'

The captain nodded, and the chaplain gazed at his
porous gray pallor of fatigue and malnutrition with a
mixture of pity and esteem. The man's body was a bony
shell inside rumpled clothing that hung on him like a
disorderly collection of sacks. Wisps of dried grass were
glued all over him; he needed a haircut badly. There
were great, dark circles under his eyes. The chaplain
was moved almost to tears by the harassed, bedraggled
picture the captain presented, and he filled with deference and compassion at the thought of the many severe
rigors the poor man had to endure daily. In a voice
hushed with humility, he said,

'Who does your laundry?'

The captain pursed his lips in a businesslike manner.
'I have it done by a washerwoman in one of the farm-
houses down the road. I keep my things in my trailer and
sneak inside once or twice a day for a clean handkerchief or a change of underwear.'

'What will you do when winter comes?'

'Oh, I expect to be back in the squadron by then,' the
captain answered with a kind of martyred confidence.
'Chief White Halfoat kept promising everyone that he
was going to die of pneumonia, and I guess I'll have to
be patient until the weather turns a little colder and
damper.' He scrutinized the chaplain perplexedly. 'Don't

you know all this? Don't you hear all the fellows talking about me?'

'I don't think I've ever heard anyone mention you.'

'Well, I certainly can't understand that.' The captain was piqued, but managed to carry on with a pretense of optimism. 'Well, here it is almost September already, so I guess it won't be too long now. The next time any of the boys ask about me, why, just tell them I'll be back grinding out those old publicity releases again as soon as Chief White Halfoat dies of pneumonia. Will you tell them that? Say I'll be back in the squadron as soon as winter comes and Chief Halfoat dies of pneumonia. Okay?'

The chaplain memorized the prophetic words solemnly, entranced further by their esoteric import. 'Do you live on berries, herbs and roots?' he asked.

'No, of course not,' the captain replied with surprise. 'I sneak into the mess hall through the back and eat in the kitchen. Milo gives me sandwiches and milk.'

'What do you do when it rains?'

The captain answered frankly. 'I get wet.'

'Where do you sleep?'

Swiftly the captain ducked down into a crouch and began backing away. 'You too?' he cried frantically.

'Oh, no,' cried the chaplain. 'I swear to you.'

'You *do* want to cut my throat!' the captain insisted.

'I give my word,' the chaplain pleaded, but it was too late, for the homely hirsute specter had already vanished, dissolving so expertly inside the blooming, dappled, fragmented malformations of leaves, light and shadows that the chaplain was already doubting that he had even been there. So many monstrous events were occurring that he was no longer positive which events *were* monstrous and which *were* really taking place. He wanted to find out about the madman in the woods as quickly as possible, to check if there ever really *had* been a Captain Flume, but his first chore, he recalled with reluctance, was to appease Corporal Whitcomb for neglecting to delegate enough responsibility to him. He plodded along the zig-zagging path through the forest listlessly, clogged with thirst and feeling almost too exhausted to go on. He was remorseful when he thought of Corporal Whitcomb. He prayed that Corporal Whitcomb would be gone when he reached the clearing so that he could undress without embarrassment, wash his arms and chest and shoulders thoroughly, drink water, lie down refreshed and perhaps even sleep for a few minutes; but he was in for still another disappointment and still another shock, for Corporal Whitcomb was *Sergeant* Whitcomb by the time he arrived and was sitting with his shirt off in the chaplain's chair sewing his new sergeant's stripes on his sleeve with the chaplain's needle and thread. Corporal Whitcomb had been promoted by Colonel Cathcart, who wanted to see the chaplain at once about the letters.

'Oh, no,' groaned the chaplain, sinking down dumbfounded on his cot. His warm canteen was empty, and he was too distraught to remember the lister bag hanging outside in the shade between the two tents. 'I can't believe it. I just can't believe that anyone would seriously believe that I've been forging Washington Irving's name.'

'Not those letters,' Corporal Whitcomb corrected, plainly enjoying the chaplain's chagrin. 'He wants to see you about the letters home to the families of casualties.'

'Those letters?' asked the chaplain with surprise.

'That's right,' Corporal Whitcomb gloated. 'He's really going to chew you out for refusing to let me send them. You should have seen him go for the idea once I reminded him the letters could carry his signature. That's why he promoted me. He's absolutely sure they'll get him into *The Saturday Evening Post*.'

The chaplain's befuddlement increased. 'But how did he know we were even considering the idea?'

'I went to his office and told him.'

'You did what?' the chaplain demanded shrilly, and charged to his feet in an unfamiliar rage. 'Do you mean to say that you actually went over my head to the colonel without asking my permission?'

355

Corporal Whitcomb grinned brazenly with scornful satisfaction. 'That's right, Chaplain,' he answered. 'And you better not try to do anything about it if you know what's good for you.' He laughed quietly in malicious defiance. 'Colonel Cathcart isn't going to like it if he finds out you're getting even with me for bringing him my idea. You know something, Chaplain?' Corporal Whitcomb continued, biting the chaplain's black thread apart contemptuously with a loud snap and buttoning on his shirt. 'That dumb bastard really thinks it's one of the greatest ideas he's ever heard.'

'It might even get me into *The Saturday Evening Post*,' Colonel Cathcart boasted in his office with a smile, swaggering back and forth convivially as he reproached the chaplain. 'And you didn't have brains enough to appreciate it. You've got a good man in Corporal Whitcomb, Chaplain. I hope you have brains enough to appreciate *that*.'

'Sergeant Whitcomb,' the chaplain corrected, before he could control himself.

Colonel Cathcart glared. 'I *said* Sergeant Whitcomb,' he replied. 'I wish you'd try listening once in a while instead of always finding fault. You don't want to be a captain all your life, do you?'

'Sir?'

'Well, I certainly don't see how you're ever going to amount to anything else if you keep on this way. Corporal Whitcomb feels that you fellows haven't had a fresh idea in nineteen hundred and forty-four years, and I'm inclined to agree with him. A bright boy, that Corporal Whitcomb. Well, it's all going to change.' Colonel Cathcart sat down at his desk with a determined air and cleared a large neat space in his blotter. When he had finished, he tapped his finger inside it. 'Starting tomorrow,' he said, 'I want you and Corporal Whitcomb to write a letter of condolence for me to the next of kin of every man in the group who's killed, wounded or taken prisoner. I want those letters to be sincere letters. I want them filled up with lots of personal details so there'll be no doubt I mean every word you say. Is that clear?'

The chaplain stepped forward impulsively to remonstrate. 'But, sir, that's impossible!' he blurted out. 'We don't even know all the men that well.'

'What difference does that make?' Colonel Cathcart demanded, and then smiled amicably. 'Corporal Whitcomb brought me this basic form letter that takes care of just about every situation. Listen: "Dear Mrs., Mr., Miss, or Mr. and Mrs.: Words cannot express the deep personal grief I experienced when your husband, son, father or brother was killed, wounded or reported missing in action." And so on. I think that opening sentence sums up my sentiments exactly. Listen maybe you'd better let Corporal Whitcomb take charge of the whole thing if you don't feel up to it.' Colonel Cathcart whipped out his cigarette holder and flexed it between both hands like an onyx and ivory riding crop. 'That's one of the things that's wrong with you, Chaplain. Corporal Whitcomb tells me you don't know how to delegate responsibility. He says you've got no initiative either. You're not going to disagree with me, are you?'

'No, sir.' The chaplain shook his head, feeling despicably remiss because he did not know how to delegate responsibility and had no initiative, and because he really had been tempted to disagree with the colonel. His mind was a shambles. They were shooting skeet outside, and every time a gun was fired his senses were jarred. He could not adjust to the sound of the shots. He was surrounded by bushels of plum tomatoes and was almost convinced that he had stood in Colonel Cathcart's office on some similar occasion deep in the past and had been surrounded by those same bushels of those same plum tomatoes. Déjà vu again. The setting seemed so familiar; yet it also seemed so distant. His clothes felt grimy and old, and he was deathly afraid he smelled.

'You take things too seriously, Chaplain,' Colonel Cathcart told him bluntly with an air of adult objectivity. 'That's another one of the things that's wrong with you.

That long face of yours gets everybody depressed. Let me see you laugh once in a while. Come on, Chaplain. You give me a belly laugh now and I'll give you a whole bushel of plum tomatoes.' He waited a second or two, watching, and then chortled victoriously. 'You see, Chaplain, I'm right. You can't give me a belly laugh, can you?'

'No, sir,' admitted the chaplain meekly, swallowing slowly with a visible effort. 'Not right now. I'm very thirsty.'

'Then get yourself a drink. Colonel Korn keeps some bourbon in his desk. You ought to try dropping around the officers' club with us some evening just to have yourself a little fun. Try getting lit once in a while. I hope you don't feel you're better than the rest of us just because you're a professional man.'

'Oh, no, sir,' the chaplain assured him with embarrassment. 'As a matter of fact, I have been going to the officers' club the past few evenings.'

'You're only a captain, you know,' Colonel Cathcart continued, paying no attention to the chaplain's remark. 'You may be a professional man, but you're still only a captain.'

'Yes, sir. I know.'

'That's fine, then. It's just as well you didn't laugh before. I wouldn't have given you the plum tomatoes anyway. Corporal Whitcomb tells me you took a plum tomato when you were in here this morning.'

'This morning? But, sir! You gave it to me.'

Colonel Cathcart cocked his head with suspicion. 'I didn't say I didn't give it to you, did I? I merely said you took it. I don't see why you've got such a guilty conscience if you really didn't steal it. Did I give it to you?'

'Yes, sir. I swear you did.'

'Then I'll just have to take your word for it. Although I can't imagine why I'd want to give you a plum tomato.' Colonel Cathcart transferred a round glass paperweight competently from the right edge of his desk to the left edge and picked up a sharpened pencil. 'Okay.

Chaplain, I've got a lot of important work to do now if your're through. You let me know when Corporal Whitcomb has sent out about a dozen of those letters and we'll get in touch with the editors of *The Saturday Evening Post*.' A sudden inspiration made his face brighten. 'Say! I think I'll volunteer the group for Avignon again. That should speed things up!'

'For Avignon?' the chaplain's heart missed a beat, and all his flesh began to prickle and creep.

'That's right,' the colonel explained exuberantly. 'The sooner we get some casualties, the sooner we can make some progress on this. I'd like to get in the Christmas issue if we can. I imagine the circulation is higher then.'

And to the chaplain's horror, the colonel lifted the phone to volunteer the group for Avignon and tried to kick him out of the officers' club again that very same night a moment before Yossarian rose up drunkenly, knocking over his chair, to start an avenging punch that made Nately call out his name and made Colonel Cathcart blanch and retreat prudently smack into General Dreedle, who shoved him off his bruised foot disgustedly and order him forward to kick the chaplain right back into the officers' club. It was all very upsetting to Colonel Cathcart, first the dreaded name *Yossarian!* tolling out again clearly like a warning of doom and then General Dreedle's bruised foot, and that was another fault Colonel Cathcart found in the chaplain, the fact that is was impossible to predict *how* General Dreedle would react each time he saw him. Colonel Cathcart would never forget the first evening General Dreedle took notice of the chaplain in the officers' club, lifting his ruddy, sweltering, intoxicated face to stare ponderously through the yellow pall of cigarette smoke at the chaplain lurking near the wall by himself.

'Well, I'll be damned,' General Dreedle had exclaimed hoarsely, his shaggy gray menacing eyebrows beetling in recognition. 'Is that a chaplain I see over there? That's really a fine thing when a man of God begins hanging around a place like this with a bunch of dirty drunks and gamblers.'

Colonel Cathcart compressed his lips primly and started to rise. 'I couldn't agree with you more, sir,' he assented briskly in a tone of ostentatious disapproval. 'I just don't know what's happening to the clergy these days.'

'They're getting better, that's what's happening to them,' General Dreedle growled emphatically.

Colonel Cathcart gulped awkwardly and made a nimble recovery. 'Yes, sir. They are getting better. That's exactly what I had in mind, sir.'

'This is just the place for a chaplain to be, mingling with the men while they're out drinking and gambling so he can get to understand them and win their confidence. How the hell else is he ever going to get them to believe in God?'

'That's exactly what I had in mind, sir, when I ordered him to come here,' Colonel Cathcart said carefully, and threw his arm familiarly around the chaplain's shoulders as he walked him off into a corner to order him in a cold undertone to start reporting for duty at the officers' club every evening to mingle with the men while they were drinking and gambling so that he could get to understand them and win their confidence.

The chaplain agreed and did report for duty to the officers' club every night to mingle with men who wanted to avoid him, until the evening the vicious fist fight broke out at the ping-pong table and Chief White Halfoat whirled without provocation and punched Colonel Moodus squarely in the nose, knocking Colonel Moodus down on the seat of his pants and making General Dreedle roar with lusty, unexpected laughter until he spied the chaplain standing close by gawking at him grotesquely in tortured wonder. General Dreedle froze at the sight of him. He glowered at the chaplain with swollen fury for a moment, his good humor gone, and turned back toward the bar disgruntledly, rolling from side to side like a sailor on his short bandy legs. Colonel Cathcart cantered fearfully along behind, glancing anxiously about in vain for some sign of help from Colonel Korn.

'That's a fine thing,' General Dreedle growled at the bar, gripping his empty shot glass in his burly hand. 'That's really a fine thing, when a man of God begins hanging around a place like this with a bunch of dirty drunks and gamblers.'

Colonel Cathcart sighed with relief. 'Yes, sir,' he exclaimed proudly. 'It certainly is a fine thing.'

'Then why the hell don't you do something about it?'

'Sir?' Colonel Cathcart inquired, blinking.

'Do you think it does you credit to have your chaplain hanging around here every night? He's in here every goddam time I come.'

'You're right, sir, absolutely right,' Colonel Cathcart responded. 'It does me no credit at all. And I *am* going to do something about it, this very minute.'

'Aren't you the one who ordered him to come here?'

'No, sir, that was Colonel Korn. I intend to punish him severely, too.'

'If he wasn't a chaplain,' General Dreedle muttered, 'I'd have him taken outside and shot.'

'He's not a chaplain, sir.' Colonel Cathcart advised helpfully.

'Isn't he? Then why the hell does he wear that cross on his collar if he's not a chaplain?'

'He doesn't wear a cross on his collar, sir. He wears a silver leaf. He's a lieutenant colonel.'

'You've got a chaplain who's a lieutenant colonel?' inquired General Dreedle with amazement.

'Oh, no, sir. My chaplain is only a captain.'

'Then why the hell does he wear a silver leaf on his collar if he's only a captain?'

'He doesn't wear a silver leaf on his collar, sir. He wears a cross.'

'Go away from mē now, you son of a bitch,' said General Dreedle. 'Or I'll have you taken outside and shot!'

'Yes, sir.'

Colonel Cathcart went away from General Dreedle with a gulp and kicked the chaplain out of the officers' club, and it was exactly the way it almost was t⋅

months later after the chaplain had tried to persuade Colonel Cathcart to rescind his order increasing the number of missions to sixty and had failed abysmally in that endeavor too, and the chaplain was ready now to capitulate to despair entirely but was restrained by the memory of his wife, whom he loved and missed so pathetically with such sensual and exalted ardor, and by the lifelong trust he had placed in the wisdom and justice of an immortal, omnipotent, omniscient, humane, universal, anthropomorphic, English-speaking, Anglo-Saxon, pro-American God, which had begun to waver. So many things were testing his faith. There was the Bible, of course, but the Bible was a book, and so were *Bleak House, Treasure Island, Ethan Frome* and *The Last of the Mohicans.* Did it then seem probable, as he had once overheard Dunbar ask, that the answers to the riddles of creation would be supplied by people too ignorant to understand the mechanics of rainfall? Had Almighty God, in all His infinite wisdom, really been afraid that men six thousand years ago would succeed in building a tower to heaven? Where the devil *was* heaven? Was it up? Down? There was no up or down in a finite but expanding universe in which even the vast, burning, dazzling, majestic sun was in a state of progressive decay that would eventually destroy the earth too. There were no miracles; prayers went unanswered, and misfortune tramped with equal brutality on the virtuous and the corrupt; and the chaplain, who had conscience and character, would have yielded to reason and relinquished his belief in the God of his fathers – would truly have resigned both his calling and his commission and taken his chances as a private in the infantry or field artillery, or even, perhaps, as a corporal in the paratroopers – had it not been for such successive mystic phenomena as the naked man in the tree at that ̶s̶e̶r̶geant's funeral weeks before and the cryptic, ̶u̶n̶m̶i̶s̶t̶a̶k̶a̶b̶l̶e̶ promise of the prophet Flume in ̶t̶h̶e̶ ̶f̶o̶r̶e̶s̶t̶ ̶t̶h̶at afternoon: '*tell them I'll be back ̶w̶i̶t̶h̶ ̶t̶h̶e̶m̶ ̶b̶y̶ ̶C̶h̶r̶i̶s̶t̶m̶a̶s̶.*'

26 Aarfy

In a way it was all Yossarian's fault, for if he had not moved the bomb line during the Big Siege of Bologna, Major — de Coverley might still be around to save him, and if he had not stocked the enlisted men's apartment with girls who had no other place to live, Nately might never have fallen in love with his whore as she sat naked from waist down in the room full of grumpy blackjack players who ignored her. Nately stared at her covertly from his over-stuffed yellow armchair, marveling at the bored, phlegmatic strength with which she accepted the mass rejection. She yawned, and he was deeply moved. He had never witnessed such heroic poise before.

The girl had climbed five steep flights of stairs to sell herself to the group of satiated enlisted men, who had girls living there all around them; none wanted her at any price, not even after she had stripped without real enthusiasm to tempt them with a tall body that was firm and full and truly voluptuous. she seemed more fatigued than disappointed. Now She sat resting in vacuous indolence, watching the card game with dull curiosity as she gathered her recalcitrant energies for the tedious chore of donning the rest of her clothing and going back to work. In a little while she stirred. A little while later she rose with an unconscious sigh and stepped lethargically into her tight cotton panties and dark skirt, then buckled on her shoes and left. Nately slipped out behind her; and when Yossarian and Aarfy entered the officers' apartment almost two hours later, there she was again, stepping into her panties and skirt, and it was almost like the chaplain's recurring sensation of having been through a situation before, except for Nately, who was moping inconsolably with his hands in his pockets.

'She wants to go now,' he said in a faint, strange voice. 'She doesn't want to stay.'

'Why don't you just pay her some money to let you spend the rest of the day with her?' Yossarian advised.

'She gave me my money back,' Nately admitted. 'She's tired of me now and wants to go looking for someone else.'

The girl paused when her shoes were on to glance in surly invitation at Yossarian and Aarfy. Her breasts were pointy and large in the thin white sleeveless sweater she wore that squeezed each contour and flowed outward smoothly with the tops of her enticing hips. Yossarian returned her gaze and was strongly attracted. He shook his head.

'Good riddance to bad rubbish,' was Aarfy's unperturbed response.

'Don't say that about her!' Nately protested with passion that was both a plea and a rebuke. 'I want her to stay with me.'

'What's so special about her?' Aarfy sneered with mock surprise. 'She's only a whore.'

'And don't call her a whore!'

The girl shrugged impassively after a few more seconds and ambled toward the door. Nately bounded forward wretchedly to hold it open. He wandered back in a heartbroken daze, his sensitive face eloquent with grief.

'Don't worry about it,' Yossarian counseled him as kindly as he could. 'You'll probably be able to find her again. We know where all the whores hang out.'

'Please don't call her that,' Nately begged, looking as though be might cry.

'I'm sorry,' murmured Yossarian.

Aarfy thundered jovially. 'There are hundreds of whores just as good crawling all over the streets. That one wasn't even pretty.' He chuckled mellifluously with resonant disdain and authority. 'Why, you rushed forward to open that door as though you were in love with her.'

'I think I am in love with her,' Nately confessed in a shamed, far-off voice.

Aarfy wrinkled his chubby round rosy forehead in comic disbelief. 'Ho, ho, ho, ho!' he laughed, patting the expansive forest-green sides of his officer's tunic prosperously. 'That's rich. You in love with her? That's really rich.' Aarfy had a date that same afternoon with a Red Cross girl from Smith whose father owned an important milk-of-magnesia plant. 'Now, that's the kind of girl you ought to be associating with, and not with common sluts like that one. Why, she didn't even look clean.'

'I don't care!' Nately shouted desperately. 'And I wish you'd shut up, I don't even want to talk about it with you.'

'Aarfy, shut up,' said Yossarian.

'Ho, ho, ho, ho!' Aarfy continued. 'I just can't imagine what your father and mother would say if they knew you were running around with filthy trollops like that one. Your father is a very distinguished man, you know.'

'I'm not going to tell him,' Nately declared with determination. 'I'm not going to say a word about her to him or Mother until after we're married.'

'Married?' Aarfy's indulgent merriment swelled tremendously. 'Ho, ho, ho, ho, ho! Now you're really talking stupid. Why, you're not even old enough to know what true love is.'

Aarfy was an authority on the subject of true love because he had already fallen truly in love with Nately's father and with the prospect of working for him after the war in some executive capacity as a reward for befriending Nately. Aarfy was a lead navigator who had never been able to find himself since leaving college. He was a genial, magnanimous lead navigator who could always forgive the other man in the squadron for denouncing him furiously each time he got lost on a combat mission and led them over concentrations of antiaircraft fire. He got lost on the streets of Rome that same afternoon and never did find the eligible Red Cross girl from Smith with the important milk-of-magnesia plant. He got lost on the mission to Ferrara the day Kraft was shot down and killed, and he got lost again on the weekly milk run to Parma and tried to lead the planes out to sea over the city of Leghorn after Yossarian had dropped his bombs on the undefended inland target and settled back against his thick wall of armor plate with his eyes closed and a fragrant cigarette in his finger tips. Suddenly there was flak, and all at once McWatt was shrieking over the intercom, 'Flak! Flak! Where the hell are we? What the hell's going on?'

Yossarian flipped his eyes open in alarm and saw the totally unexpected bulging black puffs of flak crashing down in toward them from high up and Aarfy's complacent melon-round tiny-eyed face gazing out at the approaching cannon bursts with affable bemusement. Yossarian was flabbergasted. His leg went abruptly to sleep. McWatt had started to climb and was yelping over the intercom for instructions. Yossarian sprang forward to see where they were and remained in the same place. He was unable to move. Then he realized he was sopping wet. He looked down at his crotch with a sinking, sick sensation. A wild crimson blot was crawling upward rapidly along his shirt front like an enormous sea monster rising to devour him. He was hit! Separate trickles of blood spilled to a puddle on the floor through one saturated trouser leg like countless unstoppable swarms of wriggling red worms. His heart stopped. A second solid jolt struck the plane. Yossarian shuddered with revulsion at the queer sight of his wound and screamed at Aarfy for help.

'I lost my balls! Aarfy, I lost my balls!' Aarfy didn't

hear, and Yossarian bent forward and tugged at his arm. 'Aarfy, help me,' he pleaded, almost weeping, 'I'm hit! I'm hit!'

Aarfy turned slowly with a bland, quizzical grin. 'What?'

'I'm hit, Aarfy! Help me!'

Aarfy grinned again and shrugged amiably. 'I can't hear you,' he said.

'Can't you see me?' Yossarian cried incredulously, and he pointed to the deepening pool of blood he felt splashing down all around him and spreading out underneath. 'I'm wounded! Help me, for God's sake! Aarfy, help me!'

'I still can't hear you,' Aarfy complained tolerantly, cupping his podgy hand behind the blanched corolla of his ear. 'What did you say?'

Yossarian answered in a collapsing voice, weary suddenly of shouting so much, of the whole frustrating, exasperating, ridiculous situation. He was dying, and no one took notice. 'Never mind.'

'What?' Aarfy shouted.

'I said I lost my balls! Can't you hear me? I'm wounded in the groin!'

'I still can't hear you,' Aarfy chided.

'I said *never mind!*' Yossarian screamed with a trapped feeling of terror and began to shiver, feeling very cold suddenly and very weak.

Aarfy shook his head regretfully again and lowered his obscene, lactescent ear almost directly into Yossarian's face. 'You'll just have to speak up, my friend. You'll just have to speak up.'

'Leave me alone, you bastard! You dumb, insensitive bastard, leave me alone!' Yossarian sobbed. He wanted to pummel Aarfy, but lacked the strength to lift his arms. He decided to sleep instead and keeled over sideways into a dead faint.

He was wounded in the thigh, and when he recovered consciousness he found McWatt on both knees taking care of him. He was relieved, even though he still saw

Aarfy's bloated cherub's face hanging down over McWatt's shoulder with placid interest. Yossarian smiled feebly at McWatt, feeling ill, and asked, 'Who's minding the store?' McWatt gave no sign that he heard. With growing horror, Yossarian gathered in breath and repeated the words as loudly as he could.

McWatt looked up. 'Christ, I'm glad you're still alive!' he exclaimed, heaving an enormous sigh. The good-humored, friendly crinkles about his eyes were white with tension and oily with grime as he kept unrolling an interminable bandage around the bulky cotton compress Yossarian felt strapped burdensomely to the inside of one thigh. 'Nately's at the controls. The poor kid almost started bawling when he heard you were hit. He still thinks you're dead. They knocked open an artery for you, but I think I've got it stopped. I gave you some morphine.'

'Give me some more.'

'It might be too soon. I'll give you some more when it starts to hurt.'

'It hurts now.'

'Oh, well, what the hell,' said McWatt and injected another syrette of morphine into Yossarian's arm.

'When you tell Nately I'm all right. . .' said Yossarian to McWatt, and lost consciousness again as everything went fuzzy behind a film of strawberry-strained gelatin and a great baritone buzz swallowed him in sound. He came to in the ambulance and smiled encouragement at Doc Daneeka's weevillike, glum and overshadowed countenance for the dizzy second or two he had before everything went rose-petal pink again and then turned really black and unfathomably still.

Yossarian woke up in the hospital and went to sleep. When he woke up in the hospital again, the smell of ether was gone and Dunbar was lying in pajamas in the bed across the aisle maintaining that he was not Dunbar but *a fortiori*. Yossarian thought he was cracked. He curled his lip skeptically at Dunbar's bit of news and slept on it fitfully for a day or two, then woke up while

the nurses were elsewhere and eased himself out of bed
to see for himself. The floor swayed like the floating raft
at the beach and the stitches on the inside of his thigh bit
into his flesh like fine sets of fish teeth as he limped
across the aisle to peruse the name on the temperature
card on the foot of Dunbar's bed, but sure enough,
Dunbar was right: he was not Dunbar any more but
Second Lieutenant Anthony F. Fortiori.

'What the hell's going on?'

A. Fortiori got out of bed and motioned to Yossarian to
follow. Grasping for support at anything he could reach,
Yossarian limped along after him into the corridor and
down the adjacent ward to a bed containing a harried
young man with pimples and a receding chin. The
harried young man rose on one elbow with alacrity as
they approached. A. Fortiori jerked his thumb over his
shoulder and said, 'Screw.' The harried young man
jumped out of bed and ran away. A. Fortiori climbed into
the bed and became Dunbar again.

'That was A. Fortiori,' Dunbar explained. 'They didn't
have an empty bed in your ward, so I pulled my rank and
chased him back here into mine. It's a pretty satisfying
experience pulling rank. You ought to try it sometime.
You ought to try it right now, in fact, because you look
like you're going to fall down.'

Yossarian felt like he was going to fall down. He
turned to the lantern-jawed, leather-faced middle-aged
man lying in the bed next to Dunbar's, jerked his thumb
over his shoulder and said 'Screw.' The middle-aged
man stiffened fiercely and glared.

'He's a major,' Dunbar explained. 'Why don't you aim
a little lower and try becoming Warrant Officer Homer
Lumley for a while? Then you can have a father in the
state legislature and a sister who's engaged to a champion skier. Just tell him you're a captain.'

Yossarian turned to the startled patient Dunbar had
indicated. 'I'm a captain,' he said, jerking his thumb
over his shoulder. 'Screw.'

The startled patient jumped down to the floor at

Yossarian's command and ran away. Yossarian climbed up into his bed and became Warrant Officer Homer Lumley, who felt like vomiting and was covered suddenly with a clammy sweat. He slept for an hour and wanted to be Yossarian again. It did not mean so much to have a father in the state legislature and a sister who was engaged to a champion skier. Dunbar led the way back to Yossarian's ward, where he thumbed A. Fortiori out of bed to become Dunbar again for a while. There was no sign of Warrant Officer Homer Lumley. Nurse Cramer was there, though, and sizzled with sanctimonious anger like a damp firecracker. She ordered Yossarian to get right back into his bed and blocked his path so he couldn't comply. Her pretty face was more repulsive than ever. Nurse Cramer was a good-hearted, sentimental creature who rejoiced unselfishly at news of weddings, engagements, births and anniversaries even though she was unacquainted with any of the people involved.

'Are you crazy?' she scolded virtuously, shaking an indignant finger in front of his eyes. 'I suppose you just don't care if you kill yourself, do you?'

'It's my self,' he reminded her.

'I suppose you just don't care if you lose your leg, do you?'

'It's my leg.'

'It certainly is not your leg!' Nurse Cramer retorted. 'That leg belongs to the U.S. government. It's no different than a gear or a bedpan. The Army has invested a lot of money to make you an airplane pilot, and you've no right to disobey the doctor's orders.'

Yossarian was not sure he liked being invested in. Nurse Cramer was still standing directly in front of him so that he could not pass. His head was aching. Nurse Cramer shouted at him some question he could not understand. He jerked his thumb over his shoulder and said, 'Screw.'

Nurse Cramer cracked him in the face so hard she almost knocked him down. Yossarian drew back his fist to punch her in the jaw just as his leg buckled and he began to fall. Nurse Duckett strode up in time to catch him. She addressed them both firmly.

'Just what's going on here?'

'He won't get back into his bed,' Nurse Cramer reported zealously in an injured tone. 'Sue Ann, he said something absolutely horrible to me. Oh, I can't even make myself repeat it!'

'She called me a gear,' Yossarian muttered.

Nurse Duckett was not sympathetic. 'Will you get back into bed,' she said, 'or must I take you by your ear and put you there?'

'Take me by my ear and put me there,' Yossarian dared her.

Nurse Duckett took him by his ear and put him back in bed.

27 Nurse Duckett

Nurse Sue Ann Duckett was a tall, spare, mature, straight-backed woman with a prominent, well-rounded ass, small breasts and angular ascetic New England features that came equally close to being very lovely and very plain. Her skin was white and pink, her eyes small, her nose and chin slender and sharp. She was able, prompt, strict and intelligent. She welcomed responsibility and kept her head in every crisis. She was adult and self-reliant, and there was nothing she needed from anyone. Yossarian took pity and decided to help her.

Next morning while she was standing bent over smoothing the sheets at the foot of his bed, he slipped his hand stealthily into the narrow space between her knees and, all at once, brought it up swiftly under her dress as far as it would go. Nurse Duckett shrieked and jumped into the air a mile, but it wasn't high enough, and she squirmed and vaulted and seesawed back and forth on her divine fulcrum for almost a full fifteen seconds before she wiggled free finally and retreated frantically into the aisle with an ashen, trembling face. She backed away too far, and Dunbar, who had watched from the beginning, sprang forward on his bed without warning and flung both arms around her bosom from behind.

Nurse Duckett let out another scream and twisted away, fleeing far enough from Dunbar for Yossarian to lunge forward and grab her by the snatch again. Nurse Duckett bounced out across the aisle once more like a ping-pong ball with legs. Dunbar was waiting vigilantly, ready to pounce. She remembered him just in time and leaped aside. Dunbar missed completely and sailed by her over the bed to the floor, landing on his skull with a soggy, crunching thud that knocked him cold.

He woke up on the floor with a bleeding nose and exactly the same distressful head symptoms he had been feigning all along. The ward was in a chaotic uproar. Nurse Duckett was in tears, and Yossarian was consoling her apologetically as he sat beside her on the edge of a bed. The commanding colonel was wroth and shouting at Yossarian that he would not permit his patients to take indecent liberties with his nurses.

'What do you want from him?' Dunbar asked plaintively from the floor, wincing at the vibrating pains in his temples that his voice set up. 'He didn't do anything.'

'I'm talking about you!' the thin, dignified colonel bellowed as loudly as he could. 'You're going to be punished for what you did.'

'What do you want from him?' Yossarian called out. 'All he did was fall on his head.'

'And I'm talking about you too!' the colonel declared, whirling to rage at Yossarian. 'You're going to be good and sorry you grabbed Nurse Duckett by the bosom.'

'I didn't grab Nurse Duckett by the bosom,' said Yossarian.

'*I* grabbed her by the bosom,' said Dunbar.

'Are you both crazy?' the doctor cried shrilly, backing away in paling confusion.

'Yes, he really is crazy, Doc,' Dunbar assured him. 'Every night he dreams he's holding a live fish in his hands.'

The doctor stopped in his tracks with a look of elegant amazement and distaste, and the ward grew still. '*He does what?*' he demanded.

'He dreams he's holding a live fish in his hand.'

'What kind of fish?' the doctor inquired sternly of Yossarian.

'I don't know,' Yossarian answered. 'I can't tell one kind of fish from another.'

'In which hand do you hold them?'

'It varies,' answered Yossarian.

'It varies with the fish,' Dunbar added helpfully.

The colonel turned and stared down at Dunbar suspiciously with a narrow squint. 'Yes? And how come you seem to know so much about it?'

'I'm in the dream,' Dunbar answered without cracking a smile.

The colonel's face flushed with embarrassment. He glared at them both with cold, unforgiving resentment. 'Get up off the floor and into your bed,' he directed Dunbar through thin lips. 'And I don't want to hear another word about this dream from either one of you. I've got a man on my staff to listen to disgusting bilge like this.'

'Just why do you think,' carefully inquired Major Sanderson, the soft and thickset smiling staff psychiatrist to whom the colonel had ordered Yossarian sent, 'that Colonel Ferredge finds your dream disgusting?'

Yossarian replied respectfully. 'I suppose it's either some quality in the dream or some quality in Colonel Ferredge.'

'That's very well put,' applauded Major Sanderson, who wore squeaking GI shoes and had charcoal-black hair that stood up almost straight. 'For some reason,' he confided. 'Colonel Ferredge has always reminded me of a sea gull. He doesn't put much faith in psychiatry, you know.'

'You don't like sea gulls, do you?' inquired Yossarian.

'No, not very much,' admitted Major Sanderson with a sharp, nervous laugh and pulled at his pendulous second chin lovingly as though it were a long goatee. 'I think your dream is charming, and I hope it recurs frequently so that we can continue discussing it. Would you like a cigarette?' He smiled when Yossarian declined. 'Just why do you think,' he asked knowingly, 'that you have such a strong aversion to accepting a cigarette from me?'

'I put one out a second ago. It's still smoldering in your ash tray.'

Major Sanderson chuckled. 'That's a very ingenious explanation. But I suppose we'll soon discover the true reason.' He tied a sloppy double bow in his opened shoelace and then transferred a lined yellow pad from his desk to his lap. 'This fish you dream about. Let's talk about that. It's always the same fish, isn't it?'

'I don't know,' Yossarian replied. 'I have trouble recognizing fish.'

'What does the fish remind you of?'

'Other fish.'

'And what do other fish remind you of?'

'Other fish.'

Major Sanderson sat back disappointedly. 'Do you like fish?'

'Not especially.'

'Just why do you think you have such a morbid aversion to fish?' asked Major Sanderson triumphantly.

'They're too bland,' Yossarian answered. 'And too bony.'

Major Sanderson nodded understandingly, with a smile that was agreeable and insincere. 'That's a very interesting explanation. But we'll soon discover the true reason, I suppose. Do you like this particular fish? The one you're holding in your hand?'

'I have no feelings about it either way.'

'Do you dislike the fish? Do you have any hostile or aggressive emotions toward it?'

'No, not at all. In fact, I rather like the fish.'

'Then you do like the fish.'

'Oh, no. I have no feelings toward it either way.'

'But you just said you liked it. And now you say you have no feelings toward it either way. I've just caught you in a contradiction. Don't you see?'

'Yes, sir. I suppose you have caught me in a contradiction.'

Major Sanderson proudly lettered 'Contradiction' on his pad with his thick black pencil. 'Just why do you think,' he resumed when he had finished, looking up, 'that you made those two statements expressing contradictory emotional responses to the fish?'

'I suppose I have an ambivalent attitude toward it.'

Major Sanderson sprang up with joy when he heard the words 'ambivalent attitude.' 'You do understand!' he exclaimed, wringing his hands together ecstatically. 'Oh, you can't imagine how lonely it's been for me, talking day after day to patients who haven't the slightest knowledge of psychiatry, trying to cure people who have no real interest in me or my work! It's given me such a terrible feeling of inadequacy.' A shadow of anxiety crossed his face. 'I can't seem to shake it.'

'Really?' asked Yossarian, wondering what else to say. 'Why do you blame yourself for gaps in the education of others?'

'It's silly, I know,' Major Sanderson replied uneasily with a giddy, involuntary laugh. 'But I've always depended very heavily on the good opinion of others. I reached puberty a bit later than all the other boys my age, you see, and it's given me sort of – well, all sorts of problems. I just know I'm going to enjoy discussing them with you. I'm so eager to begin that I'm almost reluctant to digress now to your problem, but I'm afraid I must. Colonel Ferredge would be cross if he knew we were spending all our time on me. I'd like to show you some ink blots now to find out what certain shapes and colors remind you of.'

'You can save yourself the trouble, Doctor. Everything reminds me of sex.'

'Does it?' cried Major Sanderson with delight, as though unable to believe his ears. 'Now we're *really* getting somewhere! Do you ever have any good sex dreams?'

'My fish dream is a sex dream.'

376

'No, I mean real sex dreams – the kind where you grab some naked bitch by the neck and pinch her and punch her in the face until she's all bloody and then throw yourself down to ravish her and burst into tears because you love her and hate her so much you don't know what else to do. *That's* the kind of sex dreams I like to talk about. Don't you ever have sex dreams like that?'

Yossarian reflected a moment with a wise look. 'That's a fish dream,' he decided.

Major Sanderson recoiled as though he had been slapped. 'Yes, of course,' he conceded frigidly, his manner changing to one of edgy and defensive antagonism. 'But I'd like you to dream one like that anyway just to see how you react. That will be all for today. In the meantime, I'd also like you to dream up the answers to some of those questions I asked you. These sessions are no more pleasant for me than they are for you, you know.'

'I'll mention it to Dunbar,' Yossarian replied.

'Dunbar?'

'He's the one who started it all. It's his dream.'

'Oh, Dunbar.' Major Sanderson sneered, his confidence returning. 'I'll bet Dunbar is that evil fellow who really does all those nasty things you're always being blamed for, isn't he?'

'He's not so evil.'

'And yet you'll defend him to the very death, won't you?'

'Not that far.'

Major Sanderson smiled tauntingly and wrote 'Dunbar' on his pad. 'Why are you limping?' he asked sharply, as Yossarian moved to the door. 'And what the devil is that bandage doing on your leg? Are you mad or something?'

'I was wounded in the leg. That's what I'm in the hospital for.'

'Oh, no, you're not,' gloated Major Sanderson maliciously. 'You're in the hospital for a stone in your salivary gland. So you're not so smart after all, are you? You don't even know what you're in the hospital for.'

'I'm in the hospital for a wounded leg,' Yossarian insisted.

Major Sanderson ignored his argument with a sarcastic laugh. 'Well, give my regards to your friend Dunbar. And you will tell him to dream that dream for me, won't you?'

But Dunbar had nausea and dizziness with his constant headache and was not inclined to co-operate with Major Sanderson. Hungry Joe had nightmares because he had finished sixty missions and was waiting again to go home, but he was unwilling to share any when he came to the hospital to visit.

'Hasn't anyone got any dreams for Major Sanderson?' Yossarian asked. 'I hate to disappoint him. He feels so rejected already.'

'I've been having a very peculiar dream ever since I learned you were wounded,' confessed the chaplain. 'I used to dream every night that my wife was dying or being murdered or that my children were choking to death on morsels of nutritious food. Now I dream that I'm out swimming in water over my head and a shark is eating my left leg in exactly the same place where you have your bandage.'

'That's a wonderful dream,' Dunbar declared. 'I bet Major Sanderson will love it.'

'That's a horrible dream!' Major Sanderson cried. 'It's filled with pain and mutilation and death. I'm sure you had it just to spite me. You know, I'm not even sure you belong in the Army, with a disgusting dream like that.'

Yossarian thought he spied a ray of hope. 'Perhaps you're right, sir,' he suggested slyly. 'Perhaps I ought to be grounded and returned to the States.'

'Hasn't it ever occurred to you that in your promiscuous pursuit of women you are merely trying to assuage your subconscious tears of sexual impotence?'

'Yes, sir, it has.'

'Then why do you do it?'

'To assuage my fears of sexual impotence.'

'Why don't you get yourself a good hobby instead?' Major Sanderson inquired with friendly interest. 'Like fishing. Do you really find Nurse Duckett so attractive? I should think she was rather bony. Rather bland and bony, you know. Like a fish.'

'I hardly know Nurse Duckett.'

'Then why did you grab her by the bosom? Merely because she has one?'

'Dunbar did that.'

'Oh, don't start that again,' Major Sanderson exclaimed with vitriolic scorn, and hurled down his pencil disgustedly. 'Do you really think that you can absolve yourself of guilt by pretending to be someone else? I don't like you, Fortiori. Do you know that? I don't like you at all.'

Yossarian felt a cold, damp wind of apprehension blow over him. 'I'm not Fortiori, sir,' he said timidly. 'I'm Yossarian.'

'You're who?'

'My name is Yossarian, sir. And I'm in the hospital with a wounded leg.'

'Your name is Fortiori,' Major Sanderson contradicted him belligerently. 'And you're in the hospital for a stone in your salivary gland.'

'Oh, come on, Major!' Yossarian exploded. 'I ought to know who I am.'

'And I've got an official Army record here to prove it,' Major Sanderson retorted. 'You'd better get a grip on yourself before it's too late. First you're Dunbar. Now you're Yossarian. The next thing you know you'll be claiming you're Washington Irving. Do you know what's wrong with you? You've got a split personality, that's what's wrong with you.'

'Perhaps you're right sir.' Yossarian agreed diplomatically.

'I know I'm right. You've got a bad persecution complex. You think people are trying to harm you.'

'People *are* trying to harm me.'

'You see? You have no respect for excessive authority

or obsolete traditions. You're dangerous and depraved, and you ought to be taken outside and shot!'

'Are you serious?'

'You're an enemy of the people!'

'Are you nuts?' Yossarian shouted.

'No, I'm not nuts,' Dobbs roared furiously back in the ward, in what he imagined was a furtive whisper. 'Hungry Joe saw them, I tell you. He saw them yesterday when he flew to Naples to pick up some black-market air conditioners for Colonel Cathcart's farm. They've got a big replacement center there and it's filled with hundreds of pilots, bombardiers and gunners on the way home. They've got forty-five missions, that's all. A few with Purple Hearts have even less. Replacement crews are pouring in from the States into the other bomber groups. They want everyone to serve overseas at least once, even administrative personnel. Don't you read the papers? We've got to kill him now!'

'You've got only two more missions to fly,' Yossarian reasoned with him in a low voice. 'Why take a chance?'

'I can get killed flying them, too,' Dobbs answered pugnaciously in his rough, quavering, overwrought voice. 'We can kill him the first thing tomorrow morning when he drives back from his farm. I've got the gun right here.'

Yossarian goggled with amazement as Dobbs pulled a gun out of his pocket and displayed it high in the air. 'Are you crazy?' he hissed frantically. 'Put it away. And keep your idiot voice down.'

'What are you worried about?' Dobbs asked with offended innocence. 'No one can hear us.'

'Hey, knock it off down there,' a voice rang out from the far end of the ward. 'Can't you see we're trying to nap?'

'What the hell are you, a wise guy?' Dobbs yelled back and spun around with clenched fists, ready to fight. He whirled back to Yossarian and, before he could speak, sneezed thunderously six times, staggering sideways on rubbery legs in the intervals and raising his elbows ineffectively to fend each seizure off. The lids of his watery eyes were puffy and inflamed.

'Who does he think,' he demanded, sniffing, spasmodically and wiping his nose with the back of his sturdy wrist, 'he is, a cop or something?'

'He's a C.I.D. man,' Yossarian notified him tranquilly. 'We've got three here now and more on the way. Oh, don't be scared. They're after a forger named Washington Irving. They're not interested in murderers.'

'Murderers?' Dobbs was affronted. 'Why do you call us murderers? Just because we're going to murder Colonel Cathcart?'

'Be quiet, damn you!' directed Yossarian. 'Can't you whisper?'

'I am whispering. I –'

'You're still shouting.'

'No, I'm not. I –'

'Hey, shut up down there, will you?' patients all over the ward began hollering at Dobbs.

'I'll fight you all!' Dobbs screamed back at them, and stood up on a rickety wooden chair, waving the gun wildly. Yossarian caught his arm and yanked him down. Dobbs began sneezing again. 'I have an allergy,' he apologized when he had finished, his nostrils running and his eyes streaming with tears.

'That's too bad. You'd make a great leader of men without it.'

'Colonel Cathcart's the murderer,' Dobbs complained hoarsely when he had shoved away a soiled, crumpled khaki handkerchief. 'Colonel Cathcart's the one who's going to murder us all if we don't do something to stop him.'

'Maybe he won't raise the missions any more. Maybe sixty is as high as he'll go.'

'He always raises the missions. You know that better than I do,' Dobbs swallowed and bent his intense face very close to Yossarian's, the muscles in his bronze, rocklike jaw bunching up into quivering knots. 'Just say it's okay and I'll do the whole thing tomorrow morning. Do you understand what I'm telling you? I'm whispering now, ain't I?'

Yossarian tore his eyes away from the gaze of burning entreaty Dobbs had fastened on him. 'Why the goddam hell don't you just go out and do it?' he protested. 'Why don't you stop talking to me about it and do it alone?'

'I'm afraid to do it alone. I'm afraid to do anything alone.'

'Then leave me out of it. I'd have to be crazy to get mixed up in something like this now. I've got a million-dollar leg wound here. They're going to send me home.'

'Are you crazy?' Dobbs exclaimed in disbelief. 'All you've got there is a scratch. He'll have you back flying combat missions the day you come out, Purple Heart and all.'

'Then I really will kill him,' Yossarian vowed. 'I'll come looking for you and we'll do it together.'

'Then let's do it tomorrow while we've still got the chance,' Dobbs pleaded. 'The chaplain says he's volunteered the group for Avignon again. I may be killed before you get out. Look how these hands of mine shake. I can't fly a plane. I'm not good enough.'

Yossarian was afraid to say yes. 'I want to wait and see what happens first.'

'The trouble with you is that you just won't do anything.' Dobbs complained in a thick infuriated voice.

'I'm doing everything I possibly can,' the chaplain explained softly to Yossarian after Dobbs had departed. 'I even went to the medical tent to speak to Doc Daneeka about helping you.'

'Yes, I can see.' Yossarian suppressed a smile. 'What happened?'

'They painted my gums purple,' the chaplain replied sheepishly.

'They painted his toes purple, too,' Nately added in outrage. 'And then they gave him a laxative.'

'But I went back again this morning to see him.'

'And they painted his gums purple again,' said Nately.

'But I did get to speak to him,' the chaplain argued in a plaintive tone of self-justification. 'Doctor Daneeka seems like such an unhappy man. He suspects that some-one is plotting to transfer him to the Pacific Ocean. All this time he's been thinking of coming to *me* for help. When I told him I needed *his* help, he wondered if there wasn't a chaplain *I* couldn't go see.' The chaplain waited in patient dejection when Yossarian and Dunbar both broke into laughter. 'I used to think it was immoral to be unhappy,' he continued, as though keening aloud in soli-tude. 'Now I don't know what to think any more. I'd like to make the subject of immorality the basis of my sermon this Sunday, but I'm not sure I ought to give any sermon at all with these purple gums. Colonel Korn was very displeased with them.'

'Chaplain, why don't you come into the hospital with us for a while and take it easy?' Yossarian invited. 'You could be very comfortable here.'

The brash iniquity of the proposal tempted and amused the chaplain for a second or two. 'No, I don't think so,' he decided reluctantly. 'I want to arrange for a trip to the mainland to see a mail clerk named Wintergreen. Doctor Daneeka told me he could help.'

'Wintergreen is probably the most influential man in the whole theater of operations. He's not only a mail clerk, but he has access to a mimeograph machine. But he won't help anybody. That's one of the reasons he'll go far.'

'I'd like to speak to him anyway. There must be some-body who will help you.'

'Do it for Dunbar, Chaplain,' Yossarian corrected with a superior air. 'I've got this million-dollar leg wound that will take me out of combat. If that doesn't do it, there's a psychiatrist who thinks I'm not good enough to be in the Army.'

'I'm the one who isn't good enough to be in the Army,' Dunbar whined jealously. 'It was my dream.'

'It's not the dream, Dunbar,' Yossarian explained. 'He likes your dream. It's my personality. He thinks it's split.'

'It's split right down the middle,' said Major Sanderson, who had laced his lumpy GI shoes for the occasion and had slicked his charcoal-dull hair down with some stiffening and redolent tonic. He smiled ostentatiously to show himself reasonable and nice. 'I'm not saying that to be cruel and insulting,' he continued with cruel and insulting delight. 'I'm not saying it because I hate you and want revenge. I'm not saying it because you rejected me and hurt my feelings terribly. No, I'm a man of medicine and I'm being coldy objective. I have very bad news for you. Are you man enough to take it?'

'God, no!' screamed Yossarian. 'I'll go right to pieces.'

Major Sanderson flew instantly into a rage. 'Can't you even do one thing right?' he pleaded, turning beet-red with vexation and crashing the sides of both fists down upon his desk together. 'The trouble with you is that you think you're too good for all the conventions of society. You probably think you're too good for me too, just because I arrived at puberty late. Well, do you know what you are? You're a frustrated, unhappy, disillusioned, undisciplined, maladjusted young man!' Major Sanderson's disposition seemed to mellow as he reeled off the uncomplimentary adjectives.

'Yes, sir,' Yossarian agreed carefully. 'I guess you're right.'

'Off course I'm right. You're immature. You've been unable to adjust to the idea of war.'

'Yes, sir.'

'You have a morbid aversion to dying. You probably resent the fact that you're at war and might get your head blown off any second.'

'I more than resent it, sir. I'm absolutely incensed.'

'You have deep-seated survival anxieties. And you don't like bigots, bullies, snobs or hypocrites. Subconsciously there are many people you hate.'

'Consciously, sir, consciously,' Yossarian corrected in an effort to help. 'I hate them consciously.'

'You're antagonistic to the idea of being robbed, exploited, degraded, humiliated or deceived. Misery

384

depresses you. Ignorance depresses you. Persecution depresses you. Violence depresses you. Slums depress you. Greed depresses you. Crime depresses you. Corruption depresses you. You know, it wouldn't surprise me if you're a manic-depressive!'

'Yes, sir. Perhaps I am.'

'Don't try to deny it.'

'I'm not denying it, sir,' said Yossarian, pleased with the miraculous rapport that finally existed between them. 'I agree with all you've said.'

'Then you admit you're crazy, do you?'

'Crazy?' Yossarian was shocked. 'What are you talking about? Why am I crazy? You're the one who's crazy!'

Major Sanderson turned red with indignation again and crashed both fists down upon his thighs. 'Calling me crazy,' he shouted in a sputtering rage, 'is a typically sadistic and vindictive paranoiac reaction! You really are crazy!'

'Then why don't you send me home?'

'And I'm going to send you home!'

'They're going to send me home!' Yossarian announced jubilantly, as he hobbled back into the ward.

'Me too!' A. Fortiori rejoiced. 'They just came to my ward and told me.'

'What about me?' Dunbar demanded petulantly of the doctors.

'You?' they replied with asperity. 'You're going with Yossarian. Right back into combat!'

And back into combat they both went. Yossarian was enraged when the ambulance returned him to the squadron, and he went limping for justice to Doc Daneeka, who glared at him glumly with misery and disdain.

'You!' Doc Daneeka exclaimed mournfully with accusing disgust, the egg-shaped pouches under both eyes firm and censorious. 'All you ever think of is yourself. Go take a look at the bomb line if you want to see what's been happening since you went to hospital.'

Yossarian was startled. 'Are we losing?'

'Losing?' Doc Daneeka cried. 'The whole military situation has been going to hell ever since we captured Paris. I knew it would happen.' He paused, his sulking ire turning to melancholy, and frowned irritably as though it were all Yossarian's fault. 'American troops are pushing into German soil. The Russians have captured back all of Romania. Only yesterday the Greeks in the Eighth Army captured Rimini. The Germans are on the defensive everywhere!' Doc Daneeka paused again and fortified himself with a huge breath for a piercing ejaculation of grief. 'There's no more Luftwaffe left!' he wailed. He seemed ready to burst into tears. 'The whole Gothic line is in danger of collapsing!'

'So?' asked Yossarian. 'What's wrong?'

'What's wrong?' Doc Daneeka cried. 'If something doesn't happen soon, Germany may surrender. And then we'll all be sent to the Pacific!'

Yossarian gawked at Doc Daneeka in grotesque dismay. 'Are you crazy? Do you know what you're saying?'

'Yeah, it's easy for you to laugh,' Doc Daneeka sneered.

'Who the hell is laughing?'

'At least you've got a chance. You're in combat and might get killed. But what about me? I've got nothing to hope for.'

'You're out of your goddam head!' Yossarian shouted at him emphatically, seizing him by the shirt front. 'Do you know that? Now keep your stupid mouth shut and listen to me.'

Doc Daneeka wrenched himself away. 'Don't you dare talk to me like that. I'm a licensed physician.'

'Then keep your stupid licensed physician's mouth shut and listen to what they told me up at the hospital. I'm crazy. Did you know that?'

'So?'

'Really crazy.'

'So?'

'I'm nuts. Cuckoo. Don't you understand? I'm off my rocker. They sent someone else home in my place by

386

mistake. They've got a licensed psychiatrist up at the hospital who examined me, and that was his verdict. I'm really insane.'

'So?'

'So?' Yossarian was puzzled by Doc Daneeka's inability to comprehend. 'Don't you see what that means? Now you can take me off combat duty and send me home. They're not going to send a crazy man out to be killed, are they?'

'Who else will go?'

28 Dobbs

McWatt went, and McWatt was not crazy. And so
did Yossarian, still walking with a limp, and when
Yossarian had gone two more times and then found himself menaced by the rumor of another mission to
Bologna, he limped determinedly into Dobb's tent early
one warm afternoon, put a finger to his mouth and said,
'Shush!'

'What are you shushing him for?' asked Kid Sampson,
peeling a tangerine with his front teeth as he perused
the dog-eared pages of a comic book. 'He isn't even saying anything.'

'Screw,' said Yossarian to Kid Sampson, jerking his
thumb back over his shoulder toward the entrance of the
tent.

Kid Sampson cocked his blond eyebrows discerningly
and rose to co-operate. He whistled upward four times
into his drooping yellow mustache and spurted away
into the hills on the dented old green motorcycle he had
purchased secondhand months before. Yossarian waited
until the last faint bark of the motor had died away in the
distance. Things inside the tent did not seem quite normal. The place was too neat. Dobbs was watching him
curiously, smoking a fat cigar. Now that Yossarian had

made up his mind to be brave, he was deathly afraid.

'All right,' he said. 'Let's kill Colonel Cathcart. We'll do it together.'

Dobbs sprang forward off his cot with a look of wildest terror. 'Shush!' he roared. 'Kill Colonel Cathcart? What are you talking about?'

'Be quiet, damn it,' Yossarian snarled. 'The whole island will hear. Have you still got that gun?'

'Are you crazy or something?' shouted Dobbs. 'Why should I want to kill Colonel Cathcart?'

'Why?' Yossarian stared at Dobbs with an incredulous scowl. 'Why? It was your idea, wasn't it? Didn't you come to the hospital and ask me to do it?'

Dobbs smiled slowly. 'But that was when I had only fifty-eight missions,' he explained, puffing on his cigar luxuriously. 'I'm all packed now and I'm waiting to go home. I've finished my sixty missions.'

'So what?' Yossarian replied. 'He's only going to raise them again.'

'Maybe this time he won't.'

'He always raises them. What the hell's the matter with you Dobbs? Ask Hungry Joe how many time she's packed his bags.'

'I've got to wait and see what happens,' Dobbs maintained stubbornly. 'I'd have to be crazy to get mixed up in something like this now that I'm out of combat.' He flicked the ash from his cigar. 'No, my advice to you,' he remarked, 'is that you fly your sixty missions like the rest of us and then see what happens.'

Yossarian resisted the impulse to spit squarely in his eye. 'I may not live through sixty,' he wheedled in a flat, pessimistic voice. 'There's a rumour around that he voluteered the group for Bologna again.'

'It's only a rumor,' Dobbs pointed out with a self-important air. 'You mustn't believe every rumor you hear.'

'Will you stop giving me advice?'

'Why don't you speak to Orr?' Dobbs advised. 'Orr got knocked down into the water again last week on that second mission to Avignon. Maybe he's unhappy enough to kill him.'

'Orr hasn't got brains enough to be unhappy.'

Orr had been knocked down into the water again while Yossarian was still in the hospital and had eased his crippled airplane down gently into the glassy blue swells off Marseilles with such flawless skill that not one member of the six-man crew suffered the slightest bruise. The escape hatches in the front and rear sections flew open while the sea was still foaming white and green around the plane, and the men scrambled out as speedily as they could in their flaccid orange Mae West life jackets that failed to inflate and dangled limp and useless around their necks and waists. The life jackets failed to inflate because Milo had removed the twin carbon-dioxide cylinders from the inflating chambers to make the strawberry and crushed-pineapple ice-cream sodas he served in the officers' mess hall and had replaced them with mimeographed notes that read: 'What's good for M & M Enterprises is good for the country.' Orr popped out of the sinking airplane last.

'You should have seen him!' Sergeant Knight roared with laughter as he related the episode to Yossarian. 'It was the funniest goddam thing you ever saw. None of the Mae Wests would work because Milo had stolen the carbon dioxide to make those ice-cream sodas you bastards have been getting in the officers' mess. But that wasn't too bad, as it turned out. Only one of us couldn't swim, and we lifted that guy up into the raft after Orr had worked it over by its rope right up against the fuselage while we were all still standing on the plane. That little crackpot sure has a knack for things like that. Then the other raft came loose and drifted away, so that all six of us wound up sitting in one with our elbows and legs pressed so close against each other you almost couldn't move without knocking the guy next to you out of the raft into the water. The plane went down about three seconds after we left it and we were out there all alone, and right after that we began unscrewing the caps on our Mae Wests to see what the hell had gone wrong and found those goddam notes from Milo telling us that what was good for him was good enough for the rest of us. That bastard! Jesus, did we curse him, all except that buddy of yours Orr, who just kept grinning as though for all he cared what was good for Milo *might* be good enough for the rest of us.

'I swear, you should have seen him sitting up there on the rim of the raft like the captain of a ship while the rest of us just watched him and waited for him to tell us what to do. He kept slapping his hands on his legs every few seconds as though he had the shakes and saying "All right now, all right," and giggling like a crazy little freak, then saying "All right now, all right again" and giggling like a crazy little freak some more. It was like watching some kind of a moron. Watching him was all that kept us from going to pieces altogether during the first few minutes, what with each wave washing over us into the raft or dumping a few of us back into the water so that we had to climb back in again before the next wave came along and washed us right back out. It was sure funny. We just kept falling out and climbing back in. We had the guy who couldn't swim stretched out in the middle of the raft on the floor, but even there he almost drowned, because the water inside the raft was deep enough to keep splashing in his face. Oh, boy!

'Then Orr began opening up compartments in the raft, and the fun really began. First he found a box of chocolate bars and he passed those around so we sat there eating salty chocolate bars while the waves kept knocking us out of the raft into the water. Next he found some bouillon cubes and aluminium cups and made us some soup. Then he found some tea. Sure, he made it! Can't you see him serving us tea as we sat there soaking wet in water up to our ass? Now I was falling out of the raft because I was laughing so much. We were all laughing. And he was dead serious, except for that goofy giggle of his and that crazy grin. What a jerk! Whatever he found he used. He found some shark repellent and he sprinkled it right out into the water. He found some market dye and he threw it into the water. The next thing he finds is a fishing line and dried bait, and his face lights up as though the Air-Sea Rescue launch had just sped up to save us before we died of exposure or before the Germans sent a boat out from Spezia to take us prisoner or machine-gun us. In no time at all, Orr had that fishing line out into the water, trolling away as happy as a lark. "Lieutenant, what do you expect to catch?" I asked him. "Cod," he told me. And he meant it. And it's a good thing he didn't catch any, because he would have eaten that codfish raw if he had caught any, and would have made us eat it, too, because he had found this little book that said it was all right to eat codfish raw.

'The next thing he found was this little blue oar about the size of a Dixie-cup spoon, and, sure enough, he began rowing with it, trying to move all nine hundred pounds of us with that little stick. Can you imagine? After that he found a small magnetic compass and a big waterproof map, and he spread the map open on his knees and set the compass on top of it. And that's how he spent the time until the launch picked us up about thirty minutes later, sitting there with that baited fishing line out behind him, with the compass in his lap and the map spread out on his knees, and paddling away as hard as he could with that dinky blue oar as though he was speeding to Majorca. Jesus!'

Sergeant Knight knew all about Majorca, and so did Orr, because Yossarian had told them often of such sanctuaries as Spain, Switzerland and Sweden where American fliers could be interned for the duration of the war under conditions of utmost ease and luxury merely by flying there. Yossarian was the squadron's leading authority on internment and had already begun plotting an emergency heading into Switzerland on every mission he flew into northernmost Italy. He would certainly have preferred Sweden, where the level of intelligence was high and where he could swim nude with beautiful girls with low, demurring voices and sire whole happy, undisciplined tribes of illegitimate Yossarians that the state would assist through parturition and launch into life without stigma; but Sweden was out of reach, too far away, and Yossarian waited for the piece of flak that would knock out one engine over the Italian Alps and provide him with the excuse for heading for Switzerland. He would not even tell his pilot he was guiding him there. Yossarian often thought of scheming with some pilot he trusted to fake a crippled engine and then destroy the evidence of deception with a belly landing, but the only pilot he really trusted was McWatt, who was happiest where he was and still got a big boot out of buzzing his plane over Yossarian's tent or roaring in so low over the bathers at the beach that the fierce wind from his propellers slashed dark furrows in the water and whipped sheets of spray flapping back for seconds afterward.

Dobbs and Hungry Joe were out of the question, and so was Orr, who was tinkering with the valve of the stove again when Yossarian limped despondently back into the tent after Dobbs had turned him down. The stove Orr was manufacturing out of an inverted metal drum stood in the middle of the smooth cement floor he had constructed. He was working sedulously on both knees. Yossarian tried paying no attention to him and limped wearily to his cot and sat down with a labored, drawn-out grunt. Prickles of perspiration were turning chilly on his forehead. Dobbs had depressed him. Doc Daneeka depressed him. An ominous vision of doom depressed him when he looked at Orr. He began ticking with a variety of internal tremors. Nerves twitched, and the vein in one wrist began palpitating.

Orr studied Yossarian over his shoulder, his moist lips drawn back around convex rows of large buck teeth. Reaching sideways, he dug a bottle of warm beer out of his foot locker, and he handed it to Yossarian after prying off the cap. Neither said a word. Yossarian sipped the bubbles off the top and tilted his head back. Orr watched him cunningly with a noiseless grin. Yossarian eyed Orr guardedly. Orr snickered with a slight, mucid sibilance and turned back to his work, squatting. Yossarian grew tense.

'Don't start,' he begged in a threatening voice, both hands tightening around his beer bottle. 'Don't start working on your stove.'

Orr cackled quietly. 'I'm almost finished.'

'No, you're not. You're about to begin.'

'Here's the valve. See? It's almost all together.'

'And you're about to take it apart. I know what you're doing, you bastard. I've seen you do it three hundred times.'

Orr shivered with glee. 'I want to get the leak in this gasoline line out,' he explained. 'I've got it down now to where it's only an ooze.'

'I can't watch you,' Yossarian confessed tonelessly. 'If you want to work with something big, that's okay. But that valve is filled with tiny parts, and I just haven't got the patience right now to watch you working so hard over things that are so goddam small and unimportant.'

'Just because they're small doesn't mean they're unimportant.'

'I don't care.'

'Once more?'

'When I'm not around. You're a happy imbecile and you don't know what it means to feel the way I do. Things happen to me when you work over small things that I can't even begin to explain. I find out that I can't stand you. I start to hate you, and I'm soon thinking seriously about busting this bottle down on your head or stabbing you in the neck with that hunting knife there. Do you understand?'

Orr nodded very intelligently. 'I won't take the valve apart now,' he said, and began taking it apart, working with slow, tireless, interminable precision, his rustic, ungainly face bent very close to the floor, picking painstakingly at the minute mechanism in his fingers with such limitless, plodding concentration that he seemed scarcely to be thinking of it at all.

Yossarian cursed him silently and made up his mind to ignore him. 'What the hell's your hurry with that stove, anyway?' he barked out a moment later in spite of himself. 'It's still hot out. We're probably going swimming later. What are you worried about the cold for.'

'The days are getting shorter,' Orr observed philosophically. 'I'd like to get this all finished for you while there's still time. You'll have the best stove in the squadron when I'm through. It will burn all night with this feed control I'm fixing, and these metal plates will radiate the heat all over the tent. If you leave a helmet full of water on this thing when you go to sleep, you'll have warm water to wash with all ready for you when you wake up. Won't that be nice? If you want to cook eggs or soup, all you'll have to do is set the pot down here and turn the fire up.'

'What do you mean, me?' Yossarian wanted to know. 'Where are you going to be?'

Orr's stunted torso shook suddenly with a muffled spasm of amusement. 'I don't know,' he exclaimed, and a weird, wavering giggle gushed out suddenly through his chattering buck teeth like an exploding jet of emotion. He was still laughing when he continued, and his voice was clogged with saliva. 'If they keep on shooting me down this way, I don't know where I'm going to be.'

Yossarian was moved. 'Why don't you try to stop flying, Orr? You've got an excuse.'

'I've only got eighteen missions.'

'But you've been shot down on almost every one. You're either ditching or crash-landing every time you go up.'

'Oh, I don't mind flying missions. I guess they're lots of fun. You ought to try flying a few with me when you're not flying lead. Just for laughs. Tee-hee.' Orr gazed up at Yossarian through the corners of his eyes with a look of pointed mirth.

Yossarian avoided his stare. 'They've got me flying lead again.'

'When you're not flying lead. If you had any brains, do

you know what you'd do? You'd go right to Piltchard and Wren and tell them you want to fly with me.'

'And get shot down with you every time you go up? What's the fun in that?'

'That's just why you ought to do it,' Orr insisted. 'I guess I'm just about the best pilot around now when it comes to ditching or making crash landings. It would be good practice for you.'

'Good practice for what?'

'Good practice in case you ever have to ditch or make a crash landing. Tee-hee-hee.'

'Have you got another bottle of beer for me?' Yossarian asked morosely.

'Do you want to bust it down on my head?'

This time Yossarian did laugh. 'Like that whore in that apartment in Rome?'

Orr sniggered lewdly, his bulging crab apple cheeks blowing outward with pleasure. 'Do you really want to know why she was hitting me over the head with her shoe?' he teased.

'I do know,' Yossarian teased back. 'Nately's whore told me.'

Orr grinned like a gargoyle. 'No she didn't.'

Yossarian felt sorry for Orr. Orr was so small and ugly. Who would protect him if he lived? Who would protect a warmhearted, simple-minded gnome like Orr from rowdies and cliques and from expert athletes like Appleby who had flies in their eyes and would walk right over him with swaggering conceit and self-assurance every chance they got? Yossarian worried frequently about Orr. Who would shield him against animosity and deceit, against people with ambition and the embittered snobbery of the big shot's wife, against the squalid, corrupting indignities of the profit motive and the friendly neighborhood butcher with inferior meat? Orr was a happy and unsuspecting simpleton with a thick mass of wavy polychromatic hair parted down the center. He would be mere child's play for them. They would take his money, screw his wife and show no kindness to his children. Yossarian felt a flood of compassion sweep over him.

Orr was an eccentric midget, a freakish, likable dwarf with a smutty mind and a thousand valuable skills that would keep him in a low income group all his life. He could use a soldering iron and hammer two boards together so that the wood did not split and the nails did not bend. He could drill holes. He had built a good deal more in the tent while Yossarian was away in the hospital. He had filed or chiseled a perfect channel in the cement so that the slender gasoline line was flush with the floor as it ran to the stove from the tank he had built outside on an elevated platform. He had constructed andirons for the fireplace out of excess bomb parts and had filled them with stout silver logs, and he had framed with stained wood the photographs of girls with big breasts he had torn out of cheesecake magazines and hung over the mantelpiece. Orr could open a can of paint. He could mix paint, thin paint, remove paint. He could chop wood and measure things with a ruler. He knew how to build fires. He could dig holes, and he had a real gift for bringing water for them both in cans and canteens from the tanks near the mess hall. He could engross himself in an inconsequential task for hours without growing restless or bored, as oblivious to fatigue as the stump of a tree, and almost as taciturn. He had an uncanny knowledge of wildlife and was not afraid of dogs or cats or beetles or moths, or of foods like scrod or tripe.

Yossarian sighed drearily and began brooding about the rumored mission to Bologna. The valve Orr was dismantling was about the size of a thumb and contained thirty-seven separate parts, excluding the casing, many of them so minute that Orr was required to pinch them tightly between the tips of his fingernails as he placed them carefully on the floor in orderly, catalogued rows, never quickening his movements or slowing them down, never tiring, never pausing in his relentless, methodical, monotonous procedure unless it was to leer at Yossarian with maniacal mischief. Yossarian tried not to watch him. He counted the parts and thought he would go clear out of his mind. He turned away, shutting his eyes, but that was even worse, for now he had only the sounds, the tiny maddening, indefatigable, distinct clicks and rustles of hands and weightless parts. Orr was breathing rhythmically with a noise that was stertorous and repulsive. Yossarian clenched his fists and looked at the long bone-handled hunting knife hanging in a holster over the cot of the dead man in the tent. As soon as he thought of stabbing Orr, his tension eased. The idea of murdering Orr was so ridiculous that he began to consider it seriously with queer whimsy and fascination. He searched the nape of Orr's neck for the probable site of the medulla oblongata. Just the daintiest stick there would kill him and solve so many serious, agonizing problems for them both.

'Does it hurt?' Orr asked at precisely that moment, as though by protective instinct.

Yossarian eyed him closely. 'Does what hurt?'

'Your leg,' said Orr with a strange, mysterious laugh. 'You still limp a little.'

'It's just a habit, I guess,' said Yossarian, breathing again with relief. 'I'll probably get over it soon.'

Orr rolled over sideways to the floor and came up on one knee, facing toward Yossarian. 'Do you remember,' he drawled reflectively, with an air of labored recollection, 'that girl who was hitting me on the head that day in Rome?' He chuckled at Yossarian's involuntary exclamation of tricked annoyance. 'I'll make a deal with you about that girl. I'll tell you why that girl was hitting me on the head with her shoe that day if you answer one question.'

'What's the question?'

'Did you ever screw Nately's girl?'

Yossarian laughed with surprise. 'Me? No. Now tell me why that girl hit you with her shoe.'

'That wasn't the question,' Orr informed him with victorious delight. 'That was just conversation. She acts like you screwed her.'

'Well, I didn't. How does she act?'

'She acts like she don't like you.'

'She doesn't like anyone.'

'She likes Captain Black, ' Orr reminded.

'That's because he treats her like dirt. Anyone can get a girl that way.'

'She wears a slave bracelet on her leg with his name on it.'

'He makes her wear it to needle Nately.'

'She even gives him some of the money she gets from Nately.'

'Listen, what do you want from me?'

'Did you ever screw my girl?'

'Your girl? Who the hell is your girl?'

'The one who hit me over the head with her shoe.'

'I've been with her a couple of times,' Yossarian admitted. 'Since when is she your girl? What are you getting at?'

'She don't like you, either.'

'What the hell do I care if she likes me or not? She likes me as much as she likes you.'

'Did she ever hit you over the head with her shoe?'

'Orr, I'm tired. Why don't you leave me alone?'

'Tee-hee-hee. How about that skinny countess in Rome and her skinny daughter-in-law?' Orr persisted impishly with increasing zest. 'Did you ever screw them?'

'Oh, how I wish I could,' sighed Yossarian honestly, imagining, at the mere question, the prurient, used, decaying feel in his petting hands of their teeny, pulpy buttocks and breasts.

'They don't like you either,' commented Orr. 'They like Aarfy, and they like Nately, but they don't like you. Women just don't seem to like you. I think they think you're a bad influence.'

'Women are crazy,' Yossarian answered, and waited grimly for what he knew was coming next.

'How about that other girl of yours?' Orr asked with a pretense of pensive curiosity. 'The fat one? The bald one? You know, that fat bald one in Sicily with the turban who kept sweating all over us all night long? Is she crazy too?'

'Didn't she like me either?'

'How could you do it to a girl with no hair?'

'How was I supposed to know she had no hair?'

'I knew it,' Orr bragged. 'I knew it all the time.'

'You knew she was bald?' Yossarian exclaimed in wonder.

'No, I knew this valve wouldn't work if I left a part out,' Orr answered, glowing with cranberry-red elation because he had just duped Yossarian again. 'Will you please hand me that small composition gasket that rolled over there? It's right near your foot.'

'No it isn't.'

'Right here,' said Orr, and took hold of something invisible with the tips of his fingernails and held it up for Yossarian to see. 'Now I'll have to start all over again.'

'I'll kill you if you do. I'll murder you right on the spot.'

'Why don't you ever fly with me?' Orr asked suddenly, and looked straight into Yossarian's face for the first time. 'There, that's the question I want you to answer. Why don't you ever fly with me?'

Yossarian turned away with intense shame and embarrassment. 'I told you why. They've got me flying lead bombardier most of the time.'

'That's not why,' Orr said, shaking his head. 'You went to Piltchard and Wren after the first Avignon mission and told them you didn't ever want to fly with me. That's why, isn't it?'

Yossarian felt his skin turn hot. 'No I didn't,' he lied.

'Yes you did,' Orr insisted equably. 'You asked them not to assign you to any plane piloted by me, Dobbs or Huple because you didn't have confidence in us at the controls. And Piltchard and Wren said they couldn't make an exception of you because it wouldn't be fair to the men who did have to fly with us.'

'So?' said Yossarian. 'It didn't make any difference then, did it?'

'But they've never made you fly with me.' Orr, working

on both knees again, was addressing Yossarian without bitterness or reproach, but with injured humility, which was infinitely more painful to observe, although he was still grinning and snickering, as though the situation were comic. 'You really ought to fly with me, you know. I'm a pretty good pilot, and I'd take care of you. I may get knocked down a lot, but that's not my fault, and nobody's ever been hurt in my plane. Yes, sir – if you had any brains, you know what you'd do? You'd go right to Piltchard and Wren and tell them you want to fly all your missions with me.'

Yossarian leaned forward and peered closely into Orr's inscrutable mask of contradictory emotions. 'Are you trying to tell me something?'

'Tee-hee-hee-hee,' Orr responded. 'I'm trying to tell you why that big girl with the shoe was hitting me on the head that day. But you just won't let me.'

'Tell me.'

'Will you fly with me?'

Yossarian laughed and shook his head. 'You'll only get knocked down into the water again.'

Orr did get knocked down into the water again when the rumored mission to Bologna was flown, and he landed his single-engine plane with a smashing jar on the choppy, windswept waves tossing and falling below the warlike black thunderclouds mobilizing overhead. He was late getting out of the plane and ended up alone in a raft that began drifting away from the men in the other raft and was out of sight by the time the Air-Sea Rescue launch came plowing up through the wind and splattering raindrops to take them aboard. Night was already falling by the time they were returned to the squadron. There was no word of Orr.

'Don't worry,' reassured Kid Sampson, still wrapped in the heavy blankets and raincoat in which he had been swaddled on the boat by his rescuers. 'He's probably been picked up already if he didn't drown in that storm. It didn't last long. I bet he'll show up any minute.'

Yossarian walked back to his tent to wait for Orr to

show up any minute and lit a fire to make things warm for him. The stove worked perfectly, with a strong, robust blaze that could be raised or lowered by turning the tap Orr had finally finished repairing. A light rain was falling, drumming softly on the tent, the trees, the ground. Yossarian cooked a can of hot soup to have ready for Orr and ate it all himself as the time passed. He hard-boiled some eggs for Orr and ate those too. Then he ate a whole tin of Cheddar cheese from a package of K rations.

Each time he caught himself worrying he made himself remember that Orr could do everything and broke into silent laughter at the picture of Orr in the raft as Sergeant Knight had described him, bent forward with a busy, preoccupied smile over the map and compass in his lap, stuffing one soaking-wet chocolate bar after another into his grinning, tittering mouth as he paddled away dutifully through the lightning, thunder and rain with the bright-blue useless toy oar, the fishing line with dried bait trailing out behind him. Yossarian really had no doubt about Orr's ability to survive. If fish could be caught with that silly fishing line, Orr would catch them, and if it was codfish he was after, then Orr would catch a codfish, even though no codfish had ever been caught in those waters before. Yossarian put another can of soup up to cook and ate that too when it was hot. Every time a car door slammed, he broke into a hopeful smile and turned expectantly toward the entrance, listening for footsteps. He knew that any moment Orr would come walking into the tent with big, glistening, rain-soaked eyes, cheeks and buck teeth, looking ludicrously like a jolly New England oysterman in a yellow oilskin rain hat and slicker numerous sizes too large for him and holding up proudly for Yossarian's amusement a great dead codfish he had caught. But he didn't.

29   Peckem

There was no word about Orr the next day, and
Sergeant Whitcomb, with commendable dispatch and
considerable hope, dropped a reminder in his tickler file
to send a form letter over Colonel Cathcart's signature
to Orr's next of kin when nine more days had elapsed.
There was word from General Peckem's headquarters,
though, and Yossarian was drawn to the crowd of officers and enlisted men in shorts and bathing trunks
buzzing in grumpy confusion around the bulletin board
just outside the orderly room.

'What's so different about this Sunday. I want to
know?' Hungry Joe was demanding vociferously of Chief
White Halfoat. 'Why won't we have a parade this Sunday
when we don't have a parade every Sunday? Huh?'

Yossarian worked his way through to the front and let
out a long, agonized groan when he read the terse
announcement there:

> *Due to circumstances beyond my control, there
> will be no big parade this Sunday afternoon.*
> Colonel Scheisskopf

Dobbs was right. They were indeed sending everyone
overseas, even Lieutenant Scheisskopf, who had resisted

the move with all the vigor and wisdom at his command and who reported for duty at General Peckem's office in a mood of grave discontent.

General Peckem welcomed Colonel Scheisskopf with effusive charm and said he was delighted to have him. An additional colonel on his staff meant that he could now begin agitating for two additional majors, four additional captains, sixteen additional lieutenants and untold quantities of additional enlisted men, type-writers, desks, filing cabinets, automobiles and other substantial equipment and supplies that would contri-bute to the prestige of his position and increase his striking power in the war he had declared against General Dreedle. He now had two full colonels; General Dreedle had only five, and four of those were combat commanders. With almost no intriguing at all, General Peckem had executed a maneuver that would eventually double his strength. And General Dreedle was getting drunk more often. The future looked wonderful, and General Peckem contemplated his bright new colonel enchantedly with an effulgent smile.

In all matters of consequence, General P.P. Peckem was, as he always remarked when he was about to criticize the work of some close associate publicly, a realist. He was a handsome, pink-skinned man of fifty-three. His manner was always casual and relaxed, and his uniforms were custom-made. He had silver-gray hair, slightly myopic eyes and thin, overhanging, sensual lips. He was a perceptive, graceful, sophisticated man who was sensitive to everyone's weaknesses but his own and found everyone absurd but himself. General Peckem laid great, fastidious stress on small matters of taste and style. He was always *augmenting* things. Approach-ing events were never *coming*, but always *upcoming*. It was not true that he wrote *memorandums* praising him-self and recommending that his authority be *enhanced* to include all combat operations; he wrote *memoranda*. And the prose in the *memoranda* of other officers was always *turgid*, *stilted*, or *ambiguous*. The errors of others were inevitably *deplorable*. Regulations were *stringent*, and his data never *was* obtained from a reliable source, but always *were* obtained. General Peckem was frequently *constrained*. Things were often *incumbent* upon him, and he frequently acted with *greatest reluctance*. It never escaped his memory that neither black nor white was a color, and he never used *verbal* when he meant *oral*. He could quote glibly from Plato, Nietzsche, Montaigne, Theodore Roosevelt, the Marquis de Sade and Warren G. Harding. A virgin audience like Colonel Scheisskopf was grist for General Peckem's mill, a stimulating opportunity to throw open his whole dazzling erudite treasure house of puns, wisecracks, slanders, homilies, anecdotes, proverbs, epigrams, apothegms, bon mots and other pungent sayings. He beamed urbanely as he began orienting Colonel Scheisskopf to his new surroundings.

'My only fault,' he observed with practiced good humor, watching for the effect of his words, 'is that I have no faults.'

Colonel Scheisskopf didn't laugh, and General Peckem was stunned. A heavy doubt crushed his enthusiasm. He had just opened with one of his most trusted paradoxes, and he was positively alarmed that not the slightest flicker of acknowledgment had moved across that impervious face, which began to remind him suddenly, in hue and texture, of an unused soap eraser. Perhaps Colonel Scheisskopf was tired, General Peckem granted to himself charitably; he had come a long way, and everything was unfamiliar. General Peckem's attitude toward all the personnel in his command, officers and enlisted men, was marked by the same easy spirit of tolerance and permissiveness. He mentioned often that if the people who worked for him met him halfway, he would meet them more than halfway, with the result, as he always added with an astute chuckle, that there was never any meeting of the minds at all. General Peckem thought of himself as aesthetic and intellectual. When people disagreed with him, he urged them to be *objective*.

And it was indeed an objective Peckem who gazed at Colonel Scheisskopf encouragingly and resumed his indoctrination with an attitude of magnanimous forgiveness. 'You've come to us just in time, Scheisskopf. The summer offensive has petered out, thanks to the incompetent leadership with which we supply our troops, and I have a crying need for a tough, experienced, competent officer like you to help produce the memoranda upon which we rely so heavily to let people know how good we are and how much work we're turning out. I hope you are a prolific writer.'

'I don't know anything about writing,' Colonel Scheisskopf retorted sullenly.

'Well, don't let that trouble you.' General Peckem continued with a careless flick of his wrist. 'Just pass the work I assign you along to somebody else and trust to luck. We call that delegation of responsibility. Somewhere down near the lowest level of this co-ordinated organization I run are people who do get the work done when it reaches them, and everything manages to run along smoothly without too much effort on my part. I suppose that's because I am a good executive. Nothing we do in this large department of ours is really very important, and there's never any rush. On the other hand, it is important that we let people know we do a great deal of it. Let me know if you find yourself short-handed. I've already put in a requisition for two majors, four captains and sixteen lieutenants to give you a hand. While none of the work we do is very important, it is important that we do a great deal of it. Don't you agree?'

'What about the parades?' Colonel Scheisskopf broke in.

'What parades?' inquired General Peckem with a feeling that his polish just wasn't getting across.

'Won't I be able to conduct parades every Sunday afternoon?' Colonel Scheisskopf demanded petulantly.

'No. Of course not. What ever gave you that idea?'

'But they said I could.'

'Who said you could?'

'The officers who sent me overseas. They told me I'd be able to march the men around in parades all I wanted to.'

'They lied to you.'

'That wasn't fair, sir.'

'I'm sorry, Scheisskopf. I'm willing to do everything I can to make you happy here, but parades are out of the question. We don't have enough men in our own organization to make up much of a parade, and the combat units would rise up in open rebellion if we tried to make them march. I'm afraid you'll just have to hold back awhile until we get control. Then you can do what you want with the men.'

'What about my wife?' Colonel Scheisskopf demanded with disgruntled suspicion. 'I'll still be able to send for her, won't I?'

'Your wife? Why in the world should you want to?'

'A husband and wife should be together.'

'That's out of the question also.'

'But they said I could send for her!'

'They lied to you again.'

'They had no right to lie to me!' Colonel Scheisskopf protested, his eyes wetting with indignation.

'Of course they had a right,' General Peckem snapped with cold and calculated severity, resolving right then and there to test the mettle of his new colonel under fire. 'Don't be such an ass, Scheisskopf. People have a right to do anything that's not forbidden by law, and there's no law against lying to you. Now, don't ever waste my time with such sentimental platitudes again. Do you hear?'

'Yes, sir,' murmured Colonel Scheisskopf.

Colonel Scheisskopf wilted pathetically, and General Peckem blessed the fates that had sent him a weakling for a subordinate. A man of spunk would have been unthinkable. Having won, General Peckem relented. He did not enjoy humiliating his men. 'If your wife were a Wac, I could probably have her transferred here. But that's the most I can do.'

'She has a friend who's a Wac,' Colonel Scheisskopf offered hopefully.

'I'm afraid that isn't good enough. Have Mrs. Scheisskopf join the Wacs if she wants to, and I'll bring her over here. But in the meantime, my dear Colonel, let's get back to our little war, if we may. Here, briefly, is the military situation that confronts us.' General Peckem rose and moved toward a rotary of enormous colored maps.

Colonel Scheisskopf blanched. 'We're not going into combat, are we?' he blurted out in horror.

'Oh, no, of course not,' General Peckem assured him indulgently, with a companionable laugh. 'Please give me *some* credit, won't you? That's why we're still down here in Rome. Certainly, I'd like to be up in Florence, too, where I could keep in closer touch with ex-P.F.C. Wintergreen. But Florence is still a bit too near the actual fighting to suit me.' General Peckem lifted a wooden pointer and swept the rubbertip cheerfully across Italy from one coast to the other. 'These, Scheisskopf, are the Germans. They're dug into these mountains very solidly in the Gothic Line and won't be pushed out till late next spring, although that isn't going to stop those clods we have in charge from trying. That gives us in Special Services almost nine months to achieve our objective. And that objective is to capture every bomber group in the U.S. Air Force. After all,' said General Peckem with his low, well-modulated chuckle, 'if dropping bombs on the enemy isn't a special service, I wonder what in the world is. Don't you agree?' Colonel Scheisskopf gave no indication that he did agree, but General Peckem was already too entranced with his own loquacity to notice. 'Our position right now is excellent. Reinforcements like yourself keep arriving, and we have more than enough time to plan our entire strategy carefully. Our immediate goal,' he said, 'is right here.' And General Peckem swung his pointer south to the island of Pianosa and tapped it significantly upon a large word that had been lettered on there with black grease pencil. The word was DREEDLE.

Colonel Scheisskopf, squinting, moved very close to

the map, and for the first time since he entered the room a light of comprehension shed a dim glow over his stolid face. 'I think I understand,' he exclaimed. 'Yes, I know I understand. Our first job is to capture Dreedle away from the enemy. Right?'

General Peckem laughed benignly. 'No, Scheisskopf. Dreedle's on our side, and Dreedle is the enemy. General Dreedle commands four bomb groups that we simply must capture in order to continue our offensive. Conquering General Dreedle will give us the aircraft and vital bases we need to carry our operations into other areas. And that battle, by the way, is just about won.' General Peckem drifted toward the window, laughing quietly again, and settled back against the sill with his arms folded, greatly satisfied by his own wit and by his knowledgeable, blasé impudence. The skilled choice of words he was exercising was exquisitely titillating. General Peckem liked listening to himself talk, like most of all listening to himself talk about himself. 'General Dreedle simply doesn't know how to cope with me,' he gloated. 'I keep invading his jurisdiction with comments and criticisms that are really none of my business, and he doesn't know what to do about it. When he accuses me of seeking to undermine him, I merely answer that my only purpose in calling attention to his errors is to strengthen our war effort by eliminating inefficiency. Then I ask him innocently if he's opposed to improving our war effort. Oh, he grumbles and he bristles and he bellows, but he's really quite helpless. He's simply out of style. He's turning into quite a souse, you know. The poor blockhead shouldn't even be a general. He has no tone, no tone at all. Thank God he isn't going to last.' General Peckem chuckled with jaunty relish and sailed smoothly along toward a favorite learned allusion. 'I sometimes think of myself as Fortinbras – ha, ha – in the play *Hamlet* by William Shakespeare, who just keeps circling and circling around the action until everything else falls apart, and then strolls in at the end to pick up all the pieces for himself. Shakespeare is –'

'I don't know anything about plays,' Colonel Scheisskopf broke in bluntly.

General Peckem looked at him with amazement. Never before had a reference of his to Shakespeare's hallowed *Hamlet* been ignored and trampled upon with such rude indifference. He began to wonder with genuine concern just what sort of shit-head the Pentagon had foisted on him. 'What *do* you know about?' he asked acidly.

'Parades,' answered Colonel Scheisskopf eagerly. 'Will I be able to send out memos about parades?'

'As long as you don't schedule any.' General Peckem returned to his chair still wearing a frown. 'And as long as they don't interfere with your main assignment of recommending that the authority of Special Services be expanded to include combat activities.'

'Can I schedule parades and then call them off?'

General Peckem brightened instantly. 'Why, that's a wonderful idea! But just send out weekly announcements *postponing* the parades. Don't even bother to schedule them. That would be infinitely more disconcerting.' General Peckem was blossoming spryly with cordiality again. 'Yes, Scheisskopf,' he said, 'I think you've really hit on something. After all, what combat commander could possible quarrel with us for notifying his men that there won't be a parade that coming Sunday? We'd be merely stating a widely known fact. But the implication is beautiful. Yes, positively beautiful. We're implying that we *could* schedule a parade if we chose to. I'm going to like you, Scheisskopf. Stop in and introduce yourself to Colonel Cargill and tell him what you're up to. I know you two will like each other.'

Colonel Cargill came storming into General Peckem's office a minute later in a furor of timid resentment. 'I've been here longer than Scheisskopf,' he complained. 'Why can't I be the one to call off the parades?'

'Because Scheisskopf has experience with parades, and you haven't. You can call off U.S.O. shows if you want to. In fact why don't you? Just think of all the places

that won't be getting a U.S.O. show on any given day.
Think of all the places each big-name entertainer won't
be visiting. Yes, Cargill, I think you've hit on something. I
think you've just thrown open a whole new area of operation for us. Tell Colonel Scheisskopf I want him to work
along under your supervision on this. And send him in to
see me when you're through giving him instructions.'

'Colonel Cargill says you told him you want me to work
along under his supervision on the U.S.O. project,'
Colonel Scheisskopf complained.

'I told him no such thing,' answered General Peckem.
'Confidentially, Scheisskopf, I'm not too happy with
Colonel Cargill. He's bossy and he's slow. I'd like you to
keep a close eye on what he's doing and see if you can't
get a little more work out of him.'

'He keeps butting in,' Colonel Cargill protested. 'He
won't let me get any work done.'

'There's something very funny about Scheisskopf,'
General Peckem agreed reflectively. 'Keep a very close
eye on him and see if you can't find out what he's up to.'

'Now he's butting into *my* business!' Colonel Scheisskopf cried.

'Don't let it worry you, Scheisskopf,' said General
Peckem, congratulating himself on how adeptly he had
fit Colonel Scheisskopf into his standard method of
operation. Already his two colonels were barely on
speaking terms. 'Colonel Cargill envies you because of
the splendid job you're doing on parades. He's afraid I'm
going to put you in charge of bomb patterns.'

Colonel Scheisskopf was all ears. 'What are bomb
patterns?'

'Bomb patterns?' General Peckem repeated, twinkling with self-satisfied good humor. 'A *bomb pattern* is
a term I dreamed up just several weeks ago. It means
nothing, but you'd be surprised at how rapidly it's
caught on. Why, I've got all sorts of people convinced I
think it's important for the bombs to explode close
together and make a neat aerial photograph. There's

411

one colonel in Pianosa who's hardly concerned any more with whether he hits the target or not. Let's fly over and have some fun with him today. It will make Colonel Cargill jealous, and I learned from Wintergreen this morning that General Dreedle will be off in Sardinia. It drives General Dreedle insane to find out I've been inspecting one of his installations while he's been off inspecting another. We may even get there in time for the briefing. They'll be bombing a tiny undefended village, reducing the whole community to rubble. I have it from Wintergreen – Wintergreen's an ex-sergeant now, by the way – that the mission is entirely unnecessary. Its only purpose is to delay German reinforcements at a time when we aren't even planning an offensive. But that's the way things go when you elevate mediocre people to positions of authority.' He gestured languidly toward his gigantic map of Italy. 'Why, this tiny mountain village is so insignificant that it isn't even there.'

They arrived at Colonel Cathcart's group too late to attend the preliminary briefing and hear Major Danby insist, 'But it is there, I tell you. It's there, it's there.'

'It's where? Dunbar demanded defiantly, pretending not to see.

'It's right there on the map where this road makes this slight turn. Can't you see this slight turn on your map?'

'No, I can't see it.'

'I can see it,' volunteered Havermeyer, and marked the spot on Dunbar's map. 'And here's a good picture of the village right on these photographs. I understand the whole thing. The purpose of the mission is to knock the whole village sliding down the side of the mountain and create a roadblock that the Germans will have to clear. Is that right?'

'That's right,' said Major Danby, mopping his perspiring forehead with his handkerchief. 'I'm glad somebody here is beginning to understand. These two armored divisions will be coming down from Austria into Italy along this road. The village is built on such a steep incline that all the rubble from the houses and other buildings you destroy will certainly tumble right down and pile upon the road.'

'What the hell difference will it make?' Dunbar wanted to know, as Yossarian watched him excitedly with a mixture of awe and adulation. 'It will only take them a couple of days to clear it.'

Major Danby was trying to avoid an argument. 'Well, it apparently makes some difference to Headquarters,' he answered in a conciliatory tone. 'I suppose that's why they ordered the mission.'

'Have the people in the village been warned?' asked McWatt.

Major Danby was dismayed that McWatt too was registering opposition. 'No, I don't think so.'

'Haven't we dropped any leaflets telling them that this time we'll be flying over to hit them?' asked Yossarian. 'Can't we even tip them off so they'll get out of the way?'

'No, I don't think so.' Major Danby was swearing some more and still shifting his eyes about uneasily. 'The Germans might find out and choose another road. I'm not sure about any of this. I'm just making assumptions.'

'They won't even take shelter,' Dunbar argued bitterly. 'They'll pour out into the streets to wave when they see our planes coming, all the children and dogs and old people. Jesus Christ! Why can't we leave them alone?'

'Why can't we create the roadblock somewhere else?' asked McWatt. 'Why must it be there?'

'I don't know,' Major Danby answered unhappily. 'I don't know. Look, fellows, we've got to have some confidence in the people above us who issue our orders. They know what they're doing.'

'The hell they do,' said Dunbar.

'What's the trouble?' inquired Colonel Korn, moving leisurely across the briefing room with his hands in his pockets and his tan shirt baggy.

'Oh, no trouble, Colonel,' said Major Danby, trying nervously to cover up. 'We're just discussing the mission.'

'They don't want to bomb the village,' Havermeyer

413

snickered, giving Major Danby away.

'You prick!' Yossarian said to Havermeyer.

'You leave Havermeyer alone,' Colonel Korn ordered Yossarian curtly. He recognized Yossarian as the drunk who had accosted him roughly at the officers' club one night before the first mission to Bologna, and he swung his displeasure prudently to Dunbar. 'Why don't you want to bomb the village?'

'It's cruel, that's why.'

'Cruel?' asked Colonel Korn with cold good humor, frightened only momentarily by the uninhibited vehemence of Dunbar's hostility. 'Would it be any less cruel to let those two German divisions down to fight with our troops? American lives are at stake, too, you know. Would you rather see American blood spilled?'

'American blood is being spilled. But those people are living up there in peace. Why can't we leave them the hell alone?'

'Yes, it's easy for you to talk,' Colonel Korn jeered. 'You're safe here in Pianosa. It won't make any difference to you when these German reinforcements arrive, will it?'

Dunbar turned crimson with embarrassment and replied in a voice that was suddenly defensive. 'Why can't we create the roadblock somewhere else? Couldn't we bomb the slope of a mountain or the road itself?'

'Would you rather go back to Bologna?' The question, asked quietly, rang out like a shot and created a silence in the room that was awkward and menacing. Yossarian prayed intensely, with shame, that Dunbar would keep his mouth shut. Dunbar dropped his gaze, and Colonel Korn knew he had won. 'No, I thought not,' he continued with undisguised scorn. 'You know, Colonel Cathcart and I have to go to a lot of trouble to get you a milk run like this. If you'd sooner fly missions to Bologna, Spezia and Ferrara, we can get those targets with no trouble at all.' His eyes gleamed dangerously behind his rimless glasses, and his muddy jowls were square and hard. 'Just let me know.'

'I would,' responded Havermeyer eagerly with another boastful snicker. 'I like to fly into Bologna straight and level with my head in the bombsight and listen to all that flak pumping away all around me. I get a big kick out of the way the men come charging over to me after the mission and call me dirty names. Even the enlisted men get sore enough to curse me and want to take socks at me.'

Colonel Korn chucked Havermeyer under the chin jovially, ignoring him, and then addressed himself to Dunbar and Yossarian in a dry monotone. 'You've got my sacred word for it. Nobody is more distressed about those lousy wops up in the hills than Colonel Cathcart and myself. *Mais c'est la guerre.* Try to remember that we didn't start the war and Italy did. That we weren't the aggressors and Italy was. And that we couldn't possibly inflict as much cruelty on the Italians, Germans, Russians and Chinese as they're already inflicting on themselves.' Colonel Korn gave Major Danby's shoulder a friendly squeeze without changing his unfriendly expression. 'Carry on with the briefing, Danby. And make sure they understand the importance of a tight bomb pattern.'

'Oh, no, Colonel,' Major Danby blurted out, blinking upward. 'Not for this target. I've told them to space their bombs sixty feet apart so that we'll have a roadblock the full length of the village instead of in just one spot. It will be a much more effective roadblock with a loose bomb pattern.'

'We don't care about the roadblock,' Colonel Korn informed him. 'Colonel Cathcart wants to come out of this mission with a good clean aerial photograph he won't be ashamed to send through channels. Don't forget that General Peckem will be here for the full briefing, and you know how he feels about bomb patterns. Incidentally, Major, you'd better hurry up with these details and clear out before he gets here. General Peckem can't stand you.'

'Oh, no, Colonel,' Major Danby corrected obligingly. 'It's General Dreedle who can't stand me.'

'General Peckem can't stand you either. In fact, no one can stand you. Finish what you're doing, Danby, and

415

disappear. I'll conduct the briefing.'

'Where's Major Danby?' Colonel Cathcart inquired, after he had driven up for the full briefing with General Peckem and Colonel Scheisskopf.

'He asked permission to leave as soon as he saw you driving up,' answered Colonel Korn. 'He's afraid General Peckem doesn't like him. I was going to conduct the briefing anyway. I do a much better job.'

'Splendid!' said Colonel Cathcart. 'No!' Colonel Cathcart countermanded himself an instant later when he remembered how good a job Colonel Korn had done before General Dreedle at the first Avignon briefing. 'I'll do it myself.'

Colonel Cathcart braced himself with the knowledge that he was one of General Peckem's favorites and took charge of the meeting, snapping his words out crisply to the attentive audience of subordinate officers with the bluff and dispassionate toughness he had picked up from General Dreedle. He knew he cut a fine figure there on the platform with his open shirt collar, his cigarette holder, and his close-cropped, gray-tipped curly black hair. He breezed along beautifully, even emulating certain characteristic mispronounciations of General Dreedle's, and he was not the least bit intimidated by General Peckem's new colonel until he suddenly recalled that General Peckem detested General Dreedle. Then his voice cracked, and all confidence left him. He stumbled ahead through instinct in burning humiliation. He was suddenly in terror of Colonel Scheisskopf. Another colonel in the area meant another rival, another enemy, another person who hated him. And this one was tough! A horrifying thought occurred to Colonel Cathcart: Suppose Colonel Scheisskopf had already bribed all the men in the room to begin moaning, as they had done at the first Avignon mission. How could he silence them? What a terrible black eye that would be! Colonel Cathcart was seized with such fright that he almost beckoned to Colonel Korn. Somehow he held himself together and synchronized the watches. When he had done that, he knew he had won, for he could end now at any time. He had come through in a crisis. He wanted to laugh in Colonel Scheisskopf's face with triumph and spite. He had proved himself brilliantly under pressure, and he concluded the briefing with an inspiring peroration that every instinct told him was a masterful exhibition of eloquent tact and subtlety.

'Now, men,' he exhorted. 'We have with us today a very distinguished guest, General Peckem from Special Services, the man who gives us all our softball bats, comic books and U.S.O. shows. I want to dedicate this mission to him. Go on out there and bomb – for me, for your country, for God, and for that great American, General P.P. Peckem. And let's see you put all those bombs on a dime!'

30 Dunbar

Yossarian no longer gave a damn where his bombs fell,
although he did not go as far as Dunbar, who dropped
his bombs hundreds of yards past the village and would
face a court-martial if it could ever be shown he had
done it deliberately. Without a word even to Yossarian,
Dunbar had washed his hands of the mission. The fall in
the hospital had either shown him the light or scrambled
his brains; it was impossible to say which.

Dunbar seldom laughed any more and seemed to be
wasting away. He snarled belligerently at superior officers, even at Major Danby, and was crude and surly and
profane even in front of the chaplain, who was afraid of
Dunbar now and seemed to be wasting away also. The
chaplain's pilgrimage to Wintergreen had proved abortive; another shrine was empty. Wintergreen was too
busy to see the chaplain himself. A brash assistant
brought the chaplain a stolen Zippo cigarette lighter as
a gift and informed him condescendingly that Wintergreen was too deeply involved with wartime activities to
concern himself with matters so trivial as the number of
missions men had to fly. The chaplain worried about
Dunbar and brooded more over Yossarian now that Orr
was gone. To the chaplain, who lived by himself in a

spacious tent whose pointy top sealed him in gloomy solitude each night like the cap of a tomb, it seemed incredible that Yossarian really preferred living alone and wanted no room-mates.

As a lead bombardier again, Yossarian had McWatt for a pilot, and that was one consolation, although he was still so utterly undefended. There was no way to fight back. He could not even see McWatt and the co-pilot from his post in the nose. All he could ever see was Aarfy, with whose fustian, moon-faced ineptitude he had finally lost all patience, and there were minutes of agonizing fury and frustration in the sky when he hungered to be demoted again to a wing plane with a loaded machine gun in the compartment instead of the precision bombsight that he really had no need for, a powerful, heavy fifty-caliber machine gun he could seize vengefully in both hands and turn loose savagely against all the demons tyrannizing him: at the smoky black puffs of the flak itself; at the German antiaircraft gunners below whom he could not even see and could not possibly harm with his machine gun even if he ever did take the time to open fire, at Havermeyer and Appleby in the lead plane for their fearless straight and level bomb run on the second mission to Bologna where the flak from two hundred and twenty-four cannons had knocked out one of Orr's engines for the very last time and sent him down ditching into the sea between Genoa and La Spezia just before the brief thunderstorm broke.

Actually, there was not much he could do with that powerful machine gun except load it and test-fire a few rounds. It was no more use to him than the bombsight. He could really cut loose with it against attacking German fighters, but there were no German fighters any more, and he could not even swing it all the way around into the helpless faces of pilots like Huple and Dobbs and order them back down carefully to the ground, as he had once ordered Kid Sampson back down, which is exactly what he did want to do to Dobbs and Huple on the hideous first mission to Avignon the moment he realized the

419

fantastic pickle he was in, the moment he found himself aloft in a wing plane with Dobbs and Huple in a flight headed by Havermeyer and Appleby. Dobbs and Huple? Huple and Dobbs? Who were they? What preposterous madness to float in thin air two miles high on an inch or two of metal, sustained from death by the meager skill and intelligence of two vapid strangers, a beardless kid named Huple and a nervous nut like Dobbs, who really did go nuts right there in the plane, running amuck over the target without leaving his co-pilots' seat and grabbing the controls from Huple to plunge them all down into that chilling dive that tore Yossarian's headset loose and brought them right back inside the dense flak from which they had almost escaped. The next thing he knew, another stranger, a radio-gunner named Snowden, was dying in back. It was impossible to be positive that Dobbs had killed him, for when Yossarian plugged his headset back in, Dobbs was already on the intercom pleading for someone to go up front and help the bombardier. And almost immediately Snowden broke in, whimpering, 'Help me. Please help me. I'm cold. I'm cold.' And Yossarian crawled slowly out of the nose and up on top of the bomb bay and wriggled back into the rear section of the plane – passing the first-aid kit on the way that he had to return for – to treat Snowden for the wrong wound, the yawning, raw, melon-shaped hole as big as a football in the outside of his thigh, the unsevered, blood-soaked muscle fibers inside pulsating weirdly like blind things with lives of their own, the oval, naked wound that was almost a foot long and made Yossarian moan in shock and sympathy the instant he spied it and nearly made him vomit. And the small, slight tail gunner was lying on the floor beside Snowden in a dead faint, his face as white as a handkerchief, so that Yossarian sprang forward with revulsion to help him first.

Yes, in the long run, he was much safer flying with McWatt, and he was not even safe with McWatt, who loved flying too much and went buzzing boldly inches off the ground with Yossarian in the nose on the way back from the training flight to break in the new bombardier in the whole replacement crew Colonel Cathcart had obtained after Orr was lost. The practice bomb range was on the other side of Pianosa, and, flying back, McWatt edged the belly of the lazing, slow-cruising plane just over the crest of mountains in the middle and then, instead of maintaining altitude, jolted both engines open all the way, lurched up on one side and, to Yossarian's astonishment, began following the falling land down as fast as the plane would go, wagging his wings gaily and skimming with a massive, grinding, hammering roar over each rocky rise and dip of the rolling terrain like a dizzy gull over wild brown waves. Yossarian was petrified. The new bombardier beside him sat demurely with a bewitched grin and kept whistling 'Whee!' and Yossarian wanted to reach out and crush his idiotic face with one hand as he flinched and flung himself away from the boulders and hillocks and lashing branches of trees that loomed up above him out in front and rushed past just underneath in a sinking, streaking blur. No one had a right to take such frightful risks with his life.

'Go up, go up, go up!' he shouted frantically at McWatt, hating him venomously, but McWatt was singing buoyantly over the intercom and probably couldn't hear. Yossarian, blazing with rage and almost sobbing for revenge, hurled himself down into the crawlway and fought his way through against the dragging weight of gravity and inertia until he arrived at the main section and pulled himself up to the flight deck, to stand trembling behind McWatt in the pilot's seat. He looked desperately about for a gun, a gray-black .45 automatic that he could cock and ram right up against the base of McWatt's skull. There was no gun. There was no hunting knife either, and no other weapon with which he could bludgeon or stab, and Yossarian grasped and jerked the collar of McWatt's coveralls in tightening fists and shouted to him to go up, go up. The land was

421

still swimming by underneath and flashing by overhead on both sides. McWatt looked back at Yossarian and laughed joyfully as though Yossarian were sharing his fun. Yossarian slid both hands around McWatt's bare throat and squeezed. McWatt turned stiff.

'Go up,' Yossarian ordered unmistakably through his teeth in a low, menacing voice. 'Or I'll kill you.'

Rigid with caution, McWatt cut the motors back and climbed gradually. Yossarian's hands weakened on McWatt's neck and slid down off his shoulders to dangle inertly. He was not angry any more. He was ashamed. When McWatt turned, he was sorry the hands were his and wished there were someplace where he could bury them. They felt dead.

McWatt gazed at him deeply. There was no friendliness in his stare. 'Boy,' he said coldly, 'you sure must be in pretty bad shape. You ought to go home.'

'They won't let me.' Yossarian answered with averted eyes, and crept away.

Yossarian stepped down from the flight deck and seated himself on the floor, hanging his head with guilt and remorse. He was covered with sweat.

McWatt set course directly back toward the field. Yossarian wondered whether McWatt would now go to the operations tent to see Piltchard and Wren and request that Yossarian never be assigned to his plane again, just as Yossarian had gone surreptitiously to speak to them about Dobbs and Huple and Orr and, unsuccessfully, about Aarfy. He had never seen McWatt look displeased before, had never seen him in any but the most lighthearted mood, and he wondered whether he had just lost another friend.

But McWatt winked at him reassuringly as he climbed down from the plane and joshed hospitably with the credulous new pilot and bombardier during the jeep ride back to the squadron, although he did not address a word to Yossarian until all four had returned their parachutes and separated and the two of them were walking side by side toward their own row of tents. Then

McWatt's sparsely freckled tan Scotch-Irish face broke suddenly into a smile and he dug his knuckles playfully into Yossarian's ribs, as though throwing a punch.

'You louse,' he laughed. 'Were you really going to kill me up there?'

Yossarian grinned penitently and shook his head. 'No I don't think so.'

'I didn't realize you got it so bad. Boy! Why don't you talk to somebody about it?'

'I talk to everybody about it. What the hell's the matter with you? Don't you ever hear me?'

'I guess I never really believed you.'

'Aren't you ever afraid?'

'Maybe I ought to be.'

'Not even on the missions?'

'I guess I just don't have brains enough.' McWatt laughed sheepishly.

'There are so many ways for me to get killed,' Yossarian commented, 'and you had to find one more.'

McWatt smiled again. 'Say, I bet it must really scare you when I buzz your tent, huh?'

'It scares me to death. I've told you that.'

'I thought it was just the noise you were complaining about.' McWatt made a resigned shrug. 'Oh, well, what the hell,' he sang. 'I guess I'll just have to give it up.'

But McWatt was incorrigible, and, while he never buzzed Yossarian's tent again, he never missed an opportunity to buzz the beach and roar like a fierce and low-flying thunderbolt over the raft in the water and the secluded hollow in the sand where Yossarian lay feeling up Nurse Duckett or playing hearts, poker or pinochle with Nately, Dunbar and Hungry Joe. Yossarian met Nurse Duckett almost every afternoon that both were free and came with her to the beach on the other side of the narrow swell of shoulder-high dunes separating them from the area in which the other officers and enlisted men went swimming nude. Nately, Dunbar and Hungry Joe would come there, too. McWatt would occasionally join them, and often Aarfy, who always arrived pudgily in full uniform and never removed any of his clothing but his shoes and his hat; Aarfy never went swimming. The other men wore swimming trunks in deference to Nurse Duckett, and in deference also to Nurse Cramer, who accompanied Nurse Duckett and Yossarian to the beach every time and sat haughtily by herself ten yards away. No one but Aarfy ever made reference to the naked men sun-bathing in full view farther down the beach or jumping and diving from the enormous white-washed raft that bobbed on empty oil drums out beyond the silt sand. Nurse Cramer sat by herself because she was angry with Yossarian and disappointed in Nurse Duckett.

Nurse Sue Ann Duckett despised Aarfy, and that was another one of the numerous fetching traits about Nurse Duckett that Yossarian enjoyed. He enjoyed Nurse Sue Ann Duckett's long white legs and supple, callipygous ass; he often neglected to remember that she was quite slim and fragile from the waist up and hurt her unintentionally in moments of passion when he hugged her too roughly. He loved her manner of sleepy acquiescence when they lay on the beach at dusk. He drew solace and sedation from her nearness. He had a craving to touch her always, to remain always in physical communication. He liked to encircle her ankle loosely with his fingers as he played cards with Nately, Dunbar and Hungry Joe, to lightly and lovingly caress the downy skin of her fair, smooth thigh with the backs of his nails or, dreamily, sensuously, almost unconsciously, slide his proprietary, respectful hand up the shell-like ridge of her spine beneath the elastic strap of the top of the two-piece bathing suit she always wore to contain and cover her tiny, long-nippled breasts. He loved Nurse Duckett's serene, flattered response, the sense of attachment to him she displayed proudly. Hungry Joe had a craving to feel Nuse Duckett up, too, and was restrained more than once by Yossarian's forbidding glower. Nurse Duckett flirted with Hungry Joe just to keep him in heat, and her round light-brown eyes glimmered with mischief every time Yossarian rapped her sharply with his elbow or fist to make her stop.

The men played cards on a towel, undershirt, or blanket, and Nurse Duckett mixed the extra deck of cards, sitting with her back resting against a sand dune. When she was not shuffling the extra deck of cards, she sat squinting into a tiny pocket mirror, brushing mascara on her curling reddish eyelashes in a birdbrained effort to make them longer permanently. Occasionally she was able to stack the cards or spoil the deck in a way they did not discover until they were well into the game, and she laughed and glowed with blissful gratification when they all hurled their cards down disgustedly and began punching her sharply on the arms or legs as they called her filthy names and warned her to stop fooling around. She would prattle nonsensically when they were striving hardest to think, and a pink flush of elation crept into her cheeks when they gave her more sharp raps on the arms and legs with their fists and told her to shut up. Nurse Duckett reveled in such attention and ducked her short chestnut bangs with joy when Yossarian and the others focused upon her. It gave her a peculiar feeling of warm and expectant well-being to know that so many naked boys and men were idling close by on the other side of the sand dunes. She had only to stretch her neck or rise on some pretext to see twenty or forty undressed males lounging or playing ball in the sunlight. Her own body was such a familiar and unremarkable thing to her that she was puzzled by the convulsive ecstasy men could take from it, by the intense and amusing need they had merely to touch it, to reach out urgently and press it, squeeze it, pinch it, rub it. She did not understand Yossarian's lust; but she was willing to take his word for it.

Evenings when Yossarian felt horny he brought Nurse Duckett to the beach with two blankets and enjoyed making love to her with most of their clothes on more than he sometimes enjoyed making love to all the vigorous bare amoral girls in Rome. Frequently they went to the beach at night and did not make love, but just lay shivering between the blankets against each other to ward off the brisk, damp chill. The ink-black nights were turning cold, the stars frosty and fewer. The raft swayed in the ghostly trail of moonlight and seemed to be sailing away. A marked hint of cold weather penetrated the air. Other men were just starting to build stoves and came to Yossarian's tent during the day to marvel at Orr's workmanship. It thrilled Nurse Duckett rapturously that Yossarian could not keep his hands off her when they were together, although she would not let him slip them inside her bathing shorts during the day when anyone was near enough to see, not even when the only witness was Nurse Cramer, who sat on the other side of her sand dune with her reproving nose in the air and pretended not to see anything.

Nurse Cramer had stopped speaking to Nurse Duckett, her best friend, because of her liaison with Yossarian, but still went everywhere with Nurse Duckett since Nurse Duckett *was* her best friend. She did not approve of Yossarian or his friends. When they stood up and went swimming with Nurse Duckett, Nurse Cramer stood up and went swimming, too, maintaining the same ten-yard distance between them, and maintaining her silence, snubbing them even in the water. When they laughed and splashed, she laughed and splashed; when they dived, she dived; when they swam to the sand bar and rested, Nurse Cramer swam to the sand bar and rested. When they came out, she came out, dried her shoulders with her own towel and seated herself aloofly in her own spot, her back rigid and a ring of reflected sunlight burnishing her light-blond hair like a halo. Nurse Cramer was prepared to begin talking to Nurse Duckett again if she repented and apologized. Nurse Duckett preferred things the way they were. For a long time she had wanted to give Nurse Cramer a rap to make her shut up.

Nurse Duckett found Yossarian wonderful and was already trying to change him. She loved to watch him

426

taking short naps with his face down and his arm thrown across her, or staring bleakly at the endless tame, quiet waves breaking like pet puppy dogs against the shore, scampering lightly up the sand a foot or two and then trotting away. She was calm in his silences. She knew she did not bore him, and she buffed or painted her fingernails studiously while he dozed or brooded and the desultory warm afternoon breeze vibrated delicately on the surface of the beach. She loved to look at his wide, long, sinewy back with its bronzed, unblemished skin. She loved to bring him to flame instantly by taking his whole ear in her mouth suddenly and running her hand down his front all the way. She loved to make him burn and suffer till dark, then satisfy him. Then kiss him adoringly because she had brought him such bliss.

Yossarian was never lonely with Nurse Duckett, who really did know how to keep her mouth shut and was just capricious enough. He was haunted and tormented by the vast, boundless ocean. He wondered mournfully, as Nurse Duckett buffed her nails, about all the people who had died under water. There were surely more than a million already. Where were they? What insects had eaten their flesh? He imagined the awful impotence of breathing in helplessly quarts and quarts of water. Yossarian followed the small fishing boats and military launches plying back and forth far out and found them unreal; it did not seem true that there were full-sized men aboard, going somewhere every time. He looked toward stony Elba, and his eyes automatically searched overhead for the fluffy, white, turnip-shaped cloud in which Clevinger had vanished. He peered at the vaporous Italian skyline and thought of Orr. Clevinger and Orr. Where had they gone? Yossarian had once stood on a jetty at dawn and watched a tufted round log that was drifting toward him on the tide turn unexpectedly into the bloated face of a drowned man; it was the first dead person he had ever seen. He thirsted for life and reached out ravenously to grasp and hold Nurse Duckett's flesh.

427

He studied every floating object fearfully for some gruesome sign of Clevinger and Orr, prepared for any morbid shock but the shock McWatt gave him one day with the plane that came blasting suddenly into sight out of the distant stillness and hurtled mercilessly along the shore line with a great growling, clattering roar over the bobbing raft on which blond, pale Kid Sampson, his naked sides scrawny even from so far away, leaped clownishly up to touch it at the exact moment some arbitrary gust of wind or minor miscalculation of McWatt's senses dropped the speeding plane down just low enough for a propeller to slice him half away.

Even people who were not there remembered vividly exactly what happened next. There was the briefest, softest *tsst!* filtering audibly through the shattering, overwhelming howl of the plane's engines, and then there were just Kid Sampson's two pale, skinny legs, still joined by strings somehow at the bloody truncated hips, standing stock-still on the raft for what seemed a full minute or two before they toppled over backward into the water finally with a faint, echoing splash and turned completely upside down so that only the grotesque toes and the plaster-white soles of Kid Sampson's feet remained in view.

On the beach, all hell broke loose. Nurse Cramer materialized out of thin air suddenly and was weeping hysterically against Yossarian's chest while Yossarian hugged her shoulders and soothed her. His other arm bolstered Nurse Duckett, who was trembling and sobbing against him, too, her long, angular face dead white. Everyone at the beach was screaming and running, and the men sounded like women. They scampered for their things in panic, stooping hurriedly and looking askance at each gentle, knee-high wave bubbling in as though some ugly, red, grisly organ like a liver or a lung might come washing right up against them. Those in the water were struggling to get out, forgetting in their haste to swim, wailing, walking, held back in their flight by the viscous, clinging sea as though by a biting wind.

Kid Sampson had rained all over. Those who spied drops of him on their limbs or torsoes drew back with terror and revulsion, as though trying to shrink away from their own odious skins. Everybody ran in a sluggish stampede, shooting tortured, horrified glances back, filling the deep, shadowy, rustling woods with their frail gasps and cries. Yossarian drove both stumbling, faltering women before him frantically, shoving them and prodding them to make them hurry, and raced back with a curse to help when Hungry Joe tripped on the blanket or the camera case he was carrying and fell forward on his face in the mud of the stream.

Back at the squadron everyone already knew. Men in uniform were screaming and running there too, or standing motionless in one spot, rooted in awe, like Sergeant Knight and Doc Daneeka as they gravely craned their heads upward and watched the guilty, banking, forlorn airplane with McWatt circle and circle slowly and climb.

'Who is it?' Yossarian shouted anxiously at Doc Daneeka as he ran up, breathless and limp, his somber eyes burning with a misty, hectic anguish. 'Who's in the plane?'

'McWatt,' said Sergeant Knight. 'He's got the two new pilots with him on a training flight. Doc Daneeka's up there, too.'

'I'm right here,' contended Doc Daneeka, in a strange and troubled voice, darting an anxious look at Sergeant Knight.

'Why doesn't he come down?' Yossarian exclaimed in despair. 'Why does he keep going up?'

'He's probably afraid to come down,' Sergeant Knight answered, without moving his solemn gaze from McWatt's solitary climbing airplane. 'He knows what kind of trouble he's in.'

And McWatt kept climbing higher and higher, nosing his droning airplane upward evenly in a slow, oval spiral that carried him far out over the water as he headed south and far in over the russet foothills when he had circled the landing field again and was flying north. He was soon up over five thousand feet. His engines were soft as whispers. A white parachute popped open suddenly in a surprising puff. A second parachute popped open a few minutes later and coasted down, like the first, directly in toward the clearing of the landing strip. There was no motion on the ground. The plane continued south for thirty seconds more, following the same pattern, familiar and predictable now, and McWatt lifted a wing and banked gracefully around into his turn.

'Two more to go,' said Sergeant Knight. 'McWatt and Doc Daneeka.'

'I'm right here, Sergeant Knight,' Doc Daneeka told him plaintively. 'I'm not in the plane.'

'Why don't they jump?' Sergeant Knight asked, pleading aloud to himelf. 'Why don't they jump?'

'It doesn't make sense,' grieved Doc Daneeka biting his lip. 'It just doesn't make sense.'

But Yossarian understood suddenly why McWatt wouldn't jump, and went running uncontrollably down the whole length of the squadron after McWatt's plane, waving his arms and shouting up at him imploringly to come down, McWatt, come down; but no one seemed to hear, certainly not McWatt, and a great, choking moan tore from Yossarian's throat as McWatt turned again, dipped his wings once in salute, decided oh, well, what the hell, and flew into a mountain.

Colonel Cathcart was so upset by the deaths of Kid Sampson and McWatt that he raised the missions to sixty-five.

31 Mrs. Daneeka

When Colonel Cathcart learned that Doc Daneeka too
had been killed in McWatt's plane, he increased the
number of missions to seventy.

The first person in the squadron to find out that Doc
Daneeka was dead was Sergeant Towser, who had been
informed earlier by the man in the control tower that
Doc Daneeka's name was down as a passenger on the
pilot's manifest McWatt had filed before taking off.
Sergeant Towser brushed away a tear and struck Doc
Daneeka's name from the roster of squadron personnel.
With lips still quivering, he rose and trudged outside
reluctantly to break the bad news to Gus and Wes,
discreetly avoiding any conversation with Doc Daneeka
himself as he moved by the flight surgeon's slight
sepulchral figure roosting despondently on his stool in
the late-afternoon sunlight between the orderly room
and the medical tent. Sergeant Towser's heart was
heavy; now he had *two* dead men on his hands – Mudd,
the dead man in Yossarian's tent who wasn't even there,
and Doc Daneeka, the new dead man in the squadron,
who most certainly was there and gave every indication
of proving a still thornier administrative problem for
him.

Gus and Wes listened to Sergeant Towser with looks of stoic surprise and said not a word about their bereavement to anyone else until Doc Daneeka himself came in about an hour afterward to have his temperature taken for the third time that day and his blood pressure checked. The thermometer registered a half degree lower than his usual subnormal temperature of 96.8. Doc Daneeka was alarmed. The fixed, vacant, wooden stares of his two enlisted men were even more irritating than always.

'Goddammit,' he expostulated politely in an uncommon excess of exasperation, 'what's the matter with you two men anyway? It just isn't right for a person to have a low temperature all the time and walk around with a stuffed nose.' Doc Daneeka emitted a glum, self-pitying sniff and strolled disconsolately across the tent to help himself to some aspirin and sulphur pills and paint his own throat with Argyrol. His downcast face was fragile and forlorn as a swallow's, and he rubbed the back of his arms rhythmically. 'Just look how cold I am right now. You're sure you're not holding anything back?'

'You're dead, sir,' one of his two enlisted men explained.

Doc Daneeka jerked his head up quickly with resentful distrust. 'What's that?'

'You're dead, sir,' repeated the other. 'That's probably the reason you always feel so cold.'

'That's right, sir. You've probably been dead all this time and we just didn't detect it.'

'What the *hell* are you both talking about?' Doc Daneeka cried shrilly with a surging, petrifying sensation of some onrushing unavoidable disaster.

'It's true, sir,' said one of the enlisted men. 'The records show that you went up in McWatt's plane to collect some flight time. You didn't come down in a parachute, so you must have been killed in the crash.'

'That's right, sir,' said the other. 'You ought to be glad you've got any temperature at all.'

Doc Daneeka's mind was reeling in confusion. 'Have

you both gone crazy?' he demanded. 'I'm going to report this whole insubordinate incident to Sergeant Towser.'

'Sergeant Towser's the one who told us about it,' said either Gus or Wes. 'The War Department's even going to notify your wife.'

Doc Daneeka yelped and ran out of the medical tent to remonstrate with Sergeant Towser, who edged away from him with repugnance and advised Doc Daneeka to remain out of sight as much as possible until some decision could be reached relating to the disposition of his remains.

'Gee, I guess he really is dead,' grieved one of his enlisted men in a low, respectful voice. 'I'm going to miss him. He was a pretty wonderful guy, wasn't he?'

'Yeah, he sure was,' mourned the other. 'But I'm glad the little fuck is gone. I was getting sick and tired of taking his blood pressure all the time.'

Mrs. Daneeka, Doc Daneeka's wife, was not glad that Doc Daneeka was gone and split the peaceful Staten Island night with woeful shrieks of lamentation when she learned by War Department telegram that her husband had been killed in action. Women came to comfort her, and their husbands paid condolence calls and hoped inwardly that she would soon move to another neighbourhood and spare them the obligation of continuous sympathy. The poor woman was totally distraught for almost a full week. Slowly, heroically, she found the strength to contemplate a future filled with dire problems for herself and her children. Just as she was growing resigned to her loss, the postman rang with a bolt from the blue – a letter from overseas that was signed with her husband's signature and urged her frantically to disregard any bad news concerning him. Mrs. Daneeka was dumfounded. The date on the letter was illegible. The handwriting throughout was shaky and hurried, but the style resembled her husband's and the melancholy, self-pitying tone was familiar, although more dreary than usual. Mrs. Daneeka was overjoyed and wept irrepressibly with relief and kissed the crinkled,

433

grubby tissue of V-mail stationery a thousand times. She dashed a grateful note off to her husband pressing him for details and sent a wire informing the War Department of its error. The War Department replied touchily that there had been no error and that she was undoubtedly the victim of some sadistic and psychotic forger in her husband's squadron. The letter to her husband was returned unopened, stamped KILLED IN ACTION.

Mrs. Daneeka had been widowed cruelly again, but this time her grief was mitigated somewhat by a notification from Washington that she was sole beneficiary of her husband's $10,000 GI insurance policy, which amount was obtainable by her on demand. The realization that she and the children were not faced immediately with starvation brought a brave smile to her face and marked the turning point in her distress. The Veterans Administration informed her by mail the very next day that she would be entitled to pension benefits for the rest of her natural life because of her husband's demise, and to a burial allowance for him of $250. A government check for $250 was enclosed. Gradually, inexorably, her prospects brightened. A letter arrived that same week from the Social Security Administration stating that, under the provisions of the Old Age and Survivors Insurance Act of 1935, she would receive monthly support for herself and her dependent children until they reached the age of eighteen, and a burial allowance of $250. With these government letters as proof of death, she applied for payment on three life insurance policies Doc Daneeka had carried, with a value of $50,000 each; her claim was honored and processed swiftly. Each day brought new unexpected treasures. A key to a safe-deposit box led to a fourth life insurance policy with a face value of $50,000, and to $18,000 in cash on which income tax had never been paid and need never be paid. A fraternal lodge to which he had belonged gave her a cemetery plot. A second fraternal organization of which he had been a member sent her a burial allowance of

$250. His county medical association gave her a burial allowance of $250.

The husbands of her closest friends began to flirt with her. Mrs. Daneeka was simply delighted with the way things were turning out and had her hair dyed. Her fantastic wealth just kept piling up, and she had to remind herself daily that all the hundreds of thousands of dollars she was acquiring were not worth a single penny without her husband to share this good fortune with her. It astonished her that so many separate organizations were willing to do so much to bury Doc Daneeka, who, back in Pianosa, was having a terrible time trying to keep his head above the ground and wondered with dismal apprehension why his wife did not answer the letter he had written.

He found himself ostracized in the squadron by men who cursed his memory foully for having supplied Colonel Cathcart with provocation to raise the number of combat missions. Records attesting to his death were pullulating like insect eggs and verifying each other beyond all contention. He drew no pay or PX rations and depended for life on the charity of Sergeant Towser and Milo, who both knew he was dead. Colonel Cathcart refused to see him, and Colonel Korn sent word through Major Danby that he would have Doc Daneeka cremated on the spot if he ever showed up at Group Headquarters. Major Danby confided that Group was incensed with all flight surgeons because of Dr. Stubbs, the busy-haired, baggy-chinned, slovenly flight surgeon in Dunbar's squadron who was deliberately and defiantly brewing insidious dissension there by grounding all men with sixty missions on proper forms that were rejected by Group indignantly with orders restoring the confused pilots, navigators, bombardiers and gunners to combat duty. Morale there was ebbing rapidly, and Dunbar was under surveillance. Group was glad Doc Daneeka had been killed and did not intend to ask for a replacement.

Not even the chaplain could bring Doc Daneeka back to life under the circumstances. Alarm changed to resignation, and more and more Doc Daneeka acquired the look of an ailing rodent. The sacks under his eyes turned hollow and black, and he padded through the shadows fruitlessly like a ubiquitous spook. Even Captain Flume recoiled when Doc Daneeka sought him out in the woods for help. Heartlessly, Gus and Wes turned him away from their medical tent without even a thermometer for comfort, and then, only then, did he realize that, to all intents and purposes, he really was dead, and that he had better do something damned fast if he ever hoped to save himself.

There was nowhere else to turn but to his wife, and he scribbled an impassioned letter begging her to bring his plight to the attention of the War Department and urging her to communicate at once with his group commander, Colonel Cathcart, for assurances that – no matter what else she might have heard – it was indeed he, her husband, Doc Daneeka, who was pleading with her, and not a corpse or some impostor. Mrs. Daneeka was stunned by the depth of emotion in the almost illegible appeal. She was torn with compunction and tempted to comply, but the very next letter she opened that day was from that same Colonel Cathcart, her husband's group commander, and began:

Dear Mrs., Mr., Miss, or Mr. and Mrs. Daneeka: Words cannot express the deep personal grief I experienced when your husband, son, father or brother was killed, wounded or reported missing in action.

Mrs. Daneeka moved with her children to Lansing, Michigan, and left no forwarding address.

32   Yo-Yo's roomies

Yossarian was warm when the cold weather came and whale-shaped clouds blew low through a dingy, slate-gray sky, almost without end, like the droning, dark, iron flocks of B-17 and B-24 bombers from the long-range air bases in Italy the day of the invasion of southern France two months earlier. Everyone in the squadron knew that Kid Sampson's skinny legs had washed up on the wet sand to lie there and rot like a purple twisted wishbone. No one would go to retrieve them, not Gus or Wes or even the men in the mortuary at the hospital; everyone made believe that Kid Sampson's legs were not there, that they had bobbed away south forever on the tide like all of Clevinger and Orr. Now that bad weather had come, almost no one ever sneaked away alone any more to peek through bushes like a pervert at the moldering stumps.

There were no more beautiful days. There were no more easy missions. There was stinging rain and dull, chilling fog, and the men flew at week-long intervals, whenever the weather cleared. At night the wind moaned. The gnarled and stunted tree trunks creaked and groaned and forced Yossarian's thoughts each morning, even before he was fully awake, back on Kid

Sampson's skinny legs bloating and decaying, as systematically as a ticking clock, in the icy rain and wet sand all through the blind, cold, gusty October nights. After Kid Sampson's legs, he would think of pitiful, whimpering Snowden freezing to death in the rear section of the plane, holding his eternal, immutable secret concealed inside his quilted, armor-plate flak suit until Yossarian had finished sterilizing and bandaging the wrong wound on his leg, and then spilling it out suddenly all over the floor. At night when he was trying to sleep, Yossarian would call the roll of all the men, women and children he had ever known who were now dead. He tried to remember all the soldiers, and he resurrected images of all the elderly people he had known when a child – all the aunts, uncles, neighbors, parents and grandparents, his own and everyone else's, and all the pathetic, deluded shopkeepers who opened their small, dusty stores at dawn and worked in them foolishly until midnight. They were all dead, too. The number of dead people just seemed to increase. And the Germans were still fighting. Death was irreversible, he suspected, and he began to think he was going to lose.

Yossarian was warm when the cold weather came because of Orr's marvelous stove, and he might have existed in his warm tent quite comfortably if not for the memory of Orr, and if not for the gang of animated roommates that came swarming inside rapaciously one day from the two full combat crews Colonel Cathcart had requisitioned – and obtained in less than forty-eight hours – as replacements for Kid Sampson and McWatt. Yossarian emitted a long, loud, croaking gasp of protest when he trudged in tiredly after a mission and found them already there.

There were four of them, and they were having a whale of a good time as they helped each other set up their cots. They were horsing around. The moment he saw them, Yossarian knew they were impossible. They were frisky, eager and exuberant, and they had all been friends in the States. They were plainly unthinkable.

They were noisy, overconfident, emptyheaded kids of twenty-one. They had gone to college and were engaged to pretty, clean girls whose pictures were already standing on the rough cement mantelpiece of Orr's fireplace. They had ridden in speedboats and played tennis. They had been horseback riding. One had once been to bed with an older woman. They knew the same people in different parts of the country and had gone to school with each other's cousins. They had listened to the World Series and really cared who won football games. They were obtuse; their morale was good. They were glad that the war had lasted long enough for them to find out what combat was really like. They were halfway through unpacking when Yossarian threw them out.

They were plainly out of the question, Yossarian explained adamantly to Sergeant Towser, whose sallow equine face was despondent as he informed Yossarian that the new officers would have to be admitted. Sergeant Towser was not permitted to requisition another six-man tent from Group while Yossarian was living in one alone.

'I'm not living in this one alone,' Yossarian said with a sulk. 'I've got a dead man in here with me. His name is Mudd.'

'Please, sir,' begged Sergeant Towser, sighing wearily, with a sidelong glance at the four baffled new officers listening in mystified silence just outside the entrance. 'Mudd was killed on the mission to Orvieto. You know that. He was flying right beside you.'

'Then why don't you move his things out?'

'Because he never even got here. Captain, please don't bring that up again. You can move in with Lieutenant Nately if you like. I'll even send some men from the orderly room to transfer your belongings.'

But to abandon Orr's tent would be to abandon Orr, who would have been spurned and humiliated clannishly by these four simple-minded officers waiting to move in. It did not seem just that these boisterous, immature young men should show up after all the work was done and be allowed to take possession of the most desirable tent on the island. But that was the law, Sergeant Towser explained, and all Yossarian could do was glare at them in baleful apology as he made room for them and volunteer helpful penitent hints as they moved inside his privacy and made themselves at home.

They were the most depressing group of people Yossarian had ever been with. They were always in high spirits. They laughed at everything. They called him 'Yo-Yo' jocularly and came in tipsy late at night and woke him up with their clumsy, bumping, giggling efforts to be quiet, then bombarded him with asinine shouts of hilarious good-fellowship when he sat up cursing to complain. He wanted to massacre them each time they did. They reminded him of Donald Duck's nephews. They were afraid of Yossarian and persecuted him incessantly with nagging generosity and with their exasperating insistence on doing small favors for him. They were reckless, puerile, congenial, naive, presumptuous, deferential and rambunctious. They were dumb; they had no complaints. They admired Colonel Cathcart and they found Colonel Korn witty. They were afraid of Yossarian, but they were not the least bit afraid of Colonel Cathcart's seventy missions. They were four cleancut kids who were having lots of fun, and they were driving Yossarian nuts. He could not make them understand that he was a crotchety old fogey of twenty-eight, that he belonged to another generation, another era, another world, that having a good time bored him and was not worth the effort, and that they bored him, too. He could not make them shut up; they were worse than women. They had not brains enough to be introverted and repressed.

Cronies of theirs in other squadrons began dropping in unashamedly and using the tent as a hangout. There was often not room enough for him. Worst of all, he could no longer bring Nurse Duckett there to lie down with her. And now that foul weather had come, he had no place else! This was a calamity he had not foreseen, and he wanted to bust his roommates' heads open with his fists or pick them up, each in turn, by the seats of their pants and the scruffs of their necks and pitch them out once and for all into the dank, rubbery perennial weeds growing between his rusty soupcan urinal with nail holes in the bottom and the knotty-pine squadron latrine that stood like a beach locker not far away.

Instead of busting their heads open, he tramped in his galoshes and black raincoat through the drizzling darkness to invite Chief White Halfoat to move in with him, too, and drive the fastidious, clean-living bastards out with his threats and swinish habits. But Chief White Halfoat felt cold and was already making plans to move up into the hospital to die of pneumonia. Instinct told Chief White Halfoat it was almost time. His chest ached and he coughed chronically. Whiskey no longer warmed him. Most damning of all, Captain Flume had moved back into his trailer. Here was an omen of unmistakable meaning.

'He had to move back,' Yossarian argued in a vain effort to cheer up the glum, barrel-chested Indian, whose well-knit sorrel-red face had degenerated rapidly into a dilapidated, calcareous gray. 'He'd die of exposure if he tried to live in the woods in this weather.'

'No, that wouldn't drive the yellowbelly back,' Chief White Halfoat disagreed obstinately. He tapped his forehead with cryptic insight. 'No, sirree. He knows something. He knows it's time for me to die of pneumonia, that's what he knows. And that's how I know it's time.'

'What does Doc Daneeka say?'

'I'm not allowed to say anything,' Doc Daneeka said sorrowfully from his seat on his stool in the shadows of a corner, his smooth, tapered, diminutive face turtle-green in the flickering candlelight. Everything smelled of mildew. The bulb in the tent had blown out several days before, and neither of the two men had been able to muster the initiative to replace it. 'I'm not allowed to practice medicine, any more,' Doc Daneeka added.

'He's dead,' Chief White Halfoat gloated, with a horse laugh entangled in phlegm. 'That's really funny.'

'I don't even draw my pay any more.'

'That's really funny,' Chief White Halfoat repeated. 'All this time he's been insulting my liver, and look what happened to him. He's dead. Killed by his own greed.'

'That's not what killed me,' Doc Daneeka observed in a voice that was calm and flat. 'There's nothing wrong with greed. It's all that lousy Dr. Stubbs' fault, getting Colonel Cathcart and Colonel Korn stirred up against flight surgeons. He's going to give the medical profession a bad name by standing up for principle. If he's not careful, he'll be black-balled by his state medical association and kept out of the hospitals.'

Yossarian watched Chief White Halfoat pour whiskey carefully into three empty shampoo bottles and store them away in the musette bag he was packing.

'Can't you stop by my tent on your way up to the hospital and punch one of them in the nose for me?' he speculated aloud. 'I've got four of them, and they're going to crowd me out of my tent altogether.'

'You know, something like that once happened to my whole tribe,' Chief White Halfoat remarked in jolly appreciation, sitting back on his cot to chuckle. 'Why don't you get Captain Black to kick those kids out? Captain Black likes to kick people out.'

Yossarian grimaced sourly at the mere mention of Captain Black, who was already bullying the new fliers each time they stepped into his intelligence tent for maps or information. Yossarian's attitude towards his roommates turned merciful and protective at the mere recollection of Captain Black. It was not their fault that they were young and cheerful, he reminded himself as he carried the swinging beam of his flashlight back through the darkness. He wished that he could be young and cheerful, too. And it wasn't their fault that they were courageous, confident and carefree. He would just have to be patient with them until one or two were killed and the rest wounded, and they they would all turn out okay. He vowed to be more tolerant and benevolent, but when he ducked inside his tent with his friendlier attitude a great blaze was roaring in the fireplace, and he gasped in horrified amazement. *Orr's beautiful birch logs were going up in smoke!* His roommates had set fire to them! He gaped at the four insensitive overheated faces and wanted to shout curses at them. He wanted to bang their heads together as they greeted him with loud convivial cries and invited him generously to pull up a chair and eat their chestnuts and roasted potatoes. What could he do with them?

And the very next morning they got rid of the dead man in his tent! Just like that, they whisked him away! They carried his cot and all his belongings right out into the bushes and simply dumped them there, and then they strode back slapping their hands briskly at a job well done. Yossarian was stunned by their overbearing vigor and zeal, by their practical, direct efficiency. In a matter of moments they had disposed energetically of a problem with which Yossarian and Sergeant Towser had been grappling unsuccessfully for months. Yossarian was alarmed – they might get rid of him just as quickly, he feared – and ran to Hungry Joe and fled with him to Rome the day before Nately's whore finally got a good night's sleep and woke up in love.

33 Nately's whore

He missed Nurse Duckett in Rome. There was not much
else to do after Hungry Joe left on his mail run.
Yossarian missed Nurse Duckett so much that he went
searching hungrily through the streets for Luciana,
whose laugh and invisible scar he had never forgotten,
or the boozy, blowzy, bleary-eyed floozy in the over-
loaded white brassière and unbuttoned orange satin
blouse whose naughty salmon-colored cameo ring Aarfy
had thrown away so callously through the window of
her car. How he yearned for both girls! He looked for
them in vain. He was so deeply in love with them, and he
knew he would never see either again. Despair gnawed
at him. Visions beset him. He wanted Nurse Duckett
with her dress up and her slim thighs bare to the hips.
He banged a thin streetwalker with a wet cough who
picked him up from an alley between hotels, but that
was no fun at all and he hastened to the enlisted men's
apartment for the fat, friendly maid in the lime-colored
panties, who was overjoyed to see him but couldn't
arouse him. He went to bed there early and slept alone.
He woke up disappointed and banged a sassy, short,
chubby girl he found in the apartment after breakfast,
but that was only a little better, and he chased her away

when he'd finished and went back to sleep. He napped till lunch and then went shopping for presents for Nurse Duckett and a scarf for the maid in the lime-coloured panties, who hugged him with such gargantuan gratitude that he was soon hot for Nurse Duckett and ran looking lecherously for Luciana again. Instead he found Aarfy, who had landed in Rome when Hungry Joe returned with Dunbar, Nately and Dobbs, and who would not go along on the drunken foray that night to rescue Nately's whore from the middle-aged military big shots holding her captive in a hotel because she would not say uncle.

'Why should I risk getting into trouble just to help her out?' Aarfy demanded haughtily. 'But don't tell Nately I said that. Tell him I had to keep an appointment with some very important fraternity brothers.'

The middle-aged big shots would not let Nately's whore leave until they made her say uncle.

'Say uncle,' they said to her.

'Uncle,' she said.

'No, no. Say uncle.'

'Uncle,' she said.

'She still doesn't understand.'

'You still don't understand, do you? We can't really make you say uncle unless you don't want to say uncle. Don't you see? Don't say uncle when I tell you to say uncle. Okay? Say uncle.'

'Uncle,' she said.

'No, don't say uncle. Say uncle.'

She didn't say uncle.

'That's good!'

'That's very good.'

'It's a start. Now say uncle.'

'Uncle,' she said.

'It's no good.'

'No, it's no good that way either. She just isn't impressed with us. There's just no fun making her say uncle when she doesn't care whether we make her say uncle or not.'

'No, she really doesn't care, does she? Say "foot." '

'Foot.'

'You see? She doesn't care about anything we do. She doesn't care about us. We don't mean a thing to you, do we?'

'Uncle,' she said.

She didn't care about them a bit, and it upset them terribly. They shook her roughly each time she yawned. She did not seem to care about anything, not even when they threatened to throw her out the window. They were utterly demoralized men of distinction. She was bored and indifferent and wanted very much to sleep. She had been on the job for twenty-two hours, and she was sorry that these men had not permitted her to leave with the other two girls with whom the orgy had begun. She wondered vaguely why they wanted her to laugh when they laughed, and why they wanted *her* to enjoy it when they made love to her. It was all very mysterious to her, and very uninteresting.

She was not sure what they wanted from her. Each time she slumped over with her eyes closed they shook her awake and made her say 'uncle' again. Each time she said 'uncle,' they were disappointed. She wondered what 'uncle' meant. She sat on the sofa in a passive, phlegmatic stupor, her mouth open and all her clothing crumpled in a corner on the floor, and wondered how much longer they would sit around naked with her and make her say uncle in the elegant hotel suite to which Orr's old girl friend, giggling uncontrollably at Yossarian's and Dunbar's drunken antics, guided Nately and the other members of the motley rescue party.

Dunbar squeezed Orr's old girl friend's fanny gratefully and passed her back to Yossarian, who propped her against the door jamb with both hands on her hips and wormed himself against her lasciviously until Nately seized him by the arm and pulled him away from her into the blue sitting room, where Dunbar was already hurling everything in sight out the window into

446

the court. Dobbs was smashing furniture with an ash stand. A nude, ridiculous man with a blushing appendectomy scar appeared in the doorway suddenly and bellowed.

'What's going on here?'

'Your toes are dirty,' Dunbar said.

The man covered his groin with both hands and shrank from view. Dunbar, Dobbs and Hungry Joe just kept dumping everything they could lift out the window with great, howling whoops of happy abandon. They soon finished with the clothing on the couches and the luggage on the floor, and they were ransacking a cedar closet when the door to the inner room opened again and a man who was very distinguished-looking from the neck up padded into view imperiously on bare feet.

'Here, you, stop that,' he barked. 'Just what do you men think you're doing?'

'Your toes are dirty,' Dunbar said to him.

The man covered his groin as the first one had done and disappeared. Nately charged after him, but was blocked by the first officer, who plodded back in holding a pillow in front of him, like a bubble dancer.

'Hey, you men!' he roared angrily. 'Stop it!'

'Stop it,' Dunbar replied.

'That's what I said.'

'That's what I said,' Dunbar said.

The officer stamped his foot petulantly, turning weak with frustration. 'Are you deliberately repeating everything I say?'

'Are you deliberately repeating everything I say?'

'I'll thrash you.' The man raised a fist.

'I'll thrash you,' Dunbar warned him coldly. 'You're a German spy, and I'm going to have you shot.'

'German spy? I'm an American colonel.'

'You don't look like an American colonel. You look like a fat man with a pillow in front of him. Where's your uniform, if you're an American colonel?'

'You just threw it out the window.'

'All right, men,' Dunbar said. 'Lock the silly bastard

447

up. Take the silly bastard down to the station house and throw away the key.'

The colonel blanched with alarm. 'Are you all crazy? Where's your badge? Hey, you! Come back in here!'

But he whirled too late to stop Nately, who had glimpsed his girl sitting on the sofa in the other room and had darted through the doorway behind his back. The others poured through after him right into the midst of the other naked big shots. Hungry Joe laughed hysterically when he saw them, pointing in disbelief at one after the other and clasping his head and sides. Two with fleshy physiques advanced truculently until they spied the look of mean dislike and hostility on Dobbs and Dunbar and noticed that Dobbs was still swinging like a two-handed club the wrought-iron ash stand he had used to smash things in the sitting room. Nately was already at his girl's side. She stared at him without recognition for a few seconds. Then she smiled faintly and let her head sink to his shoulder with her eyes closed. Nately was in ecstasy; she had never smiled at him before.

'Filpo,' said a calm, slender, jaded-looking man who had not even stirred from his armchair. 'You don't obey orders. I told you to get them out, and you've gone and brought them in. Can't you see the difference?'

'They've thrown our things out the window, General.'

'Good for them. Our uniforms too? That was clever. We'll never be able to convince anyone we're superior without our uniforms.'

'Let's get their names, Lou, and –'

'Oh, Ned, relax,' said the slender man with practiced weariness. 'You may be pretty good at moving armored divisions into action, but you're almost useless in a social situation. Sooner or later we'll get our uniforms back, and then we'll be their superiors again. Did they really throw our uniforms out? That was a splendid tactic.'

'They threw everything out.'

'The ones in the closet, too?'

'They threw the closet out, General. That was that crash we heard when we thought they were coming in to kill us.'

'And I'll throw you out next,' Dunbar threatened.

The general paled slightly. 'What the devil is he so mad about?' he asked Yossarian.

'He means it, too,' Yossarian said. 'You'd better let the girl leave.'

'Lord, take her,' exclaimed the general with relief. 'All she's done is make us feel insecure. At least she might have disliked or resented us for the hundred dollars we paid her. But she wouldn't even do that. Your handsome young friend there seems quite attached to her. Notice the way he lets his fingers linger on the inside of her thighs as he pretends to roll up her stockings.'

Nately, caught in the act, blushed guiltily and moved more quickly through the steps of dressing her. She was sound asleep and breathed so regularly that she seemed to be snoring softly.

'Let's charge her now, Lou!' urged another officer. 'We've got more personnel, and we can encircle –'

'Oh, no, Bill,' answered the general with a sigh. 'You may be a wizard at directing a pincer movement in good weather on level terrain against an enemy that has already committed his reserves, but you don't always think so clearly anywhere else. Why should we want to keep her?'

'General, we're in a very bad strategic position. We haven't got a stitch of clothing, and it's going to be very degrading and embarrassing for the person who has to go downstairs through the lobby to get some.'

'Yes, Filpo, you're quite right,' said the general. 'And that's exactly why you're the one to do it. Get going.'

'Naked, sir?'

'Take your pillow with you if you want to. And get some cigarettes, too, while you're downstairs picking up my underwear and pants will you?'

'I'll send everything up for you,' Yossarian offered.

'There, General,' said Filpo with relief. 'Now I won't have to go.'

'Filpo, you nitwit. Can't you see he's lying?'

'Are you lying?'

Yossarian nodded, and Filpo's faith was shattered. Yossarian laughed and helped Nately walk his girl out into the corridor and into the elevator. Her face was smiling as though with a lovely dream as she slept with her head still resting on Nately's shoulder. Dobbs and Dunbar ran out into the street to stop a cab.

Nately's whore looked up when they left the car. She swallowed dryly several times during the arduous trek up the stairs to her apartment, but she was sleeping soundly again by the time Nately undressed her and put her to bed. She slept for eighteen hours, while Nately dashed about the apartment all the next morning shushing everybody in sight, and when she woke up she was deeply in love with him. In the last analysis, that was all it took to win her heart – a good night's sleep.

The girl smiled with contentment when she opened her eyes and saw him, and then, stretching her long legs languorously beneath the rustling sheets, beckoned him into bed beside her with that look of simpering idiocy of a woman in heat. Nately moved to her in a happy daze, so overcome with rapture that he hardly minded when her kid sister interrupted him again by flying into the room and flinging herself down onto the bed between them. Nately's whore slapped and cursed her, but this time with laughter and generous affection, and Nately settled back smugly with an arm about each, feeling strong and protective. They made a wonderful family group, he decided. The little girl would go to college when she was old enough, to Smith or Radcliffe or Bryn Mawr – he would see to that. Nately bounded out of bed after a few minutes to announce his good fortune to his friends at the top of his voice. He called to them jubilantly to come to the room and slammed the door in their startled faces as soon as they arrived. He had remembered just in time that his girl had no clothes on.

'Get dressed,' he ordered her, congratulating himself on his alertness.

'*Perchè?*' she asked curiously.

'*Perchè?*' he repeated with an indulgent chuckle. 'Because I don't want them to see you without any clothes on.'

'*Perchè no?*' she inquired.

'*Perchè no?*' He looked at her with astonishment. 'Because it isn't right for other men to see you naked, that's why.'

'*Perchè no?*'

'Because I say no!' Nately exploded in frustration. 'Now don't argue with me. I'm the man and you have to do whatever I say. From now on, I forbid you ever to go out of this room unless you have all your clothes on. Is that clear?'

Nately's whore looked at him as though he were insane. 'Are you crazy? *Che succede?*'

'I mean every word I say.'

'*Tu sei pazzo!*' she shouted at him with incredulous indignation, and sprang out of bed. Snarling unintelligibly, she snapped on panties and strode toward the door.

Nately drew himself up with full mainly authority. 'I forbid you to leave this room that way,' he informed her.

'*Tu sei pazzo!*' she shot back at him, after he had left, shaking her head in disbelief. '*Idiota! Tu sei un pazzo imbecille!*'

'*Tu sei pazzo,*' said her thin kid sister, starting out after her in the same haughty walk.

'You come back here,' Nately ordered her. 'I forbid you to go out that way, too!'

'*Idiota!*' the kid sister called back at him with dignity after she had flounced past. '*Tu sei un pazzo imbecille.*'

Nately fumed in circles of distracted helplessness for several seconds and then sprinted out into the sitting room to forbid his friends to look at his girl friend while she complained about him in only her panties.

'Why not?' asked Dunbar.

'Why not?' exclaimed Nately. 'Because she's my girl now, and it isn't right for you to see her unless she's fully dressed.'

'Why not?' asked Dunbar.

'You see?' said his girl with a shrug. '*Lui è pazzo!*'

'*Si, è molto pazzo,*' echoed her kid sister.

'Then make her keep her clothes on if you don't want us to see her,' argued Hungry Joe. 'What the hell do you want from us?'

'She won't listen to me,' Nately confessed sheepishly. 'So from now on you'll all have to shut your eyes or look in the other direction when she comes in that way. Okay?'

'*Madonn'!*' cried his girl in exasperation, and stamped out of the room.

'*Madonn'!*' cried her kid sister, and stamped out behind her.

'*Lui è pazzo,*' Yossarian observed good-naturedly. 'I certainly have to admit it.'

'Hey, you crazy or something?' Hungry Joe demanded of Nately. 'The next thing you know you'll be trying to make her give up hustling.'

'From now on,' Nately said to his girl, 'I forbid you to go out hustling.'

'*Perchè?*' she inquired curiously.

'*Perchè?*' he screamed with amazement. 'Because it's not nice, that's why!'

'*Perchè no?*'

'Because it just isn't!' Nately insisted. 'It just isn't right for a nice girl like you to go looking for other men to sleep with. I'll give you all the money you need, so you won't have to do it any more.'

'And what will I do all day instead?'

'Do?' said Nately. 'You'll do what all your friends do.'

'My friends go looking for men to sleep with.'

'Then get new friends! I don't even want you to associate with girls like that, anyway. Prostitution is bad! Everybody knows that, even him.' He turned with confidence to the experienced old man. 'Am I right?'

'You're wrong,' answered the old man. 'Prostitution gives her an opportunity to meet people. It provides fresh air and wholesome exercise, and it keeps her out of trouble.'

'From now on,' Nately declared sternly to his girl friend, 'I forbid you to have anything to do with that wicked old man.'

'*Va fongul!*' his girl replied, rolling her harassed eyes up toward the ceiling. 'What does he want from me?' she implored, shaking her fists. '*Lasciami!*' she told him in menacing entreaty. '*Stupido!* If you think my friends are so bad, go tell your friends not to ficky-fick all the time with my friends!'

'From now on,' Nately told his friends, 'I think you fellows ought to stop running around with her friends and settle down.'

'*Madonn'!*' cried his friends, rolling their harassed eyes up toward the ceiling.

Nately had gone clear out of his mind. He wanted them all to fall in love right away and get married. Dunbar could marry Orr's whore, and Yossarian could fall in love with Nurse Duckett or anyone else he liked. After the war they could all work for Nately's father and bring up their children in the same suburb. Nately saw it all very clearly. Love had transmogrified him into a romantic idiot, and they drove him away back into the bedroom to wrangle with his girl over Captain Black. She agreed not to go to bed with Captain Black again or give him any more of Nately's money, but she would not budge an inch on her friendship with the ugly, ill-kempt, dissipated, filthy-minded old man, who witnessed Nately's flowering love affair with insulting derision and would not admit that Congress was the greatest deliberative body in the whole world.

'From now on,' Nately ordered his girl firmly, 'I absolutely forbid you even to speak to that disgusting old man.'

'Again the old man?' cried the girl in wailing confusion. '*Perchè no?*'

'He doesn't like the House of Representatives.'

'*Mamma mia!* What's the *matter* with you?'

'*È pazzo*,' observed her kid sister philosophically. 'That's what's the matter with him.'

'*Si*,' the older girl agreed readily, tearing at her long brown hair with both hands. '*Lui è pazzo*.'

But she missed Nately when he was away and was furious with Yossarian when he punched Nately in the face with all his might and knocked him into the hospital with a broken nose.

34 Thanksgiving

It was actually all Sergeant Knight's fault that Yossarian busted Nately in the nose on Thanksgiving Day, after everyone in the squadron had given humble thanks to Milo for providing the fantastically opulent meal on which the officers and enlisted men had gorged themselves insatiably all afternoon and for dispensing like inexhaustible largess the unopened bottles of cheap whiskey he handed out unsparingly to every man who asked. Even before dark, young soldiers with pasty white faces were throwing up everywhere and passing out drunkenly on the ground. The air turned foul. Other men picked up steam as the hours passed, and the aimless, riotous celebration continued. It was a raw, violent, guzzling saturnalia that spilled obstreperously through the woods to the officers' club and spread up into the hills toward the hospital and the antiaircraft-gun emplacements. There were fist fights in the squadron and one stabbing. Corporal Kolodny shot himself through the leg in the intelligence tent while playing with a loaded gun and had his gums and toes painted purple in the speeding ambulance as he lay on his back with the blood spurting from his wound. Men with cut fingers, bleeding heads, stomach cramps and broken ankles came limping penitently up to the medical tent to have their gums and toes painted purple by Gus and Wes and be given a laxative to throw into the bushes. The joyous celebration lasted long into the night, and the stillness was fractured often by wild, exultant shouts and by the cries of people who were merry or sick. There was the recurring sound of retching and moaning, of laughter, greetings, threats and swearing, and of bottles shattering against rock. There were dirty songs in the distance. It was worse than New Year's Eve.

Yossarian went to bed early for safety and soon dreamed that he was fleeing almost headlong down an endless wooden staircase, making a loud, staccato clatter with his heels. Then he woke up a little and realized someone was shooting at him with a machine gun. A tortured, terrified sob rose in his throat. His first thought was that Milo was attacking the squadron again, and he rolled off his cot to the floor and lay underneath in a trembling, praying ball, his heart thumping like a drop forge, his body bathed in a cold sweat. There was no noise of planes. A drunken, happy laugh sounded from afar. 'Happy New Year, Happy New Year!' a triumphant familiar voice shouted hilariously from high above between the short, sharp bursts of machine gun fire, and Yossarian understood that some men had gone as a prank to one of the sandbagged machine gun emplacements Milo had installed in the hills after his raid on the squadron and staffed with his own men.

Yossarian blazed with hatred and wrath when he saw he was the victim of an irresponsible joke that had destroyed his sleep and reduced him to a whimpering hulk. He wanted to kill, he wanted to murder. He was angrier than he had ever been before, angrier even than when he had slid his hands around McWatt's neck to strangle him. The gun opened fire again. Voices cried 'Happy New Year!' and gloating laughter rolled down from the hills through the darkness like a witch's glee. In moccasins and coveralls, Yossarian charged out of his tent for revenge with his .45, ramming a clip of cartridges up into the grip and slamming the bolt of the gun back to load it. He snapped off the safety catch and was ready to shoot. He heard Nately running after him to restrain him, calling his name. The machine gun opened fire once more from a black rise above the motor pool, and orange tracer bullets skimmed like low-gliding dashes over the tops of the shadowy tents, almost clipping the peaks. Roars of rough laughter rang out again between the short bursts. Yossarian felt resentment boil like acid inside him; they were endangering his life, the bastards! With blind, ferocious rage and determination, he raced across the squadron past the motor pool, running as fast as he could, and was already pounding up into the hills along the narrow, winding path when Nately finally caught up, still calling 'Yo-Yo! Yo-Yo!' with pleading concern and imploring him to stop. He grasped Yossarian's shoulders and tried to hold him back. Yossarian twisted free, turning. Nately reached for him again, and Yossarian drove his fist squarely into Nately's delicate young face as hard as he could, cursing him, then drew his arm back to hit him again, but Nately had dropped out of sight with a groan and lay curled up on the ground with his head buried in both hands and blood streaming between his fingers. Yossarian whirled and plunged ahead up the path without looking back.

Soon he saw the machine gun. Two figures leaped up in silhouette when they heard him and fled into the night with taunting laughter before he could get there. He was too late. Their footsteps receded, leaving the circle of sandbags empty and silent in the crisp and windless moonlight. He looked about dejectedly. Jeering laughter came to him again, from a distance. A twig snapped nearby. Yossarian dropped to his knees with a cold thrill of elation and aimed. He heard a stealthy rustle of leaves on the other side of the sandbags and fired two quick rounds. Someone fired back at him once, and he recognized the shot.

'Dunbar?' he called.

'Yossarian?'

The two men left their hiding places and walked forward to meet in the clearing with weary disappointment, their guns down. They were both shivering slightly from the frosty air and wheezing from the labor of their uphill rush.

'The bastards,' said Yossarian. 'They got away.'

'They took ten years off my life,' Dunbar exclaimed. 'I thought that son of a bitch Milo was bombing us again. I've never been so scared. I wish I knew who the bastards were.'

'One was Sergeant Knight.'

'Let's go kill him.' Dunbar's teeth were chattering. 'He had no right to scare us that way.'

Yossarian no longer wanted to kill anyone. 'Let's help Nately first. I think I hurt him at the bottom of the hill.'

But there was no sign of Nately along the path, even though Yossarian located the right spot by the blood on the stones. Nately was not in his tent either, and they did not catch up with him until the next morning when they checked into the hospital as patients after learning he had checked in with a broken nose the night before. Nately beamed in frightened surprise as they padded into the ward in their slippers and robes behind Nurse Cramer and were assigned to their beds. Nately's nose was in a bulky cast, and he had two black eyes. He kept blushing giddily in shy embarrassment and saying he was sorry when Yossarian came over to apologize for hitting him. Yossarian felt terrible; he could hardly bear to look at Nately's battered countenance, even though the sight was so comical he was tempted to guffaw. Dunbar was disgusted by their sentimentality, and all three were relieved when Hungry Joe came barging in unexpectedly with his intricate black camera and trumped-up symptoms of appendicitis to be near enough to Yossarian to take pictures of him feeling up Nurse Duckett. Like Yossarian, he was soon disappointed. Nurse Duckett had decided to marry a doctor – any doctor, because they all did so well in business – and would not take chances in the vicinity of the man who might someday be her husband. Hungry Joe was irate and inconsolable until – of all people – the chaplain was led in wearing a maroon corduroy bathrobe, shining like a skinny lighthouse with a radiant grin of self-satisfaction too tremendous to be concealed. The chaplain had entered the hospital with a pain in his heart that the doctors thought was gas in his stomach and with an advanced case of Wisconsin shingles.

'What in the world are Wisconsin shingles?' asked Yossarian.

'That's just what the doctors wanted to know!' blurted out the chaplain proudly, and burst into laughter. No one had ever seen him so waggish, or so happy. 'There's no such thing as Wisconsin shingles. Don't you understand? I lied. I made a deal with the doctors. I promised that I would let them know when my Wisconsin shingles went away if they would promise not to do anything to cure them. I never told a lie before. Isn't it wonderful?'

The chaplain had sinned, and it was good. Common sense told him that telling lies and defecting from duty were sins. On the other hand, everyone knew that sin was evil, and that no good could come from evil. But he did feel good; he felt positively marvelous. Consequently, it followed logically that telling lies and defecting from duty could not be sins. The chaplain had mastered, in a moment of divine intuition, the handy technique of protective rationalization, and he was exhilarated by his discovery. It was miraculous. It was almost no trick at all, he saw, to turn vice into virtue and slander into truth, impotence into abstinence, arrogance into humility, plunder into philanthropy, thievery into honor, blasphemy into wisdom, brutality into patriotism, and sadism into justice. Anybody could do it; it required no brains at all. It merely required no character. With effervescent agility the chaplain ran through the whole gamut of orthodox immoralities, while Nately sat up in bed with flushed elation, astounded by the mad gang of companions of which he found himself the

459

nucleus. He was flattered and apprehensive, certain that some severe official would soon appear and throw the whole lot of them out like a pack of bums. No one bothered them. In the evening they all trooped exuberantly out to see a lousy Hollywood extravaganza in Technicolor, and when they trooped exuberantly back in after the lousy Hollywood extravaganza, the soldier in white was there, and Dunbar screamed and went to pieces.

'He's back!' Dunbar screamed. 'He's back! He's back!'

Yossarian froze in his tracks, paralyzed as much by the eerie shrillness in Dunbar's voice as by the familiar, white, morbid sight of the soldier in white covered from head to toe in plaster and gauze. A strange, quavering, involuntary noise came bubbling from Yossarian's throat.

'He's back!' Dunbar screamed again.

'He's back!' a patient delirious with fever echoed in automatic terror.

All at once the ward erupted into bedlam. Mobs of sick and injured men began ranting incoherently and running and jumping in the aisle as though the building were on fire. A patient with one foot and one crutch was hopping back and forth swiftly in panic crying. 'What is it? What is it? Are we burning? Are we burning?'

'He's back!' someone shouted at him. 'Didn't you hear him? He's back! He's back!'

'Who's back?' shouted someone else. 'Who is it?'

'What does it mean? What should we do?'

'Are we on fire?'

'Get up and run, damn it! Everybody get up and run!'

Everybody got out of bed and began running from one end of the ward to the other. One C.I.D. man was looking for a gun to shoot one of the other C.I.D. men who had jabbed his elbow into his eye. The ward had turned into chaos. The patient delirious with the high fever leaped into the aisle and almost knocked over the patient with one foot, who accidentally brought the black rubber tip of his crutch down on the other's bare foot, crushing some toes. The delirious man with the fever and the crushed toes sank to the floor and wept in pain while other men tripped over him and hurt him more in their blind, milling, agonized stampede. 'He's back!' all the men kept mumbling and chanting and calling out hysterically as they rushed back and forth. 'He's back, he's back!' Nurse Cramer was there in the middle suddenly like a spinning policeman, trying desperately to restore order, dissolving helplessly into tears when she failed. 'Be still, please be still,' she urged uselessly through her massive sobs. The chaplain, pale as a ghost, had no idea what was going on. Neither did Nately, who kept close to Yossarian's side, clinging to his elbow, or Hungry Joe, who followed dubiously with his scrawny fists clenched and glanced from side to side with a face that was scared.

'Hey, what's going on?' Hungry Joe pleaded. 'What the hell is going on?'

'It's the same one!' Dunbar shouted at him emphatically in a voice rising clearly above the raucous commotion. 'Don't you understand? It's the same one.'

'The same one!' Yossarian heard himself echo, quivering with a deep and ominous excitement that he could not control, and shoved his way after Dunbar toward the bed of the soldier in white.

'Take it easy, fellas,' the short patriotic Texan counseled affably, with an uncertain grin. 'There's no cause to be upset. Why don't we all just take it easy?'

'The same one!' others began murmuring, chanting and shouting.

Suddenly Nurse Duckett was there, too. 'What's going on?' she demanded.

'He's back!' Nurse Cramer screamed, sinking into her arms. 'He's back, he's back!'

It was, indeed, the same man. He had lost a few inches and added some weight, but Yossarian remembered him instantly by the two stiff arms and the two stiff, thick, useless legs all drawn upward into the air almost perpendicularly by the taut ropes and the long lead weights suspended from pulleys over him and by the frayed black hole in the bandages over his mouth. He had, in fact, hardly changed at all. There was the same zinc pipe rising from the hard stone mass over his groin and leading to the clear glass jar on the floor. There was the same clear glass jar on a pole dripping fluid into him through the crook of his elbow. Yossarian would recognize him anywhere. He wondered who he was.

'There's no one inside!' Dunbar yelled out at him unexpectedly.

Yossarian felt his heart skip a beat and his legs grow weak. 'What are you talking about?' he shouted with dread, stunned by the haggard, sparking anguish in Dunbar's eyes and by his crazed look of wild shock and horror. 'Are you nuts or something? What the hell do you mean, there's no one inside?'

'They've stolen him away!' Dunbar shouted back. 'He's hollow inside, like a chocolate soldier. They just took him away and left those bandages there.'

'Why should they do that?'

'Why do they do anything?'

'They've stolen him away!' screamed someone else, and people all over the ward began screaming. 'They've stolen him away. They've stolen him away!'

'Go back to your beds,' Nurse Duckett pleaded with Dunbar and Yossarian, pushing feebly against Yossarian's chest. 'Please go back to your beds.'

'You're crazy!' Yossarian shouted angrily at Dunbar. 'What the hell makes you say that?'

'Did anyone see him?' Dunbar demanded with sneering fervor.

'You saw him, didn't you?' Yossarian said to Nurse Duckett. 'Tell Dunbar there's someone inside.'

'Lieutenant Schmulker is inside,' Nurse Duckett said. 'He's burned all over.'

'Did she see him?'

'You saw him, didn't you?'

'The doctor who bandaged him saw him.'

462

'Go get him, will you? Which doctor was it?'

Nurse Duckett reacted to the question with a startled gasp. 'The doctor isn't even here!' she exclaimed. 'The patient was brought to us that way from a field hospital.'

'You see?' cried Nurse Cramer. 'There's no one inside!'

'There's no one inside!' yelled Hungry Joe, and began stamping on the floor.

Dunbar broke through and leaped up furiously on the soldier in white's bed to see for himself, pressing his gleaming eye down hungrily against the tattered black hole in the shell of white bandages. He was still bent over staring with one eye into the lightless, unstirring void of the soldier in white's mouth when the doctors and the M.P.s came running to help Yossarian pull him away. The doctors wore guns at the waist. The guards carried carbines and rifles with which they shoved and jolted the crowd of muttering patients back. A stretcher on wheels was there, and the soldier in white was lifted out of bed skillfully and rolled out of sight in a matter of seconds. The doctors and M.P.s moved through the ward assuring everyone that everything was all right.

Nurse Duckett plucked Yossarian's arm and whispered to him furtively to meet her in the broom closet outside in the corridor. Yossarian rejoiced when he heard her. He thought Nurse Duckett finally wanted to get laid and pulled her skirt up the second they were alone in the broom closet, but she pushed him away. She had urgent news about Dunbar.

'They're going to disappear him,' she said.

Yossarian squinted at her uncomprehendingly. 'They're what?' he asked in surprise, and laughed uneasily. 'What does that mean?'

'I don't know. I heard them talking behind a door.'

'Who?'

'I don't know. I couldn't see them. I just heard them say they were going to disappear Dunbar.'

'Why are they going to disappear him?'

'I don't know.'

'It doesn't make sense. It isn't even good grammar. What the hell does it mean when they disappear somebody?'

'I don't know.'

'Jesus, you're a great help!'

'Why are you picking on me?' Nurse Duckett protested with hurt feelings, and began sniffing back tears. 'I'm only trying to help. It isn't my fault they're going to disappear him, is it? I shouldn't even be telling you.'

Yossarian took her in his arms and hugged her with gentle, contrite affection. 'I'm sorry,' he apologized, kissing her cheek respectfully, and hurried away to warn Dunbar, who was nowhere to be found.

35 Milo the militant

For the first time in his life, Yossarian prayed. He got
down on his knees and prayed to Nately not to volunteer
to fly more than seventy missions after Chief White Halfoat did die of pneumonia in the hospital and Nately had
applied for his job. But Nately just wouldn't listen.

'I've got to fly more missions.' Nately insisted lamely
with a crooked smile. 'Otherwise they'll send me home.'

'So?'

'I don't want to go home until I can take her back with
me.'

'She means that much to you?'

Nately nodded dejectedly. 'I might never see her
again.'

'Then get yourself grounded.' Yossarian urged. 'You've
finished your missions and you don't need the flight pay.
Why don't you ask for Chief White Halfoat's job, if you
can stand working for Captain Black?'

Nately shook his head, his cheeks darkening with shy
and regretful mortification. 'They won't give it to me. I
spoke to Colonel Korn, and he told me I'd have to fly more
missions or be sent home.'

Yossarian cursed savagely. 'That's just plain mean-
ness.'

'I don't mind, I guess. I've flown seventy missions without getting hurt. I guess I can fly a few more.'

'Don't do anything at all about it until I talk to someone,' Yossarian decided, and went looking for help from Milo, who went immediately afterward to Colonel Cathcart for help in having himself assigned to more combat missions.

Milo had been earning many distinctions for himself. He had flown fearlessly into danger and criticism by selling petroleum and ball bearings to Germany at good prices in order to make a good profit and help maintain a balance of power between the contending forces. His nerve under fire was graceful and infinite. With a devotion to purpose above and beyond the line of duty, he had then raised the price of food in his mess halls so high that all officers and enlisted men had to turn over all their pay to him in order to eat. Their alternative – there was an alternative, of course, since Milo detested coercion and was a vocal champion of freedom of choice – was to starve. When he encountered a wave of enemy resistance to this attack, he stuck to his position without regard for his safety or reputation and gallantly invoked the law of supply and demand. And when someone somewhere said no, Milo gave ground grudgingly, valiantly defending, even in retreat, the historic right of free men to pay as much as they had to for the things they needed in order to survive.

Milo had been caught red-handed in the act of plundering his countrymen, and, as a result, his stock had never been higher. He proved good as his word when a rawboned major from Minnesota curled his lip in rebellious disavowal and demanded his share of the syndicate Milo kept saying everybody owned. Milo met the challenge by writing the words 'A Share' on the nearest scrap of paper and handing it away with a virtuous disdain that won the envy and admiration of almost everyone who knew him. His glory was at a peak, and Colonel Cathcart, who knew and admired his war record, was astonished by the deferential humility with which Milo presented himself at Group Headquarters and made his fantastic appeal for more hazardous assignments.

'You want to fly more combat missions?' Colonel Cathcart gasped. 'What in the world for?'

Milo answered in a demure voice with his face lowered meekly. 'I want to do my duty, sir. The country is at war, and I want to fight to defend it like the rest of the fellows.'

'But, Milo, you are doing your duty,' Colonel Cathcart exclaimed with a laugh that thundered jovially. 'I can't think of a single person who's done more for the men than you have. Who gave them chocolate-covered cotton?'

Milo shook his head slowly and sadly. 'But being a good mess officer in wartime just isn't enough, Colonel Cathcart.'

'Certainly it is, Milo. I don't know what's come over you.'

'Certainly it isn't, Colonel,' Milo disagreed in a somewhat firm tone, raising his subservient eyes significantly just far enough to arrest Colonel Cathcart's. 'Some of the men are beginning to talk.'

'Oh, is that it? Give me their names, Milo. Give me their names and I'll see to it that they go on every dangerous mission the group flies.'

'No, Colonel, I'm afraid they're right,' Milo said, with his head drooping again. 'I was sent overseas as a pilot, and I should be flying more combat missions and spending less time on my duties as a mess officer.'

Colonel Cathcart was surprised but co-operative. 'Well, Milo, if you really feel that way, I'm sure we can make whatever arrangements you want. How long have you been overseas now?'

'Eleven months, sir.'

'And how many missions have you flown?'

'Five.'

'Five?' asked Colonel Cathcart.

'Five, sir.'

'Five, eh?' Colonel Cathcart rubbed his cheek

467

pensively. 'That isn't very good, is it?'

'Isn't it?' asked Milo in a sharply edged voice, glancing up again.

Colonel Cathcart quailed. 'On the contrary, that's very good, Milo,' he corrected himself hastily. 'It isn't bad at all.'

'No, Colonel,' Milo said, with a long, languishing, wistful sigh, 'it isn't very good. Although it's very generous of you to say so.'

'But it's really not bad, Milo. Not bad at all, when you consider all your other valuable contributions. Five missions, you say? Just five?'

'Just five, sir.'

'Just five.' Colonel Cathcart grew awfully depressed for a moment as he wondered what Milo was really thinking, and whether he had already got a black eye with him. 'Five is very good, Milo,' he observed with enthusiasm, spying a ray of hope. 'That averages out to almost one combat mission every two months. And I'll bet your total doesn't include the time you bombed us.'

'Yes, sir. It does.'

'It does?' inquired Colonel Cathcart with mild wonder. 'You didn't actually fly along on that mission, did you? If I remember correctly, you were in the control tower with me, weren't you?'

'But it was my mission,' Milo contended. 'I organized it, and we used my planes and supplies. I planned and supervised the whole thing.'

'Oh, certainly, Milo, certainly. I'm not disputing you. I'm only checking the figures to make sure you're claiming all you're entitled to. Did you also include the time we contracted with you to bomb the bridge at Orvieto?'

'Oh, no, sir. I didn't think I should, since I was in Orvieto at the time directing the antiaircraft fire.'

'I don't see what difference that makes, Milo. It was still your mission. And a damned good one, too, I must say. We didn't get the bridge, but we did have a beautiful bomb pattern. I remember General Peckem commenting on it. No, Milo, I insist you count Orvieto as a mission, too.'

'If you insist, sir.'

'I do insist, Milo. Now, let's see – you now have a grand total of six missions, which is damned good, Milo, damned good, really. Six missions is an increase of twenty per cent in just a couple of minutes, which is not bad at all, Milo, not bad at all.'

'Many of the other men have seventy missions,' Milo pointed out.

'But they never produced any chocolate-covered cotton, did they? Milo, you're doing more than your share.'

'But they're getting all the fame and opportunity,' Milo persisted with a petulance that bordered on sniveling. 'Sir, I want to get in there and fight like the rest of the fellows. That's what I'm here for. I want to win medals, too.'

'Yes, Milo, of course. We all want to spend more time in combat. But people like you and me serve in different ways. Look at my own record,' Colonel Cathcart uttered a deprecatory laugh. 'I'll bet it's not generally known, Milo, that I myself have flown only four missions, is it?'

'No, sir,' Milo replied. 'It's generally known that you've flown only two missions. And that one of those occurred when Aarfy accidentally flew you over enemy territory while navigating you to Naples for a black-market water cooler.'

Colonel Cathcart, flushing with embarrassment, abandoned all further argument. 'All right, Milo. I can't praise you enough for what you want to do. If it really means so much to you, I'll have Major Major assign you to the next sixty-four missions so that you can have seventy, too.'

'Thank you, Colonel, thank you, sir. You don't know what this means.'

'Don't mention it, Milo. I know exactly what it means.'

'No, Colonel, I don't think you do know what it means,' Milo disagreed pointedly. 'Someone will have to begin running the syndicate for me right away. It's very complicated, and I might get shot down at any time.'

Colonel Cathcart brightened instantly at the thought

and began rubbing his hands with avaricious zest. 'You know, Milo, I think Colonel Korn and I might be willing to take the syndicate off your hands,' he suggested in an offhand manner, almost licking his lips in savory anticipation. 'Our experience in black-market plum tomatoes should come in very useful. Where do we begin?'

Milo watched Colonel Cathcart steadily with a bland and guileless expression. 'Thank you, sir, that's very good of you. Begin with a salt-free diet for General Peckem and a fat-free diet for General Dreedle.'

'Let me get a pencil. What's next?'

'The cedars.'

'Cedars?'

'From Lebanon.'

'Lebanon?'

'We've got cedars from Lebanon due at the sawmill in Oslo to be turned into shingles for the builder in Cape Cod. C.O.D. And then there's the peas.'

'Peas?'

'That are on the high seas. We've got boatloads of peas that are on the high seas from Atlanta to Holland to pay for the tulips that were shipped to Geneva to pay for the cheeses that must go to Vienna M.I.F.'

'M.I.F.?'

'Money in Front. The Hapsburgs are shaky.'

'Milo.'

'And don't forget the galvanized zinc in the warehouse at Flint. Four carloads of galvanized zinc from Flint must be flown to the smelters in Damascus by noon of the eighteenth, terms F.O.B. Calcutta two per cent ten days E.O.M. One Messerschmitt full of hemp is due in Belgrade for a C-47 and a half full of those semi-pitted dates we stuck them with from Khartoum. Use the money from the Portuguese anchovies we're selling back to Lisbon to pay for the Egyptian cotton we've got coming back to us from Mamaroneck and to pick up as many oranges as you can in Spain. Always pay cash for *naranjas*.'

'*Naranjas*?'

'That's what they call oranges in Spain, and these are Spanish oranges. And – oh, yes. Don't forget Piltdown Man.'

'Piltdown Man?'

'Yes, Piltdown Man. The Smithsonian Institution is not in a position at this time to meet our price for a second Piltdown Man, but they are looking forward to the death of a wealthy and beloved donor and –'

'Milo.'

'France wants all the parsley we can send them, and I think we might as well, because we'll need the francs for the lire for the pfennigs for the dates when they get back. I've also ordered a tremendous shipment of Peruvian balsa wood for distribution to each of the mess halls in the syndicate on a pro rata basis.'

'Balsa wood? What are the mess halls going to do with balsa wood?'

'Good balsa wood isn't so easy to come by these days, Colonel. I just didn't think it was a good idea to pass up the chance to buy it.'

'No, I suppose not,' Colonel Cathcart surmised vaguely with the look of somebody seasick. 'And I assume the price was right.'

'The price,' said Milo, 'was outrageous – positively exorbitant! But since we bought it from one of our own subsidiaries, we were happy to pay it. Look after the hides.'

'The hives?'

'The hides.'

'The hides?'

'The hides. In Buenos Aires. They have to be tanned.'

'Tanned?'

'In Newfoundland. And shipped to Helsinki N.M.I.F. before the spring thaw begins. Everything to Finland goes N.M.I.F. before the spring thaw begins.'

'No Money in Front?' guessed Colonel Cathcart.

'Good, Colonel. You have a gift, sir. And then there's the cork.'

'The cork?'

'That must go to New York, the shoes for Toulouse, the ham for Siam, the nails from Wales, and the tangerines for New Orleans.'

'Milo.'

'We have coals in Newcastle, sir.'

Colonel Cathcart threw up his hands. 'Milo, stop!' he cried, almost in tears. 'It's no use. You're just like I am – *indispensable!*' He pushed his pencil aside and rose to his feet in frantic exasperation. 'Milo, you can't fly sixty-four more missions. You can't even fly one more mission. The whole system would fall apart if anything happened to you.'

Milo nodded serenely with complacent gratification. 'Sir, are you forbidding me to fly any more combat missions?'

'Milo, I forbid you to fly any more combat missions,' Colonel Cathcart declared in a tone of stern and inflexible authority.

'But that's not fair, sir,' said Milo. 'What about my record? The other men are getting all the fame and medals and publicity. Why should I be penalized just because I'm doing such a good job as mess officer?'

'No, Milo, it isn't fair. But I don't see anything we can do about it.'

'Maybe we can get someone else to fly my missions for me.'

'But maybe we can get someone else to fly your missions for you,' Colonel Cathcart suggested. 'How about the striking coal miners in Pennsylvania and West Virgina?'

Milo shook his head. 'It would take too long to train them. But why not the men in the squadron, sir? After all, I'm doing this for them. They ought to be willing to do something for me in return.'

'But why not the men in the squadron, Milo?' Colonel Cathcart exclaimed. 'After all, you're doing all this for them. They ought to be willing to do something for you in return.'

'What's fair is fair.'

'What's fair is fair.'

'They could take turns, sir.'

'They might even take turns flying your missions for you, Milo.'

'Who gets the credit?'

'You get the credit, Milo. And if a man wins a medal flying one of your missions, you get the medal.'

'Who dies if he gets killed?'

'Why, he dies, of course. After all, Milo, what's fair is fair. There's just one thing.'

'You'll have to raise the number of missions.'

'I might have to raise the number of missions again, and I'm not sure the men will fly them. They're still pretty sore because I jumped them to seventy. If I can get just one of the regular officers to fly more, the rest will probably follow.'

'Nately will fly more missions, sir.' Milo said. 'I was told in strictest confidence just a little while ago that he'll do anything he has to in order to remain overseas with a girl he's fallen in love with.'

'But Nately will fly more!' Colonel Cathcart declared, and he brought his hands together in a resounding clap of victory. 'Yes, Nately will fly more. And this time I'm really going to jump the missions, right up to eighty, and really knock General Dreedle's eye out. And this is a good way to get that lousy rat Yossarian back into combat where he might get killed.'

'Yossarian?' A tremor of deep concern passed over Milo's simple, homespun features, and he scratched the corner of his reddish-brown mustache thoughtfully.

'Yeah, Yossarian. I hear he's going around saying that he's finished his missions and the war's over for him. Well, maybe he had finished his missions. But he hasn't finished *your* missions, has he? Ha! Ha! Has *he* got a surprise coming to him!'

'Sir, Yossarian is a friend of mine,' Milo objected. 'I'd hate to be responsible for doing anything that would put him back in combat. I owe a lot to Yossarian. Isn't there any way we could make an exception of him?'

'Oh, no, Milo.' Colonel Cathcart clucked sententiously, shocked by the suggestion. 'We must never play favorites. We must always treat every man alike.'

'I'd give everything I own to Yossarian,' Milo persevered gamely on Yossarian's behalf. 'But since I don't own anything, I can't give everything to him, can I? So he'll just have to take his chances with the rest of the men, won't he?'

'What's fair is fair, Milo.'

'Yes, sir, what's fair is fair,' Milo agreed. 'Yossarian is no better than the other men, and he has no right to expect any special privileges, has he?'

'No, Milo. What's fair is fair.'

And there was no time for Yossarian to save himself from combat once Colonel Cathcart issued his announcement raising the missions to eighty late that same afternoon, no time to dissuade Nately from flying them or even to conspire again with Dobbs to murder Colonel Cathcart, for the alert sounded suddenly at dawn the next day and the men were rushed into the trucks before a decent breakfast could be prepared, and they were driven at top speed to the briefing room and then out to the airfield, where the clitterclattering fuel trucks were still pumping gasoline into the tanks of the planes and the scampering crews of armorers were toiling as swiftly as they could at hoisting the thousand-pound demolition bombs into the bomb bays. Everybody was running, and engines were turned on and warmed up as soon as the fuel trucks had finished.

Intelligence had reported that a disabled Italian cruiser in drydock at La Spezia would be towed by the Germans that same morning to a channel at the entrance of the harbor and scuttled there to deprive the Allied armies of deep-water port facilities when they captured the city. For once, a military intelligence report proved accurate. The long vessel was halfway across the harbor when they flew in from the west, and broke it apart with direct hits from every flight that filled them all with waves of enormously satisfying

474

group pride until they found themselves engulfed in great barrages of flak that rose from guns in every bend of the huge horseshoe of mountainous land below. Even Havermeyer resorted to the wildest evasive action he could command when he saw what a vast distance he had still to travel to escape, and Dobbs, at the pilot's controls in his formation, zigged when he should have zagged, skidding his plane into the plane alongside, and chewed off its tail. His wing broke off at the base, and his plane dropped like a rock and was almost out of sight in an instant. There was no fire, no smoke, not the slightest untoward noise. The remaining wing revolved as ponderously as a grinding cement mixer as the plane plummeted nose downward in a straight line at accelerating speed until it struck the water, which foamed open at the impact like a white water lily on the dark-blue sea, and washed back in a geyser of apple-green bubbles when the plane sank. It was over in a matter of seconds. There were no parachutes. And Nately, in the other plane was killed too.

36   The cellar

Nately's death almost killed the chaplain. Chaplain
Shipman was seated in his tent, laboring over his paper-
work in his reading spectacles, when his phone rang and
news of the mid-air collision was given to him from the
field. His insides turned at once to dry clay. His hand
was trembling as he put the phone down. His other hand
began trembling. The disaster was too immense to contemplate. Twelve men killed – how ghastly, how very,
very awful! His feeling of terror grew. He prayed
instinctively that Yossarian, Nately, Hungry Joe and his
other friends would not be listed among the victims, then
berated himself repentantly, for to pray for their safety
was to pray for the death of other young men he did not
even know. It was too late to pray; yet that was all he
knew how to do. His heart was pounding with a noise
that seemed to be coming from somewhere outside, and
he knew he would never sit in a dentist's chair again,
never glance at a surgical tool, never witness an automobile accident or hear a voice shout at night, without
experiencing the same violent thumping in his chest and
dreading that he was going to die. He would never watch
another fist fight without fearing he was going to faint
and crack his skull open on the pavement or suffer a

fatal heart attack or cerebal hemorrhage. He wondered if he would ever see his wife again or his three small children. He wondered if he ever *should* see his wife again, now that Captain Black had planted in his mind such strong doubts about the fidelity and character of all women. There were so many other men, he felt, who could prove more satisfying to her sexually. When he thought of death now, he always thought of his wife, and when he thought of his wife he always thought of losing her.

In another minute the chaplain felt strong enough to rise and walk with glum reluctance to the tent next door for Sergeant Whitcomb. They drove in Sergeant Whitcomb's jeep. The chaplain made fists of his hands to keep them from shaking as they lay in his lap. He ground his teeth together and tried not to hear as Sergeant Whitcomb chirruped exultantly over the tragic event. Twelve men killed meant twelve more form letters of condolence that could be mailed in one bunch to the next of kin over Colonel Cathcart's signature, giving Sergeant Whitcomb hope of getting an article on Colonel Cathcart into *The Saturday Evening Post* in time for Easter.

At the field a heavy silence prevailed, overpowering motion like a ruthless, insensate spell holding in thrall the only beings who might break it. The chaplain was in awe. He had never beheld such a great, appalling stillness before. Almost two hundred tired, gaunt, downcast men stood holding their parachute packs in a somber and unstirring crowd outside the briefing room, their faces staring blankly in different angles of stunned dejection. They seemed unwilling to go, unable to move. The chaplain was acutely conscious of the faint noise his footsteps made as he approached. His eyes searched hurriedly, frantically, through the immobile maze of limp figures. He spied Yossarian finally with a feeling of immense joy, and then his mouth gaped open slowly in unbearable horror as he noted Yossarian's vivid, beaten, grimy look of deep, drugged despair. He understood at

477

once, recoiling in pain from the realization and shaking his head with a protesting and imploring grimace, that Nately was dead. The knowledge struck him with a numbing shock. A sob broke from him. The blood drained from his legs, and he thought he was going to drop. Nately was dead. All hope that he was mistaken was washed away by the sound of Nately's name emerging with recurring clarity now from the almost inaudible babble of murmuring voices that he was suddenly aware of for the first time. Nately was dead: the boy had been killed. A whimpering sound rose in the chaplain's throat, and his jaw began to quiver. His eyes filled with tears, and he was crying. He started toward Yossarian on tiptoe to mourn beside him and share his wordless grief. At that moment a hand grabbed him roughly around the arm and a brusque voice demanded,

'Chaplain Shipman?'

He turned with surprise to face a stout, pugnacious colonel with a large head and mustache and a smooth, florid skin. He had never seen the man before. 'Yes. What is it?' The fingers grasping the chaplain's arm were hurting him, and he tried in vain to squirm loose.

'Come along.'

The chaplain pulled back in frightened confusion. 'Where? Why? Who are you, anyway?'

'You'd better come along with us, Father,' a lean, hawkfaced major on the chaplain's other side intoned with reverential sorrow. 'We're from the government. We want to ask you some questions.'

'What kind of questions? What's the matter?'

'Aren't you Chaplain Shipman?' demanded the obese colonel.

'He's the one,' Sergeant Whitcomb answered.

'Go on along with them,' Captain Black called out to the chaplain with a hostile and contemptuous sneer. 'Go on into the car if you know what's good for you.'

Hands were drawing the chaplain away irresistibly. He wanted to shout for help to Yossarian, who seemed too far away to hear. Some of the men nearby were beginning to look at him with awakening curiosity. The chaplain bent his face away with burning shame and allowed himself to be led into the rear of a staff car and seated between the fat colonel with the large, pink face and the skinny, unctuous, despondent major. He automatically held a wrist out to each, wondering for a moment if they wanted to handcuff him. Another officer was already in the front seat. A tall M.P. with a whistle and a white helmet got in behind the wheel. The chaplain did not dare raise his eyes until the closed car had lurched from the area and the speeding wheels were whining on the bumpy blacktop road.

'Where are you taking me?' he asked in a voice soft with timidity and guilt, his gaze still averted. The notion came to him that they were holding him to blame for the mid-air crash and the death of Nately. 'What have I done?'

'Why don't you keep your trap shut and let us ask the questions?' said the colonel.

'Don't talk to him that way,' said the major. 'It isn't necessary to be so disrespectful.'

'Then tell him to keep his trap shut and let us ask the questions.'

'Father, please keep your trap shut and let us ask the questions,' urged the major sympathetically. 'It will be better for you.'

'It isn't necessary to call me Father,' said the chaplain. 'I'm not a Catholic.'

'Neither am I, Father,' said the major. 'It's just that I'm a very devout person, and I like to call all men of God Father.'

'He doesn't even believe there are atheists in foxholes,' the colonel mocked, and nudged the chaplain in the ribs familiarly. 'Go on, Chaplain, tell him. Are there atheists in foxholes?'

'I don't know, sir,' the chaplain replied. 'I've never been in a foxhole.'

The officer in front swung his head around swiftly with a quarrelsome expression. 'You've never been in heaven either, have you? But you know there's a heaven, don't you?'

'Or do you?' said the colonel.

'That's a very serious crime you've committed, Father,' said the major.

'What crime?'

'We don't know yet,' said the colonel. 'But we're going to find out. And we sure know it's very serious.'

The car swung off the road at Group Headquarters with a squeal of tires, slackening speed only slightly, and continued around past the parking lot to the back of the building. The three officers and the chaplain got out. In single file, they ushered him down a wobbly flight of wooden stairs leading to the basement and led him into a damp, gloomy room with a low cement ceiling and unfinished stone walls. There were cobwebs in all the corners. A huge centipede blew across the floor to the shelter of a water pipe. They sat the chaplain in a hard, straight-backed chair that stood behind a small, bare table.

'Please make yourself comfortable, Chaplain,' invited the colonel cordially, switching on a blinding spotlight and shooting it squarely into the chaplain's face. He placed a set of brass knuckles and box of wooden matches on the table. 'We want you to relax.'

The chaplain's eyes bulged out incredulously. His teeth chattered and his limbs felt utterly without strength. He was powerless. They might do whatever they wished to him, he realized; these brutal men might beat him to death right there in the basement, and no one would intervene to save him, no one, perhaps, but the devout and sympathetic major with the sharp face, who set a water tap dripping loudly into a sink and returned to the table to lay a length of heavy rubber hose down beside the brass knuckles.

'Everything's going to be all right, Chaplain,' the major said encouragingly. 'You've got nothing to be afraid of if you're not guilty. What are you so afraid of? You're not guilty, are you?'

480

'Sure he's guilty,' said the colonel. 'Guilty as hell.'

'Guilty of what?' implored the chaplain, feeling more and more bewildered and not knowing which of the men to appeal to for mercy. The third officer wore no insignia and lurked in silence off to the side. 'What did I do?'

'That's just what we're going to find out,' answered the colonel, and he shoved a pad and pencil across the table to the chaplain. 'Write your name for us, will you? In your own handwriting.'

'My own handwriting?'

'That's right. Anywhere on the page.' When the chaplain had finished, the colonel took the pad back and held it up alongside a sheet of paper he removed from a folder. 'See?' he said to the major, who had come to his side and was peering solemnly over his shoulder.

'They're not the same, are they?' the major admitted.

'I told you he did it.'

'Did what?' asked the chaplain.

'Chaplain, this comes as a great shock to me,' the major accused in a tone of heavy lamentation.

'What does?'

'I can't tell you how disappointed I am in you.'

'For what?' persisted the chaplain more frantically. 'What have I done?'

'For this,' replied the major, and, with an air of disillusioned disgust, tossed down on the table the pad on which the chaplain had signed his name. 'This isn't your handwriting.'

The chaplain blinked rapidly with amazement. 'But of course it's my handwriting.'

'No it isn't, Chaplain. You're lying again.'

'But I just wrote it!' the chaplain cried in exasperation. 'You saw me write it.'

'That's just it,' the major answered bitterly. 'I *saw* you write it. You can't deny that you did write it. A person who'll lie about his own handwriting will lie about anything.'

'But who lied about my own handwriting?' demanded the chaplain, forgetting his fear in the wave of anger and indignation that welled up inside him suddenly. 'Are you crazy or something? What are you both talking about?'

'We asked you to write your name in your own handwriting. And you didn't do it.'

'But of course I did. In whose handwriting did I write it if not my own?'

'In somebody else's.'

'Whose?'

'That's just what we're going to find out,' threatened the colonel.

'Talk, Chaplain.'

The chaplain looked from one to the other of the two men with rising doubt and hysteria. 'That handwriting is mine,' he maintained passionately. 'Where else is my handwriting, if that isn't it?'

'Right here,' answered the colonel. And looking very superior, he tossed down on the table a photostatic copy of a piece of V mail in which everything but the salutation 'Dear Mary' had been blocked out and on which the censoring officer had written, 'I long for you tragically. R.O. Shipman, Chaplain, U.S. Army.' The colonel smiled scornfully as he watched the chaplain's face turn crimson. 'Well, Chaplain? Do you know who wrote that?'

The chaplain took a long moment to reply; he had recognized Yossarian's handwriting. 'No.'

'You can read, though, can't you?' the colonel persevered sarcastically. 'The author signed his name.'

'That's my name there.'

'Then you wrote it. Q.E.D.'

'But I didn't write it. That isn't my handwriting, either.'

'Then you signed your name in somebody else's handwriting again,' the colonel retorted with a shrug. 'That's all that means.'

'Oh, this is ridiculous!' the chaplain shouted, suddenly losing all patience. He jumped to his feet in a blazing fury, both fists clenched. 'I'm not going to stand for this any longer! Do you hear? Twelve men were just killed, and

482

I have no time for these silly questions. You've no right to keep me here, and I'm just not going to stand for it.'

Without saying a word, the colonel pushed the chaplain's chest hard and knocked him back down into the chair, and the chaplain was suddenly weak and very much afraid again. The major picked up the length of rubber hose and began tapping it menacingly against his open palm. The colonel lifted the box of matches, took one out and held it poised against the striking surface, watching with glowering eyes for the chaplain's next sign of defiance. The chaplain was pale and almost too petrified to move. The bright glare of the spotlight made him turn away finally; the dripping water was louder and almost unbearably irritating. He wished they would tell him what they wanted so that he would know what to confess. He waited tensely as the third officer, at a signal from the colonel, ambled over from the wall and seated himself on the table just a few inches away from the chaplain. His face was expressionless, his eyes penetrating and cold.

'Turn off the light,' he said over his shoulder in a low, calm voice. 'It's very annoying.'

The chaplain gave him a small smile of gratitude. 'Thank you, sir. And the drip too, please.'

'Leave the drip,' said the officer. 'That doesn't bother me.' He tugged up the legs of his trousers a bit, as though to preserve their natty crease. 'Chaplain,' he asked casually, 'of what religious persuasion are you?'

'I'm an Anabaptist, sir.'

'That's a pretty suspicious religion, isn't it?'

'Suspicious?' inquired the chaplain in a kind of innocent daze. 'Why, sir?'

'Well, I don't know a thing about it. You'll have to admit that, won't you? Doesn't that make it pretty suspicious?'

'I don't know, sir,' the chaplain answered diplomatically, with an uneasy stammer. He found the man's lack of insignia disconcerting and was not even sure he had

483

to say 'sir.' Who was he? And what authority had he to interrogate him?

'Chaplain, I once studied Latin. I think it's only fair to warn you of that before I ask my next question. Doesn't the word Anabaptist simply mean that you're not a Baptist?'

'Oh, no, sir. There's much more.'

'Are you a Baptist?'

'No, sir.'

'Then you *are* not a Baptist, aren't you?'

'Sir?'

'I don't see why you're bickering with me on that point. You've already admitted it. Now, Chaplain, to say you're not a Baptist doesn't really tell us anything about what you are, does it? You could be anything or anyone.' He leaned forward slightly and his manner took on a shrewd and significant air. 'You could even be,' he added, 'Washington Irving, couldn't you?'

'Washington Irving?' the chaplain repeated with surprise.

'Come on, Washington,' the corpulent colonel broke in irascibly. 'Why don't you make a clean breast of it? We know you stole that plum tomato.'

After a moment's shock, the chaplain giggled with nervous relief. 'Oh, is *that* it!' he exclaimed. 'Now I'm beginning to understand. I didn't steal that plum tomato, sir. Colonel Cathcart gave it to me. You can even ask him if you don't believe me.'

A door opened at the other end of the room and Colonel Cathcart stepped into the basement as though from a closet.

'Hello, Colonel. Colonel, he claims you gave him that plum tomato. Did you?'

'Why should I give him a plum tomato?' answered Colonel Cathcart.

'Thank you, Colonel. That will be all.'

'It's a pleasure, Colonel,' Colonel Cathcart replied, and he stepped back out of the basement, closing the door after him.

'Well, Chaplain? What have you got to say now?'

'He did give it to me!' the chaplain hissed in a whisper that was both fierce and fearful. 'He did give it to me!'

'You're not calling a superior officer a liar are you, Chaplain?'

'Why should a superior officer give you a plum tomato, Chaplain?'

'Is that why you tried to give it to Sergeant Whitcomb, Chaplain? Because it was a hot tomato?'

'No, no, no,' the chaplain protested, wondering miserably why they were not able to understand. 'I offered it to Sergeant Whitcomb because I didn't want it.'

'Why'd you steal it from Colonel Cathcart if you didn't want it?'

'I didn't steal it from Colonel Cathcart!'

'Then why are you so guilty, if you didn't steal it?'

'I'm not guilty!'

'Then why would we be questioning you if you weren't guilty?'

'Oh, I don't know,' the chaplain groaned, kneading his fingers in his lap and shaking his bowed and anguished head. 'I don't know.'

'He thinks we have time to waste,' snorted the major.

'Chaplain,' resumed the officer without insignia at a more leisurely pace, lifting a typewritten sheet of yellow paper from the open folder, 'I have a signed statement here from Colonel Cathcart asserting you stole that plum tomato from him.' He lay the sheet face down on one side of the folder and picked up a second page from the other side. 'And I have a notarized affidavit from Sergeant Whitcomb in which he states that he knew the tomato was hot just from the way you tried to unload it on him.'

'I swear to God I didn't steal it, sir,' the chaplain pleaded with distress, almost in tears. 'I give you my sacred word it was not a hot tomato.'

'Chaplain, do you believe in God?'

'Yes, sir. Of course I do.'

'That's odd, Chaplain,' said the officer, taking from the folder another typewritten yellow page, 'because I have here in my hands now another statement from Colonel Cathcart in which he swears that you refused to co-operate with him in conducting prayer meetings in the briefing room before each mission.'

After looking blank a moment, the chaplain nodded quickly with recollection. 'Oh, that's not quite true, sir,' he explained eagerly. 'Colonel Cathcart gave up the idea himself once he realized enlisted men pray to the same God as officers.'

'He did *what*?' exclaimed the officer in disbelief.

'What nonsense!' declared the red-faced colonel, and swung away from the chaplain with dignity and annoyance.

'Does he expect us to believe that?' cried the major incredulously.

The officer without insignia chuckled acidly. 'Chaplain, aren't you stretching things a bit far now?' he inquired with a smile that was indulgent and unfriendly.

'But, sir, it's the truth, sir! I swear it's the truth.'

'I don't see how that matters one way or the other,' the officer answered nonchalantly, and reached sideways again toward the open folder filled with papers. 'Chaplain, did you say you did believe in God in answer to my question? I don't remember.'

'Yes, sir. I did say so, sir. I do believe in God.'

'Then that really is very odd, Chaplain, because I have here another affidavit from Colonel Cathcart that states you once told him atheism was not against the law. Do you recall ever making a statement like that to anyone?'

The chaplain nodded without any hesitation, feeling himself on very solid ground now. 'Yes, sir, I did make a statement like that. I made it because it's true. Atheism is not against the law.'

'But that's still no reason to say so, Chaplain, is it?' the officer chided tartly, frowning, and picked up still one more typewritten, notarized page from the folder. 'And here I have another sworn statement from Sergeant Whitcomb that says you opposed his plan of sending letters of condolence over Colonel Cathcart's signature

486

to the next of kin of men killed or wounded in combat. Is that true?'

'Yes, sir, I did oppose it,' answered the chaplain. 'And I'm proud that I did. Those letters are insincere and dishonest. Their only purpose is to bring glory to Colonel Cathcart.'

'But what difference does that make?' replied the officer. 'They still bring solace and comfort to the families that receive them, don't they? Chaplain, I simply can't understand your thinking process.'

The chaplain was stumped and at a complete loss for a reply. He hung his head, feeling tongue-tied and naive.

The ruddy stout colonel stepped forward vigorously with a sudden idea. 'Why don't we knock his goddam brains out?' he suggested with robust enthusiasm to the others.

'Yes, we could knock his goddam brains out, couldn't we?' the hawk-faced major agreed. 'He's only an Anabaptist.'

'No, we've got to find him guilty first,' the officer without insignia cautioned with a languid restraining wave. He slid lightly to the floor and moved around to the other side of the table, facing the chaplain with both hands pressed flat on the surface. His expression was dark and very stern, square and forbidding. 'Chaplain,' he annouced with magisterial rigidity, 'we charge you formally with being Washington Irving and taking capricious and unlicensed liberties in censoring the letters of officers and enlisted men. Are you guilty or innocent?'

'Innocent, sir.' The chaplain licked dry lips with a dry tongue and leaned forward in suspense on the edge of his chair.

'Guilty,' said the colonel.

'Guilty,' said the major.

'Guilty it is, then,' remarked the officer without insignia, and wrote a word on a page in the folder. 'Chaplain,' he continued, looking up, 'we accuse you also of the commission of crimes and infractions we don't even know about yet. Guilty or innocent?'

'I don't know, sir. How can I say if you don't tell me what they are?'

'How can we tell you if we don't know?'

'Guilty,' decided the colonel.

'Sure he's guilty,' agreed the major. 'If they're his crimes and infractions, he must have committed them.'

'Guilty it is, then,' chanted the officer without insignia, and moved off to the side of the room. 'He's all yours, Colonel.'

'Thank you,' commended the colonel. 'You did a very good job.' He turned to the chaplain. 'Okay, Chaplain, the jig's up. Take a walk.'

The chaplain did not understand. 'What do you wish me to do?'

'Go on, beat it, I told you!' the colonel roared, jerking a thumb over his shoulder angrily. 'Get the hell out of here.'

The chaplain was shocked by his bellicose words and tone and, to his own amazement and mystification, deeply chagrined that they were turning him loose. 'Aren't you even going to punish me?' he inquired with querulous surprise.

'You're damned right we're going to punish you. But we're certainly not going to let you hang around while we decide how and when to do it. So get going. Hit the road.'

The chaplain rose tentatively and took a few steps away. 'I'm free to go?'

'For the time being. But don't try to leave the island. We've got your number, Chaplain. Just remember that we've got you under surveillance twenty-four hours a day.'

It was not conceivable that they would allow him to leave. The chaplain walked toward the exit gingerly, expecting at any instant to be ordered back by a peremptory voice or halted in his tracks by a heavy blow on the shoulder or the head. They did nothing to stop him. He found his way through the stale, dark, dank corridors to the flight of stairs. He was staggering and panting when he climbed out into the fresh air. As soon as he had escaped, a feeling of overwhelming moral outrage filled him. He was furious, more furious at the atrocities of the day than he had ever felt before in his whole life. He swept through the spacious, echoing lobby of the building in a temper of scalding and vindictive resentment. He was not going to stand for it any more, he told himself, he was simply not going to stand for it. When he reached the entrance, he spied, with a feeling of good fortune, Colonel Korn trotting up the wide steps alone. Bracing himself with a deep breath, the chaplain moved courageously forward to intercept him.

'Colonel, I'm not going to stand for it any more,' he declared with vehement determination, and watched in dismay as Colonel Korn went trotting by up the steps without even noticing him. 'Colonel Korn!'

The tubby, loose figure of his superior officer stopped, turned and came trotting back down slowly. 'What is it, Chaplain?'

'Colonel Korn, I want to talk to you about the crash this morning. It was a terrible thing to happen, terrible!'

Colonel Korn was silent a moment, regarding the chaplain with a glint of cynical amusement. 'Yes, Chaplain, it certainly was terrible,' he said finally. 'I don't know *how* we're going to write this one up without making ourselves look bad.'

'That isn't what I meant,' the chaplain scolded firmly without any fear at all. 'Some of those twelve men had already finished their seventy missions.'

Colonel Korn laughed. 'Would it be any less terrible if they had all been new men?' he inquired caustically.

Once again the chaplain was stumped. Immoral logic seemed to be confounding him at every turn. He was less sure of himself than before when he continued, and his voice wavered. 'Sir, it just isn't right to make the men in this group fly eighty missions when the men in other groups are being sent home with fifty and fifty-five.'

'We'll take the matter under consideration,' Colonel

Korn said with bored disinterest, and started away. '*Adios*, Padre.'

'What does that mean, sir?' the chaplain persisted in a voice turning shrill..

Colonel Korn stopped with an unpleasant expression and took a step back down. 'It means we'll think about it, Padre,' he answered with sarcasm and contempt. 'You wouldn't want us to do anything without thinking about it, would you?'

'No, sir, I suppose not. But you have been thinking about it, haven't you?'

'Yes, Padre, we have been thinking about it. But to make you happy, we'll think about it some more, and you'll be the first person we'll tell if we reach a new decision. And now, *adios*.' Colonel Korn whirled away again and hurried up the stairs.

'Colonel Korn!' The chaplain's cry made Colonel Korn stop once more. His head swung slowly around toward the chaplain with a look of morose impatience. Words gushed from the chaplain in a nervous torrent. 'Sir, I would like your permission to take the matter to General Dreedle. I want to bring my protests to Wing Headquarters.'

Colonel Korn's thick, dark jowls inflated unexpectedly with a suppressed guffaw, and it took him a moment to reply. 'That's all right, Padre,' he answered with mischievous merriment, trying hard to keep a straight face. 'You have my permission to speak to General Dreedle.'

'Thank you, sir. I believe it only fair to warn you that I think I have some influence with General Dreedle.'

'It's good of you to warn me, Padre. And I believe it only fair to warn you that you won't find General Dreedle at Wing.' Colonel Korn grinned wickedly and then broke into triumphant laughter. 'General Dreedle is out, Padre. And General Peckem is in. We have a new wing commander.'

The chaplain was stunned. 'General Peckem!'

'That's right, Chaplain. Have you got any influence with him?'

'Why, I don't even know General Peckem,' the chaplain protested wretchedly.

Colonel Korn laughed again. 'That's too bad, Chaplain, because Colonel Cathcart knows him very well.' Colonel Korn chuckled steadily with gloating relish for another second or two and then stopped abruptly. 'And by the way, Padre,' he warned coldly, poking his finger once into the chaplain's chest. 'The jig is up between you and Dr. Stubbs. We know very well he sent you up here to complain today.'

'Dr. Stubbs?' The chaplain shook his head in baffled protest. 'I haven't seen Dr. Stubbs, Colonel. I was brought here by three strange officers who took me down into the cellar without authority and questioned and insulted me.'

Colonel Korn poked the chaplain in the chest once more. 'You know damned well Dr. Stubbs has been telling the men in his squadron they didn't have to fly more than seventy missions.' He laughed harshly. 'Well, Padre, they do have to fly more than seventy missions, because we're transferring Dr. Stubbs to the Pacific. So *adios*, Padre. *Adios*.'

37   General Scheisskopf

Dreedle was out, and General Peckem was in, and General Peckem had hardly moved inside General Dreedle's office to replace him when his splendid military victory began falling to pieces around him.

'*General* Scheisskopf?' he inquired unsuspectingly of the sergeant in his new office who brought him word of the order that had come in that morning. 'You mean *Colonel* Scheisskopf, don't you?'

'No, sir, General Scheisskopf. He was promoted to general this morning, sir.'

'Well, that's certainly curious! Scheisskopf? A general? What grade?'

'Lieutenant general, sir, and –'

'Lieutenant general!'

'Yes, sir, and he wants you to issue no orders to anyone in your command without first clearing them through him.'

'Well, I'll be damned,' mused General Peckem with astonishment, swearing aloud for perhaps the first time in his life. 'Cargill, did you hear that? Scheisskopf was promoted way up to lieutenant general. I'll bet that promotion was intended for me and they gave it to him by mistake.'

Colonel Cargill had been rubbing his sturdy chin reflectively. 'Why is he giving orders to us?'

General Peckem's sleek, scrubbed, distinguished face tightened. 'Yes, Sergeant,' he said slowly with an uncomprehending frown. 'Why is he issuing orders to us if he's still in Special Services and we're in combat operations?'

'That's another change that was made this morning, sir. All combat operations are now under the jurisdiction of Special Services. General Scheisskopf is our new commanding officer.'

General Peckem let out a sharp cry. 'Oh, my God!' he wailed, and all his practical composure went up in hysteria. 'Scheisskopf in charge? *Scheisskopf?*' He pressed his fists down on his eyes with horror. 'Cargill, get me Wintergreen! *Scheisskopf? Not Scheisskopf!*'

All phones began ringing at once. A corporal ran in and saluted.

'Sir, there's a chaplain outside to see you with news of an injustice in Colonel Cathcart's squadron.'

'Send him away, send him away! We've got enough injustices of our own. Where's Wintergreen?'

'Sir, General Scheisskopf is on the phone. He wants to speak to you at once.'

'Tell him I haven't arrived yet. Good Lord!' General Peckem screamed, as though struck by the enormity of the disaster for the first time. '*Scheisskopf?* The man's a moron! I walked all over that blockhead, and now he's my superior officer. Oh, my Lord! Cargill! Cargill, don't desert me! Where's Wintergreen?'

'Sir, I have an ex-Sergeant Wintergreen on your other telephone. He's been trying to reach you all morning.'

'General, I can't get Wintergreen,' Colonel Cargill shouted. 'His line is busy.'

General Peckem was perspiring freely as he lunged for the other telephone.

'Wintergreen!'

'Peckem, you son of a bitch –'

'Wintergreen, have you heard what they've done?'

'– what have you done, you stupid bastard?'

'They put Scheisskopf in charge of everything!'

Wintergreen was shrieking with rage and panic. 'You and your goddam memorandums! They've gone and transferred combat operations to Special Services!'

'Oh, no,' moaned General Peckem. 'Is that what did it? My memoranda? Is that what made them put Scheisskopf in charge? Why didn't they put me in charge?'

'Because you weren't in Special Services any more. You transferred out and left him in charge. And do you know what he wants? Do you know what the bastard wants us all to do?'

'Sir, I think you'd better talk to General Scheisskopf,' pleaded the sergeant nervously. 'He insists on speaking to someone.'

'Cargill, talk to Scheisskopf for me. I can't do it. Find out what he wants.'

Colonel Cargill listened to General Scheisskopf for a moment and went white as a sheet. 'Oh, my God!' he cried, as the phone fell from his fingers. 'Do you know what he wants? He wants us to march. He wants *everybody* to march!'

38   Kid sister

Yossarian marched backward with his gun on his hip
and refused to fly any more missions. He marched backward because he was continuously spinning around as
he walked to make certain no one was sneaking up on
him from behind. Every sound to his rear was a warning,
every person he passed a potential assassin. He kept his
hand on his gun butt constantly and smiled at no one but
Hungry Joe. He told Captain Piltchard and Captain
Wren that he was through flying. Captain Piltchard and
Captain Wren left his name off the flight schedule for
the next mission and reported the matter to Group Headquarters.

Colonel Korn laughed calmly. 'What the devil do you
mean, he won't fly more missions?' he asked with a
smile, as Colonel Cathcart crept away into a corner to
brood about the sinister import of the name Yossarian
popping up to plague him once again. 'Why won't he?'

'His friend Nately was killed in the crash over Spezia.
Maybe that's why.'

'Who does he think he is – Achilles?' Colonel Korn
was pleased with the simile and filed a mental reminder
to repeat it the next time he found himself in General
Peckem's presence. 'He has to fly more missions. He has

no choice. Go back and tell him you'll report the matter
to us if he doesn't change his mind.'

'We already did tell him that, sir. It made no difference.'

'What does Major Major say?'

'We never see Major Major. He seems to have disappeared.'

'I wish we could disappear *him*!' Colonel Cathcart
blurted out from the corner peevishly. 'The way they did
that fellow Dunbar.'

'Oh, there are plenty of other ways we can handle this
one,' Colonel Korn assured him confidently, and continued to Piltchard and Wren. 'Let's begin with the
kindest. Send him to Rome for a rest for a few days.
Maybe this fellow's death really did hurt him a bit.'

Nately's death, in fact, almost killed Yossarian too,
for when he broke the news to Nately's whore in Rome
she uttered a piercing, heartbroken shriek and tried to
stab him to death with a potato peeler.

'*Bruto!*' she howled at him in hysterical fury as he
bent her arm up around behind her back and twisted
gradually until the potato peeler dropped from her
grasp. '*Bruto! Bruto!*' She lashed at him swiftly with the
long-nailed fingers of her free hand and raked open his
cheek. She spat in his face viciously.

'What's the matter?' he screamed in stinging pain and
bewilderment, flinging her away from him all the way
across the room to the wall. 'What do you want from
me?'

She flew back at him with both fists flailing and
bloodied his mouth with a solid punch before he was
able to grab her wrists and hold her still. Her hair tossed
wildly. Tears were streaming in single torrents from her
flashing, hate-filled eyes as she struggled against him
fiercely in an irrational frenzy of maddened might,
snarling and cursing savagely and screaming '*Bruto!
Bruto!*' each time he tried to explain. Her great strength
caught him off guard, and he lost his footing. She was
nearly as tall as Yossarian, and for a few fantastic,

terror-filled moments he was certain she would overpower him in her crazed determination, crush him to the ground and rip him apart mercilessly limb from limb for some heinous crime he had never committed. He wanted to yell for help as they strove against each other frantically in a grunting, panting stalemate, arm against arm. At last she weakened, and he was able to force her back and plead with her to let him talk, swearing to her that Nately's death had not been his fault. She spat in his face again, and he pushed her away hard in disgusted anger and frustration. She hurled herself down toward the potato peeler the instant he released her. He flung himself down after her, and they rolled over each other on the floor several times before he could tear the potato peeler away. She tried to trip him with her hand as he scrambled to his feet and scratched an excruciating chunk out of his ankle. He hopped across the room in pain and threw the potato peeler out the window. He heaved a huge sigh of relief once he saw he was safe.

'Now, please let me explain something you,' he cajoled in a mature, reasoning, earnest voice.

She kicked him in the groin. *Whoosh!* went the air out of him, and he sank down on his side with a shrill and ululating cry, doubled up over his knees in chaotic agony and retching for breath. Nately's whore ran from the room. Yossarian staggered up to his feet not a moment too soon, for she came charging back in from the kitchen carrying a long bread knife. A moan of incredulous dismay wafted from his lips as, still clutching his throbbing, tender, burning bowels in both hands, he dropped his full weight down against her shins and knocked her legs out from under her. She flipped completely over his head and landed on the floor on her elbows with a jarring thud. The knife skittered free, and he slapped it out of sight under the bed. She tried to lunge after it, and he seized her by the arm and yanked her up. She tried to kick him in the groin again, and he slung her away with a violent oath of his own. She slammed into the wall off

497

balance and smashed a chair over into a vanity table covered with combs, hairbrushes and cosmetic jars that all went crashing off. A framed picture fell to the floor at the other end of the room, the glass front shattering.

'What do you *want* from me?' he yelled at her in whining and exasperated confusion. 'I didn't kill him.'

She hurled a heavy glass ash tray at his head. He made a fist and wanted to punch her in the stomach when she came charging at him again, but he was afraid he might harm her. He wanted to clip her very neatly on the point of the jaw and run from the room, but there was no clear target, and he merely skipped aside neatly at the last second and helped her along past him with a strong shove. She banged hard against the other wall. Now she was blocking the door. She threw a large vase at him. Then she came at him with a full wine bottle and struck him squarely on the temple, knocking him down half stunned on one knee. His ears were buzzing, his whole face was numb. More than anything else, he was embarrassed. He felt awkward because she was going to murder him. He simply did not understand what was going on. He had no idea *what to do*. But he did know he had to save himself, and he catapulted forward off the floor when he saw her raise the wine bottle to clout him again and barreled into her midriff before she could strike him. He had momentum, and he propelled her before him backward in his driving rush until her knees buckled against the side of the bed and she fell over onto the mattress with Yossarian sprawled on top of her between her legs. She plunged her nails into the side of his neck and gouged as he worked his way up the supple, full hills and ledges of her rounded body until he covered her completely and pressed her into submission, his fingers pursuing her thrashing arm persistently until they arrived at the wine bottle finally and wrenched it free. She was still kicking and cursing and scratching ferociously. She tried to bite him cruelly, her coarse, sensual lips stretched back over her teeth like an enraged omnivorous beast's. Now that she lay captive beneath

498

him, he wondered how he would ever escape her without leaving himself vulnerable. He could feel the tensed, straddling inside of her buffeting thighs and knees squeezing and churning around one of his legs. He was stirred by thoughts of sex that made him ashamed. He was conscious of the voluptuous flesh of her firm, young-woman's body straining and beating against him like a humid, fluid, delectable, unyielding tide, her belly and warm, live, plastic breasts thrusting upward against him vigorously in sweet and menacing temptation. Her breath was scalding. All at once he realized – though the writhing turbulence beneath him had not diminished one whit – that she was no longer grappling with him, recognized with a quiver that she was not fighting him but heaving her pelvis up against him remorselessly in the primal, powerful, rhapsodic instinctual rhythm of erotic ardor and abandonment. He gasped in delighted surprise. Her face – as beautiful as a blooming flower to him now – was distorted with a new kind of torture, the tissues serenely swollen, her half-closed eyes misty and unseeing with the stultifying languor of desire.

'Caro,' she murmured hoarsely as though from the depths of a tranquil and luxurious trance. 'Ooooh, caro mio.'

He stroked her hair. She drove her mouth against his face with savage passion. He licked her neck. She wrapped her arms around him and hugged. He felt himself falling, falling ecstatically in love with her as she kissed him again and again with lips that were steaming and wet and soft and hard, mumbling deep sounds to him adoringly in an incoherent oblivion of rapture, one caressing hand on his back slipping deftly down inside his trouser belt while the other groped secretly and treacherously about on the floor for the bread knife and found it. He saved himself just in time. She still wanted to kill him! He was shocked and astounded by her depraved subterfuge as he tore the knife from her grasp and hurled it away. He bounded out of the bed to his feet. His face was agog with befuddlement and disillusion. He

499

did not know whether to dart through the door to freedom or collapse on the bed to fall in love with her and
place himself abjectly at her mercy again. She spared
him from doing either by bursting unpredictably into
tears. He was stunned again.

This time she wept with no other emotion than grief,
profound, debilitating, humble grief, forgetting all about
him. Her desolation was pathetic as she sat with her
tempestuous, proud, lovely head bowed, her shoulders
sagging, her spirit melting. This time there was no mistaking her anguish. Great racking sobs choked and shook
her. She was no longer aware of him, no longer cared.
He could have walked from the room safely then. But he
chose to remain and console and help her.

'Please,' he urged her inarticulately with his arm
about her shoulders, recollecting with pained sadness
how inarticulate and enfeebled he had felt in the plane
coming back from Avignon when Snowden kept whimpering to him that he was cold, he was cold, and all
Yossarian could offer him in return was 'There, there.
There, there.' 'Please,' he repeated to her sympathetically. 'Please, please.'

She rested against him and cried until she seemed too
weak to cry any longer, and did not look at him once until
he extended his handkerchief when she had finished.
She wiped her cheeks with a tiny, polite smile and gave
the handkerchief back, murmuring 'Grazie, grazie' with
meek, maidenly propriety, and then, without any warning whatsoever of a change in mood, clawed suddenly at
his eyes with both hands. She landed with each and let
out a victorious shriek.

'Ha! Assassino!' she hooted, and raced joyously across
the room for the bread knife to finish him off.

Half blinded, he rose and stumbled after her. A noise
behind him made him turn. His senses reeled in horror
at what he saw. Nately's whore's kid sister, of all people,
was coming after him with another long bread knife!

'Oh, no,' he wailed with a shudder, and he knocked the
knife out of her hand with a sharp downward blow on

her wrist. He lost patience entirely with the whole grotesque and incomprehensible melee. There was no telling who might lunge at him next through the doorway with another long bread knife, and he lifted Nately's whore's kid sister off the floor, threw her at Nately's whore and ran out of the room, out of the apartment and down the stairs. The two girls chased out into the hall after him. He heard their footsteps lag farther and farther behind as he fled and then cease altogether. He heard sobbing directly overhead. Glancing backward up the stair well, he spied Nately's whore sitting in a heap on one of the steps, weeping with her face in both hands, while her pagan irrepressible kid sister hung dangerously over the banister shouting 'Bruto! Bruto!' down at him happily and brandished her bread knife at him as though it were an exciting new toy she was eager to use.

Yossarian escaped, but kept looking back over his shoulder anxiously as he retreated through the street. People stared at him strangely, making him more apprehensive. He walked in nervous haste, wondering what there was in his appearance that caught everyone's attention. When he touched his hand to a sore spot on his forehead, his fingers turned gooey with blood, and he understood. He dabbed his face and neck with a handkerchief. Wherever it pressed, he picked up new red smudges. He was bleeding everywhere. He hurried into the Red Cross building and down the two steep flights of white marble stairs to the men's washroom, where he cleansed and nursed his innumerable visible wounds with cold water and soap and straightened his shirt collar and combed his hair. He had never seen a face so badly bruised and scratched as the one still blinking back at him in the mirror with a dazed and startled uneasiness. What on earth had she wanted from *him*?

When he left the men's room, Nately's whore was waiting outside in ambush. She was crouched against the wall near the bottom of the staircase and came pouncing down upon him like a hawk with a glittering silver steak knife in her fist. He broke the brunt of her assault with his upraised elbow and punched her neatly on the jaw. Her eyes rolled. He caught her before she dropped and sat her down gently. Then he ran up the steps and out of the building and spent the next three hours hunting through the city for Hungry Joe so that he could get away from Rome before she could find him again. He did not feel really safe until the plane had taken off. When they landed in Pianosa, Nately's whore, disguised in a mechanic's green overalls, was waiting with her steak knife exactly where the plane stopped, and all that saved him as she stabbed at his chest in her leather-soled high-heeled shoes was the gravel underfoot that made her feet roll out from under her. Yossarian, astounded, hauled her up into the plane and held her motionless on the floor in a double armlock while Hungry Joe radioed the control tower for permission to return to Rome. At the airport in Rome, Yossarian dumped her out of the plane on the taxi strip, and Hungry Joe took right off for Pianosa again without even cutting his engines. Scarcely breathing, Yossarian scrutinized every figure warily as he and Hungry Joe walked back through the squadron toward their tents. Hungry Joe eyed him steadily with a funny expression.

'Are you sure you didn't imagine the whole thing?' Hungry Joe inquired hesitantly after a while.

'Imagine it? You were right there with me, weren't you? You just flew her back to Rome.'

'Maybe I imagined the whole thing, too. Why does she want to kill you for?'

'She never did like me. Maybe it's because I broke his nose, or maybe it's because I was the only one in sight she could hate when she got the news. Do you think she'll come back?'

Yossarian went to the officers' club that night and stayed very late. He kept a leery eye out for Nately's whore as he approached his tent. He stopped when he saw her hiding in the bushes around the side, gripping a huge carving knife and all dressed up to look like a Pianosan farmer. Yossarian tiptoed around the back

502

noiselessly and seized her from behind.

'*Caramba!*' she exclaimed in a rage, and resisted like a wildcat as he dragged her inside the tent and hurled her down on the floor.

'Hey, what's going on?' queried one of his roommates drowsily.

'Hold her till I get back,' Yossarian ordered, yanking him out of bed on top of her and running out. 'Hold her!'

'Let me kill him and I'll ficky-fick you all,' she offered.

The other roommates leaped out of their cots when they saw it was a girl and tried to make her ficky-fick them all first as Yossarian ran to get Hungry Joe, who was sleeping like a baby. Yossarian lifted Huple's cat off Hungry Joe's face and shook him awake. Hungry Joe dressed rapidly. This time they flew the plane north and turned in over Italy far behind the enemy lines. When they were over level land, they strapped a parachute on Nately's whore and shoved her out the escape hatch. Yossarian was positive that he was at last rid of her and was relieved. As he approached his tent back in Pianosa, a figure reared up in the darkness right beside the path, and he fainted. He came to sitting on the ground and waited for the knife to strike him, almost welcoming the mortal blow for the peace it would bring. A friendly hand helped him up instead. It belonged to a pilot in Dunbar's squadron.

'How are you doing?' asked the pilot, whispering.

'Pretty good,' Yossarian answered.

'I saw you fall down just now. I thought something happened to you.'

'I think I fainted.'

'There's a rumor in my squadron that you told them you weren't going to fly any more combat missions.'

'That's the truth.'

'Then they came around from Group and told us that the rumor wasn't true, that you were just kidding around.'

'That was a lie.'

'Do you think they'll let you get away with it?'

'I don't know.'

'What will they do to you?'

'I don't know.'

'Do you think they'll court-martial you for desertion in the face of the enemy?'

'I don't know.'

'I hope you get away with it,' said the pilot in Dunbar's squadron, stealing out of sight into the shadows. 'Let me know how you're doing.'

Yossarian stared after him a few seconds and continued toward his tent.

'Pssst!' said a voice a few paces onward. It was Appleby, hiding in back of a tree. 'How are you doing?'

'Pretty good,' said Yossarian.

'I heard them say they were going to threaten to court-martial you for deserting in the face of the enemy. But that they wouldn't try to go through with it because they're not even sure they've got a case against you on that. And because it might make them look bad with the new commanders. Besides, you're still a pretty big hero for going around twice over the bridge at Ferrara. I guess you're just about the biggest hero we've got now in the group. I just thought you'd like to know that they'll only be bluffing.'

'Thanks, Appleby.'

'That's the only reason I started talking to you, to warn you.'

'I appreciate it.'

Appleby scuffed the toes of his shoes into the ground sheepishly. 'I'm sorry we had that fist fight in the officers' club, Yossarian.'

'That's all right.'

'But I didn't start it. I guess that was Orr's fault for hitting me in the face with his ping-pong paddle. What'd he want to do that for?'

'You were beating him.'

'Wasn't I supposed to beat him? Isn't that the point? Now that he's dead, I guess it doesn't matter any more whether I'm a better ping-pong player or not, does it?'

'I guess not.'

'And I'm sorry about making such a fuss about those Atabrine tablets on the way over. If you want to catch malaria, I guess it's your business, isn't it?'

'That's all right, Appleby.'

'But I was only trying to do my duty. I was obeying orders. I was always taught that I had to obey orders.'

'That's all right.'

'You know, I said to Colonel Korn and Colonel Cathcart that I didn't think they ought to make you fly any more missions if you didn't want to, and they said they were very disappointed in me.'

Yossarian smiled with rueful amusement. 'I'll bet they are.'

'Well, I don't care. Hell, you've flown seventy-one. That ought to be enough. Do you think they'll let you get away with it?'

'No.'

'Say, if they do let you get away with it, they'll have to let the rest of us get away with it, won't they?'

'That's why they can't let me get away with it.'

'What do you think they'll do?'

'I don't know.'

'Do you think they will try to court-martial you?'

'I don't know.'

'Are you afraid?'

'Yes.'

'Are you going to fly more missions?'

'No.'

'I hope you do get away with it,' Appleby whispered with conviction. 'I really do.'

'Thanks, Appleby.'

'I don't feel too happy about flying so many missions either now that it looks as though we've got the war won. I'll let you know if I hear anything else.'

'Thanks, Appleby.'

'Hey!' called a muted, peremptory voice from the leafless shrubs growing beside his tent in a waist-high clump after Appleby had gone. Havermeyer was hiding there in a squat. He was eating peanut brittle, and his pimples and large, oily pores looked like dark scales. 'How you doing?' he asked when Yossarian had walked to him.

'Pretty good.'

'Are you going to fly more missions?'

'No.'

'Suppose they try to make you?'

'I won't let them.'

'Are you yellow?'

'Yes.'

'Will they court-martial you?'

'They'll probably try.'

'What did Major Major say?'

'Major Major's gone.'

'Did they disappear him?'

'I don't know.'

'What will you do if they decide to disappear you?'

'I'll try to stop them.'

'Didn't they offer you any deals or anything if you did fly?'

'Piltchard and Wren said they'd arrange things so I'd only go on milk runs.'

Havermeyer perked up. 'Say, that sounds like a pretty good deal. I wouldn't mind a deal like that myself. I bet you snapped it up.'

'I turned it down.'

'That was dumb.' Havermeyer's stolid, dull face furrowed with consternation. 'Say, a deal like that wasn't so fair to the rest of us, was it? If you only flew on milk runs, then some of us would have to fly your share of the dangerous missions, wouldn't we?'

'That's right.'

'Say, I don't like that,' Havermeyer exclaimed, rising resentfully with his hands clenched on his hips. 'I don't like that a bit. That's a real royal screwing they're getting ready to give me just because you're too goddam yellow to fly any more missions, isn't it?'

'Take it up with them,' said Yossarian and moved his hand to his gun vigilantly.

'No, I'm not blaming you,' said Havermeyer, 'even though I don't like you. You know, I'm not too happy about flying so many missions any more either. Isn't there some way I can get out of it, too?'

Yossarian snickered ironically and joked, 'Put a gun on and start marching with me.'

Havermeyer shook his head thoughtfully. 'Nah, I couldn't do that. I might bring some disgrace on my wife and kid if I acted like a coward. Nobody likes a coward. Besides, I want to stay in the reserves when the war is over. You get five hundred dollars a year if you stay in the reserves.'

'Then fly more missions.'

'Yeah, I guess I have to. Say, do you think there's any chance they might take you off combat duty and send you home?'

'No.'

'But if they do and let you take one person with you, will you pick me? Don't pick anyone like Appleby. Pick me.'

'Why in the world should they do something like that?'

'I don't know. But if they do, just remember that I asked you first, will you? And let me know how you're doing. I'll wait for you here in these bushes every night. Maybe if they don't do anything bad to you, I won't fly any more missions either. Okay?'

All the next evening, people kept popping up at him out of the darkness to ask him how he was doing, appealing to him for confidential information with weary, troubled faces on the basis of some morbid and clandestine kinship he had not guessed existed. People in the squadron he barely knew popped into sight out of nowhere as he passed and asked him how he was doing. Even men from other squadrons came one by one to conceal themselves in the darkness and pop out. Everywhere he stepped after sundown someone was lying in wait to pop out and ask him how he was doing. People popped out at him from trees and bushes, from ditches and tall weeds, from around the corners of tents and

507

from behind the fenders of parked cars. Even one of his roommates popped out to ask him how he was doing and pleaded with him not to tell any of his other roommates he had popped out. Yossarian drew near each beckoning, overly cautious silhouette with his hand on his gun, never knowing which hissing shadow would finally turn dishonestly into Nately's whore or, worse, into some duly constituted governmental authority sent to club him ruthlessly into insensibility. It began to look as if they would have to do something like that. They did not want to court-martial him for desertion in the face of the enemy because a hundred and thirty-five miles away from the enemy could hardly be called the face of the enemy, and because Yossarian was the one who had finally knocked down the bridge at Ferrara by going around twice over the target and killing Kraft – he was always almost forgetting Kraft when he counted the dead men he knew. But they had to do something to him, and everyone waited grimly to see what horrible thing it would be.

During the day, they avoided him, even Aarfy, and Yossarian understood that they were different people together in daylight than they were alone in the dark. He did not care about them at all as he walked about backward with his hand on his gun and awaited the latest blandishments, threats and inducements from Group each time Captains Piltchard and Wren drove back from another urgent conference with Colonel Cathcart and Colonel Korn. Hungry Joe was hardly around, and the only other person who ever spoke to him was Captain Black, who called him 'Old Blood and Guts' in a merry, taunting voice each time he hailed him and who came back from Rome toward the end of the week to tell him Nately's whore was gone. Yossarian turned sorry with a stab of yearning and remorse. He missed her.

'Gone?' he echoed in a hollow tone.

'Yeah, gone.' Captain Black laughed, his bleary eyes narrow with fatigue and his peaked, sharp face sprouting as usual with a sparse reddish-blond stubble. He rubbed the bags under his eyes with both fists. 'I thought I might as well give the stupid broad another boff just for old times' sake as long as I was in Rome anyway. You know, just to keep that kid Nately's body spinning in his grave, ha, ha! Remember the way I used to needle him? But the place was empty.'

'Was there any word from her?' prodded Yossarian, who had been brooding incessantly about the girl, wondering how much she was suffering, and feeling almost lonely and deserted without her ferocious and unappeasable attacks.

'There's no one there,' Captain Black exclaimed cheerfully, trying to make Yossarian understand. 'Don't you understand? They're all gone. The whole place is busted.'

'Gone?'

'Yeah, gone. Flushed right out into the street.' Captain Black chuckled heartily again, and his pointed Adam's apple jumped up and down with glee inside his scraggly neck. 'The joint's empty. The M.P.s busted the whole apartment up and drove the whores right out. Ain't that a laugh?'

Yossarian was scared and began to tremble. 'Why'd they do that?'

'What difference does it make?' responded Captain Black with an exuberant gesture. 'They flushed them right out into the street. How do you like that? The whole batch.'

'What about the kid sister?'

'Flushed away,' laughed Captain Black. 'Flushed away with the rest of the broads. Right out into the street.'

'But she's only a kid!' Yossarian objected passionately. 'She doesn't know anybody else in the whole city. What's going to happen to her?'

'What the hell do I care?' responded Captain Black with an indifferent shrug, and then gawked suddenly at Yossarian with surprise and with a crafty gleam of prying elation. 'Say, what's the matter? If I knew this was going to make you so unhappy, I would have come right over and told you, just to make you eat your liver. Hey, where are you going? Come on back! Come on back here and eat your liver!'

39 The eternal city

Yossarian was going absent without official leave with
Milo, who, as the plane cruised toward Rome, shook his
head reproachfully and, with pious lips pursed, informed
Yossarian in ecclesiastical tones that he was ashamed
of him. Yossarian nodded. Yossarian was making an
uncouth spectacle of himself by walking around backward with his gun on his hip and refusing to fly more
combat missions, Milo said. Yossarian nodded. It was
disloyal to his squadron and embarrassing to his
superiors. He was placing Milo in a very uncomfortable
position, too. Yossarian nodded again. The men were
starting to grumble. It was not fair for Yossarian to think
only of his own safety while men like Milo, Colonel
Cathcart, Colonel Korn and ex-P.F.C. Wintergreen were
willing to do everything they could to win the war. The
men with seventy missions were starting to grumble
because they had to fly eighty, and there was a danger
some of them might put on guns and begin walking
around backward, too. Morale was deteriorating and it
was all Yossarian's fault. The country was in peril; he
was jeopardizing his traditional rights of freedom and
independence by daring to exercise them.

Yossarian kept nodding in the co-pilot's seat and tried

not to listen as Milo prattled on. Nately's whore was on his mind, as were Kraft and Orr and Nately and Dunbar, and Kid Sampson and McWatt, and all the poor and stupid and diseased people he had seen in Italy, Egypt and North Africa and knew about in other areas of the world, and Snowden and Nately's whore's kid sister were on his conscience, too. Yossarian thought he knew why Nately's whore held him responsible for Nately's death and wanted to kill him. Why the hell shouldn't she? It was a man's world, and she and everyone younger had every right to blame him and everyone older for every unnatural tragedy that befell them; just as she, even in her grief, was to blame for every man-made misery that landed on her kid sister and on all other children behind her. Someone had to do something sometime. Every victim was a culprit, every culprit a victim, and somebody had to stand up sometime to try to break the lousy chain of inherited habit that was imperiling them all. In parts of Africa little boys were still stolen away by adult slave traders and sold for money to men who disemboweled them and ate them. Yossarian marveled that children could suffer such barbaric sacrifice without evincing the slightest hint of fear or pain. He took it for granted that they did submit so stoically. If not, he reasoned, the custom would certainly have died, for no craving for wealth or immortality could be so great, he felt, as to subsist on the sorrow of children.

He was rocking the boat, Milo said, and Yossarian nodded once more. He was not a good member of the team, Milo said. Yossarian nodded and listened to Milo tell him that the decent thing to do if he did not like the way Colonel Cathcart and Colonel Korn were running the group was go to Russia, instead of stirring up trouble. Yossarian refrained from pointing out that Colonel Cathcart, Colonel Korn and Milo could all go to Russia if they did not like the way he was stirring up trouble. Colonel Cathcart and Colonel Korn had both been very good to Yossarian, Milo said; hadn't they given him a medal after the last mission to Ferrara and promoted him to captain? Yossarian nodded. Didn't they feed him and give him his pay every month? Yossarian nodded again. Milo was sure they would be charitable if he went to them to apologize and recant and promise to fly eighty missions. Yossarian said he would think it over, and held his breath and prayed for a safe landing as Milo dropped his wheels and glided in toward the runway. It was funny how he had really come to detest flying.

Rome was in ruins, he saw, when the plane was down. The airdrome had been bombed eight months before, and knobby slabs of white stone rubble had been bulldozed into flat-topped heaps on both sides of the entrance through the wire fence surrounding the field. The Colosseum was a dilapidated shell, and the Arch of Constantine had fallen. Nately's whore's apartment was a shambles. The girls were gone, and the only one there was the old woman. The windows in the apartment had been smashed. She was bundled up in sweaters and skirts and wore a dark shawl about her head. She sat on a wooden chair near an electric hot plate, her arms folded, boiling water in a battered aluminium pot. She was talking aloud to herself when Yossarian entered and began moaning as soon as she saw him.

'Gone,' she moaned before he could even inquire. Holding her elbows, she rocked back and forth mournfully on her creaking chair. 'Gone.'

'Who?'

'All. All the poor young girls.'

'Where?'

'Away. Chased away into the street. All of them gone. All the poor young girls.'

'Chased away by who? Who did it?'

'The mean tall soldiers with the hard white hats and clubs. And by our *carabinieri*. They came with their clubs and chased them away. They would not even let them take their coats. The poor things. They just chased them away into the cold.'

'Did they arrest them?'

513

'They chased them away. They just chased them away.'

'Then why did they do it if they didn't arrest them?'

'I don't know,' sobbed the old woman. 'I don't know. Who will take care of me? Who will take care of me now that all the poor young girls are gone? Who will take care of me?'

'There must have been a reason,' Yossarian persisted, pounding his fist into his hand. 'They couldn't just barge in here and chase everyone out.'

'No reason,' wailed the old woman. 'No reason.'

'What right did they have?'

'Catch-22.'

'*What?*' Yossarian froze in his tracks with fear and alarm and felt his whole body begin to tingle. '*What* did you say?'

'Catch-22' the old woman repeated, rocking her head up and down. 'Catch-22. Catch-22 says they have a right to do anything we can't stop them from doing.'

'What the hell are you talking about?' Yossarian shouted at her in bewildered, furious protest. 'How did you know it was Catch-22? Who the hell told you it was Catch-22?'

'The soldiers with the hard white hats and clubs. The girls were crying. "Did we do anything wrong?" they said. The men said no and pushed them away out the door with the ends of their clubs. "Then why are you chasing us out?" the girls said. "Catch-22," the men said. "What right do you have?" the girls said. "Catch-22," the men said. All they kept saying was "Catch-22, Catch-22." What does it mean, Catch-22? What is Catch-22?'

'Didn't they show it to you?' Yossarian demanded, stamping about in anger and distress. 'Didn't you even make them read it?'

'They don't have to show us Catch-22,' the old woman answered. 'The law says they don't have to.'

'What law says they don't have to?'

'Catch-22.'

'Oh, God damn!' Yossarian exclaimed bitterly. 'I bet it

514

wasn't even really there.' He stopped walking and glanced about the room disconsolately. 'Where's the old man?'

'Gone,' mourned the old woman.

'Gone?'

'Dead,' the old woman told him, nodding in emphatic lament, pointing to her head with the flat of her hand. 'Something broke in here. One minute he was living, one minute he was dead.'

'But he can't be dead!' Yossarian cried, ready to argue insistently. But of course he knew it was true, knew it was logical and true; once again the old man had marched along with the majority.

Yossarian turned away and trudged through the apartment with a gloomy scowl, peering with pessimistic curiosity into all the rooms. Everything made of glass had been smashed by the men with the clubs. Torn drapes and bedding lay dumped on the floor. Chairs, tables and dressers had been overturned. Everything breakable had been broken. The destruction was total. No wild vandals could have been more thorough. Every window was smashed, and darkness poured like inky clouds into each room through the shattered panes. Yossarian could imagine the heavy, crashing footfalls of the tall M.P.s in the hard white hats. He could picture the fiery and malicious exhilaration with which they had made their wreckage, and their sanctimonious, ruthless sense of right and dedication. All the poor young girls were gone. Everyone was gone but the weeping old woman in the bulky brown and gray sweaters and black head shawl, and soon she too would be gone.

'Gone,' she grieved, when he walked back in, before he could even speak. 'Who will take care of me now?'

Yossarian ignored the question. 'Nately's girl friend – did anyone hear from her?' he asked.

'Gone.'

'I know she's gone. But did anyone hear from her? Does anyone know where she is?'

'Gone.'

'The little sister. What happened to her?'

'Gone.' The old woman's tone had not changed.

'Do you know what I'm talking about?' Yossarian asked sharply, staring into her eyes to see if she were not speaking to him from a coma. He raised his voice. 'What happened to the kid sister, to the little girl?'

'Gone, gone,' the old woman replied with a crabby shrug, irritated by his persistence, her low wail growing louder. 'Chased away with the rest, chased away into the street. They would not even let her take her coat.'

'Where did she go?'

'I don't know. I don't know.'

'Who will take care of her?'

'Who will take care of me?'

'She doesn't know anybody else, does she?'

'Who will take care of me?'

Yossarian left money in the old woman's lap – it was odd how many wrongs leaving money seemed to right – and strode out of the apartment, cursing Catch-22 vehemently as he descended the stairs, even though he knew there was no such thing. Catch-22 did not exist, he was positive of that, but it made no difference. What did matter was that everyone thought it existed, and that was much worse, for there was no object or text to ridicule or refute, to accuse, criticize, attack, amend, hate, revile, spit at, rip to shreds, trample upon or burn up.

It was cold outside, and dark, and a leaky, insipid mist lay swollen in the air and trickled down the large, unpolished stone blocks of the houses and the pedestals of monuments. Yossarian hurried back to Milo and recanted. He said he was sorry and, knowing he was lying, promised to fly as many more missions as Colonel Cathcart wanted if Milo would only use all his influence in Rome to help him locate Nately's whore's kid sister.

'She's just a twelve-year-old virgin, Milo,' he explained anxiously, 'and I want to find her before it's too late.'

Milo responded to his request with a benign smile.

'I've got just the twelve-year-old virgin you're looking for,' he announced jubilantly. 'This twelve-year-old virgin is really only thirty-four, but she was brought up on a low-protein diet by very strict parents and didn't start sleeping with men until –'

'Milo, I'm talking about a little girl!' Yossarian interrupted him with desperate impatience. 'Don't you understand? I don't want to sleep with her. I want to help her. You've got daughters. She's just a little kid, and she's all alone in this city with no one to take care of her. I want to protect her from harm. Don't you know what I'm talking about?'

Milo did understand and was deeply touched. 'Yossarian, I'm proud of you,' he exclaimed with profound emotion . 'I really am. You don't know how glad I am to see that everything isn't always just sex with you. You've got principles. Certainly I've got daughters, and I know exactly what you're talking about. We'll find that girl. Don't you worry. You come with me and we'll find that girl if we have to turn this whole city upside down. Come along.'

Yossarian went along in Milo Minderbinder's speeding M & M staff car to police headquarters to meet a swarthy, untidy police commissioner with a narrow black mustache and unbuttoned tunic who was fiddling with a stout woman with warts and two chins when they entered his office and who greeted Milo with warm surprise and bowed and scraped in obscene servility as though Milo were some elegant marquis.

'Ah, Marchese Milo,' he declared with effusive pleasure, pushing the fat, disgruntled woman out the door without even looking toward her. 'Why didn't you tell me you were coming? I would have a big party for you. Come in, come in, Marchese. You almost never visit us any more.'

Milo knew that there was not one moment to waste. 'Hello, Luigi,' he said, nodding so briskly that he almost seemed rude. 'Luigi, I need your help. My friend here wants to find a girl.'

517

'A girl, Marchese?' said Luigi, scratching his face pensively. 'There are lots of girls in Rome. For an American officer, a girl should not be too difficult.'

'No, Luigi, you don't understand. This is a twelve-year-old virgin that he has to find right away.'

'Ah, yes, now I understand,' Luigi said sagaciously. 'A virgin might take a little time. But if he waits at the bus terminal where the young farm girls looking for work arrive, I –'

'Luigi, you still don't understand,' Milo snapped with such brusque impatience that the police commissioner's face flushed and he jumped to attention and began buttoning his uniform in confusion. 'This girl is a friend, an old friend of the family, and we want to help her. She's only a child. She's all alone in this city somewhere, and we have to find her before somebody harms her. Now do you understand? Luigi, this is very important to me. I have a daughter the same age as that little girl, and nothing in the world means more to me right now than saving that poor child before it's too late. Will you help?'

'*Si*, Marchese, now I understand,' said Luigi. 'And I will do everything in my power to find her. But tonight I have almost no men. Tonight all my men are busy trying to break up the traffic in illegal tobacco.'

'Illegal tobacco?' asked Milo.

'Milo,' Yossarian bleated faintly with a sinking heart, sensing at once that all was lost.

'*Si*, Marchese,' said Luigi. 'The profit in illegal tobacco is so high that the smuggling is almost impossible to control.'

'Is there really that much profit in illegal tobacco?' Milo inquired with keen interest, his rust-colored eyebrows arching avidly and his nostrils sniffing.

'Milo,' Yossarian called to him. 'Pay attention to *me*, will you?'

'*Si*, Marchese,' Luigi answered. 'The profit in illegal tobacco is very high. The smuggling is a national scandal, Marchese, truly a national disgrace.'

'Is that a fact?' Milo observed with a preoccupied

smile and started toward the door as though in a spell.

'Milo!' Yossarian yelled, and bounded forward impulsively to intercept him. 'Milo, you've got to help me.'

'Illegal tobacco,' Milo explained to him with a look of epileptic lust, struggling doggedly to get by. 'Let me go. I've got to smuggle illegal tobacco.'

'Stay here and help me find her,' pleaded Yossarian. 'You can smuggle illegal tobacco tomorrow.'

But Milo was deaf and kept pushing forward, non-violently but irresistibly, sweating, his eyes, as though he were in the grip of a blind fixation, burning feverishly, and his twitching mouth slavering. He moaned calmly as though in remote, instinctive distress and kept repeating, 'Illegal tobacco, illegal tobacco.' Yossarian stepped out of the way with resignation finally when he saw it was hopeless to try to reason with him. Milo was gone like a shot. The commissioner of police unbuttoned his tunic again and looked at Yossarian with contempt.

'What do you want here?' he asked coldly. 'Do you want me to arrest you?'

Yossarian walked out of the office and down the stairs into the dark, tomblike street, passing in the hall the stout woman with warts and two chins, who was already on her way back in. There was no sign of Milo outside. There were no lights in any of the windows. The deserted sidewalk rose steeply and continuously for several blocks. He could see the glare of a broad avenue at the top of the long cobblestone incline. The police station was almost at the bottom; the yellow bulbs at the entrance sizzled in the dampness like wet torches. A frigid, fine rain was falling. He began walking slowly, pushing uphill. Soon he came to a quiet, cozy, inviting restaurant with red velvet drapes in the windows and a blue neon sign near the door that said: TONY'S RESTAURANT. FINE FOOD AND DRINK. KEEP OUT. The words on the blue neon sign surprised him mildly for only an instant. Nothing warped seemed bizarre any more in his strange, distorted surroundings. The tops of the sheer buildings slanted in weird, surrealistic perspective, and the street seemed tilted. He raised the collar of his warm woolen coat and hugged it around him. The night was raw. A boy in a thin shirt and thin tattered trousers walked out of the darkness on bare feet. The boy had black hair and needed a haircut and shoes and socks. His sickly face was pale and sad. His feet made grisly, soft, sucking sounds in the rain puddles on the wet pavement as he passed, and Yossarian was moved by such intense pity for his poverty that he wanted to smash his pale, sad, sickly face with his fist and knock him out of existence because he brought to mind *all* the pale, sad, sickly children in Italy that same night who needed haircuts and needed shoes and socks. He made Yossarian think of cripples and of cold and hungry men and women, and of all the dumb, passive, devout mothers with catatonic eyes nursing infants outdoors that same night with chilled animal udders bared insensibly to that same raw rain. Cows. Almost on cue, a nursing mother padded past holding an infant in black rags, and Yossarian wanted to smash her too, because she reminded him of the barefoot boy in the thin shirt and thin, tattered trousers and of all the shivering, stupefying misery in a world that never yet had provided enough heat and food and justice for all but an ingenious and unscrupulous handful. What a lousy earth! He wondered how many people were destitute that same night even in his own prosperous country, how many homes were shanties, how many husbands were drunk and wives socked, and how many children were bullied, abused or abandoned. How many families hungered for food they could not afford to buy? How many hearts were broken? How many suicides would take place that same night, how many people would go insane? How many cockroaches and landlords would triumph? How many winners were losers, successes failures, rich men poor men? How many wise guys were stupid? How many happy endings were unhappy endings? How many honest men were liars, brave men cowards, loyal men traitors, how many sainted men were corrupt, how many people in positions of trust had sold their souls to blackguards for petty cash, how many had never had souls? How many straight-and-narrow paths were crooked paths? How many best families were worst families and how many good people were bad people? When you added them all up and then subtracted, you might be left with only the children, and perhaps with Albert Einstein and an old violinist or sculptor somewhere. Yossarian walked in lonely torture, feeling estranged, and could not wipe from his mind the excruciating image of the barefoot boy with sickly cheeks until he turned the corner into the avenue finally and came upon an Allied soldier having convulsions on the ground, a young lieutenant with a small, pale, boyish face. Six other soldiers from different countries wrestled with different parts of him, striving to help him and hold him still. He yelped and groaned unintelligibly through clenched teeth, his eyes rolled up into his head. 'Don't let him bite his tongue off,' a short sergeant near Yossarian advised shrewdly, and a seventh man threw himself into the fray to wrestle with the ill lieutenant's face. All at once the wrestlers won and turned to each other undecidedly, for now that they held the young lieutenant rigid they did not know what to do with him. A quiver of moronic panic spread from one straining brute face to another. 'Why don't you lift him up and put him on the hood of that car?' a corporal standing in back of Yossarian drawled. That seemed to make sense, so the seven men lifted the young lieutenant up and stretched him out carefully on the hood of a parked car, still pinning each struggling part of him down. Once they had him stretched out on the hood of the parked car, they stared at each other uneasily again, for they had no idea what to do with him next. 'Why don't you lift him up off the hood of that car and lay him down on the ground?' drawled the same corporal behind Yossarian. That seemed like a good idea, too, and they began to move him back to the sidewalk, but before they could finish, a jeep raced up with a flashing red spotlight at the side and two military policemen in the front seat.

'What's going on?' the driver yelled.

'He's having convulsions,' one of the men grappling with one of the young lieutenant's limbs answered. 'We're holding him still.'

'That's good. He's under arrest.'

'What should we do with him?'

'Keep him under arrest!' the M.P. shouted, doubling over with raucous laughter at his jest, and sped away in his jeep.

Yossarian recalled that he had no leave papers and moved prudently past the strange group toward the sound of muffled voices emanating from a distance inside the murky darkness ahead. The broad, rain-blotched boulevard was illuminated every half-block by short, curling lamp posts with eerie, shimmering glares surrounded by smoky brown mist. From a window overhead he heard an unhappy female voice pleading, 'Please don't. Please don't.' A despondent young woman in a black raincoat with much black hair on her face passed with her eyes lowered. At the Ministry of Public Affairs on the next block, a drunken lady was backed up against one of the fluted Corinthian columns by a drunken young soldier, while three drunken comrades in arms sat watching nearby on the steps with wine bottles standing between their legs. 'Pleeshe don't,' begged the drunken lady. 'I want to go home now. Pleeshe don't.' One of the sitting men cursed pugnaciously and hurled a wine bottle at Yossarian when he turned to look up. The bottle shattered harmlessly far away with a brief and muted noise. Yossarian continued walking away at the same listless, unhurried pace, hands buried in his pockets. 'Come on, baby,' he heard the drunken soldier urge determinedly. 'It's my turn now.' 'Pleeshe don't,' begged the drunken lady. 'Pleeshe don't.' At the very next corner, deep inside the dense, impenetrable shadows of a narrow, winding side street, he heard the mysterious, unmistakable sound of someone shoveling snow. The measured, labored, evocative scrape of iron shovel against concrete made his flesh crawl with terror as he stepped from the curb to cross the ominous alley and hurried onward until the haunting, incongruous noise had been left behind. Now he knew where he was: soon, if he continued without turning, he would come to the dry fountain in the middle of the boulevard, then to the officers' apartment seven blocks beyond. He heard snarling, inhuman voices cutting through the ghostly blackness in front suddenly. The bulb on the corner lamppost had died, spilling gloom over half the street, throwing everything visible off balance. On the other side of the intersection, a man was beating a dog with a stick like the man who was beating the horse with a whip in Raskolnikov's dream. Yossarian strained helplessly not to see or hear. The dog whimpered and squealed in brute, dumfounded hysteria at the end of an old Manila rope and groveled and crawled on its belly without resisting, but the man beat it and beat it anyway with his heavy, flat stick. A small crowd watched. A squat woman stepped out and asked him please to stop. 'Mind your own business,' the man barked gruffly, lifting his stick as though he might beat her too, and the woman retreated sheepishly with an abject and humiliated air. Yossarian quickened his pace to get away, almost ran. The night was filled with horrors, and he thought he knew how Christ must have felt as he walked through the world, like a psychiatrist through a ward full of nuts, like a victim through a prison full of thieves. What a welcome sight a leper must have been! At the next corner a man was beating a small boy brutally in the midst of an immobile crowd of adult spectators who made no effort to intervene. Yossarian recoiled with sickening recognition. He was certain he had witnessed that same horrible scene sometime before. *Déjà vu?* The sinister coincidence shook him and filled him with doubt and dread. It was the same scene he had witnessed a block before, although everything in it seemed quite different. What in the world was happening? Would a squat

woman step out and ask the man to please stop? Would
he raise his hand to strike her and would she retreat?
Nobody moved. The child cried steadily as though in
drugged misery. The man kept knocking him down with
hard, resounding open-palm blows to the head, then
jerking him up to his feet in order to knock him down
again. No one in the sullen, cowering crowd seemed to
care enough about the stunned and beaten boy to interfere. The child was no more than nine. One drab woman
was weeping silently into a dirty dish towel. The boy was
emaciated and needed a haircut. Bright-red blood was
streaming from both ears. Yossarian crossed quickly to
the other side of the immense avenue to escape the
nauseating sight and found himself walking on human
teeth lying on the drenched, glistening pavement near
splotches of blood kept sticky by the pelting raindrops
poking each one like sharp fingernails. Molars and broken incisors lay scattered everywhere. He circled on
tiptoe the grotesque debris and came near a doorway
containing a crying soldier holding a saturated handkerchief to his mouth, supported as he sagged by two other
soldiers waiting in grave impatience for the military
ambulance that finally came clanging up with amber fog
lights on and passed them by for an altercation on the
next block between a civilian Italian with books and a
slew of civilian policemen with armlocks and clubs. The
screaming, struggling civilian was a dark man with a
face white as flour from fear. His eyes were pulsating in
hectic desperation, flapping like bat's wings, as the
many tall policemen seized him by the arms and legs and
lifted him up. His books were spilled on the ground.
'Help!' he shrieked shrilly in a voice strangling in its own
emotion, as the policemen carried him to the open doors
in the rear of the ambulance and threw him inside.
'Police! Help! Police!' The doors were shut and bolted,
and the ambulance raced away. There was a humorless
irony in the ludicrous panic of the man screaming for
help to the police while policemen were all around him.
Yossarian smiled wryly at the futile and ridiculous cry

for aid, then saw with a start that the words were ambiguous, realized with alarm that they were not, perhaps, intended as a call for police but as a heroic warning from the grave by a doomed friend to everyone who was not a policeman with a club and a gun and a mob of other policemen with clubs and guns to back him up. 'Help! Police!' the man had cried, and he could have been shouting of danger. Yossarian responded to the thought by slipping away stealthily from the police and almost tripped over the feet of a burly woman of forty hastening across the intersection guiltily, darting furtive, vindictive glances behind her toward a woman of eighty with thick, bandaged ankles doddering after her in a losing pursuit. The old woman was gasping for breath as she minced along and muttering to herself in distracted agitation. There was no mistaking the nature of the scene; it was a chase. The triumphant first woman was halfway across the wide avenue before the second woman reached the curb. The nasty, small, gloating smile with which she glanced back at the laboring old woman was both wicked and apprehensive. Yossarian knew he could help the troubled old woman if she would only cry out, knew he could spring forward and capture the sturdy first woman and hold her for the mob of policemen nearby if the second woman would only give him license with a shriek of distress. But the old woman passed by without even seeing him, mumbling in terrible, tragic vexation, and soon the first woman had vanished into the deepening layers of darkness and the old woman was left standing helplessly in the centre of the thoroughfare, dazed, uncertain which way to proceed, alone. Yossarian tore his eyes from her and hurried away in shame because he had done nothing to assist her. He darted furtive, guilty glances back as he fled in defeat, afraid the old woman might now start following him, and he welcomed the concealing shelter of the drizzling, drifting, lightless, nearly opaque gloom. Mobs ... mobs of policemen – everything but England was in the hands of mobs, mobs, mobs. Mobs with clubs were in control everywhere.

The surface of the collar and shoulders of Yossarian's coat was soaked. His socks were wet and cold. The light on the next lamp post was out, too, the glass globe broken. Buildings and featureless shapes flowed by him noiselessly as though borne past immutably on the surface of some rank and timeless tide. A tall monk passed, his face buried entirely inside a coarse gray cowl, even the eyes hidden. Footsteps sloshed toward him steadily through a puddle, and he feared it would be another barefoot child. He brushed by a gaunt, cadaverous, tristful man in a black raincoat with a star-shaped scar in his cheek and a glossy mutilated depression the size of an egg in one temple. On squishing straw sandals, a young woman materialized with her whole face disfigured by a God-awful pink and piebald burn that started on her neck and stretched in a raw, corrugated mass up both cheeks past her eyes! Yossarian could not bear to look, and shuddered. No one would ever love her. His spirit was sick; he longed to lie down with some girl he could love who would soothe and excite him and put him to sleep. A mob with a club was waiting for him in Pianosa. The girls were all gone. The countess and her daughter-in-law were no longer good enough; he had grown too old for fun, he no longer had the time. Luciana was gone, dead, probably; if not yet, then soon enough. Aarfy's buxom trollop had vanished with her smutty cameo ring, and Nurse Duckett was ashamed of him because he had refused to fly more combat missions and would cause a scandal. The only girl he knew nearby was the plain maid in the officers' apartment, whom none of the men had ever slept with. Her name was Michaela, but the men called her filthy things in dulcet, ingratiating voices, and she giggled with childish joy because she understood no English and thought they were flattering her and making harmless jokes. Everything wild she watched them do filled her with enchanted delight. She was a happy, simple-minded, hard-working girl who could not read and was barely able to write her name. Her straight hair was the color of rotting straw.

She had sallow skin and myopic eyes, and none of the men had ever slept with her because none of the men had ever wanted to, none but Aarfy, who had raped her once that same evening and had then held her prisoner in a clothes closet for almost two hours with his hand over her mouth until the civilian curfew sirens sounded and it was unlawful for her to be outside.

Then he threw her out the window. Her dead body was still lying on the pavement when Yossarian arrived and pushed his way politely through the circle of solemn neighbors with dim lanterns, who glared with venom as they shrank away from him and pointed up bitterly toward the second-floor windows in their private, grim, accusing conversations. Yossarian's heart pounded with fright and horror at the pitiful, ominous, gory spectacle of the broken corpse. He ducked into the hallway and bolted up the stairs into the apartment, where he found Aarfy pacing about uneasily with a pompous, slightly uncomfortable smile. Aarfy seemed a bit unsettled as he fidgeted with his pipe and assured Yossarian that everything was going to be all right. There was nothing to worry about.

'I only raped her once,' he explained.

Yossarian was aghast. 'But you killed her, Aarfy! You killed her!'

'Oh, I had to do that after I raped her,' Aarfy replied in his most condescending manner. 'I couldn't very well let her go around saying bad things about us, could I?'

'But why did you have to touch her at all, you dumb bastard?' Yossarian shouted. 'Why couldn't you get yourself a girl off the street if you wanted one? The city is full of prostitutes.'

'Oh, no, not me,' Aarfy bragged. 'I never paid for it in my life.'

'Aarfy, are you insane?' Yossarian was almost speechless. 'You *killed* a girl. They're going to put you in jail!'

'Oh, no,' Aarfy answered with a forced smile. 'Not me. They aren't going to put good old Aarfy in jail. Not for killing *her*.'

'But you threw her out the window. She's lying dead in the street.'

'She has no right to be there,' Aarfy answered. 'It's after curfew.'

'Stupid! Don't you realize what you've done?' Yossarian wanted to grab Aarfy by his well-fed, caterpillar-soft shoulders and shake some sense into him. 'You've murdered a human being. They *are* going to put you in jail. They might even *hang* you!'

'Oh, I hardly think they'll do that,' Aarfy replied with a jovial chuckle, although his symptoms of nervousness increased. He spilled tobacco crumbs unconsciously as his short fingers fumbled with the bowl of his pipe. 'No, sirree. Not to good old Aarfy.' He chortled again. 'She was only a servant girl. I hardly think they're going to make too much of a fuss over one poor Italian servant girl when so many thousands of lives are being lost every day. Do you?'

'Listen!' Yossarian cried, almost in joy. He pricked up his ears and watched the blood drain from Aarfy's face as sirens mourned far away, police sirens, and then ascended almost instantaneously to a howling, strident, onrushing cacophony of overwhelming sound that seemed to crash into the room around them from every side. 'Aarfy, they're coming for you,' he said in a flood of compassion, shouting to be heard above the noise. 'They're coming to arrest you. Aarfy, don't you understand? You can't take the life of another human being and get away with it, even if she is just a poor servant girl. Don't you see? Can't you understand?'

'Oh, no,' Aarfy insisted with a lame laugh and a weak smile. 'They're not coming to arrest me. Not good old Aarfy.'

All at once he looked sick. He sank down on a chair in a trembling stupor, his stumpy, lax hands quaking in his lap. Cars skidded to a stop ouside. Spotlights hit the windows immediately. Car doors slammed and police whistles screeched. Voices rose harshly. Aarfy was green. He kept shaking his head mechanically with a queer, numb smile and repeating in a weak, hollow monotone that they were not coming for him, not for good old Aarfy, no sirree, striving to convince himself that this was so even as heavy footsteps raced up the stairs and pounded across the landing, even as fists beat on the door four times with a deafening, inexorable force. Then the door to the apartment flew open, and two large, tough, brawny M.P.s with icy eyes and firm, sinewy, unsmiling jaws entered quickly, strode across the room, and arrested Yossarian.

They arrested Yossarian for being in Rome without a pass.

They apologized to Aarfy for intruding and led Yossarian away between them, gripping him under each arm with fingers as hard as steel manacles. They said nothing at all to him on the way down. Two more tall M.P.s with clubs and hard white helmets were waiting outside at a closed car. They marched Yossarian into the back seat, and the car roared away and weaved through the rain and muddy fog to a police station. The M.P.s locked him up for the night in a cell with four stone walls. At dawn they gave him a pail for a latrine and drove him to the airport, where two more giant M.P.s with clubs and white helmets were waiting at a transport plane whose engines were already warming up when they arrived, the cylindrical green cowlings oozing quivering beads of condensation. None of the M.P.s said anything to each other either. They did not even nod. Yossarian had never seen such granite faces. The plane flew to Pianosa. Two more silent M.P.s were waiting at the landing strip. There were now eight, and they filed with precise, wordless discipline into two cars and sped on humming tires past the four squadron areas to the Group Headquarters building, where still two more M.P.s were waiting at the parking area. All ten tall, strong, purposeful, silent men towered around him as they turned toward the entrance. Their footsteps crunched in loud unison on the cindered ground. He had an impression of accelerating haste. He was terrified.

Everyone of the ten M.P.s seemed powerful enough to bash him to death with a single blow. They had only to press their massive, toughened, boulderous shoulders against him to crush all life from his body. There was nothing he could do to save himself. He could not even see which two were gripping him under the arms as they marched him rapidly between the two tight single-file columns they had formed. Their pace quickened, and he felt as though he were flying along with his feet off the ground as they trotted in resolute cadence up the wide marble staircase to the upper landing, where still two more inscrutable military policemen with hard faces were waiting to lead them all at an even faster pace down the long, cantilevered balcony overhanging the immense lobby. Their marching footsteps on the dull tile floor thundered like an awesome, quickening drum roll through the vacant center of the building as they moved with even greater speed and precision toward Colonel Cathcart's office, and violent winds of panic began blowing in Yossarian's ears when they turned him toward his doom inside the office, where Colonel Korn, his rump spreading comfortably on a corner of Colonel Cathcart's desk, sat waiting to greet him with a genial smile and said,

'We're sending you home.'

40   Catch-22

There was, of course, a catch.

'Catch-22?' inquired Yossarian.

'Of course,' Colonel Korn answered pleasantly, after he had chased the mighty guard of massive M.P.s out with an insouciant flick of his hand and a slightly contemptuous nod – most relaxed, as always, when he could be most cynical. His rimless square eyeglasses glinted with sly amusement as he gazed at Yossarian. 'After all, we can't simply send you home for refusing to fly more missions and keep the rest of the men here, can we? That would hardly be fair to them.'

'You're goddam right!' Colonel Cathcart blurted out, lumbering back and forth gracelessly like a winded bull, puffing and pouting angrily. 'I'd like to tie him up hand and foot and throw him aboard a plane on every mission. That's what I'd like to do.'

Colonel Korn motioned Colonel Cathcart to be silent and smiled at Yossarian. 'You know, you really have been making things terribly difficult for Colonel Cathcart,' he observed with flip good humor, as though the fact did not displease him at all. 'The men are unhappy and morale is beginning to deteriorate. And it's all your fault.'

'It's your fault,' Yossarian argued, 'for raising the number of missions.'

'No, it's your fault for refusing to fly them,' Colonel Korn retorted. 'The men were perfectly content to fly as many missions as we asked as long as they thought they had no alternative. Now you've given them hope, and they're unhappy. So the blame is all yours.'

'Doesn't he know there's a war going on?' Colonel Cathcart, still stamping back and forth, demanded morosely without looking at Yossarian.

'I'm quite sure he does,' Colonel Korn answered. 'That's probably why he refuses to fly them.'

'Doesn't it make any difference to him?'

'Will the knowledge that there's a war going on weaken your decision to refuse to participate in it?' Colonel Korn inquired with sarcastic seriousness, mocking Colonel Cathcart.

'No, sir,' Yossarian replied, almost returning Colonel Korn's smile.

'I was afraid of that,' Colonel Korn remarked with an elaborate sigh, locking his fingers together comfortably on top of his smooth, bald, broad, shiny brown head. 'You know, in all fairness, we really haven't treated you too badly, have we? We've fed you and paid you on time. We gave you a medal and even made you a captain.'

'I never should have made him a captain,' Colonel Cathcart exclaimed bitterly. 'I should have given him a court-martial after he loused up that Ferrara mission and went around twice.'

'I told you not to promote him,' said Colonel Korn, 'but you wouldn't listen to me.'

'No you didn't. You told me to promote him, didn't you?'

'I told you *not* to promote him. But you just wouldn't listen.'

'I should have listened.'

'You never listen to me,' Colonel Korn persisted with relish. 'That's the reason we're in this spot.'

'All right, gee whiz. Stop rubbing it in, will you?'

Colonel Cathcart burrowed his fists down deep inside his pockets and turned away in a slouch. 'Instead of picking on me, why don't you figure out what we're going to do about him?'

'We're going to send him home, I'm afraid.' Colonel Korn was chuckling triumphantly when he turned away from Colonel Cathcart to face Yossarian. 'Yossarian, the war is over for you. We're going to send you home. You really don't deserve it, you know, which is one of the reasons I don't mind doing it. Since there's nothing else we can risk doing to you at this time, we've decided to return you to the States. We've worked out this little deal to –'

'What kind of deal?' Yossarian demanded with defiant mistrust.

Colonel Korn tossed his head back and laughed. 'Oh, a thoroughly despicable deal, make no mistake about that. It's absolutely revolting. But you'll accept it quickly enough.'

'Don't be too sure.'

'I haven't the slightest doubt you will, even though it stinks to high heaven. Oh, by the way. You haven't told any of the men you've refused to fly more missions, have you?'

'No, sir,' Yossarian answered promptly.

Colonel Korn nodded approvingly. 'That's good. I like the way you lie. You'll go far in this world if you ever acquire some decent ambition.'

'Doesn't he know there's a war going on?' Colonel Cathcart yelled out suddenly, and blew with vigorous disbelief into the open end of his cigarette holder.

'I'm quite sure he does,' Colonel Korn replied acidly, 'since you brought that identical point to his attention just a moment ago.' Colonel Korn frowned wearily for Yossarian's benefit, his eyes twinkling swarthily with sly and daring scorn. Gripping the edge of Colonel Cathcart's desk with both hands, he lifted his flaccid haunches far back on the corner to sit with both short legs dangling freely. His shoes kicked lightly against the yellow oak wood, his sludge-brown socks, garterless, collapsed in sagging circles below ankles that were surprisingly small and white. 'You know, Yossarian,' he mused affably in a manner of casual reflection that seemed both derisive and sincere, 'I really do admire you a bit. You're an intelligent person of great moral character who has taken a very courageous stand. I'm an intelligent person with no moral character at all, so I'm in an ideal position to appreciate it.'

'These are very critical times,' Colonel Cathcart asserted petulantly from a far corner of the office, paying no attention to Colonel Korn.

'Very critical times indeed,' Colonel Korn agreed with a placid nod. 'We've just had a change of command above, and we can't afford a situation that might put us in a bad light with either General Scheisskopf or General Peckem. Isn't that what you mean, Colonel?'

'Hasn't he got any patriotism?'

'Won't you fight for your country?' Colonel Korn demanded, emulating Colonel Cathcart's harsh, self-righteous tone. 'Won't you give up your life for Colonel Cathcart and me?'

Yossarian tensed with alert astonishment when he heard Colonel Korn's concluding words. 'What's that?' he exclaimed. 'What have you and Colonel Cathcart got to do with my country? You're not the same.'

'How can you separate us?' Colonel Korn inquired with ironical tranquillity.

'That's right,' Colonel Cathcart cried emphatically. 'You're either for us or against us. There's no two ways about it.'

'I'm afraid he's got you,' added Colonel Korn. 'You're either for us or against your country. It's as simple as that.'

'Oh, no, Colonel. I don't buy that.'

Colonel Korn was unruffled. 'Neither do I, frankly, but everyone else will. So there you are.'

'You're a disgrace to your uniform!' Colonel Cathcart declared with blustering wrath, whirling to confront

Yossarian for the first time. 'I'd like to know how you ever got to be a captain, anyway.'

'You promoted him,' Colonel Korn reminded sweetly, stifling a snicker. 'Don't you remember?'

'Well, I never should have done it.'

'I told you not to do it,' Colonel Korn said. 'But you just wouldn't listen to me.'

'Gee whiz, will you stop rubbing it in?' Colonel Cathcart cried. He furrowed his brow and glowered at Colonel Korn through eyes narrow with suspicion, his fists clenched on his hips. 'Say, whose side are you on, anyway?'

'Your side, Colonel. What other side could I be on?'

'Then stop picking on me, will you? Get off my back, will you?'

'I'm on your side, Colonel. I'm just loaded with patriotism.'

'Well, just make sure you don't forget that.' Colonel Cathcart turned away grudgingly after another moment, incompletely reassured, and began striding the floor, his hands kneading his long cigarette holder. He jerked a thumb toward Yossarian. 'Let's settle with him. I know what I'd like to do with him. I'd like to take him outside and shoot him. That's what I'd like to do with him. That's what General Dreedle would do with him.'

'But General Dreedle isn't with us any more,' said Colonel Korn, 'so we can't take him outside and shoot him.' Now that his moment of tension with Colonel Cathcart had passed, Colonel Korn relaxed again and resumed kicking softly against Colonel Cathcart's desk. He returned to Yossarian. 'So we're going to send you home instead. It took a bit of thinking, but we finally worked out this horrible little plan for sending you home without causing too much dissatisfaction among the friends you'll leave behind. Doesn't that make you happy?'

'What kind of plan? I'm not sure I'm going to like it.'

'I know you're not going to like it.' Colonel Korn laughed, locking his hands contentedly on top of his head again. 'You're going to loathe it. It really is odious and certainly will offend your conscience. But you'll agree to it quickly enough. You'll agree to it because it will send you home safe and sound in two weeks, and because you have no choice. It's that or a court-martial. Take it or leave it.'

Yossarian snorted. 'Stop bluffing, Colonel. You can't court-martial me for desertion in the face of the enemy. It would make you look bad and you probably couldn't get a conviction.'

'But we can court-martial you now for desertion from duty, since you went to Rome without a pass. And we could make it stick. If you think about it a minute, you'll see that you'd leave us no alternative. We can't simply let you keep walking around in open insubordination without punishing you. All the other men would stop flying missions, too. No, you have my word for it. We will court-martial you if you turn our deal down, even though it would raise a lot of questions and be a terrible black eye for Colonel Cathcart.'

Colonel Cathcart winced at the words 'black eye' and, without any apparent premeditation, hurled his slender onyx-and-ivory cigarette holder down viciously on the wooden surface on his desk. 'Jesus Christ!' he shouted unexpectedly. 'I hate this goddam cigarette holder!' The cigarette holder bounced off the desk to the wall, ricocheted across the window sill to the floor and came to a stop almost where he was standing. Colonel Cathcart stared down at it with an irascible scowl. 'I wonder if it's really doing me any good.'

'It's a feather in your cap with General Peckem, but a black eye for you with General Scheisskopf,' Colonel Korn informed him with a mischievous look of innocence.

'Well, which one am I supposed to please?'

'Both.'

'How can I please them both? They hate each other. How am I ever going to get a feather in my cap from General Scheisskopf without getting a black eye from General Peckem?'

'March.'

'Yeah, march. That's the only way to please him. March. March.' Colonel Cathcart grimaced sullenly. 'Some generals! They're a disgrace to their uniforms. If people like those two can make general, I don't see how I can miss.'

'You're going to go far.' Colonel Korn assured him with a flat lack of conviction, and turned back chuckling to Yossarian, his disdainful merriment increasing at the sight of Yossarian's unyielding expression of antagonism and distrust. 'And there you have the crux of the situation. Colonel Cathcart wants to be a general and I want to be a colonel, and that's why we have to send you home.'

'Why does he want to be a general?'

'Why? For the same reason that I want to be a colonel. What else have we got to do? Everyone teaches us to aspire to higher things. A general is higher than a colonel, and a colonel is higher than a lieutenant colonel. So we're both aspiring. And you know, Yossarian, it's a lucky thing for you that we are. Your timing on this is absolutely perfect, but I suppose you took that factor into account in your calculations.'

'I haven't been doing any calculating,' Yossarian retorted.

'Yes, I really do enjoy the way you lie,' Colonel Korn answered. 'Won't it make you proud to have your commanding officer promoted to general – to know you served in an outfit that averaged more combat missions per person than any other? Don't you want to earn more unit citations and more oak leaf clusters for your Air Medal? Where's your 'sprit de corps? Don't you want to contribute further to this great record by flying more combat missions? It's your last chance to answer yes.'

'No.'

'In that case, you have us over a barrel –' said Colonel Korn without rancor.

'He ought to be ashamed of himself!'

'– and we have to send you home. Just do a few little things for us, and –'

'What sort of things?' Yossarian interrupted with belligerent misgiving.

'Oh, tiny, insignificant things. Really, this is a very generous deal we're making with you. We will issue orders returning you to the States – really, we will – and all you have to do in return is . . . '

'What? What must I do?'

Colonel Korn laughed curtly. 'Like us.'

Yossarian blinked. 'Like you?'

'Like us.'

'Like you?'

'That's right,' said Colonel Korn, nodding, gratified immeasurably by Yossarian's guileless surprise and bewilderment. 'Like us. Join us. Be our pal. Say nice things about us here and back in the States. Become one of the boys. Now, that isn't asking too much, is it?'

'You just want me to like you? Is that all?'

'That's all.'

'That's all?'

'Just find it in your heart to like us.'

Yossarian wanted to laugh confidently when he saw with amazement that Colonel Korn was telling the truth. 'That isn't going to be too easy,' he sneered.

'Oh, it will be a lot easier than you think,' Colonel Korn taunted in return, undismayed by Yossarian's barb. 'You'll be surprised at how easy you'll find it to like us once you begin.' Colonel Korn hitched up the waist of his loose, voluminous trousers. The deep black grooves isolating his square chin from his jowls were bent again in a kind of jeering and reprehensible mirth. 'You see, Yossarian, we're going to put you on easy street. We're going to promote you to major and even give you another medal. Captain Flume is already working on glowing press releases describing your valor over Ferrara, your deep and abiding loyalty to your outfit and your consummate dedication to duty. Those phrases are all actual quotations, by the way. We're going to glorify you and send you home a hero, recalled by the Pentagon for morale and public-relations purposes. You'll live like a millionaire. Everyone will lionize you. You'll have parades in your honor and make speeches to raise money for war bonds. A whole new world of luxury awaits you once you become our pal. Isn't it lovely?'

Yossarian found himself listening intently to the fascinating elucidation of details. 'I'm not sure I want to make speeches.'

'Then we'll forget the speeches. The important thing is what you say to people here.' Colonel Korn leaned forward earnestly, no longer smiling. 'We don't want any of the men in the group to know that we're sending you home as a result of your refusal to fly more missions. And we don't want General Peckem or General Scheisskopf to get wind of any friction between us, either. That's why we're going to become such good pals.'

'What will I say to the men who asked me why I refused to fly more missions?'

'Tell them you had been informed in confidence that you were being returned to the States and that you were unwilling to risk your life for another mission or two. Just a minor disagreement between pals, that's all.'

'Will they believe it?'

'Of course they'll believe it, once they see what great freinds we've become and when they see the press releases and read the flattering things you have to say about me and Colonel Cathcart. Don't worry about the men. They'll be easy enough to discipline and control when you've gone. It's only while you're still here that they may prove troublesome. You know, one good apple can spoil the rest,' Colonel Korn concluded with conscious irony. 'You know – this would really be wonderful – you might even serve as an inspiration to them to fly more missions.'

'Suppose I denounce you when I get back to the States?'

'After you've accepted our medal and promotion and all the fanfare? No one would believe you, the Army wouldn't let you, and why in the world should you want to? You're going to be one of the boys, remember? You'll enjoy a rich, rewarding, luxurious, privileged existence. You'd have to be a fool to throw it all away just for a moral principle, and you're not a fool. Is it a deal?'

'I don't know.'

'It's that or a court-martial.'

'That's a pretty scummy trick I'd be playing on the men in the squadron, isn't it?'

'Odious,' Colonel Korn agreed amiably, and waited, watching Yossarian patiently with a glimmer of private delight.

'But what the hell!' Yossarian exclaimed. 'If they don't want to fly more missions, let them stand up and do something about it the way I did. Right?'

'Of course,' said Colonel Korn.

'There's no reason I have to risk my life for them, is there?'

'Of course not.'

Yossarian arrived at his decision with a swift grin. 'It's a deal!' he announced jubilantly.

'Great,' said Colonel Korn with somewhat less cordiality than Yossarian had expected, and he slid himself off Colonel Cathcart's desk to stand on the floor. He tugged the folds of cloth of his pants and undershorts free from his crotch and gave Yossarian a limp hand to shake. 'Welcome aboard.'

'Thanks, Colonel. I –'

'Call me Blackie, John. We're pals now.'

'Sure, Blackie. My friends call me Yo-Yo. Blackie, I –'

'His friends call him Yo-Yo,' Colonel Korn sang out to Colonel Cathcart. 'Why don't you congratulate Yo-Yo on what a sensible move he's making?'

'That's a real sensible move you're making, Yo-Yo,' Colonel Cathcart said, pumping Yossarian's hand with clumsy zeal.

'Thank you, Colonel, I –'

'Call him Chuck,' said Colonel Korn.

'Sure, call me Chuck,' said Colonel Cathcart with a laugh that was hearty and awkward. 'We're all pals now.'

'Sure, Chuck.'

'Exit smiling,' said Colonel Korn, his hands on both their shoulders as the three of them moved to the door.

'Come on over for dinner with us some night, Yo-Yo,' Colonel Cathcart invited hospitably. 'How about tonight? In the group dining room.'

'I'd love to, sir.'

'Chuck,' Colonel Korn corrected reprovingly.

'I'm sorry, Blackie. Chuck. I can't get used to it.'

'That's all right, pal.'

'Sure, pal.'

'Thanks, pal.'

'Don't mention it, pal.'

'So long, pal.'

Yossarian waved goodbye fondly to his new pals and sauntered out onto the balcony corridor, almost bursting into song the instant he was alone. He was home free: he had pulled it off; his act of rebellion had succeeded; he was safe, and he had nothing to be ashamed of to anyone. He started toward the staircase with a jaunty and exhilarated air. A private in green fatigues saluted him. Yossarian returned the salute happily, staring at the private with curiosity. He looked strangely familiar. When Yossarian returned the salute, the private in green fatigues turned suddenly into Nately's whore and lunged at him murderously with a bone-handled kitchen knife that caught him in the side below his upraised arm. Yossarian sank to the floor with a shriek, shutting his eyes in overwhelming terror as he saw the girl lift the knife to strike at him again. He was already unconscious when Colonel Korn and Colonel Cathcart dashed out of the office and saved his life by frightening her away.

41 Snowden

'Cut,' said a doctor.

'You cut,' said another.

'No cuts,' said Yossarian with a thick, unwieldy tongue.

'Now look who's butting in,' complained one of the doctors. 'Another county heard from. Are we going to operate or aren't we?'

'He doesn't need an operation,' complained the other. 'It's a small wound. All we have to do is stop the bleeding, clean it out and put a few stitches in.'

'But I've never had a chance to operate before. Which one is the scalpel? Is this one the scalpel?'

'No, the other one is the scalpel. Well, go ahead and cut already if you're going to. Make the incision.'

'Like this?'

'Not there, you dope!'

'No incisions,' Yossarian said, perceiving through the lifting fog of insensibility that the two strangers were ready to begin cutting him.

'Another county heard from,' complained the first doctor sarcastically. 'Is he going to keep talking that way while I operate on him?'

'You can't operate on him until I admit him,' said a clerk.

'You can't admit him until I clear him,' said a fat, gruff

542

colonel with a mustache and an enormous pink face that pressed down very close to Yossarian and radiated scorching heat like the bottom of a huge frying pan. 'Where were you born?'

The fat, gruff colonel reminded Yossarian of the fat, gruff colonel who had interrogated the chaplain and found him guilty. Yossarian stared up at him through a glassy film. The cloying scents of formaldehyde and alcohol sweetened the air.

'On a battlefield,' he answered.

'No, no. In what state were you born?'

'In a state of innocence.'

'No, no, you don't understand.'

'Let me handle him,' urged a hatchet-faced man with sunken acrimonious eyes and a thin, malevolent mouth. 'Are you a smart aleck or something?' he asked Yossarian.

'He's delirious,' one of the doctors said. 'Why don't you let us take him back inside and treat him?'

'Leave him right here if he's delirious. He might say something incriminating.'

'But he's still bleeding profusely. Can't you see? He might even die.'

'*Good* for him!'

'It would serve the finky bastard right,' said the fat, gruff colonel. 'All right, John, let's speak out. We want to get to the truth.'

'Everyone calls me Yo-Yo.'

'We want you to co-operate with us, Yo-Yo. We're your friends and we want you to trust us. We're here to help you. We're not going to hurt you.'

'Let's jab our thumbs down inside his wound and gouge it,' suggested the hatchet-faced man.

Yossarian let his eyes fall closed and hoped they would think he was unconscious.

'He's fainted,' he heard a doctor say. 'Can't we treat him now before it's too late? He really might die.'

'All right, take him. I hope the bastard does die.'

'You can't treat him until I admit him,' the clerk said.

543

Yossarian played dead with his eyes shut while the clerk admitted him by shuffling some papers, and then he was rolled away slowly into a stuffy, dark room with searing spotlights overhead in which the cloying smell of formaldehyde and sweet alcohol was even stronger. The pleasant, permeating stink was intoxicating. He smelled ether too and heard glass tinkling. He listened with secret, egotistical mirth to the husky breathing of the two doctors. It delighted him that they thought he was unconscious and did not know he was listening. It all seemed very silly to him until one of the doctors said,

'Well, do you think we should save his life? They might be sore at us if we do.'

'Let's operate,' said the other doctor. 'Let's cut him open and get to the inside of things once and for all. He keeps complaining about his liver. His liver looks pretty small on this X ray.'

'That's his pancreas, you dope. This is his liver.'

'No it isn't. That's his heart. I'll bet you a nickel this is his liver. I'm going to operate and find out. Should I wash my hands first?'

'No operations,' Yossarian said, opening his eyes and trying to sit up.

'Another country heard from,' scoffed one of the doctors indignantly. 'Can't we make him shut up?'

'We could give him a total. The ether's right here.'

'No totals,' said Yossarian.

'Another county heard from,' said a doctor.

'Let's give him a total and knock him out. Then we can do what we want with him.'

They gave Yossarian total anesthesia and knocked him out. He woke up thirsty in a private room, drowning in ether fumes. Colonel Korn was there at his bedside, waiting calmly in a chair in his baggy, wool, olive-drab shirt and trousers. A bland, phlegmatic smile hung on his brown face with its heavy-bearded cheeks, and he was buffing the facets of his bald head gently with the palms of both hands. He bent forward chuckling when Yossarian awoke, and assured him in the friendliest tones that the deal they had made was still on if Yossarian didn't die. Yossarian vomited, and Colonel Korn shot to his feet at the first cough and fled in disgust, so it seemed indeed that there was a silver lining to every cloud, Yossarian reflected, as he drifted back into a suffocating daze. A hand with sharp fingers shook him awake roughly. He turned and opened his eyes and saw a strange man with a mean face who curled his lip at him in a spiteful scowl and bragged,

'We've got your pal, buddy. We've got your pal.'

Yossarian turned cold and faint and broke into a sweat.

'Who's my pal?' he asked when he saw the chaplain sitting where Colonel Korn had been sitting.

'Maybe I'm your pal,' the chaplain answered.

But Yossarian couldn't hear him and closed his eyes. Someone gave him water to sip and tiptoed away. He slept and woke up feeling great until he turned his head to smile at the chaplain and saw Aarfy there instead. Yossarian moaned instinctively and screwed his face up with excruciating irritability when Aarfy chortled and asked how he was feeling. Aarfy looked puzzled when Yossarian inquired why he was not in jail. Yossarian shut his eyes to make him go away. When he opened them, Aarfy was gone and the chaplain was there. Yossarian broke into laughter when he spied the chaplain's cheerful grin and asked him what in the hell he was so happy about.

'I'm happy about you,' the chaplain replied with excited candor and joy. 'I heard at Group that you were very seriously injured and that you would have to be sent home if you lived. Colonel Korn said your condition was critical. But I've just learned from one of the doctors that your wound is really a very slight one and that you'll probably be able to leave in a day or two. You're in no danger. It isn't bad at all.'

Yossarian listened to the chaplain's news with enormous relief. 'That's good.'

'Yes,' said the chaplain, a pink flush of impish pleasure

545

creeping into his cheeks. 'Yes, that is good.'

Yossarian laughed, recalling his first conversation with the chaplain. 'You know, the first time I met you was in the hospital. And now I'm in the hospital again. Just about the only time I see you lately is in the hospital. Where've you been keeping yourself?'

The chaplain shrugged. 'I've been praying a lot,' he confessed. 'I try to stay in my tent as much as I can, and I pray every time Sergeant Whitcomb leaves the area, so that he won't catch me.'

'Does it do any good?'

'It takes my mind off my troubles,' the chaplain answered with another shrug. 'And it gives me something to do.'

'Well that's good, then, isn't it?'

'Yes,' agreed the chaplain enthusiastically, as though the idea had not occurred to him before. 'Yes, I guess that is good.' He bent forward impulsively with awkward solicitude. 'Yossarian, is there anything I can do for you while you're here, anything I can get you?'

Yossarian teased him jovially. 'Like toys, or candy, or chewing gum?'

The chaplain blushed again, grinning self-consciously, and then turned very respectful. 'Like books, perhaps, or anything at all. I wish there was something I could do to make you happy. You know, Yossarian, we're all very proud of you.'

'Proud?'

'Yes, of course. For risking your life to stop that Nazi assassin. It was a very noble thing to do.'

'What Nazi assassin?'

'The one that came here to murder Colonel Cathcart and Colonel Korn. And you saved them. He might have stabbed you to death as you grappled with him on the balcony. It's a lucky thing you're alive!'

Yossarian snickered sardonically when he understood. 'That was no Nazi assassin.'

'Certainly it was. Colonel Korn said it was.'

546

'That was Nately's girl friend. And she was after me, not Colonel Cathcart and Colonel Korn. She's been trying to kill me ever since I broke the news to her that Nately was dead.'

'But how could that be?' the chaplain protested in livid and resentful confusion. 'Colonel Cathcart and Colonel Korn both saw him as he ran away. The official report says you stopped a Nazi assassin from killing them.'

'Don't believe the official report,' Yossarian advised dryly. 'It's part of the deal.'

'What deal?'

'The deal I made with Colonel Cathcart and Colonel Korn. They'll let me go home a big hero if I say nice things about them to everybody and never criticize them to anyone for making the rest of the men fly more missions.'

The chaplain was appalled and rose halfway out of his chair. He bristled with bellicose dismay. 'But that's terrible! That's a shameful, scandalous deal, isn't it?'

'Odious,' Yossarian answered, staring up woodenly at the ceiling with just the back of his head resting on the pillow. 'I think "odious" is the word we decided on.'

'Then how could you agree to it?'

'It's that or a court-martial, Chaplain.'

'Oh,' the chaplain exclaimed with a look of stark remorse, the back of his hand covering his mouth. He lowered himself into his chair uneasily. 'I shouldn't have said anything.'

'They'd lock me in prison with a bunch of criminals.'

'Of course. You must do whatever you think is right, then.' The chaplain nodded to himself as though deciding the argument and lapsed into embarrassed silence.

'Don't worry,' Yossarian said with a sorrowful laugh after several moments had passed. 'I'm not going to do it.'

'But you must do it,' the chaplain insisted, bending forward with concern. 'Really, you must. I had no right to influence you. I really had no right to say anything.'

547

'You didn't influence me.' Yossarian hauled himself over onto his side and shook his head in solemn mockery. 'Christ, Chaplain! Can you imagine that for a sin? Saving Colonel Cathcart's life! That's one crime I don't want on my record.'

The chaplain returned to the subject with caution. 'What will you do instead? You can't let them put you in prison.'

'I'll fly more missions. Or maybe I really will desert and let them catch me. They probably would.'

'And they'd put you in prison. You don't want to go to prison.'

'Then I'll just keep flying missions until the war ends, I guess. Some of us have to survive.'

'But you might get killed.'

'Then I guess I won't fly any more missions.'

'What will you do?'

'I don't know.'

'Will you let them send you home?'

'I don't know. Is it hot out? It's very warm in here.'

'It's very cold out,' the chaplain said.

'You know,' Yossarian remembered, 'a very funny thing happened – maybe I dreamed it. I think a strange man came in here before and told me he's got my pal. I wonder if I imagined it.'

'I don't think you did,' the chaplain informed him. 'You started to tell me about him when I dropped in earlier.'

'Then he really did say it. "We've got your pal, buddy," he said. "We've got your pal." He had the most malignant manner I ever saw. I wonder who my pal is.'

'I like to think that I'm your pal, Yossarian,' the chaplain said with humble sincerity. 'And they certainly have got me. They've got my number and they've got me under surveillance, and they've got me right where they want me. That's what they told me at my interrogation.'

'No, I don't think it's you he meant,' Yossarian decided. 'I think it must be someone like Nately or Dunbar. You know, someone who was killed in the war, like Clevinger, Orr, Dobbs, Kid Sampson or McWatt.'

Yossarian emitted a startled gasp and shook his head. 'I just realized it,' he exclaimed. 'They've got all my pals, haven't they? The only ones left are me and Hungry Joe.' He tingled with dread as he saw the chaplain's face go pale. 'Chaplain, what is it?'

'Hungry Joe was killed.'

'God, no! On a mission?'

'He died in his sleep while having a dream. They found a cat on his face.'

'Poor bastard,' Yossarian said, and began to cry, hiding his tears in the crook of his shoulder. The chaplain left without saying good bye. Yossarian ate something and went to sleep. A hand shook him awake in the middle of the night. He opened his eyes and saw a thin, mean man in a patient's bathrobe and pajamas who looked at him with a nasty smirk and jeered.

'We've got your pal, buddy. We've got your pal.'

Yossarian was unnerved. 'What the *hell* are you talking about?' he pleaded in incipient panic.

'You'll find out, buddy. You'll find out.'

Yossarian lunged for his tormentor's throat with one hand, but the man glided out of reach effortlessly and vanished into the corridor with a malicious laugh. Yossarian lay there trembling with a pounding pulse. He was bathed in icy sweat. He wondered who his pal was. It was dark in the hospital and perfectly quiet. He had no watch to tell him the time. He was wide-awake, and he knew he was a prisoner in one of those sleepless, bed-ridden nights that would take an eternity to dissolve into dawn. A throbbing chill oozed up his legs. He was cold, and he thought of Snowden, who had never been his pal but was a vaguely familiar kid who was badly wounded and freezing to death in the puddle of harsh yellow sunlight splashing into his face through the side gunport when Yossarian crawled into the rear section of the plane over the bomb bay after Dobbs had beseeched him on the intercom to help the gunner, please help the gunner. Yossarian's stomach turned over when his eyes first beheld the macabre scene; he was absolutely revolted, and he paused in fright a few moments before descending, crouched on his hands and knees in the narrow tunnel over the bomb bay beside the sealed corrugated carton containing the first-aid kit. Snowden was lying on his back on the floor with his legs stretched out, still burdened cumbersomely by his flak suit, his flak helmet, his parachute harness and his Mae West. Not far away on the floor lay the small tail gunner in a dead faint. The wound Yossarian saw was in the outside of Snowden's thigh, as large and deep as a football, it seemed. It was impossible to tell where the shreds of his saturated coveralls ended and the ragged flesh began.

There was no morphine in the first-aid kit, no protection for Snowden against pain but the numbing shock of the gaping wound itself. The twelve syrettes of morphine had been stolen from their case and replaced by a cleanly lettered note that said: 'What's good for M & M Enterprises is good for the country. Milo Minderbinder.' Yossarian swore at Milo and held two aspirins out to ashen lips unable to receive them. But first he hastily drew a tourniquet around Snowden's thigh because he could not think what else to do in those first tumultuous moments when his senses were in turmoil, when he knew he must act competently at once and feared he might go to pieces completely. Snowden watched him steadily, saying nothing. No artery was spurting, but Yossarian pretended to absorb himself entirely into the fashioning of a tourniquet, because applying a tourniquet was something he did know how to do. He worked with simulated skill and composure, feeling Snowden's lack-luster gaze resting upon him. He recovered possession of himself before the tourniquet was finished and loosened it immediately to lessen the danger of gangrene. His mind was clear now, and he knew how to proceed. He rummaged through the first-aid kit for scissors.

'I'm cold.' Snowden said softly. 'I'm cold.'

'You're going to be all right, kid,' Yossarian reassured him with a grin. 'You're going to be all right.'

'I'm cold,' Snowden said again in a frail, childlike voice. 'I'm cold.'

'There, there,' Yossarian said, because he did not know what else to say. 'There, there.'

'I'm cold,' Snowden whimpered. 'I'm cold.'

'There, there. There, there.'

Yossarian was frightened and moved more swiftly. He found a pair of scissors at last and began cutting carefully through Snowden's coveralls high up above the wound, just below the groin. He cut through the heavy gabardine cloth all the way around the thigh in a straight line. The tiny tail gunner woke up while Yossarian was cutting with the scissors, saw him, and fainted again. Snowden rolled his head to the other side of his neck in order to stare at Yossarian more directly. A dim, sunken light glowed in his weak and listless eyes. Yossarian, puzzled, tried not to look at him. He began cutting downward through the coveralls along the inside seam. The yawning wound – was that a tube of slimy bone he saw running deep inside the gory scarlet flow behind the twitching, startling fibers of weird muscle? – was dripping blood in several trickles, like snow melting on eaves, but viscous and red, already thickening as it dropped. Yossarian kept cutting through the coveralls to the bottom and peeled open the severed leg of the garment. It fell to the floor with a plop, exposing the hem of khaki undershorts that were soaking up blotches of blood on one side as though in thirst. Yossarian was stunned at how waxen and ghastly Snowden's bare leg looked, how loathsome, how lifeless and esoteric the downy, fine, curled blond hairs on his odd, white shin and calf. The wound, he saw now, was not nearly as large as a football, but as long and wide as his hand and too raw and deep to see into clearly. The raw muscles inside twitched like live hamburger meat. A long sigh of relief escaped slowly through Yossarian's mouth when he saw that Snowden was not in danger of dying. The blood was already coagulating inside the wound, and it was simply a matter of bandaging him up and keeping him calm until the plane landed. He removed some packets of sulfanilamide from the first-aid kit. Snowden quivered when Yossarian pressed against him gently to turn him up slightly on his side.

'Did I hurt you?'

'I'm cold,' Snowden whimpered. 'I'm cold.'

'There, there,' Yossarian said. 'There, there.'

'I'm cold. I'm cold.'

'There, there. There, there.'

'It's starting to hurt me,' Snowden cried out suddenly with a plaintive, urgent wince.

Yossarian scrambled frantically through the first-aid kit in search of morphine again and found only Milo's note and a bottle of aspirin. He cursed Milo and held two aspirin tablets out to Snowden. He had no water to offer. Snowden rejected the aspirin with an almost imperceptible shake of his head. His face was pale and pasty. Yossarian removed Snowden's flak helmet and lowered his head to the floor.

'I'm cold,' Snowden moaned with half-closed eyes. 'I'm cold.'

The edges of his mouth were turning blue. Yossarian was petrified. He wondered whether to pull the rip cord of Snowden's parachute and cover him with the nylon folds. It was very warm in the plane. Glancing up unexpectedly, Snowden gave him a wan, co-operative smile and shifted the position of his hips a bit so that Yossarian could begin salting the wound with sulfanilamide. Yossarian worked with renewed confidence and optimism. The plane bounced hard inside an air pocket, and he remembered with a start that he had left his own parachute up front in the nose. There was nothing to be done about that. He poured envelope after envelope of the white crystalline powder into the bloody oval wound until nothing red could be seen then drew a deep, apprehensive breath, steeling himself with gritted teeth as he touched his bare hand to the dangling shreds of drying flesh to tuck them up inside the wound. Quickly he covered the whole wound with a large cotton compress and jerked his hand away. He smiled nervously when his brief ordeal had ended. The actual contact with the dead flesh had not been nearly as repulsive as he had anticipated, and he found excuse to caress the wound with his fingers again and again to convince himself of his own courage.

Next he began binding the compress in place with a roll of gauze. The second time around Snowden's thigh with the bandage, he spotted the small hole on the inside through which the piece of flak had entered, a round, crinkled wound the size of a quarter with blue edges and a black core inside where the blood had crusted. Yossarian sprinkled this one with sulfanilamide too and continued unwinding the gauze around Snowden's leg until the compress was secure. Then he snipped off the roll with the scissors and slit the end down the center. He made the whole thing fast with a tidy square knot. It was a good bandage, he knew, and he sat back on his heels with pride, wiping the perspiration from his brow, and grinned at Snowden with spontaneous friendliness.

'I'm cold,' Snowden moaned. 'I'm cold.'

'You're going to be all right, kid,' Yossarian assured him, patting his arm comfortingly. 'Everything's under control.'

Snowden shook his head feebly. 'I'm cold,' he repeated, with eyes as dull and blind as stone. 'I'm cold.'

'There, there,' said Yossarian, with growing doubt and trepidation. 'There, there. In a little while we'll be back on the ground and Doc Daneeka will take care of you.'

But Snowden kept shaking his head and pointed at last, with just the barest movement of his chin, down toward his armpit. Yossarian bent forward to peer and saw a strangely colored stain seeping through the coveralls just above the armhole of Snowden's flak suit. Yossarian felt his heart stop, then pound so violently he found it difficult to breathe. Snowden was wounded inside his flak suit. Yossarian ripped open the snaps of Snowden's flak suit and heard himself scream wildly as

Snowden's insides slithered down to the floor in a soggy pile and just kept dripping out. A chunk of flak more than three inches big had shot into his other side just underneath the arm and blasted all the way through, drawing whole mottled quarts of Snowden along with it through the gigantic hole in his ribs it made as it blasted out. Yossarian screamed a second time and squeezed both hands over his eyes. His teeth were chattering in horror. He forced himself to look again. Here was God's plenty, all right, he thought bitterly as he stared – liver, lungs, kidneys, ribs, stomach and bits of the stewed tomatoes Snowden had eaten that day for lunch. Yossarian hated stewed tomatoes and turned away dizzily and began to vomit, clutching his burning throat. The tail gunner woke up while Yossarian was vomiting, saw him, and fainted again. Yossarian was limp with exhaustion, pain and despair when he finished. He turned back weakly to Snowden, whose breath had grown softer and more rapid, and whose face had grown paler. He wondered how in the world to begin to save him.

'I'm cold,' Snowden whimpered. 'I'm cold.'

'There, there,' Yossarian mumbled mechanically in a voice too low to be heard. 'There, there.'

Yossarian was cold, too, and shivering uncontrollably. He felt goose pimples clacking all over him as he gazed down despondently at the grim secret Snowden had spilled all over the messy floor. It was easy to read the message in his entrails. Man was matter, that was Snowden's secret. Drop him out a window and he'll fall. Set fire to him and he'll burn. Bury him and he'll rot, like other kinds of garbage. The spirit gone, man is garbage. That was Snowden's secret. Ripeness was all.

'I'm cold,' Snowden said. 'I'm cold.'

'There, there,' said Yossarian. 'There, there.' He pulled the rip cord of Snowden's parachute and covered his body with the white nylon sheets.

'I'm cold.'

'There, there.'

42 Yossarian

'Colonel Korn says,' said Major Danby to Yossarian with a prissy, gratified smile, 'that the deal is still on. Everything is working out fine.'

'No it isn't.'

'Oh, yes, indeed,' Major Danby insisted benevolently. 'In fact, everything is much better. It was really a stroke of luck that you were almost murdered by that girl. Now the deal can go through perfectly.'

'I'm not making any deals with Colonel Korn.'

Major Danby's effervescent optimism vanished instantly, and he broke out all at once into a bubbling sweat. 'But you do have a deal with him, don't you?' he asked in anguished puzzlement. 'Don't you have an agreement?'

'I'm breaking the agreement.'

'But you shook hands on it, didn't you? You gave him your word as a gentleman.'

'I'm breaking my word.'

'Oh, dear,' sighed Major Danby, and began dabbing ineffectually at his careworn brow with a folded white handkerchief. 'But why, Yossarian? It's a very good deal they're offering you.'

'It's a lousy deal, Danby. It's an odious deal.'

'Oh, dear,' Major Danby fretted, running his bare hand over his dark, wiry hair, which was already soaked with perspiration to the tops of the thick, close-cropped waves. 'Oh dear.'

'Danby, don't you think it's odious?'

Major Danby pondered a moment. 'Yes, I suppose it is odious,' he conceded with reluctance. His globular, exophthalmic eyes were quite distraught. 'But why did you make such a deal if you didn't like it?'

'I did it in a moment of weakness,' Yossarian wise-cracked with glum irony. 'I was trying to save my life.'

'Don't you want to save your life now?'

'That's why I won't let them make me fly more missions.'

'Then let them send you home and you'll be in no more danger.'

'Let them send me home because I flew more than fifty missions,' Yossarian said, 'and not because I was stabbed by that girl, or because I've turned into such a stubborn son of a bitch.'

Major Danby shook his head emphatically in sincere and bespectacled vexation. 'They'd have to send nearly every man home if they did that. Most of the men have more than fifty missions. Colonel Cathcart couldn't possibly requisition so many inexperienced replacement crews at one time without causing an investigation. He's caught in his own trap.'

'That's his problem.'

'No, no, no, Yossarian,' Major Danby disagreed solicitously. 'It's your problem. Because if you don't go through with the deal, they're going to institute court-martial proceedings as soon as you sign out of the hospital.'

Yossarian thumbed his nose at Major Danby and laughed with smug elation. 'The hell they will! Don't lie to me, Danby. They wouldn't even try.'

'But why wouldn't they?' inquired Major Danby, blinking with astonishment.

'Because I've really got them over a barrel now.

There's an official report that says I was stabbed by a Nazi assassin trying to kill them. They'd certainly look silly trying to court-martial me after that.'

'But, Yossarian!' Major Danby exclaimed. 'There's another official report that says you were stabbed by an innocent girl in the course of extensive black-market operations involving acts of sabotage and the sale of military secrets to the enemy.'

Yossarian was taken back severely with surprise and disappointment. 'Another official report?'

'Yossarian, they can prepare as many official reports as they want and choose whichever ones they need on any given occasion. Didn't you know that?'

'Oh, dear,' Yossarian murmured in heavy dejection, the blood draining from his face. 'Oh, dear.'

Major Danby pressed forward avidly with a look of vulturous well-meaning. 'Yossarian, do what they want and let them send you home. It's best for everyone that way.'

'It's best for Cathcart, Korn and me, not for everyone.'

'For everyone,' Major Danby insisted. 'It will solve the whole problem.'

'Is it best for the men in the group who will have to keep flying more missions?'

Major Danby flinched and turned his face away uncomfortably for a second. 'Yossarian,' he replied, 'it will help nobody if you force Colonel Cathcart to court-martial you and prove you guilty of all the crimes with which you'll be charged. You will go to prison for a long time, and your whole life will be ruined.'

Yossarian listened to him with a growing feeling of concern. 'What crimes will they charge me with?'

'Incompetence over Ferrara, insubordination, refusal to engage the enemy in combat when ordered to do so, and desertion.'

Yossarian sucked his cheeks in soberly. 'They could charge me with all that, could they? They gave me a medal for Ferrara. How could they charge me with incompetence now?'

'Aarfy will swear that you and McWatt lied in your official report.'

'I'll bet the bastard would!'

'They will also find you guilty,' Major Danby recited, 'of rape, extensive black-market operations, acts of sabotage and the sale of military secrets to the enemy.'

'How will they prove any of that? I never did a single one of those things.'

'But they have witnesses who will swear you did. They can get all the witnesses they need simply by persuading them that destroying you is for the good of the country. And in a way, it *would* be for the good of the country.'

'In what way?' Yossarian demanded, rising up slowly on one elbow with bridling hostility.

Major Danby drew back a bit and began mopping his forehead again. 'Well, Yossarian,' he began with an apologetic stammer, 'it would not help the war effort to bring Colonel Cathcart and Colonel Korn into disrepute now. Let's face it, Yossarian – in spite of everything, the group does have a very good record. If you were court-martialed and found innocent, other men would probably refuse to fly missions, too. Colonel Cathcart would be in disgrace, and the military efficiency of the unit might be destroyed. So in that way it *would* be for the good of the country to have you found guilty and put in prison, even though you *are* innocent.'

'What a sweet way you have of putting things!' Yossarian snapped with caustic resentment.

Major Danby turned red and squirmed and squinted uneasily. 'Please don't blame me,' he pleaded with a look of anxious integrity. 'You know it's not my fault. All I'm doing is trying to look at things objectively and arrive at a solution to a very difficult situation.'

'I didn't create the situation.'

'But you can resolve it. And what else can you do? You don't want to fly more missions.'

'I can run away.'

'Run away?'

'Desert. Take off. I can turn my back on the whole damned mess and start running.'

Major Danby was shocked. 'Where to? Where could you go?'

'I could get to Rome easily enough. And I could hide myself there.'

'And live in danger every minute of your life that they would find you? No, no, no, no, Yossarian. That would be a disastrous and ignoble thing to do. Running away from problems never solved them. Please believe me. I am only trying to help you.'

'That's what that kind detective said before he decided to jab his thumb into my wound,' Yossarian retorted sarcastically.

'I am not a detective,' Major Danby replied with indignation, his cheeks flushing again. 'I'm a university professor with a highly developed sense of right and wrong, and I wouldn't try to deceive you. I wouldn't lie to anyone.'

'What would you do if one of the men in the group asked you about this conversation?'

'I would lie to him.'

Yossarian laughed mockingly, and Major Danby, despite his blushing discomfort, leaned back with relief, as though welcoming the respite Yossarian's changing mood promised. Yossarian gazed at him with a mixture of reserved pity and contempt. He sat up in bed with his back resting against the headboard, lit a cigarette, smiled slightly with wry amusement, and stared with whimsical sympathy at the vivid, pop-eyed horror that had implanted itself permanently on Major Danby's face the day of the mission to Avignon, when General Dreedle had ordered him taken outside and shot. The startled wrinkles would always remain, like deep back scars, and Yossarian felt sorry for the gentle, moral, middle-aged idealist, as he felt sorry for so many people whose shortcomings were not large and whose troubles were light.

With deliberate amiability he said, 'Danby, how can you work along with people like Cathcart and Korn? Doesn't it turn your stomach?'

Major Danby seemed surprised by Yossarian's question. 'I do it to help my country,' he replied, as though the answer should have been obvious. 'Colonel Cathcart and Colonel Korn are my superiors, and obeying their orders is the only contribution I can make to the war effort. I work along with them because it's my duty. And also,' he added in a much lower voice, dropping his eyes, 'because I am not a very aggressive person.'

'Your country doesn't need your help any more,' Yossarian reasoned with antagonism. 'So all you're doing is helping them.'

'I try not to think of that,' Major Danby admitted frankly. 'But I try to concentrate on only the big result and to forget that they are succeeding, too. I try to pretend that they are not significant.'

'That's my trouble, you know,' Yossarian mused sympathetically, folding his arms. 'Between me and every ideal I always find Scheisskopfs, Peckems, Korns and Cathcarts. And that sort of changes the ideal.'

'You must try not to think of them,' Major Danby advised affirmatively. 'And you must never let them change your values. Ideals are good, but people are sometimes not so good. You must try to look up at the big picture.'

Yossarian rejected the advice with a skeptical shake of his head. 'When I look up, I see people cashing in. I don't see heaven or saints or angels. I see people cashing in on every decent impulse and every human tragedy.'

'But you must try not to think of that,' Major Danby insisted. 'And you must try not to let it upset you.'

'Oh, it doesn't really upset me. What does upset me, though, is that they think I'm a sucker. They think that they're smart, and that the rest of us are dumb. And, you know, Danby, the thought occurs to me right now, for the first time, that maybe they're right.'

'But you must try not to think of that too,' argued Major Danby. 'You must think only of the welfare of your country and the dignity of man.'

'Yeah,' said Yossarian.

'I mean it, Yossarian. This is not World War One. You must never forget that we're at war with aggressors who would not let either one of us live if they won.'

'I know that,' Yossarian replied tersely, with a sudden surge of scowling annoyance. 'Christ, Danby, I earned that medal I got, no matter what their reasons were for giving it to me. I've flown seventy goddam combat missions. Don't talk to me about fighting to save my country. I've been fighting all along to save my country. Now I'm going to fight a little to save myself. The country's not in danger any more, but I am.'

'The war's not over yet. The Germans are driving toward Antwerp.'

'The Germans will be beaten in a few months. And Japan will be beaten a few months after that. If I were to give up my life now, it wouldn't be for my country. It would be for Cathcart and Korn. So I'm turning my bombsight in for the duration. From now on I'm thinking only of me.'

Major Danby replied indulgently with a superior smile, 'But, Yossarian, suppose everyone felt that way.'

'Then I'd certainly be a damned fool to feel any other way, wouldn't I?' Yossarian sat up straighter with a quizzical expression. 'You know, I have a queer feeling that I've been through this exact conversation before with someone. It's just like the chaplain's sensation of having experienced everything twice.'

'The chaplain wants you to let them send you home,' Major Danby remarked.

'The chaplain can jump in the lake.'

'Oh, dear.' Major Danby sighed, shaking his head in regretful disappointment. 'He's afraid he might have influenced you.'

'He didn't influence me. You know what I might do? I might stay right here in this hospital bed and vegetate. I could vegetate very comfortably right here and let other people make the decisions.'

'You must make decisions,' Major Danby disagreed. 'A person can't live like a vegetable.'

'Why not?'

A distant warm look entered Major Danby's eyes. 'It must be nice to live like a vegetable,' he conceded wistfully.

'It's lousy,' answered Yossarian.

'No, it must be very pleasant to be free from all this doubt and pressure,' insisted Major Danby. 'I think I'd like to live like a vegetable and make no important decisions.'

'What kind of vegetable, Danby?'

'A cucumber or a carrot.'

'What kind of cucumber? A good one or a bad one?'

'Oh, a good one, of course.'

'They'd cut you off in your prime and slice you up for a salad.'

Major Danby's face fell. 'A poor one, then.'

'They'd let you rot and use you for fertilizer to help the good ones grow.'

'I guess I don't want to live like a vegetable, then,' said Major Danby with a smile of sad resignation.

'Danby, must I really let them send me home?' Yossarian inquired of him seriously.

Major Danby shrugged. 'It's a way to save yourself.'

'It's a way to lose myself, Danby. You ought to know that.'

'You could have lots of things you want.'

'I don't want lots of things I want,' Yossarian replied, and then beat his fist down against the mattress in an outburst of rage and frustration. 'Goddammit, Danby! I've got friends who were killed in this war. I can't make a deal now. Getting stabbed by that bitch was the best thing that ever happened to me.'

'Would you rather go to jail?'

'Would you let them send you home?'

'Of course I would!' Major Danby declared with conviction. 'Certainly I would,' he added a few moments later, in a less positive manner. 'Yes, I suppose I would let them send me home if I were in your place,' he decided uncomfortably, after lapsing into troubled contemplation. Then he threw his face sideways disgustedly

562

in a gesture of violent distress and blurted out, 'Oh, yes, of course I'd let them send me home! But I'm such a terrible coward I couldn't really be in your place.'

'But suppose you weren't a coward?' Yossarian demanded, studying him closely. 'Suppose you did have the courage to defy somebody?'

'Then I *wouldn't* let them send me home,' Major Danby vowed emphatically with vigorous joy and enthusiasm. 'But I certainly wouldn't let them court-martial me.'

'Would you fly more missions?'

'No, of course not. That would be total capitulation. And I might be killed.'

'Then you'd run away?'

Major Danby started to retort with proud spirit and came to an abrupt stop, his half-opened jaw swinging closed dumbly. He pursed his lips in a tired pout. 'I guess there just wouldn't be any hope for me, then, would there?'

His forehead and protuberant white eyeballs were soon glistening nervously again. He crossed his limp wrists in his lap and hardly seemed to be breathing as he sat with his gaze drooping toward the floor in acquiescent defeat. Dark, steep shadows slanted in from the window. Yossarian watched him solemnly, and neither of the two men stirred at the rattling noise of a speeding vehicle skidding to a stop outside and the sound of racing footsteps pounding toward the building in haste.

'Yes, there's hope for you,' Yossarian remembered with a sluggish flow of inspiration. 'Milo might help you. He's bigger than Colonel Cathcart, and he owes me a few favors.'

Major Danby shook his head and answered tonelessly. 'Milo and Colonel Cathcart are pals now. He made Colonel Carthcart a vice-president and promised him an important job after the war.'

'Then ex-P.F.C. Wintergreen will help us,' Yossarian exclaimed. 'He hates them both, and this will infuriate him.'

Major Danby shook his head bleakly again. 'Milo and

ex-P.F.C. Wintergreen merged last week. They're all partners now in M & M Enterprises.'

'Then there is no hope for us, is there?'

'No hope.'

'No hope at all, is there?'

'No, no hope at all,' Major Danby conceded. He looked up after a while with a half-formed notion. 'Wouldn't it be nice if they could disappear us the way they disappeared the others and relieve us of all these crushing burdens?'

Yossarian said no. Major Danby agreed with a melancholy nod, lowering his eyes again, and there was no hope at all for either of them until footsteps exploded in the corridor suddenly and the chaplain, shouting at the top of his voice, came bursting into the room with the elctrifying news about Orr, so overcome with hilarious excitement that he was almost incoherent for a minute or two. Tears of great elation were sparkling in his eyes, and Yossarian leaped out of bed with an incredulous yelp when he finally understood.

'*Sweden?*' he cried.

'Orr!' cried the chaplain.

'Orr?' cried Yossarian.

'Sweden!' cried the chaplain, shaking his head up and down with gleeful rapture and prancing about uncontrollably from spot to spot in a grinning, delicious frenzy. 'It's a miracle, I tell you! A miracle! I believe in God again. I really do. Washed ashore in Sweden after so many weeks at sea! It's a miracle.'

'Washed ashore, hell!' Yossarian declared, jumping all about also and roaring in laughing exultation at the walls, the ceiling, the chaplain and Major Danby. 'He didn't *wash* ashore in Sweden. He *rowed* there! He *rowed* there, chaplain, he *rowed* there.'

'Rowed there?'

'He *planned* it that way! He went to Sweden deliberately.'

'Well, I don't care!' the chaplain flung back with undiminished zeal. 'It's still a miracle, a miracle of

564

human intelligence and human endurance. Look how much he accomplished!' The chaplain clutched his head with both hands and doubled over in laughter. 'Can't you just picture him?' he exclaimed with amazement. 'Can't you just picture him in that yellow raft, paddling through the Straits of Gibraltar at night with that tiny little blue oar –'

'With that fishing line trailing out behind him, eating raw codfish all the way to Sweden, and serving himself tea every afternoon –'

'I can just see him!' cried the chaplain, pausing a moment in his celebration to catch his breath. 'It's a miracle of human perseverance, I tell you. And that's just what I'm going to do from now on! I'm going to persevere. Yes, I'm going to persevere.'

'He knew what he was doing every step of the way!' Yossarian rejoiced, holding both fists aloft triumphantly as though hoping to squeeze revelations from them. He spun to a stop facing Major Danby. 'Danby, you dope! There is hope, after all. Can't you see? Even Clevinger might be alive somewhere in that cloud of his, hiding inside until it's safe to come out.'

'What are you talking about?' Major Danby asked in confusion. 'What are you both talking about?'

'Bring me apples, Danby, and chestnuts too. Run, Danby, run. Bring me crab apples and horse chestnuts before it's too late, and get some for yourself.'

'Horse chestnuts? Crab apples? What in the world for?'

'To pop into our cheeks, of course.' Yossarian threw his arms up into the air in a gesture of mighty and despairing self-recrimination. 'Oh, why didn't I listen to him? Why wouldn't I have some faith?'

'Have you gone crazy?' Major Danby demanded with alarm and bewilderment. 'Yossarian, will you please tell me what you are talking about?'

'Danby, Orr planned it that way. Don't you understand – he planned it that way from the beginning. He even practiced getting shot down. He rehearsed for it on every mission he flew. And I wouldn't go with him! Oh, why wouldn't I listen? He invited me along, and I wouldn't go with him! Danby, bring me buck teeth too, and a valve to fix and a look of stupid innnocence that nobody would ever suspect of any cleverness. I'll need them all. Oh, why wouldn't I listen to him. Now I understand what he was trying to tell me. I even understand why that girl was hitting him on the head with her shoe.'

'Why?' inquired the chaplain sharply.

Yossarian whirled and seized the chaplain by the shirt front in an importuning grip. 'Chaplain, help me! Please help me. Get my clothes. And hurry, will you? I need them right away.'

The chaplain started away alertly. 'Yes, Yossarian, I will. But where are they? How will I get them?'

'By bullying and browbeating anybody who tries to stop you. Chaplain, get me my uniform! It's around this hospital somewhere. For once in your life, succeed at something.'

The chaplain straightened his shoulders with determination and tightened his jaw. 'Don't worry, Yossarian. I'll get your uniform. But why was that girl hitting Orr over the head with her shoe? Please tell me.'

'Because he was paying her to, that's why! But she wouldn't hit him hard enough, so he had to row to Sweden. Chaplain, find me my uniform so I can get out of here. Ask Nurse Duckett for it. She'll help you. She'll do anything she can to be rid of me.'

'Where are you going?' Major Danby asked apprehensively when the chaplain had shot from the room. 'What are you going to do?'

'I'm going to run away,' Yossarian announced in an exuberant, clear voice, already tearing open the buttons of his pajama tops.

'Oh, no,' Major Danby groaned, and began patting his perspiring face rapidly with the bare palms of both hands. 'You can't run away. Where can you run to? Where can you go?'

'To Sweden.'

'To Sweden?' Major Danby exclaimed in astonishment. 'You're going to run to Sweden? Are you crazy?'

'Orr did it.'

'Oh, no, no, no. no, no,' Major Danby pleaded. 'No, Yossarian, you'll never get there. You can't run away to Sweden. You can't even row.'

'But I can get to Rome if you'll keep your mouth shut when you leave here and give me a chance to catch a ride. Will you do it?'

'But they'll find you,' Major Danby argued desperately, 'and bring you back and punish you even more severely.'

'They'll have to try like hell to catch me this time.'

'They will try like hell. And even if they don't find you, what kind of way is that to live? You'll always be alone. No one will ever be on your side, and you'll always live in danger of betrayal.'

'I live that way now.'

'But you can't just turn your back on all your responsibilities and run away from them,' Major Danby insisted. 'It's such a negative move. It's escapist.'

Yossarian laughed with buoyant scorn and shook his head. 'I'm not running away from my responsibilities. I'm running to them. There's nothing negative about running away to save my life. You know who the escapists are, don't you, Danby? Not me and Orr.'

'Chaplain, please talk to him, will you? He's deserting. He wants to run away to Sweden.'

'Wonderful!' cheered the chaplain, proudly throwing on the bed a pillowcase full of Yossarian's clothing. 'Run away to Sweden, Yossarian. And I'll stay here and persevere. Yes. I'll persevere. I'll nag and badger Colonel Cathcart and Colonel Korn every time I see them. I'm not afraid. I'll even pick on General Dreedle.'

'General Dreedle's out,' Yossarian reminded, pulling on his trousers and hastily stuffing the tails of his shirt inside. 'It's General Peckem now.'

The chaplain's babbling confidence did not falter for an instant. 'Then I'll pick on General Peckem, and even on General Scheisskopf. And do you know what else I'm going to do? I'm going to punch Captain Black in the nose the very next time I see him. Yes, I'm going to punch him in the nose. I'll do it when lots of people are around so that he may not have a chance to hit me back.'

'Have you both gone crazy?' Major Danby protested, his bulging eyes straining in their sockets with tortured awe and exasperation. 'Have you both taken leave of your senses? Yossarian, listen –'

'It's a miracle, I tell you,' the chaplain proclaimed, seizing Major Danby about the waist and dancing him around with his elbows extended for a waltz. 'A real miracle. If Orr could row to Sweden, then I can triumph over Colonel Cathcart and Colonel Korn, if only I persevere.'

'Chaplain, will you please shut up?' Major Danby entreated politely, pulling free and patting his perspiring brow with a fluttering motion. He bent toward Yossarian, who was reaching for his shoes. 'What about Colonel –'

'I couldn't care less.'

'But this may actua –'

'To hell with them both!'

'This may actually help them,' Major Danby persisted stubbornly. 'Have you thought of that?'

'Let the bastards thrive, for all I care, since I can't do a thing to stop them but embarrass them by running away. I've got responsibilities of my own now, Danby. I've got to get to Sweden.'

'You'll never make it. It's impossible. It's almost a geographical impossibility to get there from here.'

'Hell, Danby, I know that. But at least I'll be trying. There's a young kid in Rome whose life I'd like to save if I can find her. I'll take her to Sweden with me if I can find her, so it isn't all selfish, is it?'

'It's absolutely insane. Your conscience will never let you rest.'

'God bless it.' Yossarian laughed. 'I wouldn't want to live without strong misgivings. Right, Chaplain?'

'I'm going to punch Captain Black right in the nose the

next time I see him,' gloried the chaplain, throwing two left jabs in the air and then a clumsy haymaker. 'Just like that.'

'What about the disgrace?' demanded Major Danby.

'What disgrace? I'm more in disgrace now.' Yossarian tied a hard knot in the second shoelace and sprang to his feet. 'Well, Danby, I'm ready. What do you say? Will you keep your mouth shut and let me catch a ride?'

Major Danby regarded Yossarian in silence, with a strange, sad smile. He had stopped sweating and seemed absolutely calm. 'What would you do if I did try to stop you?' he asked with rueful mockery. 'Beat me up?'

Yossarian reacted to the question with hurt surprise. 'No, of course not. Why do you say that?'

'I will beat you up,' boasted the chaplain, dancing up very close to Major Danby and shadowboxing. 'You and Captain Black, and maybe even Corporal Whitcomb. Wouldn't it be wonderful if I found I didn't have to be afraid of Corporal Whitcomb any more?'

'Are you going to stop me?' Yossarian asked Major Danby, and gazed at him steadily.

Major Danby skipped away from the chaplain and hesitated a moment longer. 'No, of course not!' he blurted out, and suddenly was waving both arms toward the door in a gesture of exuberant urgency. 'Of course I won't stop you. Go, for God sakes, and hurry! Do you need any money?'

'I have some money.'

'Well, here's some more.' With fervent, excited enthusiasm, Major Danby pressed a thick wad of Italian currency upon Yossarian and clasped his hand in both his own, as much to still his own trembling fingers as to give encouragement to Yossarian. 'It must be nice to be in Sweden now,' he observed yearningly. 'The girls are so sweet. And the people are so advanced.'

'Goodbye, Yossarian,' the chaplain called. 'And good-luck. I'll stay here and persevere, and we'll meet again when the fighting stops.'

'So long, Chaplain. Thanks, Danby.'

'How do you feel, Yossarian?'

'Fine. No, I'm very frightened.'

'That's good,' said Major Danby. 'It proves you're still alive. It won't be fun.'

Yossarian started out. 'Yes it will.'

'I mean it, Yossarian. You'll have to keep on your toes every minute of every day. They'll bend heaven and earth to catch you.'

'I'll keep on my toes every minute.'

'You'll have to jump.'

'I'll jump.'

'Jump!' Major Danby cried.

Yossarian jumped. Nately's whore was hiding just outside the door. The knife came down, missing him by inches, and he took off.

THE END

GOD KNOWS by JOSEPH HELLER

'Mr Heller is dancing at the top of his form again . . . original, sad, wildly funny and filled with roaring'
Mordecai Richler, New York Times Book Review

Joseph Heller's powerful, wonderfully funny, deeply moving new novel is the story of David – yes, *that* David: warrior king of Israel, husband of Bathsheba, father of Solomon, slayer of Goliath, and psalmist nonpareil . . . as well as the David we've known before now; David the cocky Jewish kind, David the fabulous lover, David the plagiarised poet, David the Jewish father, David the (one-time) crony of God . . .

At last, David is telling his own story, and he's holding nothing back – equally unembarrassed by his faults, his sins, his prowess, his incomparable glory . . .

God Knows is an ancient story, a modern story, a love story. It is a novel about growing up and growing old, about men and women, about fathers and sons, about man and God. It is a novel of emotional force, imaginative richness, and unbridled comic invention. It is quintessential Heller.

'Joseph Heller is the outstandingly clever ideas-man of modern fiction . . . brilliantly inventive'
Jonathan Raban, Sunday Times

'The unforgiving genius still flares, and the book is worth the price of admission for the first few pages alone'
Martin Amis, The Observer

0 552 99169 4

THE WORLD ACCORDING TO GARP
by John Irving

'It is not easy to find words in which to convey the joy, the excitement, the passion this superb novel evokes. The imagination soars as Irving draws us on inexorably into Garp's world, which is at once larger than life and as real as our own most private dreams of life and death, love, lust and fear . . . some of the most colourful characters in recent fiction'   *Publishers Weekly*

'Absolutely extraordinary . . . A roller-coaster ride that leaves one breathless, exhausted, elated and tearful'
Los Angeles Times Book Review

'Like all great works of art, Irving's novel seems always to have been there, a diamond sleeping in the dark, chipped out at last for our enrichment and delight . . . As approachable as it is brilliant, GARP pulses with vital energy'
Cosmopolitan

0 552 99205 4

THE CIDER HOUSE RULES
by JOHN IRVING

'Bound to make as vivid an impression as *The World According to Garp*' said Publishers Weekly of John Irving's magnificent new novel spanning six decades.

Set among the apple orchards of rural Maine, it is a perverse world in which Homer Wells' odyssey begins. As the oldest unadopted offspring at St. Cloud's orphanage, he learns about the skills which in one way or another, help young and not-so-young women, from Wilbur Larch, the orphanage's founder, a man of rare compassion and with an addiction to ether.

Dr. Larch loves all his orphans, especially Homer Wells. It is Homer's story we follow, from his early apprenticeship in the orphanage surgery, to his adult life running a cidermaking factory and his strange relationship with the wife of his closest friend.

'John Irving has been compared with Kurt Vonnegut and J. D. Salinger, but is arguably more inventive than either. Wry, laconic, he sketches his characters with an economy that springs from a feeling for words and mastery over his craft. This superbly original book is one to be read and remembered'   *The Times*

'The Cider House Rules is difficult to define and impossible not to admire'   *Daily Telegraph*

'Like the rest of Irving's fiction, it is often disconcerting, but always exciting and provoking'   *The Observer*

0 552 99204 6

NO LAUGHING MATTER
by JOSEPH HELLER and SPEED VOGEL

'A jubilant romp in the face of adversity'
Vanity Fair

Joseph Heller is the distinguished author of CATCH-22
and other classic novels. Speed Vogel is a retired textile
manufacturer, sometime artist and herring taster.
Together, they have written an inspiring account of a
calamitous illness – Guillain-Barré syndrome – suffered
by Joe. And while Joe fought for his life, Speed moved
into Joe's apartment, thenceforth to act as his messenger,
servant and general factotum. He not only wrote but
signed Joe's cheques, wined and dined (at Joe's expense)
his favourite nurses, and warded off the tantrums of his
paralysed buddy.

Joe's friends rallied around: Mel Brooks, arch-
hypochondriac of the Western World; Mario Puzo, the
most reluctant hospital visitor of all time, and Dustin
Hoffman, who twice came through with strokes of
imagination that helped to make Joe's time in hospital
a little easier.

But it was Speed Vogel who played the major part in
helping Joe Heller, writer and buddy extraordinaire,
through his greatest crisis, and it is their combined
efforts which have produced a story that is as wacky,
terrifying, and great-hearted as any fiction Joseph Heller
ever wrote.

'A rumpled, untidy and absolutely winning celebration . . . CATCH-22 without the cosmic despair'
Chicago Sun-Times

0 552 13032 X

A SELECTED LIST OF TITLES
AVAILABLE FROM CORGI BOOKS

THE PRICES SHOWN BELOW WERE CORRECT AT THE TIME OF
GOING TO PRESS. HOWEVER TRANSWORLD PUBLISHERS RESERVE
THE RIGHT TO SHOW NEW RETAIL PRICES ON COVERS WHICH MAY
DIFFER FROM THOSE PREVIOUSLY ADVERTISED IN THE TEXT OR
ELSEWHERE.

*All Corgi/Bantam Books are available at your bookshop or newsagent, or can be ordered from
the following address:*

Corgi/Bantam Books,
Cash Sales Department,
P.O. Box 11, Falmouth, Cornwall TR10 9EN

Please send a cheque or postal order (no currency) and allow 60p for postage and packing
for the first book plus 25p for the second book and 15p for each additional book ordered up
to a maximum charge of £1.90 in UK.

B.F.P.O. customers please allow 60p for the first book, 25p for the second book plus 15p per
copy for the next 7 books, thereafter 9p per book.

Overseas customers, including Eire, please allow £1.25 for postage and packing for the first
book, 75p for the second book, and 28p for each subsequent title ordered.